GREAT TALES
▪ OF ▪
CRIME &
DETECTION

GREAT TALES
■ OF ■
CRIME &
DETECTION

Introduction by
Robert Bloch

Foreword by
John Lutz

Compiled by
Charles Ardai

Galahad Books
New York

First Galahad Books edition published in 1991.

Galahad Books
A division of Budget Book Service, Inc.
386 Park Avenue South
New York, NY 10016

Galahad Books is a registered trademark of Budget Book Service, Inc.

Published by arrangement with Dell Magazines,
a division of Bantam Doubleday Dell.

Library of Congress Catalog Card Number: 90-8620

ISBN: 0-88365-771-6

Printed in the United States of America.

ACKNOWLEDGMENTS

Grateful acknowledgment is made to the following for permission to reprint their copyrighted material:

The Investigation of Things by Charles Ardai, Copyright © 1991 by Davis Publications, Inc. Reprinted by permission of the author; *Out The Window* by Lawrence Block, Copyright © 1977 by Davis Publications, Inc. Reprinted by permission of Henry Morrison, Inc.; *Silent Warning* by William J. Carroll, Jr., Copyright © 1990 by Davis Publications, Inc. Reprinted by permission of the author; *Major Crimes* by Loren D. Estleman, Copyright © 1986 by Davis Publications, Inc. Reprinted by permission of the author; *Till Tuesday* by Jeremiah Healy, Copyright © 1988 by Davis Publications, Inc. Reprinted by permission of International Creative Management, Inc.; *Ride The Lightning* by John Lutz, Copyright © 1984 by Davis Publications, Inc. Reprinted by permission of the author; *The Case of the Pietro Andromache* by Sara Paretsky, Copyright © 1988 by Sara Paretsky. Reprinted by permission of the author; all first appeared in ALFRED HITCHCOCK'S MYSTERY MAGAZINE.

The Cross of Lorraine by Isaac Asimov, Copyright © 1976 by Isaac Asimov. Reprinted by permission of the author; *Crime In Rhyme* by Robert Bloch, Copyright © 1957 by Mercury Publications, Inc., © renewed 1984 by Davis Publications, Inc. Reprinted by permission of the author; *SuSu and the 8:30 Ghost* by Lillian Jackson Braun, Copyright © 1964 by Davis Publications, Inc. Reprinted by permission of the author's literary agent, Blanche C. Gregory; *The Importance of Trifles* by Avram Davidson, Copyright © 1968 by Avram Davidson. Reprinted by permission of the Virginia Kidd Literary Agency; *Nameless Enemy* by Miriam Allen deFord, Copyright © 1966 by Davis Publications, Inc. Reprinted by permission of the author; *The Adventure of the Oval Window* by John H. Dirckx, Copyright © 1983 by John H. Dirckx. Reprinted by permission of the author; *Dangerous Widows* by Mignon G. Eberhardt, Copyright © 1953 by United Newspapers Corp., © renewed 1981 by Mignon G. Eberhardt. Reprinted by permission of Brandt and Brandt Literary Agents, Inc.; *The Day of the Losers* by Dick Francis, Copyright ©

1977 by Dick Francis. Reprinted by permission of the Sterling Lord Agency, Inc.; *Your Appointment is Cancelled* by Antonia Fraser, Copyright © 1983 by Antonia Fraser. Reprinted by permission of Curtis Brown, Ltd.; *The Third Man* by Graham Greene, Copyright © 1949 by Graham Greene, © renewed 1976. Reprinted by permission of International Creative Management, Inc.; *Tragedy of a Handkerchief* by Michael Innes, Copyright © 1947 by Michael Innes, © renewed 1974. Reprinted by permission of A. P. Watt, Ltd.; *Unc Foils Show Foe* by John Jakes, Copyright © 1965 by Davis Publications, Inc. Reprinted by permission of Scott Meredith Literary Agency, Inc.; *The Nine Mile Walk* by Harry Kemelman, Copyright © 1947 by the American Mercury, Inc. © renewed 1974 by Davis Publications, Inc. Reprinted by permission of Scott Meredith Literary Agency, Inc.; *Le Chateau de l'Arsenic* by Georges Simenon, Copyright © 1948 by American Mercury, Inc. © renewed 1975 by Davis Publications, Inc. Reprinted by permission of the author; all first appeared in ELLERY QUEEN'S MYSTERY MAGAZINE or an Ellery Queen Anthology.

Introduction Copyright © 1990 by Robert Bloch
Foreword Copyright © 1990 by John Lutz

CONTENTS

This generous collection of detective stories is culled from the overflowing wealth of works from the world's two leading mystery magazines, *Ellery Queen's Mystery Magazine* and *Alfred Hitchcock's Mystery Magazine*. The stories in this volume take place across the world and over ten centuries, and feature such unique and colorful detectives as Lawrence Block's Matthew Scudder, John Lutz's Alo Nudger, Loren D. Estleman's Amos Walker, Isaac Asimov's Black Widowers, and Edgar Allan Poe's C. Auguste Dupin, the great detective who started it all. The range and variety of detective fiction is tremendous, and this volume should give you a delicious sampling of it.

Several people made major contributions to this book, without whose efforts it wouldn't have existed: Cynthia Manson, who had the idea for the collection and made it happen; John Lutz and Robert Bloch, who were generous and patient throughout; and especially Eleanor Sullivan, editor of *EQMM*, and Cathleen Jordan, editor of *AHMM*, whose exceptional magazines and editorial acumen gave us these stories in the first place.

— Charles Ardai
October, 1990

Introduction

Robert Bloch

History's pages are stained with blood.

Beginning with the chronicle of Cain, our annals are a calendar of crime, in which Death takes no holiday.

Lawlessness has always been the stuff of legends and of life itself. No wonder that when fable and folklore were replaced by modern fiction, such sagas of skullduggery endured.

It was Geoffrey Chaucer who warned us, long ago, that murder will out. But Edgar Allan Poe was the one who came up with a working procedure. His character, C. Auguste Dupin, was the first major fictional detective—created before real-life detectives ever drew breath, or pensions. And it was Poe who set the pattern for countless stories and novels of detection over the past hundred and fifty years since Dupin first set foot in the Rue Morgue.

Not all such tales are as gruesome or gory as those forming a part of our actual history. Proof can be found in these pages, where Dupin uses rationination (a power Poe bestowed on him, along with the word itself) to solve a mystery which doesn't depend on body-counts.

Sir Arthur Conan Doyle's contribution, *The Man With the Twisted Lip*, also lacks a murderous *motif* but very definitely demonstrates the progress of the detective story within the first half-century of its evolution.

Poe's Dupin is a brain without a body. There's no real physical description of this shadowy figure who prefers to lead a shadowy existence. It's his mental powers that Poe illuminates, and in so doing, lights the way to come for all the puzzle-stories and the methodology employed in their solutions.

Sir Arthur Conan Doyle's puzzle-solver isn't one to dwell in shadow. No other figure in the field, and only a handful in all literature, has attained the celebrity of Doyle's detective, Sherlock Holmes. If Poe conceived the character in terms of intellect, it was Doyle who endowed the role with the qualities of humanity and—at times—superhumanity. Ironically, Holmes achieved the ultimate in success; he's found greater fame than his creator.

Other, more contemporary creations in this book help to demonstrate the growth of the genre over the years since Dupin prowled Paris and Holmes hastened through London fog. A glance at the contents-page requires no special talent for deduction to reveal how many writers have found fascination in mystery fiction. Mark Twain is an illustrious example; Abraham Lincoln a singularly appropriate one, since shrouds of secrecy still cling to accounts of his own fate.

It may come as something of a surprise to find later writers, best-known for their novels, represented here by shorter works, but Mignon G. Eberhardt and Graham Greene in their prime and authors like Dick Francis today, are examples of those for whom the short story has held a special appeal. Even that most prolific of novelists, Georges Simenon, bylines one of the tales which follow.

Mystery writers, almost without exception, are story-tellers. They prefer plot to anecdote, involvement rather than incident-reportage. Some give their readers a humorous wink and a gentle nudge; others grab them by the throat and shake them until their teeth rattle. But never does a true storyteller adopt a casual take-it-or-leave-it attitude. Readers of these tales are going to *take* them, for these masters of mystery permit no other choice.

Chroniclers of crime and detection must be extra-clever—as clever as their criminal characters who commit the crimes, and as clever as the sleuths who solve them. And—an even greater challenge—they must be able to outsmart their readers.

The last is no easy task, for readers of this sort of fiction are generally more literate than the sado-*macho* types who are interested only in sex and violence. The true devotee of detection, the connoisseur of crime, is likely to have higher standards; his tastes are more sanguine than sanguinary.

But enough of such speculations. As someone once said, the game is afoot.

No telling what you may find lurking in the pages which follow. Enter them now, armed with curiousity. And—

Good hunting!

Foreword

John Lutz

The best sort of mystery fiction is that which in one way or another involves detection, because it's the fiction that most intimately shares with and involves the reader. That intense personal involvement is the soul of all great fiction, but especially of great mystery fiction.

In the following stories the reader can, along with the main character, observe and analyze and attempt to reach conclusions about various aspects of human behavior, criminal and otherwise. People commit crimes, and people are the victims of crime, and what it boils down to is that the crime-and-detection story is more than anything else about people. The classic elements remain: the dark deed, the suspects, the motives, the planting of clues, the unexpected yet plausible ending. But, for the most part, the following stories revolve around character. Walking in the detective's shoes and reasoning with him or her, the reader is, more than in most types of fiction, almost a character within the story.

The authors within these pages are masters at creating thoroughly wrought fictional worlds that quicken pulses and involve readers emotionally as well as intellectually. In "Out The Window" Lawrence Block's Matt Scudder tries to find out why a young New York woman committed suicide—if it was suicide. In Graham Greene's classic "The Third Man" his amateur detective Rollo Martins, a British author of American western novels, investigates the circumstances surrounding the death of his much-admired old schoolfriend, Harry Lime, in post-war Vienna. In this tstory, on which the famous movie of the Fifties was based, it turns out that not everyone was wild about Harry. Present-day Boston is the scene of Jeremiah Healy's "Till Tuesday," in which John Francis Cuddy investigates the mysterious disappearance of a client's mistress. Back across the Atlantic, Dick Francis sets a suspenseful story in the world of British horse racing, in "The Day of the Losers." In Sara Paretsky's "The Case of the Pietro Andromache," a murder is committed in relation to an art theft that occurred in Europe over forty years earlier. "Major Crimes" finds Loren D. Estleman's intrepid Amos Walker looking into the violent death of a public relations executive in modern Detroit. Time and geography herein are almost as limitless as imagination.

Aside from the pleasure of reading great fiction, the reader will be able to see how this type of story, sustained by its timeless and universal appeal, has adapted to changes in society and technology. Arthur Conan Doyle's "The Man With the Twisted Lip" begins with the chime of a Victorian doorbell, while John Jakes' "Unc Foils Show Foe" starts with the descent of a jet airliner.

In these pages you're invited to travel the world of crime and detection with the greatest tour guides in the business, past and present.

So read on.

Enjoy.

Join in.

"The most beautiful thing we can experience is the mysterious."
— Albert Einstein

Major Crimes

LOREN D. ESTLEMAN

Deborah Stonesmith was a tall black woman with auburn-tinted hair sprayed into hard waves and heavy hips tastefully disguised under a tailored gray herringbone suit. The steel desk in her office just came to her knees when she rose like a man to grasp my hand. The gesture didn't seem out of place at all; but for a spray of daisies in a cut-glass vase on the desk, the room might have belonged to any of the male detectives in the squad. When we were seated, she put on a pair of gold-rimmed glasses hanging from a chain around her neck to read my I.D., then took them off and returned the folder and leaned back in her yellow leather swivel, steepling a pair of surprisingly slender hands without a ring or long nails.

"What brings you down to Major Crimes, Mr. Walker?"

Her voice fell around the middle register, a little hoarse at the edges like a saloon singer's. I said:

"I'm working for Midwest Life, Automobile & Casualty this month. Stan Draper there hired me to look into this Gendron kill that went down Tuesday. Gendron's wife stands to collect a quarter million on the double indemnity clause, and it's Midwest's policy, excuse the expression, to investigate all claims above fifty thousand. I understand it's your case."

She smiled tightly. "How *is* Stan?"

"Three sheets to the wind, same as always. You know him?"

"We pulled stakeout together once when I was in uniform. That was before they broke him for keeping a pint of Ten High in the glove compartment." She turned the chair to the left and back again. "We made a collar in the Gendron case this morning. This kid tried to buy a tape deck at a Radio Shack downtown with bills on the hot serial-number list. He's rolling over on his partners right now."

"I heard. When can I talk to him?"

"Not until after he's arraigned, and maybe not even then. The P.D. on this one's a real nutcracker, and I'm not going to stray from the book and take a chance on blowing it all over some technicality. We got a textbook arrest on a drugstore heist and the murder of an innocent bystander, and that's how it's going to stay."

I tapped a Winston out of my pack and spiked it between my lips. "I'd like to see the autopsy report on Gendron."

"So would I. We're still waiting on it. All I've got so far is the bullet that killed him, a .38. The kid didn't have a gun on him when we picked him up, and his apartment is clean, if you call a drawerful of controlled substances and a stack of naughty pictures clean. He says it was one of the others pulled the trigger. I would, too."

"Yeah. Did you ever find out what a PR consultant was doing in a drugstore in the middle of the morning on a weekday?"

"Getting cigarettes, his secretary said. Look, you think his wife sent him there to get squiffed? One of the scroats popped him in front of four witnesses on their way out the door."

"The questions have to get asked." I lit up and flipped the match into the glass ashtray on the desk. "This kid got a sheet?"

She fingered her eyeglasses, smiling the tight smile. "Three disorderlies and a shoplifting. Copped a pair of nylon panties from the downtown Hudson's, when there was a downtown Hudson's. His size. Did I say those pictures we found in his apartment were all of men?"

"Not exactly Machine Gun Kelly."

"These days you don't have to be. All it takes is an expensive hobby, like doing pills and cruising the gay bars on Woodward."

"Any provocation for the shooting?"

"Witnesses say no. Just another goodbye kill. We get them."

"Was Gendron killed instantly?"

"Twelve paces, straight through the heart."

"They're getting better."

"I've got a ballistics expert wants his autograph."

I burned some more tobacco. Then I squashed out my butt half-smoked and rose. "Thanks, inspector. I hope you get the others."

"We will. We don't see many mysteries in Major Crimes. You see Stan, tell him Deb said hi."

The Gendron house stood in St. Clair Shores a block off the lake, really just a broad spot in the Detroit River where rich people from Grosse Pointe with nothing better to do sail catamarans and worry about their putting. It was a brick colonial with a midget windmill on the front lawn and a yellow Citroën parked behind a black Camaro in the circular driveway. I parked behind the Citroën and got out, and when I rang the doorbell, a tall party with receding gray hair answered. He had on a camel-hair sport coat over a white turtleneck and black wool peg-topped pants. His face was tanned.

"I'm Amos Walker," I said, before he could say, "Yes-s?"; and handed him a card. "I'm an investigator with the late Mr. Gendron's insurance underwriters. I wonder if I might ask Mrs. Gendron a few questions."

"I doubt it." His gaze fell somewhere behind me. It was a powder-blue gaze. What color it was behind the contacts was anybody's guess.

I said, "It has to do with whether or not Midwest pays off her claim."

"Mrs. Gendron is under sedation. I'm Dr. Redding, the family— her physician." He made the change with a slight twitch of his very black eyebrows. They looked lacquered on. "Perhaps later, when the shock has worn off—"

"Did you know Mr. Gendron well?"

"Very. He was my friend before he was my patient."

"Maybe I could talk to you."

He moved his eyebrows, then stood aside to let me in. The living room was done in beige, with blond furniture and a twist of bleached driftwood resting on the mantel of a pale stone fireplace. A bloodless room, professionally decorated. He offered me the ivory-colored sofa and helped himself to a thin cigar from his inside breast pocket.

"Shocking habit, especially for a doctor." He lit it with a Zippo and got a Winston burning for me. I noticed he chewed his nails. "We're as weak as everyone else."

"Didn't I see your name in Gendron's file?"

"I conducted his physical when he applied for the policy last year."

"Was that the last time you examined him?"

"No, I gave him his annual just six weeks ago. He was in excellent condition for a man of forty, though he could've stood to lose ten pounds."

"Every doctor says that. You knew him socially?"

"Dick and I became friends when he was a freshman at Michigan and I was interning in the hospital there. I introduced him to his wife." He flipped some ash into the ashtray on the blond coffee table.

"How was he emotionally?"

"In good spirits. Maybe a little harried. Public relations is a cannibal profession. I've referred a number of Dick's colleagues to stress counseling. Not him, though. He coped."

I added some ash of my own to the pile. The ashtray contained two of his cigar stubs and a number of shredded cigarette butts with pink lipstick stains on the tips. "Would you know if he had money troubles?"

He stroked the brown underside of his chin. "Is there something suspicious about Dick's death? I thought it was established he was killed at random by some strung-out bandit."

"That's how it looks. I'm just stitching up the loose corners. People who live in nice houses like this have a tendency to go into the hole."

"I wouldn't know about that."

It sounded stiff. "Just asking," I said. "Friends usually know about those things. How were relations between him and his wife?"

"They were devoted to each other. Really, I'm curious. Does someone imagine he threw himself in front of that bullet just to cheat the insurance company?"

"It's happened."

"Not with Dick. He had too much to live for." He killed his cigar. "I think that if Lynn were standing where I am she'd be asking you to leave about now."

"He's just doing his job, Tim."

I'm some detective. I hadn't heard her entering the room through the doorway behind me. I stood and turned to look at a small brunette in her mid-thirties, wearing a pageboy haircut and a blue satin dressing gown trimmed in ruffles. Her feet were bare in flat-heeled sandals, and she was without makeup but for a touch of pink on her lips. She wouldn't need much else. Her eyes were a little puffed.

"I heard you talking," she said. "I'm Lynn Gendron, Dick's—widow."

"Then you can answer the questions I was asking Dr. Redding."

"Lynn, you should be resting."

"What does it matter? Dick's the first thing I think of when I wake up. My husband was a happy man, Mr.—?"

"Walker."

She smiled her thanks sadly. "He worked hard and it took its toll on his nerves, but he liked the work and he loved me. We had the usual debts, nothing we couldn't stay on top of. The house is mortgaged and we—I owe three more payments on the car. If that's something to panic over, this whole neighborhood should be half berserk."

"That's the Camaro you owe on?" I asked.

"Yes," offered Redding. "The Citroën is mine. All mine."

The cigarette was burning my fingers. I got rid of it. "It's good you still make house calls."

"Only in special cases. Lynn is a dear friend. Now, I really must insist you go. Despite what Lynn says, time alone is the best cure for grief."

"Alone with you, you mean."

He did the trick with the eyebrows. "I think I resent that."

"When will you know?"

"Goodbye, Mr. Walker," cut in Mrs. Gendron. She sounded more tired than angry.

I thanked her for her help and left while Redding was still making the effort to be civilized.

Hegelman Associates, advertising and public relations, occupied the twenty-second floor of the Penobscot Building, a grand old pile of granite and red marble in downtown Detroit that looked as if it was willing to tolerate all that space-age plastic going up along the riverfront, for a while longer anyway. I followed a short carpeted corridor from the elevator to a desk behind which a china doll in a stiff blouse and Max Factor directed me to Richard Gendron's offices. The woman I found there wasn't quite as pretty, but she didn't work as hard at it. I liked her slight overbite and the wisp of soft brown hair that strayed out over her forehead. She read my card and her face got drawn.

"Mr. Hegelman said someone from the insurance company would be coming by," she said quietly. "He said we should all cooperate."

Her voice broke a little. I said, "Gendron was a good boss, huh."

"He was a good *man*. When I threw out my back bending over to open a file drawer, the company tried to deny me compensation. Dick—Mr. Gendron stormed into Mr. Hegelman's office in the middle of a conference and threatened to quit if my claim wasn't honored. I got my first check two days later. He took care of his people."

"All his people, or just you?"

Her chin came up. "I'm happily married, and so was he. Ask anyone on the staff; they've all got stories just like mine. He did right by all of us, even if it meant breaking the rules."

"Sorry. I'm starting from scratch, that's all. Can I look in his office?"

She said the door was unlocked, and I went inside. It was a corner room, looking down on Griswold to the west and out on the Renaissance Center to the south, a giant poker-chip caddy with the handle gone. An original architect's drawing of the Penobscot Building hung on the east wall, and a framed studio shot of Gendron's wife Lynn shared the desk with a telephone pad and a complicated intercom. The drawers yielded pens, stationery, a paperback book, and a carton of Pall Malls.

The telephone pad was blank. I picked it up and riffled through it. A business card slid out onto the desk. I read it.

I studied the buttons on the intercom for a minute, then gave up and went back into the outer office. Gendron's secretary looked up from her typing.

"Your boss said he was going to the store for cigarettes?"

"Yes. We had an agreement: I wouldn't try to talk him into quitting, and he wouldn't send me out to maintain his habit. We—"

"What brand did he smoke?"

"What brand? Pall Malls."

"Any thoughts on why he'd go out for cigarettes when he had a carton in his desk?"

She shook her head.

I laid the business card on top of the typewriter. The legend was embossed in tasteful blue on pebbled beige stock:

RELIANCE INVESTIGATIONS
"Courtesy, Efficiency, Confidentiality"

"What business would he have had for a private investigator?"

"It must have fallen out of the Turner file," she said, and stopped. Something fluttered across her face: a confidence betrayed.

"Who's Turner?"

"I'm sorry, I can't answer that."

"Not even if it means finding out why Gendron died?"

She looked up at me with dry eyes. "Discretion was very important to Dick. He practiced it in everything he did. He'd want me to do the same no mater what."

"Okay." I left the card where I had put it. "Did he confide in you personally?"

"Such as what?"

"Such as his health." I brought out the paperback book I had found in Gendron's desk. A pastoral cover, doves circling a meadow in blossom, the title in gentle script: *Coping with Terminal Illness.*

She stared at it a long time. "Maybe it was someone he knew. His mother or father. Or his wife."

"Maybe. Have the police been here?"

"Just to talk. None of them went into the office."

"No need, for a simple robbery killing. Can I use your telephone? It's a local call."

She said go ahead and I dialed police headquarters and asked for Deborah Stonesmith in Major Crimes. After a minute her saloon-singer voice came on the line.

"Walker, inspector," I said. "Did that autopsy sheet come through?"

"On my desk. What do you need, if it's quick?"

"Gendron's physical condition at time of death. Was he suffering from cancer, heart disease, anything that would snuff him if the bullet didn't?"

"Nope. I should be so healthy."

"Okay, thanks. How's the investigation?"

"Hot as hell. We found the kid's partners right where he said we would. They're being processed now."

"Names?"

"After the arraignment tomorrow morning."

I thanked her again and we were through talking. The secretary's eyes were on me. "Gendron was sound as a rock," I said.

"Surprised?"

"Only a little."

Back in my office I removed the *Free Press* movie section from the telephone and called Hal Needham at Reliance Investigations. When I wasn't working for Midwest or following someone's husband through the after-hours places downtown or looking for someone's daughter in the Cass Corridor, I sometimes farmed myself out to

Reliance, and Hal and I had worked in tandem enough times to owe each other some favors. I recognized his Kansas twang as soon as he answered.

"Walker? Call you back."

The telephone rang a minute later. When I picked it up he said, "Sorry. Krell's got a tap on all the incoming lines. This one's clean."

"How can you work for him?"

"I got a gifted daughter and I'm starting a bail fund for my son. What's the favor?"

"Guy named Richard Gendron at Hegelman Associates did some business with Reliance a while back, something to do with someone or something named Turner. I need the details."

He whistled. "It gets back to Krell he'll play the 'Rogue's March' over the office P.A. and break my men's room key over his knee."

"He won't get it from me."

"This one's worth a dinner. At least."

"You pick the place."

"Whose sheet are you on?"

"Midwest is picking up the expenses on this one."

"In that case, make it the London Chop House. Give me a half hour."

I said okay and broke the connection. Next I tried Lee Horst downtown. Lee's an information broker, and if you're on his accepted list, he'll hand you the inside track on anyone or anything in the Detroit area, provided you meet his price. He picked up the receiver himself: no secretaries or assistants to undersell Lee.

"Timothy Redding," he repeated in his high soft voice, after I had told him what I needed. "M.D.?"

"Yeah. I want his finances, but if you find anything else juicy, I'll take that, too."

"I'll get back to you."

The counter down the street from my building served me a three-course dinner—tuna fish sandwich, coffee, and a bill—and I unlocked the door to my office again just as the telephone started ringing. It was Hal Needham.

"Turner Chemicals," he said. "They went to Hegelman looking for a better public image, and Gendron got the assignment. He observed their operation for a month and made recommendations that included a dress code for office personnel and a pink slip for the dispatcher in their Warren plant."

"How come the canning?"

"Gendron didn't think it was good business practice to keep an armed robber on the payroll. Guy's name was Phil Hardy, and he had priors going back to the riots. Also, he was driving a new red Pontiac Firebird that he didn't buy on a dispatcher's salary."

"I like that part," I said. "I like it a lot. Tomorrow night okay for the chop house?"

"'I'm not eating a bite until then." He laughed shortly and hung up.

Lee Horst didn't call back that day. I dialed my service and asked them to reroute all calls to my home telephone, then closed the office. At home I watched a little TV, dealt myself a couple of losing games of Solitaire, and turned in early. All that dialing can really take it out of you.

In the morning I showered, dressed, and turned on the radio for the news while the coffee was brewing. When the announcer had finished with Washington and the Middle East, he noted that three men had been arraigned ten minutes before in Recorder's Court in connection with Tuesday's drugstore robbery and the murder of Richard Gendron. He gave two names I didn't recognize and we pronounced the third one together. Philip Hardy.

Stonesmith was a few minutes getting rid of the reporters and coming to the telephone. I congratulated her on the arrests. She said, "Save it for the convictions. Jay Albert Matthews represented them at the arraignment."

Matthews had defended a millionaire's daughter or two and written a bestselling book, *Mistakes of Darrow* or something on that order. "Who's paying him?" I asked.

"Privileged information, *he* said. It sure isn't any of those three."

"I think I know."

"Well, spill it."

"Privileged information, inspector."

I hung up on whatever name she was calling me and lifted the receiver again and got Lee Horst just as he was entering his office. He apologized for not calling.

"Computer was down, and isn't that the most popular new lie this season?" Keys clattered on his end. "Okay, I got a readout on Dr. Redding. You want it over the phone or on paper?"

I said over the telephone was fine, and smoked two cigarettes while he was feeding it to me. When he was through, I asked him how much.

"For you, a hundred".

"You're a fraud, Lee."

"My informants like to eat, what can I say?"

I promised to get a check off to him that week. Then I went out without finishing my coffee.

The yellow Citroën was parked in the same spot behind Lynn Gendron's Camaro when I climbed out of my own crate. It might not have moved since yesterday, but Redding was too discreet for that. A discreet fellow was Dr. Redding.

"What now?"

He had shed the camel-hair for a sober blue serge suit and knitted black necktie. This time he stood across the doorway with his feet spread, a graying sentinel with a Palm Beach tan. I said, "We can go inside or we can talk out here. My voice carries."

After a beat he let me pass. Gendron's widow was sitting on the sofa in a snug-fitting black dress that caught her just below the knees. A pair of gray cotton gloves lay on the coffee table in front of her, next to a barrel glass half full of amber liquid.

"Dick's funeral is this morning." Redding closed the door. "Can't this wait until after?"

"What'd you tell him, cancer?" I said.

His lacquered eyebrows squirmed. "What?"

"Cancer, probably. It's a buzzword, bound to have the extreme effect you were after. How deep are you in debt really, Redding? My information says six figures."

"Are you drunk? You're babbling."

"This is a computer society. Everything's on record. Your house in Grosse Pointe has a third mortgage, and you dumped a ton of preferred stock at a loss to keep the loan sharks happy downtown. You're into the IRS for sixty grand, you owe every bookie between here and Miami. You told me the truth about your car, though; you own that, at least until the government or some guy named Big Tony the Hippo seizes it."

"Keep talking," he said. "You're constructing an iron-clad case for slander and invasion of privacy."

"You need that quarter-million insurance money, Redding. It means surviving or staying out of jail. Depending on which of your creditors gets to you first. Murder was a little out of your reach, and since your old friend Gendron wasn't going to accommodate you by committing suicide, you decided to supply him with a good reason. So when you gave him his last physical, you told him he had terminal cancer."

"Now I know you've been drinking. He was in excellent health."

"You knew that, but he didn't. The symptoms of stress can be made to seem like the early stages of something much more serious, and he trusted you enough not to get a second opinion from another doctor. I found a well-thumbed self-help book in his office about living with death. It didn't take, though. With your help he chose a sudden end over letting his insides rot away slowly."

Redding smiled grimly. "Very inventive, but you forgot one thing. Suicide would have voided the policy."

"Only if it looked like suicide. Being an old friend, you planted a simple idea in Gendron's head: set up your own murder. He pulled the file on a man named Phil Hardy, a man he'd persuaded a client of his to fire in the interest of a better public image, a known armed robber who would organize the hit for an inducement—something up front, say, plus whatever he got away with from the robbery and a good attorney if he got caught.

"Jay Albert Matthews is the direct link. Gendron could supply the advance payment, but you had to hire Matthews to represent Hardy and his partners because Gendron wouldn't be around to do it once he kept his appointment in that drugstore, and if you reneged on the deal, they'd spill the details. The law says Matthews doesn't have to divulge his client's name, but once it gets out you set the whole thing up, he'll turn you in to save his own reputation. Lawyers are like that. That's where you went sour, Redding. You didn't have the guts to arrange the kill yourself, so you let Gendron do it. Only in the end you had to get your hands dirty, too."

"I wasn't Dick's beneficiary, Walker. Lynn was."

I looked at her on the sofa. "He's trying to lay it off on you."

The skin of her face drew tight. "The hell he will."

"Shut up, Lynn."

"I guess she's in love with you, or thinks she is," I said. "Otherwise, she wouldn't have gone along with it. A divorce would only have given her part interest in a car with three payments to go on it and half a house with a mortgage, but her husband's death by misadventure was good for a quarter million. It would make a nice dowry when you two got married after a suitable interval. Don't move, Redding. Let's keep my gun in my belt holster and this conversation civilized."

"Don't be melodramatic. I was just reaching for a cigar."

"That's another thing. You really should have emptied the ashtray in your Citroën. I took the liberty of inspecting it on my way up to the door just now. The pink lipstick on the cigarette butts I found there isn't your shade. Bet there are more in your house."

"You're a man."

I looked again at Mrs. Gendron. Her glass was empty now, but she was still holding it, her knuckles white. "You don't know what it's like being married to a dull man in a dull job who never took a chance in his life. Dick was horridly, stultifyingly *dependable*. Try living with that."

"Don't say anything," Redding warned her. "Matthews won't talk, and Hardy and the others don't know either of us from Adam."

"You should be grateful he was so dependable." I lifted the receiver off the telephone near the door and used that same hand to dial police headquarters, keeping my gun hand free and my eyes on Redding. "Gendron took his responsibilities seriously, and hang the rules. That's why he tried to see that you got his insurance money. He took chances, all right, but not like yours. All of his were for other people."

The police switchboard put me through to Major Crimes.

"Matthews won't turn," Deborah Stonesmith said. "Why should he? He's not guilty of anything but being a lawyer. Even if he did talk, it wouldn't prove anything."

We were seated in her office, waiting for the stenographer who had taken my statement to finish typing it up so I could sign it. The inspector had on a light blue suit today, over a white ruffled blouse that on her looked like a lace doily on an armored car. She was playing with the glasses on the chain around her neck.

I said, "Keep working on the Gendron woman. She might crack."

"More likely it'll be Redding. A funny thing happens in these unequal partnerships when they go into Interrogation: they reverse roles. The strong one spills his guts, and the weak one clams up tight. If it happens at all."

"In any case, Midwest saves having to pay off. If your hunch is right and Hardy folds on Gendron, it's suicide any way you slice it."

"So why aren't you happy?" she asked.

"Why aren't you?"

She smiled. There was no joy in it. The light of a gray Detroit sort of day came through the window at her back and painted a red nimbus around her head of hard hair. "So it was just an ordinary domestic murder after all. Not a major crime."

"They're all major," I said, admiring her halo through the smoke of my Winston. "Every last one of them."

Silent Warning

WILLIAM J. CARROLL, JR.

Thirty or so miles north and east of Rapid City, a rather dilapidated sign loomed out over a stand of pine that edged the side of the road. It read SKI WHITE WOLF!—NEXT LEFT, and although I didn't ski, I did start watching for the turn.

It came about a mile farther on, just short of a concrete span which straddled a dark, fast-moving river that looked heavy with spring runoff. Another sign, the little brother of the first one and in little better shape, marked the egress, but I pulled over and stopped for a minute to check my location on a road map and to stretch my legs.

I'd been on the road for two hours, and I was feeling my age in my shoulders and lower back, which was where I always felt it. I was tired, stiff—and a little more worried now than I had been earlier.

I stood for a while outside my rental, smoking and watching the river, which flowed southwest out of a range of blue smudge hills that peaked in the distance over the top of skeletal forest to the north, and I tried to rid myself of the anxiety that had grown up in the pit of my stomach.

But it didn't work.

I was looking for someone—someone missing—and the dark, gloomy wildness of the countryside in which I was searching had begun to give me dark, gloomy, wild thoughts.

I got back into my car and, just as I did so, a noisy pickup truck rumbled up onto the highway from the road to White Wolf.

There were two men inside, and they gave me a pair of suspicious looks as the truck fishtailed onto the road and sped off. There was a rifle rack in the cab, and on the rear bumper was a sticker that read AMERICA—LOVE IT OR DIE!

It did not quell my anxiety.

The road to White Wolf was a slender ribbon of blacktop that wound itself through some heavy forest skirting the river, then turned steeply up the side of a hill. It switchbacked so sharply at some points that I barely inched along.

Eventually the road straightened and led me down into a large oval-shaped valley, across a rattling steel bridge, and abruptly into the outskirts of a small town that sprawled along the river's edge and up across the face of a mountain.

White Wolf, South Dakota.

Under six inches of new white snow, on a clear day and with the sun bright and brilliant in the sky, it was a town that at one time might have been postcard material. It might have looked picturesque, perhaps inviting, and maybe even friendly. Maybe.

As it was, however—naked, under the shadows cast by low-hanging clouds that obscured most of the mountain, and even darker skies above—it looked like a wet, shiny fungus that had grown up out of the dirty river and was spreading like ringworm throughout the valley.

It looked gritty, but without an excuse, and I was glad to be only passing through.

But then I was always only passing through.

The town's public buildings were clumped down along the river, and I found the White Wolf police station with no trouble at all.

It was a large stone building, just off the muddy town square, with several blue and white squad cars in front. I parked next to them, braving a variety of threatening signs that forbade my doing just that, but it had been a long drive from Ellsworth Air Force Base, and a longer flight from Fort Lewis before that, and I was feeling impatiently reckless.

I climbed out of my car and heard some children laughing excitedly.

Next door to the police station was a school, and in the closed alley between the buildings a group of young boys were throwing stones at a small mangy-looking dog, which they'd trapped at one end.

I watched as the dog scampered left and right, farther and farther back into the alley, avoiding the thrown rocks pretty easily at first, but then the children began to close on the animal, and I could see it tiring.

Sensing its own doom, the dog finally stopped backing up and, braving a storm of rocks, charged down one side of the alley and out onto the street, where it was pursued out of sight by the children, who howled their disappointment.

After the boys were out of sight themselves, I stood there for a minute more letting the tension ooze out of my shoulders. More dark, gloomy thoughts crossed my mind.

White Wolf, South Dakota.

It was no place to be lost in.

It was 1500 hours exactly when I entered the large outer office of the police station. A few men in uniform looked up at me from the rear of the room, then away with studied uninterest. I told a clerk at a desk near the door who I was, and she sighed wearily, told me to wait, then disappeared for a moment.

When she returned, she had a large man in tow who frowned at me over her shoulder.

"You're Warrant Officer Virginiak?" he asked.

I told him I was, and he beckoned me into an inner office.

On the door to the office was a sign that read MAXWELL R. FOWLER—CHIEF OF POLICE.

"I've been expecting you," he told me in a rather resigned way as he waved me to a chair in front of his desk. "You work for this Colonel Chavez, right?"

"Yes, sir."

Fowler seated himself behind his desk and glared at me. He was a big man—six four or five—with a shaven, bullet-shaped head and a face marked by a large hooked nose and a pair of thick, black, and very mobile eyebrows. He looked about fifty, was thirty or forty pounds overweight, and in a bad mood. "So," he said tightly, "what can I do for the army today?"

I smiled at him. "We still have a man missing, chief . . . "

"You know," he said sharply, "I'm starting to get kind of irritated at you folks."

I nodded. Chavez had warned me that the man had sounded angry on the telephone, and he was.

Fowler pointed a finger at me. "I resent the implication that we haven't been doing our job here."

"I haven't implied anything, Chief Fowler."

"Then what are *you* doing here?" he asked quickly.

I sighed. "One of our people is missing . . . "

"I know that, Mr. Virginiak, but that doesn't answer the question, does it?"

"I suppose not." I sat back in my chair and lit a cigarette. "Look,

Chief Fowler, I know—and Colonel Chavez knows—that you've done everything you could, given the limitations we placed on you. This is a funny business." I shrugged. "I think we've been just hoping he'd turn up. We didn't want to call Gilliam missing until the last possible minute."

Fowler made a face, as if to say that he'd heard all this before—which he had.

"But," I went on, "the last possible minute came and went." I shrugged again. "Now—we're concerned."

Fowler snorted. "If your Colonel Chavez was so damned concerned about this man, he just might have been a bit more cooperative."

"How so?"

"Like a description of the man, to begin with." He made a sound of disgust. "How can I even start looking for him unless I know what he looks like, for crying out loud?"

I nodded. "I understand."

He looked at me expectantly for a moment, then said, "Well, I don't understand, Mr. Virginiak. I really don't."

"It's a funny business," I told him again.

He shook his head.

"In our line of work," I explained, "descriptions of personnel are classified." I shrugged. "Maybe it's silly, maybe it's not—but that's how it is. In any case, no one is accusing you of not doing your job."

He sighed. "Well," he said, "can you tell me what the man was doing here, at least?"

"Sure," I said. "Lieutenant Gilliam was conducting a background security check on a Military Academy applicant by the name of Falk. Roger Falk."

Fowler's thick eyebrows joined suddenly.

"The boy lived here," I went on, "for a year or so, back in '87, which was when his parents were divorced. He went to live in Oregon with his mother; that's where he is now. His father, Lee Falk, is a retired sergeant major who lives here in White Wolf . . . "

"I know the man," Fowler cut in. "And I knew the boy, too."

I nodded. "Good . . . "

"Lee Falk," he told me, in a softly warning tone, "won the Congressional Medal of Honor."

"I know."

"He's a good man."

"I imagine he is."

He leaned forward over his desk and frowned at me. "What kind of check are you doing on him?"

I smiled. "It's routine," I told him. "All West Point applicants who are being considered for appointment are subject to a preliminary background investigation. Lieutenant Gilliam was conducting it."

Fowler frowned at his desk top. "And he disappeared."

"That's right."

He thought about that for a moment, then looked up at me. "Maybe he went AWOL."

"That's not likely."

He frowned a bit more and sat back. "Okay," he told me. "So, what do you want me to do?"

"I'm not sure," I admitted. "Gilliam was seen after arriving at Ellsworth Air Force Base last Sunday night. I just came from there. He rented a 1989 blue Ford Thunderbird, and wrote on the invoice his destination as being White Wolf. After that, I don't know. I assume he drove straight here, which is when he should have checked in, but he didn't, as you know."

"This is Friday," Fowler complained. "Trail's gonna be real cold by now." He shook his head. "Your colonel didn't call me until yesterday."

I nodded and shrugged. "We didn't think there was a reason to be concerned, until yesterday."

Fowler sighed. "Well . . . "

"How many hotels in town?" I asked.

"Just one," he told me, thoughtfully.

"Only one?"

He nodded. "The other ski lodges close up after the season," he explained. "Only the Good Haven stays open year round." He shook his head. "But I already checked with them. After your colonel called. No one by the name of Gilliam—or anyone else for that matter—has checked into the Good Haven for more than a week."

"You told Colonel Chavez that there've been no reported accidents in the vicinity."

He chewed his lower lip, nodding vaguely, then asked: "Would he have been in uniform like you are?"

"Yes."

He worried his lip a second more, then shook his head. "I don't think he ever came here."

I nodded. "Well," I told him, "I have to go on the assumption that he did." I stood up. "I'll start with Sergeant-Major Falk, if you could give me directions to his house."

"He has a ranch, outside of town. Him and his nephew." He seemed to be considering something. "Tell you what, Mr. Virginiak," he said, getting to his feet, "I'll give you a ride out there myself, if you'd care to wait for a few minutes."

"I'd appreciate it," I told him.

He had me wait in the outer office where I killed the time looking over wanted posters tacked inside a glass case on the wall. Murder, armed robbery, and rape were common themes. The men depicted in the posters also seemed to share a common look—a vacant yet sullen stare—as if, by it, they were issuing a sort of silent warning.

I caught a glimpse of my own face reflected in the glass, and it had somehow taken on something of the same look. It took a conscious effort to remove it.

After about ten minutes or so, Fowler came out of his office and led the way to his marked van, next to which I had parked.

There was a ticket on my windshield.

Once inside the car I asked him: "Is he home?"

"Sure is," Fowler told me, giving me a brief look. "Said to come on out."

"Did he say anything else?"

Fowler laughed shortly. "He did mention that he hadn't seen your lieutenant friend, if that's what you mean."

"That's what I meant," I replied.

Fowler drove us quickly north, through a rather rundown, jilted-looking section of the town, then deeper into the valley along a rather narrow road that clung to the edge of the moving water.

"Falk's place is clear out the other end," he told me. "Don't get out there much, myself."

"Really."

He took this as a question and said, "I've known the Falk family all my life. Went to school with Lee. Him *and* his brother. I knew Lee's father, too."

"You know him well, then? Sergeant Falk, that is."

"To tell you the truth, not that well. Lee ran off to the army way back when, you know. Right after high school. Joined up right in the middle of Vietnam."

"I know."

He looked at me, then nodded. "Oh, sure," he said. "Well, anyway, he went off to the army, and as far as I know, he didn't come back until after his pa died. That was in '86 or so." He paused as the road began to switchback along the mountain. When it straightened out finally, we were beyond the valley and into a terrain of rolling, grass-covered hills. "I've only seen him a couple of times since then," he said.

"I see."

He looked at me. "We weren't really close friends or anything, and after he came back—well, I guess we didn't have too much in common, y'know. I guess people just change," he added.

Sometimes they do.

After another ten minutes of driving, Fowler turned down a deeply rutted dirt road that led into a narrow canyon, where he had to slow down considerably. After a few more miles the road spilled out onto a broad plain at the other end. There were cattle on either side of the road in rather large numbers, and men on horseback were worrying them.

"This all used to be Falk land," Fowler told me, waving a hand at the world outside the windshield. "This whole valley. Old Man Falk was as big a rancher as they get up this way." We made another turn, winding down into a heavily wooded glen. "But that's all done with."

"What happened?"

He sighed. "Well, after the old man died, he left the place to Lee, but Lee wasn't much of a rancher."

"I see."

"Him and his brother—" he looked over at me "—that would be Clement, they worked it for a while, but then . . . " He shrugged. "They had a lot of hard luck."

We passed through the section of trees, passed a collapsed wooden fence, and turned into a gate. There was an old sign on the ground leaning against the gate that read FALK RANCH.

"We're here," Fowler announced, pointing ahead.

At the base of a small tree-covered hill, I saw a rather homely one story ranchhouse that seemed to be leaning to one side. There was a burnt-out barn to the left of the house with an old Ford pickup in front and a dilapidated corral on the right in which an old brown mare was pretending to be confined.

"What sort of hard luck did they have?" I asked.

Fowler slowed the car as we moved down through a dirty looking stream that fronted the ranch house like a poor man's moat. "Well," he told me a bit uneasily, "Lee's wife—I think her name was Mary? Anyway, she took off with the boy, which you know. And then Clement died—that was about a year ago." He shrugged. "And now Lee's just sellin' off the land. Not workin' it at all."

We drove up out of the stream and into the waist-high weeds that choked the front yard, where Fowler parked. "Never thought he'd do that, you know. I mean, sellin' off the land." He shook his head. "I expect that's why the old man left it all to Lee in the first place, and not Clement. The old man must be turnin' in his grave."

There was no one in sight, and for a moment we stayed sitting in the car.

"Right after Lee came back," Fowler continued, "I came out, just to say hello. But he didn't have too much to say." He seemed to still be a bit puzzled by it, and a bit resentful as well.

"People change," I reminded him.

He grinned at me without much humor. "That they do," he said, opening his door. "That they do."

We got out of the van, and started toward the house, but as we did so, someone cursed loudly over to our left, and out from under the pickup truck in front of the barn a figure stood up in a small cloud of dust.

"Hello, Homer," Fowler said. "Long time no see."

A young sour-faced man wearing blue coveralls and a significant amount of dirt and grease and slapping dust from his clothes stared at us slackjawed.

"Your Uncle Lee around, Homer?" Fowler asked.

Homer's face soured a little more. Scowled at me.

"This is Mr. Virginiak," Fowler explained.

I nodded and smiled at him, but neither gesture provoked much pleasure from him.

Homer was a small man who wore his dark, dirty hair long and knotted behind his neck. He looked around twenty or so but was still battling acne in what appeared to be a losing fight, and his peeled back upper lip as he looked me over showed a line of small, rather green teeth. I guessed he had a hard time making dates.

"He's inside," he said. "Said you was comin'."

"Don't see much of you around town, these days, Homer."

Homer shrugged.

"Hope you're stayin' out of trouble."

Homer smirked.

Fowler slapped the hood of the pickup. "You be sure you get this wreck in shape before you put it on the road, Homer."

"I'm workin' on it," said Homer resentfully.

"You do that, boy," Fowler told him in a hard, official voice. "You do that."

The young man gave the White Wolf chief of police that look I'd seen on the faces in the wanted posters, then ducked back underneath the truck.

Fowler snorted, gave me a grin and a shrug, and was about to say something to me when the screen door to the house banged open and a man wearing bluejeans and a black Stetson pulled low over his forehead appeared on the porch. "That you, Max?"

"Howdy, Lee," Fowler replied, as we walked to the porch. "How've you been?"

I watched as the two men shook hands.

Sergeant-Major Lee Falk, United States Army (retired), was a small man himself, though taller than his nephew and with a good show of knobby, hardlooking muscle over his upper body and arms. He sported a wild growth of white-black beard, and his eyes, even in the shadow of the hat brim, looked almost as wild as they flicked toward me.

Fowler nodded in my direction. "This is the man I told you about, Lee, Mr. Virginiak."

Falk nodded and removed his hat, revealing a head of matted dark hair that was partially obscured by a wide red-checked bandanna he wore wrapped around his forehead. "Pleased to meet ya," he told me and started to hold out a hand for me to shake, but I came to attention and saluted instead.

This seemed to surprise him, and he returned my salute with a vague, hesitant gesture. "Well . . . " he said a bit self-consciously;

then he spotted Homer, who had crawled out from under the truck again and was gaping at us. "That's my nephew, Homer," he told me.

"We've met," I said.

"Lee . . . " Fowler began.

"Let's talk inside," Falk interrupted. "I got coffee on."

We followed him inside the house, into a large, cluttered, and somewhat dirty living room, where Falk indicated a relatively clutter-free divan for us to sit on. "Sorry 'bout the mess," he told us, rather unapologetically. "No woman round the place to clean up after us, if you know what I mean."

I told him I did, though I didn't, and sat on the musty smelling couch. Fowler said nothing, and stayed standing by a large smudged window that framed the weed garden in the front of the house.

"Coffee's fresh and hot," Falk said.

I went for it, but the chief declined.

After Falk had brought me a cup from the kitchen, he seated himself on the edge of a low coffee table piled with dirty breakfast dishes and looked at Fowler. "Ain't seen you in quite a spell, Max."

Fowler shrugged. "You know how it is, Lee."

Falk nodded.

"Heard you sold off Willow Valley," the police chief said sadly.

The sergeant-major nodded again. "Got a good price for it," he replied. "Weren't doin' me any good just holdin' onto it."

Fowler looked away, out the dirty window. "Still . . . "

Falk snorted. "I know, I know," he said quickly. He glanced at me. "Folks around these parts have this sentimental attachment to land like it was blood kin, or something." He snorted again, then smiled at Fowler. "It just ain't profitable for us small-timers any more, Max. Hasn't been for years."

Falk turned to me again. "My pa thought that way, too," he said, "but he was just plain wrong."

I nodded.

Falk sighed and sipped at his own coffee, then said to me: "So, what can I do for ya? What's this about some lieutenant?"

"Lieutenant Gilliam," I told him. "He worked in my section," I explained. "We're CIC. He was conducting a background investigation on your son Roger."

Falk's eyes squinted at me. "Roger? What's he done?"

"He's applied to West Point."

His squint eased, but he still looked a bit puzzled. "Oh," he said. "You didn't know?"

"No," he replied. "My son and I . . . Well, we haven't been very close the past few years. Since his mother took off with him, you know." He sighed. "I wish him well, though."

"Well," I said, "as I was saying, Lieutenant Gilliam was assigned to conduct a background check on your son, and he seems to have disappeared."

Falk frowned at me, then at Fowler. "Oh yeah?"

I asked: "You haven't been in contact with him, have you?"

He shook his head. "Nope. Can't say as I have."

"Nor with anyone else," I went on, "in the past few days, who might have inquired about your son?"

"Nobody."

I nodded toward the door. "How about your nephew?"

"I don't think so," he told me. "Let's find out."

Back out on the porch, Falk hollered to his nephew, who reluctantly left his work and came up to us. "Hom," Falk said to him, "you talked to anybody the past coupla days? This here man's lookin' for a frienda his. A lieutenant, name of Gillian."

"Gilliam," I corrected.

Falk smiled. "Yeah. Gilliam."

Homer shook his head. "Nope."

"No one at all?" I said

Homer snapped an angry look at me. "I said no."

"No need to be rude, boy," Falk said warningly.

Homer's mouth twisted into a smirk. "Is that all?" he asked his uncle.

Falk glared down at his nephew for a second, then waved a hand at him, and watched him turn back toward the pickup truck. "That boy," he said quietly, "is a real handful."

A peal of thunder, not too distant, cracked and echoed through the hills, and then a gusty set of breezes began whipping about the yard.

"Looks like a real banshee is cookin' up," Falk said, stepping out into the weeds. He looked back at me and said, "Sorry I couldn't help ya."

"No problem, sergeant-major," I told him, then to Fowler I said, "I guess that's it."

I shook hands with Falk, then Fowler and I got back into his truck.

Fowler gave Falk a wave, and Homer, who had turned to watch us go, a nod. As he put the car in gear and started off, Fowler said, "That boy will come to no good."

"Oh?"

"Just a hunch."

I glanced out the back window and saw Falk standing on the porch looking up in the sky for his banshee. I couldn't see Homer. I said, "Has he been in any trouble before?"

"Some," Fowler said. "Back when he was in high school. But he's got a mean streak in him just like his pa."

"That would be Sergeant Falk's brother?"

"Yeah."

"You mentioned he was dead."

He nodded. "Last year. Took a fall from a horse up in the high plains." He pointed vaguely back over his shoulder. "Broke a leg. Died."

"Died of a broken leg?"

"His horse run off, and he couldn't get back down." He shrugged in a leisurely way. "Wolves got to him."

I stared at the policeman for a moment, then said, "You don't miss him, do you?"

Fowler laughed, "No," he told me, shaking his head. "I don't miss him a'tall."

It seemed as though an explanation would be forthcoming, but it didn't happen. I was tired of talk then, anyway, so I didn't press.

We drove on in silence.

I didn't know where my next move in looking for Gilliam would be, and my mind, since talking with Falk at least, seemed to have shifted into neutral. If I couldn't get a lead on him, the FBI would have to be called in, which was something both Chavez and I would prefer to avoid but I had no ideas at all. At least, not very coherent ones. The fact of the matter was, I was starting to have uncomfortably morbid thoughts.

In fact, when we were back on the valley road, just as several sharp rolls of thunder rattled the world, I had a sudden image of Gilliam lying dead in a ditch with a bullet in his back.

Which didn't mean a thing, of course, except perhaps that I was tired and hungry, and not a little frustrated.

The sky overhead was darkening and lively with storm clouds as we got close to town. We made the outskirts just as the rain started to fall. By the time we pulled up to the police station again it was pouring.

"So, what next?" Fowler asked me as he parked the van next to my car.

"I don't know," I told him. "I'll call in to my CO and see what he wants done. In the meantime I'll need a place to stay."

"That'll be the Good Haven," he said, and he gave me directions.

When we got out of the car, he spotted, then grabbed, the now soggy parking ticket from my windshield and said, pointing to the plainly visible NO PARKING sign on the sidewalk, "Don't you believe in signs, Mr. Virginiak?"

"Sure I do," I replied.

"Well?" he demanded, shaking the ticket at me in mock anger.

I shrugged. "I just don't worship them, that's all."

I found the Good Haven Inn, with no trouble.

It was a large, rambling building, cantilevered out on stone pillars in the mountainside above the town. Mammoth trees stood guard all around it, and two large red brick chimneys running up the walls at either end chugged black smoke into the black sky.

I parked my car in the mostly empty parking lot, got out my B-4 bag, and doubletimed in the rain up the flagstone steps to the front door, over which was a sign that read: WE RESERVE THE RIGHT TO REFUSE SERVICE TO *ANYONE!* Remembering my last words to Fowler, I stepped through feeling a bit nervy.

Just inside the door I was met by a floor-mounted menu that seemed to favor beef dishes. The menu guarded a well-lit but mostly empty dining room that opened to the right, and faced a darkened bar from which some country-western music was escaping to the left. Straight ahead was a wide stairwell, and beside the stairwell, behind a curved counter, was a large woman, heavily made up and leering down into the pages of *The National Enquirer*. She batted her eyelashes at me as I approached. "Table for one?" she asked.

"Probably," I told her. "I'd also like a room, if you have a vacancy."

She laughed soundlessly and turned out a registration book. "Always a vacancy here," she said, then added with practiced regret,

"This time ayear, we're always mostly empty. We do a good business, though, come the snow. You ski?"

"No, I don't."

"Me neither," she said, smiling. "I'm just too . . . uncoordinated or something. I just fall flat on my fanny when I try." She patted her rump in case I didn't know where her fanny was, and winked. "You know what I mean?"

"I think so."

She smiled dreamily, and said, "I'm Bess Dykstra, your innkeeper, by the way."

We shook hands and then I signed the register.

"Thirty-six fifty a night," she told me, after turning the register around to read my name. "Mr. . . . "

"Virginiak."

"Virginiak," she echoed. "That's not Irish."

"No, it isn't."

She smiled, then leaned forward over the counter, resting her large bosom over her folded arms so that it blossomed up through the top of her blouse. "Sounds like somebody who's crazy for virgins." Her tongue darted to the corner of her mouth. "Is that what you are?"

I laughed, and pointed to the sign on the wall behind her. "Just how selective are you?"

"Call me Bess," she said in a whispery voice, as if she'd found some double meaning in what I'd said.

"Do you refuse service often, Bess?"

She blinked, turned to look where I was pointing, laughed. "Oh, no!" she said, and shook her head. "That was my ex's idea. He was an idiot."

"How about last Sunday night?"

"Huh?"

"I'm looking for a friend of mine. It's possible that he might have been in White Wolf last Sunday night, and I was wondering if you might have seen him?"

One of her painted eyebrows arched. "Chief Fowler . . . " she said.

"Yes."

She nodded. "He came by the other day to check the register for some guy . . . " She frowned slightly, cracking the patina of makeup over her forehead.

"Lieutenant Robert Gilliam. United States Army," I said.

"That's it!" she told me, then shrugged. "But he never checked in." She moved the register back around to face me. "Look for yourself."

"What I'm asking, Bess, is it possible that he might have been refused service here? Were you full up, Sunday night?"

"We haven't been full up since March."

"I see."

"We're so strapped right now, that Jerry wouldn't have refused service to Bigfoot if he came through that door."

"Who's Jerry?"

"My son," she told me, with curious reluctance. "He works the desk here weekends."

"Is he around?"

She rolled her eyes. "No way! He tends bar till four, weekdays, and then he's gone. God forbid he should stick around to help out after four."

I picked up my bags.

"Can you find the room by yourself, honey?" she asked sweetly, dangling the room key close to her bosom.

I took the key from her hand and smiled.

"Room 22, just down the hall to the right at the top of the stairs," she said to my back. "Dinner till nine," she added hopefully.

I found my room, a large one choked with overstuffed furniture and with a window view of the valley. I showered, changed into civvies, and, after placing a call to my office back at Fort Lewis to let them know where I was, decided I was hungry.

The dining room by the time I got back downstairs held a good crowd, which, I assumed, was the mainstay of the inn's business during the off-season, and I had a good, if expensive, meal and half a bottle of a too dry Californian that made me drowsy.

I was in bed before ten, but despite the wine, sleep didn't come easily. A feeling that I'd forgotten something nagged at the corner of my mind.

A little after eleven I head a soft, tentative knocking at what could have been some other door but was probably mine. I was afraid it was Bess, so I stayed still as death and the knock was not repeated.

After that I fell asleep, and dreamed about being stoned by laughing children, who were slowly, but inexorably, turning into wolves.

* * *

A soft purring sound woke me at 0300, and it took me a moment to find the phone in the dark, strange surroundings.

It was Chavez, sounding impatient. "They found Gilliam."

"Gilliam?" I said. My mouth felt rubbery. "Where?"

"He's dead."

I stared at the glowing numbers on the face of my clock.

"Virginiak?"

I turned on a light to make sure I wasn't dreaming.

"Virginiak?"

"I'm here," I said, rubbing my face. "Did you say he's dead?"

"Some sort of accident," said Chavez irritably. "Are you anywhere near Beaumont?"

I thought about that.

"Virginiak?"

"I don't know. Hold on." I pulled out my roadmap, studied it for a moment, then said, "Yes, I am. It's about twenty miles or so north of White Wolf." I put the map away. "Is that where he is?"

"Yeah. The South Dakota state police just called the staff duty officer here. Gilliam put his car into a river somewhere." He sighed. "He's been in the water for a few days, they said."

"Oh, damn."

"Damn is right," he told me, then sighed again. "Hell, I hardly knew the kid."

"Neither did I."

"Yeah. Well . . . "

"You want me to go to Beaumont, sir?"

"Yes. He'll have some material with him we'll want back. They haven't pulled the car out yet, so I'm told."

"All right."

"And, you could identify the body."

"All right."

"Um . . . It's at the morgue which is located in something called the Beaumont County Criminal Justice Center."

"I'll find it."

"Right," he said.

And then—for just a second or two—when we should have had something to say in the way of mourning the loss of a man we worked with, we said nothing.

We hadn't really known him, so there was nothing to say—and we were both a little ashamed of that.

"Well," Chavez said finally in a rough-edged voice, "I'm going back to sleep."

"All right, sir."

"Um . . . call me, if something comes up," he added.

"Yes, sir."

"Right," he said, and then he hung up.

And for a while then, I stayed in bed, watching my travel alarm tick time on the dresser, and I tried to remember Gilliam.

But I was tired, and he was dead, and it didn't matter anyway.

I got up the next morning feeling rather irritable, and I took it out on my face while shaving. For some reason, the idea that Gilliam was dead because of some stupid traffic accident angered me more than the notion I'd had the day before of Gilliam lying sprawled in a ditch somewhere with a bullet in his back. Something about the meaninglessness of it all rubbed me the wrong way, and I nicked myself a couple of times on the chin and neck, talking to myself about it.

But then, my mood was more likely the result of an underlying self-reproach.

Lieutenant Gilliam had been the new man in the section. New in all respects, in fact. Newly commissioned and fresh out of the Field Intelligence Training School at Fort Huachuca, he had reeked of green enthusiasm—which meant, of course, that I, being the crusty old pro that I was, avoided him.

My SOP with new people on the job. Standing off. Keeping my distance. Letting them sink or swim on their own. And then—*only* then—if they showed some promise of ability and of lasting, would I stoop to help.

A tried and proven practice. Even Chavez did it.

And that was because, we would say to ourselves, we weren't in the business of winning friends. Our business was lonely stuff. Cold work—and only those who could work alone and in the cold were worth the effort of getting to know better.

And Gilliam had yet to prove himself.

And I was now remembering Gilliam, a friendly, willing, self-effacing young man whom I had not said ten words to in the six weeks he'd worked in my office.

A tried and proven practice.

How did I ever get to be such a jerk?

After getting dressed, I tried to decide whether to check out of the inn then or later. As I was fussing over that monumental problem, Fowler called.

He told me that he'd heard about Gilliam and offered to drive me to Beaumont.

I accepted the offer, and he said he was on his way.

On my way out the door I spotted a dark-haired young man behind the front desk whose eyes moved over me with a curious suspicion.

I nodded to him but got nothing back.

Good morning, White Wolf.

Outside, the rain had more or less quit, but there was a wet spring chill in the air that hunched my shoulders, and by the time Fowler pulled up and I got in, I was shivering.

"You cold?" he asked, knocking the heater up a notch.

"A bit."

"Helluva thing, isn't it?"

"Yes, it is."

Fowler moved us down the mountain road and onto the highway out of town. "We got the word this morning on the state police teletype." He glanced at me. "I'm sorry about this."

I nodded. "So's he."

We drove in silence until we came to the highway. Fowler turned left and headed north, where the countryside was less heavily wooded.

"Was Gilliam a friend of yours?" Fowler asked in a tentative way.

I sighed. "I hardly knew him," I admitted. "He'd just started with us."

"Was he married?"

"No," I replied. "He was quite young."

"Too bad."

"Yes it is."

After about a fifteen minute drive, which took us into a higher country, we crossed a bridge and turned west along a road which edged a section of the river that churned heavily and very rapidly. A bit farther on, the road turned up sharply, then down abruptly, and we came to a narrow hairpin bordered on one side by a steep, pine-shrouded hill and on the other by a hundred foot deadfall to the dark water below.

A pickup truck with police markings was parked on the shoulder, and two state policemen were standing by a flattened guard rail at the edge of the cliff, taking measurements.

Fowler pulled up beside the two men and asked for Captain Blaney.

"He's downriver," one of the men said, pointing farther west. "Where they pulled him out."

Fowler looked over the edge. "This where he went in?"

The state policeman nodded. "Sure is," he replied, then pointed to the road behind us. "Some skidmarks back there. Looks like he come over the hill too fast and just lost control."

Fowler nodded, then turned to me. "Want to take a look?"

I told him no, and he turned back to the state policeman. "How far downriver are they?"

"'Bout a half mile or so," he told Fowler. "River runs real strong all along here, y'know." He stared down at the muddy, boiling water. "Musta been a helluva ride."

Just beyond where Gilliam's car had taken its plunge, the road leveled, and ahead on the left, we could see state police vehicles and a crane down at the river's edge.

A few boats were circling in the water.

The crumpled remains of a 1989 blue Ford Thunderbird were at that moment being dragged, front end first, out of the river.

Fowler parked next to a truck, and a grayhaired man wearing a black poncho got out of it and walked over to us as we got out.

"Blaney," Fowler said, "this is Warrant Officer Virginiak."

The man nodded and stared at me. His face wore the practiced mask of a man who found himself at the scene of accidents quite often. It gave nothing away. No sympathy. No reproach.

I suspected it had nothing to give.

"We got told that only you gets the stuff in the car," he said to me.

I nodded back to him, then at the car in the river. "How did you find him?" I asked.

"Road patrol found the guardrail down yesterday afternoon," Blaney explained. "We planned to have a look-see today, but then some kids—" he pointed to a spot on the river about a hundred meters from shore where some rocks broke the surface of the brown torrent "—they was out in a dinghy last night, and they come across the car. It was hung up in them boulders." He tuned his blank-faced look back at me. "Kids pulled the body out themselves."

I nodded, and watched as Gilliam's car was pulled onto the shore, dragging a lot of mud and debris with it.

Blaney led us down to the river's edge just as one of his men opened one of the doors, spilling a lot of river out of the car in the process.

The car was in very bad shape.

"River runs real strong around here," Blaney said. "Musta pushed this thing around like a toy."

I looked in the front seat, which was a sea of oozing black mud. There was a leather lettercase on the floor, and I retrieved it.

Blaney's men dug through the rest of the car's interior but found nothing more. They popped the trunk with some difficulty and salvaged Gilliam's suitcase. We drained the briefcase and Gilliam's bag of water, cleaned them, and put them in Fowler's truck.

As we started to leave, Blaney came up to me and asked, rather apologetically: "You people will see to it that the next of kin gets notified, right?"

"We will."

"Thanks." And for just an instant the mask slipped, and his face showed weary relief.

A little before ten we arrived at the Beaumont County Criminal Justice Center, a new building situated in the center of Beaumont, which was a larger, cleaner looking town than White Wolf, about twenty miles west of the scene of Gilliam's accident.

The morgue, to which we were directed, was in a basement section of the building, and after we went through a door marked EXAMINATION ROOM: AUTHORIZED PERSONNEL ONLY at the foot of the stairs, I found Lieutenant Robert Gilliam, Counter-Intelligence Corps, United States Army.

He was lying face up on a shiny stainless steel table, opened from sternum to groin.

Fowler murmured something as we came into the room, and a man in a bloodied white smock who was poking at Gilliam's corpse looked up and said, "Can I help you?"

I held out my identification and stepped forward, looking down into the bloated face of the dead man.

"Is that him?" Fowler asked behind me. "Is *that* Gilliam?"

I nodded. "That's Gilliam," I said.

But only in a way.

Only in a way that lifeless flesh, naked bone, and bared brain could be said to be anyone.

"I'm Dr. Henke," the man in the smock said. "Did you know this man?"

"We worked together," I told him.

He put aside the bit of internal organ he was holding. "I'm sorry," he said quietly. "They wanted the autopsy hurried." He looked uncomfortable, as if we'd caught him in the act of doing something shameful. "I didn't know anyone would be coming in to . . . "

"How long's he been dead?" Fowler asked.

Henke shrugged. "Not that easy to tell," he replied. "Three or four days, at most."

"He drowned?"

"No," he said. "It looks as though his neck was broken before he hit the water." To me, as if I were the next of kin or something, he added softly, "He never felt a thing, after that."

I smiled at him.

Back upstairs I made all the arrangements for having Gilliam's body shipped and took possession of his personal effects, which included his wallet, keys, loose change, receipts—but nothing remarkable.

I called Chavez to let him know that I'd identified the body and that I would probably be on my way back to Fort Lewis that night if I could get a flight out of Ellsworth.

He seemed rather more impatient than he had sounded earlier, as if he had a thousand more important things to do than to talk with me, which, I supposed, was his way of dealing with his own feeling of guilt.

He got busy, and I got angry.

Fowler, who had been hovering around while this was going on, looked like a man with something on his mind, but he was having a hard time finding the words to tell me what it was. I didn't make it easy for him, however.

For some reason, I was taking it out on him.

When we got back in the car, and started back to White Wolf, he found his voice. "I wish you'd told me," he said harshly.

"Told you what?" I said matching his tone.

He glared at me, then floored the accelerator.

"What's the hurry?" I asked him.

He sighed with irritation. "I wish you'd mentioned that Gilliam was black."

I stared at him.

He tried to ignore me for a few seconds, then shifted on his seat uncomfortably. "I suppose you think it shouldn't make any difference."

"Does it?"

His mouth set in a grim straight line while he thought. When he spoke next, there was anger in his voice. "We've got some real hardcases in White Wolf," he said. "Real throwbacks, you know what I mean?"

"Not entirely."

He nodded. "Well, it may not mean anything, but . . . " He shook his head. "We'll see."

We got back to the Good Haven Inn at just before eleven.

Inside Fowler asked Bess Dykstra if her son was there. She gave him a startled look, then nodded toward the bar, which was closed.

We found him behind the bar, getting it ready to open.

"Hello, Jerome," Fowler said to him as we walked in.

Jerome Dykstra was the same scowling young man I'd seen at the front desk earlier, and his sneering nod at me when I entered the room behind Fowler indicated he also recalled the pleasure of our earlier meeting.

Fowler took a stool at the bar and I sat next to him. "This is Mr. Virginiak. Say hello to the man, Jerome."

Jerome looked from Fowler to me but said nothing.

Fowler sighed. "This is one of those throwbacks I was tellin' you about, Mr. Virginiak. A real diehard."

The young man began polishing shot glasses.

"Ran into an old friend of yours the other day, Jerome," Fowler said easily. "Homer Falk. He didn't say to say hello."

"He ain't no friend of mine," Jerome said quietly.

"Oh?" Fowler raised his heavy eyebrows in mock surprise, then turned to me. "Jerome here and Homer used to run together. Had them a kind of club." He frowned and bit his lip, turning back to Jerome. "What did you call yourselves, Jerome?"

The young man studied a glass he'd been rubbing.

"White Trash, wasn't it, Jerome?"

Jerome scowled at the policeman. "White First!" he corrected him.

Fowler nodded. "That's it. White First. How could I have forgotten?"

Jerome sighed and picked up another glass.

"You see," Fowler told me, "Jerome and Homer and a few other of their friends in high school, they got it into their pea brains, that they were . . . special, you know. Something about bein' white, and how that meant they were better than other folks." He paused and looked at Jerome, who still avoided the policeman's eyes. "Especially colored folks. Isn't that right, Jerome?"

Jerome didn't answer.

"In fact," Fowler continued, "it was Jerome here, and his old compadre Homer, who first saw the threat. White Wolf was bein' invaded. Mongrelized, isn't that what you called it, Jerome?"

"That's what it was," the young man confirmed matter-of-factly.

Fowler nodded. "Uh-huh."

Jerome looked at Fowler, then at me. There was a smirking grin on his face.

Fowler said: "This piece of crap and his friends used to run Saturday night raids over on the north side. Break windows, set fires—and if there were enough of them, and they happened to spot some inferior person out walkin' by himself, they'd break a few bones to get their point across." He glared at the young man, whose smile had gone. "Big brave boys, right, Jerome?"

Jerome tried not to, but he swallowed.

"Couple years back," Fowler told me, in a recovered conversational tone, "these white heroes raped a little girl. Fourteen years old. Little slip of a thing. They beat her and raped her, right outside her home."

Bess Dykstra had come in from the lobby and was hovering at the end of the bar, just within earshot.

"I arrested them," Fowler told me, "but they got away with it. The girl's parents left the state with her. I had no witnesses, so I had to let them go."

"That's ancient history!" Bess Dykstra piped up. "Jerry doesn't run with that crowd any more."

Fowler looked over at the woman and shook his head. "Bess," he said tiredly, "you don't know."

"What is all this?" Jerome whined.

Fowler turned back to the young man and said,"Last Sunday night or Monday morning a man came here, looking for a room for the night."

Jerome shrugged.

"He was a soldier. A colored soldier."

Jerome's mouth twisted. "So?"

"You turned him away, didn't you, Jerome?"

"He never did no such thing!" his mother snapped; then to her son she said, "You don't answer another question without a lawyer, Jerry. Do you hear me?"

Jerome smirked and shook his head.

"The man's dead, Jerome."

The young man's smile froze. "What?"

"Oh, God," Bess Dykstra moaned, then waved both hands at her son. "Not another word, Jerry, I'm gonna call Mr. Dennison now." She began backing slowly toward the lobby. "You got no right to question that boy any more, Maxwell Fowler. You just wait!"

We all watched her reluctant leaving, then Fowler said to Jerome: "Well?"

The young man blinked, frowned, then looked down at the bar cloth in his hands.

"Fine," Fowler snapped, and removed a pair of shiny handcuffs from his belt. He tossed them onto the bar top. "Come around the end of the bar, Jerome."

The young man looked up.

Fowler grinned at him. "Believe me, Jerome. If you make any trouble, I *will* enjoy it!"

Jerome stared at the handcuffs, swallowed, and shook his head. "I didn't do it."

"You have the right to remain silent, Jerome."

"I didn't *do* it!" the young man repeated. "I mean . . . I didn't *kill* him, for Christ sake. I just wouldn't rent him a room. Is that a crime?"

Fowler snorted. "Sounds like a crime to me." He waved a hand at the end of the bar. "Come around, Jerome."

"You know what I mean," Jerome shouted. "I just told the nigger to get out. That's all!"

"And what did he say, Jerome?"

"Nothin'! He just left."

Fowler looked at me, saw me shake my head, turned back to Dykstra. "We think you're lying, Jerome."

The young man made a sound with his lips.

"Jerome," Fowler said in a tight and genuinely angry voice. "You come around the bar, with your hands behind your head right this minute or so help me," he nudged the nightstick at his belt, "I'll come and get you the hard way."

The young man held up both hands. "Wait a sec, *will ya*!" He shook his head. "Jus' lemme think!"

"Jerome?"

"I've got witnesses!" Jerome said.

"Who?"

Jerome's eyebrows joined over his nose in a furious effort of thought. "I can't remember . . . "

"That's it," Fowler said quietly, removing his nightstick. He walked to the end of the bar, went around it, and started toward the young man. "Jerome, you worthless little turd, you are under arrest. . . . "

"I told him to go to Hacker Street," Dykstra whined, his hands up in front of him. "I told him we were full up."

Fowler paused in mid-stride and looked at me.

"Did he believe you?" I asked.

Dykstra shrugged. "How should I know?" he complained; then he saw Fowler start toward him again. "Okay! Okay!" he shouted. "He *didn't* believe me." He shrugged again. "But what could he do?" He looked from Fowler to me, then back to Fowler. "He left, and I never saw him again. I swear to God!"

"What's Hacker Street?" I asked.

"I know it," Fowler told me. He turned to Dykstra. "Did you give him directions, Jerome, or did you think he'd get there by some divine insight?"

"Huh?"

"Did you tell him how to get there, Jerome?"

He nodded. "Yeah, sure I did. I told him there was a rooming house there for . . . his kind." He looked over at me. "I really did try to help him, you know."

"I'm sure."

"I *did!*"

I slid off the bar stool and looked at Fowler.

The policeman nodded at me, then looked at Jerome, and then at his nightstick with a certain wistfulness. Finally he put it away. "I might be back, Jerome," he told the young man. "So don't make any plans."

The north side of White Wolf, which we had skirted on the way out to the Falk ranch, looked like a frayed edge of a garment that kept getting stitched back together instead of being replaced.

The buildings there were older, dirtier, with patchwork carpentry dotting the walls and graffiti everywhere, explaining the situation.

We crossed a double set of long disused railroad tracks and turned down a road that fronted what had been a riverfront train station at one time but was now a county-run shelter for the homeless. It looked as if it was doing good business. A little farther on we came to what appeared to be a warehouse, but that was where Fowler parked, next to several other cars, and we got out.

As we did so, however, the policeman tripped the siren switch on the dashboard, just for a second, so that a single but piercing *swoop* echoed down the deserted street. He looked at me and said, "Oops," then stood out in the middle of the street.

It was dead quiet.

"Woman by the name of Garbett runs this place," Fowler told me. "She doesn't like me much."

"Why not?"

He shrugged. "We've raided this place a few times." He waved an arm expansively around the area. "A lot of criminal activity going on down here. We try to clean it up. Not that it works for long."

I looked at him, standing there in the street, and he caught me staring at him. "Just a minute more," he told me, then grinned. "Gotta give 'em time to get ready for me, if you know what I mean."

I didn't at first, but then I heard a door slam somewhere deep in the building and I suddenly understood, and I started liking the big man for the first time.

"I guess they're ready now," he said finally.

We stepped through the outside door of the building. A sign bolted on the wall beside it read ROOMS TO LET FOR WORKING MEN, and a smaller, hand-painted piece of cardboard was attached to it: SEE NO. 1.

Inside the door, warm, heavy, and sour smells assaulted us.

There was a girl, about fourteen or fifteen, talking on the pay phone that hung on the wall by the entrance. She stopped talking and gaped at us as we walked past her.

Fowler knocked at the first door we came to, and it opened immediately, to the extent that it could given the heavy chain lock attached to it. A pair of wary eyes peered out at us, and the sound of a soap opera leaked into the air.

"Chief Fowler, Willa. Open up, okay?"

The eyes surveyed us for a second more, then the door closed sharply and opened again, this time all the way, revealing a thin, sharp-featured black woman of indeterminable middle to old age who stared at us with stony dislike.

"Willa," Fowler said. "How've you been?"

She made a sound with her mouth that was part raspberry, part sigh, then turned her back to us and moved into the room. We followed her and stood just inside the door while she seated herself in front of a small-screened TV in the middle of the single room apartment, next to a glowing electric heater, and ignored us.

"Willa . . . " Fowler began, but the woman waved a hand sharply at him and said, "Jus' a minute. S'almost over."

Fowler sighed, then shrugged at me and leaned against the wall by the door.

It was a very small studio, with very little furnishing. Against one wall was a narrow, metal-framed cot that was piled high with pillows; against the wall behind us were several racks of clothes, men's and women's dangling on metal hangers; on the left was a tiny kitchenette, with a tiny icebox, tiny sink, and two-burner stove. The TV, bracketed by the speakers of a disassembled stereo, was propped up on a cardboard box against the wall in front of us. Up above were two large blue-tinted windows which were partially covered by a pair of bamboo-slatted blinds. The ceiling was a maze of naked pipe, the floor littered with carpet remnants, and the walls with posters with sexual and music themes.

The tiny apartment simultaneously reminded me of factories, back alleys, storage closets, and garage sales, but it was clean, and had a fresh smell about it that didn't come from a can.

We stood and waited while the soap opera played itself out. After which the woman made a sound of disgust, then turned the set off and walked over to the kitchenette where she started a tea kettle going on the stove. She was ignoring us again.

"Willa?" Fowler said.

She stared at the wall over the stove for a second or two, then turned to face us, folding her arms defensively in front of her. She sighed wearily. "Whatchu want, Fowler?"

"This is Mr. Virginiak, of Army Counter-Intelligence," he told her, nodding at me.

"Nice to meet you, Mrs. Garbett," I said to her.

She didn't look particularly happy to meet me, however. "Okay," she said, cocking her head in my direction. "What*chu* want, then?"

I smiled. "Mrs. Garbett," I said, "did you rent a room to a man last Sunday night, or early Monday morning? An army officer by the name of Gilliam?"

She kept her arms crossed tightly. "Maybe."

"It's important," Fowler said.

"Why?"

"Because he's dead," I told her.

Her eyes widened.

"Did he stay here, Mrs. Garbett?" I asked.

"He's dead?"

"Yes."

"Oh," she said with genuine remorse. "It can't *be*!"

"It was an accident," Fowler said. "Out on Route 20."

She groaned again and went back to her chair. "That poor boy," she said. "He was so nice, too."

"He did stay here, then?"

She nodded, but her gaze had turned inward.

"How long?"

"Just the one night," she said. "Are you *sure* it was an accident?"

Fowler shrugged. "That's how it looks."

She snorted, then looked back at me. "When black folks die suddenly around this town it's always an accident."

"Come on, Willa," Fowler said.

"Come on, yourself!" she barked, then looked at me again. "You bein' a soldier. Were you a friend of that boy?"

"Yes," I told her, and felt my ears burn.

She nodded, then pointed a finger at Fowler. "Then you don't trust *any*thin' this man says, you hear?" She shook her head bitterly. "I've lived in this town more'n twenty years, and let me tell you, you don't trust the po-lice here. You just don't." She glared over at Fowler, who avoided her eyes. "I come from a cracker county in south Georgia," she continued, "and let me tell you, that was a *para*-dise compared to this stinkhole."

Fowler sighed again.

"So you don't trust that man!" she told me again. "That is, *if* you really wanna know what happened to your friend."

"I do want to know," I told her. "Could I see the room he rented?"

"Hmmph," she said, then stood up. "It's down the hall."

We followed her down to a small, cell-like room at the back of the building and went inside for a look, but there was nothing to see there except for the last steel-framed cot Lieutenant Gilliam would have slept in, the sink where he'd last shaved, and the dirty mirror over it where he had his last look at himself.

Back in the hall, I asked her if Gilliam had had any visitors.

"No," she told me, flicking a glance at Fowler. "I run a clean place here, no matter what *he* may have told you."

"How about phone calls?"

"I don't think so."

"What time did Gilliam check out?"

She shrugged. "It was around noon," she replied. "Said he was goin' to Beaumont."

"Did he say why?"

She blinked at me. "Yes," she said. "He'd asked me where the Bureau of Records was, and I told him that it was at the county seat. Over in Beaumont."

"The Bureau of Records?"

She nodded. "That's it. Said he wanted to check out births and deaths," she said, then frowned. "Does that help?"

It didn't, but I thanked her, and Fowler and I started out.

At the doorway, the girl on the telephone was just hanging up, and she gave us both a suspicious look as we let her leave the building in front of us. As she did so, I noticed the graffiti on the wall beside the telephone—doodles, obscenities, names, and numbers—one of which caught my eye.

Not that it was a number familiar to me, and not that it was written in a hand that I recognized.

But there was something about the number that caught and held my attention for a moment—triggered by a memory or idea, harbored well below the surface of my conscious mind—all I could do was stare at it stupidly for a few seconds until Fowler asked me if I was coming.

Back in Fowler's car, the policeman seemed uncomfortable. He said, "I told you she didn't like me very much."

"You were right about that."

He looked at me. "Believe it or not, I've never given her reason to think the way she does of me. The old chief might have, I don't know, but I've never done my job any more or less down here than I do above Hacker Street. Believe me."

"I do," I told him.

He looked at me and nodded. "So what now?"

"I guess that depends."

"On what?"

"On whether you think Gilliam simply had an accident, or something else."

He chewed at the inside of his lower lip and said, "You're thinking about that Dykstra kid?"

"You know him better than I."

He sighed. "Unfortunately, I do. I've been around trash like that all my life, Mr. Virginiak. Occupational hazard." He sighed again and looked at me. "But I think Jerome was telling the truth. He just isn't that good a liar, you know?"

I nodded. It had sounded like the truth to me, too.

He started the car and headed us back toward the inn.

I said, "You mentioned that Dykstra and Homer Falk had been friends."

"Right," he agreed. "Maybe not *real* friends, though. Homer is kind of a hick, if you know what I mean. Not the sort of kid a snot nose like Jerome would normally have anything to do with. But in high school their 'common interests' brought them together, I guess. They probably haven't laid eyes on one another since then."

I lit a cigarette.

Fowler looked at me. "This background investigation," he said. "On Roger, I mean. Will you be conducting it now?"

"No," I told him. "But someone will."

He nodded. "It's just that I don't want you to think that Roger Falk is anything like his cousin." He said with certainty, "Roger was a real good kid."

"Okay."

"Not like Homer at all."

It had started to rain again, and Fowler had to slow the van. "Homer'd probably be in prison if it wasn't for Lee," he said.

I looked at him.

"After Clement died," said Fowler, "Lee put a tight rein on the boy. He's hardly ever in town any more—which is a good thing. He's got some bad blood in him."

"Really."

He nodded again. "Clement—that was Homer's pa. He took off himself about a year or so after Lee went into the army." He paused to squint into the past. "I think the old man just kicked him out, but I don't know for sure. He'd always been pretty wild. Smart in a wily kind of way, but bad-tempered. Got fighting mad, real quick. Always lookin' for a fight." He maneuvered the van back onto the main street of White Wolf even more slowly. "Anyway," he went on, "next I heard, Clement was doing time in the Nevada State Penitentiary for armed robbery. After that I heard he did some time in Utah for manslaughter. When he came back, about seven, eight years ago, he had a wife and little boy with him, and the old man let them stay out at the ranch."

He paused to squint again at the memory. "Funny. I don't remember her name. Homer's ma, that is. Small woman. Pretty, I recall. I don't know why she stayed with him. We'd get a call at least once or twice a year from the county hospital about her. We'd go over and question her, and she'd be all beat up, but she wouldn't sign a complaint. I don't understand women like that. Do you?"

"Not really," I admitted. "But then I don't understand men like that either."

"Yeah. Well. She died. Then Old Man Falk died, and Homer—he was about seventeen or so—he went a little wild himself. Lee had come home by then. Brought his own wife and boy with him, but she took off after about a year."

"And then Clement fell off his horse," I said.

"That's right," he said. "It hasn't been an easy life for the Falks."

Back at the Good Haven's parking lot, I asked Fowler: "You've been doing a lot of talking about the Falk family."

"They keep coming up."

"Do they?"

He frowned at me.

"What I mean is, is there some reason they're on your mind? Something you should tell me?"

He scratched his head self-consciously. "Nah. I'm just gettin' old. Runnin' off at the mouth is gettin' to be a bad habit of mine."

I opened the car door, but he put a hand on my arm and said, "What do you think Gilliam was doing going to Beaumont?"

"Verifying the personal histories of immediate family members is a routine part of any background check. It was part of his job." I got out of the car, closed the door, then said to him through the window, "Thanks for squiring me around, chief. I guess I'll be leaving myself now."

He squinted at me, as if he might have something else to say, but then held out his hand. "Nice meeting you, Mr. Virginiak."

I shook his hand. "Same here, Chief Fowler."

After booking myself on a flight out of Ellsworth, later in the day, I checked out of the Good Haven Inn, and I had little to say to Bess Dykstra doing so. She took my money and gave me a receipt, and although I was hungry and the dining room beckoned with some heady smells, I left.

I reserved the right to refuse being *served* by anyone.

I found a coffee shop in the middle of town, and had a hamburger, fries and several cups of coffee, killing the time until the moment I would have to leave White Wolf—without having punched anyone in the face, which was what I felt like doing.

I was *not* in a good mood.

I'd brought in my briefcase, which contained Gilliam's own smaller letter case. Though still damp, it was not dripping wet and, having nothing else to do, I went through it.

Inside was a wet manila folder, containing his travel orders and the file on Roger Falk. There was the picture of the young man stapled to it. He looked as fresh and as eager as he should have.

There was also a copy of the service record and a picture of his father—the sergeant-major—a good Xerox of an eight-by-ten service photo, in full dress, his medal of honor standing by itself over his left pocket. Some water spots had puckered his face, but he had the same wild black eyes.

Falk looked a bit younger in the picture than he had in person, but the beard, and a few added years accounted for that. A few years, and a lot of grief.

I put the folder away, and looked through Gilliam's wallet again. Sticking up out of the billfold was a receipt for his rented automobile. At the bottom of the receipt he had signed his name, and added his social security number under that. . . .

I don't know how long I sat there, staring at the number, but my coffee had gone stone cold by the time I got out of there.

The street outside Willa Garbett's roominghouse seemed more alive when I drove up. There were children playing in the street, and some semi-adults lounging against the walls scowled at me as I went past.

I parked and moved by a cluster of teens who were standing in front of the rooming house "listening" to a multi-speakered ghetto blaster at full crank and stepped inside.

On the wall, above the pay phone, was the number.

I couldn't say when I might have noticed it, or why such a thing would have lodged itself in some synaptic crevice of my brain, but it was there.

At some time, on some occasion, during the short time Lieutenant Robert Gilliam had worked in our office, I had seen something, some log, some report—something—on which he had written a number referring to some quantity or time, I don't know, but that number had contained a zero, a zero, with the same diagonal curlicue as the zero on the wall above the pay phone.

There was a telephone book dangling from a chain underneath the telephone, and I looked for Lee Falk's listing first.

The number was his.

I leaned against the wall and tried to think what this told me, but beyond the fact that Gilliam had written the sergeant-major's number on the wall, nothing came to mind.

Falk had told me that Gilliam hadn't called, and there was no reason I could think of why he would lie. On the other hand, calling ahead would be what I would have done had I been Gilliam.

The door behind me opened just then, and Willa Garbett trundled through with an armful of groceries.

She blinked at me suspiciously for a second, then recognized me. "You back?"

"Yes," I said, putting down the phone book and taking one of her parcels.

She snorted and opened the door to her apartment. "You come back to make a call, boy?"

"No," I said. "Mrs. Garbett . . . "

"Willa," she said with a smile, taking her parcel back.

"Willa, did Lieutenant Gilliam mention that he might go somewhere else before going to Beaumont?"

"No," she said. "He said he'd already conducted his business here in town, and that he had to go to Beaumont to check somethin' out."

"He had gone out *earlier*, then?"

She blinked at me. "Acourse he did. Didn't I say that?" She tapped her head. "I didn't, did I? I'm sorry. I plumb forgot . . . "

"Did he say where he had gone to conduct his business?"

She frowned at me. "No," she said. "I don't think so."

I waited while she frowned a bit more, but then she shook her head. "No," she said. "He didn't say. He went out early, though, about seven or eight. Got back around eleven, just when *World* comes on."

"Did he make any calls, that you know of?"

She shook her head slowly.

Back in my car, I decided to see Fowler again. I didn't know where my thinking was headed, but I needed someone to talk to, so I drove to the police station where I was told the chief was out.

I drove around the small smudgy town for a while, then slowly made my way back out onto the highway where I turned left toward Beaumont.

Beaumont was where Gilliam had been headed. The Bureau of Records. I didn't know what I was going to do there, but that's where I decided to go.

I never made it.

At the hairpin turn where Gilliam's car had gone into the river, Captain Blaney and the two officers who'd been there earlier were walking about fifty meters up the road from the collapsed guardrail.

Blaney didn't seem surprised to see me. He wouldn't. He said, "You just missed Chief Fowler."

"He was here?"

He nodded. "Just left," he told me, pointing to a spot near a dented section of guardrail. "That's where we found the glass."

I got out of my own car and looked where he pointed. "What glass?"

"Thought you'd know." He led me to his car. From the trunk he pulled out a paper sack which held broken glass. "Chief Fowler called me about an hour or so back. Said that your friend's accident mightn'ta been one after all."

"Oh?"

He jiggled the bag of glass. "This here is glass from a headlight—but it ain't from your friend's car."

"I see."

"The T'bird's lights were covered." He put the bag away, then led me to where one of his men was measuring the faint outline of a skidmark. "Coulda been this way," Blaney told me. "Your friend was comin' down the hill and got bumped from the back." He pointed to the dented guardrail. "Looks like he slammed into that sideways. We got some paint residue outa them scratches, and it could be the same as the T'bird's."

"How about from the back of his car?"

He nodded. "I just called in to the yard and they're goin' over it now."

I looked over the scene and tried to imagine something innocent, but it was hard. "If Gilliam's car hit here, I don't see how it could have carried on through the guardrail down there."

"Neither do I," Blaney agreed. "Unless it was pushed."

I tried to imagine that, and it was easier to do so. I looked at Blaney. "This could simply be evidence from some previous accident here. Something old."

Blaney shrugged. "Maybe—but Fowler's got the scent of something." He looked at me with something approaching curiosity in his face. "You got any ideas?"

I shook my head. Not because I didn't have any ideas but because I had too many. I asked, "Did Fowler say where he was headed?"

"Not to me."

"Can you call in to his station and find out if they knew where he's gone?"

He could and he did, but Fowler had not called in.

* * *

I left Blaney and his men there in the road, and drove back to town. In front of the police station, Fowler's truck was still gone, so I took his stall, intending to go inside to wait for him, but instead I just sat where I was and tried to sort out what was likely from what was possible—but that wasn't easy.

What was most likely, I knew, was that Fowler knew something that I didn't. It was something Gilliam himself had probably known as well.

Something that made his death mandatory.

But I couldn't imagine what that was.

I did know, however, one thing that Fowler didn't—and that was the fact that Gilliam had made a trip that morning before he left for his date with the river, but there the possibilities became too vast in number.

Where had he gone?

Gilliam's letter-case was beside me on the car seat, and I spilled out its still damp contents once again.

Lee Falk's service photo caught my eye.

The water spots had dried, and where a large one had somewhat marred the grainy pixels of the Xerox, just over his left eye, I saw something I hadn't noticed before. Falk had a small, half-moon shaped scar in his forehead that cut down into the top of his eyebrow.

I stared at it for a moment—then I turned the picture over.

Homer Falk was just emerging from the ranchhouse as I drove into the yard. He was holding a suitcase in his hands, and he put it down on the porch and stared at me as I parked, got out of the car, and approached him. "Uncle Lee ain't here," he told me suspiciously.

"Do you know where I could find him?"

He shook his head. "Uh-uh."

I waved a hand at the suitcase. "Going somewhere, Homer?"

He didn't answer. Instead he picked up the suitcase, tossed it into the back of the pickup—which was parked in front of the stairs and was already piled high with various household goods—then stalked back into the house.

While he did so, I checked the front of the truck.

The front bumper and grille had clearly been caved in and then pounded back into serviceable condition. Also, the left headlight was so new it still had a price marker stuck into one corner.

Homer took his time coming out again, and when he did, he was carrying a short black tire iron in his hands. He seemed a bit impatient at finding me still there. "What do you want around here anyway?" he demanded.

"I want to ask your uncle some questions, Homer."

He shook his head. "No, you don't," he said with certainty. "You wanna just get along. Believe me."

"Where *is* your uncle, Homer?"

"I don't know."

"When is he coming back?"

"I don't know."

I nodded. "Then I'll wait."

"No," he told me, hefting the tire iron in front of his chest in a semi-threatening way. "You better just get along now, before . . . "

"Before what, Homer?" I snapped at him, feeling somewhat angry.

He blinked, swallowed, then shook his head. "You're makin' a big mistake, fella . . . "

"Really?" I said, climbing the stairs, and watching him back to the door. "I don't think so, Homer."

He swallowed again and let the tire iron drop to his side. "Look . . . "

"Have you seen Chief Fowler, Homer?"

He shook his head. "I'm tellin' you, mister . . . "

I stepped closer to him. "You're not telling me anything, Homer. Not so far. But you will. I promise you that."

The young man drew himself up and glared at me.

"There's a man dead, Homer. The man I asked you about yesterday. Remember?"

Homer's eyes narrowed.

"Somebody ran him off the road," I told him. "Somebody rammed his car from behind and he went into the river." I nodded toward the pickup. "You wouldn't know anything about that, would you, Homer?"

His brow furrowed. "You're lyin'."

I poked him then, in the chest with a stiff finger, and he stepped back, his eyes suddenly filling with tears of anger and fear. "Back off!" he said hoarsely.

I felt a little ashamed of myself, but I prodded the young man again. "The man's *dead*, Homer."

He took a few deep ragged breaths. "Okay!" he complained. "*Okay!*"

I closed on him again. "Tell me what you know about it, Homer."
He swallowed hard, and looked away from me. "Back off, will ya."
"Talk to me, Homer."
"Jesus!" he said in exasperation, moving sideways to get away
from me. "He was only a nigger, you know!"
I dropped my hands, and took a step back. "Really," I said to him.
He looked at me.
"Now, how did you know he was black, Homer?"
He swallowed, then frowned at me for a moment as his mind sifted
through the lies and tried to come up with another—but he finally
gave up. "Leave me alone," he said roughly, and he tried to get past
me to the door. "Get outa my way."
I blocked his path by putting out a hand, but he knocked it down,
then turned on me, suddenly, swinging wildly with the tire iron. I
grabbed his wrist, and turned his hand to his face as hard as I could,
and the tool spun out of his grasp and into the dirt beside the porch. I
twisted and bent the joint of his wrist until he went to his knees, and
let out a thin yelp. I said, "Where's your uncle, Homer?"
"I don't know!" he wailed. "I swear!"
"Where's Chief Fowler?"
He started to sob. "It hurts," he pleaded. "It hurts!"
"Why did you kill Lieutenant Gilliam?"
"I *didn't*!" he yelled. "I never killed *nobody*. I swear I didn't!"
I bent his wrist back a centimeter more.
"It hurts!" he screamed.
"Homer," I told him. "You don't know what hurt is—"
Just then, a car pulled up very fast into the front yard.
It was Fowler's squad car, but Fowler wasn't driving.
I released the boy, who whimpered and moved away from me, and
watched as the car stopped and Falk got out holding a pump-action
shotgun and grinning from ear to ear. He was hatless and wearing no
bandanna this time.
There was also no scar in his left eyebrow.
"Well, well, well," he said to me, motioning me away from Homer.
"Nice to see you again, Mr. Virginiak." He looked down at Homer,
who was sitting on the ground by the pickup. "Whatchu doin' down
there, boy?" he asked pleasantly. "This man here givin' you a rough
time?" He looked back at me, and motioned again with the barrel of
the gun. "Hands behind your head."

I did as he told me. "Where's Fowler, Clement?"

He peered at me, then nodded at the car. "He's in the back seat," he said "Whyn't you have a look?" He jerked his head toward the car, and I went.

Fowler was on the back seat, slumped over on his side. His face was bloodied and he was handcuffed.

"Is he dead?" I asked.

"Not yet," Falk told me, then to his son he said, "Hom, get yer ass up outa there."

"Yes, Pa," the boy replied, getting to his feet.

Clement Falk sighed. "Willow Stream was too damn low. The damn car wouldn'ta been covered." He snorted. "Damn good thing I come back when I did, eh, boy?"

"Yes, Pa."

"I had a better idea anyway," Clement said, nodding at his son. "Yer gonna have to help me."

Homer stared fearfully at his father.

"You hear me, boy?"

The young man licked his lips, looked at me, then shook his head. "Let's jus' go, Pa!"

His father glared at his son. "You'll do just as I say, boy. You hear me?"

Homer sobbed. "I don't want to kill *no*body, Pa."

Clement, still holding the barrel of the shotgun level at my chest, kicked angrily at Homer's leg. "Get aholta yourself, boy. I need you *now*."

"Don't do it, Homer," I said.

Falk's flinty eyes clicked back to me. "Shut up!"

"It's all coming apart, Clement. There's no point in getting the boy involved."

"You don't know what yer talkin' about."

"Don't I?" I looked at Homer. "You haven't killed anyone, have you, son?"

The young man blinked at me.

"It was your father who killed Lieutenant Gilliam, wasn't it?"

Homer swallowed, and looked down at the ground.

"Boy!" Clement snapped. "You pick up that tire iron."

Homer hesitated a second, then picked up the tool and looked at it.

Clement smiled and nodded. "That's right," he said. "We gotta make this all look right, Hom." He jiggled the weapon at me. "We gotta do him like I did Fowler."

Homer still stared silently at the tire iron in his hands.

"Then we take'em up to Mustang Ridge," Falk went on, "by the old boundary road—you know the one I mean, boy?"

"I know," Homer replied quietly.

Clement smiled again at me. "We gotta make it look just right."

"Like an accident?" I asked. "Another one?"

"Uh-huh," he said.

"Like your brother?"

He snorted. "You think you're pretty smart, don't ya?"

I shrugged. "It wasn't that hard to figure out," I told him. "You're not that bright. Too many accidents, Clement. First your brother to get the ranch, then Gilliam when he figured out you weren't Lee Falk, and now Fowler, and me." I looked at Homer. "He's going to get you hanged, Homer. Don't listen to him."

Falk smirked at me. "Go ahead and bash'im, boy. We gotta get goin'."

"Don't do it, Homer," I said.

Homer stood and stared at me.

"Hurry it up, boy!" Clement warned him.

"So far," I told the young man, "you haven't done any more than cover up for your father. That's something people can understand. That's something a jury could understand." I shook my head again. "But if you help him kill me, you're in it up to your neck."

"He's in it already," Clement barked, raising the shotgun to a level with my eyes. "Do it now, boy!"

"You're not involved, yet, Homer . . . "

"He is involved," Clement shouted. "Now shut up!"

Homer shook his head, still staring at the tire iron in his hand. "Pa . . . ."

"*Do* it, boy," Clement said, moving closer to his son and giving him a nudge with the stock of the shotgun. "*Do it!*"

Homer looked at his father for a second, then took a step toward me.

"Think, Homer," I told him. "Think!"

Homer stared at me, and hesitated.

"Boy," Clement snapped, moving the barrel of the gun against his son's shoulder. "Do you hear me?"

Homer blinked, looked down—then suddenly swung the tire iron up and then down on top of the shotgun's barrel. The gun went off, its blast digging a hole next to my left foot and sending a few stinging pellets into my ankle.

The gun, however, had been knocked from Falk's grasp, and the kick of the weapon sent him backward a few steps. He cursed, then lunged forward toward the weapon, but by that time I was standing on it. He tried to pull it out from under my feet, but I pushed him away.

"Don't hurt him," Homer said to me. "Okay?"

Clement roared with rage and came at me with his head down. I snapped him upright with a knee under the chin, then I put him away with an open hand to the throat, and another in the solar plexus. He collapsed in the dirt, gagging and gasping; I picked up the shotgun.

Homer knelt beside his father. "I asked you not to hurt him."

I found another set of handcuffs in Fowler's Bronco, and put them on Falk, moved him to the back seat of my car, and told him that I'd shoot to kill if he got out. He seemed to believe me.

Which is a good thing because I was still in a bad mood and I think I meant it.

I ordered Homer to the porch. He was obedient enough, and seemed a little relieved that I didn't put him with his father.

Before calling the station for help and an ambulance, I performed a little first aid on Fowler, who had a dangerous looking wound just over his eye. It appeared survivable, though. I also did some work on myself, but the pellets from the shotgun blast had merely torn up a little skin over my ankle.

By the time the ambulance and two additional squad cars had arrived, Fowler was conscious, but he remained on the back seat of the Bronco until the paramedics got him on a stretcher, and then the both of us into the ambulance.

Captain Blaney had arrived by then and took charge in his quiet, unflappable way. Homer, handcuffed and with his head down, was walked past his father to one police vehicle, and his father cursed him and his mother in a low, measured, and menacing way that made me feel sorry for the young man.

"You say that kid helped you take Clement?" Fowler asked me as we watched from the window of the ambulance.

"He did that."

Fowler sighed raggedly. "I was sure wrong about that boy."

"Not entirely, I think."

"But you don't think he knew his father killed Gilliam?"

"He had to suspect what his father had done, but he did seem surprised when I told him Gilliam was dead." I sat down on the stretcher across from Fowler. "Anyway, it fits with what we've seen. Clement Falk doesn't seem like the sort of man who'd leave serious work to someone else."

The rear door of the ambulance closed, and I lay down. My ankle was starting to throb. I looked over at Fowler and said: "Why didn't you tell me that Lee and Clement Falk were twins?"

"It didn't occur to me."

"Really?"

He turned his good eye toward me. "Really," he insisted. "The fact is, I don't recall that they looked identically alike. I remember Clement as being . . . bigger, somehow." He shook his head, wincing at the pain. "But that was twenty-some-odd years ago," he added in a soft, tired voice. "I should have figured it out."

"You did."

He laughed shortly. "Right," he said. "A little late, though." He winced at the pain, then pressed gingerly at the compress over his eye. "When Willa said that Gilliam had been on his way over to Beaumont to check on births and deaths, it got me to thinkin' about it. I don't know what Gilliam suspected—if anything—but it did get me to thinkin' about how maybe Clement had a pulled a switch." He paused. "Clement might have done Lee, too."

"It's possible. Maybe Homer knows."

Fowler took a few deep breaths. "But it was the truck that bothered me most. It had been botherin' me ever since I seen Gilliam's car. I went back to where the car went over and found some glass . . . "

"I know."

He gave me a curious look, then sighed. "Anyway, I put a call in to Blaney, and after he got there, I just had to come back and have a look at the damage on the pickup."

"Something else you didn't mention."

His good eye turned toward me again. "Hey," he said. "You're not on the city payroll."

"I did have an interest in this, you know."

"Yeah. Well. Things were coming together pretty fast." He shrugged. "I didn't want to make an accusation until I'd had a chance to talk with Homer. I never got the chance, though. Clement jumped me while I was looking over the pickup . . . " He paused suddenly and looked at me "Hey! What brought *you* out here?"

"As soon as I knew Clement and Lee were twins . . . "

"And how did you know *that*?" He had propped himself up on one elbow, so I reached over and pushed him back down. "Well?"

"A couple of things."

"Like what?"

"You remember when we came out here yesterday," I said, "and I saluted Falk?"

"Uh-huh."

"Well, that's a pretty standard military courtesy, given to CMH winners. They get a salute, regardless of rank, and Falk should have been used to it. But he seemed just a bit too surprised by it—and then he just kind of *waved* back at me. Remember?"

"Yeah. So?"

"Sergeant-Major Lee Falk had been the command sergeant-major of a basic training regiment at Fort Dix, New Jersey, for three years before his retirement. The last thing he would have gotten sloppy about is a salute, no matter how long he'd been out of uniform."

"Well?"

"Then there was Lee Falk's picture."

He frowned at me. "What picture?"

"Gilliam had one in his lettercase. When I finally looked at it closely, I could see that there was a scar in the eyebrow, just over his left eye. It was hardly noticeable, but it was there—and Clement had been wearing that bandanna pretty low on his forehead when we talked to him yesterday. Thinking back, I figured he could have been trying to hide something—something that wasn't there."

"Gilliam musta seen that there was no scar," Fowler muttered.

I nodded. "That's what probably tipped him off that the man he was talking to wasn't who he said he was." I shook my head. "He must have asked Falk about it. I don't know. But somehow Clement realized that Gilliam suspected something." I shrugged. "So Clement followed him. Back to town, waited for him to leave the rooming house and get on the highway to Beaumont, and then ran him off the road. Probably killed him before he put the car in the river."

Fowler frowned at me for a moment. "Wait a minute. All this . . . it only tells you that *maybe* the man you met yesterday wasn't Lee Falk. It doesn't tell you that Lee and Clement were twins."

"That's true."

"So? How did you figure it out?"

"Well, for one thing, if they hadn't been twins, you'd have known it was Clement we were talking to yesterday and not Lee."

"Oh. Right."

"But you didn't know, so Clement *had* to be Lee's twin to fool you."

He was quiet for a minute. "I could have been in on it with him."

I looked at him. "It never crossed my mind."

Fowler grinned. "You know an honest cop when you see one, eh?"

"Not really."

"Oh?"

I smiled. "Gilliam had written the word 'twins' with a question mark on the back of Lee Falk's picture."

Fowler stared at me for a moment, then laughed. "You're some detective, Virginiak," he told me. "Some detective."

I started to laugh with him.

But then I remembered Gilliam—the real detective—a grinning, self-effacing young man, whom I never bothered to get to know and, now, never would.

And then, all I wanted to do was to forget the whole thing.

The Third Man

GRAHAM GREENE

When I saw Rollo Martins first I made this note on him for my security police files: "In normal circumstances a cheerful fool. Drinks too much and may cause a little trouble. Has never really grown up, and perhaps that accounts for the way he worshipped Lime."

I met him first at Harry Lime's funeral. It was February, and the gravediggers had been forced to use electric drills to open the frozen ground in Vienna's Central Cemetery. It was as if even nature were doing its best to reject Lime, but we got him in at last and laid the earth back on him like bricks. He was vaulted in, and Rollo Martins walked quickly away as though his long, gangly legs wanted to break into a run, and the tears of a boy ran down his thirty-five-year-old cheeks. Rollo Martins believed in friendship, and that was why what happened later was such a shock.

If you are to understand this strange, rather sad story you must have an impression, at least, of the background—the smashed, dreary city of Vienna divided up in zones among the four powers: the Russian, the British, the American, the French zones, regions marked only by a notice board, and in the center of the city, surrounded by the Ring, with its heavy public buildings and its prancing statuary, the Inner Stadt under the control of all four powers.

In this once fashionable Inner Stadt, each power in turn, for a month at a time, takes, as we call it, "the chair," and becomes responsible for security. At night, if you were fool enough to waste your Austrian shillings on a night club, you would see the International Patrol at work—four military police, one from each power, communicating with one another, if they communicated at all, in the language of their enemy.

I never knew Vienna between the wars, and I am too young to remember the old Vienna, with its Strauss music and its bogus easy charm. To me, it is simply a city of undignified ruins which turned, that February, into great glaciers of snow and ice. The Danube was a gray, flat, muddy river a long way off across the Russian zone. The Prater lay smashed and desolate and full of weeds; only the Great

Wheel moved, revolving slowly over the foundations of merry-go-rounds like abandoned milestones, the rusting iron of smashed tanks which nobody had cleared away, the frost-nipped weeds where the snow was thin.

At night, the kidnappings occur—such senseless kidnappings they sometimes seemed to us—a Ukrainian girl without a passport, an old man beyond the age of usefulness, sometimes, of course, the technician or the traitor. This was, roughly, the Vienna to which Rollo Martins had come on February 7 of last year.

A British subject can still travel if he is content to take with him only five English pounds, which he is forbidden to spend abroad, but if Rollo Martins had not received an invitation from Lime of the International Refugee Office he would not have been allowed to enter Austria, which counts still as occupied territory. Lime had suggested that Martins might "write up" the business of looking after the international refugees, and although it wasn't Martins's usual line, he had consented.

Rollo Martins's usual line was the writing of paper-covered Westerns under the name of Buck Dexter. His public was large but unremunerative. He couldn't have afforded Vienna if Lime had not offered to pay his expenses when he got there out of some vaguely described propaganda fund. He could also, he said, keep him supplied with paper *Bafs*—the only currency in use from a penny upward in British hotels and clubs. So it was with exactly five unusable pound notes that Martins arrived in Vienna.

An odd incident had occurred at Frankfurt, where the plane from London grounded for an hour. Martins was eating a hamburger in the American canteen (a kindly air line supplied the passengers with a voucher for 65 cents' worth of food) when a man he could recognize from twenty feet away as a journalist approached.

"You Mr. Dexter?" he asked.

"Yes," Martins said, taken off his guard.

"You look younger than your photographs," the man said. "Like to make a statement? I represent the local paper here. We'd like to know what you think of Frankfurt."

"I only touched down ten minutes ago."

"Fair enough," the man said. "What about views on the American novel?"

"I don't read them," Martins said.

"The well-known acid humor," the journalist said. He pointed at a small, gray-haired man with two protruding teeth, nibbling a bit of bread. "Happen to know if that's Carey?"

"No. What Carey?"

"J. G. Carey, of course."

"I've never heard of him."

"You novelists live out of the world. He's my real assignment." And Martins watched the journalist make across the room for the great Carey.

Dexter wasn't the man's assignment, but Martins couldn't help feeling a certain pride—nobody had ever before referred to him as a novelist; and that sense of pride and importance carried him over the disappointment when Lime was not there to meet him at the airport, nor at the Hotel Astoria, where the bus landed him, and no message—only a cryptic one for Mr. Dexter from someone he had never heard of called Crabbin: "We expected you on tomorrow's plane. Please stay where you are. On the way round. Hotel room booked." But Rollo Martins wasn't the kind of man who stayed around.

Martins had been given Lime's address, and he felt no curiosity about the man called Crabbin. It was too obvious that a mistake had been made, though he didn't yet connect it with the conversation at Frankfurt. Lime had written that he could put Martins up in his own flat, a large apartment on the edge of Vienna, so Martins drove straightaway to the building lying in the third (British) zone.

How quickly one becomes aware of silence even in so silent a city as Vienna, with the snow steadily settling. Martins hadn't reached the second floor before he was convinced that he would not find Lime there, and as he reached the fourth floor and saw the big, black bow over the door handle, he knew he would not find Lime anywhere in the world. Of course, it might have been a cook who had died, a housekeeper, anybody but Harry Lime, but Martins knew that Lime, the Lime he had hero-worshipped now for twenty years, since the first meeting in a grim school corridor with a cracked bell ringing for prayers, was gone.

After he had rung the doorbell half a dozen times, a small man with a sullen expression put his head out from another flat and told him in a tone of vexation, "It's no use ringing like that. There's nobody there. He's dead."

Martins, as he told me later, asked him, "When did it happen? How?"

"He was run over by a car," the man said. "Last Thursday." He added sullenly, as if really this were none of his business, "They are burying him this afternoon. You've only just missed a couple of friends and the coffin."

"Wasn't he in a hospital?"

"There was no sense in taking him to a hospital. He was killed here on his own doorstep—instantaneously."

"Where are they burying him?"

"In the Central Cemetery."

He had no idea how to pay for his taxi, or indeed where in Vienna he could find a room in which he could live for five English pounds, but that problem had to be postponed until he had seen the last of Harry Lime. He drove straight to Central Cemetery.

It was just chance that he found the funeral in time—one patch in the enormous park where the snow had been shoveled aside and a tiny group were gathered, apparently bent on some very private business. A priest had finished speaking, and a coffin was on the point of being lowered into the ground. Two men in lounge suits were at the graveside. A girl stood a little way away with her hands over her face, and I stood twenty yards away by another grave watching with relief the last of Lime and noticing carefully who was there—just a man in a mackintosh, I was to Martins. He came up to me and said, "Could you tell me who they are burying?"

"A fellow called Lime," I said, and was astonished to see the tears start to this stranger's eyes. He didn't look like a man who wept, nor was Lime the kind of man who I thought was likely to have mourners.

Martins stood there, till the end, close beside me. He said to me later that as an old friend he didn't want to intrude on these newer ones. As soon as the affair was over, Martins strode back to his taxi; he made no attempt to speak to anyone, and the tears now were really running. I followed him. I knew the other three; I wanted to know the stranger.

I caught him up by his taxi and said, "I haven't any transport. Would you give me a lift into town?"

"Of course," he said. I knew the driver of my jeep would spot me as we came out and follow us.

I said, "My name's Calloway."

"Martins," he said.

"You were a friend of Lime?"

"Yes." Most people in the last week would have hesitated before they admitted quite so much. "I came only this afternoon from England. Harry had asked me to stay with him. I hadn't heard."

"Bit of a shock?"

"Look here," he said; "I badly want a drink, but I haven't any cash—except five pounds sterling. I'd be awfully grateful if you'd stand me one."

It was my turn to say, "Of course." I thought for a moment, and told the driver the name of a small bar in the Kärtnerstrasse.

On the door was the usual notice saying the bar opened at 6 till 10, but one just pushed the door and walked through the front rooms. We had a whole small room to ourselves.

Martins said over his second quick drink, "I'm sorry, but he was the best friend I ever had."

I couldn't resist saying, knowing what I knew, and because I was anxious to vex him—one learns a lot that way—"That sounds like a cheap novelette."

He said quickly, "I write cheap novelettes."

I said, "Tell me about yourself—and Lime."

"Look here," he said; "I badly need another drink, but I can't keep scrounging on a stranger. Could you change me a pound or two into Austrian money?"

"Don't bother about that," I said, and called the waiter. "You can treat me when I come to London on leave. You were going to tell me about Lime and how you met him?"

The glass of liqueur might have been a crystal the way he looked at it and turned it this way and that. He said, "It was a long time ago. I don't suppose anyone knows Harry the way I do." And I thought of the thick file of agents' reports in my office, each claiming the same thing.

"How long?"

"Twenty years—or a bit more. I met him my first term at school. I can see the place. I can see the notice-board and what was on it. I can hear the bell ringing. He was a year older and knew the ropes. He put me wise to a lot of things."

"Was he clever at school?"

"Not the way they wanted him to be. But what things he did think up! He was a wonderful planner. I was far better at subjects like History and English than Harry, but I was a hopeless mug when it came to carrying out his plans." He laughed; he was already beginning, with the help of drink and talk, to throw off the shock of the death. He said, "I was always the one who got caught."

"That was convenient for Lime."

"That was my fault, not his. He could have found someone cleverer if he'd chosen, but he liked me. He was endlessly patient with me."

"When did you see him last?"

"Oh, he was over in London six months ago for a medical congress. You know, he qualified as a doctor, though he never practiced. That was typical of Harry. He just wanted to see if he could do a thing, and then he lost interest. But he used to say that it often came in handy."

And that, too, was true. It was odd how like the Lime he knew was to the Lime I knew; it was only that he looked at Lime's image from a different angle or in a different light.

He said, "One of the things I liked about Harry was his humor." He gave a grin which took five years off his age. "I'm a buffoon. I like playing the silly fool, but Harry had real wit. You know, he could have been a first-class light composer if he had worked at it."

He whistled a tune—it was oddly familiar to me. "I always remember that. I saw Harry write it. Just in a couple of minutes on the back of an envelope. That was what he always whistled when he had something on his mind. It was his signature tune."

He whistled the tune a second time, and I knew then who had written it—of course, it wasn't Harry. I nearly told him so, but what was the point?

The tune wavered and went out. He stared down into his glass, drained what was left, and said, "It's a damned shame to think of him dying the way he did."

"It was the best thing that ever happened to him," I said.

"You mean there wasn't any pain?"

"He was lucky in that way, too."

It was my tone of voice and not my words that caught Martins's attention. He asked gently and dangerously—I could see his right hand tighten—"Are you hinting at something?"

There is no point at all in showing physical courage in all situations; I eased my chair far enough back to be out of reach of his fist. I said, "I mean that I had his case completed at police headquarters. He would have served a long spell—a very long spell—if it hadn't been for the accident."

"What for?"

"He was about the worst racketeer who ever made a dirty living in this city."

I could see him measuring the distance between us and deciding that he couldn't reach me from where he sat.

"You're a policeman?" he asked.

"Yes."

"I've always hated policemen. They are always either crooked or stupid."

"Is that the kind of books you write?"

I could see him edging his chair round to block my way out. I caught the waiter's eye, and he knew what I meant—there's an advantage in always using the same bar for interviews.

Martins said gently, and brought out a surface smile: "I have to call them sheriffs."

"Been in America?"

"Is this an interrogation?"

"Just interest."

"Because if Harry was that kind of racketeer, I must be one, too. We always worked together."

"I daresay he meant to cut you in—somewhere in the organization. I wouldn't be surprised if he had meant to give you the baby to hold. That was his method at school—you told me, didn't you?"

"You are running true to form, aren't you? I suppose there was some petty racket going on with petrol and you couldn't pin it on anyone, so you've picked a dead man. That's just like a policeman. You're a real policeman, I suppose?"

"Yes, Scotland Yard, but they've put me into a colonel's uniform when I'm on duty."

He was between me and the door now. I couldn't get away from the table without coming into range. I'm no fighter, and he had six inches of advantage anyway. I said, "It wasn't petrol."

"Tires, saccharins . . . why don't you policemen catch a few murderers for a change?"

"Well, you could say that murder was part of his racket."

He pushed the table over with one hand and made a dive at me with the other. The drink confused his calculations. Before he could try again my driver had his arms around him.

"Listen, Callaghan, or whatever your bloody name is—"

"Calloway. I'm English, not Irish."

"I'm going to make you look the biggest bloody fool in Vienna."

"I see. You're going to find me the real criminal?"

"You can let me go, Callaghan. I'd rather make you look the fool you are than black your eye. You'd only have to go to bed for a few days with a black eye. But when I've finished with you, you'll leave Vienna."

I took out a couple of pounds' worth of *Bafs* and stuck them in his breast pocket. "These will see you through tonight," I said, "and I'll make sure they keep a seat for you on tomorrow's London plane."

"You can't turn me out. My papers are in order."

"Yes, but this is like other cities: You need money here. If you change sterling on the black market I'll catch up on you inside twenty-four hours. . . . Let him go."

Rollo Martins dusted himself down. "I'll be seeing you again when I've got the dope," he said.

"I might come and see you off tomorrow," I said.

"I shouldn't waste your time. I won't be there."

"Paine, here, will show you the way to Sacher's. You can get a bed and dinner there. I'll see to that."

He stepped to one side as though to make way for the waiter, and slashed out at me. I just avoided him but stumbled against the table. Before he could try again, Paine had landed him on the mouth. He went bang over in the alleyway between the tables and came up bleeding from a cut lip.

I had had a long day and I was tired of Rollo Martins. I said to Paine, "See him safely into Sacher's. Don't hit him again if he behaves."

What happened next I didn't hear from Paine, but from Martins a long time afterward. Paine simply saw him to the head porter's desk and explained there, "This gentleman came in on the plane from London. Colonel Calloway says he's to have a room." Having made that clear, he said, "Good evening, sir," and left.

"Had you already got a reservation, sir?" the porter asked.

"No. No, I don't think so," Martins said in a muffled voice, holding his handkerchief to his mouth.

"I thought perhaps you might be Mr. Dexter. We had a room reserved for a week for Mr. Dexter."

Martins said, "Oh, I am Mr. Dexter." He told me later that it occurred to him that Lime might have engaged him a room in that name because perhaps it was Buck Dexter and not Rollo Martins who was to be used for propaganda purposes.

A voice said at his elbow, "I'm so sorry you were not met at the plane, Mr. Dexter. My name's Crabbin."

The speaker was a stout, middle-aged young man with one of the thickest pairs of horn-rimmed glasses that Martins had ever seen. He went apologetically on, "One of our chaps happened to ring up Frankfurt and heard you were on the plane. H. Q. made one of their usual foolish mistakes and wired you were not coming. Something about Sweden, but the cable was badly mutilated. Directly I heard from Frankfurt I tried to meet the plane, but I just missed you. You got my note?"

Martins held his handkerchief to his mouth and said obscurely, "Yes. Yes?"

"May I say at once, Mr. Dexter, how excited I am to meet you?"

"Good of you."

"Ever since I was a boy, I've thought you the greatest novelist of our century."

Martins winced; it was painful opening his mouth to protest. He took an angry look instead at Mr. Crabbin, but it was impossible to suspect that young man of a practical joke.

"You have a big Austrian public, Mr. Dexter, both for your originals and your translations. Especially for *The Curved Prow*; that's my own favorite."

Martins was thinking hard. "Did you say—room for a week?"

"Yes."

"Very kind of you."

"Mr. Schmidt, here, will give you tickets every day, to cover all meals. But I expect you'll need a little pocket money. We'll fix that. Tomorrow we thought you'd like a quiet day—to look about."

"Yes."

"Of course, any of us are at your service if you need a guide. Then, the day after tomorrow in the evening there's a little quiet discussion at the Institute—on the contemporary novel. We thought perhaps you'd say a few words."

Martins at that moment was prepared to agree to anything, to get rid of Mr. Crabbin and also to secure a week's free board and lodging. He said, "Of course, of course," into his handkerchief.

"Excuse me, Mr. Dexter, have you got a toothache?"

"No. Somebody hit me, that's all."

"Good heavens! Were they trying to rob you?"

"No, it was a soldier. I was trying to punch his colonel in the eye."

He removed the handkerchief and gave Crabbin a view of his cut mouth. He told me that Crabbin was at a complete loss for words; Martins couldn't understand why, because he had never read the work of his great contemporary, Benjamin Dexter; he hadn't even heard of him. I am a great admirer of Dexter, so that I could understand Crabbin's bewilderment.

Dexter has been ranked as a stylist with Henry James, but he has a wider feminine streak than his master—indeed, his enemies have sometimes described his subtle, complex, wavering style as old-maidish. For a man still just on the right side of 50, his passionate interest in embroidery and his habit of calming a not very tumultuous mind with tatting—a trait beloved by his disciples—certainly to others seems a little affected.

"Have you ever read a book called *The Lone Rider to Santa Fe*?" Martins asked.

"No, I don't think so."

Martins said, "This lone rider had his best friend shot by the sheriff of a town called Lost Claim Gulch. The story is how he hunted that sheriff down—quite legally—until his revenge was completed."

"I never imagined you reading Westerns, Mr. Dexter," Crabbin said.

"Well, I'm gunning just the same way for Colonel Callaghan."

"Never heard of him."

"Heard of Harry Lime?"

"Yes," Crabbin said cautiously, "but I didn't really know him. A friend of his—an actress, you know—is learning English at the Institute. He called once or twice to fetch her."

Martins remembered the girl by the grave with her hands over her face. He said, "I'd like to meet any friend of Harry's."

"She'll probably be at your lecture."

"Austrian?"

"She claims to be Austrian, but I suspect she's Hungarian. She works at the Josefstadt."

"Why claims to be Austrian?"

"The Russians sometimes get interested in the Hungarians. I wouldn't be surprised if Lime had not helped her with her papers. She calls herself Schmidt. Anna Schmidt."

Martins felt he had got all he could from Crabbin, so he pleaded tiredness, a long day, promised to ring up in the morning, accepted ten pounds' worth of *Bafs* for immediate expenses, and went to his room.

He was tired. He realized that when he stretched himself out on his bed in his boots. Within a minute he was asleep. He woke suddenly, to hear the telephone ringing by his bed.

A voice with a trace of foreign accent—only a trace—said, "Is that Mr. Rollo Martins?"

"Yes."

"You wouldn't know me," the voice said unnecessarily, "but I was a friend of Harry Lime."

It was a change, too, to hear anyone claim to be a friend of Harry's; Martins's heart warmed toward the stranger. He said, "I'd be glad to meet you."

"I'm just around the corner at the Old Vienna."

"Wouldn't you make it tomorrow?"

"Harry asked me to see that you were all right. I was with him when he died."

"I thought—" Rollo Martins said, and stopped. He was going to say, "I thought he died instantaneously," but something suggested caution. He said, instead, "You haven't told me your name."

"Kurtz," the voice said, "I'd offer to come round to you, only, you know, Austrians aren't allowed in Sacher's."

"Perhaps we could meet at the Old Vienna in the morning."

"Certainly," the voice said, "if you are quite sure that you are all right till then."

"How do you mean?"

"Harry had it on his mind that you'd be penniless." Rollo Martins lay back on his bed with the receiver to his ear and thought, "Come to Vienna to make money." This was the third stranger to stake him in less than five hours. He said cautiously, "Oh, I can carry on till I see you."

"Shall we say eleven then, at Old Vienna in the Kärtnerstrasse? I'll be in a brown suit and I'll carry one of your books."

"That's fine. How did you get hold of one?"

"Harry gave it to me."

The voice had enormous charm and reasonableness, but when Martins had said good night and rung off, he couldn't help wondering how it was that if Harry had been so conscious before he died, he had not had a cable sent to stop him. Hadn't Callaghan, too, said that Lime had died instantaneously—or without pain, was it? Or had he, himself, put the words into Callaghan's mouth?

It was then that the idea first lodged firmly in Martins's mind that there was something wrong about Lime's death, something the police had been too stupid to discover. He tried to discover it himself with the help of two cigarettes, but he fell asleep without his dinner and with the mystery still unsolved.

"What I disliked about him at first sight," Martins told me, "was his toupee. It was one of those obvious toupees—flat and yellow, with the hair cut straight at the back and not fitting close. There *must* be something phony about a man who won't accept baldness gracefully."

This conversation took place some days later—he brought out his whole story when the trail was nearly cold. It appeared that Kurtz was sitting there at the Old Vienna making a great show of reading *The Lone Rider to Santa Fe.*

Martins introduced himself and sat down. "So you were a friend of Harry's," he said.

"I think his best," but Kurtz added, with the smallest pause in which his brain must have registered the error, "except you, of course."

"Tell me how he died."

"I was with him. We came out together from the door of his flat and Harry saw a friend he knew across the road—an American called Cooler. He waved to Cooler, and started across the road to him, when a jeep came tearing round the corner and bowled him over. It was Harry's fault really—not the driver's."

"Somebody told me he died instantaneously."

"I wish he had. He died before the ambulance could reach us, though."

"He could speak then?"

"Yes. Even in his pain he worried about you."

"What did he say?"

"I can't remember the exact words, Rollo—I may call you Rollo, mayn't I? He always called you that to us. He was anxious that I should look after you when you arrived."

"But why didn't you cable to stop me?"

"We did, but the cable must have missed you."

"There was an inquest?"

"Of course."

"Did you know that the police have a crazy notion that Harry was mixed up in some racket?"

"They get rather absurd ideas sometimes," Kurtz said cautiously.

"I'm going to stay here till I prove them wrong."

"I don't see what you can do."

"I'm going to start working back from his death. You were there, and this man Cooler and the chauffeur. You can give me their addresses."

"I don't know the chauffeur's."

"I can get it from the coroner's records. And then there's Harry's girl—"

Kurtz said, "It will be painful for her."

"I'm not concerned about her. I'm concerned about Harry."

"Do you know what it is that the police suspect?"

"No. I lost my temper too soon."

"Has it occurred to you," Kurtz said gently, "that you might dig up something—well, discreditable to Harry?"

"I'll risk that."

"It will take a bit of time—and money."

"I've got time and you were going to lend me some money, weren't you?"

"I'm not a rich man," Kurtz said. "I promised Harry to see you were all right and that you got your plane back."

"You needn't worry about the money—or the plane," Martins said. "But I'll make a bet with you—in pounds sterling—five pounds against two hundred schillings—that there's something queer about Harry's death."

It was a shot in the dark, but already he had this firm, instinctive sense that there was something wrong, though he hadn't yet attached the word "murder" to the instinct. Kurtz had a cup of coffee halfway to his lips and Martins watched him. The shot apparently went wide; an unaffected hand held the cup to the mouth and Kurtz drank, a little noisily, in long sips. Then he put down the cup and said, "How do you mean—queer?"

"It was convenient for the police to have a corpse, but wouldn't it have been equally convenient, perhaps, for the real racketeers?" When he had spoken he realized that, after all, Kurtz had not been unaffected by his wild statement. The hands of the guilty don't necessarily tremble. Tension is more often shown in the studied action. Kurtz had finished his coffee as though nothing had been said.

"Well"—he took another sip—"of course, I wish you luck, though I don't believe there's anything to find. Just ask me for any help you want."

"I want Cooler's address."

"Certainly. I'll write it down for you. Here it is. In the American zone."

"And yours?"

"I've already put it—underneath. I'm unlucky enough to be in the Russian zone—so you shouldn't visit me very late. Things sometimes happen round our way." He rose, giving one of his studied Viennese smiles. "Keep in touch," he said, "and if you need help—but I still think you are very unwise."

Martins sat on a hard chair just inside the stage door of the Josefstadt Theater. He had sent up his card to Anna Schmidt after the matinee, marking it, "A friend of Harry's."

He had had time to think. He thought, "Kurtz is right. They are all right. I'm behaving like a romantic fool; I'll just have a word with Anna Schmidt, a word of commiseration, and then I'll pack and go."

A voice over his head called, "Mr. Martins," and he looked up at the face that watched him from between the curtains a few feet above his head. It wasn't a beautiful face, he firmly explained to me. Just an honest face with dark hair and eyes which looked brown; a wide forehead, a large mouth which didn't try to charm. She said, "Will you come up, please? The second door on the right."

There are some people, he explained to me carefully, whom one recognizes instantly as friends. You can be at ease with them because you know that never, never will you be in danger. "That was Anna," he said.

He said to her, "I wanted very much to see you. About Harry."

It was the dreaded moment; he could see her mouth stiffen to meet it. "Yes?"

"I was his friend. We were at school together, you know, and after that there weren't many months running when we didn't meet."

She said, "When I got your card I couldn't say no, but there's nothing, really, for us to talk about. Everything's over, finished."

"We both loved him."

"I don't know. You can't know a thing like that—afterward. I don't know anything any more except—that I want to be dead, too."

Martins told me, "Then I nearly went away. What was the good of tormenting her because of this wild idea of mine? But instead I asked her one question: 'Do you know a man called Cooler?'"

"An American?" she asked. "I think that was the man who brought me some money when Harry died. I didn't want to take it, but he said Harry had been anxious—at the last moment."

"So he didn't die instantaneously?"

"Oh, no."

Martins said to me later, "I began to wonder why I had got that idea into my head, and then I thought, it was only the man in the flat who told me so, no one else."

Martins said to Anna, "He must have been very clear in his head at the end, because he remembered about me, too. That seems to show that there wasn't really any pain."

"That's what I tell myself all the time," she said.

"Did you know the doctor?"

"Yes. Harry sent me to him once."

Martins suddenly saw in that odd chamber of the mind which constructs such pictures, instantaneously, irrationally, a desert place, a body on the ground, a group of birds gathered. He thought, "How odd that they were all there, just at that moment, all Harry's friends—Kurtz, the doctor, this man Cooler; only the two people who loved him seemed to have been missing." He said, "And the driver? Did you hear his evidence?"

"He was upset, scared. But Cooler's evidence exonerated him. No, it wasn't his fault, poor man. I've often heard Harry say what a careful driver he was."

"*He* knew Harry, too?" Another bird flapped down and joined the others round the silent figure on the sand who lay face down.

Somebody called outside the window, "Fräulein Schmidt."

She said, "They don't like one to stay too long. It uses up their electricity."

He had given up the idea of sparing her anything. He told her, "The police say they were going to arrest Harry. They'd pinned some racket on him."

She took the news in much the same way as Kurtz. "Everybody's in a racket."

"I don't believe he was in anything serious. He may have been framed. Do you know a man called Kurtz?"

"I don't think so."

"He wears a toupee."

"Oh." He could tell that that struck home. He said, "Don't you think it was odd they were all there—at the death. Everybody knew Harry. Even the driver, the doctor—"

She said, with hopeless calm, "I've thought that, too, though I didn't know about Kurtz. I wondered whether they'd murdered him, but what's the use of wondering?"

"I'm going to find out," Rollo Martins said.

"Fräulein Schmidt," the voice called again.

"I must go."

"I'll walk with you a bit of the way."

It was almost dark. The snow had ceased. The great statues of the Ring, the prancing horses, the chariots, and the eagles, were gunshot-gray with the end of evening light. "It's better to give up and forget," Anna said.

"Will you give me the doctor's address?"

They stood in the shelter of a wall while she wrote it down for him.

"And yours, too?"

"Why do you want that?"

"I might have news for you."

"There isn't any news that would do any good now."

He watched her from a distance board her tram, bowing her head against the wind.

* * *

An amateur detective has this advantage over the professional, that he doesn't work set hours. Rollo Martins was not confined to the eight-hour day; his investigations didn't have to pause for meals. In his one day he covered as much ground as one of my men would have covered in two, and he had this initial advantage over us, that he was Harry's friend.

Dr. Winkler was at home. Perhaps he would not have been at home to a police officer. Again, Martins had marked his card with the sesame phrase: "A friend of Harry Lime's."

Dr. Winkler was the cleanest doctor Martins had ever seen. He was very small and neat, in a black tail coat and a high, stiff collar; his little black mustache was like an evening tie. He said, "Mr. Martins?"

"We were both friends of Harry Lime," Martins said.

"I was his medical adviser," Dr. Winkler corrected him, and waited obstinately.

"I arrived too late for the inquest. Harry had invited me out here to help him in something. I don't quite know what. I didn't hear of his death till I arrived."

"Very sad," Dr. Winkler said.

"Naturally, under the circumstances, I want to hear all I can."

"There is nothing I can tell you that you don't know. He was knocked over by a car. He was dead when I arrived."

"Would he have been conscious at all?"

"I understand he was for a short time, while they carried him into the house."

"You are quite certain that it was an accident?"

Dr. Winkler touched his mustache. "I was not there. My opinion is limited to the cause of death. Have you any reason to be dissatisfied?"

The amateur has another advantage over the professional: He can be reckless. He can tell unnecessary truths and propound wild theories.

Martins said, "The police had implicated Harry in a very serious racket. It seemed to me that he might have been murdered—or had even killed himself."

"I am not competent to pass an opinion," Dr. Winkler said.

"Do you know a man called Cooler?"

"I don't think so."

"He was there when Harry was killed."

"Then of course I have met him. He wears a toupee."

"That was Kurtz."

Dr. Winkler was not only the cleanest, he was also the most cautious doctor that Martins had ever met. His statements were so limited that you could not for a moment doubt their veracity. He said, "There was a second man there."

"Had you been Harry's doctor for long?"

"For about a year."

"Well, it's good of you to have seen me."

Dr. Winkler bowed. When he bowed there was a very slight creak, as though his shirt were made of celluloid.

When Rollo Martins left Dr. Winkler's he was in no danger. He could have gone home to bed at Sacher's and slept with a quiet mind. He could even have visited Cooler at this stage without trouble. No one was seriously disturbed. Unfortunately for him, he chose to go back to Harry's flat. He wanted to talk to the little vexed man who said he had seen the accident.

The little man—who bore the name of Koch—was friendly and quite ready to talk. He had just finished dinner and had crumbs on his mustache. "Ah, I remember you. You are Herr Lime's friend."

He welcomed Martins in with great cordiality and introduced him to a mountainous wife.

"Did you tell me that you had actually seen the accident?" Martins asked.

Herr Koch exchanged glances with his wife. "The inquest is over, Ilse. There is no harm. You can trust my judgment. The gentleman is a friend. . . . Yes, I saw the accident, but you are the only one who knows. When I say that I saw it, perhaps I should say that I heard it. I heard the brakes put on and the sound of the skid, and I got to the window in time to see them carry the body to the house."

"But didn't you give evidence?"

"It is better not to be mixed up in such things. My office cannot spare me. We are short of staff, and of course I did not actually *see*—"

"But you told me yesterday how it happened."

"That was how they described it in the papers."

"Was he in great pain?"

"He was dead. I looked right down from my window here and I saw his face. I know when a man is dead. You see, it is, in a way, my business. I am the head clerk at the mortuary."

"But the others say that he did not die at once."

"Perhaps they don't know death as well as I do."

"I think, Herr Koch, that you should have given evidence."

"One must look after oneself, Herr Martins. I was not the only one who should have been there."

"How do you mean?"

"There were three people who helped to carry your friend to the house."

"I know—two men and the driver."

"The driver stayed where he was. He was very much shaken."

"Three men . . ." It was as though, suddenly fingering that bare wall, his fingers had encountered, not so much a crack perhaps, but at least a roughness that had not been smoothed away by the careful builders.

"Can you describe the men?"

But Herr Koch was not trained to observe the living; only the man with the toupee had attracted his eyes; the other two were just men, neither tall nor short, thick nor thin. He had seen them from far above, foreshortened, bent over their burden. They had not looked up, and he had quickly looked away and closed the window, realizing at once the wisdom of not being seen, himself. "There was no evidence I could really give, Herr Martins."

No evidence, Martins thought, no evidence! He no longer doubted that murder had been done. Why else had they lied about the moment of death? And the third man? Who was he?

He said, "Did you see Herr Lime go out?"

"No."

"Did you hear a scream?"

"Only the brakes, Herr Martins."

It occurred to Martins that there was nothing—except the word of Kurtz and Cooler and the driver—to prove that in fact Harry had been killed at that precise moment. There was the medical evidence, but that could not prove more than that he had died, say, within a half-hour, and in any case the medical evidence was only as strong as Dr. Winkler's word.

"Herr Martins, it just occurs to me, if you need accommodation and spoke to the authorities quickly, you might secure Herr Lime's flat."

"Could I see the flat?"

"Ilse, the keys."

Herr Koch led the way into the flat that had been Harry's. In the little dark hall there was still the smell of cigarette smoke—the Turkish cigarettes that Harry always smoked.

The living-room was completely bare—it seemed to Martins too bare. The chairs had been pushed up against the walls; the desk at which Harry must have written was free from dust or any papers. Herr Koch opened a door and showed the bedroom—the bed neatly made with clean sheets.

"You see," Herr Koch said, "it is quite ready for a newcomer."

"Were there no papers, Herr Koch?"

"Herr Lime was always a very tidy man. His wastepaper basket was full and his brief case, but his friend fetched that away."

"His friend?"

"The gentleman with the toupee."

It was possible, of course, that Lime had not taken the journey so unexpectedly, and it occurred to Martins that Lime had perhaps hoped he would arrive in time to help. He said to Herr Koch, "I believe my friend was murdered."

"Murdered?" Herr Koch's cordiality was snuffed out by the word. He said, "I would not have asked you in here if I had thought you would talk such nonsense."

"Why should it be nonsense?"

"We do not have murders in this zone."

"All the same, your evidence may be very valuable."

"I have no evidence. I saw nothing. I am not concerned. You must leave here at once, please. You have been very inconsiderate." He hustled Martins back through the hall; already the smell of the cigarette smoke was fading a little more. Herr Koch's last word before he slammed his own door was, "It's no concern of mine."

Poor Herr Koch! We do not choose our concerns. Later, when I was questioning Martins closely, I said to him, "Did you see anybody at all on the stairs, or in the street outside?"

"Nobody." He had everything to gain by remembering some chance passer-by, and I believed him.

"Of course, it proves nothing. There is a basement where anybody who had followed you could hide."

"Yes."

"The whole story may be phony."

"Yes."

"The trouble is I can see no motive for you to have done it. It's true you are already guilty of getting money on false pretenses: You came out here to join Lime, perhaps to help him—"

Martins said to me, "What was this racket you keep on hinting at?"

"I'd have told you all the facts when I first saw you if you hadn't lost your temper so damned quickly. Now, I don't think I shall be acting wisely to tell you. It would be disclosing official information, and your contacts, you know, don't inspire confidence. A girl with phony papers supplied by Lime, this man Kurtz—"

"Dr. Winkler—"

"I've got nothing against Dr. Winkler. No, if you are phony, you don't need the information, but it might help you to learn exactly what we know. You see, our facts are not complete."

"I bet they aren't. I could invent a better detective than you in my bath."

"Your literary style does not do your namesake justice." Whenever he was reminded of Mr. Crabbin, that poor, harassed representative of the British Council, Rollo Martins turned pink with annoyance, embarrassment, shame. That, too, inclined me to trust him.

He had certainly given Crabbin some uncomfortable hours. On returning to Sacher's Hotel after his interview with Herr Koch he had found a desperate note waiting for him from the representative.

"I have been trying to locate you all day," Crabbin wrote. "It is essential that we should get together and work out a proper program for you. This morning by telephone I have arranged lectures at Innsbruck and Salzburg for next week, but I must have your consent to the subjects, so that proper programs can be printed.

"Apart from this, there are a great many people here who would like to meet you, and I want to arrange a cocktail party for early next week. But for all this I must have a few words with you." The letter ended on a note of acute anxiety: "You will be at the discussion tomorrow night, won't you? We all expect you at 8:30, and, needless to say, look forward to your coming. I will send transport to the hotel at 8:15 sharp."

Rollo Martins read the letter and, without bothering any further about Mr. Crabbin, went to bed.

* * *

Martins spent the greater part of the following day studying the reports of the inquest, thus again demonstrating the superiority of the amateur to the professional, and making him more vulnerable to Cooler's liquor (which the professional in dutybound would have refused). It was nearly five o'clock when he reached Cooler's flat.

Again the card marked "Harry's friend" was like an entrance ticket.

Cooler, a man with tousled gray hair, a worried, kindly face, and long-sighted eyes, was in officer's uniform, but wore no badges of rank. His maid referred to him as Colonel Cooler. His warm, frank handclasp was the most friendly act that Martins had encountered in Vienna.

"Any friend of Harry is all right with me," Cooler said.

"I wondered—you were there, weren't you?—if you'd tell me about Harry's death."

"It was a terrible thing," Cooler said. "I was just crossing the road to go to Harry. He and a Mr. Kurtz were on the sidewalk. Maybe if I hadn't started across the road he'd have stayed where he was. But he saw me and stepped straight off to meet me, and this jeep—it was terrible, terrible. The driver braked, but Harry didn't stand a chance. . . . Have a drink, Mr. Martins. It's silly of me, but I get shaken up when I think of it."

"Was the other man in the car?"

Cooler took a long pull and then measured what was left with his tired, kindly eyes. "What man would you be referring to, Mr. Martins?"

"I was told there was another man there."

"I don't know how you got that idea. You'll find all about it in the inquest reports." He poured out two more generous drinks. "There were just the three of us—me and Mr. Kurtz and the driver. The doctor, of course. I expect you were thinking of the doctor."

"This man I was talking to happened to look out of a window—he has the next flat to Harry's—and he said he saw three men and the driver. That's before the doctor arrived."

"He didn't say that in court."

"He didn't want to get involved."

"You'll never teach these Europeans to be good citizens. It was his duty." Cooler brooded sadly over his glass. "It's an odd thing, Mr. Martins, with accidents. You'll never get two reports that coincide. Why, even I and Mr. Kurtz disagreed about the details. The thing happens so suddenly, you aren't concerned to notice things, until bang crash! And then you have to reconstruct, remember. I expect he got too tangled up trying to sort out what happened before and what after, to distinguish the four of us."

"The four?"

"I was counting Harry. What else did he see, Mr. Martins?"

"Nothing of interest—except he says Harry was dead when he was carried to the house."

"Well, he was dying—not much difference there. . . . Have another drink, Mr. Martins?"

"Perhaps one more—to keep you company," Martins said.

"Do you know Anna Schmidt?" he asked, while the whisky still tingled on his tongue.

"Harry's girl? I met her once, that's all. As a matter of fact, I helped Harry fix her papers. Not the sort of thing I should confess to a stranger, I suppose, but you have to break the rules sometimes. Humanity's a duty, too."

"What was wrong?"

"She was Hungarian and her father had been a Nazi, so they said. She was scared the Russians would pick her up."

"But she lives in the British zone."

"That wouldn't stop them. The streets aren't well lighted, and you haven't many police around."

"You took her some money from Harry, didn't you?"

"Yes, but I wouldn't have mentioned that affair. Did she tell you?"

The telephone rang, and Cooler drained his glass.

"Hullo," he said. . . . "Why, yes. This is Colonel Cooler." Then he sat with the receiver at his ear and an expression of sad patience, while some voice a long way off drained into the room. "Yes," he said once. "Yes." His eyes dwelt on Martins's face, but they seemed to be looking a long way beyond him; flat and tired and kind, they might have been gazing out over acres of sea. He said, "You did quite right," in a tone of commendation, and then, with a touch of asperity, "Of course they will be delivered. I gave my word. Good-bye."

He put the receiver down and passed a hand across his forehead wearily. It was as though he were trying to remember something he had to do.

Martins said, "Had you heard anything about this racket the police talk about?"

"I'm sorry. What's that?"

"They say Harry was mixed up in some racket."

"Oh, no," Cooler said, "no. That's quite impossible. He had a great sense of duty."

"Kurtz seemed to think it was possible."

"Kurtz doesn't understand how an Anglo-Saxon feels," Cooler replied.

It was nearly dark when Martins made his way along the banks of the canal; across the water lay the half-destroyed Diana Baths and in the distance the great, black circle of the Prater Wheel, stationary above the ruined houses. Coming up the Kärtnerstrasse, Martins passed the door of the Military Police station. The four men of the International Patrol were climbing into their jeep; the Russian M.P. sat beside the driver (for the Russians had that day taken over the chair for the next four weeks), and the Englishman, the Frenchman, and the American mounted behind. The third stiff whisky fumed in Martins's brain, and he moved toward the only girl he knew in Vienna.

He hadn't, of course, known that she would be in, that her play was not on that night in the Josefstadt. She was sitting alone in an unheated room, with the bed disguised as a divan.

He said awkwardly, "I thought I'd just look you up. You see, I was passing—"

"Passing? Where to?" It had been a good half-hour's walk from the Inner City to the rim of the English zone, but he always had a reply: "I had too much whisky with Colonel Cooler. I needed a walk, and I just happened to find myself this way."

"I can't give you a drink here. Except tea."

"No. No thank you." He said, "Can I stay a little?"

"I wish you would."

He slumped down on the divan, and he told me, a long time later, that there it was he took his second real look at her. She stood there as awkward as himself in a pair of old flannel trousers, with her legs firmly straddled as though she were opposing someone and was determined to hold her ground.

"One of those bad days?" he asked her.

"It's always bad about this time." She explained, "He used to look in, and when I heard your ring, just for a moment, I thought—" She sat down on a hard chair opposite him and said, "Please talk. You knew him. Just tell me anything."

And so he talked. He noticed after a while that their hands had met. He said to me, "I never meant to fall in love, not with Harry's girl."

"When did it happen?" I asked him.

"It was very cold and I got up to close the window curtains. I only noticed my hand was on hers when I took it away. As I stood up I looked down at her face, and she was looking up. It wasn't a beautiful face—that was the trouble. It was a face to live with, day in, day out. A face for wear. I felt as though I'd come into a new country where I couldn't speak the language. I had always thought it was beauty one loved in a woman.

"I stood there at the curtains, waiting to pull them, looking out. I couldn't see anything but my own face, looking back into the room, looking for her. She said, 'And what did Harry do that time?' and I wanted to say, 'Damn Harry. He's dead. We both loved him, but he's dead. The dead are made to be forgotten.' Instead, of course, all I said was, 'What do you think? He just whistled his old tune as if nothing was the matter,' and I whistled it to her as well as I could. I heard her catch her breath, and I looked round, and before I could think, is this the right way, the right card, the right gambit? I'd already said, 'He's dead. You can't go on remembering him forever.'"

She had answered, "I know, but perhaps something will happen first."

"What do you mean—something happen?" Martins had asked.

"Oh, I mean, perhaps there'll be another war, or I'll die, or the Russians will take me."

"You'll forget him in time. You'll fall in love again."

"I know, but I don't want to. Don't you see I don't want to?"

So Rollo Martins came back from the window and sat down on the divan again. When he had risen, half a minute before, he had been the friend of Harry comforting Harry's girl; now he was a man in love with Anna Schmidt, who had been in love with a man they had both once known called Harry Lime. He didn't speak again that evening about the past. Instead, he began to tell her of the people he had seen.

"I can believe anything of Winkler," he told her, "but Cooler—I liked Cooler. He was the only one of his friends who stood up for Harry. The trouble is, if Cooler's right, then Koch is wrong, and I really thought I had something there."

"Who's Koch?"

He explained how he had returned to Harry's flat, and he described his interview with Koch, the story of the third man.

"If it's true," she said, "it's very important."

"It doesn't prove anything. After all, Koch backed out of the inquest; so might this stranger."

"That's not the point," she said. "It means that *they* lied, Kurtz and Cooler."

"They might have lied so as not to inconvenience this fellow—if he was a friend."

"Yet another friend—on the spot. And where's your Cooler's honesty then?"

"What do we do? Koch clamped down like an oyster and turned me out of his flat."

"He won't turn *me* out," she said, "or his Ilse won't."

They walked up the long road to the flat together; the snow clogged on their shoes and made them move slowly. Anna Schmidt said, "Is it far?"

"Not very far now. Do you see that knot of people up the road? It's somewhere about there." The group of people up the road was like a splash of ink on the whiteness that flowed, changed shape, spread out. When they came a little nearer Martins said, "I think that is his block. What do you suppose this is—a political demonstration?"

Anna Schmidt stopped; she said, "Who else have you told about Koch?"

"Only you and Colonel Cooler. Why?"

"I'm frightened. It reminds me—" She had her eyes fixed on the crowd and he never knew what memory out of her confused past had risen to warn her. "Let's go away," she implored him.

"You're crazy. We're onto something here, something big."

"I'll wait for you."

"But you're going to talk to him."

"Find out first what all those people—" She said, strangely for one who worked behind the footlights, "I hate crowds."

He walked slowly on alone. He had the impression of heads turning to watch him come. When he reached the fringe of the little crowd he knew for certain that it was the house. A man looked hard at him and said, "Are you another of them?"

"Who do you mean?"

"The police."

"No. What are they doing?"

"They've been in and out all day."

"What's everybody waiting for?"

"They want to see him brought out."

"Who?"

"Herr Koch."

"What's he done?"

"Nobody knows that yet. They can't make their minds up in there—it might be suicide, you see, and it might be murder."

"Herr Koch?"

"Of course. There is talk of a foreigner who called on Herr Koch yesterday."

Martins walked back down the street toward Anna. He said, "Koch has been murdered. Come away from here." He walked as rapidly as the snow would, let him, turning this corner and that. He paid no attention when Anna said to him, "Then what Koch said was true. There *was* a third man."

The tram cars flashed like icicles at the end of the street; they were back at the Ring. Martins said, "You had better go home alone. I'll keep away from you a while till things have sorted out."

"But nobody can suspect you."

"They were asking about the foreigner who called on Koch yesterday. There may be some unpleasantness for a while."

"Why don't you go to the police?"

"They are so stupid. I don't trust them. See what they've pinned on Harry. And then I tried to hit this man Callaghan. They'll have it in for me. The least they'll do is send me away from Vienna. But if I stay quiet—There's only one person who can give me away: Cooler."

"And he won't want to."

"Not if he's guilty. But then I can't believe he's guilty."

Before she left him she said, "Be careful. Koch knew so very little and they murdered him. You know as much as Koch."

The warning stayed in his brain all the way to Sacher's; after nine o'clock the streets are very empty, and he would turn his head at every padding step coming up the street behind him, as though that third man whom they had protected so ruthlessly was now following him like an executioner.

At Sacher's a desk man said, "Colonel Calloway has been in, asking after you, sir. I think you'll find him in the bar."

"Back in a moment," Martins said, and walked straight out of the hotel again; he wanted time to think. But immediately he stepped outside a man came forward, touched his cap, and said firmly, "Please, sir." He flung open the door of a khaki-painted truck with a Union Jack on the windscreen and firmly urged Martins within. He surrendered without protest; sooner or later he had felt sure inquiries would be made; he had only pretended optimism to Anna Schmidt.

The driver drove too fast for safety on the frozen road, and Martins protested. All he got in reply was a sullen grunt and a muttered sentence containing the word "orders."

The car drew up before a building and the driver led the way up two flights of stairs. He rang the bell of a great double door, and Martins was aware beyond it of many voices. He turned sharply to the driver and said, "Where the—?" but the driver was halfway down the stairs, and already the door was opening. His eyes were dazzled from the darkness by the lights inside; he heard but he could hardly see the advance of Mr. Crabbin: "Oh, Mr. Dexter, we have been so anxious, but better late than never. Let me introduce you to Miss Wilbraham and the Gräfin von Meyersdorf."

A buffet laden with coffee cups; an urn steaming; a woman's face shiny with exertion; two young men with the happy, intelligent faces of sixth formers; and huddled in the background, like faces in a family album, a multitude of the old-fashioned, the dingy, the earnest and cheery features of constant readers. Martins looked behind him, but the door had closed.

He said desperately to Mr. Crabbin, "I'm sorry, but—"

"Don't think any more about it," Mr. Crabbin said. "One cup of coffee and then let's go on to the discussion."

One of the young men placed a cup in his hand, the other shoveled in sugar before he could say he preferred his coffee unsweetened.

Martins was not able to tell me very much about the meeting; his mind was still dazed with the death. He could not say how he got through the discussion. Perhaps Crabbin took the brunt; perhaps he was helped by some of the audience who got into an animated discussion about the film version of a popular American novel. He remembered very little more before Crabbin was making a final speech in his honor. Then one of the young men led him to a table stacked with books and asked him to sign them.

Martins took his pen and wrote: "From B. Dexter, author of *The Lone Rider from Santa Fe*," and the young man read the sentence and blotted it, with a puzzled expression.

Suddenly in a mirror Martins saw my driver, Sgt. Paine. He seemed to be having an argument with one of Crabbin's young henchmen. Martins thought he caught the sound of his own name. It was then he lost his nerve, and with it any relic of common sense. The young man, Crabbin, and Paine stood together at the entrance.

"And this gentleman?" Sgt. Paine asked.

"It's Mr. Benjamin Dexter," the young man said.

Paine said respectfully, "We were looking for you, sir. Colonel Calloway wants a word with you."

I had kept a very careful record of Martins's movements from the moment I knew that he had not caught the plane home. Events had taken a disquieting turn, and it seemed to me that the time had come for another interview.

I put a good, wide desk between us and gave him a cigarette. I found him sullen but ready to talk, within strict limits. I asked him about Kurtz, and he seemed to me to answer satisfactorily. I then asked him about Anna Schmidt, and I gathered from his reply that he must have been with her after visiting Colonel Cooler. That filled in one of the missing points. I tried him with Dr. Winkler, and he answered readily enough.

"You've been getting around," I said, "quite a bit. And have you found out anything about your friend?"

"Oh, yes," he said. "It was under your nose but you didn't see it."

"What?"

"That he was murdered." That took me by surprise; I had at one time played with the idea of suicide, but I had ruled even that out.

"Go on," I said. He tried to eliminate from his story all mention of Koch, talking about an informant who had seen the accident. This made his story rather confusing, and I couldn't grasp at first why he attached so much importance to the third man.

"He didn't turn up at the inquest, and the others lied to keep him out."

"I don't see much importance in that. If it was a genuine accident, all the evidence needed was there. Why get the other chap into trouble?"

"There was more to it than that," he said. "The little chap who told me about the third man—they've murdered him. You see, they obviously didn't know what else he had seen."

"Now we have it," I said. "You mean Koch."

"Yes."

"As far as we know you were the last person to see him alive. The Austrian police are anxious to pin this on you. Frau Koch told them how disturbed her husband was by your visit. Who else knew about it?"

"I told Cooler." He said excitedly, "Suppose immediately I left he telephoned the story to someone—to the third man. They had to stop Koch's mouth."

"When you told Colonel Cooler about Koch, the man was already dead. That night he got out of bed, hearing someone, and went downstairs."

"Well, that rules me out. I was in Sacher's."

"But he went to bed very early. Your visit brought on a headache. It was soon after nine that he got up. You returned to Sacher's at nine-thirty. Where were you before that?"

He said gloomily, "Wandering round and trying to sort things out."

I wanted to frighten him, so there was no point in telling him that he had been followed all the time. I knew that he hadn't cut Koch's throat, but I wasn't sure that he was quite so innocent as he made out.

He said, "How did you know that I went to Koch's? That was why you pulled me here, wasn't it?"

"Immediately you left Colonel Cooler's, he telephoned to me."

"Then that let him out. If he had been concerned, he wouldn't have wanted me to tell you my story—to tell Koch's story, I mean."

"He might assume that you were a sensible man and would come to me with your story as soon as you learned of Koch's death. By the way, how did you learn of it?"

He told me promptly, and I believed him. It was then I began to believe him altogether. He said, "I still can't believe Cooler's concerned. I'd stake anything on his honesty. He's one of those Americans with a real sense of duty."

"Yes," I said, "he told me about that when he phoned. He apologized for it. He said it was the worst of having been brought up to believe in citizenship. He said it made him feel a prig. To tell you the truth, Cooler irritates me. Of course, he doesn't know that I know about his tire deals."

"Is he in a racket too, then?"

"Not a very serious one. I daresay he's salted away $25,000."

"I see." He said thoughtfully, "Is that the kind of thing Harry was up to?"

"No. It was not so harmless."

He said, "You know, this business—Koch's death—has shaken me. Perhaps Harry did get mixed up in something pretty bad. Perhaps he was trying to clear out again, and that's why they murdered him."

"Or perhaps," I said, "they wanted a bigger cut of the spoils. Thieves fall out."

He took it this time without any anger at all. He said, "We won't agree about motives, but I think you check your facts pretty well. I'm sorry about the other day."

"That's all right." There are times when one has to make a flash decision—this was one of them. I owed him something in return for the information he had given me. I said, "I'll show you enough of the facts in Lime's case for you to understand. But don't fly off the handle. It's going to be a shock."

It couldn't help being a shock. The war and the peace let loose a great number of rackets, but none more vile than this one. The black marketeers in food did at least supply food, and the same applied to all the other racketeers who provided articles in short supply at extravagant prices. But the penicillin racket was a different affair altogether. Penicillin in Austria was supplied only to the military hospitals; no civilian doctor, not even a civilian hospital, could obtain it by legal means.

As the racket started, it was relatively harmless. Penicillin would be stolen by military orderlies and sold to Austrian doctors for very high sums—a phial would fetch anything up to $300.

This racket went on quite happily for a while. Occasionally an orderly was caught and punished, but the danger simply raised the price of penicillin. Then the racket began to get organized. The big men saw big money in it, and while the original thief got less for his spoils, he received, instead, a certain security.

This, I have sometimes called stage two. Stage three was when the organizers decided that the profits were not large enough. Penicillin would not always be impossible to obtain legitimately; they wanted more money and quicker money while the going was good. They began to dilute the penicillin with colored water, and in the case of penicillin dust, with sand.

I keep a small museum in one drawer in my desk, and I showed Martins examples. He wasn't enjoying the talk, but he hadn't yet grasped the point. He said, "I suppose that makes the stuff useless."

I said, "We wouldn't worry so much if that was all, but just consider that you can be immunized from the effects of penicillin. At the best, you can say that the use of this stuff makes a penicillin treatment for the particular patient ineffective in the future. That isn't so funny, of course, if you are suffering from V.D. Then the use of sand on a wound that requires penicillin—well, it's not healthy. Men have lost their legs and arms that way—and their lives. But perhaps what horrified me most was visiting the children's hospital here. They had bought some of this penicillin for use against meningitis. A number of children simply died, and a number went off their heads. You can see them now in the mental ward."

He sat on the other side of the desk scowling into his hands.

I said, "It doesn't bear thinking about very closely, does it?"

"You haven't shown me any evidence yet that Harry—"

"We are coming to that now," I said. "Just sit still and listen." I opened Lime's file and began to read.

I am not going to bother the reader now, as I bothered Martins then, with all the stages—the long tussle to win the confidence of the go-between, a man called Harbin. At last we had the screws on Harbin, and we twisted them until he squealed. "But he led us only as far as Kurtz," I said.

"Kurtz!" Martins exclaimed. "But why haven't you pulled him in?"

"Zero hour is almost here," I said.

Kurtz was a great step forward, for Kurtz was in direct communication with Lime—he had a small outside job in connection with international relief. With Kurtz, Lime sometimes put things on paper, if he was pressed. I showed Martins the photostat of a note. "Can you identify that?"

"It's Harry's hand." He read it through. "I don't see anything wrong."

"No, but now read this note from Harbin to Kurtz, which we dictated. Look at the date. This is the result."

He read them both through twice.

"You see what I mean?"

If one watched a world come to an end, a planet dive from its course, I don't suppose one would chatter, and a world for Martins had certainly come to an end, a world of easy friendship, hero-worship, confidence, which had begun twenty years before.

While he sat there, looking at his hands and saying nothing, I fetched a precious bottle of whisky out of a cupboard and poured out two large doubles. "Go on," I said, "drink that," and he obeyed me as though I were his doctor. I poured him out another.

He said slowly, "Are you certain that he was the real boss?"

"It's as far back as we have got so far."

"Suppose," he said, "someone had got a line on him, forced him into this racket, as you forced Harbin to double-cross."

"It's possible."

"And they murdered him in case he talked when he was arrested."

"It's not impossible."

"I'm glad they did," he said. "I wouldn't have liked to hear Harry squeal." He made a curious little dusting movement of his hand on his knee, as much as to say, "That's that." He said, "I'll be getting back to England."

"I'd rather you didn't just yet. The Austrian police would make an issue if you tried to leave Vienna at the moment. You see, Cooler's sense of duty made him call them up, too."

"I see," he said hopelessly.

"When we've found the third man—" I said.

"I'd like to hear *him* squeal," Martins said.

After he left me Martins went straight off to drink himself silly. By the time the spots were swimming in front of his eyes he was op-pressed by a sense of loneliness. The trams had stopped, and he set out obstinately on foot to find Harry's girl.

It must have been about three in the morning when he climbed the stairs to Anna's room. He was nearly sober by that time and had only one idea in his head—that she must know about Harry, too. He felt that somehow this knowledge would pay the mortmain that memory levies on human beings, and he would stand a chance with Harry's girl.

When Anna opened the door to him, with astonishment at the sight of him, tousled, on the threshold, he never imagined that she was opening the door to a stranger.

He said, "Anna, I've found out everything."

"Come in," she said. "You don't want to wake the house." She was in a dressing gown; the divan had become a bed.

"Now," she said, while he stood there, fumbling for words, "what is it? I thought you were going to keep away. Are the police after you?"

"No."

"You didn't really kill that man, did you?"

"Of course not."

"You're drunk, aren't you?"

"I am a bit," he said sulkily. The meeting seemed to be going on the wrong lines. "I've been with the British police. They are satisfied I didn't do it. But I've learned everything from them. Harry was in a racket—a bad racket." He said hopelessly, "He was no good at all. We were both wrong."

"You'd better tell me," Anna said.

She sat down on the bed and he told her.

"They really proved it?" Anna asked.

"Yes."

"I'm glad he's dead now," she said. "I wouldn't have wanted him to rot for years in prison."

"But can you understand how Harry—your Harry, my Harry—could have got mixed up—?" He said hopelessly, "I feel as though he had never really existed, that we'd dreamed him. Was he laughing at fools like us all the time?"

"He may have been. What does it matter?" she said. "Sit down. Don't worry." He had pictured himself comforting *her*, not this other way about. She said, "If he was alive now, he might be able to explain, but we've got to remember him as he was to us. There are always so many things one doesn't know about a person, even a person one loves—good things, bad things. We have to leave plenty of room for them."

"Those children—"

She said angrily, "For heaven's sake stop making people in *your* image. Harry was real. He wasn't just your hero. He was Harry. He was in a racket. He did bad things. What about it? He was the man we knew."

He said, "Don't talk such bloody wisdom. Don't you see that I love you?"

She looked at him with astonishment. "You?"

"Yes, me. I don't kill people with fake drugs. I'm not a hypocrite who persuades people that I'm the greatest—I'm just a bad writer who drinks too much and falls in love with girls—"

She said, "But I don't even know what color your eyes are. If you'd rung me up just now and asked me whether you were dark or fair or wore a mustache, I wouldn't have known."

"Can't you get him out of your head?"

"No."

He said, "As soon as they've cleared up this Koch murder I'm leaving Vienna. I can't feel interested any longer in whether Kurtz killed Harry—or the third man. Whoever killed him, it was a kind of justice. Maybe I'd kill him myself under those circumstances. But you still love him. You love a cheat, a murderer."

"I loved a man," she said. "I told you—a man doesn't alter because you find out more about him. He's still the same man."

"I hate the way you talk. I've got a splitting headache, and you talk and talk."

Suddenly she laughed. She said, "You are so comic. You come here at three in the morning—a stranger—and say you love me. Then you get angry and pick a quarrel. What do you expect me to do—or say?"

"I haven't seen you laugh before. Do it again. I like it."

"There isn't enough for two laughs," she said.

He took her by the shoulders and shook her gently. He said, "I'd make comic faces all day long. I'd learn a lot of jokes from the books on After-Dinner Speaking."

"Come away from the window. There are no curtains."

"There's nobody to see." But automatically checking his statement, he wasn't quite so sure; a long shadow that had moved, perhaps with the movement of clouds over the moon, was motionless again. He said, "You still love Harry, don't you?"

"Yes."

"Perhaps I do. I don't know." He dropped his hands and said, "I'll be pushing off."

He walked rapidly away. He didn't bother to see whether he was being followed, to check up on the shadow. But passing by the end of the street, he happened to turn, and there, just around the corner, pressed against a wall to escape notice, was a thick, stocky figure. Martins stopped and stared. There was something familiar about that figure. "Perhaps," he thought, "I've grown unconsciously used to him during these last twenty-four hours; perhaps he is one of those who have so assiduously checked my movements."

Martins stood there, twenty yards away, staring at the silent, motionless figure in the dark side street who stared back at him. A police spy, perhaps, or an agent of those other men, those men who had corrupted Harry first and then killed him. Even possibly the third man?

It was not the face that was familiar, for he could not make out so much as the angle of the jaw; nor a movement, for the body was so still that he began to believe that the whole thing was an illusion caused by shadow. He called sharply, "Do you want anything?" and there was no reply. He called again: "Answer, can't you?" And an answer came, for a window curtain was drawn petulantly back by some sleeper he had awakened and the light fell straight across the narrow street and lit up the features of Harry Lime.

"Do you believe in ghosts?" Martins asked of me.

"Do *you*?"

He hadn't come to me at once with his story—only the danger to Anna Schmidt tossed him back into my office, like something the sea has washed up, tousled, unshaven, haunted by an experience he couldn't understand.

He said, "If it had been just the face, I wouldn't have worried. I'd been thinking about Harry, and I might easily have mistaken a stranger. . . . The light was turned off again at once, you see; I only got one glimpse, and the man made off down the street—if he was a man. There was no turning for a long way, but I was so startled I gave him another thirty yards' start. He came to one of those newspaper kiosks, and for a moment moved out of sight. I ran after him. It only took me ten seconds to reach the kiosk, and he must have heard me running, but the strange thing was he never appeared again. I reached the kiosk. There wasn't anybody there. The street was empty. He couldn't have reached a doorway without my seeing him. He'd simply vanished."

"What did you do then?"

"I had to have another drink. My nerves were all to pieces."

"Didn't that bring him back?"

"No, but it sent me back to Anna's . . . But Anna was gone."

I think he would have been ashamed to come to me with his absurd story if it had not been for the attempt on Anna Schmidt. My theory when he did tell me his story was that there had been a watcher, though it was drink and hysteria that had pasted on the man's face the features of Harry Lime. That watcher had noted his visit to Anna, and the member of the ring—the penicillin ring—had been warned by telephone.

Events that night moved fast. Kurtz lived in the Russian zone, on a wide, empty, desolate street that runs down to the Prater Platz.

What happened was this: Russia, you remember, was in the chair as far as the Inner Stadt was concerned, and when Russia was in the chair you expected certain irregularities. On this occasion, halfway through the patrol, the Russian policeman pulled a fast one on his colleagues and directed the car to the street where Anna Schmidt lived. The British M.P. that night was new to his job; he didn't realize till his colleagues told him that they had entered a British zone. He spoke a little German and no French, and the Frenchman, a cynical, hard-bitten Paris *flic*, gave up the attempt to explain to him.

The American took on the job. "It's all right by me," he said, "but is it all right by you?" The British M.P. tapped the Russian's shoulder, who turned his Mongol face and launched a flood of incomprehensible Slav on him. The car drove on.

Outside Anna Schmidt's block the American took a hand in the game and demanded in German what it was all about. The Frenchman leaned against the bonnet and lit a stinking cigarette. France wasn't concerned, and nothing that didn't concern France had any genuine importance to him. The Russian dug out a few words of German and flourished some papers. As far as they could tell, a Russian national wanted by the Russian police was living there without proper papers.

They went upstairs and the Russian tried Anna's door. It was flimsily bolted, but he put his shoulder to it without giving the occupant an opportunity of letting them in. Anna was in bed, though I don't suppose, after Martins's visit, that she was asleep.

While Anna was dressing, the British M.P., a Corporal Starling, phoned through to me, and I gave my instructions.

When he went back to Anna's room a dispute was raging. Anna

had told the American that she had Austrian papers (which was true) and that they were quite in order (which was rather stretching the truth). The American told the Russian in bad German that they had no right to arrest an Austrian citizen. He asked Anna for her papers, and when she produced them the Russian snatched them from her hand.

"Hungarian," he said, pointing at Anna. "Hungarian," and then, flourishing the papers, "Bad, bad."

The American, whose name was O'Brien, said, "Give the girl back her papers," which the Russian, naturally, didn't understand. The American put his hand on his gun, and Corporal Starling said gently, "Let it go, Pat."

"If those papers are not in order we got a right to look."

"Just let it go. We'll see the papers at H.Q."

"If we get to H.Q. You can't trust these Russian drivers. As like as not he'll drive straight through to the Russian zone."

They got back into the car with Anna, who sat in the front with the Russian, dumb with terror.

After they had gone a little way the American touched the Russian on his shoulder. "Wrong way. H.Q. that way," he said.

The Russian chattered back in his own tongue, making a conciliatory gesture, while they drove on.

"Just as I figured it," O'Brien told Starling. "They're taking her to the Russian zone." Anna stared out with terror through the windscreen. "Don't worry," O'Brien said, "I'll fix this all right." His hand was fidgeting round his gun again.

The driver put on his brakes suddenly; there was a road block. You see, I knew they would have to pass this military post if they did not make their way to the international H.Q. in the Inner City. I put my head in at the window and said to the Russian, haltingly, in his own tongue, "What are you doing in the British zone?"

He grumbled that it was "Orders."

"Whose orders? Let me see them." I noted the signature—it was useful information. I said, "This tells you to pick up a certain Hungarian national and war criminal who is living with faulty papers in the British zone. Let me see the papers."

He started on a long explanation, but I saw the papers sticking in his pocket and I pulled them out. He made a grab at his gun, and I punched his face—I felt really mean at doing so, but it's the conduct they expect from an angry officer and it brought him to reason—that and seeing three British soldiers approaching his headlights.

I said, "These papers look to me quite in order, but I'll investigate them and send a report of the result to your colonel. He can, of course, ask for the extradition of this lady at any time. All we want is proof of her criminal activities. I'm afraid we don't regard Hungarian in itself as Russian nationality."

He goggled at me (my Russian was probably half incomprehensible), and I said to Anna, "Get out of the car." She couldn't get by the Russian, so I had to pull him out first. Then I put a packet of cigarettes in his hand, said "Have a good smoke," waved my hand to the others, gave a sigh of relief, and that incident was closed.

While Martins told me how he went back to Anna's and found her gone, I did some hard thinking. I wasn't satisfied with the ghost story or the idea that the man with Harry Lime's features had been an illusion. Keeping Martins silent with a glass of whisky, I rang up my assistant and asked him if he had located Harbin yet. He said no; he understood he'd left Klagenfurt a week ago to visit his family in the adjoining zone.

"All right," I said; "go on trying to get hold of him."

"I'm sorry, sir."

Martins was right; I had made a complete fool of myself, but remember that police work in an occupied city is not like police work at home. Everything is unfamiliar—the methods of one's foreign colleagues; the rules of evidence; even the procedure at inquests. I suppose I had got into the state of mind where one trusts too much to one's personal judgment. I had been immensely relieved by Lime's death. I was satisfied with the accident.

I said to Martins, "Did you look inside the newspaper kiosk, or was it locked?"

"Oh, it wasn't exactly a newspaper kiosk," he said. "It was one of those solid iron kiosks you see everywhere plastered with posters."

"You'd better show me the place."

"But is Anna all right?"

"The police are watching the flat. They won't try anything else yet."

I didn't want to make a fuss and stir in the neighborhood with a police car, so we took trams—several trams, changing here and there, and came into the district on foot.

"This is the turning," Martins said, and led me down a side street. We stopped at the kiosk. "You see, he passed behind here and simply vanished—into the ground."

"That was exactly where he did vanish to," I said.

"How do you mean?"

An ordinary passer-by would never have noticed that the kiosk had a door, and of course it had been dark when the man disappeared. I pulled the door open and showed to Martins the little curling iron staircase that disappeared into the ground.

He said, "Then I didn't imagine him."

"It's one of the entrances to the main sewer."

"And anyone can go down?"

"Anyone. For some reason, the Russians object to these being locked."

"How far can one go?"

"Right across Vienna. People used them in air raids; some of our prisoners hid for two years down there. Deserters have used them—and burglars. If you know your way about you can emerge again almost anywhere in the city through a manhold or a kiosk like this one. The Austrians have to have special police for patrolling these sewers." I closed the door of the kiosk again. I said, "So that's how Harry disappeared."

"You really believe it was Harry?"

"The evidence points that way."

"Then whom did they bury?"

"I don't know yet, but we soon shall, because we are digging him up again. I've got a shrewd idea, though, that Koch wasn't the only inconvenient man they murdered."

Martins said, "What are you going to do about it?"

"I don't know. It's no good applying to the Russians, and you can bet Lime's hiding out now in the Russian zone. We have no line now on Kurtz, for Harbin's gone."

"But it's odd, isn't it, that Koch didn't recognize the dead man's face from the window?"

"The window was a long way up, and I expect the face had been damaged before they took the body out of the car."

Martins said thoughtfully, "I wish I could speak to him. You see, there's so much I simply can't believe."

"Perhaps you are the only one who could speak to him. It's risky, though, because you do know too much."

"I still can't believe . . . I only saw the face for a moment." He said, "What shall I do?"

"He won't leave the Russian zone now. Perhaps that's why he tried to have the girl taken over. Because he loves her? Because he doesn't feel secure? I don't know. I do know that the only person who could persuade him to come over would be you—or her, if he still believes you are his friend. But first you've got to speak to him. I can't see the line."

"I could go and see Kurtz."

I said, "Remember. Lime may not want you to leave the Russian zone when once you are there, and I can't protect you there."

"I want to clear the whole damned thing up," Martins said, "but I'm not going to act as a decoy. I'll talk to him. That's all."

Martins gave Mr. Kurtz no warning of his visit. Better to find him out than a reception prepared for him. He was careful to carry with him all his papers, including the *laissez-passer* of the four powers that on the face of it allowed him to move freely through all the zones of Vienna.

He had no difficulty in finding Mr. Kurtz's block, and when he rang the bell the door was opened quickly by Mr. Kurtz himself.

"Oh," Mr. Kurtz said. "It's you, Rollo," and made a perplexed motion with his hand to the back of his head.

Martins had been wondering why he looked so different, and now he knew. Mr. Kurtz was not wearing his toupee, and yet his head was not bald. He had a perfectly normal head of hair cut close.

Kurtz said, "It would have been better to have telephoned me. You nearly missed me; I was going out."

In the hall a cupboard door stood open, and Martins saw Mr. Kurtz's overcoat, his raincoat, a couple of soft hats, and, hanging sedately on a peg like a wrap, Mr. Kurtz's toupee. He said, "I'm glad to see your hair has grown," and was astonished to see, in the mirror on the cupboard door, the hatred flame and blush on Mr. Kurtz's face.

When Martins turned, Mr. Kurtz smiled at him like a conspirator and said vaguely, "It keeps the head warm."

"Whose head?" Martins asked, for it had suddenly occurred to him how useful that toupee might have been on the day of the accident. "Never mind," he went quickly on, for his errand was not with Mr. Kurtz. "I'm here to see Harry."

"Are you mad?"

"I'm in a hurry, so let's assume that I am. Just make a note of my madness. If you should see Harry—or his ghost—let him know that I want to talk to him. I'll be waiting in the Prater by the Big Wheel for the next two hours—if you can get in touch with the dead, hurry." He added, "Remember, I was Harry's friend."

Kurtz said nothing, but somewhere, in a room off the hall, somebody cleared his throat. Martins threw open a door; he had half expected to see the dead rise yet again, but it was only Dr. Winkler who rose from a chair in front of the kitchen stove, and bowed very stiffly and correctly, with the same celluloid squeak.

Martins turned to Kurtz: "Tell the doctor about my madness. He might be able to make a diagnosis. And remember the place by the Great Wheel. Or do ghosts only rise by night?" He left the flat.

For an hour he waited, walking up and down to keep warm, inside the enclosure of the Great Wheel. The smashed Prater, with its bones sticking crudely through the snow, was nearly empty. A few courting couples would be packed together in a single car of the Wheel and revolve slowly above the city surrounded by empty cars.

Martins wondered who would come for him. Was there enough friendship left in Harry for him to come alone, or would a squad of police arrive? It was obvious from the raid on Anna Schmidt's flat that he had a certain pull. And then as his watch hand passed the hours, he wondered, "Was it all an invention of my mind? Are they digging up Harry's body now in the Central Cemetery?"

Somewhere behind the cake stall a man was whistling, and Martins knew the tune. He turned and waited. Was it fear or excitement that made his heart beat—or just the memories that tune ushered in, for life had always quickened when Harry came, came just as he came now, as though nothing much had happened, nobody had been lowered into a grave or found with cut throat in a basement, came with his amused, deprecating take-it-or-leave-it manner—and of course one always took it.

"Harry."

"Hullo, Rollo."

Don't picture Harry Lime as a smooth scoundrel. He wasn't that. The picture I have of him on my files is an excellent one: He is caught by a street photographer with his stocky legs apart, big shoulders a little hunched, a belly that has known too much good food too long, and on his face a look of cheerful rascality, a geniality, a recognition that *his* happiness will make the world's day. Now he didn't make the mistake of putting out a hand—which might have been rejected—but instead just patted Martins on the elbow and said, "How are things?"

"We've got to talk, Harry."

"Of course."

He had always known the ropes, and even in the smashed pleasure park he knew them, tipping the woman in charge of the Wheel, so that they might have a car to themselves.

Very slowly on one side of them the city sank; very slowly on the other the great cross girders of the Wheel rose into sight. As the horizon slid away, the Danube became visible, and the piers of the Kaiser Friedrich Brucke lifted above the houses.

"Well," Harry said, "it's good to see you, Rollo."

"I was at your funeral."

"That was pretty smart of me, wasn't it?"

"Not so smart for your girl. She was there, too—in tears."

"She's a good little thing," Harry said; "I'm very fond of her."

"I didn't believe the police when they told me about you."

Harry said, "I wouldn't have asked you to come if I'd known what was going to happen, but I didn't think the police were onto me."

"Were you going to cut me in on the spoils?"

"I've never kept you out of anything, old man, yet."

He stood with his back to the door as the car swung upward, and smiled back at Rollo Martins, who could remember him in just such an attitude in a secluded corner of the school quad, saying, "I've learnt the way to get out at night. It's absolutely safe. You are the only one I'm letting in on it."

For the first time Rollo Martins looked back through the years without admiration, as he thought, "He's never grown up." Evil was like Peter Pan—it carried with it the horrifying and horrible gift of eternal youth.

Martins said, "Have you ever visited the children's hospital? Have you seen any of your victims?"

Harry took a look at the toy landscape below and came away from the door. "I never feel quite safe in these things," he said. He felt the back of the door with his hand, as though he were afraid that it might fly open and launch him into space.

"Victims?" he asked. "Don't be melodramatic, Rollo; look down there," he went on, pointing through the window at the people moving like black flies at the base of the Wheel. "Would you really feel any pity if one of those dots stopped moving—forever? If I said you can have twenty thousand pounds for every dot that stops, would you really, old man, tell me to keep my money—without hesitation? Or would you calculate how many dots you could afford to spare? Free of income tax, old man. Free of income tax."

"Couldn't you have stuck to tires?"

"Like Cooler? No, I've always been ambitious."

"You are finished now. The police know everything."

"But they can't catch me, Rollo; you'll see. I'll pop up again. You can't keep a good man down."

The car swung to a standstill at the highest point of the curve, and Harry turned his back and gazed out of the window.

Martins thought, "One good shove and I could break the glass," and he pictured the body falling, falling, through the iron struts, a piece of carrion dropping down among the flies.

He said, "You know the police are planning to dig up your body. What will they find?"

"Harbin," Harry replied with simplicity.

"Why did the Russians try to take Anna Schmidt?" Martins asked.

"She had false papers, old man."

"Who told them?"

"The price of living in this zone, Rollo, is service. I have to give them a little information now and then."

"I thought perhaps you were just trying to get her here—because she was your girl? Because you wanted her?"

Harry smiled. "I haven't all that influence."

"What would have happened to her?"

"Nothing very serious. She'd have been sent back to Hungary. There's nothing against her, really. A year in a labor camp, perhaps. She'd be infinitely better off in her own country than being pushed around by the British police."

"She loves you."

"Well, I gave her a good time while it lasted."

"And I love her."

"That's fine, old man. Be kind to her. She's worth it. I'm glad." He gave the impression of having arranged everything to everybody's satisfaction.

"I'd like to knock you through the window."

"But you won't, old man. I'd trust you anywhere, Rollo. Kurtz tried to persuade me not to come, but I know you. Then he tried to persuade me to, well, arrange an accident. He told me it would be quite easy in this car."

"Except that I'm the stronger man."

"But I've got the gun. You don't think a bullet wound would show when you hit *that* ground?"

Again the car began to move, sailing slowly down, until the flies were midgets, were recognizable human beings.

"What fools we are, Rollo, talking like this, as if I'd do that to you—or you to me." He turned his back and leaned his face against the glass. "In these days, old man, nobody thinks in terms of human beings. Governments don't, so why should we? They talk of the people and the proletariat, and I talk of the mugs. It's the same thing."

As the car reached the platform and the face of the doomed-to-be-victims, the tired, pleasure-hoping Sunday faces, peered in at them, he said, "I could cut you in, you know. I have no one left in the Inner City."

"Except Cooler? And Winkler?"

"You really mustn't turn policeman, old man." They passed out of the car and he put his hand again on Martins's elbow. "That was a joke; I know you won't. I've got to leave you here. We'll see each other—some time. If you are in a jam, you can always get me at Kurtz's."

He moved away and, turning, waved the hand he had the tact not to offer; it was like the whole past moving off under a cloud.

Martins called after him, "Don't trust me, Harry," but there was too great a distance now between them for the words to carry.

"Anna was at the theater," Martins told me, "for the Sunday matinee. I had to see the whole dreary comedy through a second time. About a middle-aged composer and an infatuated girl and an understanding—a terribly understanding—wife. Anna acted very badly; she wasn't much of an actress at the best of times. I saw her afterward in her dressing-room.

"I told her Harry was alive—I thought she'd be glad and that I would hate to see how glad she was, but she sat in front of her make-up mirror and let the tears streak the grease paint, and I wished, after all, that she had been glad. She looked awful and I loved her. Then I told her about my interview with Harry, but she wasn't really paying much attention, because when I'd finished she said, 'I wish he was dead.'"

"He deserves to be," Martins had answered.

"I mean, he would be safe then—from everybody," Anna had said.

I asked Martins, "Did you show her the photographs I gave you—of the children?"

"Yes. I thought, it's got to be kill or cure this time. She's got to get Harry out of her system. I propped the pictures up among the pots of grease. She couldn't avoid seeing them. I said, 'The police can't arrest Harry unless they get him into this zone, and we've got to help do it.'

"She said, 'Thought he was your friend.' I said, 'He *was* my friend.' She said, 'I'll never help you to get Harry. I don't want to see him again, I don't want to be touched by him, but I won't do a thing to harm him.'

"I felt bitter—I don't know why, because, after all, I had done nothing for her. I just got up and left her then. Now it's your turn to work on me, Colonel. What do you want me to do?"

"I want to act quickly," I told Martins. "It was Harbin's body in the coffin, so we can pick up Winkler and Cooler right away. Kurtz is out of our reach for the time being, and so is the driver. We'll put in a formal request to the Russians for permission to arrest Kurtz and Lime. It makes our files tidy. If we are going to use you as our decoy, your message must go to Lime straight away—not after you've hung around in this zone for twenty-four hours.

"As I see it, you were brought here for a grilling almost as soon as you got back into the Inner City; you heard then from me about Harbin; you put two and two together, and you go and warn Cooler. We'll let Cooler slip for the sake of the bigger game; we have no evidence he was in on the penicillin racket. He'll escape into the Russian zone to Kurtz, and Lime will know you've played the game. Three hours later you send a message that the police are after you; you are in hiding and must see him."

"He won't come."

"I'm not so sure. We'll choose our hiding place carefully—when he'll think there's a minimum of risk. It's worth trying. It would appeal to his pride and his sense of humor if he could scoop you out. And it would stop your mouth."

He said, "I told Harry not to trust me, but he didn't hear."

"Do you agree to this plan?"

"Yes," he said, "I agree."

All the first arrangements went well. We delayed arresting Winkler, who had returned from the Russian zone, until after Cooler had been warned.

Martins enjoyed his short interview with Cooler. Cooler greeted him without embarrassment and with considerable patronage: "Why, Mr. Martins, it's good to see you. Sit down. I'm glad everything went off all right between you and Colonel Calloway. A very straight chap, Calloway."

"It didn't," Martins said.

"You don't bear any ill will, I'm sure, about my letting him know about you seeing Koch. The way I figured it was this: If you were innocent you'd clear yourself right away, and if you were guilty, well, the fact that I liked you oughtn't to stand in the way. A citizen has his duties."

"Like giving false evidence at an inquest."

Cooler said, "Oh, that old story. I'm afraid you are riled at me, Mr. Martins. Look at it this way—you as a citizen, owing allegiance to—"

"The police have dug up the body. They'll be after you and Winkler. I want you to warn Harry."

"I don't understand."

"Oh, yes, you do." And it was obvious that he did.

Martins left him abruptly. He wanted no more of that kindly, humanitarian face.

It only remained then to bait the trap. After studying the map of the sewer system I came to the conclusion that a café anywhere near the main entrance of the great sewer, which was placed in what Martins had mistakenly called a newspaper kiosk, would be the most likely spot to tempt Lime. He had only to rise once again through the ground, walk fifty yards, bring Martins back with him, and sink again into the obscurity of the sewers.

He had no idea that his method of evasion was known to us. He probably knew that one patrol of the sewer police ended before midnight, and the next did not start till two; and so, at midnight, Martins sat in the little cold café in sight of the kiosk drinking coffee after coffee. I had given him a revolver; I had men posted as close to the kiosk as I could, and the sewer police were ready, when zero hour struck, to close the manholes and start sweeping the sewers inward from the edge of the city.

There was no heating in the café, and Martins sat warming each hand in turn on a cup of ersatz coffee—innumerable cups. There was usually one of my men in the café with him, but I changed them every twenty minutes or so irregularly. More than an hour passed. Martins had long given up hope, and so had I where I waited at the end of a phone several streets away, with a party of the sewer police ready to go down.

My telephone rang. It was Martins. He said, 'I'm perishing with cold. It's a quarter past one. Is there any point in going on with this?"

"He can't delay much longer if he's coming. He won't want to run into the two-o'clock patrol. Stick it another quarter of an hour, but keep away from the telephone."

Martins's voice said suddenly, "He's here. He's—" And then the telephone went dead.

I said to my assistant, "Give the signal to guard all manholes," and to my sewer police, "We are going down."

What had happened was this: Martins was still on the telephone, still talking to me, when Harry Lime came into the café. I don't know what he heard, if he heard anything. The mere sight of a man wanted by the police and without friends in Vienna speaking on the telephone would have been enough to warn him. He was out of the café again before Martins had put down the receiver. It was one of those rare moments when none of my men were in the café. One had just left and another was about to come in.

Harry Lime brushed by him and made for the kiosk. Martins came out of the café and saw my man. If he had called out then it would have been easy to shoot, but it was not, I suppose, Lime, the penicillin racketeer, who was escaping down the street; it was Harry. He hesitated just long enough for Lime to put the kiosk between them; then he called out, "That's him," but Lime had already gone to ground.

What a strange world unknown to most of us lies under our feet; we live above a cavernous land of waterfalls and rushing rivers, where tides ebb and flow as in the world above.

The main sewer, half as wide as the Thames, rushes by under a huge arch, fed by tributary streams. These streams have fallen in waterfalls from higher levels and have been purified in their fall, so that only in these side channels is the air foul. The main stream smells sweet and fresh, with a faint tang of ozone, and everywhere in the darkness is the sound of rushing water.

It was just past high tide when Martins and the policeman reached the river. First the curving iron staircase, then a short passage so low they had to stoop, and then the shallow edge of the water lapped at their feet. My man shone his light along the edge of the current and said, "He's gone that way," for just as a deep stream when it shallows at the rim leaves an accumulation of debris, so the sewer left in the quiet water against the wall a scum of orange peel, old cigarette butts, and the like, and in this scum Lime had left his trail.

My policeman shone his light ahead with his left hand and carried his gun in his right. He said to Martins, "Keep behind me, sir; he may shoot."

The water came halfway up their legs as they walked. The policeman kept his light pointing down and ahead at the disturbed trail at the sewer's edge. He said, "The silly thing is he doesn't stand a chance. The manholes are all guarded and we've cordoned off the way into the Russian zone. All our chaps have to do now is to sweep inward down the side passage from the manholes."

He took a whistle out of his pocket and blew, and very far away there came the notes of the reply. He said, "They are all down here now. The sewer police, I mean."

He lifted his light for the moment to shine it ahead, and at that moment the shot came. The light flew out of his hand and fell on the stream. He said, "Dod blast it!"

"Are you hurt?" Martins asked.

"Scraped my hand, that's all. A week off work. Here, take this other flashlight, sir, while I tie my hand up. Don't shine it. He's in one of the side passages."

For a long time the sound of the shot went on reverberating; when the last echo died, a whistle blew ahead of them, and Martins's companion blew an answer.

Martins said, "Let me come in front. I don't think he'll shoot at me, and I want to talk to him."

"I had orders to look after you, sir."

"That's all right." Martins edged round, plunging a foot deeper in the stream as he went. When he was in front he called out, "Harry," and the name set up an echo, "Harry, Harry, Harry," which traveled down the stream and woke a whole chorus of whistles in the darkness.

A voice startlingly close made them hug the wall. "Is that you, old man?" it called. "What do you want me to do?"

"Come out. And put your hands above your head."

"I haven't a light, old man. I can't see a thing."

"Be careful, sir," the policeman said.

"Get flat against the wall. He won't shoot at me," Martins said. He called, "Harry, I'm going to shine the light. Play fair and come out. You haven't got a chance."

He flashed the light on, and twenty feet away, at the edge of the light and the water, Harry stepped into view. "Hands above the head, Harry."

Harry raised his hand and fired. The shot ricocheted against the wall a foot from Martins's head, and he heard the policeman cry out. At the same moment a searchlight from fifty yards away lit the whole channel, caught Harry in its beams, Martins, the staring eyes of the policeman slumped at the water's edge with the sewage washing to his waist.

Martins stood above the policeman's body, with Harry Lime half-way between us. We couldn't shoot for fear of hitting Martins, and the light of the searchlight dazzled Lime. We moved slowly on, our revolvers trained for a chance, and Lime turned this way and that way, like a rabbit dazzled by headlights. Then suddenly he took a flying jump into the deep central rushing stream. When we turned the searchlight after him he was submerged, and the current of the sewer carried him rapidly on, past the body of the policeman, out of the range of the searchlight into the dark.

Martins stood at the outer edge of the searchlight beam, staring downstream. He had his gun in his hand now, and he was the only one of us who could fire with safety. I thought I saw a movement, and called out to him, "There. There. Shoot."

He lifted his gun and fired. A cry of pain came tearing back; a reproach, an entreaty.

"Well done," I called.

I looked up, and Martins was out of sight in the darkness. I called his name, and it was lost in a confusion of echoes, in the rush and the roar of the underground river. Then I heard a third shot.

Martins told me later: "I walked upstream to find Harry, but I must have missed him in the dark. I was afraid to lift the torch; I didn't want to tempt him to shoot again. He must have been struck by my bullet just at the entrance of a side passage. Then I suppose he crawled up the passage to the foot of the iron stairs. Thirty feet above his head was the manhole, but he wouldn't have had the strength to lift it, and even if he had succeeded, the police were waiting above.

"He must have known all that, but he was in great pain, and just as an animal creeps into the dark to die, so I suppose a man makes for the light. He wants to die at home, and the darkness is never home to *us*. He began to pull himself up the stairs, but then the pain took him and he couldn't go on. What made him whistle that absurd scrap of a tune I'd been fool enough to believe he had written himself?

"Anyway, I heard his whistle and came back along the edge of the stream, and felt the wall end and found my way up the passage where he lay. I said, 'Harry,' and the whistling stopped, just above my head. I put my hand on an iron handrail and climbed. I was still afraid he might shoot. Then, only three steps up, my foot stamped down on his hand.

"I shone my light on him; he didn't have a gun; he must have dropped it when my bullet hit him. For a moment I thought he was dead, but then he whimpered with pain. I said, 'Harry,' and he swiveled his eyes with a great effort to my face. He was trying to speak, and I bent down to listen.

"'Bloody fool,' he said—that was all: I don't know whether he meant that for himself or for me. Then he began to whimper again. I couldn't bear it any more, and I put a bullet through him."

"We'll forget that bit," I said.

Martins said, "I never shall."

* * *

A thaw set in that night, and all over Vienna the snow melted, and the ugly ruins came to light again: steel rods hanging like stalactites and rusty girders thrusting like bones through the gray slush. Burials were much simpler than they had been a week before, when electric drills had been needed to break the frozen ground. It was almost as warm as a spring day when Harry Lime had his second funeral. I was glad to get him under earth again. But it had taken two men's deaths. The group by the grave was smaller now; Kurtz wasn't there, nor Winkler—only the girl and Rollo Martins and myself. And there weren't any tears.

After it was over, the girl walked away, without a word to either of us, down the long avenue of trees that led to the main entrance and the tram stop, splashing through the melted snow.

I said to Martins, "I've got transport. Can I give you a lift?"

"No," he said, "I'll take a tram back."

"You win; you've proved me a bloody fool."

"I haven't won," he said. "I've lost."

I watched him striding off after the girl. He caught up with her and they walked side by side. I don't think he said a word to her. It was like the end of a story, except that before they turned out of my sight her hand was through his arm—which is how a story usually begins.

And Crabbin? Oh, Crabbin is still arguing with the British Council about Dexter's expenses. They say they can't pass simultaneous payments in Stockholm and Vienna. Poor Crabbin. . . . Poor all of us, when you come to think of it.

The Cross of Lorraine

ISAAC ASIMOV

Emmanuel Rubin did not, as a general rule, ever permit a look of relief to cross his face. Had one done so, it would have argued a prior feeling of uncertainty or apprehension, sensations he might feel but would certainly never admit to.

This time, however, the relief was unmistakable. It was monthly banquet time for the Black Widowers. Rubin was the host and it was he who was supplying the guest. And here it was twenty minutes after seven and only now—with but ten minutes left before dinner was to start—only now did his guest arrive.

Rubin bounded toward him, careful, however, not to spill a drop of his second drink.

"Gentlemen," he said, clutching the arm of the newcomer, "my guest, The Amazing Larri—spelled L-A-R-R-I." And in a lowered voice, over the hum of pleased-to-meet-yous, "Where the hell were you?"

Larri muttered, "The subway train stalled." Then he returned smiles and greetings.

"Pardon me," said Henry, the perennial—and nonpareil—waiter at the Black Widower banquets, "but there is not much time for the guest to have his drink before dinner begins. Would you state your preference, sir?"

"A good notion, that," said Larri gratefully. "Thank you, waiter, and let me have a dry martini, but not too darned dry—a little damp, so to speak."

"Certainly, sir," said Henry.

Rubin said, "I've told you, Larri, that we members all have our *ex officio* doctorates, so now let me introduce them in nauseating detail. This tall gentleman with the neat mustache, black eyebrows, and straight back is Dr. Geoffrey Avalon. He's a lawyer and he never smiles. The last time he tried, he was fined for contempt of court."

Avalon smiled as broadly as he could and said, "You undoubtedly know Manny well enough, sir, not to take him seriously."

"Undoubtedly," said Larri. As he and Rubin stood together, they looked remarkably alike. Both were the same height—about five feet

140

five—both had active, inquisitive faces, both had straggly beards, though Larri's was longer and was accompanied by a fringe of hair down both sides of his face as well.

Rubin said, "And here, dressed fit to kill anyone with a *real* taste for clothing, is our artist-expert, Dr. Mario Gonzalo, who will insist on producing a caricature of you in which he will claim to see a resemblance.—Dr. Roger Halsted inflicts pain on junior high-school students under the guise of teaching them what little he knows of mathematics.—Dr. James Drake is a superannuated chemist who once conned someone into granting him a Ph.D.—And finally, Dr. Thomas Trumbull, who works for the government in an unnamed job as a code expert and who spends most of his time hoping Congress doesn't find out."

"Manny," said Trumbull wearily, "if it were possible to cast a retroactive blackball, I think you could count on five."

And Henry said, "Gentlemen, dinner is served."

It was one of those rare Black Widower occasions when lobster was served, rarer now than ever because of the increase in price.

Rubin, who as host bore the cost, shrugged it off. "I made a good paperback sale last month and we can call this a celebration."

"We can celebrate," said Avalon, "but lobster tends to kill conversation. The cracking of claws and shells, the extraction of meat, the dipping in melted butter—all that takes one's full concentration." And he grimaced with the effort he was putting into the compression of a nutcracker.

"In that case," said the Amazing Larri, "I shall have a monopoly of the conversation," and he grinned with satisfaction as a large platter of prime rib-roast was dexterously placed before him by Henry.

"Larri is allergic to seafood," said Rubin.

Conversation was indeed subdued, as Avalon had predicted, until the various lobsters had been clearly worsted in culinary battle, and then, finally, Halsted asked, "What makes you Amazing, Larri?"

"Stage name," said Larri. "I am a prestidigitator, and escapist extraordinary, and the greatest living exposer."

Trumbull, who was sitting to Larri's right, formed ridges on his bronzed forehead. "What the devil do you mean by 'exposer'?"

Rubin beat a tattoo on his water glass at this point and said, "No grilling till we've had our coffee."

"For God's sake," said Trumbull, "I'm just asking for the definition of a word."

"Host's decision is final," said Rubin.

Trumbull scowled in Rubin's direction. "Then I'll *guess* the answer. An exposer is one who exposes fakes—people who, using trickery of one sort or another, pretend to produce effects they attribute to supernatural or paranatural forces."

Larri thrust out his lower lip, raised his eyebrows, and nodded. "Very good for a guess. I couldn't have put it better."

Gonzalo said, "You mean that whatever someone did by what he claimed was real magic, you could do by stage magic?"

"Exactly," said Larri. "For instance, suppose that some mystic claimed he had the capacity to bend spoons by means of unknown forces. I can do the same by using natural force, this way." He lifted his spoon and, holding it by its two ends, he bent it half an inch out of shape.

Trumbull said, "That scarcely counts. Anyone can do it that way."

"Ah," said Larri, "but this spoon you saw me bend is not the amazing effect at all. That spoon you were watching merely served to trap and focus the ethereal rays that did the real work. Those rays acted to bend *your* spoon, Dr. Trumbull."

Trumbull looked down and picked up his spoon, which was bent nearly at right angles. "How did you do this?"

Larri shrugged. "Would you believe ethereal forces?"

Drake laughed, and pushing his dismantled lobster toward the center of the table, lit a cigarette. He said, "Larri did it a few minutes ago, with his hands, when you weren't looking."

Larri seemed unperturbed by exposure. "When Manny banged his glass, Dr. Trumbull, you looked away. I had rather hoped you all would."

Drake said, "I know better than to pay attention to Manny."

"But," said Larri, "if no one had seen me do it, would you have accepted the ethereal forces?"

"Not a chance," said Trumbull.

"Even if there had been no other way in which you could explain the effect?—Here, let me show you something. Suppose you wanted to flip a coin—"

He fell silent for a moment while Henry passed out the strawberry shortcake, pushed his own serving out of the way, and said, "Suppose

you wanted to flip a coin without actually lifting it and turning it—
this penny, for instance. There are a number of ways it could be done.
The simplest would be merely to touch it quickly, because, as you all
know, a finger is always slightly sticky, especially at meal time, so
that the coin lifts up slightly as the finger is removed and can easily
be made to flip over. It is tails now, you see. Touch it again and it is
heads."

Gonzalo said, "No prestidigitation there, though. We see it flip."

"Exactly," said Larri, "and that's why I won't do it that way. Let's
put something over it so that it can't be touched. Suppose we use a—"
He looked around the table for a moment and seized a salt shaker.
"Suppose we use this."

He placed the salt shaker over the coin and said, "Now it's showing
heads—"

"Hold on," said Gonzalo. "How do we know it's showing heads? It
could be tails and then, when you reveal it later, you'll say it flipped,
when it was tails all along."

"You're perfectly right," said Larri, "and I'm glad you raised the
point.—Dr. Drake, you have eyes that caught me before. Would you
check this on behalf of the assembled company? I'll lift the salt
shaker and you tell me what the coin shows."

Drake looked and said, "Heads," in his softly hoarse voice.

"You'll all take Dr. Drake's word, I hope, gentlemen?—Please,
watch me place the salt shaker back on the coin and make sure it
doesn't flip in the process—"

"It didn't," said Drake.

"Now to keep my fingers from slipping while performing this trick,
I will put this paper napkin over the salt shaker."

Larri folded the paper napkin neatly and carefully around the salt
shaker, then said, "But, in manipulating this napkin, I caused you all
to divert your attention from the penny and you may think I have
flipped it in the process." He lifted the salt shaker with the napkin
around it, and said, "Dr. Drake, will you check the coin again?"

Drake leaned toward it. "Still heads," he said.

Very carefully and gently Larri put back the salt shaker, the paper
napkin still folded around it, and said, "The coin remained as is?"

"Still heads," said Drake.

"In that case, I now perform the magic." Larri pushed down on the
salt shaker and the paper napkin collapsed. There was nothing inside.

There was a moment of shock, and then Gonzalo said, "Where's the salt shaker?"

"In another plane of existence," said Larri airily.

"But you said you were going to flip the coin."

"I lied."

Avalon said, "There's no mystery. He had us all concentrating on the coin as a diversion tactic. When he picked up the salt shaker with the napkin around it to let Jim look at the coin, he just dropped the salt shaker into his hand and placed the empty, folded napkin over the coin."

"Did you see me do that, Dr. Avalon?" asked Larri.

"No. I was looking at the coin, too."

"Then you're just guessing," said Larri.

Rubin, who had not participated in the demonstration at all, but who had eaten his strawberry shortcake instead, said, "The tendency is to argue these things out logically and that's impossible. Scientists and other rationalists are used to dealing with the universe, which fights fair. Faced with a mystic who does not, they find themselves maneuvered into believing nonsense and, in the end, making fools of themselves.

"Magicians, on the other hand," Rubin went on, "know what to watch for, are experienced enough not to be misdirected, and are not impressed by the apparently supernatural. That's why mystics generally won't perform if they know magicians are in the audience."

Coffee had been served and was being sipped, and Henry was quietly preparing the brandy, when Rubin sounded the water glass and said, "Gentlemen, it is time for the official grilling, assuming you idiots have left anything to grill. Jeff, will you do the honors tonight?"

Avalon cleared his throat portentously and frowned down on The Amazing Larri from under his dark and luxuriant eyebrows. Using his voice in the deepest of its naturally deep register, he said, "It is customary to ask our guests to justify their existences, but if today's guest exposes phony mystics even occasionally, I, for one, consider his existence justified and will pass on to another question.

"The temptation is to ask you how you performed your little disappearing trick of a few moments ago, but I quite understand that the ethics of your profession preclude your telling us—even though everything said here is considered under the rose, and though nothing has ever leaked, I will refrain from that question.

"Let me instead ask about your failures.—Sir, you describe yourself as an exposer. Have there been any supposedly mystical demonstrations you have not been able to account for by natural means?"

Larri said, "I have not attempted to explain all the effects I have ever encountered or heard of, but where I have studied an effect and made an attempt to duplicate it, I have succeeded in every case."

"No failures?"

"None."

Avalon considered that, but as he prepared for the next question, Gonzalo broke in. His head was leaning on one palm, but the fingers of that hand were carefully disposed in such a way as not to disarray his hair. He said, "Now, wait, Larri, would it be right to suggest that you tackled only easy cases? The really puzzling cases you might have made no attempts to explain?"

"You mean," said Larri, "that I shied away from anything that might spoil my perfect record or that might upset my belief in the rational order of the universe?—If so, you're quite wrong, Dr. Gonzalo. Most reports of apparent mystical powers are dull and unimportant, crude and patently false. I ignore those. The cases I do take on are precisely the puzzling ones that have attracted attention because of their unusual nature and their apparent divorce from the rational. So, you see, the ones I take on are precisely those you suspect I avoid."

Gonzalo subsided and Avalon said, "Larri, the mere fact that you can duplicate a trick by prestidigitation doesn't mean that it couldn't also have been performed by a mystic through supernatural means. The fact that human beings can build machines that fly doesn't mean that birds are man-made machines."

"Quite right," said Larri, "but mystics lay their claims to supernatural powers on the notion, either expressed or implicit, that there is no other way of producing the effect. If I show that the same effect *can* be produced by natural means, the burden of proof then shifts to them to show that the effect can be produced after the natural means are made impossible. I don't know of any mystic who has accepted the conditions set by professional magicians to guard against trickery and who then succeeded."

"And nothing has ever baffled you? Not even the tricks other magicians have developed?"

"Oh, yes, there are effects produced by some magicians that baffle me in the sense that I don't know quite how they do it. I might duplicate the effect by perhaps using a different method. In any case, that's not the point. As long as an effect is produced by natural means, it doesn't matter whether I can reproduce it or not. I am not the best magician in the world. I am just a better magician than any mystic is."

Halsted, his high forehead flushed, and stuttering slightly in his eagerness to speak, said, "But then nothing would startle you? No disappearance like the one involving the salt shaker?"

"You mean that one?" asked Larri, pointing. There was a salt shaker in the middle of the table, but no one had seen it placed there.

Halsted, thrown off a moment, recovered and said, "Have you ever been *startled* by any disappearance? I heard once that magicians have made elephants disappear."

"Actually, making an elephant disappear is childishly simple. I assure you there's nothing puzzling about disappearances performed in a magic act." And then a peculiar look crossed Larri's face, a flash of sadness and frustration. "Not in a magic act. Just—"

"Yes?" said Halsted. "Just what?"

"Just in real life," said Larri, smiling and attempting to toss off the remark lightheartedly.

"Just a minute," said Trumbull, "we can't let that pass. If there has been a disappearance in real life you can't explain, we want to hear about it."

Larri shook his head. "No, no, Dr. Trumbull. It is not a mysterious disappearance or an inexplicable one. Nothing like that at all. I just—well, I lost something and can't find it and it—saddens me."

"The details," said Trumbull.

"It wouldn't be worth your attention," said Larri, embarrassed. "It's a—silly story and somewhat—" He fell into silence.

"Damn it," thundered Trumbull, "we all sit here and voluntarily refrain from asking anything that might result in your being tempted to violate your ethics. Would it violate the ethics of the magician's art for you to tell this story?"

"It's not that at all—"

"Well, then sir, I repeat what Jeff has told you. Everything said here is in absolute confidence, and the agreement surrounding these monthly dinners is that all questions must be answered.—Manny?"

Rubin shrugged. "That's the way it is, Larri. If you don't want to answer the question we'll have to declare the meeting at an end."

Larri sat back in his chair and looked depressed. "I can't very well allow that to happen, considering the fine hospitality I've been shown. I will tell you the story, but you'll find there's not much to it. I met a woman quite accidentally; I lost touch with her; I can't locate her. That's all there is."

"No," said Trumbull, "that's not all there is. Where and how did you meet her? Where and how did you lose touch with her? Why can't you find her again? We want to know the details."

Gonzalo said, "In fact, if you tell us the details, we may be able to help you."

Larri laughed sardonically. "I think not."

"You'd be surprised," said Gonzalo. "In the past—"

Avalon said, "Quiet, Mario. Don't make promises we might not be able to keep.—Would you give us the details, sir? I assure you we'll do our best to help."

Larri smiled wearily. "I appreciate your offer, but you will see that there is nothing you can do merely by sitting here."

He adjusted himself in his seat and said, "I was done with my performance in an upstate town—I'll give you the details when and if you insist, but for the moment they don't matter, except that this happened about a month ago. I had to get to another small town some hundred and fifty miles away for a morning show and that presented a little transportation problem.

"My magic, unfortunately, is not the kind that can transport me a hundred and fifty miles in a twinkling, or even conjure up a pair of seven-league boots. I did not have my car with me—just as well, for I don't like to travel strange roads at night when I am sleepy—and the net result was that I would have to take a bus that would take nearly four hours. I planned to catch some sleep while on wheels and thus make the trip serve a double purpose.

"But when things go wrong, they go wrong in battalions, so you can guess that I missed my bus and that the next one would not come along for two more hours. There was an enclosed station in which I could wait, one that was as dreary as you could imagine—with no reading matter except some fly-blown posters on the wall—no place to buy a paper or a cup of coffee. I thought grimly that it was fortunate it wasn't raining, and settled down to drowse, when my luck changed.

"A woman walked in. I've never been married, gentlemen, and I've never even had what young people today call a 'meaningful relation-ship.' Some casual attachments, perhaps, but on the whole, though it seems trite to say so, I am married to my art and find it much more satisfying than women, generally.

"I had no reason to think that this woman was an improvement on the generality, but she had a pleasant appearance. She was something over thirty, and was just plump enough to have a warm, comfortable look about her, and she wasn't too tall.

"She looked about and said, smiling, 'Well, I've missed my bus, I see.'

"I smiled with her. I liked the way she said it. She didn't fret or whine or act annoyed at the universe. It was a good-humored state-ment of fact, and just hearing it cheered me up tremendously because actually I myself was in the mood to fret and whine and act annoyed. Now I could be as good-natured as she and say, "Two of us, madam, so you don't even have the satisfaction of being unique.'

"'So much the better,' she said. 'We can talk and pass the time that much faster.'

"I was astonished. She did not treat me as a potential attacker or as a possible thief. God knows I am not handsome or even particularly respectable in appearance, but it was as though she had casually penetrated to my inmost character and found it satisfactory. You have no idea how flattered I was. If I were ten times as sleepy, I would have stayed up to talk to her.

"And we did talk. Inside of fifteen minutes I knew I was having the pleasantest conversation in my life—in a crummy bus station at midnight. I can't tell you all we talked about, but I can tell you what we *didn't* talk about. We didn't talk about magic.

"I can interest anyone by doing tricks, but then it isn't me they're interested in; it's the flying fingers and the patter they like. And while I'm willing to buy attention that way, you don't know how pleasant it is to get the attention without purchasing it. She apparently just liked to listen to me, and I know I liked to listen to her.

"Fortunately, my trip was not an all-out effort, so I didn't have my large trunk with the show-business advertising all over it, just two rather large valises. I told her nothing personal about myself, and asked nothing about her. I gathered briefly that she was heading for her brother's place, that it was right on the road, that she would have to wake him up because she had carelessly let herself be late—but she only told me that in order to say that she was glad it had happened. She would buy my company at the price of inconveniencing her brother. I liked that.

"We didn't talk politics or world affairs or religion or the theater. We talked people—all the funny and odd and peculiar things we had observed about people. We laughed for two hours, during which not one other person came to join us. I had never had anything like that happen to me, had never felt so alive and happy, and when the bus finally came at 1:50 A.M., it was amazing how sorry I was. I didn't want the night to end.

"When we got onto the bus, of course, it was no longer quite the same thing, even though we found a double seat we could share. After all, we had been alone in the station and there we could talk loudly and laugh. On the bus people were sleeping.

"Of course it wasn't all bad. It was a nice feeling to have her so close to me. Despite the fact that I'm rather an old horse, I felt like a teenager—enough like a teenager, in fact, to be embarrassed at being watched.

"Immediately across the way was a woman and her young son. He was about eight years old, I should judge, and *he* was awake. He kept watching me with his sharp little eyes. I could see those eyes fixed on us every time a street light shone into the bus and it was very inhibiting. I wished he were asleep but, of course, the excitement of being on a bus, perhaps, was keeping him awake.

"The motion of the bus, the occasional whisper, the feeling of being quite out of reality, the pressure of her body against mine—it was like confusing dream and fact, and the boundary between sleep and wakefulness just vanished. I didn't intend to sleep, and I started awake once or twice, but then finally, when I started awake one more time, it was clear there had been a considerable period of sleep, and the seat next to me was empty."

Halstead said, "I take it she had gotten off."

"I didn't think she had disappeared into thin air," said Larri. "Naturally, I looked about. I couldn't call her name, because I didn't know her name. She wasn't in the rest room, because its door was swinging open.

"The little boy across the aisle spoke in a rapid high treble—in French. I can understand French reasonably well, but I didn't have to make any effort, because his mother was now awakened and she translated. She spoke English quite well. She said, 'Pardon me, sir, but is it that you are looking for the woman that was with you?'

"'Yes,' I said. 'Did you see where she got off?'

"'Not I, sir. I was sleeping. But my son says that she descended at the place of the Cross of Lorraine.'

"'At the what?'

"She repeated it, and so did the child, in French.

"She said, 'You must excuse my son, sir. He is a great hero worshipper of President Charles de Gaulle and though he is young he knows the tale of the Free French forces in the war very well. He would not miss a sight like a Cross of Lorraine. If he said he saw it, he did.'

"I thanked them and then went forward to the bus driver and asked him, but at that time of night the bus stops wherever a passenger would like to get off, or get on. He had made numerous stops and let numerous people on and off, and he didn't know for sure where he had stopped and whom he had let off. He was rather churlish, in fact."

Avalon cleared his throat. "He may have thought you were up to no good and was deliberately withholding information to protect the passenger."

"Maybe," said Larri despondently, "but what it amounted to was that I had lost her. When I came back to my seat, I found a little note tucked into the pocket of the jacket I had placed in the rack above. I managed to read it by a streetlight at the next stop, where the French mother and son got off. It said, "Thank you so much for a delightful time. Gwendolyn.'"

Gonzalo said, "You have her first name anyway."

Larri said, "I would appreciate having had her last name, her address, her telephone number. A first name is useless."

"You know," said Rubin, "she may deliberately have withheld information because she wasn't interested in continuing the acquaintanceship. A romantic little interlude is one thing; a continuing danger is another. She may be a married woman."

"Have you done anything about trying to find her?" asked Gonzalo.

"Certainly," said Larri sardonically. "If a magician is faced with a disappearing woman he must understand what has happened. I have gone over the bus route twice by car, looking for a Cross of Lorraine.

If I had found it, I would have gone in and asked if anyone there knew a woman by the name of Gwendolyn. I'd have described her. I'd have gone to the local post office or the local police station."

"But you haven't found a Cross of Lorraine, I take it," said Trumbull.

"I have not."

Halsted said, "Mathematically speaking, it's a finite problem. You could try every post office along the whole route."

Larri sighed. "If I get desperate enough, I'll try. But, mathematically speaking, that would be so inelegant. Why can't I find the Cross of Lorraine?"

"The youngster might have made a mistake," said Trumbull.

"Not a chance," said Larri. "An adult, yes, but a child, never. Adults have accumulated enough irrationality to be very unreliable eyewitnesses. A bright eight-year-old is different. Don't try to pull any trick on a bright kid; he'll see through it.

"Just the same," he went on, "nowhere on the route is there a restaurant, a department store, or anything else with the name Cross of Lorraine. I've checked every set of yellow pages along the entire route."

"Now wait a while," said Avalon, "that's wrong. The child wouldn't have seen the words because they would have meant nothing to him. If he spoke and read only French, as I suppose he did, he would know the phrase as 'Croix de Lorraine.' The English would have never caught his eyes. He must have seen the symbol, the cross with the two horizontal bars, like this." He reached out and Henry obligingly handed him a menu.

Avalon turned it over and on the blank back drew the following:

"Actually," he said, "it's more properly called the Patriarchal Cross or the Archiepiscopal Cross since it symbolized the high office of patriarchs and archbishops by doubling the bars. You will not be surprised to hear that the Papal Cross has three bars. The Patriarchal Cross was used as a symbol of Godfrey of Bouillon, who was one of the leaders of the First Crusade, and since he was Duke of Lorraine, it came to be called the Cross of Lorraine. As we all know, it was adopted as the emblem of the Free French during the Hitlerian War." He coughed slightly and tried to look modest.

Larri said, a little impatiently, "I understand about the symbol, Dr. Avalon, and I didn't expect the youngster to note words. I think you'll agree, though, that any establishment calling itself the Cross of Lorraine would surely display the symbol along with the name. I looked for the name in the yellow pages and for the symbol on the road."

"And you didn't find it?" said Gonzalo.

"As I've already said, I didn't. I was desperate enough to consider things I didn't think the kid could possibly have seen at night. I thought, who knows how sharp young eyes are and how readily they may see something that represents an overriding interest? So I looked at signs in windows, at street signs—even at graffiti."

"If it were a graffito," said Trumbull, "which happens to be the singular form of graffiti, by the way, then, of course, it could have been erased between the time the child saw it and the time you came to look for it."

"I'm not sure of that," said Rubin. "It's my experience that graffiti are never erased. We've got some on the outside of our apartment house—"

"That's New York," said Trumbull. "In smaller towns there's less tolerance for these evidences of anarchy."

"Hold on," said Gonzalo, "what makes you think graffiti are necessarily signs of anarchy? As a matter of fact—"

"Gentlemen! Gentlemen!" And as always, when Avalon's voice was raised to its full baritone, a silence fell. "We are not here to argue the merits and demerits of graffiti. The question is: how can we find this woman who disappeared? Larri has found no restaurant or other establishment with the name of Cross of Lorraine; he has found no evidence of the symbol along the route taken. Can we help him?"

Drake held up his hand and squinted through the curling smoke of his cigarette. "Hold on, there's no problem. Have you ever seen a Russian Orthodox Church? Do you know what its cross is like?" He made quick marks on the back of the menu and shoved it toward the center of the table. "Here—"

He said, "The kid, being hipped on the Free French, would take a quick look at that and see it as the Cross of Lorraine. So what you have to do, Larri, is look for a Russian Orthodox Church en route. I doubt there would be more than one."

Larri thought about it, but did not seem overjoyed. "The cross with that second bar set at an angle would be on the top of the spire, wouldn't it?"

"I imagine so."

"And it wouldn't be floodlighted, would it? How would the child be able to see it at three or four o'clock in the morning?"

Drake stubbed out his cigarette. "Well, now, churches usually have a bulletin board near the entrance. There could have been a Russian Orthodox cross on the—"

"I would have seen it," said Larri firmly.

"Could it have been a Red Cross?" asked Gonzalo feebly. "You know, there might be a Red Cross headquarters along the route."

"The Red Cross," said Rubin, "is a Greek Cross with all four arms equal. I don't see how that could possibly be mistaken for a Cross of Lorraine by a Free French enthusiast. Look at it—"

Halsted said, "The logical thing, I suppose, is that you simply missed it, Larri. If you insist that, as a magician, you're such a trained observer that you *couldn't* have missed it, then maybe it was a symbol on something movable—on a truck in a driveway, for instance—and it moved on after sunrise."

"The boy made it quite clear that it was at the *place* of the Cross of Lorraine," said Larri. "I suppose even an eight-year-old can tell the difference between a place and a movable object."

"He spoke French. Maybe you mistranslated."

"I'm not that bad at the language," said Larri, "and besides, his mother translated and French is her native tongue."

"But English isn't. *She* might have gotten it wrong. The kid might have said something else. He might not even have said the Cross of Lorraine at all."

Avalon raised his hand for silence and said, "One moment, gentlemen, I see Henry, our esteemed waiter, smiling. What is it, Henry?"

Henry, from his place at the sideboard, said, "I'm afraid that I am amused at your doubting the child's evidence. It is quite certain, in my opinion, that he did see the Cross of Lorraine."

There was a moment's silence and Larri said, "How can you tell that, Henry?"

"By not being too subtle, sir."

Avalon's voice boomed out. "I knew it! We're being too complicated. Henry, how is it possible for us to achieve greater simplicity?"

"Why, Mr. Avalon; the incident took place at night. Instead of looking at all signs, all places, all varieties of cross, why not begin by asking ourselves what very few things *can* be easily seen on a highway at night?"

"A Cross of Lorraine?" asked Gonzalo incredulously.

"Certainly," said Henry, "among other things. Especially if we don't call it a Cross of Lorraine. What the youngster saw as a Cross of Lorraine, out of his special interest, we would see as something else so clearly that its relationship to the Cross of Lorraine would be invisible. What has been happening just now has been precisely what happened earlier with Mr. Larri's trick with the coin and the salt shaker. We concentrated on the coin and didn't watch the salt shaker, and now we concentrate on the Cross of Lorraine and don't look for the alternative."

Trumbull said, "Henry, if you don't stop talking in riddles, you're fired. What the hell is the Cross of Lorraine, if it isn't the Cross of Lorraine?"

Henry said gravely, "What is this?" and carefully he drew on the back of the menu—

Trumbull said, "A Cross of Lorraine—tilted."

"No, sir, you would never have thought so, if we hadn't been talking about the Cross of Lorraine. Those are English letters and a very common symbol on highways if you add something to it—" He wrote quickly and the tilted Cross became:

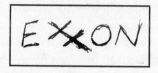

"The one thing," said Henry, "that is designed to be seen without trouble, day or night, on any highway, is a gas-station sign. The child saw the Cross of Lorraine in this one, but Mr. Larri, retracing the route, sees only a double X, since he reads the entire sign as Exxon. All signs showing this name, whether on the highway, in advertisements, or on credit cards, show the name in this fashion."

Now Larri caught fire. "You mean, Henry, that if I go into the Exxon stations en route and ask for Gwendolyn—"

"The proprietor of one of them is likely to be her brother, and there would not be more than a half dozen or so at most to inqure at."

"Good God, Henry," said Larri, "you're a magician."

"Merely simple-minded," said Henry, "though not, I hope, in the pejorative sense."

Nameless Enemy

MIRIAM ALLEN DEFORD

This story begins 30 years before its ending. In 1935 Wilson Blayn was young, rich, and ambitious. He was a graduate *magna cum laude* of a great law school, and like most young men of his antecedents and connections he had started low in a blue-ribbon law firm, expecting and being expected to rise rapidly—always concerned with civil and corporation cases, never with practice in the criminal courts. He had married a girl from the right circles, he lived in the right kind of house in the right kind of suburb, unostentatiously and frugally as frugality is understood among the more Puritanical rich—and any prophet could have foretold his future.

When he died in 1965, Wilson Blayn—though he still had most of his inherited fortune, carefully invested in the safest bonds—was an embittered, lonely man, ostracized by the people among whom he had grown up, disregarded or avoided by such formal associates as he had left, wifeless, childless, homeless (he had holed up in a second-class residential hotel for the last years of his life), and with only one burning ambition left—to identify, expose, and destroy the man who had caused his downfall.

In 1935 Blayn's ambition had been not for vengeance, but for political achievement. His road was carefully mapped out—District Attorney, State Attorney General, Governor, perhaps even President. He belonged to the right party for his state and district, he had the money to conduct effective campaigns, he knew the people who mattered and who could help. He thought of himself much as a young Roman of good family might have thought in the days of the Republic: civic leadership was his natural duty and responsibility as well as his path to eminence. The state primary was in June; he was a candidate for the nomination of District Attorney by the party in power, and nomination was tantamount to election. He had every right to expect success; his only opponent was a longtime deputy who was getting beyond the useful age and was rumored to be too fond of the bottle.

A single night changed it all.

On the night of April 15, 1935, Wilson Blayn went to bed a very happy man. He had spent the afternoon with the County Central Committee, and everything had gone well. He had spent the evening in a private room in a hospital, where two days before his wife had given birth to their son.

He let himself in at about ten o'clock to an empty house, for the three servants and the housekeeper, a Mrs. Schoff, slept out; he and Mary preferred their privacy. But Mrs. Schoff had, as usual, left sandwiches for him on a plate in the dining room; he poured himself a nightcap to drink while he ate, and by eleven he was in bed. He fell asleep almost at once, remembering fondly Mary's smile as she bent over the baby, and the thrill of feeling the tiny hand curl around his finger.

He was awakened from deep slumber by a pounding on the front door and intermittent ringing of the doorbell. He looked sleepily at the bedside clock and saw that it was 2:45. He got himself into a dressing gown and slippers and stumbled downstairs, his eyes half shut and his hair ruffled.

He opened the door on the chain, and there on the step stood a woman—young and slender, from what he could see, and a complete stranger.

"Oh!" she gasped as the door opened, "Thank heaven I woke somebody at last!"

"What's the matter?" asked Blayn, his voice thick with sleep.

"My car's broken down, and I want to phone the Association."

Peering out, Blayn could see a car parked at the curb.

"Please just let me use your phone!" the woman pleaded. "I was afraid I'd have to sit in the car till daylight, and anything could happen."

Blayn shook his head to waken himself fully. A thousand thoughts darted through his mind. Was there a confederate hidden in the thick bushes of the front garden? If he let the woman in, would he be rushed, overpowered, burgled, perhaps shot if he resisted?

"Why pick on me?" he growled. "There are plenty of other houses on the block." He caught himself before he added that he was alone in the house.

The girl began to cry.

"Oh, *please*," she sobbed. "I only want to use your phone. I don't know what's wrong—I'm not out of gas, but the car stopped dead, right in front here, and I can't get it going. I was afraid to try anywhere else—these houses are so far apart and they all have grounds around them. The Association will send someone to tow me away, if I can just call them, and I can wait in the car if you'll turn a light on or keep an eye on me till they come."

Then Blayn thought of something else—the kind of people who "don't want to get involved," who like Pharisees pass by on the other side. He was not that kind of person. Perhaps, too, he remembered that if this girl was really in trouble and he turned her down, the story might injure his nomination. And it was true that it would be dangerous for her to sit even in a locked car, and even in this neighborhood, at three o'clock in the morning.

He made up his mind and unlatched the chain.

The woman stepped into the front hall. "The phone's right here," he started to say.

It all happened too fast to register clearly.

With one motion the girl threw off her long coat, and to his horror Blayn saw that under it she wore nothing whatever. She wound her arms around his neck, pushing his head upward, and pressed herself tightly against him. Instantly, in the darkness outside, a flashbulb went off twice. And then, before he could get his breath, she had darted down for her coat, run out of the house, and half a minute later the engine in the "stalled" car started and the car was speeding down the street.

Blayn ran to the open door, but all he could see was the vanishing tail-light. The photographer must have raced to the car with her, but Blayn caught only a half-glimpsed shadow of movement.

He did not go to bed again. He sat with a bottle of whiskey beside him, smoking many cigarettes, trying to figure things out.

It was a beautiful frameup. What could he do to counter it? And who had done it to him, and why?

The "why" seemed obvious enough. Somebody wanted to kill his nomination. As for the "who," all he could be sure of at the moment was that somebody knew he was alone in the house and vulnerable. But that was no secret—the papers had carried the news yesterday of the baby's birth. And anybody could find out without much effort that the servants left every evening after cleaning up from dinner and did not return until eight o'clock the following morning.

The Deputy District Attorney who was challenging him for the nomination? Not that old hack; he hadn't the astuteness for such a plot, nor the courage to take such a risk.

What other enemies had he? He searched his mind. None that he could think of in the party. None in the law office. None among his social acquaintances. None from his past, or from school. He had no family; he was an only child, and an orphan. Both his parents had been killed in an automobile accident before he was three years old, and he had been reared under the depersonalized guardianship of an officer of the bank which was acting as executor of his parents' estate.

He remembered neither of his parents; his unemotional childhood and youth had turned him into a self-sufficient, rather self-centered man, whose only weakness was an occasionally uncontrollable temper. He had never had a friend close enough to quarrel with, or felt really close to anybody.

Could his enemy, then, be someone who had wanted Mary, and was seeking revenge? It seemed unlikely. Mary had gone to school in France and had returned to America only a few months before he met her. From the beginning he had monopolized her, and she was not the sort to encourage a jealous rival. Theirs was a marriage of cool affection and suitability rather than of ardent love.

For a while he toyed with the idea that some lunatic envious of his good luck—his money, his health and youth and good looks, his contented marriage, even his infant son—was trying to ruin him; but he dimissed that with a shrug. This was obviously a cold, sane plot.

As for counteraction, there was nothing he could do until his antagonist made his next move. That would probably be soon enough.

It came the very next afternoon, in a sensational evening tabloid of the political opposition, which had a big surreptitious circulation even in this sedate suburb of a big city.

Does Brook County Want a Playboy As D.A.?

His startled grimace in the photograph could have passed for lechery. The hands with which by reflex he had pushed the woman from him seemed glued to her naked body. She was leaning a little backward, and even from a rear view she was voluptuously beautiful.

More so than poor Mary, who was a bit on the skinny side.

Driving to the hospital, the horrible paper crushed beside him, Blayn could only pray that he would have a chance to tell Mary the real story before somebody passed this one on to her. Phrases and

innuendoes from the smirking newspaper account echoed sickeningly
in his mind.

He was too late. Mary had heard the nurses giggling together and
had insisted on knowing the joke. Her special nurse met him at the
door of her room. "I'm so sorry, Mr. Blayn," she murmured, struggling to keep from smiling. "Mrs. Blayn isn't feeling so well today.
She said to tell you she didn't feel up to seeing you right now."

He pushed by her angrily. Mary was lying on her back, her eyes
closed, her face pale.

"Oh, my dear!" he cried. "I'm so sorry. I wanted to get here and tell
you about this first."

What he had loved in Mary was her coolness, her calm. They had
never pretended to be passionately in love, but to him at least it had
been the perfect partnership he had wanted. Now she opened her eyes
and her look was cold, not cool. She spoke, scarcely moving her lips,
and her tone was harsh.

"To do this to me!" she said. "I wouldn't have minded so much if
you had been discreet—but to disgrace me like this! I'm ashamed to
look my family and my friends in the face. And my poor little
baby!"

"My"—not "our."

His tenderness turned to boiling rage; he felt his face flush and the
veins in his temples swell. He did not recognize his own voice.

"So that's how much you trust me, is it? You'd rather believe that
filthy yellow rag than your own husband! They framed me, Mary. I
thought you at least would stand by me."

Here eyes filled with tears and they ran down her cheeks. She made
no effort to wipe them away. But her voice did not change.

"I've always suspected you didn't really care for me, not really,"
she said icily. "Now I understand a lot of things."

"That story's a dirty lie!" Blayn protested. "I'm going to sue that
paper for enough to put it out of business. Somebody did this to me,
and I'm going to find out who. Listen, Mary. Last night I was sound
asleep when—"

"Please, Will. I can't—I'm feeling too ill to talk. Later—not now.
Please go now, Will—please."

She turned her back on him. He wheeled abruptly and strode from
the room. The nurse opened the door.

"You bitch!" he growled. Her scared face made him feel like

laughing. He almost ran out of the hospital; he drove away savagely, twice just missed a collision, and reached his office full of helpless fury.

They all knew, down to the office boy; he could tell from their averted glances. On his desk he found a note from his secretary: "Mr. Mackintosh wants to see you as soon as you come in."

Old Phineas Mackintosh, the senior member of the firm. The old man was embarrassed.

"Of course I realize this is all nonsense, my boy," he mumbled. "But I think it would be wise if you'd take a short leave till you can clear it up and the talk dies down. I've felt right along you were devoting too much time to politics, anyway."

That was untrue. Up to now Mackintosh had been encouraging him. Anger overcame Blayn again.

"That won't be necessary," he said roughly. "I'm tendering my resignation, as of now."

Against the old man's sputtering he slammed the door, dictated his resignation, stood over his secretary while she typed it, signed it, and ordered her to take it to Mackintosh. Then without another word he cleaned his desk of personal belongings and left the office.

He dared not trust himself to go in person to *The Daily Intelligencer*. He went home to draw up papers for a suit for defamation of character. The paper had been careful about direct libel.

Mrs. Schoff had left a note on the desk in his study: "My daughter is sick and I have to look after her. I don't know when I can be back. Please send check for wages due to my address."

He wrote the check at once and enclosed it in a note informing Mrs. Schoff that he was giving her a month's wages in lieu of notice. In the kitchen he found the two maids gossiping with the gardener; he paid them all off on the spot.

He packed a bag and took a room in a downtown hotel. There he sent for a public stenographer and dictated a letter to the County Central Committee withdrawing his candidacy.

Notice of his suit brought all the other news media down upon him. It did not help him much when he broke a persistent TV photographer's camera, and punched a tenacious reporter on the nose.

The suit was heard much sooner than he had ever been able to get other suits on the trial docket in behalf of the law firm. He acted as his own attorney. The defense attorney was a flamboyant lawyer, a master of publicity, whose clients were usually the accused in sensational murder cases.

The Daily Intelligencer's defense was that the picture and story had been published in good faith and without malice as legitimate news about a candidate for public office. They had not taken the photograph; it had been brought to the city editor's desk. Both the editor and the reporter who wrote the story refused to name their source; they were sentenced for contempt and spent a widely publicized week in jail—that was one of the duties of employees of *The Daily Intelligencer*.

All Blayn could plead was his hitherto unblemished reputation and his unverified account of the grotesque affair in his front hall. "In twenty years at the bar," exclaimed the defendant's lawyer dramatically, "I have never heard so imbecilic and incredible a story! My honorable colleague is wasted in our profession. With an imagination like his, he should be writing soap operas!"

The judge smiled and several of the jury laughed. The audience had to be quieted. Blayn lost his temper again and shouted abuse at his opponent. Then he too was threatened with contempt and had to make a grudging apology.

The jury took just half an hour to bring in a verdict against him, though it smugly deplored the sensationalism of the paper—which undoubtedly most of them read regularly.

A week later Blayn was served with notice of a hearing for disbarment proceedings, based on "moral turpitude and consequent notoriety." He did not even appear, and was duly disbarred.

By this time he had ceased to care; his life was in ruins.

Mary had gone from the hospital back to her parents' home, taking the baby with her. There was one dreadful scene there, when he shouted and she refused to speak to him and her father ordered him out of the house. After that she hung up on him when he phoned her, and the day he was disbarred he was served with divorce papers. To save her own dignity she gave the grounds as cruelty, not adultery, but the papers, TV, and radio had another field day.

He did not contest the divorce, and he paid heavy alimony without protest. He was given the most meagre visiting privileges for his son. A year later Mary remarried and moved to another city with her new husband, and the only communication he ever had with her again was a letter, which he never answered, telling him that her husband had adopted the baby legally and given him his name.

All Wilson Blayn had left was his inherited fortune and his bitter determination to track down and punish his enemy.

For a while he drank heavily and brooded alone in his hotel room. He sold the house in the suburban town and the furniture; Mary had stripped it of all her own possessions. He saw no one and hung up on the few who called him.

He was saved from utter disintegration by Pearl Harbor. He enlisted at once, was soon transferred to Officers' Training School, was posted in the South Pacific, and for three years was in the thick of combat. It became a hiatus in his crusade for revenge; he visited on the public enemy his rage at his private foe.

He emerged from the war unscathed, a Lieutenant Colonel with three medals and a rainbow of campaign ribbons. For a while he thought of remaining in the army. But with peace his obsession for revenge came back to him; he thirsted to return to civilian life and renew his pursuit of the unknown man who had wrecked his life.

He made only one more attempt to reinstate himself in the world of normal people. He began to cast about for something to occupy his time. He still avoided company, and he wanted no occupation that would force him to mingle with other people. Finally he settled on accounting, and signed up for courses in City College.

His mind was as good as ever, and he passed with distinction. He had some difficulty in taking the examination for certification, because of his disbarment; but his war record saved him.

He was certified, and opened an office as a public accountant. He could afford to pick and choose his clients; what he wanted was big impersonal firms where he would have few direct personal contacts. He was more bitter and more desirous of solitude than ever. His leisure he gave to the patient hunt for his enemy.

Three years later Blayn had built up a flourishing business and a solid reputation. What setbacks he had were because of his low boiling point and his rude arrogance. The whole sorry affair of the frameup and the disastrous suit seemed to have faded from everybody's consciousness—except his own.

And then calamity struck again.

Suddenly, within a week, all his biggest customers abruptly terminated their connection with him. Most of them refused to give any reason except that they were "no longer satisfied" and had decided to employ another accountant. Three told him stiffly that "on confidential and reliable information received" they no longer considered him an asset. All of them flatly refused to say more, and it only made things worse when in each case he stormed into the offices and made an angry scene. He wound up his business, and thenceforth confined himself to the care of his own investments.

In a last effort to distract himself, Blayn set out on a world tour that in two years took him to almost every country on the globe. He tried to sink himself into travel, to think of nothing but the places he visited—their history, their points of interest, their natural beauties. It did no good. Underneath, there was always the festering sore, the consciousness of frustration.

Until he met Katherine Wilmot.

That was in Egypt, and appropriately they met at the buried feet of the Sphinx. Katherine was English, no longer a young girl, handsome rather than pretty, a woman with an independence to match his own. She had never married. For the first time since Mary, Wilson Blayn felt a stirring of interest in a woman.

The fierce hostility with which he had been greeting his fellow beings had calmed a bit under the influence of time and change of environment. Almost without knowing it, against his conscious desire and for the first time in his life, he fell deeply in love. When Katherine went home he followed her. Six months later they were engaged to be married.

Katherine was Somebody, connected by blood with important people. The newspapers played up the engagement, and an enterprising correspondent sent a notice to America. The papers in his home city caught it and gave it front-page attention. *The Daily Intelligencer* ran the notorious picture again, and rehashed the whole nauseating story.

It was most unlikely that Katherine or anyone she knew would ever see *The Daily Intelligencer*. But two copies did go to England, sent anonymously. One went to him, one to her.

She listened to his account calmly, and she believed it. But she was proud and fastidious. To marry a divorced American was bad enough; but she could not face involving herself in this kind of background. Sadly but implacably she broke their engagement.

Now Blayn knew definitely that somewhere he had a relentless ruthless enemy, who would never allow him to build up an endurable life for himself.

He returned to his home city with only one objective—find out who, and why, and to strike him down.

He became a fanatic. He combed his memory for every episode of his past that could conceivably have caused affront to anyone. There were plenty of them; he had always had a hot temper, badly disciplined. He followed up every name he could dig out of the recesses of recollection—college classmates, political associates, clients and opponents in legal cases, girls he had gone around with before he met Mary (though it seemed most unlikely that this was a feminine plot), every member of Mary's family and her close friends in the days of his courtship.

He made long journeys to distant cities to consult records; he followed up every name to the point where it was impossible to consider it further. Some were dead, some had left the city many years ago and had lost all contact with it, some—a judge, a senator, a clergyman, a professor—even to his jaundiced eye were improbable in the role.

Years crept by, and his hopeless search became Wilson Blayn's only interest in life. He hid himself in his shabby hotel, ate sparingly, grew careless of his appearance, ceased to have any but the most cursory relations with other human beings. He was undoubtedly a little mad. But he was safe from interference, for he still could and did manage his financial affairs sensibly, and he became richer rather than poorer.

So the years went on—five, ten, fifteen. Still the search continued, though his adversary had made no further move against a ruined man. Perhaps a professional detective could have accomplished more; and if he had had a good lead he would have hired one, but he shrank from even that invasion of his privacy.

And at last, almost by accident, he struck pay dirt.

He was getting near the end of his list of possible suspects. In desperation he began to think of his own family.

He knew very little about them, from the circumstances of his alienated boyhood. When he grew old enough to be curious and asked his legal guardian, the bank official was of little help. Blayn knew his father's given names—Lucius Edwin—and his mother's maiden name—Harriet Wilson. He had had a grandfather who had been the founder of the family fortune, and from old directories he discovered a few Blayns, with that unusual spelling (Wilsons were hopeless; there were too many of them), for 70-odd years back. He began a systematic survey of the city records.

He found odd bits of information, and significant bits of lack of information. From the latter he gathered that his father must have been an only child. That stood to reason, anyway—if there had been aunts or uncles or even first cousins on either side, surely one of *them* would have been made his guardian, or at the very least would have come forward after his parents' death.

The clerk in the Hall of Records was used by now to his almost daily presence. The records were open to the public, but only Wilson Blayn was so constant an inquirer. To avoid curiosity, Blayn had told the clerk that he was a professional genealogist, looking up data for clients.

He was down to futile, desperate measures by now, having exhausted all others. He started methodically with the year of his own birth and plodded through all the volumes of births from A to Z, in the hope of finding a clue—a name he would recognize that he had forgotten. He himself knew that this was sheer insanity—his persecutor, whose very name he hoped might activate a new train of memories, might have been born anywhere, at any time.

But he couldn't stop—by this time, to stop would have been to die. This ceaseless hunt at least kept him alive.

And then, two years after he had been born, all the way into the S's, he suddenly caught sight of his father's name.

It was in the record of birth of one Julian Snow, son of Claribelle Snow and Lucius Edwin Blayn. Illegitimate, but acknowledged.

With the blinding certainty of a lightning stroke, Wilson Blayn realized now what must have been the true nature of that fatal "accident" which had cost him both his parents before he was three years old. He could visualize the bitterness, the anger, the quarrels. In that last drive together, whose hand was on the steering wheel, or whose hand snatched the other away and headed the car over the cliff? He would never know; but he was convinced the deaths of his mother and father were murder and suicide.

Now he understood, too, the reason for the inexorable persecution. It became crystal clear when he got the report of the expensive, efficient detective he employed.

Julian Snow had not been difficult to trace. Blayn was given his address, his history, his physical description—everything except the least shred of legal evidence against him.

After all, they were sons of the same father; they had personality traits in common. In Snow's place, Blayn would have felt the same way, perhaps acted the same way, though his natural response would have been violence rather than deviousness: they shared ambition and pride and deep-seated resentment of wrong.

Blayn had no doubt that the father who had acknowledged an illegitimate son must at the time have provided financially for the mother, made some kind of settlement on them. Perhaps he had intended to leave, discreetly, a sufficient sum to insure Julian's welfare and education. But he had not had time; the will he had made out at Wilson's birth still stood. Perhaps it was a quarrel over that which had led to the final catastrophe. Blayn had no idea what Claribelle Snow had meant to Lucius Blayn—whether he loved her and wanted a divorce from his wife to marry her, or whether Julian was the result of a casual indiscretion.

So Wilson Blayn had spent his boyhood at exclusive boarding schools, with conducted tours and cruises during the long vacations; he had gone to the very best college and law school; he had never had to give a moment's thought to the cost of food or lodging or clothing or any other need. He had had no trouble in finding a place in an important law firm. He had married a girl from the same social and financial circles in which he had always lived, and she bore him a son. He had bought a house in a gilt-edge suburb, and if he lived modestly it was by his own taste and not from necessity. When his ambition turned to politics, he had every prospect of complete success. Even after he had been disgraced, he had easily become an officer in the army. And he was tall, good-looking, well-built, athletic. He had had everything.

But Julian Snow, with an equally fine mind and an equally proud spirit, had had the bad public schooling of a slum district. He had never been able to go beyond high school; he had had to find a job to support his mother, an invalid for years before she died. He had never been able to put anything aside beyond bare subsistence: what small ambitions he had achieved had been at the expense of grueling toil. He had married a girl as poor as he was; the marriage had not been successful—she had divorced him after three years, and he had never remarried. They had no children. He lived in one room in a cheap boarding house. He had inherited brains and personality from the senior Blayn, but physically he was a Snow—and the Snows were short, running to unhealthy obesity, suffering frequently from an asthmatic tendency. He had been rejected at his medical examination in the draft. He had had nothing.

And the only difference between the two half brothers was that one of them was legitimate.

Was it any wonder, then, that he had hated with a brooding jealousy the brother he had never seen, or that his warped mind had plotted revenge as tortuous as it was surreptitious?

There were other indications too of Julian Snow's having been the author of all Wilson Blayn's misfortunes. For Snow was by trade a free-lance news photographer. He had in consequence a wide acquaintance among newspaper people, and doubtless often earned extra sums for supplying news tips or gossip to sheets like The Daily Intelligencer. And he could have found out through his contacts which firms were employing Blayn.

The indictment was complete—but there was not one bit of proof to substantiate it. And even if there had been, or if it could be discovered, what good would it do now, when one brother's mind was as sick as the other's, to smear their father's name in a court of law?

There were no damages to be had from Julian Snow. There were no damages to be had from anyone for 30 years of a devastated life. The revelation to which Wilson Blayn had devoted nearly half his years had after all brought him nothing worth having.

If Blayn had learned his father's secret early in life, when he was young and optimistic, he would in all probability have acted very differently. His lonely boyhood had cooled and hardened him, but he would still have been capable then of understanding and compassion. He was too proud and too ambitious ever to have acknowledged his half brother openly, but he would have felt it a debt to his father to see that Julian Snow was well provided for.

But it was too late now. Their father had eaten sour grapes, and both his children's teeth were set on edge.

It was almost a disappointment to know the truth. Life had lost its savor for Blayn now that he no longer had the stimulus of the constant search. The only interest it held any more was to plan a perfect punishment and revenge.

Then suddenly he became obsessed by the fear that Snow would die before him, and so triumph over him again. Snow was two years younger, but for many reasons he was more liable to disease or accident. And they were both in late middle-age by now—58 and 56. He must hurry.

Blayn had been disbarred long ago, but he still retained his legal ability. He knew how to draw up a will that could not be broken in any court in the country.

He read it over with profound satisfaction before putting it in the hands of the bank that, like his father's, was his executor.

It left his whole fortune to "my brother, Julian Snow"—let them enjoy the scandal once he was dead, to make sure it would rebound on Snow himself, with his own name cleared.

But it was left on one condition.

"He is to make a sworn affidavit to the following effect: that in 1935 he was solely responsible for a frameup by which I was photographed in a compromising position with a woman unknown to me, in consequence of which and as a result of the ensuing publicity I lost my wife and child, was disbarred by the State Bar Association, and forfeited any aspiration to political office; that in 1940 he furnished false information which resulted in the collapse of my career as an accountant; that in 1950 he inspired further damaging publicity which caused the breaking of my engagement to remarry; that his activating motive in all these actions was resentment and jealousy arising from the fact that I was the legitimate and he the illegitimate son of Lucius Edwin Blayn, and that in consequence I had received means and opportunities which had been denied him; that we never met and that until recently I was even unaware of his existence.

"This affidavit is to be inserted in every newspaper of this city as a paid advertisement, in bold-face type, and particularly in *The Daily Ingelligencer*; and certified copies of it are to be sent to my former wife, now Mary Hallimund, to my son, now known as Edwin Hallimund, and to Katherine Wilmot, all of whose addresses will be given to him by my executor.

"If the said Julian Snow does not fulfill in every detail this condition of this, my last will and testament, my entire estate is to revert to the government, since there is no charitable or other organization which I care to have benefit by it."

There was one more thing.

Blayn went to the most outstanding psychiatrist he could learn of, and requested a complete and exhaustive mental examination. He paid for and got a signed statement that he was entirely competent mentally to dispose of his property. He filed this statement with his will.

Now, he reflected triumphantly, let Julian Snow struggle between pride and greed! He was sure greed (or even, he thought callously, pure need) would win. Wilson Blayn would be vindicated. Mary and their son, and Katherine, would know the truth and be shamed for their lack of faith and loyalty.

All that remained was to make certain that he died before Julian.

The chambermaid found him in bed the next morning, his head under a pillow to muffle the sound, a bullet through his brain.

For the first time in all the years she had seen him daily, he seemed to be smiling.

Tragedy of a Handkerchief

MICHAEL INNES

The curtain rose on the last scene of Shakespeare's *Othello*, the dreadful scene in which Desdemona is smothered, the scene which Dr. Johnson declared is not to be endured. But by this audience, it seemed to Inspector Appleby, it was going to be endured tolerably well. For one thing, the smothering was apparently to be staged in the reticent way favored by touring companies that depend on the support of organized parties of school children. Not that the school children, probably, would take a thoroughly Elizabethan robustness at all amiss. But headmistresses are different. If their charges must, in the sovereign name of Shakespeare, be taken to see a horrid murder, let it at least be committed in hugger-mugger in a darkened corner of the stage.

But if the audience was not going to be horrified, neither—so far—had it been gripped. Whatever currents of emotion had been liberated behind this proscenium arch, they were not precisely those intended by the dramatist. Or rather, Inspector Appleby thought, it was as if across the main torrent of feeling as Shakespeare had designed it, there were drifting eddies of private passion muddying and confusing the whole.

One was familiar with something of the sort in amateur theatricals, in which the jealousies and spites of rival performers occasionally reveal themselves as absurdly incongruous with the relationships designed by the story. But it is a thing less common on the professional stage, and during the preceding act the audience had been growing increasingly restless and unconvinced. Perhaps only Appleby himself, who had dropped into this dilapidated provincial theater merely to fill an empty evening in a strange town, was giving a steadily more concentrated attention to the matters transacting themselves on the stage.

Around him were the gigglings of bored children and the rustling of stealthily opened paper bags. Appleby, however, studied Desdemona's bedchamber with a contracted brow.

Othello was about to enter with a taper and announce that *"It is the cause, it is the cause, my soul . . ."*

But there was a hitch. For one of those half-minute intervals which can seem an eternity in terms of theatrical time, Othello failed to appear. The stage stood empty, with the sleeping Desdemona scarcely visible in her curtained and shadowy bed at the rear. And this delay was only one of several signs that all was not well behind the scenes.

Most striking had been the blow—that public indignity to which Othello subjects his wife in the fourth act. The crack of an open palm across a face is a thing easily simulated on the stage; the assailant makes his gesture, his victim staggers back, and at the same time someone watching from the wings smartly claps his hands together. But on this occasion there had been the sound of *two* blows—one from the wings and one from the stage itself. And as Desdemona fell back it had been just possible to discern first a cheek unnaturally flushed and then a trickle of blood from a nostril. Almost as if *Othello* were the brutal pot-house tragedy which some unfriendly critics have accused it of being, the hero had given his wife a bloodied nose.

And the ensuing twenty lines had been uncommonly ticklish, with Desdemona playing out her shock and horror while covertly dabbing at her face with a handkerchief. No doubt an actor may be carried away. But an Othello who allowed himself this artistic excess would be decidedly dangerous. What if he permitted himself a similar wholeheartedness when the moment for smothering Desdemona came?

Still staring at the empty stage, Inspector Appleby shook his head. There had been other hints that private passions were percolating through the familiar dramatic story. *Othello* is a tragedy of suspicion, of suspicion concentrated in Othello himself—the hero who, not easily jealous, is yet brought by the triumphant cunning of the villain Iago to kill his wife because of a baseless belief in her adultery. But among the people on this stage, suspicion was not concentrated but diffused. Behind the high dramatic poetry, behind the traditional business of the piece, an obscure and pervasive wariness lurked, as if in every mind were a doubtful speculation as to what other minds knew.

Desdemona, Appleby could have sworn, was more frightened than Shakespeare's heroine need be; Iago was indefinably on the defensive, whereas his nature should know nothing but ruthless if oblique attack; Iago's wife, Emilia, although she played out the honest, impercipient waiting-woman efficiently scene by scene, was perceptibly wishing more than one of her fellow-players to the devil. As for Michael Cassio, he was harassed—which is no doubt what Cassio should chiefly be. But this Cassio was harassed behind the mask as well as across it. Appleby, knowing nothing of these strolling players without name or fame, yet suspected that Cassio was the company's manager, and one despairingly aware that the play was misfiring badly.

On one side of Appleby a small girl massively exhaled an odor of peppermint drops. On the other side an even smaller boy entertained himself by transforming his program into paper pellets and flicking them at the audience in the seats below.

And now here was Othello at last—a really black Othello of the kind fashionable since Paul Robeson triumphed in the part. Only about this fellow there had been a faint flavor of minstrel from the start and it had long been plain that there was nothing approaching great acting in him. Yet the theater fell suddenly silent.

The man stood there, framed in a canvas doorway, the customary lighted taper in his hand. His eyes rolled, fixed themselves, rolled again. His free hand made exaggerated clawing gestures before him. As far as any elevated conception of his role went, he was violating almost every possible canon of the actor's art. And yet the effect was queerly impressive—startling, indeed. The child on Appleby's left gulped and regurgitated, as if all but choked by peppermint going down the wrong way. The boy on the right let his ammunition lie idle before him. From somewhere higher up another child cried out in fright.

Othello stepped forward into a greenish limelight which gave him the appearance of a rather badly decomposed corpse.

Some forty-five seconds behind schedule, the unbearable scene had begun.

"It is the cause, it is the cause, my soul—
Let me not name it to you, you chaste stars!—
It is the cause . . ."

The mysterious words rolled out into the darkness of the auditorium. And, of course, they were indestructible. Not even green limelight, not even an Othello who made damnable faces as he talked, could touch them.

"Yet I'll not shed her blood,

Nor scar that whiter skin of hers than snow . . ."

To the dreadful threat Desdemona awoke. Propped up on the great bed, she edged herself into another limelight which again offended all artistic decorum.

"Will you come to bed, my lord?"

With mounting tension, the scene moved inexorably forward. Othello—who at least had inches—was towering over the woman on the bed.

"That handkerchief which I so loved and gave thee

Thou gavest to Cassio . . ."

The Tragedy of the Handkerchief, this play had been contemptuously called. And the French translator, Inspector Appleby remembered, had preferred the more elevated word, *bandeau*.

"By heaven, I saw my handkerchief in 's hand.

O perjured woman! thou dost stone my heart,

And makest me call what I intend to do

A murder, which I thought a sacrifice;

I saw the handkerchief . . ."

The limelights faded, sparing the susceptibilities of the schoolmistresses. It was just possible to discern Othello as taking up a great pillow in his hands. His last words to Desdemona rang out. There followed only horrible and inarticulate sounds. For, as if to give the now appalled children their money's worth after all, the players in their almost invisible alcove were rendering these final moments with ghastly verisimilitude: the panting respirations of the man pressing the pillow home; the muffled groans and supplications of the dying woman. And then from a door hard by the bedhead came the cries of Emilia demanding admission. Othello drew the bed-hangings to, reeled backwards like a drunken man, plunged into rambling speech as Emilia's clamor grew:

"My wife! my wife! what wife? I have no wife."

From despairing realization, his voice swelled in volume, swelled into its vast theatrical rhetoric, and from behind the hangings the dying Desdemona could be heard to moan anew.

"O, insupportable! O heavy hour!

Me thinks it should be now a huge eclipse

Of sun and moon, and that the affrighted globe

Should yawn at alteration . . ."

Emilia was calling again. Othello drew the hangings closer to, staggered to the door and unlocked it. The woman burst in with her news of disaster and in rapid colloquy Othello learned that his plot for the death of Cassio had failed. Again his voice rang out in despair:

"Not Cassio kill'd! then murder's out of tune,
And sweet revenge grows harsh . . ."

And suddenly there was absolute silence on the stage. Othello and Emilia were standing still—waiting. Again, and with a different note of anxiety, Othello cried out:

"And sweet revenge grows harsh . . ."

Inspector Appleby shivered. For again there was silence, the repeated cue producing nothing. It was now that Desdemona should call out, that Emilia should wrench back the hangings upon the heroine's death-agony and her last sublime attempt to free her lord from blame. But only silence held the boards.

With a swift panicky bump, the curtain fell, blotting out the stage.

"Their names?" asked Inspector Appleby. "We'll stick to Shakespeare for the moment and avoid confusion. And I think Cassio is the man who runs the show?"

The sergeant of police nodded. He was uncertain whether to be relieved or annoyed that a Detective-Inspector from Scotland Yard had emerged helpfully but authoritatively from the audience. "That's so, sir. And here he is."

Chill drafts blew across the stage. The great curtain stirred uneasily, and from behind it there could still be heard the tramp and gabble of bewildered children being shepherded out. Here amid the scenes and tawdry properties everything showed shadowy and insubstantial. The dead woman lay on what had seemed a bed and beneath its grease paint her face showed as black as Othello's. The players, still in costumes, wigs, and beards to which theatrical illusion no longer attached, hovered in a half world between fantasy and fact. And Cassio stood in the midst of them, his hand nervously toying with the hilt of a rapier, his weak and handsome face a study in despair. Inspector Appleby nodded to him.

"This is your company?" he asked. "And Desdemona's death means pretty well the end of it?"

Cassio groaned. "That is so. And it is an unimaginable disaster, as well as being"—he glanced fearfully towards the bed—"unspeakably horrible and painful."

"In fact, if somebody wanted to smash you, this would have been a thoroughly effective way of going about it?"

The actor-manager looked startled. "It certainly would. The sort of audience we get will never book a seat with my company again. But I don't think—"

"Quite so. It is a possible motive but not a likely one. Now, please tell me of the relationships existing between your different members."

The man hesitated, "I am myself married to Bianca."

"A fellow," thought Appleby, "almost damned in a fair wife." Aloud he said: "And the dead woman was actually married to Othello?"

"Yes. And so too are Iago and Emilia."

"I see. In fact, your private relations are quite oddly akin to those in the play? And you may be said to be an isolated community, moving from town to town, with the rest of your company not much more than extras?"

Cassio licked his lips. "That is more or less true. We can't afford much."

"You certainly can't afford murder." Appleby's glance swept the players who were now ranged in a semicircle round him. "I suppose you know that your performance this evening was all at sixes and sevens? Even the children were at a loss." His finger shot out at Othello. "Why did you strike your wife?"

"Yes, why did you strike her?" Emilia had stepped foward. Her eyes, though red with weeping, snapped fire. "And why did you murder her, too?"

"Strike her?" Othello, his face a blotched pallor beneath its paint, had been glaring at Iago. Now he swung round upon Iago's wife. "You foul-mouthed—"

"That will do." Appleby's voice, although quiet, echoed in this resonant space. "There were six of you: Othello and Desdemona, Iago and Emilia, Cassio and Bianca. Your emotional relationships were a sordid muddle and tonight they got out of hand. Well, I'm afraid we must have them into the limelight. And if you won't confess to what was troubling you, I expect there are minor members of your company who can be informative enough."

"But this is outrageous!" It was Bianca who spoke—a beautiful girl with every appearance of self-control. "You can't bully us like that, no matter what has happened." She looked defiantly at the still figure on the bed and then turned to her husband, "Isn't that so?"

But it was Iago, not Cassio, who answered. He was a dark man with a constantly shifting eye and a lip which twitched nervously as he spoke. "Certainly it is so. In interrogating possible witnesses in such an affair, the police are bound by the strictest rules. And until a solicitor—"

"Rubbish!" Unexpectedly and with venom, Emilia had turned on her husband. "Let the man go his own way and it will be the sooner over."

"But at least there are the mere physical possibilities to consider first." Cassio was at once agitated and reasonable. "Just when did the thing happen? And is it possible therefore to rule anyone out straight away?"

Inspector Appleby nodded. "Very well. Opportunity first and motive second . . . At line 83 Desdemona was alive." Appleby glanced up from the text which had been handed to him. "And at line 117 she was dead. Throughout this interval she was invisible, since at first she was lying within heavy shadow and subsequently the bed-hangings were drawn to by Othello. It is clear that Othello himself may simply have smothered her when the action required that he should appear to do so. But there are other possibilities.

"The bed is set in a recess which is accessible not from the main stage alone. Behind the bed-head there is only a light curtain, and it would thus be accessible to anybody behind the scenes who was passing forward towards the wings. Othello ceased to have Desdemona under his observation at about line 85. There are then nearly twenty lines before Emilia enters. These lines are taken up partly by Othello in desperate soliloquy and partly by Emilia calling from 'without.' When Emilia does enter, it is by the door close by the bed-head. And it follows from this that Emilia could have smothered Desdemona during these twenty lines, some five or six of which she had to speak herself. It would be a procedure requiring considerable nerve, but that is no convincing argument against it.

"A third possibility, however, remains. After Emilia has entered, and until the moment that Desdemona cries out that she has been murdered, there are some twelve broken lines, with a certain amount of time-consuming mime increasing the suspense. During this period, any other actor standing near the wings might have slipped to the bed-head and committed the murder. So the position is this: Othello and Emilia are definitely suspects, so far as opportunity goes. And so is anybody else who could have approached the bed-head unobserved during the twelve lines after Emilia's entry."

"Which rules me out." Cassio spoke without any apparent relief and it was clear that with him the disaster which had befallen his company overshadowed everything else. "I was on the opposite side with the electrician when we heard the cue for Emilia's going on. I just couldn't have made it."

"But your wife could." And Emilia, who had broken in, turned with venom on Bianca. "For I saw you not far behind me when I stepped onstage."

"No doubt you did. And I saw your husband." Bianca, still perfectly calm, turned a brief glance of what was surely cold hatred on Iago. "I saw him standing in the wings there and wondered what he was about."

Iago's lip twitched more violently than before. Then he laughed harshly. "This will get the police nowhere. And what about all the other conventional questions, like who last saw the victim alive?"

Suddenly Othello exclaimed. "My God!" he cried, and whirled on Emilia. "*You* know whether I smothered her. Everyone knows what your habit is."

"What do you mean?" Emilia's hand had flown to her bosom and beneath the grease paint she was very pale.

"When waiting to come on, you have always parted the curtain at the bed-head and had a look at her and perhaps whispered a word. I can't tell why, for you weren't all that friendly. But that's what you always did, and you must have done it tonight. Well, how was it? Was she alive or dead?"

"She was alive." It was after a moment's hesitation that Emilia spoke. "She didn't say anything. And of course it was almost dark. But I could see that she—that she was weeping."

"As she very well might be, considering that her husband had actually struck her on the open stage." The police sergeant spoke for the first time. "Now, if you'll—"

But Appleby brusquely interrupted. "Weeping?" he said. "Had she a handkerchief?"

Emilia looked at him with dilated eyes. "But of course."

Appleby strode to the body on the bed and in a moment was back holding a small square of cambric, wringing wet. "Quite true," he said. "And it was right under the body. But this can't be her ordinary handkerchief, which was blood-stained as a result of the blow and will be in her dressing-room now. So perhaps this is—"

Cassio took a stride forward. "Yes!" he said, "it's the love-token— Othello's magic handkerchief which Desdemona loses."

And Inspector Appleby nodded sombrely. "'Sure,'" he said slowly, "'there's some wonder in this handkerchief.'"

Remorselessly the investigation went on. Cassio was the last person in whose hand the handkerchief was seen—but on going offstage Cassio had tossed it on a chair from which anyone might have taken it up. And it seemed likely that a Desdemona overcome with grief had done so.

Emilia's story then was plausible, and if believed it exonerated both Othello and herself. What followed from this? It appeared that of the rest of the company only Iago and Bianca had possessed a reasonable opportunity of slipping from the wings to the bed-head and there smothering Desdemona in that twelve-line interval between Emilia's going onstage and the play's coming to its abrupt and disastrous end. But further than this it was hard to press. Appleby turned from opportunity to motive.

Othello and his wife Desdemona, Iago and his wife Emilia, Cassio and his wife Bianca: these were the people concerned. Desdemona had been murdered. Cassio was not the murderer. And upon the stage, just before the fatality, there had been perceptible an obscure interplay of passion and resentment. What situation did these facts suggest?

Not, Appleby thought, a situation which had been common property long. For it was unlikely that the company had been playing night after night in this fashion; either matters would have come to a head or private passions would have been brought under control, at least during the three hours' traffic on the stage. Some more or less abrupt revelation, therefore, must be the background of what had happened tonight.

Three married couples living in a substantially closed group and with the standards of theatrical folk of the seedier sort. The picture was not hard to see. Adultery, or some particularly exacerbating drift taken by a customary promiscuity, was the likely background to this Desdemona's death. And Appleby felt momentarily depressed. He turned abruptly back to them. Detective investigation requires more than the technique of reading fingerprints and cigarette ends. It requires the art of reading minds and hearts. How, then, did these people's emotions stand now?

Othello was horrified and broken; with him as with Cassio—but more obscurely—things had come to an end. Well, his wife had been horribly killed, shortly after he had struck her brutally in the face. In a sense, then, Othello's immediate emotions were accounted for.

What of Iago? Iago was on the defensive still—and defensiveness means a sense of guilt. He was like a man, Appleby thought, before whom there has opened more evil than he intended or knew. And in whatever desperation he stood, he seemed likely to receive small succor or comfort from his wife. Emilia hated him. Was it a settled hate? Appleby judged that it had not that quality. It was a hatred, then, born of shock. Born of whatever abrupt revelation had preluded the catastrophe.

There remained Bianca, Cassio's wife. She, perhaps, was the enigma in the case, for her emotions ran deep. And her husband was out of it. Cassio was the type of chronically worried man; he expended his anxieties on the business of keeping his company financially afloat and emerged from this only to play subsidiary roles. As a husband he would not be very exciting. And Bianca required excitement. That hidden sort did.

The analysis was complete. Appleby thought a little longer and then spoke. "I am going to tell you," he said quietly, "what happened. But only the principal actors need remain."

There was a sigh from the people gathered round. Like shadows they melted into the wings—some with the alacrity of relief, others with the shuffle of fatigue. It had grown very cold. The curtain stirred and swayed, like a great shroud waiting to envelop those who remained.

"It began with Desdemona's seduction, or with the revelation of it. Is that not so?" Appleby looked gravely round. There was absolute silence. "Is that not so?" he repeated gently. But the silence prolonged itself. And Appleby turned to Othello. "You struck her because of that?"

And abruptly Othello wept. His blotched black face crumpled. "Yes," he said, "I struck her because I had discovered that."

Appleby turned to Iago. "You seduced this man's wife. And the result has been wilful murder. But did you know the truth was out? Or was it you yourself who smothered her to prevent confession and disclosure?"

Iago stepped back, snarling. "You've got nothing on me," he said. "And I won't say a word."

"From this time forth I never will speak word . . ." But Appleby was now facing Emilia. "Your husband had betrayed you. You had discovered he was sleeping with this man's wife. Did you, in the frenzy of your jealousy, smother her?"

Emilia's face had hardened. "These accusations mean nothing. Nobody knows who smothered her. And you will never find out."

There was a pause. Appleby turned slowly to Bianca. "And you?" he asked. "For how long had you been Iago's mistress? And what did you do when you found he had cast you off?"

"Nothing! I did nothing! And she's right. Nobody saw. Nobody can tell anything."

"And so the mystery will be unsolved?" Appleby nodded seriously. "It is not impossible that you are right. But we shall know in the morning." He turned to Cassio. "Did Desdemona have a dressing-room of her own? I'll just look in there before I go . . ."

"They probably won't hang her," Appleby said next day to the police sergeant. "It was a crime of sudden impulse, after all. And of course there was provocation in the adultery she had discovered." He paused. "Will it be any consolation to her in prison to know that she has made history in forensic medicine? I suppose not."

The sergeant sighed. "It's been neat enough," he said, "and something quite beyond our range, I must admit. But how did you first tumble to its being Emilia?"

"It was because she changed her mind about whom to blame. At first she had resolved to plant it on Othello, simply as the likeliest person. 'And why did you murder her, too?' she had asked him. But later on she told a story that pointed to either Bianca or her own husband, Iago. Desdemona, she said, had been alive and weeping when she looked through the curtain at the bed-head. And that, of course, let Othello out, as he had no subsequent opportunity for the murder.

"I asked myself what this change of front meant. Was it simply that Emilia had no grudge against Othello and altered her story in order to implicate her unfaithful husband whom she now hated? Somehow, I didn't think it was that. And then I recalled a gesture she had made. Do you remember? It was when Othello revealed that she was accustomed to draw back the curtain behind the bed and speak to Desdemona before going onstage."

The sergeant considered. "I seem to remember her hand going to her bodice. I thought it a bit theatrical—the conventional gesture of an agitated woman."

Appleby shook his head. "It wasn't quite that. What you saw was a hand flying up to where something should be—something that was now lost. And that something was a handkerchief. I saw the truth in a flash. *She had lost a handkerchief—a tear-soaked handkerchief—while smothering Desdemona.* And my guess was confirmed seconds later when she made her change of front and declared that she had seen Desdemona alive and weeping. For of course her change of story came from a sudden feeling that she must somehow account for the presence of the handkerchief beside the corpse."

"I see." The sergeant shook his head. "It was clever enough. But it was dangerous, being an unnecessary lie."

"It was fatal, as it turned out. But first I saw several things come together. A man may weep, but he won't weep into a small cambric handkerchief. Emilia showed signs of weeping, whereas another suspect, Bianca, was entirely self-controlled. So what had happened was pretty clear. Emilia had discovered her husband's infidelity and had been under strong stress of emotion. She had snatched up the handkerchief—Othello's magic handkerchief—perhaps while running to her dressing-room, and there she had wept into it. When her call came, she thrust it into her bodice. Later, when she yielded to an overwhelming impulse and smothered Desdemona, the handkerchief was dropped in the struggle and the body rolled on top of it.

"But how could all this be proved? Perhaps, as those people said, it couldn't be, and we should never get further than suspicion. But there was one chance—once chance of proving that Emilia had lied.

"A substantial proportion of people are what physiologists call secretors. And this means, among other things, that there is something special about their tears. From their tears, just as well as from their blood, you can determine their blood-group. Well, I had Desdemona's blood on one handkerchief and I had tears on another. I went straight to your local Institute of Medical Research. And they told me what I hoped to learn. *Those tears could not have come from a person of Desdemona's blood-group.*"

The sergeant sighed again. "Yes," he said, "it's neat—very neat, indeed."

"And we shall certainly learn, as soon as the law allows us to make a test, that the tears could have been Emilia's. And as Bianca, who has allowed herself to be blood-grouped, is ruled out equally with Desdemona, the case is clear."

Inspector Appleby rose. "Incidentally there is a moral attached to all this."

"A moral?"

"The moral that one savage old critic declared to be all there is to learn from Shakespeare's play. Housewives, he said, should look to their linen. In other words, it's dangerous to drop a handkerchief— and particularly in the neighborhood of a dead body."

Unc Foils Show Foe

JOHN JAKES

In-flight flix came to sharp halt as pilot announced midst midnight bouncings that a navigation gizmo had defuncted, resulting in letdown of big jet at airport I discovered was Cincy., O.

Plane was theoretically Gotham nonstopper, carrying me back from latest road stand for *GALORE, The Newspaper of Amusement.* But as it was already Sat. and I was not due in shop until Mon. ayem, seemed ideal setup for quick wheel-over to Weevers, Ind., home grounds for my only relatives, who raised me after my folks passed on.

Same burg is located in hills north of O. River. Yearly vacations and side trips are pleasant changes of pace after nights spent lamping stars in saloons.

A toothsome airport chick skedded me on flight out of Indpls. late Sun. eve. Then I ascertained rental car was available. Before claiming, I went into the lounge for a quick cleanup, only to discover my shave bomb in emptysville. I would have to surprise Weevers kin sans smootho cheeks.

Midmorning Sat. discovered me tooling down Main Street, Weevers, in warm June sun. Quick pause and park revealed odd circumstance. My Uncle Pinkerton was not present in his hardware store. Also noted hand-scrawled placard in window flacking *Annual Rummage Sale!* being staged Fri. and all day today by Ladies' Aid of Presbyterian Church. Doubtless Aunt Ellen would be attending event.

I hopped back in car while groups of farm folks shopping ogled continental cut of my threads and cast glances askance. Weevers has lofty suspicions of Insidious East Coast.

Wondering about Unc's whereabouts, I headed for Elm Street, location of big, old white house belonging to Unc and Aunt E. On left I saw a large, gabled joint with neon sign frontmost. Recalled this was Unc's lodge hall. In the side parking lot spotted a County Sheriff's cruiser and Unc's old, straight-stick Chev coupe.

This promised mystery. Unc is considered a double-dome in Weevers—viz., he knows what blvd. *Lullaby of Broadway* is named after. Rural constabulary invariably consult him on matters criminologic.

I pulled in and ascended the lodge hall steps. A card inside a glass bulletin case read: *Saturday Night Only—STAR-STUDDED VARIETY SHOW! Tickets $1.50. Benefit Fluoridation Referendum Publicity Committee.*

Puzzling over unique teaming of music and molars, I was unprepared for sudden opening of door. Got glowers from middle-aged Deputy Sheriff standing guard.

"Sheriff Gumley says no newspaper reporters allowed until the trouble's cleared up, buddy."

"The name's not buddy, and I'm not exactly a newspaper reporter."

Beaucoup ogling of my strictly uptown wardrobe. "Well, I know for a fact the manager don't talk to liquor peddlers on week-ends. Beat it, bub."

Luckily I espied Unc passing across corridor within.

"Unc! Hey, Unc, it's me!"

In act of putting bandanna back into wash-pants pocket, Unc peered. "Good land! Woodrow! What on earth are you doing here? Otis, let him in. That's my nephew, Woodrow Ennis. You remember, my sister Nella's boy."

Deputy did goggle. "You're joshing me, Pinkerton. I recollect Woodrow Ennis when he was just a shaver shooting marbles in front of the courthouse. This fella looks like a Chicago sharpie."

"Tempus fugits, Clyde," I said, but Deputy didn't flip over in-type levity.

"My, Woodrow," said Unc as I bypassed guard, "I surely am glad to see you. I know your Aunt will be, too. She's over at the church rummage sale this morning, by the way."

Following Unc down long stuffy hall, I heard from chamber on left ahead a soprano caterwaul, as of young chick doing bathos bit. Unc was thinking of something else.

"By the way, Woodrow, the snapshot you sent in your last letter from San Francisco sort of upset your Aunt. Now I appreciate you have to visit night clubs for your entertainment newspaper, but your Aunt was mighty worried by the picture of those girls wearing not much more than their good intentions. Also, they appeared to be gyrating some."

"Gosh, Unc," I said, "I thought Aunt E. would dig a scene of authentic SF discotheque dansapation."

"Unfortunately, Woodrow, your Aunt doesn't fathom the customs of the entertainment trades. Which is why you have to sort of shift mental gears when you visit Weevers." But he grinned and punched my shoulder. Pleasantry was short-lived, however. Caterwauling burst out afresh from room ahead.

"Say, Unc, what's that racket? And why the fuzzmobile parked outside?"

"Someone," said Unc with grim glance, "did a mean underhanded thing last night. Sneaked in here—well, I shouldn't say sneaked, exactly. He walked in and out bold as brass, and he—see for yourself."

He aimed mitt at big open doors on right, entrance to small lodge auditorium. Rows of folding chairs were set up show-style. There were musical instruments, mikes, juggler's clubs, other vaude apparati on stage. The piece of equipment nearest the blacked-out foots was a large marimba, mostly colored green.

"Wow, that's a real smear job, Unc."

"Yes, somebody came in here last night and threw a quart or so of green paint all over Wanda Jean Finch's perfectly good $500 marimba. Ruined it for fair. Oh, we've got the culprit, but he won't talk. And we don't know how he managed it. Worse, I'm pretty certain about who's really responsible, but I'm jiggered if I can figure out how to prove it. You know how Sheriff Gus Gumley is, Woodrow. A mite of mystery and he sends out for help. Namely me. This time I'm stumped. Well, let's see if Wanda Jean has calmed down any."

As we ankled for chamber from which the howls issued, I asked, "Is that musical gear for the variety show I saw advertised outside?"

"Yes, 'tis."

"But what's it got to do with tooth decay?"

Further eludication was prevented by our entrance into chamber where four persons were assembled. First was 7-yr.-old juve all dolled up in banana curls and sobbing heart out. Mother, a young jane, was attempting to console her.

Also present was older gent in Oshkosh B'gosh work togs. He sat in a chair pulled out in room's center. He had several stogies sticking out of his shirt pocket. He was scratching stubbly chin and looking vacant in gray cells dept. I pegged him as lodge hall handyman, harmless old coot named Luther Small. Standing over Small was fatty in Sam Browne belt who failed to recognize me.

"Pinkerton," cried Sheriff, "I won't stand for those fluoridation folks sending a hotshot lawyer in here to bedevil us!"

"Woodrow, take off those sunglasses. Gus, it's my nephew."

"What's he wearing that sissified suit for?" Gumley retorted.

Was no time to comment on lack of knowledgeability of stix hix re notched lapels and side vents. Couldn't have anyway, as tot burst out afresh, wailing, "Oh, mummy, mummy, you promised I could play for the peoples tonight."

Gumley glared at his captive. "See what you caused, Luther?"

Old Luther had a guilty puss, but he was stubborn. "I di'nt do nothin', and I'm not sayin' nothin' more."

"Now Luther," Unc said, "if somebody has bulldozed you into clamming up, you ought to realize that Sheriff Gumley here exerts a lot more influence, relatively speaking."

Luther Small scuffed work brogans on flooring. He looked trembly and scared, but he had plenty of ginger left. "Di'nt do it. If you think I did, where's the paint can, hannh? Where's the paint I shoulda had all over my fingers, hannh?"

He held up mitts, which showed no traces of green. I had my notepad out, scribbling away. Variety show tie-in possibly meant hotsy copy for *GALORE*.

Unc sighed. "Gus, I'm afraid he's got us licked. Are you positive your boys searched the lodge hall top to bottom?"

"Yes, Pinky, I am. No empty cans of green paint anywhere. And Luther didn't have nary a stain or smudge when Deputy Booth picked him up after he came out of the lodge hall at 11:30 last night."

"Oh, mummy," tot burst out, "I wanna play for the peoples, I wanna, I wanna!"

Young mom feverishly attempted to soothe offspring. "Hush, Wanda Jean, we'll get you a new marimba, I promise. You can play *I'm Putting All My Eggs in One Basket* another time. Oh, I wish they'd never brought up that awful fluoride business anyway! Come on, Wanda Jean. We'll come back later and see if the big thinkers have found the guilty person."

Mother cradled tot to bosom and team exited. Words "big thinkers" caused Gumley to sigh and Unc to shake his head in mystified way. Wanda Jean went baaw in distance. Door slammed.

"Psst, Unc," I said. "Fill me in?"

Unc nodded in his absent-minded way and said, "Gus, I want to have another look in the basement. That's where I ran into you-know-who Thursday night." Luther seemed to know who too. He gave a shudder like extra in Karloff pic.

"Luther's scared to death," Unc muttered after he had shut the door behind us. "And I know who's scaring him. But proving it is something else again."

I urged Unc to take it from the top as we tramped down into musty basement occupied by large workbench, tools, junk, oil containers, big coal furnace out of use now that June had arrived, and a janitor's closet. I stood scrivening in my notebook while Unc gave synopsis of action thus far.

Two elements in Weevers were warring over a big issue—viz., whether to add fluoride to drinking water supply come fall. Some locals were for it. Other, and more vociferous element, was equally strong against, considering it part of subversive plot to poison U.S. body fluids. Pro-fluoride folks had decided to mount pub-rel campaign in local paper and on Radio Station WEEV. This took cash nut. Hence variety show, to feature terping, thesping, vaude acts by fluoride proponents and their small fry. However, very rental of lodge hall to this group had touched off brouhaha.

"We had a lively go-round at the lodge board meeting Thursday night. Those of us who thought there was no harm in renting the hall outvoted the others four to two. The one loudest against renting is the sanctimonious windbag I suspect has got Luther Small buffaloed—namely, our chairman of the Buildings and Grounds Committee, C. Harold Bixby. Remember him?"

"Think so. Premium pusher?"

Unc cocked an eyebrow. "In exactly what tongue are you speaking, Woodrow?"

"'Scuse me, Unc. Bixby's in the insurance rack—business."

"Right. He's not only anti-fluoride, he's anti almost anything you can name, from nicotine to *I Love You Truly* at weddings. I don't object to him being against things, mind you—that's his right. But I surely do object to his talking poor Luther into an act of vandalism designed to sabotage the fund-raising show. I know he did it—feel it in my bones. It's logical, too. Being chairman of buildings and grounds at the lodge, he can throw Luther out of a job overnight. And Luther, being Luther, couldn't come by another job very easy."

"Bixby against everything," I muttered, writing. "O.o.b.b."

"Beg pardon, Woodrow?"

"Optics of beholder bit."

Unc cast eyes heavenward, then gazed at old pine workbench upon which reposed tin lunch pail bearing initials *LS* scratched in side with knife point.

Unc stared at the initials, finally said, "Proving Bixby twisted Luther's arm so he'd throw paint on the marimba is only half the problem, Woodrow. Bixby has an alibi—tight as a drum. He was down at the rummage sale last evening helping his wife out till they closed. Then he and his missus invited some friends over till way past 11:30, which is when Deputy Booth caught Luther sneaking out of here. Gus Gumley made some phone inquiries this morning." Unc stopped running index digit aimlessly round and round brown ring stain left on pine surface. Puss glum, he wound up, "Bixby's alibi is solid."

"How come the deputy picked up Small? I mean, being handyman, doesn't he have the right to be in the lodge hall at night?"

"Yes, but his behavior roused Deputy Booth's suspicions. On the nights when Deputy Booth is on duty, he usually parks his car right across the street to keep an eye on Main Street. The lodge hall closes up about 11:00. Last night Deputy Booth saw nobody go in or come out after that hour until Luther showed up at 11:25. Luther seemed to be sort of sneaking into the building around the side, but Deputy Booth spotted him. And he recollected that Luther had been in a scrape a couple of years ago."

"What kind of scrape?"

"Luther got pressed for funds and dipped into the lodge cash box one night after hours. He got off that time because everybody in Weevers felt sorry for him. Last night Deputy Booth remembered the scrape when Luther came sneaking back out of here, exactly five minutes after he went in. Deputy Booth jumped out of his car and yelled to Luther, who jackrabbited off."

"Then what happened?"

"Oh, Booth collared him easy enough. And poor Luther, caught flat, bleated out a lame story. According to the deputy, Luther said he'd just come back for his lunch things, which he maintained he forgot. All right, said the deputy, then where are your lunch things? Well, Luther wasn't carrying anything at all, so it was pretty obvious he was scared, muddled, and saying the first thing that came into his head. So with Luther still yowling, they went back inside, just for a check. And there, all over the marimba, was fresh green paint, wet as a tadpole in a pond."

Possibility of *GALORE* copy under my *Woody* byline caused me to exclaim, "Socko! Unreel the next skein quick!"

Next skein was nub of other half of problem. To bedaub marimba, Luther had to have a can of paint. He was carrying nothing with him when he went into lodge and, as reported, nothing when he came out. Outer apparel consisted of just a skimpy jacket as it was a warm pleasant evening. No possibility of concealing can on person. And there was not a stain or smudge of green on his hands.

"Now it certainly seems likely, Woodrow, that a man is going to spill just a spot or two somewhere on his person if he opens a can of paint and lets fly. But not Luther. Deputy Booth and his men searched this place all over. No paint cans or lids anywhere. Not in that furnace—not in the trash barrels out back—not even in Luther's lunch pail here on the bench. Not in any place big enough to hold an empty paint can. So where did Luther get the paint and how did he get rid of the can?"

Big sigh. Unc ran finger along edge of the workbench, where a half-dollar-size blob of dried green paint contrasted with light pinewood. Unc stared at green blob.

"I didn't notice that before. Wonder if Luther came down here last night and spilled some of his paint on the workbench getting the can open? Then where's the can? Oh, fiddlesticks! Come along, Woodrow. I spent enough time in this basement Thursday night, and I'm fed up."

So saying, he led march back upstairs. We looked into quiz chamber, discovered Gumley alone and morose in facial dept.

"Pinky, you got to come up with something. Luther absolutely won't talk."

"'Knows he's got us over a barrel," Unc opined.

"How about a little rubber hose scene?" I suggested.

"In those films you are required to sit through for your work, Woodrow, maybe. But we folks in Weevers don't do things in that way. Your Aunt should be home from the rummage sale about now. She'll fix us some lunch. Gus, I'll phone you if I get a hot flash."

"Yow!" I said. "Scheme snags tooth tuner."

"Has he drunk some intoxicating beverage, Pinky?" Sheriff said.

"No, Gus. A tuner is, I believe, a musical show. Woodrow is just composing another of those headlines in his paper's peculiar lingo." Unc grinned, but sans heart. Many frixamples could be given of how Unc had saved local police bacon, and he was doubtless feeling current failure keenly as we took his Chev coupe out Elm to the digs.

On the way, per my request, Unc explained earlier reference to activities Thurs. eve. in lodge cellar.

Seems that after rent-or-not-to-rent vote, C. Harold Bixby had stalked out, refusing to sit in meeting any longer with "parlor pink named Pinkerton." Meeting broke up about an hour later. Unc, who is stanch Repub., was still doing slow burn over Bixby crack. He located Bixby in dingy cellar where "self-important frog" had gone to "make routine weekly inspection."

Unc filled in scene, picturing C. Harold Bixby as portly do-gooder garbed in size 46 blue pinstripe and size 13 shoes.

"There he was, leaning back against that workbench puffing a cloud of cigar smoke in my face and telling me to go jump in the lake. I said anybody who walked out of a meeting the way he did was a crybaby. But he just stood planted there with his elbows resting on the workbench and kept puffing away. He promised to make sure I was voted off the lodge hall board because I was a dangerous radical. I don't often get the urge to punch anybody in the nose, but I got it then, so I walked out."

"That's real gutsy meller material, Unc," I said as we swung in drive.

"Now Woodrow, try to control your racy jargon. Aunt Ellen's home."

As we entered kitchen, Aunt E. turned, did double take and flustered bit, patting her gray bun and fiddling with specs. "Woodrow! Mercy on us, what are you doing here long before your vacation?"

Following buss and squeezes, I scenarioed stranding at Cincy airport.

"Sit down, Woodrow. There's cherry pie just coming out of the oven." Aunt E. paused for sad-but-loving expresh. "You look undernourished. Have you been consorting too much with those loose-living theatrical persons?"

"Been in Vegas covering a preem of a Blighty rocker troupe, Aunt."

"If I interpret my free subscription copies correctly," Unc put in, "that means he was attending the first performance of some English music group with soup-bowl haircuts."

Aunt Ellen pulled out her freshly heated pie. "Well, I do wish you'd go to bed a little earlier. Somehow it doesn't seem quite American rising at noon like you do. And that reminds me. That picture you sent of those girls dancing—was that in public?"

"Natch," I grinned. "Frisco diskery nitery."

"Oh, dear. And I still remember when you used to raise mushrooms in flats in the basement. You be careful, young man! Sleep under that comforter I sent you. Pinkerton! Are you falling asleep?"

Unc blinked, chin resting on palms, elbows on table. He screwed up his face in that thoughtful way of his. "No, I was just wondering what I'm missing. I think I've got all the pieces, yet I can't put 'em together. Meanwhile, C. Harold Bixby is getting away scot-free, Wanda Jean Finch's marimba is ruined, and Gus Gumley can't make Luther Small talk."

Rapidly Unc described latest developments to Aunt E. as we attacked chow. He mentioned Bixby alibi.

"Well," Aunt E. said, "I can vouch that Harold Bixby was present at the rummage sale from seven until ten last night, Pinkerton. He was helping his wife Grace the way he does every year. The place was packed, too. As for the Bixby party later, I wasn't invited. Grace Bixby is obviously mad as a hornet because of your row with Harold at the lodge. I met her at the door as she was bringing in some men's clothes last night and she cut me dead. Not that I care a fig. I must say Harold acted a mite peculiar too. He dropped in a while this morning and he was still acting the same way."

Unc dropped fork with clatter. "Peculiar? Explain yourself, woman."

"Nervous. Fidgety as a tick. He was watching the folks buying the dishes and clothes and books. This morning he kept whizzing around the church basement like an express train."

"Thunderation, that's it!" Unc jumped up, did nifty jig.

"Pinkerton! Have you got the St. Vitus dance?"

"Ellen, I see how he—oh." Unc's shoulders slumped. "I believe I have Bixby, but that's not enough. I still don't know how Luther hid the paint or kept his hands clean. Think I'll drive over and discuss it with Gus some more. Coming, Woodrow?"

"You bet."

Escaped house before Aunt E. could press extra glass of cow extract into my hand. As Unc drove, I recalled being out of shv. crm. He doubleparked at Atwater's Drug Store while I ran in. He seemed off in outer spheres when I slid back into seat.

"What's that you have, Woodrow?"

"Just the shave bomb I bought in the pill parlor, Unc."

"Shave cream. Drug store. *My* store! Right under my own nose all the time. Woodrow, quick! Park the car and meet me at the hardware store. I'm going to phone Gus. At last I've got that sneaky Bixby red—er, green-handed." Out he hopped.

Fearing Unc had really flipped this time, I ditched lather on car seat, parked per order, and awaited his return. I leaned against the hardware frontage while rurals gave the o.o. to tassels on my cordovans. In about 10 mins. Unc came racing up sidewalk, a bulgy paper sack tucked under arm.

"What's in the bag, Unc?"

"Something which absolutely had to be around the lodge someplace, Woodrow, even though I never actually saw it myself."

"What is—?"

"Let's not waste time. Gus Gumley will meet us at Bixby's. If I can crack Harold, that'll make Luther talk."

I wondered about nature of fadeout if Bixby were innocent as lamb and sued for false arrest. However, following Unc allowed no time for speculation. He plunged inside a first-floor office door featuring cornball copy—BIXBY INSURANCE, "*C. Harold*" *For Your Coverage*.

Overstuffed sec'y. babe did not immediately think I was with Unc, announced that presence of "hawkers" was discouraged. Unc said I was in party and was Bixby in back office? Babe started to say nix when Gumley arrived, puffing.

"Pinky, what in fire are you up to?"

"Just follow me, Gus. Don't announce us, Rosemary, we'll go right in." Unc pushed through swing gate.

With Gumley looking worried, me feeling same, we charged ahead into large office. Human mastodon in blue pinstripe of Ringling tent proportions ceased shuffling papers behind desk. Mastodon scowled while tiny eyes glared at Unc amidst lotsa flesh.

"Pinkerton, I resent your barging in here. I have nothing more to say to anarchists."

"But I've got a lot to say, Harold, concerning a mean act of vandalism rigged up to ruin the variety show."

"Oh, I did hear something about that," said C. Harold. "But only in passing. Say, who's this debauched-looking lad? Some egghead agitator?"

"This is my nephew Woodrow Ennis."

C. Harold clutched paunch. "Woodrow Ennis! He used to roll a hoop past here every night on the way home from school. He was clean-cut and wholesome. This specimen has obviously had his bodily fluids poisoned by the conspiracy which is now sweeping—"

"Be quiet, Harold," Unc said. "You have a right to your opinions, but when you start cat's-pawing poor Luther Small to spoil a show put on by people who happen to disagree with you, I get mad."

"Pinky," Gumley stage-whispered, "don't make rash accusations."

"Did you make that phone call, Gus?"

"Yes, but I'll be switched if I see why."

"Let me worry about that, Gus."

"Just a minute here," said Bixby, big sneer on map. "Do you propose to give me a lecture on fluoridation, Pinkerton? I suppose you think it's healthful."

"When I render an opinion, Harold, I'll do it in the ballot box, not after dark using a poor fuzzy-witted janitor as a dupe."

C. Harold turned ripe red in jowl dept. Gumley looked petrified as Unc went on, "Specifically, Harold, I think you decided when you lost the rent vote that you had to stop the fund-raising show. After you stalked out of the board meeting, I think you went home and got the particular can of green paint. Then you came back to the lodge with your scheme fully hatched. I think you found Luther Small puttering around in the basement, and you threatened to have him fired unless he helped out. That's when I came downstairs to give you what-for."

Premium pusher puffed in pump-organ fashion, "Nothing but a pack of outrageous—"

"Do me the courtesy of letting me finish, Harold. When I found you in the lodge basement, I think you were putting Luther through his paces—showing him what to do with the paint so he wouldn't get caught by leaving evidence behind. Folks in Weevers know you're against vice of every sort, as I mentioned to my nephew earlier today. You're against sin, gin, and also nicotine. And yet there you were

Thursday night, leaning against the workbench and blowing cigar smoke in my face.

"It's my opinion you grabbed that cigar out of Luther's pocket and lit up when you heard me coming. You hate products of the weed. But Luther doesn't—in fact, he had some cigars in his shirt pocket this morning. You heard me coming downstairs, shoved Luther into the janitor's closet, sacrificed your principles, and puffed up a real smokescreen. I was so riled it didn't dawn on me then—you don't smoke but you *had* to Thursday night. Because, Harold, you'd been showing Luther how to use the paint. *And paint smells.*"

What a performance! I'd eyeballed smokeys in Luther's togs pocket also, but failed to link same with earlier anti-nicotine fact stated by Unc. Bixby gnawed liver lips and rolled eyes as if seeking escape hatch.

Unc pressed on. "Further, Harold, in demonstrating how Luther was to do the job you got some green paint on the edge of the workbench. So you leaned against the bench kind of nonchalant-like and didn't move the whole time I was there. Otherwise I'd have seen that paint which I did see, dried, this very morning."

"Then where's the paint can?" snapped C.H.B. "The way I hear it, Gumley's boys couldn't find it anywhere in the lodge hall."

"That's where we got temporarily snookered," replied Unc. "Gus's boys searched every cranny in the lodge that might have hidden a round, squat, ordinary-type paint can of quart size or less. But like everything else these days, cans have changed. There's another style of paint can for sale most everywhere. You probably had one around home. I sell 'em right in my own hardware store. I was reminded about it when Woodrow stopped in at the drugstore. Y'see, Harold, I'm old-fashioned—I still use shaving soap in a mug. But Woodrow here is modern. He buys those lather bombs. Those spray cans. And today, Harold, *paint comes in spray cans too.*"

"Of all the crazy—!"

"Tall, thin, round cans, Harold. With a nice, neat spray nozzle that you just press. Hold a can like that far enough away from you and if you're careful you don't get a single drop on your clothes. Or even on your hands."

"But we didn't find any new-fangled aerosol paint cans neither, Pinky," protested Sheriff G.

"'Course you didn't. You didn't search in the right-shaped place."

"In the what?"

"You said your boys looked in lots of odd places, like Luther Small's lunch pail down in the basement. But they passed up something else which I found just a while ago, tucked way back in a corner of the janitor's closet." Unc waved paper bag.

"No fair!" I said. "We didn't look in the closet before."

"Now, Woodrow, don't be thick. I told you I didn't have to look. The evidence not only said what the hiding place had to be, but exactly what it looked like, too. We know Luther couldn't have carried it out, so it was just a matter of finding it. If your boys spotted it at all, Gus, they must have passed it up because of the shape problem."

Shaking dome vigorously, I said, "Beats me."

"Remember," Unc said, "the first thing Luther hollered when Deputy Booth caught him was that he'd forgot his lunch things. Luther was making up a story, all right. But he was blurting out the truth too, in a kind of slantwise way. He was guilty as sin, and when he thought up that excuse quick, he also automatically thought about the hiding place of the evidence against him. Luther definitely said lunch things, *plural*. Deputy Booth even repeated it. Now Woodrow, what goes along with a packed lunch and, if it spills, leaves a brown ring like the one we saw on the workbench plain as day?"

"Yipes. Jamoko!"

"I guess you're trying to say coffee. You're right. Now, what one thing on earth holds coffee, but could also hold a tall, thin, round spray can of paint, and goes with a lunch pail—lunch things plural— as surely as eggs are the other half of ham?"

Presto! Unc whipped open paper bag and took out an old, battered qt. Thermos.

Bottle had red plastic drinking cup screwed upside down onto top. Unc unscrewed this, pulled plastic jug plug, then unscrewed top part of outside cylinder. He lifted off this smaller upper part, turned over larger bottom cylinder—and bingo! out dropped not a shiny glass liner but a tall, round aerosol can of *E-Z-Glos Spra-E-Namel,* 314 *Leafy Bower Green.*

Bixby lamped can on carpet like it was tarantula.

"Neat fit," Unc said. "Nice hideout, too. Luther gets the paint out of the Thermos bottle, ruins the marimba, puts the can back for disposal later. And it almost worked, except for Woodrow needing a shave."

Right then Bixby zipped around from behind the desk, shaking fist. "You rotten, radical meddler—you still haven't got a nickel's worth of proof."

"Not here—no, that's right, I haven't."

Mother! thought I. Here's where Unc's carpet gets pulled.

"You admit there's no proof?" Bixby said, suddenly narrow in eye region.

Unc fielded fast. "I said I don't have any proof *here*, Harold. I have a notion the proof is over at the Presbyterian Church rummage sale. I phoned Gus, and he has a deputy looking for it now. I'm speaking of one blue pinstripe suitcoat, the only kind you wear. This one probably has a green stain down around the seat of the coat—a stain you got leaning up against the workbench so I couldn't see the spill Thursday night.

"The way I figure it, Harold, maybe you didn't know how to get rid of that coat without rousing suspicion. You couldn't, for example, throw it in your furnace, or in the one at the lodge hall. This being June, and warm, and all furnaces shut down, anything burning in a furnace would be noticed right off. Or maybe you didn't realize right away that the coat was stained.

"I bet you sneaked the coat home. Then lo and behold, in typical fashion, as a lot of men with wives can testify, your wife went through your things yesterday, looking for rummage when you weren't around. She found the paint-stained coat and took it to the church. My wife saw Grace bringing in some men's clothes. The suitcoat being in the batch would certainly explain why you acted, as I get it, so dang nervous at the sale last night. Why you watched to see who bought what. Why you went back this morning to see if the coat was still there.

"Because I guess you know, Harold, there isn't much of a market in Weevers for size 46 suits, not since Chubby Henderson moved away, anyhow. With so many people milling around, you'd have to wait until tonight—until the sale was over—to get that suit back and dispose of it. Taking one of your own garments off the rack during the sale would just have called attention to it. Yes, I'll wager you've been pretty nervous, Harold, waiting for that rummage sale to wind up so you could destroy the evidence we're going to use to make Luther Small confess."

Loud confabbing in outer office caused all parties to rotate heads.

Deputy Sheriff bearing clothing item had entered premium pusher's premises. Even from inner office, green stain on blue pinstripe was highly visible.

Bixby wilted instanter. Gumley collared him.

"Come along, Harold. You should be ashamed of yourself."

"Second that," said Unc with nod.

"Take your hands off me!" Bixby jerked arm from Sheriff's grip. "As for you, Pinkerton—I hope you're satisfied, and will continue to be satisfied when the fluorides of which you are in favor poison all your bodily fluids. I'll get a lawyer. I'll fight this, don't you think I won't."

So mouthing, guilty party was taken away. Faithful sec'y. appeared ready to expire from shock.

Unc hitched up his wash pants, bent down, retrieved the paint can. He deposited same in paper bag again with parts of Thermos. "Let's be going, Woodrow. I haven't put in a lick of work at the store today. I have several things to wind up before we go out to eat."

We ankled to street. "Eating any place special, Unc?"

"Yes, I'm treating you and your Aunt Ellen to cube steaks and all the trimmings at Hadley's Hickory Heaven before the show. I also have to pick up an extra—ducat, is it?—for you. I'll bet little Wanda Jean electrifies the folks tonight."

"But her marimba's kaput!"

"Oh, Wanda Jean also studies the novelty tap. She's a real trouper though only age seven."

"Unc, I thought tonight's gig had already done El Foldo!"

"What ever gave you that idea?"

"You mean the amateur show must go on?"

Eyes a-twinkle, Unc said, "Certainly, Woodrow. That's show biz."

Dangerous Widows

MIGNON G. EBERHART

One of my widows telephoned me at one o'clock Friday, and the other telephoned me at three o'clock Friday, and both of them invited me urgently to spend the weekend at their country place.

Neither, however, was a social invitation; each widow said frankly she was in need of my advice. In fact, it was an invitation to murder.

In literal fact, too, neither woman was my widow in the accepted sense. They were Henry Briggs's widows. Both, however, were very likely to fall within my scope of duty, for I am a banker, elderly enough to be entrusted with the somewhat difficult chore of advising, coaxing, cajoling, and generally acting as nursemaid to widows who seem strangely determined to invest in nonexistent uranium ore deposits and dry oil wells.

The two Mrs. Briggs were Henry's wives; one was his first wife, Frances Briggs, divorced and never remarried; the other, Eloise Briggs, was his second and the official Mrs. Briggs. Henry Briggs was one of my old clients. And the country house each referred to was the same country house, for it had been left to them, jointly, by his will.

Consequently a rather delicate situation was in the making. I took the 5:30 train to Stamford.

While Henry Briggs had been a client of the bank's for a long time, especially during his last illness, and I had had much to do with his affairs, I had never met either of his wives.

I cannot say that I faced the prospect with any pleasure. I do not like strife or emotions, and both were far too likely to develop. As I got out of the train and looked down the long platform I wondered which one would meet me and thus possibly endeavor to get in her claims first.

Neither did. A thickset, red-faced man, done to a turn in flagrantly country clothes, approached me and said with a hearty manner, "Mr. Wickwire?"

I nodded. He put out a large red hand. His face was jovial and friendly; he had shrewd, cold-blue eyes. "I'm Al Muller—friend of Henry's. The station wagon is this way."

I said, "Quite so," and followed him.

He put my bag in the station wagon, and wedged himself, puffing, behind the wheel. "I'm staying at the house. Thought I might be of some service to them." He negotiated a turn amid traffic.

I said, "Indeed."

His blue eyes shot me a rather narrow glance. "Yes. Frances—that's the first wife—arrived Thursday night by train. Henry was buried that afternoon, you'll remember. Eloise—that's the second wife—was here, of course."

I said, perhaps rather dryly, "And when did you arrive, Mr. Muller?"

He paused to examine a road sign rather deliberately. "Oh, I came up later Thursday night. Seemed to me I owed it to Henry. It's an odd situation, leaving the property like that. Do you know either of the Mrs. Briggs?"

Something about his manner went against my grain. I said stiffly that I hadn't had that pleasure.

He chuckled. "They're as like as two peas in a pod—extremely attractive women. You'll see. And there's a fight brewing there, mark my words. Neither is the sort to give up easily. I don't envy you, Mr. Wickwire."

"I am in no sense an arbiter. That is for the lawyers." I spoke coldly enough to penetrate even Mr. Al Muller's hide. We concluded our ride along the winding country roads in silence.

The house and grounds, when we reached them, proved to be on a rather lavish scale, with velvety lawns, swimming pool, tennis court, gardens. It represented, I knew, the whole of Henry Briggs's property; he had had a fairly large income, but had lived up to it. I had arrived at an approximate sum which I thought the property might fetch and was deducting, in my mind, such things as possible capital gains and taxes when we drew up at the white-columned entrance.

Here two women stood, waiting; both advanced to greet me as I got out of the car. And at least in one instance Muller was right; allowing for possibly fifteen years' difference in age they were very much alike. Both slender, fine-featured, blonde, and extremely attractive.

The younger—the official Mrs. Briggs—spoke to me first, putting out a jeweled hand toward mine; she introduced me to the first Mrs. Briggs, while Al Muller stood watching with a rather stupid grin on his red face and a very watchful look in those shrewd eyes. We went at once into the house.

A maid took my bag upstairs. Cocktails were set out on a tray in the spacious living room. It was an imposing room, full of what might be called objects of art and dominated by a huge portrait of Henry Briggs, done apparently when he was a rather young man, at least twenty years before his death.

Eloise, the younger Mrs. Briggs, in her proper role of hostess, saw to it that I was comfortably seated, and asked me my preference as to cocktails. In the soft light from the table lamps the likeness between the two women diminished. They were the same general type—that was all.

The first Mrs. Briggs, Frances, was thinner and finer-drawn than the second, with darker hair but penetrating blue eyes. She wore a simple, inexpensive white cotton dress and no jewelry beyond her wedding ring.

Eloise was almost beautiful, with a magnolia skin, soft red mouth, and a rather luxuriant figure. Her dress was simple, too, but even my bachelor eyes perceived that it was an expensive simplicity; a diamond bracelet sparkled on her wrist.

It was Eloise who, again assuming her unquestionably correct position of authority, said that, if I agreed, both she and the other Mrs. Briggs preferred to postpone our discussion of business until morning. I agreed, most sincerely. Al Muller helped himself to another drink, at which both Mrs. Briggs looked at him coldly. The maid who had taken my bag announced dinner.

Aside from the fact that Al Muller became talkative in a jovial, rallying way, it was a quiet and merely social dinner. Not a word that was said, not a gesture, suggested potential strife between the two Mrs. Briggs. They were, in short, perfect ladies.

The evening was an early one. Eloise showed me to my room. "I hope you'll not mind coming down to breakfast," she said. "The maid lives in the village and goes home at night."

I assured her that it didn't matter. "By the way, Mrs. Briggs, exactly why did you ask me to come here?"

She hesitated for a second. Then she came close to me; her lovely mouth smiled invitingly. She put both hands appealingly on my arm. "Because I need your help."

Perfume wafted toward me; there was a deep glow in her eyes. I recoiled slightly. "I'm afraid the only help I can give you is to advise you to put the settlement of the estate in the hands of your lawyer."

Her hands, of necessity, dropped. She eyed me for a moment. Then she said, "Of course. Good night, Mr. Wickwire . . ."

It was all very calm, all very polite, But there was something very wrong in the house. I was obliged to wait, however, until the house was quiet before I went quietly downstairs again and out the door. I took the road to the village. It was a dark night, with scudding clouds.

The village was still lighted, and the drugstore had a pay telephone booth.

There are certain shortcuts to certain kinds of information which a banker knows. Nevertheless, since it was by then rather late, it took some time to accomplish my purpose.

Fortunately, in a way, I was under the interested observation of the young man behind the soda fountain the whole time, and indeed, I bought several magazines and an ice-cream soda from him. He had, however, told me that he'd have to shut up shop in another ten minutes when my New York call came through.

He turned off the lights as I left the drugstore and took my way back to the Briggs house. It seemed a rather short walk for I was thinking deeply, and it was with a sense of surprise that I turned in at the gates.

I stopped there, struck with another kind of surprise. The house was ablaze with lights. And then I heard the thud of automobiles. Indeed, I ducked out of the driveway barely in time as the first one took the curve and shot up to the entrance.

Other cars and motorcycles followed it. By the time I had run across the grass and reached the house the entire village constabulary as well as state troopers were swarming into the house, where Al Muller lay dead of a revolver shot on the rug below Henry's portrait.

I pushed my way in, passing Eloise and Frances, white and frightened, in the hall.

Al Muller's thick body lay apparently as it had fallen. His too-fancy country oxfords were sprawled wide apart. His brightly checked jacket was crumpled. A gun lay near his hand.

It was dawn when the police at last went away. Both Mrs. Briggs, exhausted and tense with strain, went upstairs as the last police car disappeared down the drive. I watched them go. And I wondered which one had murdered him.

Not that the police called it murder. The inquiry had been a long one and their questions had been many; they had taken our finger-prints; they had determined the ownership of the gun, which had belonged to Henry. But they had been guarded and reticent. They had not—as yet—called it murder.

They had listened to my own story, which luckily the young man in the drugstore could substantiate. They had listened to the stories of the two Mrs. Briggs, which were identical. Each had been awakened, she said, by the sound of the shot; each had waited a few moments, questioning it; they had come into the hall at almost the same time and then downstairs together to find Al Muller dead.

They had telephoned for the police. They had tried to arouse me and discovered my absence. They had been afraid that I, too, had been a victim of some robber who might still be about the grounds. When asked if either of them believed that Al Muller had been depressed by Henry's death to the point of suicide both appeared doubtful.

It was not suicide. It was murder.

But I didn't know which one had murdered him. I listened as their light footsteps, the whisper of their movements, died away above. Then I went back to the living room. Al Muller's body had been removed but the room still seemed to hold his presence, and it was not a pleasant one.

The room was in considerable disorder—chairs pushed around, the rug upon which Al Muller had died rolled up into a corner, small tables and lamps shoved aside carelessly; the portrait of Henry Briggs hung slightly askew on the wall.

I preferred not to touch the rug, or even approach it, but being a banker and a bachelor and somewhat finicky in habits of tidiness, I straightened the chairs and tables. No clues of course; I hadn't really expected there would be. I went to Henry's huge portrait with its heavy frame and straightened that, too. It seemed rather oddly out of place. Someone's shoulder must have brushed against it.

I measured, rather absently, my own shoulder height below the portrait. I am not a tall man, but the lower corner of the gilded frame was at least a foot above my own shoulder. So someone's hand had pushed it aside. I stood looking at Henry for a moment. Then I got a chair and climbed on it and looked behind the portrait.

Some time later I straightened the portrait carefully, got down from the chair, restored it to its place, and sat down in it. Something was going to happen, and it would happen soon.

I cannot say it was a pleasant wait. I hoped there was not another gun in the house. Somewhere a clock was ticking with an ominous, warning note as if to remind me of the fleeting quality of time.

It had run out swiftly for Al Muller. I am not a brave man; when I heard the faint rustle of a woman's garment on the stairway, and the very soft whisper of footsteps, I had to force myself to remain—waiting.

She must have seen the light in the room; still she thought it was empty for when she appeared as quietly as a ghost in the doorway and saw me she caught her breath and flung both hands to her throat. It was Frances, the first Mrs. Briggs.

After a moment she came toward me, her negligee gathered around her. Her fine eyes were very bright. "I didn't know you were here. I came to—to look. I had to see if there was anything the police didn't see. Mr. Wickwire—Eloise killed him."

It was, of course, in the cards. One of them would accuse the other; indeed, each might accuse the other of being the murderess—one because she must shield herself with a lie, the other because she must shield herself with the truth.

I said, "Why?"

Her hands moved toward each other. "I don't know. But I think it had something to do with money. Al Muller was simply not the kind of man to come here out of sympathy. He wanted something."

"Mrs. Briggs, why did you send for me?"

Her bright eyes didn't waver. "Because Muller was here. I didn't trust him. I was going to ask you to get rid of him. But I know Eloise killed him because I didn't. And there was no one else."

"I didn't kill him," Eloise said clearly from the doorway. "So it must have been you!" She was wearing a long floating negligee, and she had a gun in her hand.

Violence has never been, so to speak, my dish. I felt a kind of creeping chill up my backbone. But I had to get both women and myself out of the room and, of course, I'd have to get that gun.

I said, "We are all very tired. I suggest that you two ladies—er—dress while I prepare some sort of breakfast for us." I went to Eloise. "Whose gun is that?"

"Mine. Henry got it for me."

"What were you going to do with it?"

She looked at me. "I don't know," she said blankly and, I think, truthfully.

"You'd better give it to me."

She did so at once which both surprised and pleased me. I then said briskly, "Now I'll see to coffee," and went out of the room and through the dining room to the kitchen where I made a great clatter about cupboard doors and pots and pans. I made a mistake, however, when for safety's sake I dropped the gun into the flour bin.

I gave them barely time to dress and to accomplish what one of them had to accomplish in the living room, and consequently burned the toast while I was watching the clock. But as I took it and coffee into the dining room, Frances Briggs came in, charming and fresh in blue linen. After a moment Eloise, lovely and fresh in pink, entered also.

Both seized upon coffee. Neither spoke, and I was rather uneasily aware of stored-up dynamite. A very slight jar was all that was necessary to induce an explosion, and I was not ready for that. So when I spoke I did so cautiously.

"In view of the circumstances I'd like to suggest that we postpone our business talk. But I have a request to make. I was an old friend of Henry's. If neither of you wishes to keep the portrait of him, I wonder if you would be so kind as to give it to me."

Eloise's eyes leaped to me above the rim of her coffee cup. She put the cup down, and put her handkerchief to her eyes. She said from behind it, "Of course. I didn't realize that you felt that way about Henry. I have other pictures of Henry. He—he would want you to have it." She dabbed at her eyes with her handkerchief.

"Thank you," I said and turned to Frances, who had risen.

She said, "I'm sorry. I'll not pretend that I was in love with Henry when he met you, Eloise. I was not heartbroken when he asked me for a divorce; I agreed to it. But once, when Henry and I were young, when that portrait was made, I loved him. I'm sorry, Mr. Wickwire, I want the portrait."

So I knew what I had to know. I said something about understanding it, made an excuse, and left the room.

I let myself out, cautiously, through the back door. A grape arbor ran along there toward the garage, and I took shelter behind it. I reached the garage and was opening the door of the station wagon when Eloise ran into the garage.

"Mr. Wickwire, where are you going?"

"To the state police. Will you drive? I'm not accustomed to this car. Besides, it might be safer."

"Safer! Do you mean she—" She gave a kind of quick gasp and then slid behind the wheel. "Take the back way down to the road," I said. "The trees and shrubbery will shield us from the house."

The sun was up, streaking across shrubbery and lawns and making a bright path of the country road. She knew the way to the state police headquarters. She went in with me, and the young lieutenant who had directed the night's inquiry was at his desk using the telephone when we were shown into his office. He looked pleased and relaxed; his revolver lay on the desk.

"Oh, there you are. I was about to phone you. The fingerprints on the gun are Al Muller's. So it was probably suicide."

Fingerprints of course can be placed on guns after death, but I didn't care to argue with him about that. I gave one longing thought toward the gun in the flour bin and said, "I'm afraid I have evidence to the contrary. If you'll search the Briggs house you'll find a package of notes, given for loans advanced by Al Muller and signed by Henry Briggs. The signatures are forgeries. And in the meantime—" I cleared my throat "—kindly arrest this Mrs. Briggs at once and charge her—"

I couldn't finish because Eloise was too quick; she snatched the officer's revolver. Two shots went wild, a third crashed through the window, and then the young lieutenant had her tight in his arms, but it was not a loverlike embrace.

He released her when other troopers rushed in. I crawled out from under the desk with such dignity as I could summon. The young lieutenant was also very quick. "The notes." he said, panting and blushing deeply, "are probably on her. Get the matron from the village, Sergeant."

He was right. The notes, a rather bulky package, were concealed in her brassiere. I must say I was relieved to see them; she had had neither the time nor the chance to destroy them.

Later, back at the house, I had a conversation with the young lieutenant and with Frances Briggs. "So Muller loaned her all that money," the lieutenant said. "I take it that he thought he was loaning it to Henry during his illness, but she forged Henry's signatures."

I nodded. "Muller probably discovered, or knew from the begining, that it was forgery. After Henry's death he—er—"

"Put the screws on," the lieutenant said. "He must have demanded quite a price. So she shot him."

"Then she had to get out of the room and up the backstairs in a hurry. She got the notes out of his pocket, shoved them behind the portrait, put his fingerprints on the gun, and ran up the back way. Frances Briggs came into the hall at about that time."

"But how did you know?"

"I found the notes. I didn't know which woman had shot him or which one had forged the notes and thus must get possession of them again. I gave both women time—I was afraid too much time—but, at any rate, I then asked for Henry's portrait.

"I knew that the woman who had shot Muller would not want the portrait: she wouldn't want any association with so strong a reminder of guilt. So a rejection of the portrait would be an indication of guilt—and an indication that the notes were gone.

"Eloise leaped at the chance to get rid of the portrait. Frances did not."

I added, "I must tell you that I made some inquiries by telephone as to Eloise. She was wearing jewelry; she was dressed expensively. In short, I found that she had staggering charge accounts and had spent far more money than Henry—remember, I am in a position to know—could have given her. So where was she getting the money? Why was Al Muller there?"

But the lieutenant said astutely, "You must have more solid evidence—basis for suspicion."

I told the lieutenant, "When anybody urgently wishes to see any banker, he—she—wants to borrow money. Frances Briggs had a different reason which was sound and sensible. But Eloise—"

"She wanted to borrow enough money on the property to pay off Muller!" the lieutenant cried. "Did she ask you for a loan?"

"Not," I said, "precisely."

"Oh, I see. But you weren't having any—I mean to say, you were not—that is, her charm—that is—" He blushed, looked apologetic, and tired to stop grinning.

"Oh, Mr. Wickwire!" Frances Briggs leaned toward me with a lovely smile, her magnificent eyes warm. "You are a detective! And a very courageous man."

There are more ways than one in which an attractive widow may be dangerous. I rose rather quickly and said I had to return to town. Indeed, when another widow invited me to her house on Long Island the next weekend I sent a subordinate in my place.

Ride the Lightning

JOHN LUTZ

A slanted sheet of rain swept like a scythe across Placid Cove Trailer Park. For an instant, an intricate web of lightning illumined the park. The rows of mobile homes loomed square and still and pale against the night, reminding Nudger of tombs with awnings and TV antennas. He held his umbrella at a sharp angle to the wind as he walked, putting a hand in his pocket to pull out a scrap of paper and double-check the address he was trying to find in the maze of trailers. Finally, at the end of Tranquility Lane, he found Number 307 and knocked on its metal door.

"I'm Nudger," he said when the door opened.

For several seconds the woman in the doorway stood staring out at him, rain blowing in beneath the metal awning to spot her corn-flowered dress and ruffle her straw-blonde hair. She was tall but very thin, fragile-looking, and appeared at first glance to be about twelve years old. Second glance revealed her to be in her mid-twenties. She had slight crow's feet at the corners of her luminous blue eyes when she winced as a raindrop struck her face, a knowing cast to her oversized, girlish, full-lipped mouth, and slightly buck teeth. Her looks were hers alone. There was no one who could look much like her, no middle ground with her; men would consider her scrawny and homely, or they would see her as uniquely sensuous. Nudger liked coltish girl-women; he catalogued her as attractive.

"Whoeee!" she said at last, as if seeing for the first time beyond Nudger. "Ain't it raining something terrible?"

"It is," Nudger agreed. "And on me."

Her entire thin body gave a quick, nervous kind of jerk as she smiled apologetically. "I'm Holly Ann Adams, Mr. Nudger. And you are getting wet, all right. Come on in."

She moved aside and Nudger stepped up into the trailer. He expected it to be surprisingly spacious; he'd once lived in a trailer and remembered them as such. This one was cramped and confining. The furniture was cheap and its upholstery was threadbare; a portable black and white TV on a tiny table near the Scotch-plaid sofa was

209

blaring shouts of ecstasy emitted by "The Price is Right" contestants. The air was thick with the smell of something greasy that had been fried too long.

Holly Ann cleared a stack of *People* magazines from a vinyl chair and motioned for Nudger to sit down. He folded his umbrella, left it by the door, and sat. Holly Ann started to say something, then jerked her body in that peculiar way of hers, almost a twitch, as if she'd just remembered something not only with her mind but with her blood and muscle, and walked over and switched off the noisy television. In the abrupt silence, the rain seemed to beat on the metal roof with added fury. "Now we can talk," Holly Ann proclaimed, sitting opposite Nudger on the undersized sofa. "You a sure-enough private investigator?"

"I'm that," Nudger said. "Did someone recommend me to you, Miss Adams?"

"Gotcha out of the Yellow Pages. And if you're gonna work for me, it might as well be Holly Ann without the Adams."

"Except on the check," Nudger said.

She grinned a devilish twelve-year-old's grin. "Oh, sure, don't worry none about that. I wrote you out a check already, just gotta fill in the amount. That is, if you agree to take the job. You might not."

"Why not?"

"It has to do with my fiancé, Curtis Colt."

Nudger listened for a few seconds to the rain crashing on the roof. "The Curtis Colt who's going to be executed next week?"

"That's the one. Only he didn't kill that liquor store woman; I know it for a fact. It ain't right he should have to ride the lightning."

"Ride the lightning?"

"That's what convicts call dying in the electric chair, Mr. Nudger. They call that chair lotsa things: Old Sparky . . . The Lord's Frying Pan. But Curtis don't belong sitting in it wired up, and I can prove it."

"It's a little late for that kind of talk," Nudger said. "Or did you testify for Curtis in court?"

"Nope. Couldn't testify. You'll see why. All them lawyers and the judge and jury don't even know about me. Curtis didn't want them to know, so he never told them." She crossed her legs and swung her right calf jauntily. She was smiling as if trying to flirt him into wanting to know more about the job so he could free Curtis Colt by a governor's reprieve at the last minute, as in an old movie.

Nudger looked at her gauntly pretty, country-girl face and said, "Tell me about Curtis Colt, Holly Ann."

"You mean you didn't read about him in the newspapers or see him on the television?"

"I only scan the media for misinformation. Give me the details."

"Well, they say Curtis was inside the liquor store, sticking it up—him and his partner had done three other places that night, all of 'em gas stations, though—when the old man that owned the place came out of a back room and seen his wife there behind the counter with her hands up and Curtis holding the gun on her. So the old man lost his head and ran at Curtis, and Curtis had to shoot him. Then the woman got mad when she seen that and ran at Curtis, and Curtis shot her. She's the one that died. The old man, he'll live, but he can't talk nor think nor even feed himself."

Nudger remembered more about the case now. Curtis Colt had been found guilty of first degree murder, and because of a debate in the legislature over the merits of cyanide gas versus electricity, the state was breaking out the electric chair to make him its first killer executed by electricity in over a quarter of a century. Those of the back-to-basics school considered that progress.

"They're gonna shoot Curtis full of electricity next Saturday, Mr. Nudger," Holly Ann said plaintively. She sounded like a little girl complaining that the grade on her report card wasn't fair.

"I know," Nudger said. "But I don't see how I can help you. Or, more specifically, help Curtis."

"You know what they say thoughts really are, Mr. Nudger?" Holly Ann said, ignoring his professed helplessness. Her wide blue eyes were vague as she searched for words. "Thoughts ain't really nothing but tiny electrical impulses in the brain. I read that somewheres or other. What I can't help wondering is, when they shoot all that electricity into Curtis, what's it gonna be like to his thinking? How long will it seem like to him before he finally dies? Will there be a big burst of crazy thoughts along with the pain? I know it sounds loony, but I can't help laying awake nights thinking about that, and I feel I just gotta do whatever's left to try and help Curtis."

There was a sort of check-out-line tabloid logic in that, Nudger conceded; if thoughts were actually weak electrical impulses, then high-voltage electrical impulses could become exaggerated, horrible thoughts. Anyway, try to disprove it to Holly Ann.

"They never did catch Curtis's buddy, the driver who sped away and left him in that service station, did they?" Nudger asked.

"Nope. Curtis never told who the driver was, neither, no matter how much he was threatened. Curtis is a stubborn man."

Nudger was getting the idea. "But you know who was driving the car."

"Yep. And he told me him and Curtis was miles away from that liquor store at the time it was robbed. When he seen the police closing in on Curtis in that gas station where Curtis was buying cigarettes, he hit the accelerator and got out of the parking lot before they could catch him. The police didn't even get the car's license plate number."

Nudger rubbed a hand across his chin, watching Holly Ann swing her leg as if it were a shapely metronome. She was barefoot and wearing no nylon hose. "The jury thought Curtis not only was at the liquor store, but that he shot the old man and woman in cold blood.

"That ain't true, though. Not according to—" she caught herself before uttering the man's name.

"Curtis's friend," Nudger finished.

"That's right. And he ought to know," Holly Ann said righteously, as if that piece of information were the trump card and the argument was over.

"None of this means anything unless the driver comes forward and substantiates that he was with Curtis somewhere other than at the liquor store when it was robbed."

Holly Ann nodded and stopped swinging her leg. "I know. But he won't. He can't. That's where you come in."

"My profession might enjoy a reputation a notch lower than dognapper," Nudger said, "but I don't hire out to do anything illegal."

"What I want you to do *is* legal," Holly Ann said in a hurt little voice. Nudger looked past her into the dollhouse kitchen and saw an empty gin bottle. He wondered if she might be slightly drunk. "It's the eyewitness accounts that got Curtis convicted," she went on. "And those people are wrong. I want you to figure out some way to convince them it wasn't Curtis they saw that night."

"Four people, two of them customers in the store, picked Curtis out of a police lineup."

"So what? Ain't eyewitnesses often mistaken?"

Nudger had to admit that they were, though he didn't see how they could be in this case. There were, after all, four of them. And yet, Holly Ann was right; it was amazing how people could sometimes be so certain that the wrong man had committed a crime just five feet in front of them.

"I want you to talk to them witnesses," Holly Ann said. "Find out *why* they think Curtis was the killer. Then show them how they might be wrong and get them to change what they said. We got the truth on our side, Mr. Nudger. At least one witness will change his story when he's made to think about it, because Curtis wasn't where they said he was."

"Curtis has exhausted all his appeals," Nudger said. "Even if all the witnesses changed their stories, it wouldn't necessarily mean he'd get a new trial."

"Maybe not, but I betcha they wouldn't kill him. They couldn't stand the publicity if enough witnesses said they was wrong, it was somebody else killed the old woman. Then, just maybe, eventually, he'd get another trial and get out of prison."

Nudger was awed. Here was foolish optimism that transcended even his own. He had to admire Holly Ann.

The leg started pumping again beneath the cornflower-colored dress. When Nudger lowered his gaze to stare at it, Holly Ann said, "So will you help me, Mr. Nudger?"

"Sure. It sounds easy."

"Why should I worry about it any more?" Randy Gantner asked Nudger, leaning on his shovel. He didn't mind talking to Nudger; it meant a break from his construction job on the new Interstate 170 cloverleaf. "Colt's been found guilty and he's going to the chair, ain't he?"

The afternoon sun was hammering down on Nudger, warming the back of his neck and making his stomach queasy. He thumbed an antacid tablet off the roll he kept in his shirt pocket and popped one of the white disks into his mouth. With his other hand, he was holding up a photograph of Curtis Colt for Gantner to see. It was a snapshot Holly Ann had given him of the wiry, shirtless Colt leaning on a fence post and holding a beer can high in a mock toast: this one's for Death!

"This is a photograph you never saw in court. I just want you to look at it closely and tell me again if you're sure the man you saw in the liquor store was Colt. Even if it makes no difference in whether he's executed, it will help ease the mind of somebody who loves him."

"I'd be a fool to change my story about what happened now that the trial's over," Gantner said logically.

"You'd be a murderer if you really weren't sure."

Gantner sighed, dragged a dirty red handkerchief from his jeans pocket, and wiped his beefy, perspiring face. He peered at the photo, then shrugged. "It's him, Colt, the guy I seen shoot the man and woman when I was standing in the back aisle of the liquor store. If he'd known me and Sanders was back there, he'd have probably zapped us along with them old folks."

"You're positive it's the same man?"

Gantner spat off to the side and frowned; Nudger was becoming a pest, and the foreman was staring. "I said it to the police and the jury, Nudger; that little twerp Colt did the old lady in. Ask me, he deserves what he's gonna get."

"Did you actually see the shots fired?"

"Nope. Me and Sanders was in the back aisle looking for some reasonable-priced bourbon when we heard the shots, then looked around to see Curtis Colt back away, turn, and run out to the car. Looked like a black or dark green old Ford. Colt fired another shot as it drove away."

"Did you see the driver?"

"Sort of. Skinny dude with curly black hair and a mustache. That's what I told the cops. That's all I seen. That's all I know."

And that was the end of the conversation. The foreman was walking toward them, glaring. *Thunk!* Gantner's shovel sliced deep into the earth, speeding the day when there'd be another place for traffic to get backed up. Nudger thanked him and advised him not to work too hard in the hot sun.

"You wanna help?" Gantner asked, grinning sweatily.

"I'm already doing some digging of my own," Nudger said, walking away before the foreman arrived.

The other witnesses also stood by their identifications. The fourth and last one Nudger talked with, an elderly woman named Iris Langeneckert, who had been walking her dog near the liquor store and had seen Curtis Colt dash out the door and into the getaway car, said something that Gantner had touched on. When she'd described the getaway car driver, like Gantner she said he was a thin man with curly black hair and a beard or mustache, then she had added, "Like Curtis Colt's hair and mustache."

Nudger looked again at the snapshot Holly Ann had given him. Curtis Colt was about five foot nine, skinny, and mean-looking, with a broad bandito mustache and a mop of curly, greasy black hair. Nudger wondered if it was possible that the getaway car driver had been Curtis Colt himself, and his accomplice had killed the shopkeeper. Even Nudger found that one hard to believe.

He drove to his second-floor office in the near suburb of Maplewood and sat behind his desk in the blast of cold air from the window unit, sipping the complimentary paper cup of iced tea he'd brought up from Danny's Donuts directly below. The sweet smell of the doughnuts was heavier than usual in the office; Nudger had never quite gotten used to it and what it did to his sensitive stomach.

When he was cool enough to think clearly again, he decided he needed more information on the holdup, and on Curtis Colt, from a more objective source than Holly Ann Adams. He phoned Lieutenant Jack Hammersmith at home and was told by Hammersmith's son Jed that Hammersmith had just driven away to go to work on the afternoon shift, so it would be a while before he got to his office.

Nudger checked his answering machine, proving that hope did indeed spring eternal in a fool's breast. There was a terse message from his former wife Eileen demanding last month's alimony payment; a solemn-voiced young man reading an address where Nudger could send a check to help pay to form a watchdog committee that would stop the utilities from continually raising their rates; and a cheerful man informing Nudger that with the labels from ten packages of a brand name hot dog he could get a Cardinals ballgame ticket at half price. (That meant eating over eighty hot dogs. Nudger calculated that baseball season would be over by the time he did that.) Everyone seemed to want some of Nudger's money. No one wanted to pay Nudger any money. Except for Holly Ann Adams. Nudger decided he'd better step up his efforts on the Curtis Colt case.

He tilted back his head, downed the last dribble of iced tea, then tried to eat what was left of the crushed ice. But the ice clung stubbornly to the bottom of the cup, taunting him. Nudger's life was like that.

He crumpled up the paper cup and tossed it, ice and all, into the wastebasket. Then he went downstairs where his Volkswagen was parked in the shade behind the building and drove east on Manchester, toward downtown and the Third District station house.

Police Lieutenant Jack Hammersmith was in his Third District office, sleek, obese, and cool-looking behind his wide metal desk. He was pounds and years away from the handsome cop who'd been Nudger's partner a decade ago in a two-man patrol car. Nudger could still see traces of a dashing quality in the flesh-upholstered Hammersmith, but he wondered if that was only because he'd known Hammersmith ten years ago.

"Sit down, Nudge," Hammersmith invited, his lips smiling but his slate-gray, cop's eyes unreadable. If eyes were the windows to the soul, his shades were always down.

Nudger sat in one of the straight-backed chairs in front of Hammersmith's desk. "I need some help," he said.

"Sure," Hammersmith said, "you never come see me just to trade recipes or to sit and rock." Hammersmith was partial to irony; it was a good thing, in his line of work.

"I need to know more about Curtis Colt," Nudger said.

Hammersmith got one of his vile greenish cigars out of his shirt pocket and stared intently at it, as if its paper ring label might reveal some secret of life and death. "Colt, eh? The guy who's going to ride the lightning?"

"That's the second time in the past few days I've heard that expression. The first time was from Colt's fiancée. She thinks he's innocent."

"Fiancées think along those lines. Is she your client?"

Nudger nodded but didn't volunteer Holly Ann's name.

"Gullibility makes the world go round," Hammersmith said. "I was in charge of the Homicide investigation on that one. There's not a chance Colt is innocent, Nudge."

"Four eyewitness I.D.'s is compelling evidence," Nudger admitted. "What about the getaway car driver? His description is a lot like Colt's. Maybe he's the one who did the shooting and Colt was the driver."

"Colt's lawyer hit on that. The jury didn't buy it. Neither do I. The man is guilty, Nudge."

"You know how inaccurate eyewitness accounts are," Nudger persisted.

That seemed to get Hammersmith mad. He lit the cigar. The office immediately fogged up.

Nudger made his tone more amicable. "Mind if I look at the file on the Colt case?"

Hammersmith gazed thoughtfully at Nudger through a dense greenish haze. He inhaled, exhaled; the haze became a cloud. "How come this fiancée didn't turn up at the trial to testify for Colt? She could have at least lied and said he was with her that night."

"Colt apparently didn't want her subjected to taking the stand."

"How noble," Hammersmith said. "What makes this fiancée think her prince charming is innocent?"

"She knows he was somewhere else when the shopkeepers were shot."

"But not with her?"

"Nope."

"Well, that's refreshing."

Maybe it was refreshing enough to make up Hammersmith's mind. He picked up the phone and asked for the Colt file. Nudger could barely make out what he was saying around the fat cigar, but apparently everyone at the Third was used to Hammersmith and could interpret cigarese.

The file didn't reveal much that Nudger didn't know. Fifteen minutes after the liquor store shooting, officers from a two-man patrol car, acting on the broadcast description of the gunman, approached Curtis Colt inside a service station where he was buying a pack of ciagarettes from a vending machine. A car that had been parked near the end of the dimly lighted lot had sped away as they'd entered the station office. The officers had gotten only a glimpse of a dark green old Ford; they hadn't made out the license plate number but thought it might start with the letter "L."

Colt had surrendered without a struggle, and that night at the Third District station the four eyewitnesses had picked him out of a lineup. Their description of the getaway car matched that of the car the police had seen speeding from the service station. The loot from the holdup, and several gas station holdups committed earlier that night, wasn't on Colt, but probably it was in the car.

"Colt's innocence just jumps out of the file at you, doesn't it, Nudge?" Hammersmith said. He was grinning a fat grin around the fat cigar.

"What about the murder weapon?"

"Colt was unarmed when we picked him up."

"Seems odd."

"Not really," Hammersmith said. "He was planning to pay for the cigarettes. And maybe the gun was still too hot to touch so he left it in the car. Maybe it's still hot; it got a lot of use for one night."

Closing the file folder and laying it on a corner of Hammersmith's desk, Nudger stood up. "Thanks, Jack. I'll keep you tapped in if I learn anything interesting."

"Don't bother keeping me informed on this one, Nudge. It's over. I don't see how even a fiancée can doubt Colt's guilt."

Nudger shrugged, trying not to breathe too deeply in the smoke-hazed office. "Maybe it's an emotional thing. She thinks that because thought waves are tiny electrical impulses, Colt might experience time warp and all sorts of grotesque thoughts when all that voltage shoots through him. She has bad dreams."

"I'll bet she does," Hammersmith said. "I'll bet Colt has bad dreams, too. Only he deserves his. And maybe she's right."

"About what?"

"About all that voltage distorting thought and time. Who's to say?"

"Not Curtis Colt," Nudger said. "Not after they throw the switch."

"It's a nice theory, though," Hammersmith said. "I'll remember it. It might be a comforting thing to tell the murder victim's family."

"Sometimes," Nudger said, "you think just like a cop who's seen too much."

"Any of it's too much, Nudge," Hammersmith said with surprising sadness. He let more greenish smoke drift from his nostrils and the corners of his mouth; he looked like a stone Buddha seated behind the desk, one in which incense burned.

Nudger coughed and said goodbye.

"Only two eyewitnesses are needed to convict," Nudger said to Holly Ann the next day in her trailer, "and in this case there are four. None of them is at all in doubt about their identification of Curtis Colt as the killer. I have to be honest; it's time you should face the fact that Colt is guilty and that you're wasting your money on my services."

"All them witnesses know what's going to happen to Curtis," Holly

Ann said. "They'd never want to live with the notion they might have made a mistake, killed an innocent man, so they've got themselves convinced that they're positive it was Curtis they saw that night."

"Your observation on human psychology is sound," Nudger said, "but I don't think it will help us. The witnesses were just as certain three months ago at the trial. I took the time to read the court transcript; the jury had no choice but to find Colt guilty, and the evidence hasn't changed."

Holly Ann drew her legs up and clasped her knees to her chest with both arms. Her little-girl posture matched her little-girl faith in her lover's innocence. She believed the white knight must arrive at any moment and snatch Curtis Colt from the electrical jaws of death. She believed hard. Nudger could almost hear his armor clank when he walked.

She wanted him to believe just as hard. "I see you need to be convinced of Curtis's innocence," she said wistfully. There was no doubt he'd forced her into some kind of corner. "If you come here tonight at eight, Mr. Nudger, I'll convince you."

"How?"

"I can't say. You'll understand why tonight."

"Why do we have to wait till tonight?"

"Oh, you'll see."

Nudger looked at the waif-like creature curled in the corner of the sofa. He felt as if they were playing a childhood guessing game while Curtis Colt waited his turn in the electric chair. Nudger had never seen an execution; he'd heard it took longer than most people thought for the condemned to die. His stomach actually twitched.

"Can't we do this now with twenty questions?" he asked.

Holly Ann shook her head. "No, Mr. Nudger."

Nudger sighed and stood up, feeling as if he were about to bump his head on the trailer's low ceiling even though he was barely six feet tall.

"Make sure you're on time tonight, Mr. Nudger," Holly Ann said as he went out the door. "It's important."

At eight on the nose that evening Nudger was sitting at the tiny table in Holly Ann's kitchenette. Across from him was a thin, nervous man in his late twenties or early thirties, dressed in a longsleeved shirt despite the heat, and wearing sunglasses with silver mirror lenses.

Holly Ann introduced the man as "Len, but that's not his real name," and said he was Curtis Colt's accomplice and the driver of their getaway car on the night of the murder.

"But me and Curtis was nowhere near the liquor store when them folks got shot," Len said vehemently.

Nudger assumed the sunglasses were so he couldn't effectively identify Len if it came to a showdown in court. Len had lank, dark brown hair that fell to below his shoulders, and when he moved his arm Nudger caught sight of something blue and red on his briefly exposed wrist. A tattoo. Which explained the longsleeved shirt.

"You can understand why Len couldn't come forth and testify for Curtis in court," Holly Ann said.

Nudger said he could understand that. Len would have had to incriminate himself.

"We was way on the other side of town," Len said, "casing another service station, when that liquor store killing went down. Heck, we never held up nothing but service stations. They was our speciality."

Which was true, Nudger had to admit. Colt had done time for armed robbery six years ago after sticking up half a dozen service stations within a week. And all the other holdups he'd been tied to this time around were of service stations. The liquor store was definitely a department in his M.O., one not noted in court during Curtis Colt's rush to judgment.

"Your hair is in your favor," Nudger said to Len.

"Huh?"

"Your hair didn't grow that long in the three months since the liquor store killing. The witnesses described the getaway car driver as having shorter, curlier hair, like Colt's, and a mustache."

Len shrugged. "I'll be honest with you—it don't help at all. Me and Curtis was kinda the same type. So to confuse any witnesses, in case we got caught, we made each other look even more alike. I'd tuck up my long hair and wear a wig that looked like Curtis's hair. My mustache was real, like Curtis's. I shaved it off a month ago. We did look alike at a glance; sorta like brothers."

Nudger bought that explanation; it wasn't uncommon for a team of holdup men to play tricks to confuse witnesses and the police. Too many lawyers had gotten in the game; the robbers, like the cops, were taking the advice of their attorneys and thinking about a potential trial even before the crime was committed.

"Is there any way, then, to prove you were across town at the time of the murder?" Nudger asked, looking at the two small Nudgers staring back at him from the mirror lenses.

"There's just my word," Len said, rather haughtily.

Nudger didn't bother telling him what that was worth. Why antagonize him?

"I just want you to believe Curtis is innocent," Len said with desperation. "Because he is! And so am I!"

And Nudger understood why Len was here, taking the risk. If Colt was guilty of murder, Len was guilty of being an accessory to the crime. Once Curtis Colt had ridden the lightning, Len would have hanging over him the possibility of an almost certain life sentence, and perhaps even his own ride on the lightning, if he were ever caught. It wasn't necessary to actually squeeze the trigger to be convicted of murder.

"I need for you to try extra hard to prove Curtis is innocent," Len said. His thin lips quivered; he was near tears.

"Are you giving Holly Ann the money to pay me?" Nudger asked.

"Some of it, yeah. From what Curtis and me stole. And I gave Curtis's share to Holly Ann, too. Me and her are fifty-fifty on this."

Dirty money, Nudger thought. Dirty job. Still, if Curtis Colt happened to be innocent, trying against the clock to prove it was a job that needed to be done.

"Okay. I'll stay on the case."

"Thanks," Len said. His narrow hand moved impulsively across the table and squeezed Nudger's arm in gratitude. Len had the look of an addict; Nudger wondered if the longsleeved shirt was to hide needle tracks as well as the tattoo.

Len stood up. "Stay here with Holly Ann for ten minutes while I make myself scarce. I gotta know I wasn't followed. You understand it ain't that I don't trust you; a man in my position has gotta be sure, is all."

"I understand. Go."

Len gave a spooked smile and went out the door. Nudger heard his running footfalls on the gravel outside the trailer. Nudger was forty-three years old and ten pounds overweight; lean and speedy Len needed a ten minute head start like Sinatra needed singing lessons.

"Is Len a user?" Nudger asked Holly Ann.

"Sometimes. But my Curtis never touched no dope."

"You know I have to tell the police about this conversation, don't you?"

Holly Ann nodded. "That's why we arranged it this way. They won't be any closer to Len than before."

"They might want to talk to you, Holly Ann."

She shrugged. "It don't matter. I don't know where Len is, nor even his real name nor how to get in touch with him. He'll find out all he needs to know about Curtis by reading the papers."

"You have a deceptively devious mind," Nudger told her, "considering that you look like Barbie Doll's country kid cousin."

Holly Ann smiled, surprised and pleased. "Do you find me attractive, Mr. Nudger?"

"Yes. And painfully young."

For just a moment Nudger almost thought of Curtis Colt as a lucky man. Then he looked at his watch, saw that his ten minutes were about up, and said goodbye. If Barbie had a kid cousin, Ken probably had one somewhere, too. And time was something you couldn't deny. Ask Curtis Colt.

"It doesn't wash with me," Hammersmith said from behind his desk, puffing angrily on his cigar. Angrily because it did wash a little bit; he didn't like the possibility, however remote, of sending an innocent man to his death. That was every good homicide cop's nightmare. "This Len character is just trying to keep himself in the clear on a murder charge."

"You could read it that way," Nudger admitted.

"It would help if you gave us a better description of Len," Hammersmith said gruffly, as if Nudger were to blame for Curtis Colt's accomplice still walking around free.

"I gave you what I could," Nudger said. "Len didn't give me much to pass on. He's streetwise and scared and knows what's at stake."

Hammersmith nodded, his fit of pique past. But the glint of weary frustration remained in his eyes.

"Are you going to question Holly Ann?" Nudger said.

"Sure, but it won't do any good. She's probably telling the truth. Len would figure we'd talk to her; he wouldn't tell her how to find him."

"You could stake out her trailer."

"Do you think Holly Ann and Len might be lovers?"

"No."

Hammersmith shook his head. "Then they'll probably never see each other again. Watching her trailer would be a waste of manpower."

Nudger knew Hammersmith was right. He stood up to go.

"What are you going to do now?" Hammersmith asked.

"I'll talk to the witnesses again. I'll read the court transcript again. And I'd like to talk with Curtis Colt."

"They don't allow visitors on Death Row, Nudge, only temporary boarders."

"This case is an exception," Nudger said. "Will you try to arrange it?"

Hammersmith chewed thoughtfully on his cigar. Since he'd been the officer in charge of the murder investigation, he'd been the one who'd nailed Curtis Colt. That carried an obligation.

"I'll phone you soon," he said, "let you know."

Nudger thanked Hammersmith and walked down the hall into the clear, breathable air of the booking area.

That day he managed to talk again to all four eyewitnesses. Two of them got mad at Nudger for badgering them. They all stuck to their stories. Nudger reported this to Holly Ann at the Right-Steer Steakhouse, where she worked as a waitress. Several customers that afternoon got tears with their baked potatoes.

Hammersmith phoned Nudger that evening.

"I managed to get permission for you to talk to Colt," he said, "but don't get excited. Colt won't talk to you. He won't talk to anyone, not even a clergyman. He'll change his mind about the clergyman, but not about you."

"Did you tell him I was working for Holly Ann?"

"I had that information conveyed to him. He wasn't impressed. He's one of the stoic ones on Death Row."

Nudger's stomach kicked up, growled something that sounded like a hopeless obscenity. If even Curtis Colt wouldn't cooperate, how could he be helped? Absently Nudger peeled back the aluminum foil on a roll of antacid tablets and slipped two chalky white disks into his mouth. Hammersmith knew about his nervous stomach and must have heard him chomping the tablets. "Take it easy, Nudge. This isn't your fault."

"Then why do I feel like it is ?"

"Because you feel too much of everything. That's why you had to quit the department."

"We've got another day before the execution," Nudger said. "I'm going to go through it all again. I'm going to talk to each of those witnesses even if they try to run when they see me coming. Maybe somebody will say something that will let in some light."

"There's no light out there, Nudge. You're wasting your time. Give up on this one and move on."

"Not yet," Nudger said. "There's something elusive here that I can't quite grab."

"And never will," Hammersmith said. "Forget it, Nudge. Live your life and let Curtis Colt lose his."

Hammersmith was right. Nothing Nudger did helped Curtis Colt in the slightest. At eight o'clock Saturday morning, while Nudger was preparing breakfast in his apartment, Colt was put to death in the electric chair. He'd offered no last words before two thousand volts had turned him from something into nothing.

Nudger heard the news of Colt's death on his kitchen radio. He went ahead and ate his eggs, but he skipped the toast.

That afternoon he consoled a numbed and frequently sobbing Holly Ann and apologized for being powerless to stop her true love's execution. She was polite, trying to be brave. She preferred to suffer alone. Her boss at the Right-Steer gave her the rest of the day off, and Nudger drove her home.

Nudger slept a total of four hours during the next two nights. On Monday, he felt compelled to attend Curtis Colt's funeral. There were about a dozen people clustered around the grave, including the state-appointed clergyman and pallbearers. Nudger stood off to one side during the brief service. Holly Ann, looking like a child playing dress-up in black, stood well off to the other side. They didn't exchange words, only glances.

As the coffin was lowered into the earth, Nudger watched Holly Ann walk to where a taxi was waiting by a weathered stone angel. The cab wound its way slowly along the snaking narrow cemetery road to tall iron gates and the busy street. Holly Ann never looked back.

That night Nudger realized what was bothering him, and for the first time since Curtis Colt's death, he slept well.

In the morning he began watching Holly Ann's trailer.

At seven-thirty she emerged, dressed in her yellow waitress uniform, and got into another taxi. Nudger followed in his battered Volkswagen Beetle as the cab drove her the four miles to her job at the Right-Steer Steakhouse. She didn't look around as she paid the driver and walked inside through the molded plastic Old-West-saloon swinging doors.

At six that evening another cab drove her home, making a brief stop at a grocery store.

It went that way for the rest of the week, trailer to work to trailer. Holly Ann had no visitors other than the plain brown paper bag she took home every night.

The temperature got up to around ninety-five and the humidity rose right along with it. It was one of St. Louis's legendary summer heat waves. Sitting melting in the Volkswagen, Nudger wondered if what he was doing was really worthwhile. Curtis Colt was, after all, dead, and had never been his client. Still, there were responsibilities that went beyond the job. Or perhaps they were actually the essence of the job.

The next Monday, after Holly Ann had left for work, Nudger used his Visa card to slip the flimsy lock on her trailer door, and let himself in.

It took him over an hour to find what he was searching for. It had been well hidden, in a cardboard box inside the access panel to the bathroom plumbing. After looking at the box's contents—almost seven hundred dollars in loot from Curtis Colt's brief life of crime, and another object Nudger wasn't surprised to see—Nudger resealed the box and replaced the access panel.

He continued to watch and follow Holly Ann, more confident now.

Two weeks after the funeral, when she left work one evening, she didn't go home.

Instead her taxi turned the opposite way and drove east on Watson Road. Nudger followed the cab along a series of side streets in South St. Louis, then part way down a dead-end alley to a large garage, above the door of which was lettered "Clifford's Auto Body."

Nudger backed out quickly onto the street, then parked the Volkswagen near the mouth of the alley. A few minutes later the cab drove by without a passenger. Within ten minutes, Holly Ann drove past in a shiny red Ford. Its license plate number began with an L.

When Nudger reached Placid Cove Trailer Park, he saw the Ford nosed in next to Holly Ann's trailer.

On the way to the trailer door, he paused and scratched the Ford's hood with a key. Even in the lowering evening light he could see that beneath the new red paint the car's color was dark green.

Holly Ann answered the door right away when he knocked. She tried a smile when she saw it was him, but she couldn't quite manage her facial muscles, as if they'd become rigid and uncoordinated. She appeared ten years older. The little-girl look had deserted her; now she was an emaciated, grief-eroded woman, a country Barbie doll whose features some evil child had lined with dark crayon. The shaded crescents beneath her eyes completely took away their innocence. She was holding a glass that had once been a jelly jar. In it were two fingers of a clear liquid. Behind her on the table was a crumpled brown paper bag and a half-empty bottle of gin.

"I figured it out," Nudger told her.

Now she did smile, but it was fleeting, a sickly bluish shadow crossing her taut features. "You're like a dog with a rag, Mr. Nudger. You surely don't know when to let go." She stepped back and he followed her into the trailer. It was warm in there; something was wrong with the air conditioner. "Hot as hell, ain't it," Holly Ann commented. Nudger thought that was apropos.

He sat down across from her at the tiny Formica table, just as he and Len had sat facing each other two weeks ago. She offered him a drink. He declined. She downed the contents of the jelly jar glass and poured herself another, clumsily striking the neck of the bottle on the glass. It made a sharp, flinty sound, as if sparks might fly.

"Now, what's this you've got figured out, Mr. Nudger?" She didn't want to, but she had to hear it. Had to share it.

"It's almost four miles to the Right-Steer Steakhouse," Nudger told her. "The waitresses there make little more than minimum wage, so cab fare to and from work has to eat a big hole in your salary. But then you seem to go everywhere by cab."

"My car's been in the shop."

"I figured it might be, after I found the money and the wig."

She bowed her head slightly and took a sip of gin. "Wig?"

"In the cardboard box inside the bathroom wall."

"You been snooping, Mr. Nudger." There was more resignation than outrage in her voice.

"You're sort of skinny, but not a short girl," Nudger went on.

"With a dark curly wig and a fake mustache, sitting in a car, you'd resemble Curtis Colt enough to fool a dozen eyewitnesses who just caught a glimpse of you. It was a smart precaution for the two of you to take."

Holly Ann looked astounded. "Are you saying I was driving the getaway car at the liquor store holdup?"

"Maybe. Then maybe you hired someone to play Len and convince me he was Colt's accomplice and that they were far away from the murder scence when the trigger was pulled. After I found the wig, I talked to some of your neighbors, who told me that until recently you'd driven a green Ford sedan."

Holly Ann ran her tongue along the edges of her protruding teeth. "So Curtis and Len used my car for their holdups."

"I doubt if Len ever met Curtis. He's somebody you paid in stolen money or drugs to sit there where you're sitting now and lie to me."

"If I was driving that getaway car, Mr. Nudger, and *knew* Curtis was guilty, why would I have hired a private investigator to try to find a hole in the eyewitnesses' stories?"

"That's what bothered me at first," Nudger said, "until I realized you weren't interested in clearing Curtis. What you were really worried about was Curtis Colt talking in prison. You didn't want those witnesses' stories changed, you wanted them verified. And you wanted the police to learn about not-his-right-name Len."

Holly Ann raised her head to look directly at him with eyes that begged and dreaded. She asked simply, "Why would I want that?"

"Because you were Curtis Colt's accomplice in all of his robberies. And when you hit the liquor store, he stayed in the car to drive. You fired the shot that killed the old woman. He was the one who fired the wild shot from the speeding car. Colt kept quiet about it because he loved you. He never talked, not to the police, not to his lawyer, not even to a priest. Now that he's dead you can trust him forever, but I have a feeling you could have anyway. He loved you more than you loved him, and you'll have to live knowing he didn't deserve to die."

She looked down into her glass as if for answers and didn't say anything for a long time. Nudger felt a bead of perspiration trickle crazily down the back of his neck. Then she said, "I didn't want to shoot that old man, but he didn't leave me no choice. Then the old woman came at me." She looked up at Nudger and smiled ever so slightly. It was a smile Nudger hadn't seen on her before, one he didn't like. "God help me, Mr. Nudger, I can't quit thinking about shooting that old woman."

"You murdered her," Nudger said, "and you murdered Curtis Colt by keeping silent and letting him die for you."

"You can't prove nothing," Holly Ann said, still with her ancient-eyed, eerie smile that had nothing to do with amusement.

"You're right," Nudger told her, "I can't. But I don't think legally proving it is necessary, Holly Ann. You said it: thoughts are actually tiny electrical impulses in the brain. Curtis Colt rode the lightning all at once. With you, it will take years, but the destination is the same. I think you'll come to agree that his way was easier."

She sat very still. She didn't answer. Wasn't going to.

Nudger stood up and wiped his damp forehead with the back of his hand. He felt sticky, dirty, confined by the low ceiling and near walls of the tiny, stifling trailer. He had to get out of there to escape the sensation of being trapped.

He didn't say goodbye to Holly Ann when he walked out. She didn't say goodbye to him. The last sound Nudger heard as he left the trailer was the clink of the bottle on the glass.

Till Tuesday

JEREMIAH HEALY

Cambridge, Massachusetts, is home to Harvard University, boutique restaurants, and people who believe that Anthony Lewis editorials really make a difference. The two men sitting across from me lived there, but I pictured them more as *Wall Street Journal* than New York *Times*.

The one on the right was an architect, Michael Atlee. Atlee was lanky and angular; his brown hair showed licks of white at the temples. He fit poorly into an expensive blue tweed sports jacket and red rooster tie over slacks a little too pale to contrast correctly with his coat. Atlee held a pipe by its bowl in his hand, but made no effort to light it.

The man next to him spelled and smelled lawyer through and through. Thayer Lane, Esq., was on his business card, followed by his firm's four named partners and an upscale address. Slim, with black hair, Lane wore a charcoal pinstriped uniform of power and a muted paisley tie.

I guessed both men to be perched on the far side of forty-five. Neither seemed especially comfortable having a conference on the Wednesday after Labor Day in a one room office with JOHN FRANCIS CUDDY, CONFIDENTIAL INVESTIGATIONS on the door.

After the introductions, Lane said, "Mr. Cuddy, we are here on a matter which cannot be discussed with the police. You come highly recommended, especially in the categories of loyalty and discretion."

"Thank you."

"I should say that while Mr. Atlee will be your client in this regard, he is uncomfortable with speaking at length. Hence, he asked me to accompany him here today."

I looked at Atlee. "What seems to be the problem?"

Atlee said, "Thayer?"

Lane took his cue. "Mr. Atlee—Michael—is a designer of buildings. Perhaps you're familiar with some of his works?"

Lane ticked off five recent commercial towers. I recognized two of them. I thought they looked like I-beams wearing Tina Turner dresses, but I kept it to myself. "Is the difficulty related to one of the buildings?"

"No, Mr. Cuddy," said Lane. "Let me try to outline the situation for you."

"Go ahead. And please call me John."

"John." Lane spoke as if he might otherwise forget the name. "John, are you married?"

"Widower."

"Ah, sorry. Well . . ." Lane took a deep breath. "Michael is married. However, he has been engaged in an affair for three years with a woman, Gina Fiore. Michael believes that Ms.—Gina, has disappeared, and he would like you to find her."

I looked over to Atlee, who sucked on his unlit pipe and blew imaginary smoke at me. His facial movements masked any emotion.

"How long has she been missing?"

"That's uncertain. Michael last saw her this past Thursday but couldn't reach her yesterday."

Atlee said, "Tell him all of it."

Lane glanced at Atlee and sighed. "Every Labor Day Michael hosts a family retreat at his summer home on Parker Pond in Maine. We all go up on Thursday night, scour and spruce the place up with paint and so forth against the elements, then relax and shoot skeet Sunday and Monday."

"You shoot skeet on a lake on Labor Day weekend?"

Atlee said, "I've got ten acres. It's private enough."

I said to Atlee, "So she could be gone for as long as six days."

"Right."

"Or as little as twenty hours."

Lane stuck in, "My point precisely."

Atlee said, "Doesn't matter. She's gone."

"Where does Gina live?"

Atlee nodded to Lane, who took over again. "Gina lives in a condominium on Revere Beach that Michael purchased as an investment. Part of their, ah, arrangement is that she is to be available at all times. By telephone and in person."

Lovely. I said to Lane, "A few minutes ago you said 'we'?"

"I'm sorry?"

"You were talking about the lake thing being a family event but you said 'we all went up to the summer place.'"

"Oh, quite. Michael is a client of my firm, but we're also best friends. Roomed together at Harvard and prepped at Choate before that. My wife and I are like family to Michael and Winnie, and Seth's my godson."

I said to Atlee, "Winnie's your wife and Seth's your son?"

He nodded and bit down on the pipestem.

"Any reason for Gina to take off?"

"None." Decisively.

"Who else knows about your relationship with Gina?"

Lane said, "A woman named Marla—I'm afraid we don't have her last name—lives in the next unit in Gina's building and is aware of, ah . . ."

"Anybody else?"

Atlee fidgeted in his chair, I thought at first from impatience. Then he said, "Seth knows, or suspects. Same damned thing, I guess. Saw us once together a couple of years ago in a bar over there. Slumming with one of his swim-team chums. Damned bad luck, but there it is."

I had the impression I'd been treated to Atlee's longest speech of the decade. "Any point in my talking with him?"

"No." Case closed.

Lane said, "That would be rather difficult anyway, John."

"Why is that?"

"You see, Seth is a junior at Stanford this year, and he always leaves the morning after Labor Day to head out there."

Atlee said, "Damned fool has to drive his Jeep three-thousand miles. Can't take the plane like a normal person."

"In any case," said Lane, "I had a call from him last night. He was near Pittsburgh and wasn't sure of his next destination."

I said, "He called you?"

Lane seemed affronted. "I am his godfather."

"All right. I'll need a photo of Gina and her address over in Revere."

Atlee said, "Don't have a photo."

"I'm sure you understand," said Lane.

Before I could reply, Atlee leaned forward, tapping his pipe on my desk for emphasis. "Just understand this. I really care for that girl. I may not show it, but I do. And I want you to find her."

TWO

Revere Beach is an incongruous strip of old clamshacks and new highrise towers along a slightly polluted stretch of sand and ocean about ten miles north of Boston. I flashed the key Atlee had given me at the security guard, who smiled deferentially and used his magazine to wave me into the lobby. I took an elevator to the ninth floor.

Unit 9A was at the end of the hall. I had a little trouble with the lock, rattled it and the knob twice before the tumbler would turn. Inside, the apartment was airy, with a striking view of the Atlantic through sliding glass doors to a narrow balcony. Versatile sectional furniture for couch and chairs. Track lighting overhead, a wall unit with stereo, color TV, and even a few books.

I entered the bedroom and had been drawn toward some framed photos on the bureau when I thought I heard the snap and creak of a quick entry at the front door. I managed two steps before a perfectly tanned woman in a European string bikini appeared in the doorway to the living room. She leveled a tiny automatic at me and said, "My boyfriend told me to just keep firing until the guy falls."

I got the hint.

"Gina and me watch each other's places, you know?"

"Good system."

"Look, at least I can make you a drink or something, huh?"

She was trying hard, a little too hard, to make up for the gun scene. My investigator's I.D. had convinced her I wasn't a "real" burglar, and she was pleased to introduce herself as Marla, the girl next door. I'd seen everything except the bedroom closet with nothing to show for it. Now she was watching me rummage through Gina's dresses, slacks, and shoes.

"So Mikey figures Gina's flown on him, huh?"

I liked her using "Mikey." I said over my shoulder, "That the way you see it?"

"Without telling me? And leaving all her stuff like this?" She paused. "Hard to say for sure, though. Gina's been a little restless lately."

I stopped searching and turned around. "Restless?"

"Yeah, well, it's not so easy being somebody's sweet harbor, you know? Waiting for a phone call, planning your life around a lunch here or there and some afternoon delight."

Somehow the phrase sounded sweeter in the song. "Would she have left on her own?"

"Not likely. Gina enjoyed being took care of, even by a creep like Mikey."

"How do you mean?"

"Aw, we double-dated a coupla months ago. Her and Mikey and this guy called himself 'Jim.' We drove up to Swampscott to go sailing, like they was afraid to do the class thing and go all the way to Marblehead, maybe one of their bigshot friends sees them there with two bimbettes from Revere."

"You ever see this Jim again?"

"No, but like I said, that wasn't his real name. Stupid guy, he drives us all up there in this big green Mercedes, like we're too dumb to know how to run a plate at the registry."

"You ran his license plate?"

"Yeah. Turns out he's another Cambridge highroller with, get this, the name 'Thayer Lane.'"

Ah, Mr. Lane. "This Lane seemed interested in Gina?"

"Coulda been. I kept him pretty interested that day, I'll tell you. Never did hear back from him, though. Good old 'Jim.'"

"Gina ever mention Atlee's son?"

"Not really. Just that the father and him didn't get along too well."

"Some families are like that."

"Boy, you got that right." Her tone changed. "You got any pressing commitments after this here?"

I stuck my head back into the closet. There were three matching pieces of luggage; the size just up from the smallest seemed to be missing.

"Well, do you?"

"Marla," I said, pointing, "does Gina have a full set of these bags?"

She came over, pressing and rubbing more than my request required. "Uh-huh. Gina uses the other one for day-hops." She was wearing some kind of coconut-scented lotion.

"Meaning not overnight?"

Marla stepped back without answering. She kept going until her calves touched the bed, then sat back and onto her elbows, in one languid motion. She hooded her eyes. "Doesn't have to take all night, sugar."

Walking to the bureau, I picked up one of the photos. A girl about Marla's age, long frosted curls, winking at the lens.

"This Gina?"

She licked her lips. "Uh-huh."

"Recent?"

"Hair's a little shorter now. Let's talk about you. And me."

I think she was laughing as I went through the front door.

I stood up, put my hands in my pockets. "Mrs. Feeney told me what they were, but it was some Latin name, and I forgot it."

What happened to that elaborate altar boy training?

I looked at the purplish flowers with yellowish petals, then at her stone. Elizabeth Mary Devlin Cuddy. "Won't help me much with this one, Beth."

What's the problem?

I told her.

An architect's mistress. Sordid.

"It's about to get worse."

How?

"Tomorrow I intend to see his wife about their son."

THREE

The next morning I stopped at the office to hoke up a manila file folder and some documents, then took Memorial Drive to Cambridge. The Atlees' home was on one of those short streets off Brattle. An aggressively traditional mini-manse, it was surrounded by an outside fence nearly as tall as the trees behind it. I tapped a button on the intercom at the wrought-iron entrance and a minute later received a metallic, female "Yes?"

"Mrs. Atlee?"

"Yes."

"My name is John Cuddy. I'm a private investigator and I'm here about your son."

"My son? Is there some kind of problem?"

"No, no, ma'am. It's just that, well, it would be easier if I could show you the file."

Hesitation, then the grating buzz and click that tell you to push on the gate.

"And you say my son witnessed an accident?"

"Yes, ma'am." I slid the folder over to her, holding my index finger on the document in the middle of the Acco-clipped bunch till she held the place for herself and began reading it.

She was about Atlee's age, with strawberry-blonde hair pulled severely behind her head. A peasant dress heightened the sense of bony strength about her. Striking, not beautiful, she probably sat an English saddle well, given some of the bronzed trophies on shelves in the den. The other statuettes looked like awards for swimming and shooting.

"But this isn't even my son's handwriting."

"No, ma'am. That's the handwriting of our Mr. Green, who's no longer our Mr. Green because he fouled up so much, like here when he took down your son's statement then forgot to have him date or sign it over . . . there."

She shook her head and handed me back the file. "Well, I'm sure if Seth were here he'd be glad to help you, but he left for California on Tuesday."

I let my face fall. "Gee, Mrs. Atlee, this case is coming up for trial and all. Do you have a number where I can reach him?"

"Yes. Well, no. Not for a few more days. You see, he drives there, to return to Stanford, and he rather dawdles really, taking roads that interest him and stopping wherever."

"Does he call you?"

"Sometimes. Other times no. If we hear from him, we could ask him to call you, but it would probably be late at night and perhaps not at all."

"Is there anyone else he might call?"

She considered it. "Yes. His friend Doug Cather. Seth and Doug were on the swim team together at prep school. Doug's at Harvard now."

I looked past her to a photo on the mantel. A family portrait of a younger Atlee and wife behind a seated teenager.

"Is that Seth?"

She twisted around and looked back at me. "Yes." She darkened. "Is there something else?"

"No, no. He looks like a fine boy."

Doug Cather lived in Kirkland House, part of the not-quite-quadrangle of more-than-dorms nestled near the Charles River. He was tall, broad-shouldered, and completely hairless.

"We shave our heads."

"Why?"

"For swimming. Cuts down on the drag effect in the water."

Anything for dear old Harvard, I guess. Cather accepted my bogus accident story.

"No, I haven't heard from Seth, which is kind of funny."

"You two stay in touch that closely?"

"Not really. It's just that he always calls me when he leaves for school, and I kind of waited around for it yesterday morning. Cut classes and all."

"Wait a minute. I thought Seth left for California on Tuesday. Yesterday was Wednesday."

Cather's face clouded over.

I said, "There's something you're not telling me."

"There's something I don't think is any of your business."

"Something about Seth?"

"Yeah."

"Look, I'm not going to give you a long song and dance about confidentiality. You don't know me at all, so you don't know if you can trust me."

"That's right."

"Okay. Here's my problem. I've got to find your friend. You can help me, or I can do it the hard way. Go see other people, his dad, whoever. That might mean I find out worse things than I need to know. All I can say is if you tell me what's going on, I'll try to keep it to myself."

Cather didn't speak.

"We want Seth as a witness for us on this collision. I'm not about to spread rumors that would make him look bad."

"It's not . . ." He seemed to search inside for a moment. "I want your promise anyway. You won't tell anybody?"

"Promise."

He blew out a breath. "Okay, it's like this. After we graduated from Choate, Seth and I bounced around for the summer. One day we decide to go to Revere Beach, kind of scope out the other half, you know? Well, we dare each other to go into this bar. I mean, we're way underage and nobody's ever gonna serve us without I.D., but we try it anyway. Right off, I spot Seth's father in one of the booths, with a real tough . . . a really sharp-looking chick just a couple of years older than us. So I start to say something, and Seth sees them and gets all uptight. He's kind of impulsive anyhow, and he bolts out of there and like won't even talk with me all the way home."

"What's that got to do with his driving to California?"

"Well, it didn't take a genius to see what his dad was doing there, and I guess Seth and him had a real blow-up over it. Anyway, Seth decides not to go out for swimming at Stanford, like to punish his dad, I guess. But every year his family has this Labor Day thing to please his mom. So, okay, after Seth gets home from the weekend each year, he goes back up there."

"Seth goes back?"

"Right. He tells his parents he's leaving for school, and he does, sort of, but first he drives up to Parker Pond and does the swim."

"The swim."

"Yeah. He swims out from their property to this little island and back. It's like a ritual, I guess, to prove he can still go the distance. And maybe to think about when he was younger and he didn't, well, know about his dad."

"Would Seth sleep over in Maine on that Tuesday night?"

"Definitely. It's almost four hours to get there, and he probably wouldn't leave his parents in Cambridge much before lunchtime."

"You ever been to this Parker Pond house?"

"Sure. Lots of times."

"Can you draw me a map?"

FOUR

Even with Doug Cather's sketch, I had to stop at an inn on the main road for supplemental directions. A turnoff went from paved to gravel to hard-packed dirt. Then I saw rutted tracks curve off the road, a primitive driveway running under a white tollgate. Leaving the car, I walked up to the gate. A single horizontal bar, very freshly painted, was hinged on one of two posts and swung inward freely.

The day was warm, the only sounds the wind in the trees and a woodpecker pocking away nearby. I decided to approach more quietly than my old Fiat would allow. I tossed my sport coat into the front seat and switched on the hazard lights. Ducking under the gate bar, I started walking.

The driveway doglegged right to insure privacy and squiggled here and there to avoid particularly substantial pines. Passing the last big tree, I spotted the back of the house.

A black Jeep Wrangler was parked at the mouth of an adjoining shed.

I moved through the underbrush and approached the shed, keeping it between me and the large chalet-style house behind it. I stopped at the side of the shed to listen. No noise from inside.

Edging toward the front, I looked through the webby pane at the shed's door. Paint buckets, rake and lawnmower, gasoline can, etc. The Jeep was stuffed to the roof with the oddlot cartons and containers students use to return to college.

I circled around the house. Every door and window seemed sealed tight. The wind was really howling lakeside, kicking whitecaps against the shoreline.

At the back door, I knocked, waited, and knocked again louder. Inside I could see the kitchen area. Using a rock to break the glass, I was hit with the stench as I opened the door itself. I gagged and tried to close off my nasal passages with the back of my tongue. Grabbing a dish rag off the rack over the sink, I took it to the shed and doused it with gasoline. I held the rag to my face and went back inside.

He was lying on the floor of the great room, cathedral ceiling above him. A dry pair of swim trunks and a beach towel lay on a chair next to him. At his side, a carefully carved and scrolled double-barreled shotgun, one hand around the trigger mechanism. His face was bloated, the head connected only by the few tendons the blast had left of his neck. Seth Atlee, a marionette past all mending.

Gina was on the open, slatted staircase leading to the upper level. Naked, she'd taken the other barrel between the shoulder blades and would have been dead before her nose struck the tenth step.

The house was twenty degrees hotter than the ambient temperature outside. I didn't think my gasoline filter would support a telephone call indoors.

I pulled the door closed and walked slowly down the driveway. At the gate, I noticed what seemed to be a grass stain on the house side of the swing bar, stark against the gleaming white. Like someone had scraped the inner edge of the bar against a car.

I started the Fiat and drove to the inn to learn about law enforcement in Maine.

FIVE

The funeral was scheduled for Saturday afternoon, beginning from a mortuary on Massachusetts Avenue in Cambridge. I got there early and parked a block away. Even announced murder/suicides draw large numbers of sincere mourners these days. I watched the arrivals of Michael and Winnie Atlee, Doug Cather, and Thayer Lane with a woman I took to be his wife.

Forty minutes later, the crowd came back out, repairing to private cars to form the procession. I left the Fiat. Pausing at Lane's Mercedes, I could see the lawyer on the porch of the funeral home, bending slightly at the waist and using both hands to shake hands gently with a short, elderly woman. I caught his eye. He glared at me. I smiled and beckoned. He excused himself, moving stifflegged over to me.

"Counselor."

"Mr. Cuddy, don't you think it a bit tasteless for you to appear here?"

"What I think is that Seth didn't kill Gina or himself."

Lane stopped fussing.

I said, "How long did you figure it'd take before they were found?"

"I beg your pardon?"

"The bodies. Buttoned up in the house and all. Seth would be reported missing by his college after a while, but who would think to check the lake place?"

"What in the world kind of question is that?"

"You see, the longer the wait, the tougher to peg time of death. After a couple of weeks, no one would swear to anything shorter than a few, bracketed, days."

"Mr. Cuddy, I really must get back."

"You didn't want me searching for Gina so quickly after Atlee couldn't raise her. You double-dated with him, Gina, and Marla once. Gina was restless, maybe you caught each other's fancy."

"Preposterous."

"But Atlee's a big client and an old friend. So you needed a safe place to try your luck. None safer than the summer home you helped close up the day before."

"I'm not going to—"

"Listen any more? You've listened too much as it is, Lane. An innocent man would have walked already."

He clenched his teeth. "Finish it then."

"You didn't know about Seth's ritual swim. I'm guessing you were in the sack with Gina when Seth burst in downstairs. He would have seen your car. Did he call out to you? 'Hey, Uncle Thayer, you upstairs?'"

Lane looked clammy, unsteady.

"You jump out of bed, try to pull some clothes on. Seth's in good shape, though, takes the steps two at a time. Sees you in the nearly altogether with the woman he recognizes as his dad's mistress. He goes nuts, runs back downstairs, gets a skeet gun. He loads it and comes back, back to purge the stain from the one place he still thought was family inviolate."

"No, no."

"You try to reason with him in the great room, Gina following you down the stairs. A struggle, the gun wavers toward Seth as somebody hits the trigger. Seth goes down, Gina yells, 'You murdered him!' Or maybe she just starts screaming, screaming till you lock onto her as a target and she—"

"You can't prove a word of this!"

"No?" I gestured toward the hood of his Mercedes. "Those gouge marks. You put them there when you swung the gate in to leave the place on Tuesday."

He blinked, trying to make the scratches go away. "They . . . they . . ."

"Freshly painted gate, two days before. If you'd taken a piece out of the car driving back Monday, the missus would remember it. The kind of thing that would spoil the whole weekend."

"Seth, he called me . . ."

I shook my head. "Nobody called you Tuesday night, because Seth didn't call his friend Wednesday morning. I'm betting the medical examiner saw the bodies soon enough to place both deaths on Tuesday afternoon. The phone alibi would have been perfect in a few more weeks. Now it's going to hang you."

"Thayer? Thayer!"

We both turned.

Michael Atlee was chopping his hand toward the lead limousine. For the godfather.

Lane whispered. "What are you . . ."

"Going to do? I'm going to give you a chance here, Thayer. Mikey there is your best friend, right?"

"I . . . yes he is, but—"

"Then sometime in the next two days you're going to tell him all about it."

"Money. You want money."

"I don't want money, Thayer. I was hired to find Gina Fiore. I found her and was paid. Now you're going to do your job. You're going to be the first to tell your best friend how his mistress and son really died."

"Thayer!" called Atlee, striding determinedly toward us.

Lane said, "But for God's sake, Cuddy, that's not how it happened! The way you said, it wasn't like that."

"Maybe not. You've got till Tuesday to come up with a better version."

I walked back to my car.

The Day of the Losers

DICK FRANCIS

Austin Dartmouth Glenn set off to the Grand National with three hundred pounds in his pocket and a mixture of guilt and bravado in his mind. Austin Dartmouth Glenn knew perfectly well that he had promised on his immortal soul and his mother's sainted memory (and other similar trifles) that he would not, he would positively not, put into premature circulation various banknotes which were of intense interest to the police.

Not for five years; he had been sternly warned. Five years would see the heat off. In five years the multimillion robbery would be ancient history; the police would be chasing more recent villains; the hot serial numbers would have faded into fly-blown obscurity on out-of-date lists. In five years it would be safe to spend the fifteen thousand smackers he had been paid for his part in springing the big bold bank-robbing boss out of unwelcome jail.

That was all very well, Austin told himself aggrievedly, looking out of the train window at the flying countryside. What about inflation? What about that, then? In five years' time, fifteen thousand might not be worth the paper it was printed on. Or they might even, as in the past, change the colour and size of fivers; he'd heard of a frantic safe-blower who'd done twelve years and gone home to a cache full of the old thin white stuff. All that time served for a load of out-of-date uncashable rubbish. Austin Glenn's mouth twisted in sympathy at the thought. It wasn't going to happen to *him*, he promised himself. Not ruddy well likely.

Austin had paid for his train ticket with ordinary currency, and ditto for the cans of beer, packages of cellophaned sandwiches, and copy of the *Sporting Life*, with which he passed the journey. The hot three hundred were stowed away safely in an inner pocket, not to be risked before he reached the bustling anonymity of the huge crowd converging on Aintree racecourse, Liverpool, England. He was no fool, of course, he thought complacently. A neat pack of sixty fivers, crisp, new, and consecutive, might catch the most incurious eye: but

242

no one would look twice now that he had shuffled them thoroughly and crinkled them well with hands especially dirtied for the purpose.

He wiped beer off his mouth with the back of his hand: a scrawny fortyish man with neat, thin grey-black hair, restless eyes, and an overall air of self-importance. A life spent on the fringes of crime had given him hundreds of dubious acquaintances, an intricate memory-bank of information, and a sound knowledge of how to solicit bribes without actually cupping the palm. No one liked him very much, but Austin Dartmouth Glenn was not sensitive enough to notice.

Nearer the front of the same train Jerry Springwood sat and sweated on three counts. For one thing, he was an outdoor man, and found the train heat excessive, and for another, owing to alcohol and sex, he had no time to spare and would very likely lose his job if he arrived late; but above all, he sweated from fear.

Jerry Springwood, at thirty-two, had lost his nerve, and was trying to carry on the trade of steeplechase jockey without anyone finding out. The old days, when he used to ride with a cool brain and discount intermittent bangs as merely a nuisance, were long gone. For months now he had travelled with dread to the meetings, imagining sharp ends of bone protruding from his skin; imagining a smashed face or a severed spine; imagining pain.

For months he had been unable to take risks he would once not have seen as risks at all. For months he had been unable to urge his mounts forward into gaps, when only such urging would win; and unable to stop himself steadying his mounts to jump, when only kicking them on would do. The skill which had taken him to the top was now used to cover the cracks, and the soundness of his longtime reputation bolstered the explanations for defeat which he gave to owners and trainers. Only the most discerning saw the disguised signs of disintegration, and fewer still had put private doubts into private words. The great British public, searching the list of Grand National runners for inspiration, held good old Jerry Springwood to be a plus factor in favour of the third favourite, Haunted House.

A year ago, he reflected drearily, as he stared out at the passing March fields, he would have known better than to go to a sultry party in London on the night before the big race. A year ago he had stayed near the course, drank maybe a couple of beers, gone to bed early, slept alone. He wouldn't have dreamed of making a four-hour dash south in the evening after Friday's racing, or getting drunk, or going to bed at two with a girl he'd known three hours. He hadn't needed to blot out the thought of Saturday afternoon's marathon, but had looked forward to it with zest, excitement, and unquenchable hope.

Oh God, he thought despairingly, what has happened to me?

He was small and strong, with wiry mid-brown hair, deep-set eyes, and a nose flattened by too much fast contact with the ground. A farmer's son, natural with animals, and with social manners sophisticated by success. People usually liked Jerry Springwood, but he was too unassuming to notice.

The crowds poured cheerfully into Aintree racecourse, primed with hope, faith, and cash. Austin peeled off the first of the hot fivers at the turnstiles, and contentedly watched it being sucked into the anonymity of the gate receipts. He safely got change for another in a crowded bar, and for a third from a stall selling form sheets. Money for old rope, he thought sardonically. It didn't make sense, holding on to the stuff for five years.

The Tote, as usual, had opened its windows an hour before the first race to take bets on the Grand National, because there was not time after the second to sell tickets to all who wanted to buy for the big third. There were long queues already when Austin went along to back his fancy, for like him they knew from experience that it was best to bet early if one wanted a good vantage point on the stands. He waited in the shorter queue for the five-pound window, writing his proposal on his racecard.

When his turn came he said, "Fifty to win, number twelve," and counted off the shuffled fivers without a qualm.

The busy woman behind the window gave him his tickets with barely a glance.

"Next?" she said enquiringly, looking over his shoulder to the man behind.

Dead easy, thought Austin smugly, stuffing his tickets into his jacket pocket. Fifty on number twelve, to win. No point in messing about with place money, he always said. Mind you, he was a pretty good judge of form: he always prided himself on that. Nothing in the race had a better chance than the third favourite. Haunted House, and you couldn't want a better jockey than Springwood, now could you? He strolled with satisfaction back to the bar and bought another beer.

In the changing-room Jerry Springwood had no difficulty in disguising either his hangover or his fear. The other jockeys were gripped with the usual pre-National tension, finding their mouths a little dry, their thoughts a little abstracted, their flow of ribald jokes slowed to a trickle. Twice over Becher's, Jerry thought hopelessly: the Canal Turn: the Chair: how in God's name am I going to face it?

The Senior Steward of the Jockey Club was lunching a party of eminent overseas visitors in a private dining-room when Chief Superintendent Crispin interrupted the roast saddle of lamb.

"I want to speak to you urgently, sir," the policeman said, bending down to the Turf's top ear.

Sir William Westerland rested his bland gaze briefly on the amount of brass on the navy-blue uniform.

"You're in charge here?"

"Yes, sir. Can we talk privately?"

"I suppose so, if it's important." Sir William rose, glanced regretfully at his half-eaten lunch, and led the policeman through double glass doors to the outdoor section of his private box high in the grandstand. The two men stood hunched in the chilly air, and spoke against the background noise of the swelling crowd and the shouts of the bookmakers offering odds on the approaching first race.

Crispin said, "It's about the Birmingham bank robbery, sir."

"But that happened more than a year ago," Westerland protested.

"Some of the stolen notes have turned up here today, on the racecourse."

Westerland frowned, not needing to be told details. The blasting open of the supposed-to-be-impregnable vault, the theft of upwards of three and a half million, the violent getaway of the thieves, all had been given wider coverage than the death of Nelson. Four men, a small boy, and a dog had been killed by the explosion outwards of the bank wall, and three housewives and two young policemen had been gunned down later. The thieves had arrived in a fire engine before the crashing echoes died, had dived immediately into the ruins to carry out all the vault's contents for "safekeeping," and driven clear away with the loot, suspected only at the very last moment by a puzzled constable, whose orders to halt had been answered by a spray of machine-gun bullets.

Only one of the gang had been recognized, caught, tried, and sentenced to thirty years; and of that he had served precisely thirty days before making a spectacular escape. Recapturing him, and catching his confederates, was still a number one police priority, coast to coast.

"It's the first lead we've had for months," Crispin said earnestly. "If we can catch whoever came here with the hot money . . ."

Westerland looked down at the scurrying thousands. "Pretty hopeless, I'd have thought," he said.

"No, sir," Crispin shook his neat greying head. "A sharp-eyed checker in the Tote stopped one of the notes, and now they've found nine more. One of the sellers in the five pound windows remembers selling fifty pounds worth of tickets early on to a man who paid in fivers which *felt* new although they had been roughly creased and wrinkled."

"But even so . . ."

"She remembers he backed only one horse to win, which is unusual on Grand National day."

"Which horse?"

"Haunted House, sir. And so, sir, if Haunted House wins, our fellow will bring his batch of fifty quid's worth of winning tickets to the pay-out, and we will have him."

"But," Westerland objected, "what if Haunted House *doesn't* win?"

Crispin gazed at him steadily. "We want you to arrange that Haunted House *does* win, sir. We want you to fix the Grand National."

Down in Tattersall's enclosure Austin Dartmouth Glenn passed two hot fivers to a bookmaker who stuffed them busily into his satchel without looking. A tenner to win Spotted Tulip, at eight to one. In the noise, haste, and flurry of the last five minutes before the first race, Austin was as unnoticeable as an ant. He elbowed his way up the stands to find the best view of his money on the hoof, smirking with satisfaction.

In the changing-room Jerry Springwood reluctantly climbed into his thin white breeches and fumbled with the buttons of his shiny red and white striped colours. His mind was filling like a well with panic, the terrible desire to cut and run growing deeper and deadlier with every passing minute. He had difficulty in concentrating and virtually did not hear when anyone spoke to him. His hands trembled. He felt cold. There was another hour to live through before he would have to force himself out to the parade ring, on to the horse, down to the start, and right round those demanding four and a half miles and over thirty huge fences. I can't do it, he thought numbly. I can't face it. Where can I hide?

The four Stewards in charge of the meeting sat gloomily round their large table, reacting with varying degrees of incredulity and uneasiness to the urgings of Chief Superintendent Crispin.

"There's no precedent," said one. "It's out of the question."

"There isn't time," said another.

"You'd never get the trainers to agree," said a third.

"And what about the owners?" asked the fourth.

Crispin held racing in as little esteem as crooked politicians and considered that catching the Birmingham mob was of greater social importance than any particular horse finishing first. His inner outrage at the obstructive reaction of the Stewards seeped unmistakably into his voice.

"The Birmingham robbers murdered ten people," he said forcefully. "Everyone has a public duty to help the police catch them."

"Surely not to the extent of ruining the Grand National," insisted the Stewards.

"I understand," Crispin said, "that in steeplechasing in general few stud values are involved, and in this year's National the horses are all geldings. It is not as if we were asking you to spoil the Stud Book by fixing the Derby."

"All the same, it would be unfair on the betting public," said the Stewards.

"The people who died were part of the betting public. The next people to die, in the next violent bank raid, will also be the betting public."

Sir William Westerland listened to the arguments with his bland expression unimpaired. He had gone far in life by not declaring his views before everyone else had bared their breasts, their opinions, and their weaknesses. His mild subsequent observations had a way of being received as revealed truth, when they were basically only unemotional common sense.

He watched Crispin and his fellow Stewards heat up into emphasis and hubbub, and begin to slide towards prejudice and hostility. He sighed internally, looked at his watch, and noisily cleared his throat.

"Gentlemen," he said calmly and distinctly. "Before we reach a decision, I think we should consider the following points. First, possibility. Second, secrecy. Third, consequences."

Stewards and policeman looked at him with united relief.

"Jump jockeys," Westerland said, "are individualists. Who do you think is going to persuade them to fix the race?"

No answer.

"How is anyone to guarantee that Haunted House will not fall?"

No answer.

"How long do you suppose it would be before someone told the Press? Do we want the uproar which would follow?"

No answer, but a great shaking of stewardly heads.

"But if we refuse Chief Superintendent Crispin's request, how do we feel if another bank is blown apart, and more innocent people are killed, and we took no action to prevent it?"

The meeting looked at him in silence, awaiting his lead.

Jerry Springwood's head felt like a balloon floating somewhere above his uncoordinated body. The call of "Jockeys out, please" had found him still unable to think of a way of escape. Too many people knew him. How can I run, he thought; how can I scramble to the gate and find a taxi when everyone knows I should be walking out to ride Haunted House?

Can I faint, he thought? Can I say I'm ill?

He found himself going out with the others, his leaden legs trudging automatically while his spirit wilted. He stood in the parade ring with his mouth dry and his eyes feeling like gritty holes in his skull, not hearing the nervously hearty pre-race chit-chat of owner and trainer.

I can't, he thought.

I *can't*.

The Senior Steward of the Jockey Club, Sir William Westerland, walked up to him as he stood rigidly in his hopeless hell.

"A word in your ear, Jerry," he said.

Jerry Springwood looked at him blankly, with eyes like smooth grey pebbles. Westerland, who had seen that look on other faces and knew what it foreboded, suffered severe feelings of misgiving. He had come to the conclusion (and in spite of Crispin's agonized opposition, had secured the Stewards' wholehearted agreement) that not even to catch murderers could racing's top authorities secretly organize the outcome of the Grand National. Both practically and morally, it was impossible. The police would just have to keep a sharper check on future meetings, and one day soon, perhaps, they would catch their fish as he swam again to the Tote.

All the same, Westerland had seen no harm in wishing Jerry Springwood success; but he perceived now that Crispin had no chance of catching his man today. No jockey in this state of frozen fear could win the National. The backers of Haunted House would be fortunate if their fancy lasted half a mile before he pulled up, or ran out, or refused to jump because of the stranglehold on his reins.

"Good luck," said Westerland lamely, with regret.

Jerry made no answer, even ordinary politeness being beyond him.

Up on his vantage point on the stands, Austin Glenn watched the long line of runners walk down the course. Ten minutes to race time, with half the bookies suffering from sore throats and the massed crowds buzzing with rising excitement. Austin Glenn, who had lost his tenner on Spotted Tulip in the first, and fifteen more to bookmakers on the second, was biting his knuckles over Haunted House.

Jerry Springwood sat like a sack in the saddle, shoulders hunched. The horse, receptive to his rider's mood, plodded along in confusion, not able to sort out whether or not he should respond to the crowd instead. To Austin Glenn and many others horse and rider looked like a grade one losing combination. William Westerland shook his head ruefully, and Crispin wondered irritably why that one horse, of all of them, looked half asleep.

Jerry Springwood got himself lined up for the start by blotting out every thought. The well of panic was full and trying to flood over. Jerry, white and clammily sweating, knew that in a few more minutes he would have to dismount and run.

Have to.

When the starter let them go, Haunted House was standing flat-footed. Getting no signal from the saddle, he started hesitantly after the departing field, knowing his job, knowing that he was there to run and jump and get his head in front of all the rest, but feeling rudderless, without the help and direction he was used to. His jockey stayed on board by instinct, the long years of skill coming to his aid, the schooled muscles acting in a pattern that needed no conscious thought.

Haunted House jumped last over the first fence, and was still last five fences later, approaching Becher's. Jerry Springwood saw the horse directly in front of him fall, and knew remotely that if he went straight on he would land on top of him. Almost without thinking he twitched his right hand on the rein, and Haunted House, taking fire from this tiniest sign of life, swerved a yard, bunched his quarters, and put his great equine soul into clearing the danger.

Haunted House knew the course: had won there, with Jerry Springwood up, in shorter races. His sudden surge over Becher's melted his jockey's defensive blankness and thrust him into freshly vivid fear. Oh God, Jerry thought, as Haunted House took him inexorable towards the Canal Turn, how can I? How can I?

He sat there, fighting his panic, while Haunted House carried him surefootedly round the Turn, and over Valentine's, and all the way to the Chair. Two miles done; two and a half to go. Jerry thought forever after that he'd shut his eyes as his mount took the last few strides towards the most testing steeplechase fence in the world, but Haunted House met it perfectly and cleared the huge spread without the slightest stumble.

Over the water jump in front of the stands, and out again towards Becher's, with the whole course to jump again. Jerry thought, if I pull up now, I'll have done enough. How can I go on? Surely I've done enough?

Horses beside him tired and stopped or slid and fell, but Haunted House galloped at a steady thirty miles an hour with scant regard for his fate, and took heart from the signals reaching him from his rider's hands and heels and knees, however faint they might be. Haunted House, like all great 'chasers, positively loved to race.

Austin Glenn on the stands, and William Westerland in his private box, and Chief Superintendent Crispin tense in front of a television set, all watched with faster pulses as Haunted House made his progress through the field. By the time he reached Becher's on the second circuit he lay tenth, and seventh at the Canal Turn, and fifth after the third last fence, a mile from home.

Jerry Springwood saw a gap on the rails and didn't take it, and checked his mount before the second last fence so that they jumped it safely but lost two lengths. On the stands William Westerland groaned aloud, but on Haunted House Jerry Springwood just shrivelled inside at his own fearful cowardice. It's useless, he thought, I'd be better off dead.

The leader of the field had sprinted a long way ahead, and Jerry saw him rise over the last fence while Haunted House was a good forty lengths in the rear. One more, Jerry thought. Only one more fence. I'll never ride another race. Never.

He locked his jaw as Haunted House gathered his muscles and launched his half-ton weight at the green-faced birch. If he rolls on me, Jerry thought . . . if I fall and he crashes on top of me . . . Oh God, he thought, take me safely over this fence.

The horse in front, well-backed and high in the handicap, took the last flat half-mile at a spanking gallop. Jerry Springwood and Haunted House, still on their feet, had left it too late to make a serious bid to catch them, but with a surge of what Jerry knew to be release from purgatory they raced past everything else in a flatout dash to the post.

Austin Glenn watched Haunted House finish second by twenty lengths. Cursing himself a little for not bothering about place money, he took out his tickets, tore them philosophically across, and let the pieces flutter away to the four winds.

William Westerland rubbed his chin and wondered whether Jerry Springwood could have won if he'd tried sooner. Chief Superintendent Crispin bitterly cursed the twenty lengths by which his quarry would escape.

Sir William took his eminent foreign visitors down to watch the scenes of jubilation round the winner in the unsaddling enclosure, and was met by flurried officials with horrified faces.

"The winner can't pass the scales," they said.

"What do you mean?" Westerland demanded.

"The winner didn't carry the right weight! The trainer left the weight-cloth hanging in the saddling box when he put the saddle on his horse. The winner ran all the way with ten pounds less than he should have . . . and we'll have to disqualify him."

Forgetting the weight-cloth was done often enough; but in the National! . . . Westerland took a deep breath and told the aghast officials to relay the facts to the public over the tannoy system.

Jerry Springwood heard the news while he was himself sitting on the scales and watching the pointer swing around to the right mark. He felt, not joyful, but overwhelmingly ashamed, as if he'd won the prize by cheating. I don't deserve it, he thought painfully. Haunted House won the race, but I failed.

Crispin stationed his men strategically, and alerted all the Tote pay-out windows to signal them immediately the tell-tale tickets were presented.

Up on the stands, Austin Glenn searched for the pieces in a fury, picking up every torn and trampled scrap and peering at it anxiously. He was not alone in having disregarded the punters' rule of not throwing tickets away until after the all-clear from the weigh-in, but to see others searching as hard as he was gave him no pleasure. What if someone else picked up his tickets, and claimed his winnings? The idea enraged him; and what was more, he couldn't stay on the course indefinitely because he had to catch his return train. He couldn't afford to be late; he had work to do that night.

Crispin's men shifted from foot to foot as time went by, and were left there growing more and more conspicuous while the crowd thinned and trooped out through the gates. When the Tote closed for the day the Chief Superintendent called them off in frustrated rage, and conceded they would have to wait for another day.

In the weighing-room Jerry Springwood bore the congratulations as best he could, and announced to surprised television millions that he would be hanging up his boots in a few weeks, at the end of the season. He didn't realize that he had ridden the bravest race of his life, and when the plaudits were over he locked himself in the lavatory and wept for his lost courage.

Austin Dartmouth Glenn travelled home empty-handed and in a vile mood. He cursed his wife and kicked the cat, and after a hasty supper he put on his neat navy-blue uniform and went off scowling to work his usual night shift as a warder in the nearby high-security jail.

The Case of the Pietro Andromache

SARA PARETSKY

"You only agreed to hire him because of his art collection. Of that I'm sure." Lotty Herschel bent down to adjust her stockings. "And don't waggle your eyebrows like that—it makes you look like an adolescent Groucho Marx."

Max Loewenthal obediently smoothed his eyebrows, but said, "It's your legs, Lotty; they remind me of my youth. You know, going into the Underground to wait out the air raids, looking at the ladies as they came down the escalators. The updraft always made their skirts billow."

"You're making this up, Max. I was in those Underground stations, too, and as I remember the ladies were always bundled in coats and children."

Max moved from the doorway to put an arm around Lotty. "That's what keeps us together, *Lottchen*: I am a romantic and you are severely logical. And you know we didn't hire Caudwell because of his collection. Although I admit I am eager to see it. The board wants Beth Israel to develop a transplant program. It's the only way we're going to become competitive—"

"Don't deliver your publicity lecture to me," Lotty snapped. Her thick brows contracted to a solid black line across her forehead. "As far as I am concerned he is a cretin with the hands of a Caliban and the personality of Attila."

Lotty's intense commitment to medicine left no room for the mundane consideration of money. But as the hospital's executive director, Max was on the spot with the trustees to see that Beth Israel ran at a profit. Or at least at a smaller loss than they'd achieved in recent years. They'd brought Caudwell in part to attract more paying patients—and to help screen out some of the indigent who made up twelve percent of Beth Israel's patient load. Max wondered how long the hospital could afford to support personalities as divergent as Lotty and Caudwell with their radically differing approaches to medicine.

253

He dropped his arm and smiled quizzically at her. "Why do you hate him so much, Lotty?"

"*I* am the person who has to justify the patients I admit to this— this troglodyte. Do you realize he tried to keep Mrs. Mendes from the operating room when he learned she had AIDS? He wasn't even being asked to sully his hands with her blood and he didn't want me performing surgery on her."

Lotty drew back from Max and pointed an accusing finger at him. "You may tell the board that if he keeps questioning my judgment they will find themselves looking for a new perinatologist. I am serious about this. You listen this afternoon, Max, you hear whether or not he calls me 'our little baby doctor.' I am fifty-eight years old, I am a Fellow of the Royal College of Surgeons besides having enough credentials in this country to support a whole hospital, and to him I am a 'little baby doctor.'"

Max sat on the daybed and pulled Lotty down next to him. "No, no, *Lottchen*: don't fight. Listen to me. Why haven't you told me any of this before?"

"Don't be an idiot, Max: you are the director of the hospital. I cannot use our special relationship to deal with problems I have with the staff. I said my piece when Caudwell came for his final interview. A number of the other physicians were not happy with his attitude. If you remember, we asked the board to bring him in as a cardiac surgeon first and promote him to chief of staff after a year if everyone was satisfied with his performance."

"We talked about doing it that way," Max admitted. "But he wouldn't take the appointment except as chief of staff. That was the only way we could offer him the kind of money he could get at one of the university hospitals or Humana. And, Lotty, even if you don't like his personality you must agree that he is a first-class surgeon."

"I agree to nothing." Red lights danced in her black eyes. "If he patronizes me, a fellow physician, how do you imagine he treats his patients? You cannot practice medicine if—"

"Now it's my turn to ask to be spared a lecture," Max interrupted gently. "But if you feel so strongly about him, maybe you shouldn't go to his party this afternoon."

"And admit that he can beat me? Never."

"Very well then." Max got up and placed a heavily-brocaded wool shawl over Lotty's shoulders. "But you must promise me to behave.

This is a social function we are going to, remember, not a gladiator contest. Caudwell is trying to repay some hospitality this afternoon, not to belittle you."

"I don't need lessons in conduct from you: Herschels were attending the emperors of Austria while the Loewenthals were operating vegetable stalls on the Ring," Lotty said haughtily.

Max laughed and kissed her hand. "Then remember these regal Herschels and act like them, *Eure Hoheit.*"

II

Caudwell had bought an apartment sight unseen when he moved to Chicago. A divorced man whose children are in college only has to consult with his own taste in these matters. He asked the Beth Israel board to recommend a realtor, sent his requirements to them—twenties construction, near Lake Michigan, good security, modern plumbing—and dropped seven hundred and fifty thousand for an eight-room condo facing the lake at Scott Street.

Since Beth Israel paid handsomely for the privilege of retaining Dr. Charlotte Herschel as their perinatologist, nothing required her to live in a five room walkup on the fringes of Uptown, so it was a bit unfair of her to mutter "Parvenu" to Max when they walked into the lobby.

Max relinquished Lotty gratefully when they got off the elevator. Being her lover was like trying to be companion to a Bengal tiger: you never knew when she'd take a lethal swipe at you. Still, if Caudwell were insulting her—and her judgment—maybe he needed to talk to the surgeon, explain how important Lotty was for the reputation of Beth Israel.

Caudwell's two children were making the obligatory Christmas visit. They were a boy and a girl, Deborah and Steve, within a year of the same age, both tall, both blond and poised, with a hearty sophistication born of a childhood spent on expensive ski slopes. Max wasn't very big, and as one took his coat and the other performed brisk introductions, he felt himself shrinking, losing in self-assurance. He accepted a glass of special *cuvee* from one of them—was it the boy or the girl, he wondered in confusion—and fled into the melee.

He landed next to one of Beth Israel's trustees, a woman in her sixties wearing a grey textured mini-dress whose black stripes were constructed of feathers. She commented brightly on Caudwell's art collection, but Max sensed an undercurrent of hostility: wealthy trustees don't like the idea that they can't out-buy the staff.

While he was frowning and nodding at appropriate intervals, it dawned on Max that Caudwell did know how much the hospital needed Lotty. Heart surgeons do not have the world's smallest egos: when you ask them to name the world's three leading practitioners, they never can remember the names of the other two. Lotty was at the top of her field, and she, too, was used to having things her way. Since her confrontational style was reminiscent more of the Battle of the Bulge than the Imperial Court of Vienna, he didn't blame Caudwell for trying to force her out of the hospital.

Max moved away from Martha Gildersleeve to admire some of the paintings and figurines she'd been discussing. A collector himself of Chinese porcelains, Max raised his eyebrows and mouthed a soundless whistle at the pieces on display. A small Watteau and a Charles Demuth watercolor were worth as much as Beth Israel paid Caudwell in a year. No wonder Mrs. Gildersleeve had been so annoyed.

"Impressive, isn't it."

Max turned to see Arthur Gioia looming over him. Max was shorter than most of the Beth Israel staff, shorter than everyone but Lotty. But Gioia, a tall muscular immunologist, loomed over everyone. He had gone to the University of Arkansas on a football scholarship and had even spent a season playing tackle for Houston before starting medical school. It had been twenty years since he last lifted weights, but his neck still looked like a redwood stump.

Gioia had led the opposition to Caudwell's appointment. Max had suspected at the time that it was due more to a medicine man's not wanting a surgeon as his nominal boss than from any other cause, but after Lotty's outburst he wasn't so sure. He was debating whether to ask the doctor how he felt about Caudwell now that he'd worked with him for six months when their host surged over to him and shook his hand.

"Sorry I didn't see you when you came in, Loewenthal. You like the Watteau? It's one of my favorite pieces. Although a collector shouldn't play favorites any more than a father should, eh, sweetheart?" The last remark was addressed to the daughter, Deborah, who had come up behind Caudwell and slipped an arm around him.

Caudwell looked more like a Victorian seadog than a surgeon. He had a round red face under a shock of yellow-white hair, a hearty Santa Claus laugh, and a bluff, direct manner. Despite Lotty's vituperations, he was immensely popular with his patients. In the short time he'd been at the hospital, referrals to cardiac surgery had increased fifteen percent.

His daughter squeezed his shoulder playfully. "I know you don't play favorites with us, Dad, but you're lying to Mr. Loewenthal about your collection; come on, you know you are."

She turned to Max. "He has a piece he's so proud of he doesn't like to show it to people—he doesn't want them to see he's got vulnerable spots. But it's Christmas, Dad, relax, let people see how you feel for a change."

Max looked curiously at the surgeon, but Caudwell seemed pleased with his daughter's familiarity. The son came up and added his own jocular cajoling.

"This really is Dad's pride and joy. He stole it from Uncle Griffen when Grandfather died and kept Mother from getting her mitts on it when they split up."

Caudwell did bark out a mild reproof at that. "You'll be giving my colleagues the wrong impression of me, Steve. I didn't steal it from Grif. Told him he could have the rest of the estate if he'd leave me the Watteau and the Pietro."

"Of course he could've bought ten estates with what those two would fetch," Steve muttered to his sister over Max's head.

Deborah relinquished her father's arm to lean over Max and whisper back, "Mom, too."

Max moved away from the alarming pair to say to Caudwell, "A Pietro? You mean Pietro d'Alessandro? You have a model, or an actual sculpture?"

Caudwell gave his staccato admiral's laugh. "The real McCoy, Loewenthal. The real McCoy. An alabaster."

"An alabaster?" Max raised his eyebrows. "Surely not. I thought Pietro worked only in bronze and marble."

"Yes, yes," chuckled Caudwell, rubbing his hands together. "Everyone thinks so, but there were a few alabasters in private collections. I've had this one authenticated by experts. Come take a look at it— it'll knock your breath away. You come, too, Gioia," he barked at the immunologist. "You're Italian, you'll like to see what your ancestors were up to."

"A Pietro alabaster?" Lotty's clipped tones made Max start—he hadn't noticed her joining the little group. "I would very much like to see this piece."

"Then come along, Dr. Herschel, come along." Caudwell led them to a small hallway, exchanging genial greetings with his guests as he passed, pointing out a John William Hill miniature they might not have seen, picking up a few other people who for various reasons wanted to see his prize.

"By the way, Gioia, I was in New York last week, you know. Met an old friend of yours from Arkansas. Paul Nierman."

"Nierman?" Gioia seemed to be at a loss. "I'm afraid I don't remember him."

"Well, he remembered you pretty well. Sent you all kinds of messages—you'll have to stop by my office on Monday and get the full strength."

Caudwell opened a door on the right side of the hall and let them into his study. It was an octagonal room carved out of the corner of the building. Windows on two sides looked out on Lake Michigan. Caudwell drew salmon drapes as he talked about the room, why he'd chosen it for his study even though the view kept his mind from his work.

Lotty ignored him and walked over to a small pedestal which stood alone against the paneling on one of the far walls. Max followed her and gazed respectfully at the statue. He had seldom seen so fine a piece outside a museum. About a foot high, it depicted a woman in classical draperies hovering in anguish over the dead body of a soldier lying at her feet. The grief in her beautiful face was so poignant that it reminded you of every sorrow you had ever faced.

"Who is it meant to be?" Max asked curiously.

"Andromache," Lotty said in a strangled voice. "Andromache mourning Hector."

Max stared at Lotty, astonished equally by her emotion and her knowledge of the figure—Lotty was totally uninterested in sculpture.

Caudwell couldn't restrain the smug smile of a collector with a true coup. "Beautiful, isn't it? How do you know the subject?"

"I should know it." Lotty's voice was husky with emotion. "My grandmother had such a Pietro. An alabaster given her great-grand-father by the Emperor Joseph the Second himself for his help in consolidating imperial ties with Poland."

She swept the statue from its stand, ignoring a gasp from Max, and turned it over. "You can see the traces of the imperial stamp here still. And the chip on Hector's foot which made the Hapsburg wish to give the statue away to begin with. How came you to have this piece? Where did you find it?"

The small group that had joined Caudwell stood silent by the entrance, shocked at Lotty's outburst. Gioia looked more horrified than any of them, but he found Lotty overwhelming at the best of times—an elephant confronted by a hostile mouse.

"I think you're allowing your emotions to carry you away, doctor." Caudwell kept his tone light, making Lotty seem more gauche by contrast. "I inherited this piece from my father, who bought it— legitimately—in Europe. Perhaps from your—grandmother, was it? But I suspect you are confused about something you may have seen in a museum as a child."

Deborah gave a high-pitched laugh and called loudly to her brother, "Dad may have stolen it from Uncle Grif, but it looks like Grandfather snatched it to begin with anyway."

"Be quiet, Deborah," Caudwell barked sternly.

His daughter paid no attention to him. She laughed again and joined her brother to look at the imperial seal on the bottom of the statue.

Lotty brushed them aside. "*I* am confused about the seal of Joseph the Second?" she hissed at Caudwell. "Or about this chip on Hector's foot? You can see the line where some Philistine filled in the missing piece. Some person who thought his touch would add value to Pietro's work. Was that you, *doctor?* Or your father?"

"Lotty." Max was at her side, gently prising the statue from her shaking hands to restore it to its pedestal. "Lotty, this is not the place or the manner to discuss such things."

Angry tears sparkled in her black eyes. "Are you doubting my word?"

Max shook his head. "I'm not doubting you. But I'm also not supporting you. I'm asking you not to talk about this matter in this way at this gathering."

"But, Max: either this man or his father is a thief!"

Caudwell strolled up to Lotty and pinched her chin. "You're working too hard, Dr. Herschel. You have too many things on your mind these days. I think the board would like to see you take a leave of absence for a few weeks, go someplace warm, get yourself relaxed. When you're this tense, you're no good to your patients. What do you say, Loewenthal?"

Max didn't say any of the things he wanted to—that Lotty was insufferable and Caudwell intolerable. He believed Lotty, believed that the piece had been her grandmother's. She knew too much about it, for one thing. And for another, a lot of artworks belonging to European Jews were now in museums or private collections around the world. It was only the most god-awful coincidence that the Pietro had ended up with Caudwell's father.

But how dare she raise the matter in the way most likely to alienate everyone present? He couldn't possibly support her in such a situation. And at the same time, Caudwell's pinching her chin in that condescending way made him wish he were not chained to a courtesy that would have kept him from knocking the surgeon out even if he'd been ten years younger and ten inches taller.

"I don't think this is the place or the time to discuss such matters," he reiterated as calmly as he could. "Why don't we all cool down and get back together on Monday, eh?"

Lotty gasped involuntarily, then swept from the room without a backward glance.

Max refused to follow her. He was too angry with her to want to see her again that afternoon. When he got ready to leave the party an hour or so later, after a long conversation with Caudwell that taxed his sophisticated urbanity to the utmost, he heard with relief that Lotty was long gone. The tale of her outburst had of course spread through the gathering at something faster than the speed of sound; he wasn't up to defending her to Martha Gildersleeve who demanded an explanation of him in the elevator going down.

He went home for a solitary evening in his house in Evanston. Normally such time brought him pleasure, listening to music in his study, lying on the couch with his shoes off, reading history, letting the sounds of the lake wash over him.

Tonight, though, he could get no relief. Fury with Lotty merged into images of horror, the memories of his own disintegrated family, his search through Europe for his mother. He had never found anyone who was quite certain what became of her, although several people told him definitely of his father's suicide. And stamped over these wisps in his brain was the disturbing picture of Caudwell's children, their blond heads leaning backward at identical angles as they gleefully chanted "Grandpa was a thief, Grandpa was a thief," while Caudwell edged his visitors out of the study.

By morning he would somehow have to reconstruct himself enough to face Lotty, to respond to the inevitable flood of calls from outraged trustees. He'd have to figure out a way of soothing Caudwell's vanity, bruised more by his children's behavior than anything Lotty had said. And find a way to keep both important doctors at Beth Israel.

Max rubbed his grey hair. Every week this job brought him less joy and more pain. Maybe it was time to step down, to let the board bring in a young MBA who would turn Beth Israel's finances around. Lotty would resign then, and it would be an end to the tension between her and Caudwell.

Max fell asleep on the couch. He awoke around five muttering, "By morning, by morning." His joints were stiff from cold, his eyes sticky with tears he'd shed unknowingly in his sleep.

But in the morning things changed. When Max got to his office he found the place buzzing, not with news of Lotty's outburst but word that Caudwell had missed his early morning surgery. Work came almost completely to a halt at noon when his children phoned to say they'd found the surgeon strangled in his own study and the Pietro Andromache missing. And on Tuesday, the police arrested Dr. Charlotte Herschel for Lewis Caudwell's murder.

III

Lotty would not speak to anyone. She was out on two hundred fifty thousand dollars' bail, the money raised by Max, but she had gone directly to her apartment on Sheffield after two nights in County Jail without stopping to thank him. She would not talk to reporters, she remained silent during all conversations with the police, and she emphatically refused to speak to the private investigator who had been her close friend for many years.

Max, too, stayed behind an impregnable shield of silence. While Lotty went on indefinite leave, turning her practice over to a series of colleagues, Max continued to go to the hospital every day. But he, too, would not speak to reporters: he wouldn't even say, "No comment." He talked to the police only after they threatened to lock him up as a material witness, and then every word had to be pried from him as if his mouth were stone and speech Excalibur. For three days V. I. Warshawski left messages which he refused to return.

On Friday, when no word came from the detective, when no reporter popped up from a nearby urinal in the men's room to try to trick him into speaking, when no more calls came from the state's attorney, Max felt a measure of relaxation as he drove home. As soon as the trial was over he would resign, retire to London. If he could only keep going until then, everything would be—not all right, but bearable.

He used the remote release for the garage door and eased his car into the small space. As he got out he realized bitterly he'd been too optimistic in thinking he'd be left in peace. He hadn't seen the woman sitting on the stoop leading from the garage to the kitchen when he drove in, only as she uncoiled herself at his approach.

"I'm glad you're home—I was beginning to freeze out here."

"How did you get into the garage, Victoria?"

The detective grinned in a way he usually found engaging. Now it seemed merely predatory. "Trade secret, Max. I know you don't want to see me, but I need to talk to you."

He unlocked the door into the kitchen. "Why not just let yourself into the house if you were cold? If your scruples permit you into the garage, why not into the house?"

She bit her lip in momentary discomfort but said lightly, "I couldn't manage my picklocks with my fingers this cold."

The detective followed him into the house. Another tall monster; five foot eight, athletic, light on her feet behind him. Maybe American mothers put growth hormones or steroids in their children's cornflakes. He'd have to ask Lotty. His mind winced at the thought.

"I've talked to the police, of course," the light alto continued behind him steadily, oblivious to his studied rudeness as he poured himself a cognac, took his shoes off, found his waiting slippers, and padded down the hall to the front door for his mail.

"I understand why they arrested Lotty—Caudwell had been doped with a whole bunch of Xanax and then strangled while he was sleeping it off. And, of course, she was back at the building Sunday night. She won't say why, but one of the tenants I.D.'d her as the woman who showed up around ten at the service entrance when he was walking his dog. She won't say if she talked to Caudwell, if he let her in, if he was still alive."

Max tried to ignore her clear voice. When that proved impossible he tried to read a journal which had come in the mail.

"And those kids, they're marvelous, aren't they? Like something out of the *Fabulous Furry Freak Brothers*. They won't talk to me but they gave a long interview to Murray Ryerson over at the *Star*.

"After Caudwell's guests left, they went to a flick at the Chestnut Street Station, had a pizza afterwards, then took themselves dancing on Division Street. So they strolled in around two in the morning— confirmed by the doorman—saw the light on in the old man's study. But they were feeling no pain and he kind of overreacted—their term—if they were buzzed, so they didn't stop in to say goodnight. It was only when they got up around noon and went in that they found him."

V. I. had followed Max from the front hallway to the door of his study as she spoke. He stood there irresolutely, not wanting his private place desecrated with her insistent, air-hammer speech, and finally went on down the hall to a little-used living room. He sat stiffly on one of the brocade armchairs and looked at her remotely when she perched on the edge of its companion.

"The weak piece in the police story is the statue," V. I. continued.

She eyed the Persian rug doubtfully and unzipped her boots, sticking them on the bricks in front of the fireplace.

"Everyone who was at the party agrees that Lotty was beside herself. By now the story has spread so far that people who weren't even in the apartment when she looked at the statue swear they heard her threaten to kill him. But if that's the case, what happened to the statue?"

Max gave a slight shrug to indicate total lack of interest in the topic.

V. I. ploughed on doggedly. "Now some people think she might have given it to a friend or a relation to keep for her until her name is cleared at the trial. And these people think it would be either her Uncle Stefan here in Chicago, her brother Hugo in Montreal, or you. So the Mounties searched Hugo's place and are keeping an eye on his mail. And the Chicago cops are doing the same for Stefan. And I presume someone got a warrant and went through here, right?"

Max said nothing, but he felt his heart beating faster. Police in his house, searching his things? But wouldn't they have to get his permission to enter? Or would they? Victoria would know, but he couldn't bring himself to ask. She waited for a few minutes, but when he still wouldn't speak, she plunged on. He could see it was becoming an effort for her to talk, but he wouldn't help her.

"But I don't agree with those people. Because I know that Lotty is innocent. And that's why I'm here. Not like a bird of prey, as you think, using your misery for carrion. But to get you to help me. Lotty won't speak to me, and if she's that miserable I won't force her to. But surely, Max, you won't sit idly by and let her be railroaded for something she never did."

Max looked away from her. He was surprised to find himself holding the brandy snifter and set it carefully on a table beside him.

"Max!" Her voice was shot with astonishment. "I don't believe this. You actually think she killed Caudwell."

Max flushed a little, but she'd finally stung him into a response. "And you are God who sees all and knows she didn't?"

"I see more than you do," V. I. snapped. "I haven't known Lotty as long as you have, but I know when she's telling the truth."

"So you are God." Max bowed in heavy irony. "You see beyond the facts to the innermost souls of men and women."

He expected another outburst from the young woman, but she gazed at him steadily without speaking. It was a look sympathetic enough that Max felt embarrassed by his sarcasm and burst out with what was on his mind.

"What else am I to think? She hasn't said anything, but there's no doubt that she returned to his apartment Sunday night."

It was V. I.'s turn for sarcasm. "With a little vial of Xanax that she somehow induced him to swallow? And then strangled him for good measure? Come on, Max, you know Lotty: honesty follows her around like a cloud. If she'd killed Caudwell, she'd say something like, 'Yes, I bashed the little vermin's brains in.' Instead she's not speaking at all."

Suddenly the detective's eyes widened with incredulity. "Of course. She thinks you killed Caudwell. You're doing the only thing you can to protect her—standing mute. And she's doing the same thing. What an admirable pair of archaic knights."

"No!" Max said sharply. "It's not possible. How could she think such a thing? She carried on so wildly that it was embarrassing to be near her. I didn't want to see her or talk to her. That's why I've felt so terrible. If only I hadn't been so obstinate, if only I'd called her Sunday night. How could she think I would kill someone on her behalf when I was so angry with her?"

"Why else isn't she saying anything to anyone?" Warshawski demanded.

"Shame, maybe," Max offered. "You didn't see her on Sunday. I did. That is why I think she killed him, not because some man let her into the building."

His brown eyes screwed shut at the memory. "I have seen Lotty in the grip of anger many times, more than is pleasant to remember, really. But never, never have I seen her in this kind of—uncontrolled rage. You could not talk to her. It was impossible."

The detective didn't respond to that. Instead she said, "Tell me about the statue. I heard a couple of garbled versions from people who were at the party, but I haven't found anyone yet who was in the study when Caudwell showed it to you. Was it really her grandmother's, do you think? And how did Caudwell come to have it if it was?"

Max nodded mournfully. "Oh, yes. It was really her family's, I'm convinced of that. She could not have known in advance about the details, the flaw in the foot, the imperial seal on the bottom. As to how Caudwell got it, I did a little looking into that myself yesterday. His father was with the Army of Occupation in Germany after the war. A surgeon attached to Patton's staff. Men in such positions had endless opportunities to acquire artworks after the war."

V. I. shook her head questioningly.

"You must know something of this, Victoria. Well, maybe not. You know the Nazis helped themselves liberally to artwork belonging to Jews everywhere they occupied Europe. And not just to Jews—they plundered Eastern Europe on a grand scale. The best guess is that they stole sixteen million pieces—statues, paintings, altarpieces, tapestries, rare books. The list is beyond reckoning, really."

The detective gave a little gasp. "Sixteen million! You're joking."

"Not a joke, Victoria. I wish it were so, but it is not. The U.S. Army of Occupation took charge of as many works of art as they found in the occupied territories. In theory, they were to find the rightful owners and try to restore them. But in practice few pieces were ever traced, and many of them ended up on the black market.

"You only had to say that such-and-such a piece was worth less than five thousand dollars and you were allowed to buy it. For an officer on Patton's staff, the opportunities for fabulous acquisitions would have been endless. Caudwell said he had the statue authenticated, but of course he never bothered to establish its provenance. Anyway, how could he?" Max finished bitterly. "Lotty's family had a deed of gift from the Emperor, but that would have disappeared long since with the dispersal of their possessions."

"And you really think Lotty would have killed a man just to get this statue back? She couldn't have expected to keep it. Not if she'd killed someone to get it, I mean."

"You are so practical, Victoria. You are too analytical, sometimes, to understand why people do what they do. That was not just a statue. True, it is a priceless artwork, but you know Lotty, you know she places no value on such possessions. No, it meant her family to her, her past, her history, everything that the war destroyed forever for her. You must not imagine that because she never discusses such matters that they do not weigh on her."

V. I. flushed at Max's accusation. "You should be glad I'm analytical. It convinces me that Lotty is innocent. And whether you believe it or not I'm going to prove it."

Max lifted his shoulders slightly in a manner wholly European. "We each support Lotty according to our lights. I saw that she met her bail, and I will see that she gets expert counsel. I am not convinced that she needs you making her innermost secrets public."

V. I's grey eyes turned dark with a sudden flash of temper. "You're dead wrong about Lotty. I'm sure the memory of the war is a pain that can never be cured, but Lotty lives in the present, she works in hope for the future. The past does not obsess and consume her as, perhaps, it does you."

Max said nothing. His wide mouth turned in on itself in a narrow line. The detective laid a contrite hand on his arm.

"I'm sorry, Max. That was below the belt."

He forced the ghost of a smile to his mouth.

"Perhaps it's true. Perhaps it's why I love these ancient things so much. I wish I could believe you about Lotty. Ask me what you want to know. If you promise to leave as soon as I've answered and not to bother me again, I'll answer your questions."

IV

Max put in a dutiful appearance at the Michigan Avenue Presbyterian Church Monday afternoon for Lewis Caudwell's funeral. The surgeon's former wife came, flanked by her children and her husband's brother Griffen. Even after three decades in America Max found himself puzzled sometimes by the natives' behavior: since she and Caudwell were divorced, why had his ex-wife draped herself in black? She was even wearing a veiled hat reminiscent of Queen Victoria.

The children behaved in a moderately subdued fashion, but the girl was wearing a white dress shot with black lightning forks which looked as though it belonged at a disco or a resort. Maybe it was her only dress or her only dress with black in it, Max thought, trying hard to look charitably at the blonde Amazon—after all, she had been suddenly and horribly orphaned.

Even though she was a stranger both in the city and the church, Deborah had hired one of the church parlors and managed to find someone to cater coffee and light snacks. Max joined the rest of the congregation there after the service.

He felt absurd as he offered condolences to the divorced widow: did she really miss the dead man so much? She accepted his conventional words with graceful melancholy and leaned slightly against her son and daughter. They hovered near her with what struck Max as a stagey solicitude. Seen next to her daughter, Mrs. Caudwell looked so frail and undernourished that she seemed like a ghost. Or maybe it was just that her children had a hearty vitality that even a funeral couldn't quench.

Caudwell's brother Griffen stayed as close to the widow as the children would permit. The man was totally unlike the hearty seadog surgeon. Max thought if he'd met the brothers standing side by side he would never have guessed their relationship. He was tall, like his niece and nephew, but without their robustness. Caudwell had had a thick mop of yellow-white hair; Griffen's domed head was covered by thin wisps of grey. He seemed weak and nervous, and lacked Caudwell's outgoing *bonhomie*; no wonder the surgeon had found it easy to decide the disposition of their father's estate in his favor. Max wondered what Griffen had gotten in return.

Mrs. Caudwell's vague, disoriented conversation indicated that she was heavily sedated. That, too, seemed strange. A man she hadn't lived with for four years and she was so upset at his death that she could only manage the funeral on drugs? Or maybe it was the shame of coming as the divorced woman, not a true widow? But then why come at all?

To his annoyance, Max found himself wishing he could ask Victoria about it. She would have some cynical explanation—Caudwell's death meant the end of the widow's alimony and she knew she wasn't remembered in the will. Or she was having an affair with Griffen and was afraid she would betray herself without tranquilizers. Although it was hard to imagine the uncertain Griffen as the object of a strong passion.

Since he had told Victoria he didn't want to see her again when she left on Friday, it was ridiculous of him to wonder what she was doing, whether she was really uncovering evidence that would clear Lotty. Ever since she had gone he had felt a little flicker of hope in the bottom of his stomach. He kept trying to drown it, but it wouldn't quite go away.

Lotty, of course, had not come to the funeral, but most of the rest of the Beth Israel staff was there, along with the trustees. Arthur Gioia, his giant body filling the small parlor to the bursting point, tried finding a tactful balance between honesty and courtesy with the bereaved family; he made heavy going of it.

A sable-clad Martha Gildersleeve appeared under Gioia's elbow, rather like a furry football he might have tucked away. She made bright, unseemly remarks to the bereaved family about the disposal of Caudwell's artworks.

"Of course, the famous statue is gone now. What a pity. You could have endowed a chair in his honor with the proceeds from that piece alone." She gave a high, meaningless laugh.

Max sneaked a glance at his watch, wondering how long he had to stay before leaving would be rude. His sixth sense, the perfect courtesy that governed his movements, had deserted him, leaving him subject to the gaucheries of ordinary mortals. He never peeked at his watch at functions, and at any prior funeral he would have deftly pried Martha Gildersleeve from her victim. Instead he stood helplessly by while she tortured Mrs. Caudwell and other bystanders alike.

He glanced at his watch again. Only two minutes had passed since his last look. No wonder people kept their eyes on their watches at dull meetings: they couldn't believe the clock could move so slowly.

He inched stealthily toward the door, exchanging empty remarks with the staff members and trustees he passed. Nothing negative was said about Lotty to his face, but the comments cut off at his approach added to his misery.

He was almost at the exit when two newcomers appeared. Most of the group looked at them with indifferent curiosity, but Max suddenly felt an absurd stir of elation. Victoria, looking sane and modern in a navy suit, stood in the doorway, eyebrows raised, scanning the room. At her elbow was a police sergeant Max had met with her a few times. The man was in charge of Caudwell's death, too: it was that unpleasant association that kept the name momentarily from his mind.

V. I. finally spotted Max near the door and gave him a discreet sign. He went to her at once.

"I think we may have the goods," she murmured. "Can you get everyone to go? We just want the family, Mrs. Gildersleeve, and Gioia."

"*You* may have the goods," the police sergeant growled. "I'm here unofficially and reluctantly."

"But you're here." Warshawski grinned, and Max wondered how he ever could have found the look predatory. His own spirits rose enormously at her smile. "You know in your heart of hearts that arresting Lotty was just plain dumb. And now I'm going to make you look real smart. In public, too."

Max felt his suave sophistication return with the rush of elation that an ailing diva must have when she finds her voice again. A touch here, a word there, and the guests disappeared like the hosts of Sennacherib. Meanwhile he solicitously escorted first Martha Gildersleeve, then Mrs. Caudwell to adjacent armchairs, got the brother to fetch coffee for Mrs. Gildersleeve, the daughter and son to look after the widow.

With Gioia he could be a bit more ruthless, telling him to wait because the police had something important to ask him. When the last guest had melted away, the immunologist stood nervously at the window rattling his change over and over in his pockets. The jingling suddenly was the only sound in the room. Gioia reddened and clasped his hands behind his back.

Victoria came into the room beaming like a governess with a

delightful treat in store for her charges. She introduced herself to the Caudwells.

"You know Sergeant McGonnigal, I'm sure, after this last week. I'm a private investigator. Since I don't have any legal standing, you're not required to answer any questions I have. So I'm not going to ask you any questions. I'm just going to treat you to a travelogue. I wish I had slides, but you'll have to imagine the visuals while the audio track moves along."

"A private investigator!" Steve's mouth formed an exaggerated "O"; his eyes widdened in amazement. "Just like Bogie."

He was speaking, as usual, to his sister. She gave her high-pitched laugh and said, "We'll win first prize in the 'How I Spent My Winter Vacation' contests. Our daddy was murdered. Zowie. Then his most valuable possession was snatched. Powie. But he'd already stolen it from the Jewish doctor who killed him. Yowie! And then a P.I. to wrap it all up. Yowie! Zowie! Powie!"

"Deborah, please," Mrs. Caudwell sighed. "I know you're excited, sweetie, but not right now, okay?"

"Your children keep you young, don't they, ma'am?" Victoria said. "How can you ever feel old when your kids stay seven all their lives?"

"Oo, ow, she bites, Debbie, watch out, she bites!" Steve cried.

McGonnigal made an involuntary movement, as though restraining himself from smacking the younger man. "Ms. Warshawski is right: you are under no obligation to answer any of her questions. But you're bright people, all of you: you know I wouldn't be here if the police didn't take her ideas very seriously. So let's have a little quiet and listen to what she's got on her mind."

Victoria seated herself in an armchair near Mrs. Caudwell's. McGonnigal moved to the door and leaned against the jamb. Deborah and Steve whispered and poked each other until one or both of them shrieked. They then made their faces prim and sat with their hands folded on their laps, looking like bright-eyed choirboys.

Griffen hovered near Mrs. Caudwell. "You know you don't have to say anything, Vivian. In fact, I think you should return to your hotel and lie down. The stress of the funeral—then these strangers—"

Mrs. Caudwell's lips curled bravely below the bottom of her veil. "It's all right, Grif; if I managed to survive everything else, one more thing isn't going to do me in."

"Great." Victoria accepted a cup of coffee from Max. "Let me just sketch events for you as I saw them last week. Like everyone else in Chicago, I read about Dr. Caudwell's murder and saw it on television. Since I know a number of poeple attached to Beth Israel, I may have paid more attention to it than the average viewer, but I didn't get personally involved until Dr. Herschel's arrest on Tuesday."

She swallowed some coffee and set the cup on the table next to her with a small snap. "I have known Dr. Herschel for close to twenty years. It is inconceivable that she would commit such a murder, as those who know her well should have realized at once. I don't fault the police, but others should have known better: she is hot-tempered. I'm not saying killing is beyond her—I don't think it's beyond any of us. She might have taken the statue and smashed Dr. Caudwell's head in in the heat of rage. But it beggars belief to think she went home, brooded over her injustices, packed a dose of prescription tranquilizer, and headed back to the Gold Coast with murder in mind."

Max felt his cheeks turn hot at her words. He started to interject a protest but bit it back.

"Dr. Herschel refused to make a statement all week, but this afternoon, when I got back from my travels, she finally agreed to talk to me. Sergeant McGonnigal was with me. She doesn't deny that she returned to Dr. Caudwell's apartment at ten that night—she went back to apologize for her outburst and to try to plead with him to return the statue. He didn't answer when the doorman called up, and on impulse she went around to the back of the building, got in through the service entrance, and waited for some time outside the apartment door. When he neither answered the doorbell nor returned home himself, she finally went away around eleven o'clock. The children, of course, were having a night on the town."

"*She* says," Gioia interjected.

"Agreed." V. I. smiled. "I make no bones about being a partisan: I accept her version. The more so because the only reason she didn't give it a week ago was that she herself was protecting an old friend. She thought perhaps this friend had bestirred himself on her behalf and killed Caudwell to avenge deadly insults against her. It was only when I persuaded her that these suspicions were as unmerited as—well, as accusations against herself—that she agreed to talk."

Max bit his lip and busied himself with getting more coffee for the three women. Victoria waited for him to finish before continuing.

"When I finally got a detailed account of what took place at

Caudwell's party, I heard about three people with an axe to grind. One always has to ask, what axe and how big a grindstone? That's what I've spent the weekend finding out. You might as well know that I've been to Little Rock and to Havelock, North Carolina."

Gioia began jingling the coins in his pockets again. Mrs. Caudwell said softly, "Grif, I am feeling a little faint. Perhaps—"

"Home you go, Mom," Steve cried out with alacrity.

"In a few minutes, Mrs. Caudwell," the sergeant said from the doorway. "Get her feet up, Warshawski."

For a moment Max was afraid that Steve or Deborah was going to attack Victoria, but McGonnigal moved over to the widow's chair and the children sat down again. Little drops of sweat dotted Griffen's balding head; Gioia's face had a greenish sheen, foliage on top of his redwood neck.

"The thing that leapt out at me," Victoria continued calmly, as though there had been no interruption, "was Caudwell's remark to Dr. Gioia. The doctor was clearly upset, but people were so focused on Lotty and the statue that they didn't pay any attention to that.

"So I went to Little Rock, Arkansas, on Saturday and found the Paul Nierman whose name Caudwell had mentioned to Gioia. Nierman lived in the same fraternity with Gioia when they were undergraduates together twenty-five years ago. And he took Dr. Gioia's anatomy and physiology exams his junior year when Gioia was in danger of academic probation, so he could stay on the football team.

"Well, that seemed unpleasant, perhaps disgraceful. But there's no question that Gioia did all his own work in medical school, passed his boards, and so on. So I didn't think the board would demand a resignation for this youthful indiscretion. The question was whether Gioia thought they would, and if he would have killed to prevent Caudwell making it public."

She paused, and the immunologist blurted out, "No. No. But Caudwell—Caudwell knew I'd opposed his appointment. He and I—our approaches to medicine were very opposite. And as soon as he said Nierman's name to me, I knew he'd found out and that he'd torment me with it forever. I—I went back to his place Sunday night to have it out with him. I was more determined than Dr. Herschel and got into his unit through the kitchen entrance; he hadn't locked that.

"I went to his study, but he was already dead. I couldn't believe it. It absolutely terrified me. I could see he'd been strangled and—well, it's no secret that I'm strong enough to have done it. I wasn't thinking straight. I just got clean away from there—I think I've been running ever since."

"You!" McGonnigal shouted. "How come we haven't heard about this before?"

"Because you insisted on focusing on Dr. Herschel," V. I. said nastily. "I knew he'd been there because the doorman told me. He would have told you if you'd asked."

"This is terrible," Mrs. Gildersleeve interjected. "I am going to talk to the board tomorrow and demand the resignations of Dr. Gioia and Dr. Herschel."

"Do," Victoria agreed cordially. "Tell them the reason you got to stay for this was because Murray Ryerson at the *Herald-Star* was doing a little checking for me here in Chicago. He found out that part of the reason you were so jealous of Caudwell's collection is that you're living terribly in debt. I won't humiliate you in public by telling people what your money has gone to, but you've had to sell your husband's art collection and you have a third mortgage on your house. A valuable statue with no documented history would have taken care of everything."

Martha Gildersleeve shrank inside her sable. "You don't know anything about this."

"Well, Murray talked to Pablo and Eduardo. . . . Yes, I won't say anything else. So anyway, Murray checked whether either Gioia or Mrs. Gildersleeve had the statue. They didn't, so—"

"You've been in my house?" Mrs. Gildersleeve shrieked.

V. I. shook her head. "Not me. Murray Ryerson." She looked apologetically at the sergeant. "I knew you'd never get a warrant for me, since you'd made an arrest. And you'd never have got it in time, anyway."

She looked at her coffee cup, saw it was empty and put it down again. Max took it from the table and filled it for her a third time. His fingertips were itching with nervous irritation; some of the coffee landed on his trouser leg.

"I talked to Murray Saturday night from Little Rock. When he came up empty here, I headed for North Carolina. To Havelock, where Griffen and Lewis Caudwell grew up and where Mrs. Caudwell still lives. And I saw the house where Griffen lives, and talked to the doctor who treats Mrs. Caudwell, and—"

"You really are a pooper snooper, aren't you," Steve said.

"Pooper snooper, pooper snooper," Deborah chanted. "Don't get enough thrills of your own so you have to live on other people's shit."

"Yeah, the neighbors talked to me about you two." Victoria looked at them with contemptuous indulgence. "You've been a two-person wolfpack terrifying most of the people around you since you were three. But the folks in Havelock admired how you always stuck up for your mother. You thought your father got her addicted to tranquilizers and then left her high and dry. So you brought her newest version with you and were all set—you just needed to decide when to give it to him. Dr. Herschel's outburst over the statue played right into your hands. You figured your father had stolen it from your uncle to begin with— why not send it back to him and let Dr. Herschel take the rap?"

"It wasn't like that," Steve said, red spots burning in his cheeks.

"What was it like, son?" McGonnigal had moved next to him.

"Don't talk to them—they're tricking you," Deborah shrieked. "The pooper snooper and her gopher gooper."

"She—Mommy used to love us before Daddy made her take all this shit. Then she went away. We just wanted him to see what it was like. We started putting Xanax in his coffee and stuff; we wanted to see if he'd fuck up during surgery, let his life get ruined. But then he was sleeping there in the study after his stupid-ass party, and we thought we'd just let him sleep through his morning surgery. Sleep forever, you know, it was so easy, we used his own Harvard necktie. I was so fucking sick of hearing 'Early to bed, early to rise' from him. And we sent the statue to Uncle Grif. I suppose the pooper snooper found it there. He can sell it and Mother can be all right again."

"Grandpa stole it from Jews and Daddy stole it from Grif, so we thought it worked out perfectly if we stole it from Daddy," Deborah cried. She leaned her blonde head next to her brother's and shrieked with laughter.

V

Max watched the line of Lotty's legs change as she stood on tiptoe to reach a brandy snifter. Short, muscular from years of racing at top speed from one point to the next, maybe they weren't as svelte as the long legs of modern American girls, but he preferred them. He waited until her feet were securely planted before making his announcement.

"The board is bringing in Justin Hardwick for a final interview for chief of staff."

"Max!" She whirled, the Bengal fire sparkling in her eyes. "I know this Hardwick and he is another like Caudwell, looking for cost-cutting and no poverty patients. I won't have it."

"We've got you and Gioia and a dozen others bringing in so many non-paying patients that we're not going to survive another five years at the present rate. I figure it's a balancing act. We need someone who can see that the hospital survives so that you and Art can practice medicine the way you want to. And when he knows what happened to his predecessor, he'll be very careful not to stir up our resident tigress."

"Max!" She was hurt and astonished at the same time. "Oh. You're joking, I see. It's not very funny to me, you know."

"My dear, we've got to learn to laugh about it: it's the only way we'll ever be able to forgive ourselves for our terrible misjudgments." He stepped over to put an arm around her. "Now where is this remarkable surprise you promised to show me."

She shot him a look of pure mischief, Lotty on a dare as he first remembered meeting her at eighteen. His hold on her tightened and he followed her to her bedroom. In a glass case in the corner, complete with a humidity-control system, stood the Pietro Andromache.

Max looked at the beautiful, anguished face. I understand your sorrows, she seemed to say to him. I understand your grief for your mother, your family, your history, but it's all right to let go of them, to live in the present and hope for the future. It's not a betrayal.

Tears pricked his eyelids, but he demanded, "How did you get this? I was told the police had it under lock and key until lawyers decided on the disposition of Caudwell's estate."

"Victoria," Lotty said shortly. "I told her the problem and she got it for me. On the condition that I not ask how she did it. And Max, you know—*damned* well that it was not Caudwell's to dispose of."

It was Lotty's. Of course it was. Max wondered briefly how Joseph the Second had come by it to begin with. For that matter, what had Lotty's great-great-grandfather done to earn it from the emperor? Max looked into Lotty's tiger eyes and kept such reflections to himself. Instead he inspected Hector's foot where the filler had been carefully scraped away to reveal the old chip.

SuSu and the 8:30 Ghost

LILIAN JACKSON BRAUN

When my sister and I returned from our vacation and learned that our eccentric neighbor in the wheel chair had been removed to a mental hospital, we were sorry but hardly surprised. He was a strange man, not easy to like, and no one in our apartment building seemed to be concerned about his departure—except our Siamese cat. The friendship between SuSu and Mr. Van was so close it was alarming.

If it had not been for SuSu, we would never have made the man's acquaintance, for we were not too friendly with our neighbors. Our apartment house was very large and full of odd characters who, we thought, were best ignored. On the other hand, the old building had advantages: large rooms, moderate rents, a thrilling view of the river, and a small waterfront park at the foot of the street. It was there that we first noticed Mr. Van.

One Sunday afternoon my sister Gertrude and I were walking SuSu in the park, which was barely more than a strip of grass alongside an old wharf. Barges and tugs sometimes docked there, and SuSu—wary of these monsters—preferred to stay away from the water's edge. It was one of the last nice days in November. Soon the river would freeze over, icy winds would blow, and the park would be deserted for the winter.

SuSu loved to chew grass, and she was chewing industriously when something diverted her attention and drew her toward the river. Tugging at her leash, she insisted on moving across the grass to the boardwalk, where a middle-aged man sat in a most unusual wheel chair.

It was made almost entirely of cast iron, like the base of an old-fashioned sewing machine, and it was upholstered in worn plush. With its high back and elaborate ironwork, it looked like a mobile throne, and the man who occupied this regal wheel chair presided with the imperious air of a monarch. It conflicted absurdly with his shabby clothing.

To our surprise this was the attraction that lured SuSu. She chirped at the man, and the man leaned over and stroked her fur.

She recognizes me," he explained to us, speaking with a haughty accent that sounded vaguely Teutonic. "I was-s-s a cat myself in a former existence."

I rolled my eyes at Gertrude, but she accepted the man's statement without blinking.

He was far from attractive, having a sharply pointed chin, ears set too high on his head, and eyes that were merely slits, and when he smiled he was even less appealing. Nevertheless, SuSu found him irresistible. She rubbed his ankles, and he scratched her in the right places. They made a most unlikely pair—SuSu with her luxurious blonde fur, looking fastidious and expensive, and the man in the wheel chair with his rusty coat and moth-eaten laprobe.

In the course of a fragmentary conversation with Mr. Van we learned that he and the companion who manipulated his wheel chair had just moved into a large apartment on our floor, and I wondered why the two of them needed so many rooms. As for the companion, it was hard to decide whether he was a mute or just unsociable. He was a short thick man with a round knob of a head screwed tight to his shoulders and a flicker of something unpleasant in his eyes, and he stood behind the wheel chair in sullen silence.

On the way back to the apartment Gertrude said, "How do you like our new neighbor?"

"I prefer cats before they're reincarnated as people," I said.

"But he's rather interesting," said my sister in the gentle way she had.

A few evenings later we were having coffee after dinner, and SuSu—having finished her own meal—was washing up in the downglow of a lamp. As we watched her graceful movements, we saw her hesitate with one paw in mid-air. She held it there and listened. Then a new and different sound came from her throat, like a melodic gurgling. A minute later she was trotting to the front door with intense purpose. There she sat, watching and waiting and listening, although we ourselves could hear nothing.

It was a full two minutes before our doorbell rang. I went to open the door and was somewhat unhappy to see Mr. Van sitting there in his lordly wheel chair.

SuSu leaped into his lap—an unprecedented overture for her to make—and after he had kneaded her ears and scratched her chin, he smiled a thin-lipped, slit-eyed smile at me and said, "*Goeden avond.* I was-s-s unpacking some crates, and I found something I would like to give to you."

With a courtly flourish he handed me a small framed picture, whereupon I was more or less obliged to invite him in. He wheeled his ponderous chair into the apartment with some difficulty, the rubber tires making deep gouges in the pile of the carpet.

"How do you manage that heavy chair alone?" I asked. "It must weigh a ton."

"But it is-s-s a work of art," said Mr. Van, rubbing appreciative hands over the plush upholstery and the lacy ironwork of the wheels.

Gertrude had jumped up and poured him a cup of coffee, and he said, "I wish you would teach that man of mine to make coffee. He makes the worst *zootje* I have ever tasted. In Holland we like our coffee *sterk* with a little chicory. But that fellow, he is-s-s a *smeerlap*. I would not put up with him for two minutes if I could get around by myself."

SuSu was rubbing her head on the Dutchman's vest buttons, and he smiled with pleasure, showing small square teeth.

"Do you have this magnetic attraction for cats?" I asked with a slight edge to my voice. SuSu was now in raptures because he was twisting the scruff of her neck.

"It is-s-s only natural," he said. "I can read their thoughts, and they read mine of course. Do you know that cats are mind readers? You walk to the icebox to get a beer, and the cat she will not budge, but walk to the icebox to get out her dinner, and she will come bouncing into the kitchen from any place she happens to be. Your thought waves have reached her, even though she seems to be asleep."

Gertrude agreed it was probably true.

"Of course it is-s-s true," said Mr. Van, sitting tall. "Everything I say is-s-s true. Cats know more than you suspect. They can not only read your mind, they can plant ideas in your head. And they can sense something that is-s-s about to happen."

My sister said, "You must be right. SuSu knew you were coming here tonight, long before you rang the bell."

"Of course I am right. I am always right," said Mr. Van. "My grandmother in Vlissingen had a tomcat called Zwartje that she was-s-s very fond of, and after she died my grandmother came back every night to pet the cat. Every night Zwartje stood in front of *Grootmoeder*'s chair and stretched and purred, although there was-s-s no one there. Every night at half-past eight."

After that visit with Mr. Van, I referred to him as Grandmother's Ghost, for he too made a habit of appearing at 8:30 several times a week. He would say, "I was-s-s feeling lonesome for my little sweetheart," and SuSu would make an extravagant fuss over the man. I was pleased that he never stayed long, although Gertrude usually encouraged him to linger.

The little framed picture he had given us was not exactly to my taste. It was a silhouette of three figures—a man in top hat and frock coat, a woman in hoop skirt and sunbonnet, and a cat carrying his tail like a lance. To satisfy my sister, however, I hung it over the kitchen sink.

One evening Gertrude, who is a librarian, came home from work in great excitement. "There's a signature on that silhouette," she said, "and I looked it up at the library. Auguste Edouart was a famous artist, and our silhouette is over a hundred years old. It might be valuable."

"I doubt it," I said. "We used to cut silhouettes like that in the third grade."

Eventually, at my sister's urging, I took the object to an antique shop, and the dealer said it was a good one, probably worth $150.

When Gertrude heard this, she said, "If the dealer quoted $150, it's worth $250. I think we should give it back to Mr. Van. The poor man doesn't know what he's giving away."

"Yes," I agreed, "maybe he could sell it and buy himself a decent wheel chair."

At 8:30 that evening SuSu began to gurgle and prance.

"Here comes Grandmother's Ghost," I said, and shortly afterward the doorbell rang.

"Mr. Van," I said, as soon as Gertrude had poured his coffee, "remember that silhouette you gave us? We've found out it's very valuable, and you must take it back."

"Of course it is-s-s valuable," he said. "Would I give it to you if it was-s-s nothing but *rommel*?"

"Do you know something about antiques?"

"My dear *Mevrouw*, I have a million dollars' worth of antiques in my apartment. Tomorrow evening you ladies must come and see my treasures. I will get rid of that *smeerlap*, and the three of us will enjoy a cup of coffee."

"By the way, what is a *smeerlap*?" I asked.

"It is not very nice," said Mr. Van. "If somebody called me a *smeerlap*, I would punch him in the nose . . . Bring my little sweetheart when you come, ladies. She will find some fascinating objects to explore."

Our cat seemed to know what he was saying.

"SuSu will enjoy it," said Gertrude. "She's locked up in this apartment all winter."

"Knit her a sweater and take her to the park in cold weather," the Dutchman said in the commanding tone that always irritated me. "I often bundle up in a blanket and go to the park in the evening. It is-s-s good for insomnia."

"Susu is not troubled with insomnia," I informed him. "She sleeps twenty hours a day."

Mr. Van looked at me with scorn. "You are wrong. Cats never sleep. You think they are sleeping, but cats are the most wakeful creatures on earth. That is-s-s one of their secrets."

After he had gone, I said to Gertrude, "He must be off his rocker."

"He's just a little eccentric," she said.

"If he has a million dollars' worth of antiques, which I doubt, why is he living in this run-down building? And why doesn't he buy a wheel chair that's easier to operate?"

"Because he's a Dutchman, I suppose."

"And how about all those ridiculous things he says about cats?"

"I'm beginning to think they're true," said Gertrude.

"And who is this fellow that lives with him? Is he a servant, or a nurse, or a keeper, or what? I see him coming and going on the elevator, but he never speaks—not one word. He doesn't even seem to have a name, and Mr. Van treats him like a slave. I'm not sure we should go tomorrow night. The whole situation is too strange."

Nevertheless, we went. The Dutchman's apartment, we found, was jammed with furniture and bric-a-brac, and Mr. Van shouted at his companion, "Move that *rommel* so the ladies can sit down."

Sullenly the fellow removed some paintings and tapestries from the seat of a carved sofa.

"Now get out of here," Mr. Van shouted at him. "Get yourself a beer," and he threw the man a crumpled dollar bill with less grace than one would throw a bone to a dog.

We sat on the sofa to drink our coffee, while SuSu explored the premises, and then Mr. Van showed us his treasures, propelling his

wheel chair through a maze of furniture. He pointed out Chippendale-
this and Affleck-that and Newport-somthing-else. Perhaps they were
treasures to him, but to me they were musty relics of a dead past.

"I am in the antique business," Mr. Van explained. "Before I
was-s-s chained to this stupid wheel chair, I had a shop and exhibited
at all the major shows. Then . . . I was-s-s in a bad auto accident, and
now I sell from the apartment. By appointment only."

"Can you do that successfully?" Gertrude asked.

"And why not? The museum people know me, and collectors come
here from all over the country. I buy. I sell. And my man Frank does
the legwork. He is-s-s the perfect assistant for an antique dealer—
strong in the back, weak in the head."

"Where did you find him?"

"On a junk heap. I have taught him enough to be useful to me, but
not enough to be useful to himself. A smart arrangement, eh?"
Mr. Van winked, "He is-s-s a *smeerlap*, but I am helpless without him
. . . Hoo! Look at my little sweetheart! She has-s-s made a discovery."

SuSu was sniffing at a silver bowl with two handles.

Mr. Van nodded approvingly. It is-s-s a caudle cup made by Jeremiah Dummer of Boston in the late 17th century—for a certain lady
in Salem. They said she was-s-s a witch. Look at my little sweetheart!
She knows!"

I coughed and said, "Yes, indeed, you're lucky to have Frank."

"You think I do not know it?" said Mr. Van. "That is-s-s why I
keep him poor. If I gave him wages, he would get ideas."

"How long ago was your accident?"

"Five years, and it was-s-s that idiot's fault! He did it! He did this
to me!" The Dutchman's voice rose to a shout, and his face turned
red as he pounded the arms of his wheel chair with his fists. Then
SuSu rubbed against his ankles, and he stroked her and began to
calm down. "Yes, five years ago," he said. "Five years in this miserable chair. We were driving to an antique show in the station wagon.
That *smeerlap* went through a red light—fifty miles an hour—and hit
a truck. A gravel truck!"

"How terrible!" Gertrude said, putting both hands to her face.

"I still remember packing the wagon for that trip. I was-s-s complaining all the time about sore arches. Hah! What I would give for
some sore arches today yet!"

"Wasn't Frank hurt?"

Mr. Van made an impatient gesture. "His-s-s head only. They picked Waterford crystal out of his-s-s cranium for six hours. He has-s-s been *gek* ever since." The Dutchman tapped his temple.

"Where did you find your unusual wheel chair?" I asked.

"My dear *Mevrouw*, never ask a dealer where he found something," said Mr. Van. "This chair is-s-s unique. It was-s-s made for a railroad millionaire in 1872. It has-s-s the original plush. If you must spend your life in a wheel chair, have one that gives some pleasure. And now we come to the purpose of tonight's visit. Ladies, I want you to do something for me."

He wheeled himself to a desk, and Gertrude and I exchanged anxious glances.

"Here in this desk is-s-s a new will I have written, and I need witnesses. I am leaving a few choice items to museums, then everything else is-s-s to be sold and the proceeds used to establish a Foundation."

"What about Frank?" asked Gertrude, who is always genuinely concerned about others.

"Bah! Nothing for that *smeerlap!* . . . But before you ladies sign the paper, there is-s-s one thing I must write down. What is-s-s my little sweetheart's full name?"

Gertrude and I both hesitated, and I finally said, "SuSu's registered name is Superior Suda of Siam."

"Good! I will call it the Superior Suda Foundation. That gives me pleasure. Making a will is-s-s a dismal business, like a wheel chair, so give yourself some pleasure."

"What—ah—will be the purpose of the Foundation?" I asked.

Mr. Van blessed us with a benevolent smile. "It will sponsor research," he said. "I want the universities to study the highly developed mental perception of the domestic feline and apply this knowledge to the improvement of the human mind. Ladies, there is-s-s nothing better I could do with my fortune. Man is-s-s eons behind the smallest fireside grimalkin." He gave us a canny look, and his pupils seemed to narrow. "I am in a position to know," he added.

We signed the papers. What else could we do? A few days later we left on our vacation and never saw Mr. Van again.

Gertrude and I always went south for three weeks in winter, taking SuSu with us, and when we returned, the sorry news about our eccentric neighbor was thrown at us without ceremony.

We met Frank on the elevator, and for the first time he spoke! That in itself was a shock.

He said, "They took him away."

"What's that? What did you say?" We both clamored at once.

"They took him away." It was surprising to find that the voice of this chunky man was high-pitched and rasping.

"What happened to Mr. Van?" my sister demanded.

"He cracked up. His folks come from Pennsylvania and took him back home to a nut hospital."

I saw Gertrude wince, and she said, "Is it serious?"

Frank shrugged.

"What will happen to all his antiques?"

"His folks told me to dump the junk."

"But they're valuable things, aren't they?"

"Nah. Junk. He give everybody that guff about museums and all." Frank shrugged again and tapped his head. "He was *gek!*"

Wonderingly my sister and I returned to our apartment, and I could hardly wait to say it: "I told you the Dutchman was unbalanced."

"It's such a pity," she said.

"What do you think of the sudden change in Frank? He acts like a free man. It must have been terrible living with that old Scrooge."

"I'll miss Mr. Van," Gertrude said. "He was very interesting. SuSu will miss him, too."

But SuSu, we observed later that evening, was not willing to relinquish her friend in the wheel chair as easily as we had done.

We were unpacking the vacation luggage after dinner when SuSu staged her demonstration. She started to gurgle and prance, exactly as she had done all winter whenever Mr. Van was approaching our door. Gertrude and I stood there watching her, waiting for the bell to ring. When SuSu trotted expectantly to the front door, we followed. She was behaving in an extraordinary manner. She craned her neck, made weaving motions with her head, rolled over on her back and stretched luxuriously, all the while purring her heart out; but the doorbell never rang.

Looking at my watch, I said, "It's eight thirty. SuSu remembers."

"It's quite touching, isn't it?" said Gertrude.

That was not the end of SuSu's demonstrations. Almost every night at half-past eight she performed the same ritual.

"Cats hate to give up a habit," I remarked, recalling how SuSu had continued to sleep in the guest room long after we had moved her bed to another place. "But she'll forget after a while."

SuSu did not forget. A few weeks passed. Then we had a foretaste of spring and a sudden thaw. People went without coats prematurely, convertibles cruised with their tops down, and a few hopeful fishermen appeared down on the wharf at the foot of our street, although the river was still patched with ice.

On one of these warm evenings we walked SuSu down to the park for her first spring outing, expecting her to go after last year's dried weeds with snapping jaws. But the weeds did not tempt her. Instead, she tugged at her leash, pulling toward the boardwalk. Out of curiosity we let her go, and there on the edge of the wharf she staged her weird performance once more—gurgling, arching her back, craning her neck with joy.

"She's doing it again," I said. "I wonder what the reason could be."

Gertrude said softly, "Remember what Mr. Van said about cats and ghosts?"

"Look at that animal! You'd swear she was rubbing someone's ankles. I wish she'd stop."

"I wonder," said my sister very slowly, "if Mr. Van is really in a mental hospital."

"What do you mean?"

"Or is he—down there?" Gertrude pointed uncertainly over the edge of the wharf. "I think Mr. Van is dead, and SuSu knows."

"That's too fantastic," I said. "How could that happen?"

"I think Frank pushed the poor man off the wharf, wheel chair and all—perhaps one dark night when Mr. Van couldn't sleep and insisted on being wheeled to the park."

"Really, Gertrude—"

"Can't you see it? . . . A cold night. The riverfront deserted. Mr. Van trussed in his wheel chair with a blanket. Why, that chair would sink like lead! What a terrible thing! That icy water. That poor helpless man."

"I just can't—"

"Now Frank is free, and he has all those antiques, and nobody cares enough to ask questions. He can sell them and be set up for life. Do you know what a Newport blockfront chest is worth? I've been looking it up in the library. A chest like the one we saw in Mr. Van's apartment was sold for $40,000 at some auction in the east."

"But what about the relatives in Pennsylvania?"

"I'm sure Mr. Van had no relatives—in Pennsylvania or anywhere else."

"Well, what do you propose we should do?" I said in exasperation. "Report it to the manager of the building? Notify the police? Tell them we think the man has been murdered because our cat sees his ghost every night at eight thirty? We'd look like a couple of middle-aged ladies who are getting a little *gek*."

As a matter of fact, I was beginning to worry about Gertrude—that is, until the morning paper arrived.

I skimmed through it at the breakfast table, and there—at the bottom of page seven—one small item leaped off the paper at me. Could I believe my eyes?

"Listen to this!" I said to Gertrude. "The body of an unidentified man has been washed up on a downriver island. Police say the body apparently has been held underwater for several weeks by the ice . . . About fifty-five years old and crippled . . . No one fitting that description has been reported to the Missing Persons Bureau."

For a moment my sister sat staring at the coffee pot. Then she rose from her chair and went to the telephone.

"Now all the police have to do," she said with a slight quiver in her voice, "is to look for an antique wheel chair in the river at the foot of the street. Cast iron. With the original plush." She blinked at the phone. "Will you dial?" she asked me. "The numbers are blurred."

The Investigation Of Things (An Eleventh Century Murder Mystery)

CHARLES ARDAI

"The extension of knowledge lies in the investigation of things. For only when things are investigated is knowledge extended . . ."
— Ta Hsueh, *The Great Learning*

Ch'eng I sat in the Grove of the Ninth Bamboo studying tea. He had twenty-four varieties on a great wooden palette, spread out before him like a portrait artist's paints. Each was labelled in meticulous calligraphy and kept in place with a bit of paste. Ch'eng I noted the subtle variations in the contours and textures of the leaves, labeling salient points directly on the wood with a fine-point brush.

Next to him, his brother, Ch'eng Hao, sipped from a teacup and watched in silence.

Ch'eng I selected a pouch from among the twenty-four at his feet. He pulled out a pinch of tea and spread it on his palette, separating the leaves with the end of his brush. "You see, brother," he said without looking up from his task, "the lung-ching is flat, like the edge of a fine sword, and slick, like wet hair."

"It tastes excellent," Ch'eng Hao said, tossing back the last of his tea, "not at all like wet hair. Beyond that I know nothing. What else matters about tea? How it tastes, whether it pleases one, that is all. You are not a tea farmer, to worry about the plant. You are not Lu Yu, to write another *Ch'a Ch'ing*. You ruin your eyes peering at tea when you should be drinking it."

Ch'eng I pulled a pinch from another pouch and spread it on his board. "Pi lo-chun dries in a spiral. It is the smallest of all the teas I have examined." He scratched a few more notes onto the wood, then laid the brush aside and looked up at his brother. "Please try not to be so selfish. Tea is not merely a flavor in your mouth. Tea exists even if your mouth does not. You must not understand tea in terms of yourself. You must understand yourself in terms of tea."

286

Ch'eng Hao shook his head. "You do not understand yourself. You do not understand tea. You spend your days picking things apart, but there will always be more things than there are days. Your tea, your pouch, your brush, your tunic—these are all tools. You shouldn't study them. You should use them: drink your tea, write with your brush, wear your tunic. When you sit down to think, you should think about *this*." Ch'eng Hao tapped a finger against his forehead.

Ch'eng I gathered his materials, wrapping the palette in its silk case and stringing the pouches along his belt. "No, brother, you are mistaken." He tapped his head. "This is the tool. You should use it to think about this—" He swept his free hand around him in an open gesture. "About this—" He lifted one of the pouches and let it fall to his side again. "And this—" He ran his hand along the trunk of a tree. "Grow until your mind is the size of the world. Do not try to compress the world to make it fit inside your mind."

"But there is more in the world than you can ever hope to know," Ch'eng Hao said.

"So you would argue that I shouldn't try to know anything?"

"I say only, as Chuang Tzu says, that 'To pursue that which is unlimited with that which is limited is to know sorrow.' The world is huge; we are small and have short lives."

"When did you become a Taoist," Ch'eng I said, "that you quote Chuang Tzu?"

"Not a Taoist, I, a realist." Ch'eng Hao tried to wave the whole discussion away. "You will have to learn this for yourself. It is at least possible for one to fully understand oneself. That is a finite task. Through this understanding, one can understand everything else in the world."

"No, brother. The *Great Learning* says that self-perfection must come from the Investigation of Things, not the Investigation of Self."

"All things can be found in the self," Ch'eng Hao said.

"Now," said Ch'eng I, "you sound like a Buddhist."

"If you weren't my brother," Ch'eng Hao said, "I would demand an apology."

"If I weren't your brother," Ch'eng I said, "I might give you one."

Ch'eng Hao was about to answer when a scuffle of footsteps arose and a messenger burst into the grove. The messenger bowed deeply. The two brothers returned the courtesy, their argument temporarily set aside.

"Forgive me, please, for intruding," the messenger said, "but you are the brothers Ch'eng, are you not? Hao and I?"

Ch'eng I nodded. "We are."

"Then you must come. The Seventh Patriarch has requested your presence."

The brothers exchanged surprised glances. The Seventh Patriarch was the leader of the district's Ch'an Buddhist temple, and rarely one to invite outsiders into his sanctuary. Especially Confucian outsiders.

"He wants to see us?" Ch'eng Hao said. "Why?"

The messenger tried to look Ch'eng Hao in the eye and failed. His eyes fell on the ground and remained there, his chin pressed against his chest.

"What is it, man?"

The messenger spoke quietly: "There has been a murder."

The Temple of the Seventh Patriarch rose out of the flat land it was built on like a needle piercing upwards through a piece of fabric. It was a tower five times the height of a man, roughly pointed at the top, with walls of packed earth supported by wooden beams. The structure looked unstable and precarious, yet Ch'eng Hao knew that it was older than he was.

The messenger, who had identified himself as Wu Han-Fei, led them to the entrance and then stepped aside. "I may not enter," he said, in answer to the unasked question.

Ch'eng Hao and Ch'eng I stepped inside cautiously.

A body lay on the ground, its feet toward them. It was clearly that of a Buddhist monk—there was no mistaking the coarse robe or the waxy pallor of the skin, so deathlike in life, how much more so in death! Ch'eng I knelt beside the corpse to examine it more closely while Ch'eng Hao looked around the inside of the room.

The neck of the monk's robe was soaked with a liquid Ch'eng I knew to be blood—indeed, the entire front of the robe was. When he opened the robe, Ch'eng I discovered a ragged hole in the man's throat. He lifted the head and pulled off the hood. The monk's head was neatly shaved, as Ch'eng I had known it would be. The wound in his throat penetrated cleanly, ending in a round, puckered hole on the other side. The ground beneath the body was coated with blood, by now nearly dry, and the beams in the far wall were spattered with brown spots. Ch'eng I laid the man's head back down and replaced the hood.

Ch'eng Hao paced around the room's perimeter. It was not a large room, though it took on a sense of space because of the high roof. Other than the body and themselves, the room was completely empty and devoid of decoration. There was no more mistaking a Ch'an meditation room than there was a Ch'an monk. Only prisons were this spare in the outside world . . . and graves.

Ch'eng I left the monk's body and walked over to the far wall, where the spray of blood had struck. He examined it closely, inching his way down from eye level until he stopped about two feet above the floor. He pulled his drawing brush from his belt and knelt to his work, using the handle to pry something out from a tiny hole in the wall. Ch'eng I had to be careful not to break the brush, but he worked as quickly as he dared. Ch'eng Hao stood behind him, watching.

"What have you found?" Ch'eng Hao asked.

"I do not know yet. I will have to investigate."

Ch'eng I scraped around the edges of the hole, coaxing out the object that was lodged inside. Finally, it fell to the ground and Ch'eng I picked it up. He tested it with a fingernail. "It is a piece of soft metal," he said, holding it out on his palm for his brother to see. It was a dark, flattened lump slightly larger than a cashew. Then he held up his thumbnail. "Coated with blood, as you can see. This little ball seems to have killed the unfortunate man at our feet."

"This ball?" Ch'eng Hao was incredulous. "How can that be?"

Ch'eng I stepped over to the open entryway. "Through here. It came in, struck the monk in the throat, and killed him."

"But that is impossible!" Ch'eng Hao said. "Think of the force required! Think how hard it would have had to have been thrown in order to pierce the man's neck!"

Ch'eng I shook his head. "It is worse than that. The metal was thrown with enough force to pierce the monk's neck and then continue its flight to the opposite wall, where it lodged itself three finger-widths deep. But you are wrong to say it is impossible. The evidence of our senses demonstrates that it has happened."

Ch'eng Hao looked at the bloody metal and at the corpse and said nothing.

Wu Han-Fei reappeared at the entrance. "The Seventh Patriarch will see you now," he said.

"Will he?" Ch'eng I took the murder weapon back from his brother and found an empty pouch for it on his belt. "How good of him." He left the temple. Ch'eng Hao followed.

Ch'eng I scanned the landscape more carefully than he had before. The temple was the only building in sight, surrounded at a distance of ten yards by a dense forest; it stood like an obelisk in the center of a flat and empty meadow. "Where will we find the Seventh Patriarch?" he asked.

"You will follow me," Wu Han-Fei said. He started off for the forest.

"Hold on," Ch'eng I shouted. Wu Han-Fei stopped and turned around. "I realize that we will follow you. What I asked is *where* we will find him, not *how* we will."

Wu Han-Fei was confused. "There." He pointed in the direction he had started to walk.

"In the forest?"

He shook his head. "In a clearing. Like this."

"How far?"

He shrugged uncomfortably. "Not far. You will see."

"Yes, I imagine I will see. But first—"

"Never mind," Ch'eng Hao interrupted. "There will be plenty of time for your questions later." Then to Wu Han-Fei: "You will have to forgive my brother. He wants to know everything there is to know."

This explanation apparently satisfied the messenger, who turned around again and continued into the forest.

"I will not interfere with your investigation," Ch'eng I said as they followed their guide, "and I will ask you kindly not to interfere with mine."

"Brother," Ch'eng Hao said, "if I hadn't interfered, you would still be badgering this poor man with your questions. You'd have kept at it until we all died of old age out there."

"Perhaps," Ch'eng I said. "Perhaps I would have found the truth sooner than that."

"The truth? You were asking him how far it was to where we are going! Of what possible consequence—"

"You think truth is limited to thought and reason and motive," Ch'eng I said calmly, "and that is a mistake. Truth is also distance, and size, and weight, and force. You can seek truth in your way. I will seek it in mine."

"Sirs," Wu Han-Fei interrupted. "We are here."

They had passed through about forty feet of dense forest and were now in another clearing. A dozen small buildings were clustered in the center. The messenger pointed to one of them. "You will find the Patriarch there."

"And you?" Ch'eng I looked closely at the man for the first time. This was no Buddhist—he had a fine head of long, black hair and a dark, earthy complexion; and if his robe was coarse it was due to poverty, not piety. Most telling, a respect for the public authority Ch'eng I and Ch'eng Hao represented was clear in the way he never met their eyes for more than a second; a devoted Buddhist would stare down the Emperor himself, even if it meant death. It was indeed as Hui-Yuan had written: "A monk does not bow down before a king."

"I will go no further," Wu Han-Fei said.

"What are you doing here?" Ch'eng Hao asked, suddenly curious. "You are not one of them."

"No," Wu Han-Fei said. "I am their link with the secular world."

"I thought they did not need one," Ch'eng Hao said.

"They thought so, too." Wu Han-Fei spread his hands before him. "Murder changes such things."

"Tell me again," Ch'eng Hao said, "exactly how you found Kung." He paced as he spoke and did not turn to face the Patriarch when the old man answered.

"Kung was meditating," the Patriarch said. He had a voice that rumbled softly like a running stream. Ch'eng Hao was not insensible to beauty; he appreciated the sound of a wise and serene voice. But he listened with a suspicious ear to hear the silences, the words that remained unspoken. "Kung had grave matters on his conscience. Very grave."

"What were these grave matters?" Ch'eng Hao asked.

"Kung would not say." The Patriarch looked genuinely saddened by his monk's death, but Hao was aware that such apparent sadness might be no more than a mask. Men conceal, as he had often told his brother, in a way that nature does not. Honesty is a path only infrequently followed, and even then not without straying.

"Why would he not?"

The Patriarch caught Hao's eye and held it. "Ssu-ma Ch'ien was offered suicide but chose castration. He felt an honorable death would impair his mission on earth. So he sacrificed personal honor for the greater good."

"And . . .?"

The Patriarch said nothing more.

"I want none of your *koans*," Ch'eng Hao said sharply. "Speak plainly or not at all."

"Silence is the sound of a man speaking plainly," the Patriarch said. And silence fell.

After the strained quiet had stretched out for a minute, Ch'eng I spoke. "It would be helpful if you would describe the circumstances under which Kung's body was discovered."

The Patriarch nodded. "Kung left for the temple early in the morning. Before an hour had passed, Lin-Yu came to see me. He told me that he had gone to the temple and found Kung's body, in the condition that you observed."

"Who might have killed him?" Ch'eng Hao asked.

"Any one of us," the Patriarch said, "myself included."

"Did you?"

The Patriarch favored Ch'eng Hao with a condescending smile. "I do not think so . . . do you?"

Hao shook his head. "No. Had you killed him you could easily have arranged to rid yourself of the body without any attention. The outside world is unaware of what goes on here—even apathetic. If I had an illustrious ancestor for every time someone has said to me, 'Let the monks starve to death, we do not care,' I would be the most favored man under heaven. You would have had no reason to ask us to investigate, for that could only call punishment down on your head. No, you did not kill Kung. But," and here Ch'eng Hao paused for a bit to let his words have their full effect, "I would be very surprised if you did not know why he was killed."

The old man shook his head. "Then I will have the pleasure of surprising you, Ch'eng Hao. For I know nothing of this matter beyond the fact that I was unfortunate enough not to be able to prevent it. One of my men killed another: a son has murdered a brother. I want to know who and I want to know why."

"And how." This from Ch'eng I.

The Patriarch nodded slowly. "'How' and 'why' are such similar questions, so fundamentally intertwined. You will not find one answer without the other."

"Then the investigation commences," Ch'eng I said. He stepped out of the room abruptly and headed toward the forest.

"If I might speak with the monks," Ch'eng Hao said, "all of them at once, it might give me the perspective necessary to understand the murderous act."

The Patriarch stood. "It shall be so."

Ch'eng I measured the distance from the edge of the forest to the temple using his own footsteps for a standard. Forty paces brought him from the nearest trees to the entrance.

It was extraordinary, he thought, that such a thing was possible. For surely the attacker had concealed himself in the forest—Kung had been facing his attacker when he had been hit in the throat after all, and he would not have stood still had he seen that an attack was imminent. But for a pellet of metal, even a small one, to be propelled forty paces through the air, then through a man's neck, then for this pellet to penetrate three finger widths deep into a solid earthen wall . . . It was extraordinary indeed.

But more extraordinary things had happened in history. Had not the Yellow Emperor fought off an army single-handedly? Had not the Duke of Chou braved the fury of heaven and lived? A metal ball had been propelled with great force? So be it. It remained only to determine how it had been accomplished.

No arm could be strong enough, Ch'eng I decided quickly, or at least no *human* arm could. An inhuman arm was a possibility he did not care to contemplate. But murder, he knew, was not a tool of the spirits. Murder was an act of man against man.

This knowledge reassured Ch'eng I. If a man had done it, a man *could* do it, as impossible as it appeared to be. And if a man could do it, then Ch'eng I could figure out how. It was that simple.

The monks under the Seventh Patriarch's tutelage drew together in their largest building, one they normally used for the preparation and service of meals. Ch'eng Hao stood next to the Patriarch, who instructed the monks to answer all of the investigator's questions.

There appeared to be no resistance to this order; Ch'eng Hao had feared there might be. But then resistance, he knew, like dishonesty, does not always appear on a man's face when it burns in his heart. It remained to be seen whether the monks actually *would* answer his questions, or whether they would dance around him with elaborate riddles and pointless anecdotes as their Master had done.

"A man has been murdered," Ch'eng Hao said to the assembled

monks. It was best to get the basic information out of the way immediately. "As most of you know, it was your fellow monk, Kung." It
galled Ch'eng Hao to refer to the dead man only by his chosen name;
the man had once had two names like everyone else, and neither had
been 'Kung.' But Kung was the name he had taken when he had
severed his ties with his earthly family, and Kung was the name by
which his fellows knew him. Ch'eng Hao swallowed his contempt and
went on. "Kung was killed in a most unusual manner. My esteemed
brother, Ch'eng I, is investigating this aspect of his death. I am concerned with only one question. That question is, *Who killed Kung?*"
Knowing the positive effect of a weighty pause, Ch'eng Hao paused.

"It was almost certainly someone in this room."

No one moved. It was unnerving, Ch'eng Hao thought, the stoicism
with which they received this accusation. Any other roomful of
people would have been fidgeting with anxiety and outrage. Not these
men. They would not fidget if their own parents accused them of
murdering their children. Of course, for that they would have had to
have children, as most—shamefully enough—did not.

"I will speak with each of you in turn," Ch'eng Hao said. "If any of
you know anything about Kung's death, I strongly suggest you
divulge it without hesitation." Still no response. "You," he said,
picking a fellow out of the front row at random. "You will be first."

Ch'eng I bent over the corpse and inhaled deeply. It was not only
death he smelled, though that scent was powerful; there was an acrid
edge to the still air in the temple, a smell of fire and ashes. Incense was
Ch'eng I's first thought, but he found no sign that an incense burner
had been in the temple: the ground was unbroken and the walls showed
no smoke stains. Then, too, the smell lacked the pungent sweetness of
incense. But something, he was convinced, had been burning.

He put that thought aside and began a meticulous study of Kung's
body. Ch'eng I searched it inch by inch, making mental notes as he
went. The monk had been relatively healthy, he saw—somewhat
undernourished, perhaps, but then who these days was not?

The first curious observation Ch'eng I made was when he came to
Kung's right hand. The fleshy pads of his fingers were singed—not so
severely burned as to destroy the flesh, but burned all the same, as
though Kung had taken hold of something burning and had not let
go. This corroborated Ch'eng I's earlier suspicion, but beyond cor-
roboration it offered little other than puzzlement.

The second curious observation was this: Kung's head was scarred in two places, at the base of his skull and under his chin. The scarring had evidently occurred many years before, appearing now only as raised, white scar tissue against the dark tan of the rest of Kung's head. But the scarring was clearly not the result of an accident, since the two scars were identical—the shape was that of the character *wang*, three short horizontal lines intersected by a vertical.

Ch'eng I considered this for some time, deciding eventually that it was most likely the result of early childhood scarification, a common enough practice among the families of the plains. Kung's father would have placed the mark on his son, as his father's father must have done before him, and his great-grandfather before that. Ch'eng I could not help but wonder if this brutal tradition had influenced the young Kung in his decision to abandon his family for the monastery.

This thought, too, Ch'eng I set aside for further consideration at another time. Soon the body would start to decompose in earnest and at that point no further study would be possible. Ch'eng I focused his attention on the wound. It was at this point that he made his third curious observation: the neck of Kung's robe had no hole in it.

"Would you say that Kung was a well-liked man?" Ch'eng Hao asked.

"I would say that Kung was a man." A heavyset monk named Tso sat across from Ch'eng Hao, looking and acting like a stone wall.

"Had Kung no enemies?"

"Is one who bears you ill will an enemy?"

"I would say so."

"Then evidently he had at least one enemy," Tso said.

"But you have no idea who that might be."

Tso said nothing. He was well trained, Ch'eng Hao thought. Half the art of Buddhism is appearing to have all the answers and the other half is being sure never to give them. Even the Patriarch had been more helpful than this.

"You may go," Ch'eng Hao said. Tso was difficult on purpose, but then so were all the other monks he had interviewed. He had no reason to believe that Tso knew anything about Kung's death.

On his way out, Tso sent the next man in.

Bo-Tze was the oldest of the monks, by at least ten years. If he was not quite as old as the Patriarch, it was only because *no one* else was that old. The Patriarch was four hundred and three, rumor said; and even if rumor exaggerated, the Patriarch had certainly seen the tail end of ninety and was moving up on the century mark. Bo-Tze, Ch'eng Hao guessed, was about sixty.

His face had the texture of a hide left too long out in the sun and his robe was more worn than the others Ch'eng Hao had seen. He looked well weathered, a point Ch'eng Hao knew Bo-Tze would have prided himself on if monks permitted themselves pride. Unlike the other monks Ch'eng Hao had spoken to, Bo-Tze sat in front of him without even a trace of nervousness.

"Mister Ch'eng," Bo-Tze said, stressing the family name with disdain, "Kung was an undisciplined man. This was quite a serious problem. Do you know anything about Ch'an Buddhism, Mister Ch'eng? Ch'an is not what people in the world outside the monasteries think it is. Ch'an means 'meditation,' and meditation is our practice. Silent meditation: internal quiet, external harmony." The old monk took a raspy breath. Ch'eng Hao waited for him to continue.

"Kung was a dreamer and a visionary. We do *not* have visions, Mister Ch'eng. We are not the navel-staring mystics you think we are."

"I think no such thing," Ch'eng Hao said. Then: "Kung had visions?"

"Irrepressible visions," Bo-Tze said. "Or *irrepressed*, in any event. All men pray, in their fashion; Kung thought that his prayers were answered. When he meditated, he saw visions. He turned these visions into art—into art and into artifice. Then Heaven saw fit to strike him down. Surely this tells us something."

"What does it tell us?"

"That Kung's visions were not favored by . . ." Bo-Tze seemed to be groping for a concept.

"By . . . ?" Ch'eng Hao prodded.

"By a force powerful enough to do to him what was done to him."

"Which was?"

"I do not know, Mister Ch'eng." Bo-Tze kept up his placid facade, but Ch'eng Hao sensed a vein of anger in his voice. "But it killed him. I regret his death, of course—" of course, Ch'eng Hao thought "—but only because he died unenlightened. He will return to plague this world again and again until he achieves Nirvana, which he never will if he keeps on like this. *Visions!*" Bo-Tze spat the word out like a plum pit.

Vituperation aside, this was the most information Ch'eng Hao had gotten about the dead man from anyone. Kung had had visions? At last, a line of inquiry to pursue.

"Where is this 'art' you referred to," Ch'eng Hao asked, "in which Kung recorded his visions?"

Bo-Tze waved the question away. "In his cell, I am sure. But you do not understand. Kung was doing things he should not have been doing. This is why he died."

"You mean it is why you killed him," Ch'eng Hao ventured.

Bo-Tze absorbed the remark with a slow blink of his eyelids. "I did not kill Kung," he said. "A monk does not kill."

Monks *do* kill, Ch'eng Hao wanted to say, or at least one monk did, since a monk is now dead and it does not look as though suicide is a plausible explanation. But he said none of this. "You may go."

Bo-Tze rose calmly and exited. Only Lin-Yu remained for Ch'eng Hao to see.

A grotesque figure, Lin-Yu moved painfully and with great difficulty. His legs were withered almost to the point of uselessness, but somehow they just managed to keep his great bulk from collapsing. One sleeve of his robe flapped empty at his side and he was missing an eye. The empty socket stared at Ch'eng Hao. He looked aside.

"Bo-Tze tells me that Kung had visions," Ch'eng Hao said. "Do you know anything about this?"

"Bo-Tze is an old man. He talks too much and thinks too little." Lin-Yu's voice was soft, almost feminine. "Kung was a fortunate man, possessed of life's most generous curse: a creative soul. He created in a night's sleep works of greater ingenuity than most men create in a lifetime of waking hours. Kung was the best man here."

"What were the visions visions *of*?" Ch'eng Hao asked.

"Everything." Ch'eng Hao had expected this: a typically obscure Ch'an answer. But Lin-Yu explained, "Sometimes, merely images. Mandalas, with a thousand buddhas in the eye of the thousand-and-first. You can see some of these—the Patriarch keeps them in his cell. He appreciated Kung's talent."

"But surely there was more to it than mandalas—"

"Oh, of course!" Excitement lit Lin-Yu's face. "He dreamt machines and tools—why do you think we are able to farm on such poor land as we have? Kung created tools for us. The universal buddha nature spoke through him, gave him knowledge of the unknown . . . For instance—"

Lin-Yu stood and lifted the skirts of his robe. His withered legs were bound in metal-and-leather braces with fabric joints at the knees. "Kung made these for me. Mister Ch'eng, please understand, Kung was a genius and a compassionate soul. This is a very rare and special combination."

Ch'eng Hao noticed that when Lin-Yu said 'Mister Ch'eng' the words carried no tone of disapproval.

"I believe you," Ch'eng Hao said. "I only wish the others had been as open with me as you are."

"The others are performing for you, Mister Ch'eng," Lin-Yu said. "How often do they have the pleasure of an outsider's presence? They want to show each other how good they can be at the game. They have much to learn. But then, don't we all?"

Much to learn. Yes, Ch'eng Hao thought, we have much to learn. I, for instance, have to learn who killed this compassionate, visionary monk—so far I have made little progress. "Thank you," Ch'eng Hao said. He hoped he sounded more appreciative than he knew he usually did. "You may go."

"One moment please!" Ch'eng I dashed into the room through the parted tapestry that hung over the entrance. He put a hand on Lin-Yu's shoulder. "There are questions *I* must ask, brother." Ch'eng Hao nodded his assent.

"What can I tell you?" Lin-Yu asked.

Ch'eng I helped Lin-Yu once more to a seated position. "Please describe for me the condition in which you found Kung's body."

"Kung was dead," Lin-Yu said. The words came haltingly and tears formed in Lin-Yu's single eye. "He had a wound in his throat. There was blood all over the ground."

"You say 'throat,'" Ch'eng I said. "Do you not mean 'neck'?"

Lin-Yu considered this. "I suppose 'neck' is as good. I said 'throat' because he was on his back."

"He was on his back," Ch'eng I repeated. "Fascinating. And he was not wearing his hood?"

"No," Lin-Yu said, "he was. His hood was on."

"Brother," Ch'eng Hao said, "have you gone mad? You know all this. This is how he was when *we* saw the body."

Ch'eng I turned to his brother. "You must be less cavalier with your accusations, Hao. I am not mad, merely curious. You see," here he turned back to Lin-Yu, "when we saw him, Kung *was* as you describe. But this is not how he was when he was killed."

Lin-Yu arched an eyebrow; it was the one above the empty socket and Ch'eng Hao had to look away again.

"I have spent a good deal of time examining Kung's body," Ch'eng I said. "He was hit with this." He pulled the lump of metal from its pouch and showed it to Lin-Yu. "But he was not hit in the throat. He was hit in the back of the neck. He did not fall backward; he fell forward. And he was not wearing his hood at the time."

"How do you know all this?" Ch'eng Hao asked, caught between admiration and disbelief.

"Simple." Ch'eng I ticked off points on his fingers. "The pellet penetrated Kung's neck and continued to the opposite wall. Yet there was no hole in Kung's hood. How can this be? Kung was not wearing his hood.

"Next: the front of Kung's robe was soaked with blood as well as the back. If the force of the attack had knocked him backwards, the front of his robe would have received very little blood. If, on the other hand, he fell forward, into his pooling blood, it would account for the condition of his robe. Therefore, he fell forward.

"Finally: the wound on the back of his neck was smaller and more contained than the wound in his throat. This suggests that the latter was the exit wound, not the entry wound. Therefore, he was hit in the back of the neck."

"Very well," Ch'eng Hao said. "I accept your analysis. But why then was Kung not on his chest with his hood off when Lin-Yu found him?"

"Someone changed the position of Kung's body," Ch'eng I said. "Turned him over and covered his head." Also, he said to himself, took away whatever had been burning in the temple and erased all signs of his presence. "Why someone would do this is a mystery. However, we do know now that there was someone with Kung when he died."

"Yes, the murderer," Ch'eng Hao said. "We already knew that."

"No," said Ch'eng I, "a third man. Because the murderer was at the edge of the forest directly across from the temple entrance—where I searched and found this." He undid the strings of the largest pouch on his belt and poured two objects out onto the floor: a small metal mallet and a flattened metal capsule not much larger than the murder weapon.

"What is this?" Lin-Yu asked. He picked up the mallet and turned it over in his hands. The head was remarkably heavy for a tool so small.

"It is part of the murderer's device," Ch'eng I said. "I am still trying to piece together just how the device operated. It would help if I had it in its entirety. However, these pieces give us a starting point. Smell the capsule."

Ch'eng Hao picked up the dented metal packet. "You mean this?" Ch'eng I nodded. Ch'eng Hao sniffed at it. "It smells like . . ." He hesitated. "I cannot place it. But I know I have smelled it before." He handed the capsule to Lin-Yu.

"Black powder," Lin-Yu said as soon as he put the piece to his nose. "We use it from time to time for certain ceremonies. In explosive pyrotechnics."

Ch'eng I nodded enthusiastically; his suspicions had been confirmed. "A bamboo tube," he recited, "packed with black powder. One end open, the other closed except for a tiny hole. A fuse is attached to the latter. An explosive projectile is placed in the tube above the powder. The fuse is lit. The ignition of the powder ejects the projectile, which in turn explodes in mid-air. Am I correct?"

"That is how the fireworks work, yes," Lin-Yu said, "although I cannot imagine how you found out. It is a secret among monks—"

"I have experimented on my own," Ch'eng I said abruptly. "The principles are readily apparent. What is not so clear is how they were adapted to destructive ends." He thought the problem through aloud. "A narrower tube to suit the smaller projectile, I imagine . . . and, of course, the tube would be aimed at a target rather than at the sky . . . and in place of a fuse, this capsule . . . the capsule containing a small amount of black powder, which when compressed by a blow from the mallet explodes, igniting the main load of powder in the tube . . . and, finally, a tripod to steady the apparatus, to account for the three circular indentations in the soil where I found the mallet and the capsule." Ch'eng I folded his arms and waited for his brother's reaction.

"Fireworks as a weapon," Ch'eng Hao whispered. "Ingenious." Then he realized what he had said and he shot a glance at Lin-Yu, whose expression betrayed that he had had the same thought. Ch'eng Hao voiced it for both of them. "One of Kung's inventions."

"No one else could have invented it," Lin-Yu said.

Ch'eng I was taken back. "You think Kung invented the weapon that killed him? I find that unlikely—"

Ch'eng Hao silenced him. "I will tell you what *I* have learned while you were away," he said. "In the meantime, we should see Kung's cell. I will fill you in on the way."

* * *

The cells they passed on the way to Kung's were as bare as the temple. Wooden cots with no matting were the only furniture the brothers saw and the walls were unadorned. But Kung's cell was different. He, too, had the painful-looking cot—but every inch of his walls was covered with ink drawings and elaborate calligraphy.

As Lin-Yu had said, much of the art was religious. One entire wall, for instance, was devoted to images of the Buddha and his boddhisatvas in intricate interrelations. The painting was flat and monochromatic, but somehow deeply hypnotic.

It was the other walls that revealed Kung's true genius, however, for it was there that he had composed dozens of sketches for tools and devices of mind-boggling complexity. Lin-Yu's braces were on the wall, along with drawings of the special plows and wells Kung had designed for the monks—as well as plenty of drawings of objects at whose function the brothers could only guess. The one drawing that was conspicuously absent from the wall was that of the murder weapon. None of the sketches looked similar to the machine Ch'eng I had described.

"All of these," Lin-Yu said when Ch'eng Hao asked, "are devices that Kung actually finished and gave to us. Perhaps the weapon was not perfected yet."

"It certainly worked well enough," Ch'eng Hao said.

"We do *not* know that for certain," Ch'eng I corrected his brother. "We do not yet know what happened."

"If these are Kung's finished inventions," Ch'eng Hao asked Lin-Yu, "where did he sketch ideas for new projects?"

"On the floor," Lin-Yu said. He indicated a sharp stick leaning against the cot and then a particularly scarred portion of the dirt floor. It did look as though Kung had used the space for this purpose—Ch'eng I was able to make out a character here and there—but trying to "read" it would have been futile.

"Had he no more permanent record?" Ch'eng I asked.

Lin-Yu knelt in front of the cot and reached under it. After groping for a few seconds he pulled out a flat metal board. "He used this from time to time. When he wanted to show an idea to the Patriarch, for instance. He would stretch a piece of fabric over it and then draw on it." Lin-Yu pointed to four hook-shaped protrusions at the corners of the board. "He designed this, too."

"So there may be a fabric sketch of the weapon somewhere . . ." Ch'eng Hao began—but Ch'eng I was already out of the room.

Ch'eng Hao ran after him. Lin-Yu followed as quickly as he could. They caught up with him outside Bo-Tze's cell. Ch'eng I burst in before they could restrain him.

Bo-Tze was seated in the lotus position on his cot, his legs crossed tightly over one another, his hands outstretched on his knees. As Ch'eng I entered, Bo-Tze opened his eyes with a start and dropped his hands to his sides.

"You were contemptuous of your fellow monk," Ch'eng I said without preamble. Then, in answer to the confusion in the old man's eyes, "My brother told me what you said about Kung. That he had 'visions'—and that you hated him for it. That you feel the world looks down on *you* because of men like him. That on some level you were obsessively jealous of him."

"I was never jealous of that man," Bo-Tze snarled. In the heat of confrontation, he did not even try to hide his anger. "He was a disgrace to us."

"Why?" Lin-Yu asked. There was pain and loss in his voice. "Because of his imagination?"

"Yes," Bo-Tze said, "if you want to call it that. But that is not all. He was dealing with the outside world!"

Lin-Yu shook his head. "That is ludicrous."

"I agree," Bo-Tze said. "It is ludicrous. It is also a fact. Kung was not just creating things for our use. He was also selling his creations in the secular world. He was not a monk—he was a merchant!"

"No," Lin-Yu insisted. "You know he never left the grounds. How could he—"

"Are you *completely* blind now?" Bo-Tze shouted. "*Wu* sold Kung's goods for him."

"Wu Han-Fei?" Ch'eng Hao asked. "The messenger?"

"Our 'link to the secular world,'" Bo-Tze said sarcastically. "It was a mistake to employ him, as I predicted it would be. But who talked the Patriarch into it? Kung did! Do you not see? *Do none of you see?*"

"It is clear that you want desperately to prove yourself right," Ch'eng I said. "Is that why you went to the temple this morning when you knew Kung was there?"

Bo-Tze's guard went up at last. "I was nowhere near the temple," he said.

Ch'eng I reached out and grabbed Bo-Tze's right hand. Bo-Tze resisted but Ch'eng I was by far the stronger man. Slowly, Ch'eng I turned the monk's hand palm upwards. The pads of Bo-Tze's fingers were seared red. "Note the singed fingers," Ch'eng I said. "Compare them to the seared fingers of Kung's body. Identical."

Bo-Tze pulled his hand away. "Yes," he said, breaking down at last, "yes, I was there! I was there because it was my last chance to expose Kung to the lot of you!" Ch'eng Hao was surprised—it was hard to believe that this was the same man he had interrogated unsuccessfully so recently. Corner a lion in the field and it attacks, he reminded himself, but corner one in its den and it falls at your feet.

"I cornered Wu outside the dining hall," Bo-Tze said furiously. "He is a coward! I threatened to expose him, and he turned on Kung like this." Bo-Tze snapped his trembling fingers. "Wu said that Kung had gone to the temple to burn all the evidence of their dealings. I went there to get this evidence for myself. Sure enough, Kung was there. There was a sheet of cloth stretched out on that metal board of his and he had already set it on fire. I grabbed it; he grabbed it, too. We struggled over it—then, all of a sudden, there was a loud explosion and Kung fell forward with blood spurting all over his face and I ran out of there as quickly as I could . . ." Bo-Tze was crying and out of breath; his chest heaved and his head sank forward until it almost touched his ankles.

Ch'eng Hao pulled his brother and Lin-Yu out of the room. Bo-Tze was not the murderer they sought, Ch'eng Hao knew; and at an exposed moment like this even a Buddhist deserved his privacy.

The Patriarch's cell was no larger than any of the others. He slept on the same cot. But like Kung's, his walls were not bare. Also like Kung's, his walls were covered with Kung's art: complex ink drawings, passionate attempts to render the transcendent universe accessible to the human eye—Ch'eng Hao would have found it all very moving if he had been a Buddhist. As it was, he could only marvel at the artist's skill.

"We all have our failings," the Patriarch said. He was staring at Kung's largest image and his voice betrayed the rapture he felt. "Kung was an artist at heart, I a connoisseur. Neither is appropriate for a monk: a monk must lose all attachments to the things of this world, because such things, in their impermanence, can only produce suffering. The more beautiful a thing is, the more pain it will bring by its inevitable absence." The Patriarch sighed. "Yet if life is suffering, can we not take from it what little pleasure there is to be had? How could I tell Kung not to paint? That would have increased his suffering—surely our purpose is not *that*."

"There is more to this matter than the art," Ch'eng Hao said.

"Yes," the Patriarch said. "The tools. I should let my men starve rather than use the tools Kung devised? This is Bo-Tze's position, but he is a fool. If we cannot use Kung's tools, from the same argument we should not use any tools at all. We should dig in the dirt with our hands as our ancestors did. Perhaps we should not farm at all, since our oldest ancestors did not. Innovation is not evil; new tools are not worse than old. And heaven knows it is easier to meditate with a full belly than an empty one. Gautama himself said so—the Buddha himself! Starvation is not for Buddhists any more than decadence is."

"I understand," Ch'eng Hao said, "and I agree. But there remains the question of Kung's trade with the outside world."

For a long time, the Patriarch was silent.

"Bo-Tze says—"

"He is correct," the Patriarch whispered. "I looked the other way."

"You knew—"

"Ch'eng Hao, how could I not know?" At this moment the Patriarch looked very old and helpless. "I simply chose to tolerate it. Kung was too special a man, and too valuable to our lives, for me to risk losing him over such a minor point. So he sent his creations to people like yourself? There are graver sins. Perhaps it even made some Confucians think twice before cursing us. Surely it did no harm."

"No harm," Ch'eng Hao said, "but now Kung is dead."

"Yes," the Patriarch said. "That is so. And this is what comes of forming attachments to things of this world—now that we have lost him, we suffer."

Ch'eng Hao considered for a moment. "When we first spoke, you indicated that Kung had grave matters on his conscience. But if he knew that you tolerated his dealings with the outside world, surely he was not anxious about that?" The Patriarch shook his head. "What then?"

"I repeat what I told you before: I do not know."

Ch'eng Hao let this pass. "Just one more question," he said. "When Kung traded his goods through Wu Han-Fei, what did he get in return? Not money, obviously; he had no use for that."

The Patriarch shrugged. "It is a question I never considered." Ch'eng Hao could see from the Patriarch's face that he really *hadn't* considered it. "Perhaps he simply received the satisfaction of knowing his creations were being put to good use."

To good use. The phrase resonated for Ch'eng Hao. Yes, he thought, good use. But surely that was not all?

Lin-Yu directed Ch'eng I to a small building on the outskirts of the monastery complex. It was no more than a hut, really, but a solid and well-constructed one as huts went. Lin-Yu stood guard outside the door while Ch'eng I went inside.

A few minutes later, Ch'eng I emerged carrying a scorched square of fabric and a bamboo tube.

Ch'eng I steadied the tripod he had brought by pressing it down in the damp soil at the edge of the forest. The bamboo tube was clamped in place, the repaired capsule inserted in the tube's smaller hole. Lin-Yu had procured the necessary black powder and, what was equally important, the spare monk's robe that knelt, stuffed to over-flowing with straw and twigs, just inside the temple entrance. Ch'eng Hao held back the small crowd of onlookers he had gathered: the Patriarch, Bo-Tze, Tso, and a handful of other monks. Wu Han-Fei was not among the group.

"I am ready," Ch'eng I announced.

Lin-Yu moved to join the others. They all turned to face the dummy Ch'eng I had erected.

Ch'eng I aimed the bamboo tube carefully, sighting along its length. Then he inserted the small white stone he had selected as a projectile and took several test swings with the mallet. He steadied himself with two deep breaths.

"Proceed," Ch'eng Hao said.

Ch'eng I swung the mallet again. This time it connected with a sharp crack, squeezing the capsule flat. This tiny explosion was followed by a much larger one, one that startled all the spectators. Even Bo-Tze, who knew what to expect, started at the noise.

But the dummy did not fall. After the cloud of smoke around him cleared, Ch'eng I inspected the tube. The projectile *had* been ejected. He ran to the temple and made a quick search of the far wall. The white stone he had choosen expressly for this reason stood out clearly against the brown of the packed earth in which it was now embedded.

"Come here," he said. The others crowded into the temple, pushing the dummy aside. They stared at the stone in the wall as though it was a religious relic and worthy of their rapt attention. Ch'eng I pushed his way back through the crowd until he was able to join his brother outside the temple.

"You missed," Ch'eng Hao said.

"Indeed. It was the strike of the mallet that ruined my aim. I had not taken it into account."

"Never mind," Ch'eng Hao said. "It is of no consequence. You will never need to use that cursed instrument again."

"I do not doubt that you are right," Ch'eng I said, "but I disagree that it is of no consequence. You see—"

But at that moment Bo-Tze and the Patriarch exited the temple and intruded on the brothers' conversation.

"So that is how the murder was accomplished," the Patriarch said, clapping a hand to the small of Ch'eng I's back.

"Wu used Kung's own machine against him when he thought Kung might expose him," Bo-Tze said, his voice once again thick with disdain. "In a thief's camp, no man sleeps with both eyes closed. Kung should have known Wu would silence him if it ever proved necessary."

"How and why the murder was committed," Ch'eng Hao agreed. "You now have your answers. And we must give full credit to Ch'eng I for the greater part of this investigation—his methods proved most fruitful."

"Esteemed brother," Ch'eng I said, holding up his hand for silence, "I do not deserve your praise, or indeed any man's, if I allow the investigation to end here."

"What do you mean?" the Patriarch said. "We have seen proof—or do you, of all people, think that this was not the murder weapon?" He gestured toward the distant tripod.

"It was the murder weapon," Ch'eng I agreed.

"And did you not find the weapon, together with other incriminating evidence, in the hut of Wu Han-Fei?" Bo-Tze added.

"I did," Ch'eng I said.

Even Ch'eng Hao was confused. "And did you not put Wu Han-Fei in restraints? Surely you would not have done that unless you were as convinced as we are that he is the murderer."

"I did and I am," Ch'eng I said, "but that is only the beginning of an answer to what went on here this morning. You wrongly indict a man if you credit him with motives he did not hold."

Ch'eng Hao put a hand on Ch'eng I's shoulder. "Brother, I bow to your expertise in matters scientific, but do me the courtesy of acknowledging my insight into human character. It has to be as I explained it to you.

"Kung distributed his creations as widely as he could out of sheer good will. Lin-Yu testifies to this. Wu Han-Fei, on the other hand, had a more concrete motive for getting involved with Kung: he sold Kung's inventions for personal profit." The word 'profit' always wore a sneer the way Ch'eng Hao said it, and this time was no exception.

"Recently," Ch'eng Hao continued, "Kung dreamt up the extraordinary weapon you just demonstrated. In his initial enthusiasm he gave a working model to Wu. But Kung was a compassionate man, dedicated to the easing of life's sufferings—consider his other inventions: implements to improve farming, Lin-Yu's leg braces, and so forth. Now, for the first time, he had created a weapon. This horrible realization, combined with the fact that he had placed it in the hands of an unscrupulous man, preyed mightily on his conscience. This is why he went to the temple: to destroy the plans for this device. The murderer stole the plans from the scene of Kung's death—and are they not the very same half-burned plans you found in Wu Han-Fei's hut?

"There is nothing more to know about this murder."

"Nothing?" Ch'eng I directed this remark at all three men, but his next was reserved for his brother. "I am disappointed in you, Hao. If Wu Han-Fei planned Kung's murder, why did he send Bo-Tze to the temple to witness it? You might argue that Bo-Tze *forced* Wu Han-Fei to tell him where Kung was—but if this was the case, why didn't Wu delay the murder until a more propitious time? And how do you explain the change in the position of Kung's body after his death?"

Ch'eng Hao said nothing.

"There can be only one answer," Ch'eng I said. "Wu Han-Fei knew Bo-Tze wanted to expose Kung's dealings with him, so he lured Bo-Tze to the temple with a story about Kung's 'destroying evidence.' Then he hid in the forest, intending to use Kung's weapon to silence Bo-Tze." Bo-Tze drew a sharp breath. "Kung was not Wu Han-Fei's intended target. Bo-Tze was."

"I bow to your superior perception," Ch'eng Hao said, grasping Ch'eng I's reasoning. "So you would argue that Wu Han-Fei wanted to kill Bo-Tze—but that from a distance of forty paces, two men in brown robes looked too similar to tell apart and as a result he killed the wrong man."

"No," Ch'eng I said. "Trust your own eyes. Do you not see that Bo-Tze's robe is considerably more worn than Kung's and that his skin looks visibly older? You will recall that at least one man was not wearing his hood."

"Very likely neither man was," Ch'eng Hao said. "But one bald head looks much like another—"

Ch'eng I shook his head. "They look entirely different."

"But from a distance of forty paces—"

"Entirely different," Ch'eng I said firmly. "It is not only that Bo-Tze's head looked older—Kung's bore a highly visible mark. A prominent scar at the top of his neck. Am I correct?" This question was directed to the Patriarch.

"You are," the Patriarch said.

"A scar?" Ch'eng Hao asked.

"Not just any scar," Ch'eng I said, "a family brand. Clearly visible at forty paces, particularly if one is looking for it. As I believe Wu Han-Fei was. Consider this: suppose you were right that Wu-Han Fei could not tell the two men apart—do you think under those circumstances that he would have used the weapon?"

After a moment, Ch'eng Hao slowly shook his head. "Then how do you account for what happened?"

"The device was not perfected," Ch'eng I said gravely. "Wu Han-Fei knew which man he wanted to hit. *He simply missed.*"

They stood outside Wu Han-Fei's hut, Ch'eng I and Ch'eng Hao, Bo-Tze and the Seventh Patriarch. They stood outside because none of them wanted to enter.

"If what you have said is true," Bo-Tze said, "then we have been victims of an even greater deception than I feared."

"It cannot be," the Patriarch said.

"There is only one demonstration that will convince you," said Ch'eng I. He stepped into the hut.

The other men followed. Inside, Wu Han-Fei was in a seated position, his wrists and ankles bound behind him. The room was furnished better than the monks' cells: there were small windows with mullioned glass panes and swing shutters controlled from the inside; a mattress padded with layers of reed matting; and a stool whose top opened to reveal a bowl and a set of utensils. Ch'eng I pointed all this out while Wu Han-Fei watched in silence.

"This is the extent of Wu Han-Fei's personal profit," Ch'eng I said. "Things Kung created especially for him. If he did sell Kung's goods for money, he kept none of it. Perhaps it was all sent back to . . . his family."

Ch'eng I walked behind Wu Han-Fei and put his hand on the kneeling man's head. "A fine head of hair. He is not a Buddhist, so he can keep his hair—and can live here at a distance from the monks. A neat arrangement. When they need something from the outside world—such as men to investigate a murder—he brings it. Otherwise, he is left to himself.

"But why would a man who is not a Buddhist attach himself to a monastery in this way? It is the worst of lives, surely, caught with one leg in each of two worlds that despise one another. One must have a compelling reason to choose such a life. Why," Ch'eng I asked Wu Han-Fei, "did you?"

Wu Han-Fei said nothing.

"This was one of the questions that bothered me." Ch'eng I said. "Why would he live here? And: why would he kill to protect a monk? What was the worst the monks could do to him if his activities were exposed—send him away? Hardly a severe punishment for a man who has no ties to the monastic life anyway. No, the man they could punish was Kung—but why would a mercenary secularist care?

"A fine head of hair," Ch'eng I said again, running his fingers through Wu Han-Fei's black locks. "A lifetime of growth concealing a scalp that hasn't seen the sun in thirty years." He turned to Ch'eng Hao. "You know, when we first met Wu, I thought he lowered his eyes out of respect for us, or perhaps fear. But then I realized it was neither—it was for want of a beard."

He bent forward over Wu's shoulder. "Look up," he commanded.

Wu Han-Fei shot a sullen glance at the ceiling.

"No," Ch'eng I said, "turn your head up." Wu Han-Fei did not respond. "Your *head*, Mister Wu . . ." —Ch'eng I took a tight grip on the young man's hair and pulled his head back— ". . . or should I say Mister *Wang*?"

Bo-Tze stared at the character carved in white relief on the underside of Wu Han-Fei's chin. The Patriarch sat on the edge of the mattress and put his head in his hands. Ch'eng I released Wu Han-Fei's head. "What was Kung's real name," he asked, "his birth name?"

"Wang," the Patriarch said, nodding, his voice rumbling like the largest and saddest of gongs. "Wang Deng-Mo."

"Wang Deng-Mo," Ch'eng I repeated. "And this, we can assume, is *Wang*, not Wu, Han-Fei."

"I do not understand," the Patriarch said. "Why . . . ?"

"Why?" Ch'eng I said. "Because family is a more powerful bond than you give it credit for being. Kung took on a new identity when he joined your monastery—and so did his . . . brother?"

Wang Han-Fei let a single word escape through his clenched teeth. "Yes."

"His brother," Ch'eng I said. "As I thought. To maintain the family tie despite all else; to send resources back home, to help the rest of the family survive; to live and die and kill for a brother *because* he is a brother—*this* is 'why.'"

"But brother," Ch'eng Hao said, his face red with chagrin, "how could you possibly have known? What started you thinking in this direction?"

"The question that was at once the simplest and the most complex," Ch'eng I said. "Why had Kung's body been moved? Bo-Tze would not have done it, not when it would have meant returning to the scene of the murder. Lin-Yu might have done it but he would not have concealed it from us if he had. This meant it had to have been the murderer who had done it. But why would the murderer have moved Kung's body? I asked myself this question again and again.

"Then all at once I understood. Kung's body had not merely been moved. You will recall that Bo-Tze said Kung's blood spurted all over his face when he was hit—yet when we found the body, Kung's face was clean; his hood was neatly arranged; and he was lying on his back in a dignified position. It is no way for a man to be found, lying face down in his own blood—but that a killer recognizes this is most unusual. That is how I knew that the killer had compassion for his victim. More than compassion, even—love, and more than love, a sense of duty."

Ch'eng Hao had more questions to ask, and he asked them; Ch'eng I answered them in more detail than was absolutely necessary; Bo-Tze and the Patriarch left as quickly as they could; and no one noticed when off in his corner, his head hung low, Wang Han-Fei began to weep.

* * *

Ch'eng Hao sipped from a cup of bone-stock soup that Ch'eng I had prepared. Was that the faint flavor of tea he tasted, whispering under the rich marrow? Perhaps it was. Ch'eng Hao knew his brother was wont to experiment in the oddest directions. He set the cup down. "I would not have released him," he said.

Ch'eng I paused at the fire then went on stirring. "Why, brother? Because he was a killer and killers should not go unpunished?"

"No," Ch'eng Hao said. "He killed his brother. That was punishment enough for both of them."

"Why, then?"

"Because you should have known he would kill himself."

Ch'eng I tipped the stock pot forward to fill his cup. The thick soup steamed and he held his hands in the steam to warm them. "Forcing him to live would have been the most cruel of punishments. He could not have escaped the voice of censure no matter where he fled under heaven. A man's greatest freedom," Ch'eng I said, "is the freedom to hoard or spend his life as he chooses."

Ch'eng Hao could not disagree. "The tragedy of it is that a man such as Kung had to lie to live as he chose, that his brother had to lie to be near him, and that these lies accumulated until a killing became inevitable. A pointless killing . . ." He turned to other thoughts, less troubling for being more abstract. "I still do not understand, brother, how you knew to investigate Wu—Wang—in the first place. Even granting that you suspected that the killer was a family member—why him?"

"You were investigating the monks and making no progress," Ch'eng I said. "I trusted that had there been progress to be made, you would have made it. So I operated on the assumption that you were looking in the wrong direction entirely. As you were."

"But my approach was the logical one—"

"Yes, it was," Ch'eng I said, "but not the correct one. Therein lies one of life's great mysteries."

Ch'eng Hao bent once more to his soup. November winds were beginning to roar on the plains and the small warmth was welcome. The chill in his soul was not to be so easily dispelled. "I," he said, "If it came to that, would you kill to defend me?"

Ch'eng I looked up from his task. "I am your brother," he said. He brought the cup to his lips. "Heaven grant me good aim."

The Trailor Murder Mystery

ABRAHAM LINCOLN

One of the most important discoveries made by Howard Haycraft in his history of the detective story, MURDER FOR PLEASURE, *is the fact that Abraham Lincoln was "the first of the countless eminent men who have turned to the detective story for stimulation and solace." Lincoln was "pleased with the absolute and logical method of Poe's tales and sketches, in which the problem of mystery is given, and wrought out into everyday facts by processes of cunning analysis." It was said, on unimpeachable authority, that Lincoln permitted no year to pass without rereading Poe's tales of ratiocination.*

But while it is now established that Abraham Lincoln was a detective-story fan, it is not so well-known that he also wrote at least one mystery story, in which Lincoln himself was the detective. Biographers of Lincoln have mentioned the story without, of course, actually characterizing Abraham Lincoln as a detective. Ward H. Lamon for example, wrote in his LIFE OF LINCOLN: *"In the summer of 1841, Mr. Lincoln was engaged in a curious case. The circumstances impressed him very deeply with the insufficiency and danger of 'circumstantial evidence,' so much so, that he not only wrote the account of it to Speed, but another more extended one, which was printed in a newspaper published at Quincy, Ill. His mind was full of it; he could think of nothing else."*

But it was left for Roger W. Barrett, of Chicago, to dig into musty old newspaper files and find the actual story written by Abraham Lincoln. It is the tale of four men who went out for a walk in the spring of 1841—and only three came back. Five years later Abraham Lincoln wrote the story of this mysterious disappearance and of the murder trial that followed. Lincoln was no mere spectator of the events; he did not get his facts at secondhand. As Mr. Barrett described it: on the arrest of the three men who came back, "a lanky young lawyer of the town stretched his long legs under a wooden table at the Butler boarding house, snuffed his tallow candle, whittled his turkey quill to a clean pen point," and with Logan, his law partner at that time, Lincoln became the defense attorney and in the course

312

of the trial became the legal detective who might be said to have paved the way for Mr. Tutt and Perry Mason.

Abraham Lincoln's story of "The Trailor Murder Mystery" was published in the Quincy, Illinois "Whig" of April 15, 1846—five years, almost to the day, after the magazine appearance of the world's first detective story, "The Murders in the Rue Morgue," by Edgar A. Poe; three years after the first book appearance of THE MURDERS IN THE RUE MORGUE; *and only one year after the publication of Poe's* TALES. *So Abraham Lincoln, one of our greatest presidents and one of the truly great men in the history of the world, was also one of the our earliest detective writers!*

In the year 1841, there resided, at different points in the State of Illinois, three brothers by the name of Trailor. Their Christian names were William, Henry and Archibald. Archibald resided at Springfield, then as now the seat of Government of the State. He was a sober, retiring, and industrious man, of about thirty years of age; a carpenter by trade, and a bachelor, boarding with his partner in business—a Mr. Myers. Henry, a year or two older, was a man of like retiring and industrious habits; had a family, and resided with it on a farm, at Clary's Grove, about twenty miles distant from Springfield in a north-westerly direction.—William, still older, and with similar habits, resided on a farm in Warren county, distant from Springfield something more than a hundred miles in the same North-westerly direction. He was a widower, with several children.

In the neighborhood of William's residence, there was, and had been for several years, a man by the name of Fisher, who was somewhat above the age of fifty; had no family, and no settled home; but who boarded and lodged a while here and a while there, with persons for whom he did little jobs of work. His habits were remarkably economical, so that an impression got about that he had accumulated a considerable amount of money.

In the latter part of May, in the year mentioned, William formed the purpose of visiting his brothers at Clary's Grove and Springfield; and Fisher, at the time having his temporary residence at his house, resolved to accompany him. They set out together in a buggy with a single horse. On Sunday evening they reached Henry's residence, and stayed over night. On Monday morning, being the first Monday of June, they started on to Springfield, Henry accompanying them on horseback. They reached town about noon, met Archibald, went with him to his boarding house, and there took up their lodgings for the time they should remain.

After dinner, the three Trailors and Fisher left the boarding house in company, for the avowed purpose of spending the evening together in looking about the town. At supper, the Trailors had all returned, but Fisher was missing, and some inquiry was made about him. After supper, the Trailors went out professedly in search of him. One by one they returned, the last coming in after late tea time, and each stating that he had been unable to discover anything of Fisher.

The next day, both before and after breakfast, they went professedly in search again, and returned at noon, still unsuccessful. Dinner again being had, William and Henry expressed a determination to give up the search, and start for their homes. This was remonstrated against by some of the boarders about the house, on the ground that Fisher was somewhere in the vicinity, and would be left without any conveyance, as he and William had come in the same buggy. The remonstrance was disregarded, and they departed for their homes respectively.

Up to this time, the knowledge of Fisher's mysterious disappearance had spread very little beyond the few boarders at Myers', and excited no considerable interest. After the lapse of three or four days, Henry returned to Springfield, for the ostensible purpose of making further search for Fisher. Procuring some of the boarders, he, together with them and Archibald, spent another day in ineffectual search, when it was again abandoned, and he returned home.

No general interest was yet excited.

On the Friday a week after Fisher's disappearance, the Postmaster at Springfield received a letter from the Postmaster nearest William's residence, in Warren county, stating that William had returned home without Fisher, and was saying, rather boastfully that Fisher was dead, and had willed him his money, and that he had got about fifteen hundred dollars by it. The letter further stated that William's story and conduct seemed strange, and desired the Postmaster at Springfield to ascertain and write what was the truth in the matter.

The Postmaster at Springfield made the letter public, and at once, excitement became universal and intense. Springfield, at that time, had a population of about 3,500, with a city organization. The Attorney General of the State resided there. A purpose was forthwith formed to ferret out the mystery, in putting which into execution, the Mayor of the city and the Attorney General took the lead. To make search for, and, if possible, find the body of the man supposed to be murdered, was resolved on as the first step.

In pursuance of this, men were formed into large parties, and marched abreast, in all directions, so as to let no inch of ground in the vicinity remain unsearched. Examinations were made of cellars, wells, and pits of all descriptions, where it was thought possible the body might be concealed. All the fresh, or tolerably fresh graves in the graveyard, were pried into, and dead horses and dead dogs were disintered, where, in some instances, they had been buried by their partial masters.

This search, as has appeared, commenced on Friday. It continued until Saturday afternoon without success, when it was determined to despatch officers to arrest William and Henry, at their residences, respectively. The officers started on Sunday morning, meanwhile, the search for the body was continued, and rumors got afloat of the Trailors having passed, at different times and places, several gold pieces, which were readily supposed to have belonged to Fisher.

On Monday, the officers sent for Henry, having arrested him, arrived with him. The Mayor and Attorney Gen'l took charge of him, and set their wits to work to elicit a discovery from him. He denied, and denied, and persisted in denying. They still plied him in every conceivable way, till Wednesday, when, protesting his own innocence, he stated that his brothers, William and Archibald, had murdered Fisher; that they had killed him, without his (Henry's) knowledge at the time, and made a temporary concealment of his body; that, immediately preceding his and William's departure from Springfield for home, on Tuesday, the day after Fisher's disappearance, William and Archibald communicated the fact to him, and engaged his assistance in making a permanent concealment of the body; that, at the time he and William left professedly for home, they did not take the road directly, but, meandering their way through the streets, entered the woods at the North West of the city, two or three hundred yards to the right of where the road they should have travelled, entered them; that, penetrating the woods some few hundred yards, they halted and Archibald came a somewhat different route, on foot, and joined them; that William and Archibald then stationed him (Henry) on an old and disused road that ran near by, as a sentinel, to give warning of the approach of any intruder; that William and Archibald then removed the buggy to the edge of a dense brush thicket, about forty yards distant from his (Henry's) position, where, leaving the buggy, they entered the thicket, and in a few minutes returned with the body, and placed it in the buggy; that from his station he could and did distinctly see that the object placed in the buggy was a dead man, of the general appearance and size of Fisher; that William and Archibald then moved off with the buggy in the direction of Hickox's mill pond, and after an absence of half an hour, returned, saying they had put him in a safe place; that Archibald then left for town, and he and William found their way to the road, and made for their homes.

At this disclosure, all lingering credulity was broken down, and excitement rose to an almost inconceivable height. Up to this time, the well-known character of Archibald had repelled and put down all suspicions as to him. Till then, those who were ready to swear that a murder had been committed, were almost as confident that Archibald had had no part in it. But now, he was seized and thrown into jail; and indeed, his personal security rendered it by no means objectionable to him.

And now came the search for the brush thicket, and the search of the mill pond. The thicket was found, and the buggy tracks at the point indicated. At a point within the thicket, the signs of a struggle were discovered, and a trail from thence to the buggy track was traced. In attempting to follow the track of the buggy from the thicket, it was found to proceed in the direction of the mill pond, but could not be traced all the way. At the pond, however, it was found that a buggy had been backed down to, and partially into the water's edge.

Search was now to be made in the pond; and it was made in every imaginable way. Hundreds and hundreds were engaged in raking, fishing, and draining. After much fruitless effort in this way, on Thursday morning the mill dam was cut down, and the water of the pond partially drawn off, and the same processes of search again gone through with.

About noon of this day, the officer sent for William, returned having him in custody; and a man calling himself Dr. Gilmore, came in company with them. It seems that the officer arrested William at his own house, early in the day on Tuesday, and started to Springfield with him; that after dark awhile, they reached Lewiston, in Fulton county, where they stopped for the night; that late in the night this Dr. Gilmore arrived, stating that Fisher was alive at his house, and that he had followed on to give the information, so that William might be released without further trouble; that the officer, distrusting Dr. Gilmore, refused to release William, but brought him on to Springfield, and the Dr. accompanied them.

On reaching Springfield, the Dr. re-asserted that Fisher was alive, and at his house. At this, the multitude for a time, were utterly confounded. Gilmore's story was communicated to Henry Trailor, who without faltering, reaffirmed his own story about Fisher's murder. Henry's adherence to his own story was communicated to the crowd, and at once the idea started, and became nearly, if not quite universal, that Gilmore was a confederate of the Trailors, and had invented the tale he was telling, to secure their release and escape.

Excitement was again at its zenith.

About three o'clock the same evening, Myers, Archibald's partner, started with a two-horse carriage, for the purpose of ascertaining whether Fisher was alive, as stated by Gilmore, and if so, of bringing him back to Springfield with him.

On Friday a legal examination was gone into before two Justices, on the charge of murder against William and Archibald. Henry was introduced as a witness by the prosecution, and on oath re-affirmed his statements, as heretofore detailed, and at the end of which he bore a thorough and rigid cross-examination without faltering or expo-sure. The prosecution also proved, by a respectable lady, that on Monday evening of Fisher's disappearance, she saw Archibald, whom she well knew, and another man whom she did not then know, but whom she believed at the time of testifying to be William, (then present,) and still another, answering the description of Fisher, all enter the timber at the North West of town, (the point indicated by Henry,) and after one or two hours, saw William and Archibald return without Fisher.

Several other witnesses testified, that on Tuesday, at the time William and Henry professedly gave up the search for Fisher's body, and started for home, they did not take the road directly, but did go into the woods, as stated by Henry. By others, also, it was proved, that since Fisher's disappearance, William and Archibald had passed rather an unusual number of gold pieces. The statements heretofore made about the thicket, the signs of a struggle, the buggy tracks, &c., were fully proven by numerous witnesses.

At this the prosecution rested.

Dr. Gilmore was then introduced by the defendants. He stated that he resided in Warren county, about seven miles distant from William's residence; that on the morning of William's arrest, he was out from home, and heard of the arrest, and of its being on a charge of the murder of Fisher; that on returning to his own house, he found Fisher there; that Fisher was in very feeble health, and could give no rational account as to where he had been during his absence; that he (Gilmore) then started in pursuit of the officer, as before stated; and that he should have taken Fisher with him, only that the state of his health did not permit. Gilmore also stated that he had known Fisher for several years, and that he had understood he was subject to temporary derangement of mind, owing to an injury about his head received early in his life.

There was about Dr. Gilmore so much of the air and manner of truth, that his statement prevailed in the minds of the audience and of the court, and the Trailors were discharged, although they attempted no explanation of the circumstances proven by the other witnesses.

On the next Monday, Myers arrived in Springfield, bringing with him the now famed Fisher, in full life and proper person.

Thus ended this strange affair and while it is readily conceived that a writer of novels could bring a story to a more perfect climax, it may well be doubted whether a stranger affair ever really occurred. Much of the matter remains in mystery to this day. The going into the woods with Fisher, and returning without him, by the Trailors; their going into the woods at the same place the next day, after they professed to have given up the search; the signs of a struggle in the thicket, the buggy tracks at the edge of it; and the location of the thicket, and the signs about it, corresponding precisely with Henry's story, are circumstances that have never been explained. William and Archibald have both died since—William in less than a year, and Archibald in about two years after the supposed murder. Henry is still living, but never speaks of the subject.

It is not the object of the writer of this to enter into the many curious speculations that might be indulged upon the facts of this narrative; yet he can scarcely forbear a remark upon what would, almost certainly, have been the fate of William and Archibald, had

Fisher not been found alive. It seems he had wandered away in mental derangement, and, had he died in this condition, and his body been found in the vicinity, it is difficult to conceive what could have saved the Trailors from the consequence of having murdered him. Or, if he had died, and his body never found, the case against them would have been quite as bad, for, although it is a principle of law that a conviction for murder shall not be had, unless the body of the deceased be discovered, it is to be remembered, that Henry testified that he saw Fisher's dead body.

The Importance of Trifles

AVRAM DAVIDSON

Jacob Hays, High Constable of the City of New-York, had eaten his usual breakfast of fried eggs and beefsteak, broiled fish (shad, this time), a heap of pan-cakes, a pair of chickens' wings, hot buttered rolls and tea. More and more people were drinking coffee, as the nineteenth Century rolled into its fourth decade, but Jacob Hays still imbibed hyson rather than java.

"Promise me, Mr. Hays," his wife demanded, as he rose to leave, "that if it commences rain you'll take the Broad-way caravan."

"Mrs. Hays, good morning," said her husband briefly. And walked out of the house with brisk strides.

The day was dark, but it would be darker than it had ever been before he would spend eight cents to ride a mile. Many a mickle makes a muckle, his mother used to say; and his father's advice had been: Take care of the pennies and the pounds will take care of you. Besides, did it befit the holder of his office to cram into a crowded caravan like a commission-merchant or a law-clerk? Would the people not think he was doddering if they saw him in an omnibus? He, who patrolled the city afoot by day and by night? Just so.

Presumably, it had been a quiet night, for no message had come to pull him out from his featherbed. No riots or major fires—a mercy.

It had been twenty-six years since old Governor De Witt Clinton, then Mayor of New-York, had appointed him High Constable, and in all that time the City had never ceased to grow—nor had crime ever ceased to keep pace with commerce and culture. Jacob Hays had come to relish quiet nights, though scarcely even one of these passed in which he did not awaken, straining his ears for some sound—near or far—betokening a conflagration in South-street or a murderous "hooley" in the Five-Points. And yet there were citizens who still expected him to undertake the functions of a hog-warden!

The very thought of it made him snort. He looked around challengingly—then smiled. There was no trouble in the Broad-way at this time of morning, or, indeed, at any other time of day. The wide, clean street, lined with fashionable hotels and shops and busy office buildings, stretched along for almost three miles, the wonder of the country—proud New-Yorkers said, of the world. And all along it,

320

from the Battery to Twentieth-street, looked upon from wooden shacks and towering five-storey brick buildings alike, a press of carts, drays, wagons, carriages, cabs, and omnibuses filled the eighty-foot width of the road with a ceaseless rumbling.

"Good-morning, High Constable," said a dry-goods merchant, setting out open boxes of new percales and nankeens for passers-by to examine at pleasure. "Good-morning, Mr. Hays," said an admiralty-lawyer, on his way to visit the forest of masts along the lower East-River. "Good-morning, Jacob," said old Alderman Ter Williger.

And two young bloods, of the sort which had begun to infest the Bowery-road, hats cocked as sharply over carefully-soaped locks of hair as gravity would allow, nudged one the other sharply, and hissed, "Old Hays!"

Their expression, as they met his cold, knowledgeable eye, changed from one of studied insolence to a mixture of uneasiness and would-be defiance. He gave his high-constabular staff, which he always carried with him, a slight shake in their direction, and they lowered their gaze and slunk by. No, they were just strutting, and would make no trouble in the Broad-way.

The unpaven, narrow, pig-ridden and stinking side-streets of the lower city, ill-lit and under-patrolled (but try to obtain additional money for more constables from the Board of Aldermen!)—these were the places they would choose for crime. And it was in the Bowery, with its popular theatres and pleasure gardens, that they would seek their amusement: jostling citizens, insulting ladies, and causing commotions in general.

Once in his office Hays ignored the view of the City Hall Park, and dealt rapidly with that portion of the day's new business which responded to rapid treatment. Then he looked over his correspondence—runaway daughters and fugitive sons; complaints of bogus lotteries and similar frauds which seemed to go on forever—like "The Spanish Prisoner" swindle, the "English-Estate-in-Chancery-to-which-you-are-heir" swindle.

"Any new 'cards'?" he asked his assistant. There were—there always were. Bank robbery in Portland, green-goods merchant hastily departed from Philadelphia, murder in Albany, funds embezzled from London, cargo of rum stolen in Boston, shipment of cotton made off with in Georgia, eleven absconded apprentices, two fugitive slaves, piracy in the Gulph of Mexico.

"Post those with descriptions," he directed. "What's next?"

"Next" was a young Colored man whose bright red shirt, wide-bottomed trousers, and glazed hat—the last held respectfully in his hands—told Hays of the man's profession before he even looked at the paper held out to him.

WHEREAS, an ACT of the CONGRESS of the Year 1818, intitled *AN ACT TO DEFINE AND PROTECT THE STATUS OF SEAMEN* [Hays read], does not mention the Status of Seamen who are Persons of Color, and WHEREAS, the *Legislature* of the *STATE OF NEW-YORK* in the Year 1820 has authorized the Certification of Seamen domiciled or denizened in the State of New-York who are Free Persons of Color, now, THEREFORE, be it known that I, *Jefferson Van Der Wett, a Clerk of the CITY OF NEW-YORK*, do hereby certify that the bearer, *Lucas Oaks*, a Seaman of this City, and a Man of Color, is known to me on good evidence to be a FREE MAN, and I do further Enjoin all Men of whatsoever Cities, States, Territories, and Nations, to recognize him in such Status and not to Hold, Use, nor Dispose of him, the aforesaid *Lucas Oaks*, a FREE MAN of Color, as if he were not in Fact *FREE*.

"Anything against him?" Hays asked. The Constable shook his head. Hays dipped his quill, wrote *No Criminal Record. J. Hays. High Constable, C. of N-Y.*, scattered sand, and handed it to the Negro who departed with thanks.

And so the day proceeded. The Five-Points—that foul and teeming human rookery where Cross, Anthony, Littlewater, Orange, and Mulberry meet—had had its usual murder. The usual sailor had been found dead by violence. This time the almost nightly occurrence was not the same, though often enough it was a sailor found dead in the Five-Points; often in its black and filthy heart—the swarming, putrefying tenement called the Old Brewery.

There was little chance of discovering the killers at the moment, if ever. The night had witnessed their deeds, and as little as the night would testify, so little would the furtive inhabitants of the criminal world testify. Until and unless, of course, the cut-throats had a falling out. In which case there might be a dirty, illiterate note some morning on Hays's desk—a whisper in the ear of the Watch (as the Constabulary was also called)—notes and whispers which might lead to arrest or conviction. Or might not.

It sometimes seemed to Jacob Hays that the work-houses, paupers' wards, and felon-cells of all the world, European as well as American, were pouring their wretched contents into New-York; although he knew well enough that most of the ever-increasing stream of immigrants were good people. It would ill behoove him to rail against "foreigners," as some were doing. Had not his own mother been born abroad? And his father's parents? When you came down to it, whose stock *was* entirely "Native American"?—except for the Indians. And there were those who claimed (Hays recalled a recent sermon at Scotch Presbyterian Church) that the Indians themselves were none other than the Lost Tribes of Israel!

It was Hays's custom, if the affairs of the morning permitted, to take some light refreshment about ten o'clock, and then to read through all the newspapers. That is, not to read every word, but to have a look at the items marked for him by his assistant, Constable Moore, who had standing instructions to check off any bit of news referring to crime or the police. It was always amusing—sometimes instructive—to observe the way in which the same incident was treated in different newspapers, and to see how they agreed (or, more often, disagreed) with the official report of the same incident.

In the staid *Commercial Gazette* of this morning, for example, there was the single line: *The body of a man, as yet unidentified, was found yesterday in Dunstan-Slip.* That was all. *A man.* Not, Hays noted, *a gentleman.* In the lives or deaths of the lower orders of society the *Commercial Gazette* was supremely uninterested.

The *News-Letter* had this to say: *Yesterday afternoon the body of a man was discerned floating in the River at Dunstan-Slip by a woman of the neighborhood. The dead person, who, by his dress, was evidently a member of the sea-faring class, had not long been exposed to the briny element, and appeared to be in his middle years. It is opined that he came to his death by natural causes. His name has not yet been learned.*

The recently-established *True Citizen and Temperance Advocate,* however, had learned—or said it had learned—his name. *An intelligent and respectable female identified the remains to this journal as that of one Gorman or Gormby, a sailingman, much given to the prevalent vice of his class (though not only of his class) vide licet, imbibing large quantities of alcoholic liquors—we do not denominate them 'beverages'. Whilst in a condition of intoxication, the dead man, we adduce, fell into the Slip and drowned. Within four blocks of the fatal scene our reporter counted no less than thirty-nine dram-stores, grog-shops, gin-mills, brandy-houses, and so-called "grocery"*

*establishments, these last entirely devoted to purveying raw spirits to
the ignorant. When will a supine administration awaken to the menace, et cetera, et cetera.*

And the *Register* devoted a full column to what it called a
*dastardly crime, undoubtedly committed by a gang of crimps, bent
on conveying the innocent seaman against his will to the cruel mer-
cies of a conscienceless master-mariner bound for foreign ports
where the writ of the American Republic runs not. It was doubtless
owing to his reluctance to be forced into a berth he did not desire that
the unfortunate Jack-Tar resisted so vigorously that his kidnappers
decided on his Death. He was tossed into the brackish waters of
Dunstan-Slip where, being like the generality of sea-farers, unable to
swim, he expired by drowning.*

Old Hays snorted. "Catch any crimps tossing twenty dollars worth
of two-footed merchandise away! Those they don't dope, they bash—
but, one way or another, they get them aboard alive. Any wounds on
him, Neddy?"

"Few bruises, Mr. High—but no wounds," said Constable Edward
Moore. "Course he wasn't no Gorman nor Gormby, any more than
he was crimped." His tone of voice indicated that he realized he was
not telling his superior anything the latter didn't know.

Hays nodded, picked up the official constabulary report, mumbled
the words to himself, adding his own comments. "Bruises on breast,
abdomen, and face; also, back of neck. Couldn't have gotten them all
by falling down: been fighting. Clothes worn and dirty—been on
shore a long time. Not known to the Watch or any of our waterfront
friends—didn't ship out of the port of New-York. Shoes show signs
of recent hard use—walked from his last port."

"Wasn't killed for his fortune, we may be sure," said Moore.

"The Coroner's inquisition?"

"Dead before he hit the water, seems like. Neck broke. Lungs dry.
Hardly swollen, scarcely a mark on him from fish or crabs." Hays
thought about his breakfast shad, but he had a strong stomach
(twenty-six years as High Constable) and didn't think about it long.
"He was found in mid-afternoon, and conjecture is that he'd been dead
since the night before. Woman emptying a slop-bucket spied him."

The two men mused on this unusual fastidiousness in a district
where slops were emptied, usually, out the nearest window. Then
Moore continued: "Noteworthy features? Had a great swelling of the
left ear-lobe. Forget what you call it. Key-something."

But Hays remembered. "A keloid. Scarred over and swelled when he had it pierced for an earring, I expect. Sometimes happens so. We'd know he was a sailor from that alone. Potter's Field?" Constable Moore nodded.

Hays started to put the report down, then sensed, rather than saw, that his assistant had something else to tell him; and waited.

"He had this in his mouth." The Constable held out a screw of paper, unwrapped it. Inside lay a piece of fibre, yellowish-brown in color. "Cotton—raw cotton. A trifle, but I thought I'd save it for you. What do you think?"

Hays shook his head. "No idea. But glad you kept it. File it with the report. What's next?"

"Lady robbed of a diamond heirloom ring wants to see you about it, personal. Englishman with letter of introduction from Lord Mayor of London. Three candidates for the Watch. Man from Eagle Hotel with information about the gang of baggage-thieves. A—"

The High Constable raised his hand. "That'll do for the while. Lady first." . . .

Two nights later there was a wild fight involving the crews of three ships moored in South-street. The Night Constable-in-charge was new to the post and, not trusting to his own ability to discriminate between riots major and minor, sent for Hays. He came quickly enough, though the brawl was over by then; most of the men had either stumbled aboard their vessels or staggered away for further entertainment. The few who insisted upon continuing the affair had been hauled off to the Watch-house to meditate on their sins. And several of the spectators vanished the instant they saw the High Constable's well-known figure come in sight.

But by that time something else had developed.

"Hold up your lanterns," Hays directed his men. "The gas-light from the street is so dim I—that's better. Ah, me. More sailors must die ashore than at sea, I think."

The alley was wide enough to accommodate only two men, and one of these was dead. Hays patted the pockets of the pea-coat, was rewarded with a jingle, and thrust a hand inside. "Thirty cents."

For thirty cents a man could eat well and drink himself into a stupor and still have enough left for a night's lodging if he was sober enough to want more than the floor of the city to sleep on. Men were killed for much less than thirty cents. Therefore—

Word had gotten around, and a knot of night-crawlers, still excited from the fight, crowded into the alley, pressing and craning for a glimpse. Hays rose and looked at them; at once several caps were pulled low and faces sunk into collars. He held out his staff. "Clear the alley, citizens. Just so. Constables, take the body out. Has a cart been summoned? Lay him down here. No, don't cover his face. I want him identified, if possible."

It proved easily possible. The dead man was identified before his coat touched the sidewalk. "Tim Scott. Everyone knew Tim Scott. Poor Tim. Poor Tim's a-cold." (This last from a gentleman later identified as a play-actor at the Park Theatre.) "Spent his money like a gentleman. Who saw him last alive? Well . . ." A reluctance to be identified in this capacity was at once apparent.

But other information continued to come forth. "Not so long ago Tim bought wine for everyone at Niblo's Gardens. And segars. Yes, segars, too, for all the gentlemen. Did this more than once a night, and for more than a few nights, too . . . Enemies? Not a one in the world."

"I suppose his friends killed him, then?" Silence again. Cart-wheels rattled, and the crowd, gathered from all the dram-cellars whose yellow lights beckoned dimly through dirty window-panes, parted. As the body was lifted into the cart Hays removed his hat, and—one by one—reluctance evidently springing not so much from contumacy as from ignorance that this little gesture was customary or expected—one by one the greasy hats and dirty caps came off. Then the cart clattered away again. The crowd, still eager for excitement, stirred restlessly.

"All good citizens," said Hays, "will now go home." He did not expect the suggestion to be taken literally. If "home" was a lumpy, dirty pallet on a filthy floor it naturally had no appeal to match that of a brandy-shop or an oyster-stall, where some of the "good citizens" were even now heading to satisfy newly-awakened or previously-ungratified appetites; even if "home" was the streets, the mud, filth, and dim lights were no deterrents—there was nothing better at home. In the streets there were at least company and excitement. But the crowd dissolved, and this was all Hays had hoped for.

The next day Hays paid a further visit to Tim Scott, now naked on scrubbed pine-boards. Constables Breakstone and Onderdonk accompanied him. Both young Watch-officers had taken to heart Hays's almost constant insistence on the importance of "trifles", which was more than could be said for most of the Watch, to whom a crime was insoluable if not accompanied by a knife with the knifer's name burned in the hilt.

"How much would it take to treat the house at Niblo's to wine and segars several times a night, several nights running?" Hays asked, looking at the dead man's face. The death pallor could not dispel entirely the tokens of sun and wind.

"More than a sailingman would be likely to make on a coasting voyage," Constable Breakstone said. He was the son of a ship-chandler, had grown up along the water-front, and knew its ways. At Hays's look of inquiry he continued, "Tim had said his last trip was on a coaster, but he didn't say where to. Besides, he hadn't been gone long enough for an overseas voyage. But that money in his pocket, sir, it wasn't the last of what he'd had."

"You mean there's more somewheres?"

"No, sir. I mean that he'd spent it all some time ago. He'd been cadging off the lads since then. Then the other day he said he was going to get some more. He turned up at Barney Boots's gin-parlor last night with a dollar, and the thirty cents was the last of that. And he was heard to say that this was just the beginning—that he was going to get more very soon. I asked did he have a particular friend, and it seems he did—Billy Walters. Some think they'd sailed together on this last trip. But no one has seen Billy lately. And that's all I know, sir."

Hays nodded. "That's a good bit to go on. Meanwhile—" He lowered the sheet. "Just so. I thought these would show up better today." On the dead man's muscular throat were two sets of small and ugly marks. "Strangled, you see. And strangled from behind, too. Either someone crept up on him unbeknownst, or he knew the man behind him and wasn't expecting violence. Mr. Breakstone, hold the body up. Now you, Mr. Onderdonk, stand behind him. Let's have your hands. Big ones, a wide spread—just like these. Let your fingers rest where I place them."

One by one he placed the young man's fingers so that each rested on one of the finger marks, or as near to it as possible. Leaving them so, he peered at the skin of the dead man's back. "Just so. Jabbed up his knee, used it as a lever, grabbed the throat, and squeezed. Tim Scott was a strong man. This fellow was stronger. Had finicking ways, though. All right, let him down."

Breakstone covered the face. "'Finicking ways', Mr. High?"

"Yes," said Hays thoughtfully. "Let the little finger of his left hand stick out whilst he was doing his evil work. Like he was drinking a dish of tea. Mr. Breakstone—"

"Sir?"

"You might see that the word is passed among those who enjoyed the late Tim Scott's hospitality at Niblo's—and those who enjoyed his business anywhere else, like Barney Boots, for instance—that it would be the mark of a good citizen and good Christian to contribute for funeral expenses."

"I'll do that."

"Let it be known," said Jacob Hays reflectively, "that I particularly favor such contributions. Yes. Just so."

Crime never sleeps, but it is no coincidence that in warmer weather it is more restless than commonly. As the shad run dropped off and Spring, on its way into Summer, continued to crowd the trees with green, the residents of those districts in which few trees grew seemed more and more to fall into those lawless ways from which they had taken a partial vacation during the Winter months. Which often proved unfortunate for visitors to those districts. Mrs. Jacob Hays, however, was unsympathetic.

"Do not tell me, Mr. Hays," she said, "that you intend to spend the greater part of yet another night on patrol." Her husband, as if obedience itself, did not tell her that, nor anything else—but addressed himself to his supper. "I cannot believe," she continued presently, "that these people who get themselves into trouble are truly innocent of improper intention. What is a respectable person *doing* in the Five-Points? Tell me *that*, if you please, Mr. Hays."

Evidently he did not please, for he said, "Mrs. Hays, good-evening," rose, and departed. He had doubled the patrol in the Five-Points these nights, and that meant taking men away from other places. Wall-street and South-street would howl; well, let them. Or, rather, let them come out in favor of higher taxes to pay for the extra protection the city needed. Let them pave the streets, too, while they were at it; and put up more gas-lamps. Let them—

He stopped. There was some one very near at hand, some one who did not wish to be seen, some one in the pool of darkness which was the space between two buildings at his left. "I know you are there," said Jacob Hays.

And from the darkness a low voice said, "There is a body in the Old Brewery."

"There usually is. What floor?"

"Second."

"Just so. What else?" But there was nothing else. His ears had heard no sound of departure, but he knew that whoever it was had gone. And he walked faster.

On Anthony-street he found Constables Breakstone and Onderdonk, gestured them with his staff to follow him. As he approached the looming hulk of the Old Brewery, the neighborhood was in its usual uproar—screams, shouts, obscenities, drunken songs, the raucous cries which would go on almost till dawn, and then begin again almost at once. Then—from somewhere—not in a shout or scream, not in any tone of hate, but with a sharp note of warning—"Old Hays!"—and silence fell.

That is, comparative silence: quiet enough to hear his own and his men's feet on the muddy sidewalk and then, as they entered the building, on the rotten wood of the floor, or, rather, on the accumulated filth of years which lay inches thick over the rotten wood except where the flooring had given way and left ugly, dangerous holes.

"Turn up your lamps," he directed. It was small enough light they gave at best, though enough to keep them from breaking a leg. It was a wonder that the tiny lamps burned at all in here, the air was so foul. There was no railing on the sloping stairs, but still the three men gave the walls a wide enough berth, alive and rippling with vermin as they were.

And all the time there was a murmuring, a muttering, a whispering, a hissing from the darkness. Doors were ajar and dim lights shone and bodies slunk past, but no faces were seen. Rat's claws scrabbled. The stench grew more fearful, more noisome. Doors closed softly as they approached, opened after they passed. But the door at the end of the first corridor did not move, and behind it Hays found what he had come for.

The dead man was sprawled in a chair at the table, head backwards and upwards. A bottle had been spilled recently—the sharp odor of "brandy" (as the raw, white whiskey was called) filled the room and the liquor itself was still damp; but of the bottle there was no trace. Gift horses were seldom looked long in the mouth at the Old Brewery. The dead man's face was bruised, and blood welled from his nose and from a cut over one eye, an eye which stared in fierce amazement at the shadowy ceiling.

In his ribs on the left side a knife had been driven. It was still there.

They examined the floor carefully, but nothing was there except blood and dirt. In one corner was a foul-looking bed whose greasy rags yielded nothing. A cracked water-jug. An empty ditty-bag. And that was all.

As Hays ended his scrutiny of the room he saw that young Breakstone was intently looking at the dead man's face. The Constable caught his eye, and nodded. "I've seen him before, sir. He came into my father's place a few times, on and off, when his ships were in port, to sell his adventures. But I can't put my mind on his name or his ships! Maybe they will come to me, by and by."

"Any big adventures?"

Breakstone shook his head. "I don't think so. A chest of tea. A few sacks of coffee or wool. A barrel of sugar or molasses. That sort of thing. Once, I think, he had a bale of cotton—that was the biggest."

"Ah, well. Let me hold the lanterns while you get a grip on him. I'll go ahead and light your way. Mind your—" He stopped and bent over just as they passed through the door. Something was on the floor. He picked it up, stuffed it in his pocket, and straightened. "Mind your step. Careful, now."

Slowly and gingerly they made their way down the corridor, down the stairs, and out to the street. And all the while, moved by invisible hands, doors closed as they approached and opened after they passed, and all the while there was a murmuring, a muttering, a whispering, a hissing from the fetid darkness, and the scrabbling of rats in the walls.

Of course Hays found out nothing when, the body having been carted away, he returned to question the inhabitants—particularly those in rooms adjoining the one in which the dead man was found. No one had seen any thing, heard any thing; no one knew any thing, or suspected any thing. By the time he had finished, his head was reeling from the foul air, and the street seemed deliciously cool and fresh in comparison.

As Hays and his men left the Five-Points they heard the unexpected quiet broken by what seemed like a howl from hundreds of throats—a howl of defiance, execration, an utterly evil triumph.

Breakstone half-turned, but his superior's hand kept him steady. "The water-front is no sabbath-school," Breakstone said. "But it was never like that. At least you have the clean winds from the harbor, and the people give you a smile and a laugh and mostly folks try to keep themselves a bit decent in some ways, anyway. But those in the Old Brewery now—what makes them like that?"

They walked on in silence. Then Hays said, "I don't know, Mr. Breakstone. There's a whole green continent before them, wide-open under the sweet air of Heaven. But they choose to dwell in the dark and the mire. Why are they like that? As well ask the mole and the mudfish, I suppose."

It was past mid-night when he reached home. And next day there was no time for speculation on social philosophy. The baggage-gang had extended their depredations, and complaints of thefts poured in from the docks around Jay-street, where Hudson-River boats put in, and from the Battery, whence the ferries plied to Jersey, Staten-Island, Brooklyn, and from the great packet-ships in the Upper Harbor. From mere sneak-thieves the ring had advanced to a pretense of being regular baggage-porters and hotel-runners. A genuine rustic, parted from his old cow-hide trunk, was apt to set up an immediate clamor—in which case there was a chance, though a slim one, of its recovery. But a visitor from a small town, with just enough polish to desire not to be known for what he was, would delay out of embarrassment; in which case there was usually no hope for his luggage.

The problems of taking men from elsewhere to patrol the docks, of uncovering information about who was "fencing" (and where), in addition to routine duties of a sort which could neither be postponed nor delegated, kept Hays from seeing Constable Breakstone until late in the afternoon.

"Try as I would," the young man said, "I couldn't remember that sailor's name. So I looked up old Poppie Vanderclooster, who used to help Father in the shop at one time, and took him along to the dead-house. And he knew the face at once. Henry Roberts. They called him Roaring Roberts; he had a big, booming voice. I've asked around, and it seems he'd turned to the bad of late years. Some of the adventures he sold weren't his to sell. He had a lot of money not so long ago, and was throwing it around like a drunken sailor—which, of course, is just what he was. I guess he must have spent it all, or else what would he have been doing in that hole of the Old Brewery?"

The two of them were on their way back to the dead-house. Hays gave an exclamation, and began patting his pockets. "Ah, here it is," he said. "I found it just outside the door of the room, last night, there in the Five-Points. What do you make of it? Not the sort of thing generally worn in the Old Brewery, is it?"

"A gentleman's glove? No—and not the sort of thing Roaring Roberts would've worn, generally, either. Though he might, when he was spending all that money, have bought himself a pair."

"Just so. Well, we'll see."

White-haired old Whitby, the dead-house keeper, surveyed them reproachfully through red-rimmed eyes as they came over to Roberts' body. "You're late," he said. "The inquisition's been over for hours. We're about set to coffin him. Coroner's jury reached the verdict that Deceased had come to his death through haemorrhage caused by forcible entry of a knife, length of the blade four and one-half inches, between the fourth and fifth ribs, thus occasioning the severance of veins and arteries—"

"All right, Whit, we know that—hold up your left hand, Constable." The glove slipped on easily enough; if anything, it was a size too large. "It might be his," said Hays reflectively. "Then again, it might not have anything to do with the matter. I did find it outside the room."

As he slipped the glove off, something fell to the floor. Old Whitby bent down and picked it up.

"Flax? Wool?" he asked, rolling the fibre between his fingers.

"Give it here, Whit," Hays said shortly. At the door he stopped, handed the glove to Breakstone. "Check all the haberdashers," he said. "See what you can find."

Alderman Nicholas Ter Williger had his counting-house in the same building as his ware-house. Once, when business was smaller and Ter Williger (not yet an alderman) younger, he and his family had lived up stairs. But that old Knickerbocker fashion was going out of style nowadays. Besides, his children—and some of his grand-children—had their own establishments, and Mrs. Ter Williger was dead.

The clerks looked at Hays from their high stools with unabashed astonishment, but his cold gray eyes stared them back to their ledgers. He stalked through the count-house to the office in the back where, as expected, he found the proprietor.

"Hello, Jacob," said Ter Williger. "It's been too long. I meant to stop and say a few words the other morning, but you seemed preoccupied with deep thoughts. Mrs. Hays is well, I trust?"

"Quite well."

"Capital. Convey my respects. And now. I have a piece of nice, clean Saugerties ice here and I was about to compound a sherry-cobbler. I shall compound two."

"'Take a little wine for thy stomach's sake, and for thine often infirmities,' eh, Nick?"

The old gentleman cut lemons, broke off pieces of sugar-loaf. "Exactly. You may worship Scotch Presbyterian instead of Dutch Reformed, but you're a fellow-Calvinist and know that 'Man born of woman is born to sorrow as the sparks fly upwards,' and hence pre-destined to a multitude of 'often infirmities,' for some of which—my long years have taught me—sherry-cobbler is a sovereign remedy." He nodded, pounded ice.

The drink was cool and gratifying. It was quiet in the office, with its dark walls, from which engravings of President and Lady Washington looked down with stern benignancy. After a long moment Nicholas Ter Williger sighed. "I know you and your Caledonian conscience too well, Jacob," he said, "to believe it would allow you to pay a purely social call in the daytime. What aspect of rogue-catching brings you to the office of a respectable, if almost super-annuated, cotton-broker?"

"Cotton brings me here," said Hays. He produced two tiny paper packets, unfolded them, pushed them across the desk. At once Ter Williger's hooded eyes grew sharp. "Nankeen," he said instantly. Then he took up the pieces, pulled the fibres, compared them. "Same crop, too, I'd say. Good quality Nankeen . . . Where does it grow? Well, China, originally. Nankeen or Nanking, that's a city over there. But we grow it here in our own South nowadays, more than enough for our own uses. 'Slave cotton', they call it, too, sometimes."

Hays considered. Then, "What do you mean, 'slave cotton'? Isn't most cotton grown by slaves?"

Ter Williger nodded. "Yes, but—well, here's how it works, Jacob. Some of the plantations allow their people to grow a little cotton on their own, after quitting time in the big fields, and when this cotton is sold the people get to keep the money. They use it, oh, say, to buy some relish to add to their victuals—salt-fish, maybe, as a change from pork and corn-meal—or perhaps a piece of bright cloth for a shirt or a dress. Maybe some trumpery jewelry. Well, just to keep temptation out of their way, because, being property himself, the slave doesn't have much sense of property—here, let me show you."

From the shelf behind him Ter Williger took some sample lengths of fibre. "This is what we call Sea-Island. And this is Uplands. See how much different they are in color from Nankeen? How much lighter, whiter? No slave would be foolish enough to steal some of his master's cotton and try and mix it with his own yellow Nankeen. I don't deal in it myself. Jenkins does, but he's not here now."

Something stirred in Hays's mind. "I had a card not so long ago— large quantity of cotton stolen from Georgia, somewheres."

Ter Williger nodded rapidly. "Yes, I know about that. But that was Sea-Island, not Nankeen. Planter named Remington was holding back quite some bales, hoping for a rise in the market. St. Simon's-Island. Cotton was already balled and in a shed by the wharf. Came morning they found the Negro watchman dead and the bales gone. Sea-Island, you know, fetches top price. Not Nankeen, though." He took up his glass, but it was empty, and he set it down again, regretfully.

Hays rose. "Then Nankeen doesn't grow in any one particular locality?"

The older man pursed his mouth. Then he said, "I tell you what. Why not ask Jenkins? He'd be able to give you better answers . . . Who's he? Well, not exactly a partner. An associate. We have an understanding, and he uses my premises, too. An up-and-coming young man. Pushes a bit more than I care to. When you get old— matter of fact, Jacob, why don't you come along with me and talk to him? I'm going to his boarding-house now. A dicty place near Greenwich-Village."

Ter Williger reached for his hat, chuckled. "Matter of fact, I live there myself. Jeremiah Gale keeps it, with his wife. She orders the help around and he plays whist with the guests. A well-spread table, and a brightly-furnished house. Just the thing for old moss-backs like me—*and* for young couples like the Jenkinses. House property is high, and so are house-rents and servants' wages. Time enough for them to set up for themselves when they have a few children."

In a few minutes they were sitting in a cab and old Ter Williger rambled on about the fashion for boarding-house living, the prices of butcher's meat, game, fish, wine, clothing; and how much cheaper every thing had been twenty, thirty-five, and fifty years ago.

"Nicholas, I need more men," Hays said presently. "I can't even keep up with crime with my present force, let alone keep ahead of it. I need more men, and the Board of Aldermen has got to give me the money to pay for them."

The City had cooled off as late afternoon faded into early evening.

The cab rolled along between rows of neat brick houses, freshly-painted red, with trim white lines drawn to simulate mortar. Green-clad tree branches arched over the street. There was not a pig in sight. It was quite a change from the hustle of the Broad-way, or the squalor of the Five-Points.

Nicholas Ter Williger sighed. "What can *I* do, Jacob? I'm just an old Federalist who's hung on past his time, and they all know it down at City Hall. I shall not run again, and they all know that, too. It's a Tammany-man you should be talking to about this. Am I right?"

He tipped his hat to a passing lady, and Hays followed suit. "Yes," the High Constable agreed, "but if I talk to a Tammany-man about needing more men, he'll smile like a bucketful of chips, say he agrees with me completely, and knows just the men. Two of them will be his nephews, three of them will be his cousins, and the rest of them will be broken-down oystermen or some thing of that sort, unfit for any sort of work, but all from his ward, and all deserving Democrats. Damnation, Nick, I like to hire my own men! I—oh, are we here now? Just so."

Jeremiah Gale's establishment for paying guests was undistinguishable, with its scrubbed-white stoop and its bright green shutters, from any of the other houses in the row. A neatly-dressed Irish maid opened the door to them. Her manner was staid and respectful, but there was a look in her eye which convinced Hays that she would not always be content to take gentlemen's hats, to say, "Yes, sir," and "Yes, ma'm," to haul firewood, coal and hot water up three and four flights of stairs, and to toil fourteen hours a day for the $5 a month which was the most she could hope for. Servants did not stay servants long—at least, not in New York.

The house of Jeremiah Gale was richly, almost sumptuously furnished. Silken draperies, satin-upholstered furniture, mahogany, rosewood, marble, and gilt were everywhere. Jeremiah Gale himself came forward to greet them, a short and rosy gentleman of full habit, in claret-colored coat, pepper-and-salt trousers, and white silk stockings contrasting with the black sheen of his highly-polished shoes. There was a hum of conversation from inside, in which female voices predominated, and some one was playing on the pianoforte.

"Mr. Alderman Ter Williger!" One might have thought it had been last year instead of this morning that they had parted. "I trust I see you well, and not overly fatigued from the duties of the day?" A genteel bow, and then another genteel bow. "Mr. High Constable

Hays! Delighted to meet you again!" (To the best of Hays's recollection they had never met before.) "How very happy I am that Mr. Alderman Ter Williger has honored us by bringing you to dinner. You will do us the pleasure of taking dinner, sir? My cook has dressed a pair of turkey-hens with bread-sauce—"

But Hays pleaded his wife's discomfiture, were he to spoil the edge of his appetite for her supper by partaking of Mr. Gale's cook's pair of turkey-hens; and Mr. Gale was obliged to smile ruefully, and express a hope amounting to certainty that the High Constable would honor them on another occasion. Then he led them into the parlor.

The pianoforte had ceased, but the lady seated at it was talking busily to another, who had evidently been turning the music for her. She raked the new-comers with a swift glance, but kept on talking.

"Ah, *mais non, mais non!*" she exclaimed. "Two months in England and two weeks in France? *Incroyable! Au contraire*—that is to say, on the contrary; you must revise your plans and spend two months in France and only two weeks in England. Do you not agree with me, Mr. Jenkins?"

"Perfectly, my dear."

"If, indeed, it is absolutely necessary to visit England at all! The land of our fathers it may be, call it the Old Home, but—oh, my dear, so cold, so coarse! That fat old king and his ugly wife! And so unwelcoming to Americans, are they not, Mr. Jenkins?"

"Alas, my dear, we found it so."

"*Mais, ooh, la belle France*! There you have civilization—fashion—*ton*. We will give you the names of dear friends we visited, Mr. James Jenkins and I, two years ago—people of the finest quality, the most exquisite manners, the epitome of elegance, *mais oui;* and here I see dear Alderman Ter Williger with a distinguished-looking guest. Who can it be?"

And at this point the lady (presumably Mrs. Jenkins) arose from the pianoforte and took what Hays was absolutely certain was her first breath since she had begun speaking.

Mrs. Jenkins was as expensively dressed as it was morally possible for a lady to be, and quite handsome, too. Mr. James Jenkins was a larged-framed man with a red, smooth-shaven, and smiling face. Mrs. Van Dam (the unwise would-be spender of two months in England) was thin and sallow. Mr. Van Dam—a whale-oil commission-merchant—was thinner and sallower. Miss Cadwallader was a boney lady of a certain age and of overpoweringly aristocratic family. Mr. O'Donovan made it known at once that he was from *Northern* Ireland and a Protestant as well. Mr. Blessington was superintendent of an assurance agency and evidently had nothing to say when away from the premises of that essential if unromantic business. And Mrs. Bladen was a widow-woman with a lap-dog and two fat, unmarried daughters.

Such, with the addition of Alderman Ter Williger, were Mr. Jeremiah Gale's paying guests.

In the small sitting-room to which Mr. Gale showed them, Mr. Jenkins listened with the greatest good-nature to Hays's questions. "Nankeen grows over a wide area," he said, "and while there *are* people who'll insist—particularly down South—that they can tell from what location a given staple comes, even from which plantation or field, I must regard a claim to such close knowledge as rather— well, pretentious . . . Have I been in the South? Frequently."

The Alderman, who had been listening with some small signs of impatience for the dinner-bell, said now, "Mr. Jenkins made a trip South not long ago to buy Nankeen." The High Constable asked where it had been stored in New-York, and Jenkins said it had not been stored there at all, but had been trans-shipped immediately.

The Liverpool packet-boat was about to sail, he explained, it being the first of the month, the traditional sailing date for packets; and he had heard that the Captain not only had cargo space aboard but was looking for an adventure—the private cargo which all ships' personnel were entitled to take aboard in amounts varying according to rank. The Captain had bought Mr. Jenkins's entire shipment.

The dinner-bell rang, and all three rose. "So there is not, then," Hays inquired, "any way to trace a small amount of this cotton?"

"None that I know of. It comes in to the City all the time, lays on the wharves, and anyone can draw a handful from a bale; samples are pulled in the Exchange and discarded—why, sir, the wind blows it about the streets. Can we trace the wind?"

So much for that, Hays thought, as the cab rolled its way downtown. The two murdered men had been sailors and probably had access to baled cotton, at sea or on shore, a hundred times a year— though why one would put it in his mouth and another in his glove was a question which baffled him completely. Perhaps Breakstone had discovered some thing about the glove itself.

But the Constable hadn't. It was an ordinary gentleman's glove, the haberdashers all said, sold by the dozens and the gross.

Hays sighed, tossed the glove to his desk, and looked at it discontentedly. "I can't believe," he said at last, "that it isn't a clew. Gentleman's gloves in the Old Brewery? No, my boy, it *has* to signify. Of course some one might have stolen a pair—no one would steal just one—but he'd not have carried them all the way back home with him; he'd have sold them for a half-dime to the first fence he came across—yes, and drunk up the half-dime directly, too. I am convinced that this glove was dropped by the man who killed Roberts. In which case it does have some thing to tell me. Perhaps I've not been listening. Hmm."

He picked up the glove and began to examine it carefully, inch by inch, holding it close to his eyes. Suddenly his frown vanished, gave way to a look in which astonishment vied with self-reproach.

"Ahh!" he exclaimed. "Here's something I hadn't noticed before— and shame upon me, too. Do *you* see it, Mr. Breakstone? No? Fie upon you! Look here."

Hays began to turn the glove inside-out, poking at the fingers with the small end of a pen-holder until they were all reversed. "See it now? Eh?"

Breakstone said, "I see these few wisps of cotton here, sir. But we knew there was cotton in the glove. I still don't see why. Do you?"

But Hays did not answer the question directly. "I want you to set to work on a riddle: What connection is there between Roaring Roberts and Tim Scott? And what connection between those two and the man found dead in Dunstan-Slip? What connections in life?—and in death?"

It was at this moment that the steam-tug *Unicorn* happened to ram the ferry-boat *Governor Tompkins* half-way between New-York and Brooklyn. Twenty passengers were thrown overboard, and only nine picked up from the water alive. Hays was no better with a boat-hook than any one else, but his presence on the river served to discourage the presence of those "volunteers" who were more interested in the contents of water-soaked pockets than in seeing the dead brought ashore for Christian burial.

Five of the missing eleven were found, by and by; and Hays retired from the scene. Experience told him that the rest wouldn't show up for some time.

As Breakstone, himself rather wet about the sleeves and shirt-front, made his way along South-street early that evening, he overheard this point discussed. Some thought the full moon would "draw" the dead to the surface, while others insisted that only the concussion of water-borne cannonry could dislodge them.

Meanwhile, the life of the city roared along. Cargo was laden aboard many of the vessels whose bow-sprits pointed toward the top storeys of the South-street buildings, and cargo was taken ashore from many others. Men with blackened clothes and faces poured coal into the holds of new-fangled steamers. "Cream! Cream! D'licious ice-cream!" shouted the peddlers, not even ceasing their hoarse cries when setting down their wooden pails to serve a clerk or apprentice, safely out of employer's sight.

Wine by the pipe, sugar and tobacco by the hogshead, pot-ash by the barrel, rum by the puncheon, nails by the keg, tea by the chest, cotton by the bale, and wool by the bag; shouting supercargoes, cursing carters, hoarse auctioneers, brokers scurrying between ship and shore and sale; grave old merchants and hard young sea-captains, red-faced dray- and barrow-men, pale-faced clerks and fresh faced 'prentice-boys; the reek of salt-fish, the cloying odor of molasses, the spicy scent of cinnamon-bark, the healthy smell of horses, and the sharp tang of new leather—all this was South-street, the city's premier water-front and the focal point of all New-York's commerce.

"Leatherhead! Leatherhead!" yelled a barefooted, dirty-legged boy, passing on the run. Breakstone paid no attention. The leather helmet he wore may not have been pretty, and it was often hot and heavy in the summertime, but—besides the protection it offered from brick-bars, stones, and clubs—it was the only article of uniform the New-York City Watch wore, and he was proud of it.

Otterburne's West-India Coffee-House was where Hays had said he would meet him, and there, in an upstairs room overlooking the East-River and Upper Harbor, was the High Constable himself, dipping his mahogany-colored face, for a change, into a mug of Mocha and milk.

"Have you got the answer to my riddle?" Hays asked, wiping his mouth on the back of one huge hand.

"Parts of it—I think." Then Breakstone abandoned his reserve and leaned forward eagerly. "I found out quite a bit when I was out in the boats. Do you know a Captain Lemuel Pierce, who has the *Sarah* coasting-sloop?" Hays considered for a second, then nodded. "Well, here's what it comes to: Roaring Roberts, who we found dead in the Old Brewery, had been seen more than once in company with Tim Scott—who we found in the alley three streets up from here. I'd mentioned to you that Scott had spoken of a mate named Billy Walters? Yes, and Billy Walters—who hasn't been seen of late!—had a great keloid on his left ear-lobe—"

Hays blew out his cheeks. "So *he* was the man they pulled out of Dunstan-Slip! This ties all three together with a second cord. And Lem Pierce—?" Billy Walters was said to have sailed with Captain Lem on their last voyage; Pierce's sloop was a coaster, and Tim Scott's last voyage was also on a coaster. "Lem has a wicked reputation," Hays said thoughtfully. "Coercion, crimping, blackmail, barratry, usurpation . . . I dare say he's turned his hand to a touch of piracy in his time, too. Where does the *Sarah* lie now, Constable? You've done well," he added, before Breakstone could answer. "Many a mickle makes a muckle—go on, you were saying?"

Breakstone said that the *Sarah* sloop had been down in Perth-Amboy, being over-hauled. Report was that she was on her way to the City, with only the Captain and a man from the ship-yard handling her, and should arrive just before sundown at Bayard's Wharf.

"Over-hauling costs money," Hays observed. "Scott and Roberts had been spending a lot of money, too. Bound together with a third cord, you see. And 'a three-fold cord is not easily broken', says the Proverbs of King Solomon. Come to think of it, there's another king mentioned in the Book of Proverbs. Yes. Just so. King Lemuel! Well, late to-night, about ten or so, we'll go down and visit this Lemuel and discuss Scripture—and other things!"

But when they visited that Lemuel they found him dead.

They had picked their way along the wharf through heaps of firewood the sawyers had prepared and left for galley-stoves. It was well past the farthest zone of gaslight and neither the dim ships'-lamps nor the tiny Watch-lanterns that Hays's men had did much more than make the ambient darkness seem darker.

"Ahoy, there!" Hays hailed a dim figure enjoying a pipe in the cool of above-decks. "Where's the *Sarah*? A sloop, just came in early this evening?"

Afterwards, he was to regret that hail. Then—"*Sarah*? Don't know the name, but a sloop made fast a few hours back, to the forward end of the wharf."

Her lamp was trim and bright, her paint fresh, her name bold and red. Captain Lemuel Pierce had clearly not been trying to hide. But no one answered the call and they boarded the vessel in silence. The cabin-door swung open and inside, on the deck, with his scabbard empty at his belt and his knife deep into his throat, lay the sloop's Captain.

"He's still bleeding!" Breakstone exclaimed.

"Search the ship," said Hays tersely. And then they heard it—a scrabble, a clatter, a thump, and the sound of running feet. They rushed top-side in time to see a man on the next wharf vanish into the darkness. Pursuit proved vain.

"He must have hopped over onto the ship behind this one," Hays said as they returned, winded and chagrined, "when he heard me hail and ask for the *Sarah*. Ah, well, let's do as we were about to do, anyway—search the ship."

But aside from water-ballast and a very small amount of stores, there was nothing to be found in the hold. Captain Pierce had bought a deal of new clothes, and in one coat-pocket there was a handful of gold eagles.

"A hundred dollars," Hays said, slipping the ten coins back. "A fortune for a sailor, but not so for a master. Did we scare off a robber before he could find it? Or was he a robber at all? The log—"

The log, however, listed nothing between the voyage from Perth-Amboy and one of six months previously to Wilmington, with a mixed cargo of linen, wine, rice, and flour; which was much too early for *the* voyage.

"Not an honest man at all, you see," said Hays, almost sorrowfully. "Didn't keep a proper log. Even so—to murder a master of craft under my very nose, as it were! There's insolence for you! Ahum. What is that behind your feet, Mr. Breakstone?"

The Constable tried to move forward and look backward at the same time, and before he had even completed the movement he answered that it was "Just a scrap of paper." He blinked at Hays's steady gaze and air of still waiting, then he blushed. He stooped and picked it up, looked at it, handed it over. Hays gave it a quick glance.

"*Just* a scrap of paper? Look again—Leatherhead!"

The scrap was straight on one edge and jagged on the other, and it had a few words or parts of words on one side.

a
known to
do further
es, Territor
Status and

"It seems to be part of some kind of legal paper," Breakstone said, after a moment.

"Just so." Hays's tone was almost grudging. "You ought to have seen it at once and handed it to me to find out *what* kind of legal paper. Trifles, trifles—but it's trifles that count! I sign this kind of legal paper by the dozen. Had I a quarter-of-a-dollar fee for each one—which I don't—I could have bought a summer-cottage up at Spikin-Duyvil by now. Well, listen: I'll emphasize the words you see here:

"'. . . *a* Seaman of this city, and a Man of Color, is *known* to me on good evidence to be a FREE MAN, and I *do further* Enjoin all Men of whatsoever Cities, States, Territories, and Nations, to recognize him in such *Status and*—', and so forth. We give these to the Black seamen in case they put in to a port of a slave state or a slave-holding colony or country, to keep them from being seized and sold. Now, what does it tell you?"

"That the man who killed the Captain was a Black seaman?"

"Not necessarily—but it hints at that, very powerfully, yes. Some one who wanted the papers of a free Negro sailor was here to see Pierce—he grabbed for it—but Pierce held on tight—it tore. Let's follow the obvious trail first. We know that Captain Lem had come into money lately. We know the same of Tim Scott and Roaring Roberts. Pierce spent his on the sloop. The other two poured it out like wine. Now. Do you know of any Colored sailors who've been known to spend lavishly of late?"

The wake of a passing vessel rocked the sloop. The cabin-lamp stayed level in its gimbals, but its light trembled a bit just the same, sending shadows across the High Constable's craggy face.

"No, not lavishly—that's to say, not foolishly. But now that I think about it," Breakstone mused aloud, "Cudjo Washington used to sail, on and off. And just a little while ago he opened an oyster-cellar in lower Collect-street, not far south of Anthony. A dicty place, as I think of it now—dicty for an oyster-cellar in Collect-street, that is. It must have cost him something."

Hays summoned the two Night Constables who had been standing guard at the foot of Bayard's Wharf and the one next to it, told one to rattle at the Coroner's shutters, and the other one to stand by the body—a task he plainly had no fancy for, but plainly he had even less fancy to refuse Old Hays.

"And now," said Old Hays, "We'll call on Cudjo Washington. I could relish a basin of little-necks or cherry-stones, I believe. But I'd relish information even more."

There were more men about that night than was usual for the hour, and presently some one called out from a little group which was gathered under a lamp-post.

"Jacob! Hello, there! Stop a bit." Hays crossed over and recognized Alderman Ter Williger, Mr. Jenkins, Mr. Jonathan Goodhue the fancy dry-goods importer, and his partner, Mr. Perit.

"These are late hours, gentlemen," Hays commented, "for merchants who must be up early to-morrow."

"Ah, it's to-morrow that keeps us up so late to-night," said Ter Williger genially. "To-morrow is the first of the month—that means to-night is packet-night—we've all been staying late at our counting-houses getting everything in order against the packet-vessels' sailing in the morning. Come and take a glass of lager-beer with us, Jacob: join us in a well-earned quarter-hour of ease." And, with a *Yes, yes,* and a *Do, sir,* Messrs. Goodhue and Perit seconded the invitation.

But Hays shook his head. "I'm off to Collect-street on business. And while lager is available there, I'll not invite you to join me. An ugly business and an ugly neighborhood."

Ter Williger, Goodhue, and Perit pursed their lips and raised their eyebrows. Jenkins drew out a segar, a match, and a piece of glassed paper, struck fire and lit up.

"Is that one of the new Congreve matches?" Mr. Perit asked. Jenkins, his mouth occupied with drawing smoke, didn't answer.

"Yes, it is," said Goodhue. "A great improvement over the old acid bottle. Well, well, then, Mr. Hays, we daren't detain you. Another time, perhaps."

"To be sure. Yes, we must go now. A good-night, gentlemen."

Collect-street, below Anthony-street, while not offering the amenities of, say, Washington-square, was still a cut or two above the Five-Points. A stranger might be lured into a room here, and beaten and robbed, and he might die of it; but he was not likely to be murdered in the open street for fun.

Several fences operated almost openly, ready to buy anything from a dead man's dirty shirt for a penny to a nob's gold watch for a dollar. There were the usual saloons and "grocery" stores, including that of the infamous Rosanna Spears. But to-night only one place of business on the street interested Jacob Hays. It was easy enough to spot; its lights were brighter and its paint fresher than the rest.

The Great Republic Oyster-Cellar, by C. Washington, stated a sign-board; and continued, *Fresh and Pickled Oysters, Clams, Hard-shell and Soft-shell Crabs, Garnished Lobsters. Fringed Hams. Fresh Country Fruit.*

The interior was neat and clean and contained several tables, a row of booths along one wall, and even the unusual glory of a glass-fronted show-case in which reposed half of a fringed ham, a huge platter heaped high with fried soft-shell crabs, bowls of fruit, and part of a roasted pig with a lemon in its mouth. A whitewashed keg displayed the necks of bottles of ginger-beer, porter, lager-beer, and mead, the rest of the bottles being concealed by cracked ice. On the rear wall were large steel engravings of Generals Washington and Jackson, and a smaller one of Governor Clinton.

It was, indeed, "rather a dicty place for Collect-street." It could not very well have been furnished and provisioned on the savings from a seaman's wages.

Present in the room were a Negro couple, evidently the proprietor and his wife, and several white couples, the men and women dressed in clothes which managed to look at the same time both flashy and bedraggled. The customers glanced up from their refreshments, sat for a moment transfixed at the sight of Hays and Breakstone, tensed, exchanged glances, and then as it was made obvious that the door was not being blocked and that none of them was engaging the attention of the law—relaxed somewhat: that is, if slouching in their seats and hiding their faces with arms propped on elbows may be considered relaxing.

The proprietor, a powerfully built man in his early middle years, pressed himself back against the wall with something clenched in his fist. His wife retreated wordlessly to a corner.

"Cudjo Washington," said Hays, advancing and holding out his staff, "I call upon you, as a citizen of this city, to lay down that oyster-knife." The implement fell with a clatter.

After a second Washington said, "Before the Lord, I didn't know it was you, gentlemen. I thought—" He ran his tongue over his lips, then came forward to the counter with a mechanical smile and an attitude of well-practised deference. "What will you gentlemen be pleased to have?" he asked.

"A few words with you in your back-room. Your wife can stay here to wait on the patrons." Breakstone posted himself outside.

"Well?" asked Hays. It was dark in the room. Only a small piece of candle burned in a saucer.

"I didn't know what they was up to, Mr. High Constable. I never found out until it was too late." The man's voice was low, but it came from a huge chest and throat, and rumbled out into the shadows. As to what he meant by what he had said, Jacob Hays had no idea at all. He generally avoided opening a conversation with a suspected man in terms of accusing him of a specific crime. *Well?* was usually opening enough. Often the single syllable put mind and tongue to something quite different from what the High Constable had been thinking of, something of which the High Constable had known nothing. One could, after all, always take up later the matter which had prompted the inquiry in the first place.

"He hadn't no right to keep hold of my papers. No right-a-tall," Cudju was saying. But this was not exactly what Hays was expecting him to say. Ah, well, wait a bit. Let the man talk. But all the talk, it became obvious, was on lines other than the first comment. Had Cudjo realized that he had started to give himself away? And, so considering, Hays realized that he himself was no longer thinking in terms of a simple murder.

He *would* have to lead the conversation, after all. Well, so be it. "What were they up to, Cudjo, and just when did you find it out?"

The man's eyes seemed red in the candle-light. Was there cunning in them? "You says—what, sir?" Hays repeated his words. "I mean to say," Cudjo evaded, "what was he up to, keeping my papers? Now, they was mine, legal. So—"

"So you killed him."

A confident laugh. "Cap'n Pierce? No, sir! He too mean to die!"

"Not when he'd gotten a knife in his throat, he wasn't." The laugh ebbed away, the man scanned Hays's face. His huge chest swelled. He shook his head dumbly. "Mr. Breakstone! Send the woman in here . . . Now, what time did your husband come back to-night?"

"Why 'twas about—" She checked herself and looked at her husband. But he sat still, utterly still. Her voice dropped a notch, became uncertain. "Why, master, he was here all night. He never go out." She looked from Hays to her husband, pleadingly. But neither offered aught for her comfort. She began to wail.

Cudjo accompanied them quietly to the Watch-house.

"If you didn't kill Captain Pierce," Hays asked, and asked over and over again, "then why were you so afraid when we walked in? Why did you pick up the oyster-knife? You said, 'I didn't know it was you. I thought—' *What* did you think? Who were you expecting? Who are the 'they' you talked about? What was it you 'found out they were up to?' Why was it 'too late' by then?"

Then, still getting no response, Hays put to him the brutally suggestive, but terribly pertinent, question, "Cudjo, have you ever seen a man hanged?"

Sweat popped out on the man's broad face. He began to shake his head—and continued to shake it. It seemed he could not stop. Soon his whole body was shaking from side to side. He essayed speech, but his voice clicked in his throat. Hays brought him a mug of water, and he swallowed it greedily.

"I will tell you, master," he said, after a moment. "I see there is no help for it. I will tell you everything. It begin two, three months ago."

Two or three months previously, Cudjo had been living in a corner of a room in the Shambles tenement on Cherry-street, in the Fourth Ward. He had had no job in a long time, and only the pittance which his wife earned by peddling hot-roasted corn through the streets kept them from actual starvation. Captain Lemuel Pierce came and offered him a berth for a coasting voyage, and Cudjo had jumped at it.

"You got your free papers, don't you, Cudj?" There had been no slaves in New-York State since the Emancipation of 1827, and Cudjo had been free even before then, for his owner had brought him North and manumitted him. He knew that Captian Pierce must be referring to his seaman's papers.

"Yes, sir. I got'm. We going South, Cap'n?"

Pierce smiled, showed yellow teeth. "We ain't goin' to Nova-Scoshy. Better hand them papers over to me for safe-keeping, Cudj. That way, I c'n take care."

Pierce was obliging enough to advance $2 on wages, which were given to Phoebe Washington, and to promise warm clothes as soon as they got aboard. The two proceeded to Staten-Island, where the *Sarah* was lying off a small creek which emptied into the Kill-Van-Kull. Roaring Roberts was first mate. Tim Scott and Billy Walters made up the rest of the crew. They put out to sea on the next tide.

"He never come out of the cabin till the second day," said Cudjo. "But I knew his face."

"Whose?" Hays asked.

"Mr. Jones's." And who was he and what did he look like? He was a big man with a red face. Cudjo had "seen him around"; more he knew not. Mentally Hays ran over all the Joneses he could think of, from Ap Jones the cow-keeper to Zimri Jones, who sold woollens. None fitted the picture.

The *Sarah* was dirty, but Captain Pierce had kept her in good shape otherwise. He and Mr. Jones had had words right from the start. Jones, who apparently had chartered the slope, objected to any one's—particularly the Captain's—drinking "until the job's done." Pierce had said that he was master aboard his own vessel and would drink what and when he pleased; forthwith he applied himself to his demijohn.

Neither Cudjo nor any of the three White sailors had any idea of where they were bound, except that it was, in Pierce's words, "Somewhere South and warm." It was after they had passed Cape Fear that Pierce and Jones revealed their destination to him. "They had to," Washington said. "They needed me. Cap'n Pierce knew I was born in Brunswick and had sailed all those waters."

"You ought to know St. Simon's Sound pretty well, I guess," said Pierce.

"Oh, yes, sir. My old master—"

"Damn your old master!" said Pierce. "Do you know where Remington's Landing is? You do. All right. You'll pilot us there."

They lay well off shore till dark, then entered St. Simon's Sound, then Tuppah Cove. Remington's Landing lay up an inlet into the Cove. The moon was full and bright. Captain Pierce, aided by the winds, had planned well.

"Take care, Cudj," he said; and then a while before they came up to the wharf, "you—no noise!"

The ship's-lamps were extinguished. Silent as a ghost ship, the sloop moored. The shed by the wharf was full of baled cotton. Without words, directed by gestures, they all set to work loading it aboard. Even Pierce and Jones took off their coats and pitched in.

After a while—Cudjo didn't know how long—they became aware that some one was looking at them. It was the Negro watchman.

Evidently he had been taking a nap on one of the bales. He stared at the scene—and an eerie scene it must have been, too—the six strange men toiling silently in the pool of moonlight. His voice, when he spoke, was tremulous.

"What—what are you White men doing with that there cotton? It belongs to Master Remington, and I know it ain't done been sold!"

They could have told him some lie and kept him silent, Cudjo said, recounting the story to Hays. Tied him up, maybe. But Jones pulled out a knife and at the sight of it the watchman turned and was off like the wind. He had no chance, of course. They were on him before he could cry out. Cudjo, standing aghast, saw an arm rise and fall twice. Then the five men dragged the body aside into the grass. Cudjo was still standing, numbly, when they returned, and gestured him back to work.

They were at sea again by dawn.

"What happened to the cotton?" Hays asked.

It was hot in the Watch-house; the wick in the whale-oil lamp needed trimming, but somehow he could not put his mind to asking the Night Constable-in-charge to take care of it. Here, then, was the story of the theft of the Sea-Island cotton in Georgia, of which he had been notified weeks back. It had been carried out by men recruited under his very nose, so to speak: Billy Walters, Roaring Roberts, Tim Scott, Captain Pierce, Cudjo Washington. Who had been behind it? Mr. Jones. Which ones were still alive? Cudjo Washington and Mr. Jones.

"What happened to the cotton?" Hays asked again. He knew well enough what had happened to the men.

The proprietor of The Great Republic Oyster-Cellar shook his head. "I don't know, Mr. High Constable. We put in to Philadelphia—didn't tie up, though, just lay out in the river—and Mr. Jones and Captain Pierce rowed ashore. They come back inside of an hour and Mr. Jones had a sight of money with him. I expect he'd been to the bank. They paid us off and told us to get our gear together and go ashore. Not to come back. He warned us—Mr. Jones, I mean. "Don't let me see you in New-York,' he said. 'I'm paying you extra for that,' he said, 'so you better not try to fool me.' Said to me, 'Send for your wife. Don't go back to her.' He had a mean look to him. A hard man."

"And you took the money? The proceeds of the stolen cotton? For you knew that's what it was, for all he paid you in advance."

Cudjo nodded. "He said I had to take it. Said he'd kill me if I didn't. 'You're in this, too,' he said, 'the same as the rest of us. If I were you I'd go far away.' So I took it. And I was afraid to say any thing. I could've thrown it away, all but my wages. But it was more money than I'd ever seen, almost. I thought, I'll hold on to it for a while and study this. Then—'Send for your wife,' he said. I can't write and she can't read. I come up here to see her and study what to do. And when I saw that rat's-hole we were living in—in the Shambles—and her tired out from crying hot-roasting-ears up and down the streets—"

He had succumbed to the temptation and had used the money to fit up the oyster-cellar. A sailor's life was hard, and usually, not a long one. The rest of the story was easy enough—in part—for Hays to imagine. One by one the three other sailors made their way back to New-York in defiance of "Mr. Jones's" warning. One of them must have preferred to spend his share of the crime in Philadelphia, or—Hays remembered the worn, worn shoes found on another's feet—or in some other place no closer to New-York.

"Jones" must have been a fool to think they would stay away. As soon as their money was spent they must have tried to blackmail him—tried alone, almost certainly, not in concert, for each had been killed alone and separately. Perhaps Jones hadn't even known that Cudjo had returned to New-York.

"What happened on the sloop to-night?" Hays asked. Somewhere off in the city a church-bell sounded the hour. How quickly the night was passing!

Washington had forgotten to ask for his free papers in Philadelphia. Presently he remembered, but did nothing. If he needed them, by some dire chance, to go to sea again, he could get another set. Chiefly, though, he worried about their remaining in the hands of Captain Pierce—Captain Pierce, whose evil reputation he knew as well as Hays did, and whose evil nature he knew even better, having sailed under him. But Pierce was off in Perth-Amboy, having the *Sarah* over-hauled.

"Are you going to wait in your cellar till he picks his own time and comes to kill you, like he did the others? Well, I'm not," Pierce had said. "You'd think he'd know better than to threaten me, wouldn't you? You'd think he'd speak sweet to me, but, no. 'Stay out of New-York, Pierce. I warn you!'" Cap'n Lem had mimicked "Jones". Cap'n Lem had been drinking, in his little cabin there in the sloop at Bayard's Wharf. "Well, I don't fancy staying out of New-York, see? And I don't relish the idea of being killed on some dark night. No, Cudj, I tell you: there's only this—*kill him before he kills us!*"

But Cudjo had had enough of that. Four men were already killed, including the slave watchman down on St. Simon's-Island. It was Cudjo's belief that the White men would still be living if they hadn't tried to get more money out of "Jones". All that Cudjo wanted was his free papers back. And Captain Lemuel Pierce refused to deliver them. He showed them, he laughed, he drew them back. They were to be the price of Cudjo's assistance in the death of "Jones." They had quarreled, the master of the *Sarah* grew ugly, Cudjo had snatched at papers and torn them from Pierce's grasp. Then he had run off. That was all. That was his story.

Hays was rather inclined to believe him.

But who was "Jones"?

A few hours' sleep, and the High Constable was up and on duty again. As soon as breakfast was over he stalked down-town, on his way to Ter Williger's place of business. Old Nick would be pleased to know that the matter of theft of the Sea-Island cotton from St. Simon's had been solved.

And then, as if his thoughts had become tangible, the word "Gloves" appeared in front of his eyes. Hays stopped short, looked carefully. There it was, in the window of that little shop. *D. MacNab, Leather and Leather-Findings. Cobbler's Supplies. Saddlery and Harness. Books Bound. Gloves Mended. Fire-men's and Watch-men's Helmets.*

Hays passed under the wooden awning and walked up three steps. A bell tinkled as he opened the door.

"What can you tell me any thing about this glove?" he asked.

"That it's no' yours, Mr. Hays."

The High Constable laughed shortly. "I know that. And if *you* do, it must mean that you know whose it is, Mr. MacNab."

"Och aye? Must it? It's nae muckle thing to ken whose hand fits a glove, and whose doesna." And, as Hays digested this, and ruefully admitted the man was right, Mac Nab said, "But it sae happens that I do ken whose it is, for I mended it masel'. And what's mare, I mended another for the same mon—slashed across the palm it was—and handed it back not an hour syne."

Not trying to conceal his excitement, Hays leaned across the counter. "What's his name, MacNab?"

But MacNab said, "Och, that I dinna ken. A big man, wi' a sonsy red face on him. He didna come in himsel', this time, he sent the coachman wi' the money. 'Mak' haste', says the coachie, 'for he's complainin' we won't get to the Battery in time to catch the packet-ship.' So I took the siller and gave over the glove, and that's all I ken aboot it."

Calling his thanks over his shoulder, Hays ran out.

It took three cabs, one after the other, to get him to the Battery without the horses foundering. And all the clocks along the route displayed each a truly Republican and Democratic spirit of independence, no two agreeing. He was in constant agony that he might not make his destination in time. He pondered, not for the first time, on the absurdity of the head of the only effective police-force in the State (if not the nation!) being dependent on common carriers to convey him wherever his own feet could not. He allowed himself the uncommon luxury of a dream: a light carriage, the property of the Watch, drawn by a team of swift and strong horses, ditto. But it was only a dream. "Economy in government" was the official policy—except, of course, where official corruption was the cord. So far, at any rate, the sachems of the Tammany Wigwam had refrained from taking over the Watch. Which meant economy.

Blocks before the Battery he began to groan, for the crowds streaming away meant that all the farewells had been said and the ferry for the packet-ships had already left. The spectacle of the speeding cab (though devilish little speed could it manage in these crowded streets despite the fact that Hays was standing half-up and gesturing other vehicles aside) attracted the attention of the crowd, and there were loud comments—most of which contained the words *Old Hays!*

He leapt from the cab as soon as it drew up at the wharf, and dashed through the lingering groups of people. A corner of his eye observed three known pick-pockets, but he did not stop. That is, he did not stop until he saw that the ferry had gone, gone so definitely that he could not even pick it out amidst the thronged shipping of the harbor. As he drew up short, dismay large and plain upon his rugged face, a fierce and stalwart young man, with cold blue eyes and a rather hard-looking mouth, appeared out of the crowd and demanded, "What's up?"

"Oh, Corneel—I've got to get aboard the packet-ship before she leaves—"

"Which one? Two bound for Liverpool, two for New Orleans, and one each for London, Havre, and Charleston. Take your pick, I've got a steam launch."

Which one, indeed? Liverpool was the cotton-port of England, and Jenkins had done business with the Captain of *one* of the Liverpool packets, at any rate. But, through the noise and clamor, he heard, as if in his ear, the voice of Mrs. Jenkins: *Mais, ooh, la belle France!*

"The Havre packet, Corneel! That'll be it! But can we make it in time?"

With a flurry of oaths Corneel declared that he would soon put Hays aboard her, and ripped out orders. Almost at once a small, trim steam-launch appeared and they tumbled into it. Corneel took the wheel himself, and in another minute the paddles were thrashing and the whistle was screaming.

"Damn my tripes!" Corneel shouted. "This is like the old days! Remember when I was Captain of old Gibbons' steamer, hey?"

Hays nodded. "In open violation of the monopoly that New-York State had given Livingstone and Fulton," he pointed out. "Wherefore, it was my plain duty to arrest you. I told you I'd do it if I had to carry you ashore. I *did* do it and I *did* have to carry you ashore!"

Corneel roared with laughter, damned his tripes again, and various other things, swore luridly at the pilots of any vessels which did not instantly veer out of his way at the sound of his whistle; and in very short time they had beaten a white, frothy path across the blue waters and were in the cool shadow of the huge ocean-goer.

"Ahoy, the *Hannibal* packet!" Corneel shouted, his crew-man seizing the ladder—which was still down to let the pilot off—with the boat-hook; then quickly fastening on with the line.

A row of curious faces looked down at them from above. Corneel and Hays clambered up the ladder and confronted the somewhat astonished Captain. Hays lifted his staff of office. His eyes picked out one face from the crowd, and a thickly-packed crowd it was too; for few had chosen to go below and miss the passage down the Bay and through the Narrows. It was a face easy to pick out, once it had been described. "A big man with a red face," Cudjo had said. "A sonsy red face," was MacNab's description. Hays wondered at his never having made the connection.

"What brings you aboard, Mr. Hays?" asked Captain Delano.

"A desire to ask a question or two of your passenger, here—" Hays stopped in front of the man, who greeted him with the same affable smile he had worn at their previous meeting.

"Good morning, Mr. Hays. Have you had any success in your quest for information about Nankeen?" he inquired.

"Good morning, Mr. Jenkins. Yes, I have. Do you know this glove?" For just a fleeting second the smile seemed to slip. "No, I'm afraid I don't."

"Try it on," said Hays. "Let me have your left hand."

Jenkins drew the hand away and Hays caught it. For a moment they stood face to face, breast to breast, hand in hand. A little breeze blew across the deck. No one else spoke. Jenkins was a large man and a powerful one. But, still, slowly but surely, inch by inch, Hays drew his right hand back, and clenched in his right hand was the left hand of Mr. James Jenkins.

Suddenly Jenkins laughed. "An odd jest, sir. But I'm willing to oblige you."

His resistance ceased, and he held out the reluctant hand, clad in a fawn-colored glove. For all his amiability he moved slowly, but the fawn-colored glove came off and the glove Hays held out—one of gray leather—went on.

"Now, sir, are you content?" Jenkins demanded, still smiling.

"Perfectly." Hays held out his High Constable's staff. "James Jenkins, alias Jones," he said, "I take you into custody on a charge of having murdered Billy Walters, Tim Scott, Henry Roberts, and Lemuel Pierce, all in the City of New-York; and one Negro man, a slave, name unknown to me, on St. Simon's-Island in the State of Georgia."

The smile entirely left Jenkins's face, which had gone white—then the color came flooding back, but not the smile.

"Captain Delano," said Hays, "I trust you will render whatever aid may be necessary."

Jenkins had found his tongue, and turned it glibly on the Captain. "I've never heard of any of these men, sir," he said stoutly. "Nor have I ever been to St. Simon's-Island. What is this nonsense about gloves and murders? I know many passengers will vouch for my character."

"There are those ashore," said Hays, "who can vouch for it, too! Went South not long ago to buy Nankeen, did you? Never a bit of it! Chartered Lem Pierce's sloop to go South and fill it full of stolen Sea-Island cotton, is what you did! And killed the poor Negro who was guarding it! No wonder you got rid of the bales so fast—sold them to the master of the outward-bound Liverpool packet just by good luck? Never a bit of it! Planned, planned! Every step of the way!

"But you hadn't planned on your accomplices returning to blackmail you, did you? Still, you drew up a plan soon enough for that: you lured them to dark places under pretense of payment, and there you killed them. Billy Walters was the first one. He was found with a piece of cotton in his mouth. Raw cotton—Nankeen—such as you dealt in, Jenkins. What was the cotton doing in a dead man's mouth? Here—"

Hays plucked the gray glove from the hand in which Jenkins, having taken it off, was holding it.

"Roaring Roberts, another of the lot, was found dead in the Old Brewery, and this glove at the entrance to his room. And Tim Scott, the third sailor of the crew of the sloop, was strangled to death in an alley off South-street. What is the connection in the circumstances of their deaths? Why, this—on Scott's neck were the marks of only nine fingers. Where was the tenth?"

In an instant Hays had seized the left hand of James Jenkins and held it up for all to see.

"There is no tenth," he said. "*Jenkins has only four fingers on his left hand!* That is why he always wears gloves! Look at the little finger of this glove: it has no creases. If I were to turn it inside out you'd see how the leather is darkened by use on the other four digits—but not on this one! And to hide the fact of his missing finger even more, Jenkins always stuffs the empty digit with raw cotton fibre. Look at this—"

Hays held out the fawn-colored glove. Four of its fingers hung loosely, but the fifth stayed as plump as if it had a flesh-and-blood finger inside it. Hays fished inside and the little finger went limp as he pulled out a piece of cotton stuffing.

Some thing like a sigh went up from the crowd.

"Now, examine the little finger of this first glove again," Hays continued. "See how the thread at the end is a lighter color? Why? The end had been mended and the thread hadn't yet worn as dark as the rest. But why did it need mending? Because when you, Jenkins, attacked Walters, he bit your hand, tearing the glove open and forcing the cotton stuffing out through the rip his teeth made! And before he could spit it out, his neck was broken, and he was a dead man! And in your fight with Roberts you lost the glove and were afraid to go back for it, weren't you?"

Jenkins, unsmiling now, said nothing.

"You had Duncan MacNab mend the first glove. He did his job well, so when you killed Captain Lem Pierce and found the palm of the glove that you had on then had been slashed by Pierce's knife, you took it to MacNab, too. And just got it back to-day. Let's see the other glove to this fawn-colored pair, Jenkins."

Jenkins thrust both hands deep into his pockets. There was a hard, ugly expression upon his face. "Let's see your warrant—Leatherhead!" he demanded.

Hays shook his head. "None needed to apprehend a fugitive fleeing the State to avoid prosecution."

Jenkins sneered. "You don't know much law, Leatherhead. Your jurisdiction ended back at the Battery."

Hays said calmly that they were still in New-York State waters, and that if it became necessary, he was prepared to make a citizen's arrest. Jenkins had something to say about that, but there was an interruption.

"Damn my tripes! Are you trying to keep us talking till we're out past the three-mile limit? Belay that!" And Corneel rushed forward, seized Jenkins around the waist and threw him over the side of the ship. He fell, screaming and kicking, while the ladies shrieked and swooned. Without even waiting for the splash, Corneel clattered down the ladder, Hays behind him.

Jenkins surfaced, and screamed in terror. "I can't swim! Help me, I can't swim!" He grabbed at and caught the boat-hook and was hoisted aboard the launch, where he lay, sodden and sobbing.

"If he makes any trouble, Corneel, hit him with the boat-hook—the blunt end." Hays craned his neck upward. "If Mrs. Jenkins wishes to come ashore," he called, "we'll wait for her." They waited several minutes. Then a steward pushed his head over.

"She won't come, sir. She's locked the door of her cabin and she says she won't come out."

Jenkins's face swelled.

"Cast off," Corneel directed.

"The trull!" Jenkins said, his voice thick. "The slut! I'd never have done it if it weren't for her. 'When are we going to have a house of our own, Mr. Jenkins? When are we going to have a carriage of our own?' And now the dirty—"

But Corneel told him to mind his tongue and not speak that way of ladies. Jenkins looked at him with his red eyes. "Who in the devil's name are you?" he asked.

"Cornelius Vanderbilt. *Not* at your service, except as the High Constable directs. Killed five men, did he, Hays?"

"Three sailors and a sea-captain in New-York and a slave down in Georgia."

Corneel took off his cap. "May the Lord have mercy on their

souls." He clapped it back on again and blew his whistle and damned the eyes of the pilot of the New-Brunswick ferry. There were death and evil in Jenkins's face as he looked at them, but Hays held the boat-hook, and all around them were the deep, deep waters.

The crowd at the Battery, far from having dispersed, was larger than it had been. Word of the High Constable's chase and his dash across the harbor had evidently gotten around. No one could any more believe that Old Hays had gone jaunting off to Europe than they could believe it of the Battery itself. Every spy-glass in town seemed to have followed the steam-launch, and there were cheers as they stepped on shore.

They'll cheer at the hanging too, Hays thought, for hanged Jenkins would certainly be. Not even a member of the Cotton Exchange could get away with four local murders. Cudjo would get off, though, if he turned State's evidence; as he would have to in order to avoid extradition on the Georgia charge.

There were four Constables waiting to take the prisoner into custody. One of them was young Breakstone. "Now we know the answer," he said, "to who has nine fingers and kills sailors." But Jenkins said not one word.

An officious, well-dressed, and over-fed man slapped Hays on the back. "A marvelous job of work, High Constable!" he crowed, as if he had directed it himself. "You may well congratulate yourself that it's done. Now it's up to the judge and jury—your job is over."

Hays looked at the man's pompous and moon-like face. Then he looked out over the teeming harbor, and then back to the city almost hid behind the forest of masts along the water-front; the city ever growing, thronged with new-comers from Europe and America.

As he thought of its swarming and wretched tenements and its corrupt administration, the High Constable reflected that crime—as witness Jenkins—was found in high places as well as low, and that greed and vice would go always hand in hand. Hays shook his head sadly.

"No," he said, "it's not done. It's not even begun."

The plump citizen seemed to feel a response was expected of him. He chuckled. But a slight blankness on his bland countenance seemed to indicate that he did not quite take in the High Constable Hays's meaning.

A Double-Barrelled Detective Story

MARK TWAIN

PART ONE

We ought never to do wrong
when people are looking

I

The first scene is in the country, in Virginia; the time, 1880. There has been a wedding, between a handsome young man of slender means and a rich young girl—a case of love at first sight and a precipitate marriage; a marriage bitterly opposed by the girl's widowed father.

Jacob Fuller, the bridegroom, is twenty-six years old, is of an old but unconsidered family which had by compulsion emigrated from Sedgemoor, and for King James's purse's profit, so everybody said—some maliciously, the rest merely because they believed it. The bride is nineteen and beautiful. She is intense, high-strung, romantic, immeasurably proud of her Cavalier blood, and passionate in her love for her young husband. For its sake she braved her father's displeasure, endured his reproaches, listened with loyalty unshaken to his warning predictions, and went from his house without his blessing, proud and happy in the proofs she was thus giving of the quality of the affection which had made its home in her heart.

The morning after the marriage there was a sad surprise for her. Her husband put aside her proffered caresses, and said:

"Sit down. I have something to say to you. I loved you. That was before I asked your father to give you to me. His refusal is not my grievance—I could have endured that. But the things he said of me to you—that is a different matter. There—you needn't speak; I know quite well what they were; I got them from authentic sources. Among other things he said that my character was written in my face; that I

357

was treacherous, a dissembler, a coward, and a brute without sense of pity or compassion: the 'Sedgemoor trademark,' he called it—and 'white-sleeve badge.' Any other man in my place would have gone to his house and shot him down like a dog. I wanted to do it, and was minded to do it, but a better thought came to me: to put him to shame; to break his heart; to kill him by inches. How to do it? Through my treatment of you, his idol! I would marry you; and then— Have patience. You will see."

From that moment onward, for three months, the young wife suffered all the humiliations, all the insults, all the miseries that the diligent and inventive mind of the husband could contrive, save physical injuries only. Her strong pride stood by her, and she kept the secret of her troubles. Now and then the husband said, "Why don't you go to your father and tell him?" Then he invented new tortures, applied them, and asked again. She always answered, "He shall never know by my mouth," and taunted him with his origin; said she was the lawful slave of a scion of slaves, and must obey, and would—up to that point, but no further; he could kill her if he liked, but he could not break her; it was not in the Sedgemoor breed to do it. At the end of three months he said, with a dark significance in his manner, "I have tried all things but one"—and waited for her reply. "Try that," she said, and curled her lip in mockery.

That night he rose at midnight and put on his clothes, then said to her, "Get up and dress!"

She obeyed—as always, without a word. He led her half a mile from the house, and proceeded to lash her to a tree by the side of the public road; and succeeded, she screaming and struggling. He gagged her then, struck her across the face with his cowhide, and set his bloodhounds on her. They tore the clothes off her, and she was naked. He called the dogs off, and said:

"You will be found—by the passing public. They will be dropping along about three hours from now, and will spread the news—do you hear? Goodbye. You have seen the last of me."

He went away then. She moaned to herself.

"I shall bear a child—to *him!* God grant it may be a boy!"

The farmers released her by and by—and spread the news, which was natural. They raised the country with lynching intentions, but the bird had flown. The young wife shut herself up in her father's house; he shut himself up with her, and thenceforth would see no one. His pride was broken, and his heart; so he wasted away, day by day, and even his daughter rejoiced when death relieved him.

Then she sold the estate and disappeared.

II

In 1886 a young woman was living in a modest house near a secluded New England village with no company but a little boy about five years old. She did her own work, she discouraged acquaintance-ships, and had none. The butcher, the baker, and the others that served her could tell the villagers nothing about her further than that her name was Stillman, and that she called the child Archy. Whence she came they had not been able to find out, but they said she talked like a Southerner. The child had no playmates and no comrade, and no teacher but the mother. She taught him diligently and intelli-gently, and was satisfied with the results—even a little proud of them. One day Archy said,

"Mamma, am I different from other children?"

"Well, I suppose not. Why?"

"There was a child going along out there and asked me if the postman had been by and I said yes, and she said how long since I saw him and I said I hadn't seen him at all, and she said how did I know he'd been by, then, and I said because I smelt his track on the sidewalk, and she said I was a dum fool and made a mouth at me. What did she do that for?"

The young woman turned white, and said to herself, "It's a birth-mark! The gift of the bloodhound is in him." She snatched the boy to her breast and hugged him passionately, saying, "God has appointed the way!" Her eyes were burning with a fierce light and her breath came short and quick with excitement. She said to herself: "The puzzle is solved now; many a time it has been a mystery to me, the impossible things the child has done in the dark, but it is all clear to me now." She set him in his small chair, and said:

"Wait a little till I come, dear; then we will talk about the matter."

She went up to her room and took from her dressing table several small articles and put them out of sight: a nail file on the floor under the bed; a pair of nail scissors under the bureau; a small ivory paper knife under the wardrobe. Then she returned, and said:

"There! I have left some things which I ought to have brought down." She named them, and said, "Run up and bring them, dear."

The child hurried away on his errand and was soon back again with the things.

"Did you have any difficulty, dear?"

"No, Mamma; I only went where you went."

During his absence she had stepped to the bookcase, taken several books from the bottom shelf, opened each, passed her hand over a page, noting its number in her memory, then restored them to their places. Now she said:

"I have been doing something while you have been gone, Archy. Do you think you can find out what it was?"

The boy went to the bookcase and got out the books that had been touched, and opened them at the pages which had been stroked.

The mother took him in her lap, and said:

"I will answer your question now, dear. I have found out that in one way you are quite different from other people. You can see in the dark, you can smell what other people cannot, you have the talents of a bloodhound. They are good and valuable things to have, but you must keep the matter a secret. If people found it out, they would speak of you as an odd child, a strange child, and children would be disagreeable to you, and give you nicknames. In this world one must be like everybody else if he doesn't want to provoke scorn or envy or jealousy. It is a great and fine distinction which has been born to you, and I am glad; but you will keep it a secret, for Mamma's sake, won't you?"

The child promised, without understanding.

All the rest of the day the mother's brain was busy with excited thinkings; with plans, projects, schemes, each and all of them uncanny, grim, and dark. Yet they lit up her face; lit it with a fell light of their own; lit it with vague fires of hell. She was in a fever of unrest; she could not sit, stand, read, sew; there was no relief for her but in movement. She tested her boy's gift in twenty ways, and kept saying to herself all the time, with her mind in the past: "He broke my father's heart, and night and day all these years I have tried, and all in vain, to think out a way to break his. I have found it now—I have found it now."

When night fell, the demon of unrest still possessed her. She went on with her tests; with a candle she traversed the house from garret to cellar, hiding pins, needles, thimbles, spools, under pillows, under carpets, in cracks in the walls, under the coal in the bin; then sent the little fellow in the dark to find them; which he did, and was happy and proud when she praised him and smothered him with caresses.

From this time forward life took on a new complexion for her. She said, "The future is secure—I can wait, and enjoy the waiting." The most of her lost interests revived. She took up music again, and languages, drawing, painting, and the other long-discarded delights of her maidenhood. She was happy once more, and felt again the zest of life. As the years drifted by she watched the development of her boy, and was contented with it. Not altogether, but nearly that. The soft side of his heart was larger than the other side of it. It was his only defect, in her eyes. But she considered that his love for her and worship of her made up for it. He was a good hater—that was well; but it was a question if the materials of his hatreds were of as tough and enduring a quality as those of his friendships—and that was not so well.

The years drifted on. Archy was become a handsome, shapely, athletic youth, courteous, dignified, companionable, pleasant in his ways, and looking perhaps a trifle older than he was, which was sixteen. One evening his mother said she had something of grave importance to say to him, adding that he was old enough to hear it now, and old enough and possessed of character enough and stability enough to carry out a stern plan which she had been for years contriving and maturing. Then she told him her bitter story, in all its naked atrociousness. For a while the boy was paralyzed; then he said:

"I understand. We are Southerners; and by our custom and nature there is but one atonement. I will search him out and kill him."

"Kill him? No! Death is release, emancipation; death is a favor. Do I owe him favors? You must not hurt a hair of his head."

The boy was lost in thought a while; then he said:

"You are all the world to me, and your desire is my law and my pleasure. Tell me what to do and I will do it."

The mother's eyes beamed with satisfaction, and she said: "You will go and find him. I have known his hiding place for eleven years; it cost me five years and more of inquiry, and much money, to locate it. He is a quartz miner in Colorado, and well-to-do. He lives in Denver. His name is Jacob Fuller. There—it is the first time I have spoken it since that unforgettable night. Think! That name could have been yours if I had not saved you that shame and furnished you a cleaner one. You will drive him from that place; you will hunt him down and drive him again; and yet again, and again, and again, persistently, relentlessly, poisoning his life, filling it with mysterious terrors, loading it with weariness and misery, making him wish for death, and that he had a suicide's courage; you will make of him another wandering Jew; he shall know no rest any more, no peace of mind, no placid sleep; you shall shadow him, cling to him, persecute him, till you break his heart, as he broke my father's and mine."

"I will obey, Mother."

"I believe it, my child. The preparations are all made; everything is ready. Here is a letter of credit; spend freely, there is no lack of money. At times you may need disguises. I have provided them; also some other conveniences." She took from the drawer of the typewriter table several squares of paper. They all bore these typewritten words:

$10,000 REWARD.

It is believed that a certain man who is wanted in an Eastern State is sojourning here. In 1880, in the night, he tied his young wife to a tree by the public road, cut her across the face with a cowhide, and made his dogs tear her clothes from her, leaving her naked. He left her there, and fled the country. A blood-relative of hers has searched for him for seventeen years. Address . . . , . . . , post office. The above reward will be paid in cash to the person who will furnish the seeker, in a personal interview, the criminal's address.

"When you have found him and acquainted yourself with his scent, you will go in the night and placard one of these upon the building he occupies, and another one upon the post office or in some other prominent place. It will be the talk of the region. At first you must give him several days in which to force a sale of his belongings at something approaching their value. We will ruin him by and by, but gradually; we must not impoverish him at once, for that could bring him to despair and injure his health, possibly kill him."

She took three or four more typewritten forms from the drawer—duplicates—and read one:

. . . . , ... , 18 . . . .

To Jacob Fuller:

You have . . . . . . days in which to settle your affairs. You will not be disturbed during that limit, which will expire at . . . . . . M., on the

. . . . . . of . . . . . . You must then MOVE ON. If you are still in the place after the named hour, I will placard you on all the dead walls, detailing your crime once more, and adding the date, also the scene of it, with all names concerned, including your own. Have no fear of bodily injury—it will in no circumstances ever be inflicted upon you. You brought misery upon an old man, and ruined his life and broke his heart. What he suffered, you are to suffer.

"You will add no signature. He must receive this before he learns of the reward-placard—before he rises in the morning—lest he lose his head and fly the place penniless."

"I shall not forget."

"You will need to use these forms only in the beginning—once may be enough. Afterward, when you are ready for him to vanish out of a place, see that he gets a copy of *this* form, which merely says:

MOVE ON. You have . . . . . . days.

"He will obey. That is sure."

III

Extracts from Letters to the Mother.

DENVER, *April* 3, 1897.

I have now been living several days in the same hotel with Jacob Fuller. I have his scent; I could track him through ten divisions of infantry and find him. I have often been near him and heard him talk. He owns a good mine, and has a fair income from it; but he is not rich. He learned mining in a good way—by working at it for wages. He is a cheerful creature and his forty-three years sit lightly upon him; he could pass for a younger man—say thirty-six or thirty-seven. He has never married again—passes himself off for a widower. He stands well, is liked, is popular, and has many friends. Even I feel a drawing toward him—the paternal blood in me making its claim. How blind and unreasoning and arbitrary are some of the laws of nature—the most of them, in fact! My task is become hard now—you realize it? you comprehend, and make allowances?—and the fire of it has cooled, more than I like to confess to myself. But I will carry it out. Even with the pleasure paled, the duty remains, and I will not spare him.

And for my help, a sharp resentment rises in me when I reflect that he who committed that odious crime is the only one who has not suffered by it. The lesson of it has manifestly reformed his character, and in the change he is happy. He, the guilty party, is absolved from all suffering; you, the innocent, are borne down with it. But be comforted—he shall harvest his share.

SILVER GULCH, *May* 19.

I placarded Form No. 1 at midnight of April third; an hour later I slipped Form No. 2 under his chamber door, notifying him to leave Denver at or before eleven fifty the night of the fourteenth.

Some late bird of a reporter stole one of my placards, then hunted the town over and found the other one, and stole that. In this manner he accomplished what the profession call a "scoop"—that is, he got a valuable item, and saw to it that no other paper got it. And so his paper—the principal one in the town—had it in glaring type on the editorial page in the morning, followed by a Vesuvian opinion of our wretch a column long, which wound up by adding a thousand dollars to our reward on the *paper's* account! The journals out here know how to do the noble thing—when there's business in it.

At breakfast I occupied my usual seat—selected because it afforded a view of Papa Fuller's face, and was near enough for me to hear the talk that went on at his table. Seventy-five or a hundred people were in the room, and all discussing that item, and saying they hoped the seeker would find that rascal and remove the pollution of his presence from the town—with a rail, or a bullet, or something.

When Fuller came in he had the Notice to Leave—folded up—in one hand, and the newspaper in the other; and it gave me more than half a pang to see him. His cheerfulness was all gone, and he looked old and pinched and ashy. And then—only think of the things he had to listen to! Mamma, he heard his own unsuspecting friends describe him with epithets and characterizations drawn from the very dictionaries and phrasebooks of Satan's own authorized editions down below. And more than that, he had to *agree* with the verdicts and applaud them. His applause tasted bitter in his mouth, though; he could not disguise that from me; and it was observable that his appetite was gone; he only nibbled; he couldn't eat. Finally a man said:

"It is quite likely that that relative is in the room and hearing what this town thinks of that unspeakable scoundrel. I hope so."

Ah, dear, it was pitiful the way Fuller winced, and glanced around scared! He couldn't endure any more, and got up and left.

During several days he gave out that he had bought a mine in Mexico, and wanted to sell out and go down there as soon as he could, and give the property his personal attention. He played his cards well; said he would take forty thousand dollars—a quarter in cash, the rest in safe notes; but that as he greatly needed money on account of his new purchase, he would diminish his terms for cash in full. He sold out for thirty thousand dollars. And then, what do you think he did? He asked for *greenbacks*, and took them, saying the man in Mexico was a New Englander, with a head full of crotchets, and preferred greenbacks to gold or drafts. People thought it queer, since a draft on New York could produce greenbacks quite conveniently. There was talk of this odd thing, but only for a day; that is as long as any topic lasts in Denver.

I was watching, all the time. As soon as the sale was completed and the money paid—which was on the eleventh—I began to stick to Fuller's track without dropping it for a moment. That night—no, twelfth, for it was a little past midnight—I tracked him to his room, which was four doors from mine in the same hall, then I went back and put on my muddy day-laborer disguise, darkened my complexion, and sat down in my room in the gloom, with a gripsack handy, with a change in it, and my door ajar. For I suspected that the bird would take wing now. In half an hour an old woman passed by, carrying a grip; I caught the familiar whiff and followed, with my grip, for it was Fuller. He left the hotel by a side entrance, and at the corner he turned up an unfrequented street and walked three blocks in a light rain and a heavy darkness, and got into a two-horse hack, which, of course, was waiting for him by appointment. I took a seat (uninvited) on the trunk platform behind, and we drove briskly off. We drove ten miles, and the hack stopped at a way station and was discharged. Fuller got out and took a seat on a barrow under the awning, as far as he could get from the light; I went inside, and watched the ticket office. Fuller bought no ticket; I bought none. Presently the train came along, and he boarded a car; I entered the same car at the other end, and came down the aisle and took the seat behind him. When he paid the conductor and named his objective point, I dropped back several seats, while the conductor was changing a bill, and when he came to me I paid to the same place—about a hundred miles westward.

From that time for a week on end he led me a dance. He traveled here and there and yonder—always on a general westward trend—but he was not a woman after the first day. He was a laborer, like myself, and wore bushy false whiskers. His outfit was perfect, and he could do the character without thinking about it, for he had served the trade for wages. His nearest friend could not have recognized him. At last he located himself here, the obscurest little mountain camp in Montana; he has a shanty, and goes out prospecting daily; is gone all day, and avoids society. I am living at a miner's boarding house, and it is an awful place: the bunks, the food, the dirt—everything.

We have been here four weeks, and in that time I have seen him but once; but every night I go over his track and post myself. As soon as he engaged a shanty here I went to a town fifty miles away and telegraphed that Denver hotel to keep my baggage till I should send for it. I need nothing here but a change of army shirts, and I brought that with me.

SILVER GULCH, *June* 12.

The Denver episode has never found its way here, I think. I know the most of the men in camp, and they have never referred to it, at least in my hearing. Fuller doubtless feels quite safe in these conditions. He has located a claim, two miles away, in an out-of-the-way place in the mountains; it promises very well, and he is working it diligently. Ah, but the change in him! He never smiles, and he keeps quite to himself, consorting with no one—he who was so fond of company and so cheery only two months ago. I have seen him passing along several times recently—drooping, forlorn, the spring gone from his step, a pathetic figure. He calls himself David Wilson.

I can trust him to remain here until we disturb him. Since you insist, I will banish him again, but I do not see how he can be unhappier than he already is. I will go back to Denver and treat myself to a little season of comfort, and edible food, and endurable beds, and bodily decency; then I will fetch my things, and notify poor Papa Wilson to move on.

DENVER, *June* 19.

They miss him here. They all hope he is prospering in Mexico, and they do not say it just with their mouths, but out of their hearts. You know you can always tell. I am loitering here overlong, I confess it. But if you were in my place you would have charity for me. Yes, I know what you will say, and you are right: if I were in *your* place, and carried your scalding memories in my heart—

I will take the night train back tomorrow.

DENVER, *June* 20.

God forgive us, Mother, we are hunting the *wrong man!* I have not slept any all night. I am now waiting at dawn, for the *morning* train— and how the minutes drag, how they drag!

This Jacob Fuller is a *cousin* of the guilty one. How stupid we have been not to reflect that the guilty one would never again wear his own name after that fiendish deed! The Denver Fuller is four years younger than the other one; he came here a young widower in '79, aged twenty-one—a year before you were married; and the documents to prove it are innumerable. Last night I talked with familiar friends of his who have known him from the day of his arrival. I said nothing, but a few days from now I will land him in this town again, with the loss upon his mine made good; and there will be a banquet, and a torchlight procession, and there will not be any expense on anybody but me. Do you call this "gush"? I am only a boy, as you well know; it is my privilege. By and by I shall not be a boy any more.

SILVER GULCH, *July* 3.

Mother, he is gone! Gone, and left no trace. The scent was cold when I came. Today I am out of bed for the first time since. I wish I were not a boy, then I could stand shocks better. They all think he went west. I start tonight, in a wagon—two or three hours of that, then I get a train. I don't know where I'm going, but I must go; to try to keep still would be torture.

Of course he has effaced himself with a new name and a disguise. This means that *I may have to search the whole globe to find him.* Indeed it is what I expect. Do you see, Mother? It is *I* that am the wandering Jew. The irony of it! We arranged that for another.

Think of the difficulties! And there would be none if I only could advertise for him. But if there is any way to do it that would not frighten him, I have not been able to think it out, and I have tried till my brains are addled. "If the gentleman who lately bought a mine in Mexico and sold one in Denver will send his address to" (to whom, Mother?), "it will be explained to him that it was all a mistake; his forgiveness will be asked, and full reparation made for a loss which he sustained in a certain matter." Do you see? He would think it a trap. Well, anyone would. If I should say, "It is now known that he was not the man wanted, but another man—a man who once bore the same name, but discarded it for good reasons"—would that answer? But the Denver people would wake up then and say "Oho!" and they would remember about the suspicious greenbacks, and say, "Why did he run away if he wasn't the right man?—it is too thin." If I failed to find him he would be ruined there—there where there is no taint upon him now. You have a better head than mine. Help me.

I have one clue, and only one. I know his handwriting. If he puts his new false name upon a hotel register and does not disguise it too much, it will be valuable to me if I ever run across it.

SAN FRANCISCO, *June* 28, 1898.

You already know how well I have searched the States from Colorado to the Pacific, and how nearly I came to getting him once. Well, I have had another close miss. It was here, yesterday. I struck his trail, *hot*, on the street, and followed it on a run to a cheap hotel. That was a costly mistake; a dog would have gone the other way. But I am only part dog, and can get very humanly stupid when excited. He had been stopping in that house ten days; I almost know, now, that he stops long nowhere, the past six or eight months, but is restless and has to keep moving. I understand that feeling! and I know what it is to feel it. He still uses the name he had registered when I came so near catching him nine months ago—"James Walker"; doubtless the same he adopted when he fled from Silver Gulch. An unpretending man, and has small taste for fancy names. I recognized the hand easily, through its slight disguise. A square man, and not good at shams and pretences.

They said he was just gone, on a journey; left no address; didn't say where he was going; looked frightened when asked to leave his address; had no baggage but a cheap valise; carried it off on foot—a "stingy old person and not much loss to the house." *"Old!"* I suppose he is, now. I hardly heard; I was there but a moment. I rushed along his trail, and it led me to a wharf. Mother, the smoke of the steamer he had taken was just fading out on the horizon! I should have saved half an hour if I had gone in the right direction at first. I could have taken a fast tug, and should have stood a chance of catching that vessel. She is bound for Melbourne.

HOPE CANYON, CALIFORNIA,
October 3, 1900.

You have a right to complain. "A letter a year" *is* a paucity; I freely acknowledge it; but how can one write when there is nothing to write about but failures? No one can keep it up; it breaks the heart.

I told you—it seems ages ago, now—how I missed him at Melbourne, and then chased him all over Australasia for months on end.

Well, then, after that I followed him to India; almost *saw* him in Bombay; traced him all around—to Baroda, Rawal-Pindi, Lucknow, Lahore, Cawnpore, Allahabad, Calcutta, Madras—oh, everywhere; week after week, month after month, through the dust and swelter—always approximately on his track, sometimes close upon him, yet never catching him. And down to Ceylon, and then to—Never mind, by and by I will write it all out.

I chased him home to California, and down to Mexico, and back again to California. Since then I have been hunting him about the state from the first of last January down to a month ago. I feel almost sure he is not far from Hope Canyon; I traced him to a point thirty miles from here, but there I lost the trail; someone gave him a lift in a wagon, I suppose.

I am taking a rest, now—modified by searchings for the lost trail. I was tired to death, Mother, and low-spirited, and sometimes coming uncomfortably near to losing hope; but the miners in this little camp are good fellows, and I am used to their sort this long time back; and their breezy ways freshen a person up and make him forget his troubles. I have been here a month. I am cabining with a young fellow named "Sammy" Hillyer, about twenty-five, the only son of his mother—like me—and loves her dearly, and writes to her every week—part of which is like me. He is a timid boy, and in the matter of intellect—well, he cannot be depended upon to set a river on fire; but no matter, he is well liked; he is good and fine, and it is meat and bread and rest and luxury to sit and talk with him and have a comradeship again. I wish "James Walker" could have it. He had friends; he liked company. That brings up that picture of him, the time that I saw him last. The pathos of it! It comes before me often and often. At that very time, poor thing, I was girding up my conscience to make him move on again!

Hillyer's heart is better than mine, better than anybody's in the community, I suppose, for he is the one friend of the black sheep of the camp—Flint Buckner—and the only man Flint ever talks with or allows to talk with him. He says he knows Flint's history, and that it is trouble that has made him what he is, and so one ought to be as charitable toward him as one can. Now, none but a pretty large heart could find space to accommodate a lodger like Flint Buckner, from all I hear about him outside. I think that this one detail will give you a better idea of Sammy's character than any labored-out description I could furnish you of him. In one of our talks he said something about like this: "Flint's a kinsman of mine, and he pours out all his troubles to me—empties his breast from time to time, or I reckon it would burst. There couldn't be any unhappier man, Archy Stillman; his life has been made up of misery of mind—he isn't near as old as he looks. He has lost the feel of reposefulness and peace—oh, years and years ago! He doesn't know what good luck is—never has had any; often says he wishes he was in the other hell, he is so tired of this one."

IV

*No real gentleman will tell the naked
truth in the presence of ladies*

It was a crisp and spicy morning in early October. The lilacs and laburnums, lit with the glory-fires of autumn, hung burning and flashing in the upper air, a fairy bridge provided by kind Nature for the wingless wild things that have their homes in the treetops and would visit together; the larch and the pomegranate flung their purple and yellow flames in brilliant broad splashes along the slanting sweep of the woodland; the sensuous fragrance of innumerable deciduous flowers rose upon the swooning atmosphere; far in the empty sky a solitary oesophagus slept upon motionless wing; everywhere brooded stillness, serenity, and the peace of God.

October is the time—1900; Hope Canyon is the place, a silver mining camp away down in the Esmeralda region. It is a secluded spot, high and remote; recent as to discovery; thought by its occupants to be rich in metal—a year or two's prospecting will decide that matter one way or the other. For inhabitants, the camp has about two hundred miners, one white woman and child, several Chinese washermen, five squaws, and a dozen vagrant buck Indians in rabbitskin robes, battered plug hats, and tin-can necklaces. There are no mills as yet; there is no church, no newspaper. The camp has existed but two years; it has made no big strike; the world is ignorant of its name and place.

On both sides of the canyon the mountains rise wall-like, three thousand feet, and the long spiral of straggling huts down in its narrow bottom gets a kiss from the sun only once a day, when he sails over at noon. The village is a couple of miles long; the cabins stand well apart from each other. The tavern is the only "frame" house— the only house, one might say. It occupies a central position, and is the evening resort of the population. They drink there, and play seven-up and dominoes; also billiards, for there is a table, crossed all over with torn places repaired with court-plaster; there are some cues, but no leathers; some chipped balls which clatter when they run, and do not slow up gradually, but stop suddenly and sit down; there is part of a cube of chalk, with a projecting jag of flint in it; and the man who can score six on a single break can set up the drinks at the bar's expense.

Flint Buckner's cabin was the last one of the village, going south; his silver claim was at the other end of the village, northward, and a little beyond the last hut in that direction. He was a sour creature, unsociable, and had no companionships. People who had tried to get acquainted with him had regretted it and dropped him. His history was not known. Some believed that Sammy Hillyer knew it; others said no. If asked, Hillyer said no, he was not acquainted with it. Flint had a meek English youth of sixteen or seventeen with him, whom he treated roughly, both in public and private, and of course this lad was applied to for information, but with no success. Fetlock Jones—name of the youth—said that Flint picked him up on a prospecting tramp, and as he had neither home nor friends in America, he had found it wise to stay and take Buckner's hard usage for the sake of the salary, which was bacon and beans. Further than this he could offer no testimony.

Fetlock had been in this slavery for a month now, and under his meek exterior he was slowly consuming to a cinder with the insults and humiliations which his master had put upon him. For the meek suffer bitterly from these hurts; more bitterly, perhaps, than do the manlier sort, who can burst out and get relief with words or blows when the limit of endurance has been reached. Goodhearted people wanted to help Fetlock out of his trouble, and tried to get him to leave Buckner; but the boy showed fright at the thought, and said he "dasn't." Pat Riley urged him, and said:

"You leave the damned hunks and come with me; don't you be afraid. I'll take care of *him*."

The boy thanked him with tears in his eyes, but shuddered and said he "dasn't risk it"; he said Flint would catch him alone, some time, in the night, and then—"Oh, it makes me sick, Mr. Riley, to think of it."

Others said, "Run away from him; we'll stake you; skip out for the coast some night." But all these suggestions failed; he said Flint would hunt him down and fetch him back, just for meanness.

The people could not understand this. The boy's miseries went steadily on, week after week. It is quite likely that the people would have understood if they had known how he was employing his spare time. He slept in an out-cabin near Flint's; and there, nights, he nursed his bruises and his humiliations, and studied and studied over a single problem—how he could murder Flint Buckner and not be found out. It was the only joy he had in life; these hours were the only ones in the twenty-four which he looked forward to with eagerness and spent in happiness.

He thought of poison. No—that would not serve; the inquest would reveal where it was procured and who had procured it. He thought of a shot in the back in a lonely place when Flint would be homeward-bound at midnight—his unvarying hour for the trip. No—somebody might be near, and catch him. He thought of stabbing him in his sleep. No—he might strike an inefficient blow, and Flint would seize him. He examined a hundred different ways—none of them would answer; for in even the very obscurest and secretest of them there was always the fatal defect of a *risk*, a chance, a possibility that he might be found out. He would have none of that.

But he was patient, endlessly patient. There was no hurry, he said to himself. He would never leave Flint till he left him a corpse; there was no hurry—he would find the way. It was somewhere, and he would endure shame and pain and misery until he found it. Yes, somewhere there was a way which would leave not a trace, not even the faintest clue to the murderer—there was no hurry—he would find that way, and then—oh, then, it would just be good to be alive! Meantime he would diligently keep up his reputation for meekness; and also, as always theretofore, he would allow no one to hear him say a resentful or offensive thing about his oppressor.

Two days before the before-mentioned October morning Flint had bought some things, and he and Fetlock had brought them home to Flint's cabin: a fresh box of candles, which they put in the corner; a tin can of blasting powder, which they placed upon the candle box; a keg of blasting powder, which they placed under Flint's bunk; a huge coil of fuse, which they hung on a peg. Fetlock reasoned that Flint's mining operations had outgrown the pick, and that blasting was about to begin now. He had seen blasting done, and he had a notion of the process, but he had never helped in it. His conjecture was right—blasting time had come. In the morning the pair carried fuse, drills, and the powder-can to the shaft; it was now eight feet deep; and to get into it and out of it a short ladder was used. They descended, and by command Fetlock held the drill—without any instructions as to the right way to hold it—and Flint proceeded to strike. The sledge came down; the drill sprang out of Fetlock's hand, almost as a matter of course.

"You mangy—, is that any way to hold a drill? Pick it up! Stand it up! There—hold fast. D—— you! *I'll* teach you!"

At the end of an hour the drilling was finished.

"Now, then, charge it."

The boy started to pour in the powder.

"Idiot!"

A heavy bat on the jaw laid the lad out.

"Get up! You can't lie snivelling there. Now, then, stick in the fuse *first. Now* put in the powder. Hold on, hold on! Are you going to fill the hole *all* up? Of all the sap-headed milksops I— Put in some dirt! Put in some gravel! Tamp it down! Hold on, hold on! Oh, great Scott! get out of the way!" He snatched the iron and tamped the charge himself, meantime cursing and blaspheming like a fiend. Then he fired the fuse, climbed out of the shaft, and ran fifty yards away, Fetlock following. They stood waiting a few minutes, then a great volume of smoke and rocks burst high into the air with a thunderous explosion; after a little there was a shower of descending stones; then all was serene again.

"I wish to God you'd been in it!" remarked the master.

They went down the shaft, cleaned it out, drilled another hole, and put in another charge.

"Look here! How much fuse are you proposing to waste? Don't you know how to time a fuse!"

"No, sir."

"You *don't!* Well, if you don't beat anything *I* ever saw!"

He climbed out of the shaft and spoke down:

"Well, idiot, are you going to be all day? Cut the fuse and light it!"

The trembling creature began, "If you please, sir, I—"

"You talk back to *me?* Cut it and light it!"

The boy cut and lit.

"Ger-reat Scott! a one-minute fuse! I wish you were in—"

In his rage he snatched the ladder out of the shaft and ran. The boy was aghast.

"Oh, my God! Help! Help! Oh, save me!" he implored. "Oh, what can I do! What *can* I do!"

He backed against the wall as tightly as he could; the sputtering fuse frightened the voice out of him; his breath stood still; he stood gazing and impotent; in two seconds, three seconds, four, he would be flying toward the sky torn to fragments. Then he had an inspiration. He sprang at the fuse and severed the inch of it that was left above the ground, and was saved.

He sank down limp and half lifeless with fright, his strength all gone; but he muttered with a deep joy:

"He has learnt me! I knew there was a way, if I would wait."

After a matter of five minutes Buckner stole to the shaft, looking worried and uneasy, and peered down into it. He took in the situation; he saw what had happened. He lowered the ladder, and the boy dragged himself weakly up it. He was very white. His appearance added something to Buckner's uncomfortable state, and he said, with a show of regret and sympathy which sat upon him awkwardly from lack of practice:

"It was an accident, you know. Don't say anything about it to anybody; I was excited, and didn't notice what I was doing. You're not looking well; you've worked enough for today; go down to my cabin and eat what you want, and rest. It's just an accident, you know, on account of my being excited."

"It scared me," said the lad, as he started away; "but I learnt something, so I don't mind it."

"Damned easy to please!" muttered Buckner, following him with his eye. "I wonder if he'll tell? Mightn't he? . . . I wish it *had* killed him."

The boy took no advantage of his holiday in the matter of resting; he employed it in work, eager and feverish and happy work. A thick growth of chaparral extended down the mountainside clear to Flint's cabin; the most of Fetlock's labor was done in the dark intricacies of that stubborn growth; the rest of it was done in his own shanty. At last all was complete, and he said:

"If he's got any suspicions that I'm going to tell on him, he won't keep them long, tomorrow. He will see that I am the same milksop as I always was—all day and the next. And the day after tomorrow night there'll be an end of him, and nobody will ever guess who finished him up nor how it was done. He dropped me the idea his own self, and that's odd."

V

The next day came and went.

It is now almost midnight, and in five minutes the new morning will begin. The scene is in the tavern billiard room. Rough men in rough clothing, slouch hats, breeches stuffed into boot-tops, some with vests, none with coats, are grouped about the boiler-iron stove, which has ruddy cheeks and is distributing a grateful warmth; the billiard balls are clacking; there is no other sound—that is, within; the wind is fitfully moaning without. The men look bored; also expectant. A hulking, broad-shouldered miner, of middle age, with grizzled whiskers and an unfriendly eye set in an unsociable face, rises, slips a coil of fuse upon his arm, gathers up some other personal properties, and departs without word or greeting to anybody. It is Flint Buckner. As the door closes behind him a buzz of talk breaks out.

"The regularest man that ever was," said Jake Parker, the blacksmith; "you can tell when it's twelve just by him leaving, without looking at your Waterbury."

"And it's the only virtue he's got, as fur as I know," said Peter Hawes, miner.

"He's just a blight on this society," said Wells-Fargo's man, Ferguson. "If I was running this shop I'd make him say something, *some* time or other, or vamos the ranch." This with a suggestive glance at the barkeeper, who did not choose to see it, since the man under discussion was a good customer, and went home pretty well set up, every night, with refreshments furnished from the bar.

"Say," said Ham Sandwich, miner, "does any of you boys ever recollect of him asking you to take a drink?"

"*Him?* Flint *Buckner?* Oh, Laura!"

This sarcastic rejoinder came in a spontaneous general outburst in one form of words or another from the crowd. After a brief silence, Pat Riley, miner, said:

"He's the fifteen-puzzle, that cuss. And his boy's another one. *I* can't make them out."

"Nor anybody else," said Ham Sandwich; "and if they are fifteen-puzzles, how are you going to rank up that other one? When it comes to A-1 right-down solid mysteriousness, he lays over both of them. *Easy*—don't he?"

"You bet!"

Everybody said it. Every man but one. He was the newcomer— Peterson. He ordered the drinks all round, and asked who No. 3 might be. All answered at once, "Archy Stillman!"

"Is he a mystery?" asked Peterson.

"Is *he* a mystery? Is Archy *Stillman* a mystery?" said Wells-Fargo's man, Ferguson. "Why, the fourth dimension's foolishness to *him*."

For Ferguson was learned.

Peterson wanted to hear all about him; everybody wanted to tell him; everybody began. But Billy Stevens, the barkeeper, called the house to order, and said one at a time was best. He distributed the drinks, and appointed Ferguson to lead. Ferguson said:

"Well, he's a boy. And that is just about all we know about him. You can pump him till you are tired; it ain't any use; you won't get anything. At least about his intentions, or line of business, or where he's from, and such things as that. And as for getting at the nature and get-up of his main big chief mystery, why, he'll just change the subject, that's all. You can *guess* till you're black in the face—it's your privilege—but suppose you do, where do you arrive at? Nowhere, as near as I can make out."

"What *is* his big chief one?"

"Sight, maybe. Hearing, maybe. Instinct, maybe. Magic, maybe. Take your choice—grownups, twenty-five; children and servants, half price. Now I'll tell you what he can do. You can start here, and just disappear; you can go and hide wherever you want to, I don't care where it is, nor how far—and he'll go straight and put his finger on you."

"You don't mean it!"

"I just do, though. Weather's nothing to him—elemental conditions is nothing to him—he don't even take notice of them."

"Oh, come! Dark? Rain? Snow? Hey?"

"It's all the same to *him*. *He* don't give a damn."

"Oh, *say*—including *fog*, per'aps?"

"*Fog!* he's got an eye 't can plunk through it like a bullet."

"Now, boys, honor bright, what's he giving me?"

"It's a fact!" they all shouted. "Go on, Wells-Fargo."

"Well, sir, you can leave him here, chatting with the boys, and you can slip out and go to any cabin in this camp and open a book—yes, sir, a dozen of them—and take the page in your memory, and he'll start out and go straight to that cabin and open every one of them books at the right page, and call it off, and never make a mistake."

"He must be the devil!"

"More than one has thought it. Now I'll tell you a perfectly wonderful thing that he done. The other night he—"

There was a sudden great murmur of sounds outside, the door flew open, and an excited crowd burst in, with the camp's one white woman in the lead and crying:

"My child! my child! she's lost and gone! For the love of God help me to find Archy Stillman; we've hunted everywhere!"

Said the barkeeper:

"Sit down, sit down, Mrs. Hogan, and don't worry. He asked for a bed three hours ago, tuckered out tramping the trails the way he's always doing, and went upstairs. Ham Sandwich, run up and roust him out; he's in No. 14."

The youth was soon downstairs and ready. He asked Mrs. Hogan for particulars.

"Bless you, dear, there ain't any; I wish there was. I put her to sleep at seven in the evening, and when I went in there an hour ago to go to bed myself, she was gone. I rushed for your cabin, dear, and you wasn't there, and I've hunted for you ever since, at every cabin down the gulch, and now I've come up again, and I'm that distracted and scared and heartbroke; but, thanks to God, I've found you at last, dearheart, and you'll find my child. Come on! come quick!"

"Move right along; I'm with you, madam. Go to your cabin first."

The whole company streamed out to join the hunt. All the southern half of the village was up, a hundred men strong, and waiting outside, a vague dark mass sprinkled with twinkling lanterns. The mass fell into columns by threes and fours to accommodate itself to the narrow road, and strode briskly along southward in the wake of the leaders. In a few minutes the Hogan cabin was reached.

"There's the bunk," said Mrs. Hogan; "there's where she was; it's where I laid her at seven o'clock; but where she is now, God only knows."

"Hand me a lantern," said Archy. He set it on the hard earth floor and knelt by it, pretending to examine the ground closely. "Here's her track," he said, touching the ground here and there and yonder with his finger. "Do you see?"

Several of the company dropped upon their knees and did their best to see. One or two thought they discerned something like a track; the others shook their heads and confessed that the smooth hard surface had no marks upon it which their eyes were sharp enough to discover. One said, "Maybe a child's foot could make a mark on it, but *I* don't see how."

Young Stillman stepped outside, held the light to the ground, turned leftward, and moved along three steps, closely examining; then said, "I've got the direction—come along; take the lantern, somebody."

He strode off swiftly southward, the files following, swaying and bending in and out with the deep curves of the gorge. Thus a mile, and the mouth of the gorge was reached; before them stretched the sagebrush plain, dim, vast, and vague. Stillman called a halt, saying, "We mustn't start wrong, now; we must take the direction again." He took a lantern and examined the ground for a matter of twenty yards; then said, "Come on; it's all right," and gave up the lantern. In and out among the sagebrushes he marched, a quarter of a mile, bearing gradually to the right; then took a new direction and made another great semicircle; then changed again and moved due west nearly half a mile—and stopped.

"She gave it up, here, poor little chap. Hold the lantern. You can see where she sat."

But this was in a slick alkali flat which was surfaced like steel, and no person in the pary was quite hardy enough to claim an eyesight that could detect the track of a cushion on a veneer like that. The bereaved mother fell upon her knees and kissed the spot, lamenting.

"But where is she, then?" someone said. "She didn't stay here. We can see *that* much, anyway."

Stillman moved about in a circle around the place, with the lantern, pretending to hunt for tracks. "Well!" he said presently, in an annoyed tone, "I don't understand it." He examined again. "No use. She was here—that's certain; she never *walked* away from here—and that's certain. It's a puzzle; I can't make it out."

The mother lost heart then.

"Oh, my God! oh, blessed Virgin! some flying beast has got her. I'll never see her again!"

"Ah, *don't* give up," said Archy. "We'll find her—don't give up."

"God bless you for the words, Archy Stillman!" and she seized his hand and kissed it fervently.

Peterson, the newcomer, whispered satirically in Ferguson's ear:

"Wonderful performance to find this place, wasn't it? Hardly worthwhile to come so far, though; any other supposititious place would have answered just as well—hey?"

Ferguson was not pleased with the innuendo. He said, with some warmth:

"Do you mean to insinuate that the child hasn't been here? I tell you the child *has* been here! Now if you want to get yourself into as tidy a little fuss as—"

"All right!" sang out Stillman. "Come, everybody, and look at this! It was right under our noses all the time, and we didn't see it."

There was a general plunge for the ground at the place where the child was alleged to have rested, and many eyes tried hard and hopefully to see the thing that Archy's finger was resting upon. There was a pause, then a several-barrelled sigh of disappointment. Pat Riley and Ham Sandwich said, in the one breath:

"What is it, Archy? There's nothing here."

"Nothing? Do you call *that* nothing?" and he swiftly traced upon the ground a form with his finger. "There—don't you recognize it now? It's Injun Billy's track. He's got the child."

"God be praised!" from the mother.

"Take away the lantern. I've got the direction. Follow!"

He started on a run, racing in and out among the sagebushes a matter of three hundred yards, and disappeared over a sand wave; the others struggled after him, caught him up, and found him waiting. Ten steps away was a little wickieup, a dim and formless shelter of rags and old horse blankets, a dull light showing throughout its chinks.

"You lead, Mrs. Hogan," said the lad. "It's your privilege to be first."

All followed the sprint she made for the wickieup, and saw, with her, the picture its interior afforded. Injun Billy was sitting on the ground; the child was asleep beside him. The mother hugged it with a wild embrace, which included Archy Stillman, the grateful tears running down her face, and in a choked and broken voice she poured out a golden stream of that wealth of worshipping endearments which has its home in full richness nowhere but in the Irish heart.

"I find her bymeby it is ten o'clock," Billy explained. "She 'sleep out yonder, ve'y tired—face wet, been cryin', 'spose; fetch her home, feed her, she heap much hungry—go 'sleep 'gin."

In her limitless gratitude the happy mother waived rank and hugged him too, calling him "the angel of God in disguise."

And he probably was in disguise if he was that kind of an official. He was dressed for the character.

At half past one in the morning the procession burst into the village, singing "When Johnny Comes Marching Home," waving its lanterns, and swallowing the drinks that were brought out all along its course. It concentrated at the tavern, and made a night of what was left of the morning.

PART TWO

I

The next afternoon the village was electrified with an immense sensation. A grave and dignified foreigner of distinguished bearing and appearance had arrived at the tavern, and entered this formidable name upon the register:

Sherlock Holmes.

The news buzzed from cabin to cabin, from claim to claim; tools were dropped, and the town swarmed toward the center of interest. A man passing out at the northern end of the village shouted it to Pat Riley, whose claim was the next one to Flint Buckner's. At that time Fetlock Jones seemed to turn sick. He muttered to himself:

"Uncle *Sherlock!* The mean luck of it!—that *he* should come just when . . ." He dropped into a reverie, and presently said to himself: "But what's the use of being afraid of *him?* Anybody that knows him the way I do knows he can't detect a crime, except when he plans it all out beforehand and arranges the clues and hires some fellow to commit it according to instructions. . . . Now there ain't going to *be* any clues this time—so, what show has he got? None at all. No, sir; everything's ready. If I was to risk putting it off . . . No, I won't run any risk like that. Flint Buckner goes out of this world tonight, for sure." Then another trouble presented itself. "Uncle Sherlock'll be wanting to talk home matters with me this evening, and how am I going to get rid of him? for I've *got* to be at my cabin a minute or two about eight o'clock." This was an awkward matter, and cost him much thought. But he found a way to beat the difficulty. "We'll go for a walk, and I'll leave him in the road a minute, so that he won't see what it is I do: the best way to throw a detective off the track, anyway, is to have him along when you are preparing the thing. Yes, that's the safest—I'll take him with me."

Meantime the road in front of the tavern was blocked with villagers waiting and hoping for a glimpse of the great man. But he kept his room, and did not appear. None but Ferguson, Jake Parker the blacksmith, and Ham Sandwich had any luck. These enthusiastic admirers of the great scientific detective hired the tavern's detained-baggage lockup, which looked into the detective's room across a little alleyway ten or twelve feet wide, ambushed themselves in it, and cut some peepholes in the window blind. Mr. Holmes's blinds were down; but by and by he raised them. It gave the spies a hair-lifting but pleasurable thrill to find themselves face to face with the Extraordinary Man who had filled the world with the fame of his more-than-human ingenuities. There he sat—not a myth, not a shadow, but real, alive, compact of substance, and almost within touching distance with the hand.

"Look at that head!" said Ferguson, in an awed voice. "By gracious! *that's* a head!"

"You bet!" said the blacksmith, with deep reverence. "Look at his nose! look at his eyes! Intellect? Just a battery of it!"

"And that paleness," said Ham Sandwich. "Comes from thought—that's what it comes from. Hell! duffers like us don't know what real thought *is*."

"No more we don't," said Ferguson. "What we take for thinking is just blubber and slush."

"Right you are, Wells-Fargo. And look at that frown—that's *deep* thinking—away down, down, forty fathom into the bowels of things. He's on the track of something."

"Well, he is, and don't you forget it. Say—look at that awful gravity—look at that pallid solemness—there ain't any corpse can lay over it."

"No, sir, not for dollars! And it's his'n by hereditary rights, too; he's been dead four times a'ready, and there's history for it. Three times natural, once by accident. I've heard say he smells damp and cold, like a grave. And he—"

"'Sh! Watch him! There—he's got his thumb on the bump on the near corner of his forehead, and his forefinger on the off one. His think-works is just a-*grinding* now, you bet your other shirt."

"That's so. And now he's gazing up toward heaven and stroking his mustache slow, and—"

"Now he has rose up standing, and is putting his clues together on his left fingers with his right finger. See? he touches the forefinger—now middle finger—now ring finger—"

"Stuck!"

"Look at him scowl! He can't seem to make out *that* clue. So he—"

"See him smile!—like a tiger—and tally off the other fingers like nothing! He's got it, boys; he's got it sure!"

"Well, I should *say!* I'd hate to be in that man's place that he's after."

Mr. Holmes drew a table to the window, sat down with his back to the spies, and proceeded to write. The spies withdrew their eyes from the peepholes, lit their pipes, and settled themselves for a comfortable smoke and talk. Ferguson said, with conviction:

"Boys, it's no use talking, he's a wonder! He's got the signs of it all over him."

"You hain't ever said a truer word than that, Wells-Fargo," said Jake Parker. "Say, wouldn't it 'a' been nuts if he'd a-been here last night?"

"Oh, by George, but wouldn't it!" said Ferguson. "Then we'd have seen *scientific* work. Intellect—just pure intellect—away up on the upper levels, dontchuknow. Archy is all right, and it don't become anybody to belittle *him*, I can tell you. But his gift is only just eyesight, sharp as an owl's, as near as I can make it out just a grand natural animal talent, no more, no less, and prime as far as it goes, but no intellect in it, and for awfulness and marvelousness no more to be compared to what this man does than—than— Why, let me tell you what *he'd* have done. He'd have stepped over to Hogan's and glanced—just *glanced*, that's all—at the premises, and that's enough. See everything? Yes, sir, to the last little *de*tail; and he'd know more about that place than the Hogans would know in seven years. Next, he would sit down on the bunk, just as ca'm and say to Mrs. Hogan—*Say*, Ham, consider that you are Mrs. Hogan. I'll ask the questions; you answer them."

"All right; go on."

"Madam, if you please—attention—do not let your mind wander. Now then—sex of the child?"

"Female, your Honor."

"Um—female. Very good, very good. Age?"

"Turned six, your Honor."

"Um—young, weak—two miles. Weariness will overtake it then. It will sink down and sleep. We shall find it two miles away, or less. Teeth?"

"Five, your Honor, and one a-coming."

"Very good, very good, *very* good indeed. You see, boys, *he* knows a clue when he sees it, when it wouldn't mean a dern thing to anybody else. Stockings, madam? Shoes?"

"Yes, your Honor—both"

"Yarn, perhaps? Morocco?"

"Yarn, your Honor. And kip."

"Um—kip. This complicates the matter. However, let it go—we shall manage. Religion?"

"Catholic, your Honor."

"Very good. Snip me a bit from the bed blanket, please. Ah, thanks. Part wool—foreign make. Very well. A snip from some garment of the child's, please. Thanks. Cotton. Shows wear. An excellent clue, excellent. Pass me a pellet of the floor dirt, if you'll be so kind. Thanks, many thanks. Ah, admirable, admirable! *Now* we know where we are, I think. You see, boys, he's got all the clues he wants now; he don't need anything more. Now, then, what does this Extraordinary Man do? He lays those snips and that dirt out on the table and leans over them on his elbows, and puts them together side by side and studies them—mumbles to himself, 'Female'; changes them around—mumbles, 'Six years old'; changes them this way and that—again mumbles: 'Five teeth—one a-coming—Catholic—yarn—cotton—kip—damn that kip.' Then he straightens up and gazes toward heaven, and ploughs and ploughs, muttering, 'Damn that kip!' Then he stands up and frowns, and begins to tally off his clues on his fingers—and gets stuck at the ring finger. But only just a minute—then his face glares all up in a smile like a house afire, and he straightens up stately and majestic, and says to the crowd, 'Take a lantern, a couple of you, and go down to Injun Billy's and fetch the child—the rest of you go 'long home to bed; good night, madam; good night, gents.' And he bows like the Matterhorn, and pulls out for the tavern. That's *his* style, and the *Only*—scientific, intellectual—all over in fifteen minutes—no poking around all over the sagebrush range an hour and a half in a mass-meeting crowd for *him*, boys—you hear *me!*"

"By Jackson, it's grand!" said Ham Sandwich. "Wells-Fargo, you've got him down to a dot. He ain't painted up any exacter to the life in the books. By George, I can just see him—can't you, boys?"

"You bet you! It's just a photograft, that's what it is."

Ferguson was profoundly pleased with his success, and grateful. He sat silently enjoying his happiness a little while, then he murmured, with a deep awe in his voice,

"I wonder if God made him?"

There was no response for a moment; then Ham Sandwich said, reverently, "Not all at one time, I reckon."

II

At eight o'clock that evening two persons were groping their way past Flint Buckner's cabin in the frosty gloom. They were Sherlock Holmes and his nephew.

"Stop here in the road a moment, Uncle," said Fetlock, "while I run to my cabin; I won't be gone a minute."

He asked for something—the uncle furnished it—then he disappeared in the darkness, but soon returned, and the talking-walk was resumed. By nine o'clock they had wandered back to the tavern. They worked their way through the billiard room, where a crowd had gathered in the hope of getting a glimpse of the Extraordinary Man.

A royal cheer was raised. Mr. Holmes acknowledged the compliment with a series of courtly bows, and as he was passing out his nephew said to the assemblage,

"Uncle Sherlock's got some work to do, gentlemen, that'll keep him till twelve or one, but he'll be down again then, or earlier if he can, and hopes some of you'll be left to take a drink with him."

"By George, he's just a duke, boys! Three cheers for Sherlock Holmes, the greatest man that ever lived!" shouted Ferguson. "Hip, hip, hip—"

"Hurrah! hurrah! hurrah! Tiger!"

The uproar shook the building, so hearty was the feeling the boys put into their welcome. Upstairs the uncle reproached the nephew gently, saying,

"What did you get me into that engagement for?"

"I reckon you don't want to be unpopular, do you, Uncle? Well, then, don't you put on any exclusiveness in a mining camp, that's all. The boys admire you; but if you was to leave without taking a drink with them, they'd set you down for a snob. And, besides, you said you had home talk enough in stock to keep us up and at it half the night."

The boy was right, and wise—the uncle acknowledged it. The boy was wise in another detail which he did not mention—except to himself: "Uncle and the others will come handy—in the way of nailing an *alibi* where it can't be budged."

He and his uncle talked diligently about three hours. Then, about midnight, Fetlock stepped downstairs and took a position in the dark a dozen steps from the tavern, and waited. Five minutes later Flint Buckner came rocking out of the billiard room and almost brushed him as he passed.

"I've *got* him!" muttered the boy. He continued to himself, looking after the shadowy form: "Goodbye—goodbye for good, Flint Buckner; you called my mother a—well, never mind what; it's all right, now; you're taking your last walk, friend."

He went musing back into the tavern. "From now till one is an hour. We'll spend it with the boys; it's good for the *alibi*."

He brought Sherlock Holmes to the billiard room, which was jammed with eager and admiring miners; the guest called the drinks, and the fun began. Everybody was happy; everybody was complimentary; the ice was soon broken; songs, anecdotes, and more drinks followed, and the pregnant minutes flew. At six minutes to one, when the jollity was at its highest—

Boom!

There was silence instantly. The deep sound came rolling and rumbling from peak to peak up the gorge, then died down, and ceased. The spell broke, then, and the men made a rush for the door, saying,

"Something's blown up!"

Outside, a voice in the darkness said,

"It's away down the gorge; I saw the flash."

The crowd poured down the canyon—Holmes, Fetlock, Archy Stillman, everybody. They made the mile in a few minutes. By the light of a lantern they found the smooth and solid dirt floor of Flint Buckner's cabin; of the cabin itself not a vestige remained, not a rag nor a splinter. Nor any sign of Flint. Search parties sought here and there and yonder, and presently a cry went up.

"Here he is!"

It was true. Fifty yards down the gulch they had found him—that is, they had found a crushed and lifeless mass which represented him. Fetlock Jones hurried thither with the others and looked.

The inquest was a fifteen minute affair. Ham Sandwich, foreman of the jury, handed up the verdict, which was phrased with a certain unstudied literary grace, and closed with this finding, to wit: that "deceased came to his death by his own act or some other person or persons unknown to this jury not leaving any family or similar effects behind but his cabin which was blown away and God have mercy on his soul amen."

Then the impatient jury rejoined the main crowd, for the storm-center of interest was there—Sherlock Holmes. The miners stood silent and reverent in a half-circle, enclosing a large vacant space which included the front exposure of the site of the late premises. In this considerable space the Extraordinary Man was moving about, attended by his nephew with a lantern. With a tape he took measurements of the cabin site; of the distance from the wall of chaparral to the road; of the height of the chaparral bushes; also various other measurements. He gathered a rag here, a splinter there, and a pinch of earth yonder, inspected them profoundly, and preserved them. He took the "lay" of the place with a pocket compass, allowing two seconds for magnetic variation. He took the time (Pacific) by his watch, correcting it for local time. He paced off the distance from the cabin site to the corpse, and corrected that for tidal differentiation. He took the altitude with a pocket aneroid, and the temperature with a pocket thermometer. Finally he said, with a stately bow: "It is finished. Shall we return, gentlemen?"

He took up the line of march for the tavern, and the crowd fell into his wake, earnestly discussing and admiring the Extraordinary Man, and interlarding guesses as to the origin of the tragedy and who the author of it might be.

"My, but it's grand luck having him here—hey, boys?" said Ferguson.

"It's the biggest thing of the century," said Ham Sandwich. "It'll go all over the world; you mark my words."

"*You* bet!" said Jake Parker the blacksmith. "It'll boom this camp. Ain't that so, Wells-Fargo?"

"Well, as you want my opinion—if it's any sign of how *I* think about it, I can tell you this: yesterday I was holding the Straight Flush claim at two dollars a foot; I'd like to see the man that can get it at sixteen today."

"Right you are, Wells-Fargo! It's the grandest luck a new camp ever struck. Say, did you see him collar them little rags and dirt and things? What an eye! He just can't overlook a clue—'tain't *in* him."

"That's so. And they wouldn't mean a thing to anybody else; but to him, why, they're just a book—large print at that."

"Sure's you're born! Them odds and ends have got their little old secret, and they think there ain't anybody can pull it; but, land! when he sets his grip there they've got to squeal, and don't you forget it."

"Boys, I ain't sorry, now, that he wasn't here to roust out the child; this is a bigger thing, by a long sight. Yes, sir, and more tangled up and scientific and intellectual."

"I reckon we're all of us glad it's turned out this way. Glad? 'George! it ain't any name for it. Dontchuknow, Archy could've *learnt* something if he'd had the nous to stand by and take notice of how that man works the system. But no; he went poking up into the chaparral, and just missed the whole thing."

"It's true as gospel; I seen it myself. Well, Archy's young. He'll know better one of these days."

"Say, boys, who do you reckon done it?"

That was a difficult question, and brought out a world of unsatisfying conjecture. Various men were mentioned as possibilities, but one

by one they were discarded as not being eligible. No one but young
Hillyer had been intimate with Flint Buckner; no one had really had
a quarrel with him; he had affronted every man who had tried to
make up to him, although not quite offensively enough to require
bloodshed. There was one name that was upon every tongue from the
start, but it was the last to get utterance—Fetlock Jones's. It was Pat
Riley that mentioned it.

"Oh, well," the boys said, "of course we've all thought of him,
because he had a million rights to kill Flint Buckner, and it was just
his plain duty to do it. But all the same there's two things we can't get
around: for one thing, he hasn't got the sand; and for another, he
wasn't anywhere near the place when it happened."

"I know it," said Pat. "He was there in the billiard room with us
when it happened."

"Yes, and was there all the time for an hour *before* it happened."

"It's so. And lucky for him, too. He'd have been suspected in a
minute if it hadn't been for that."

III

The tavern dining room had been cleared of all its furniture save
one six foot pine table and a chair. This table was against one end of
the room; the chair was on it; Sherlock Holmes, stately, imposing,
impressive, sat in the chair. The public stood. The room was full. The
tobacco smoke was dense, the stillness profound.

The Extraordinary Man raised his hand to command additional
silence; held it in the air a few moments; then, in brief, crisp terms he
put forward question after question, and noted the answers with
"Um-ums," nods of the head, and so on. By this process he learned all
about Flint Buckner, his character, conduct, and habits, that people
were able to tell him. It thus transpired that the Extraordinary Man's
nephew was the only person in the camp who had a killing-grudge
against Flint Buckner. Mr. Holmes smiled compassionately upon the
witness, and asked, languidly—

"Do any of you gentlemen chance to know where the lad Fetlock
Jones was at the time of the explosion?"

A thunderous response followed—

"In the billiard room of this house!"

"Ah. And had he just come in?"

"Been there all of an hour!"

"Ah. It is about—about—well, about how far might it be to the scene of the explosion?"

"All of a mile!"

"Ah. It isn't *much* of an alibi, 'tis true, but—"

A storm-burst of laughter, mingled with shouts of, "By jiminy, but he's chain-lightning!" and, "Ain't you sorry you spoke, Sandy?" shut off the rest of the sentence, and the crushed witness drooped his blushing face in pathetic shame. The inquisitor resumed:

"The lad Jones's somewhat *distant* connection with the case" (*laughter*) "having been disposed of, let us now call the *eye*-witnesses of the tragedy, and listen to what they have to say."

He got out his fragmentary clues and arranged them on a sheet of cardboard on his knee. The house held its breath and watched.

"We have the longitude and the latitude, corrected for magnetic variation, and this gives us the exact location of the tragedy. We have the altitude, the temperature, and the degree of humidity prevailing— inestimably valuable, since they enable us to estimate with precision the degree of influence which they would exercise upon the mood and disposition of the assassin at that time of the night." (*Buzz of admiration; muttered remark, "By George, but he's deep!"*) He fingered his clues. "And now let us ask these mute witnesses to speak to us.

"Here we have an empty linen shot-bag. What is its message? This: that robbery was the motive, not revenge. What is its further message? This: that the assassin was of inferior intelligence—shall we say light-witted, or perhaps approaching that? How do we know this? Because a person of sound intelligence would not have proposed to rob the man Buckner, who never had much money with him. But the assassin might have been a stranger? Let the bag speak again. I take from it this article. It is a bit of silver-bearing quartz. It is peculiar. Examine it, please—you—and you—and you. Now pass it back, please. There is but one lode on this coast which produces just that character and color of quartz; and that is a lode which crops out for nearly two miles on a stretch, and in my opinion is destined, at no distant day, to confer upon its locality a globe-girdling celebrity, and upon its two hundred owners riches beyond the dreams of avarice. Name that lode, please."

"The Consolidated Christian Science and Mary Ann!" was the prompt response.

A wild crash of hurrahs followed, and every man reached for his neighbor's hand and wrung it, with tears in his eyes; and Wells-Fargo Ferguson shouted, "The Straight Flush is on the lode, and up she goes to a hundred and fifty a foot—you hear *me*!"

When quiet fell, Mr. Holmes resumed:

"We perceive, then, that three facts are established, to wit: the assassin was approximately light-witted; he was not a stranger; his motive was robbery, not revenge. Let us proceed. I hold in my hand a small fragment of fuse, with the recent smell of fire upon it. What is its testimony? Taken with the corroborative evidence of the quartz, it reveals to us that the assassin was a miner. What does it tell us further? This, gentlemen: that the assassination was consummated by means of an explosive. What else does it say? This: that the explosive was located against the side of the cabin nearest the road—the front side—for within six feet of that spot I found it.

"I hold in my fingers a burnt Swedish match—the kind one rubs on a safety-box. I found it in the road, six hundred twenty-two feet from the abolished cabin. What does it say? This: that the train was fired from that point. What further does it tell us? This: that the assassin was left-handed. How do I know this? I should not be able to explain to you, gentlemen, how I know it, the signs being so subtle that only long experience and deep study can enable one to detect them. But the signs are here, and they are reinforced by a fact which you must have often noticed in the great detective narratives—that *all* assassins are left-handed."

"By Jackson, *that's* so!" said Ham Sandwich, bringing his great hand down with a resounding slap upon his thigh; "blamed if I ever thought of it before."

"Nor I!" "Nor I!" cried several. "Oh, there can't anything escape *him*—look at his eye!"

"Gentlemen, distant as the murderer was from his doomed victim, he did not wholly escape injury. This fragment of wood which I now exhibit to you struck him. It drew blood. Wherever he is, he bears the telltale mark. I picked it up where he stood when he fired the fatal train." He looked out over the house from his high perch, and his countenance began to darken; he slowly raised his hand, and pointed—

"There stands the assassin!"

For a moment the house was paralyzed with amazement; then twenty voices burst out with:

"Sammy Hillyer? Oh, *hell*, no! *Him?* It's pure foolishness!"

"Take care, gentlemen—be not hasty. Observe—he has the blood-mark on his brow."

Hillyer turned white with fright. He was near to crying. He turned this way and that, appealing to every face for help and sympathy; and held out his supplicating hands toward Holmes and began to plead:

"*Don't*, oh, don't! I never did it; I give my word I never did it. The way I got this hurt on my forehead was—"

"Arrest him, constable!" cried Holmes. "I will swear out the warrant."

The constable moved reluctantly forward—hesitated—stopped.

Hillyer broke out with another appeal. "Oh, Archy, don't let them do it; it would kill Mother! *You* know how I got the hurt. Tell them, and save me, Archy; save me!"

Stillman worked his way to the front, and said:

"Yes, I'll save you. Don't be afraid." Then he said to the house, "Never mind how he got the hurt; it hasn't anything to do with this case, and isn't of any consequence."

"God bless you, Archy, for a true friend!"

"Hurrah for Archy! Go in, boy, and play 'em a knock-down flush to their two pair 'n' a jack!" shouted the house, pride in their home talent and a patriotic sentiment of loyalty to it rising suddenly in the public heart and changing the whole attitude of the situation.

Young Stillman waited for the noise to cease; then he said,

"I will ask Tom Jeffries to stand by that door yonder, and Constable Harris to stand by the other one here, and not let anybody leave the room."

"Said and done. Go on, old man!"

"The criminal is present, I believe. I will show him to you before long, in case I am right in my guess. Now I will tell you all about the tragedy, from start to finish. The motive *wasn't* robbery; it was revenge. The murderer *wasn't* light-witted. He *didn't* stand six hundred twenty-two feet away. He *didn't* get hit with a piece of wood. He *didn't* place the explosive against the cabin. He *didn't* bring a shot-bag with him, and he *wasn't* left-handed. With the exception of these errors, the distinguished guest's statement of the case is substantially correct."

A comfortable laugh rippled over the house; friend nodded to friend, as much as to say, "That's the word, with the bark *on* it. Good lad, good boy. *He* ain't lowering his flag any!"

The guest's serenity was not disturbed. Stillman resumed:

"I also have some witnesses; and I will presently tell you where you can find some more." He held up a piece of coarse wire; the crowd craned their necks to see. "It has a smooth coating of melted tallow on it. And here is a candle which is burned halfway down. The remaining half of it has marks cut upon it an inch apart. Soon I will tell you where I found these things. I will now put aside reasonings, guesses, the impressive hitching of odds and ends of clues together, and the other showy theatricals of the detective trade, and tell you in a plain, straightforward way just how this dismal thing happened."

He paused a moment, for effect—to allow silence and suspense to intensify and concentrate the house's interest; then he went on:

"The assassin studied out his plan with a good deal of pains. It was a good plan, very ingenious, and showed an intelligent mind, not a feeble one. It was a plan which was well calculated to ward off all suspicion from its inventor. In the first place, he marked a candle into spaces an inch apart, and lit it and timed it. He found it took three hours to burn four inches of it. I tried it myself for half an hour, a while ago, upstairs here, while the inquiry into Flint Buckner's character and ways was being conducted in this room, and I arrived in that way at the rate of a candle's consumption when sheltered from the wind. Having proved his trial candle's rate, he blew it out—I have already shown it to you—and put his inch-marks on a fresh one.

"He put the fresh one into a tin candlestick. Then at the five-hour mark he bored a hole through the candle with a red-hot wire. I have already shown you the wire, with a smooth coat of tallow on it—tallow that had been melted and had cooled.

"With labor—very hard labor, I should say—he struggled up through the stiff chaparral that clothes the steep hillside back of Flint Buckner's place, tugging an empty flour barrel with him. He placed it in that absolutely secure hiding-place, and in the bottom of it he set the candlestick. Then he measured off about thirty-five feet of fuse— the barrel's distance from the back of the cabin. He bored a hole in the side of the barrel—there is the large gimlet he did it with. He went on and finished his work; and when it was done, one end of the fuse was in Buckner's cabin, and the other end, with a notch chipped in it to expose the powder, was in the hole in the candle—timed to blow the place up at one o'clock this morning, provided the candle was lit about eight o'clock yesterday evening—which I am betting it

was—and provided there was an explosive in the cabin and connected with that end of the fuse—which I am also betting there was,
though I can't prove it. Boys, the barrel is there in the chaparral, the
candle's remains are in it in the tin stick; the burnt-out fuse is in the
gimlet-hole, the other end is down the hill where the late cabin stood.
I saw them all an hour or two ago, when the professor here was
measuring off unimplicated vacancies and collecting relics that
hadn't anything to do with the case."

He paused. The house drew a long, deep breath, shook its strained
cords and muscles free, and burst into cheers.

"Dang him!" said Ham Sandwich, "that's why he was snooping
around in the chaparral, instead of picking up points out of the
p'fessor's game. Looky here—*he* ain't no fool, boys."

"No, sir! Why, great Scott—"

But Stillman was resuming:

"While we were out yonder an hour or two ago, the owner of the
gimlet and the trial candle took them from a place where he had
concealed them—it was not a good place—and carried them to what
he probably thought was a better one, two hundred yards up in the
pine woods, and hid them there, covering them over with pine
needles. It was there that I found them. The gimlet exactly fits the
hole in the barrel. And now—"

The Extraordinary Man interrupted him. He said, sarcastically:

"We have had a very pretty fairytale, gentlemen—very pretty indeed. Now I would like to ask this young man a question or two."

Some of the boys winced, and Ferguson said,

"I'm afraid Archy's going to catch it now."

The others lost their smiles and sobered down. Mr. Holmes said:

"Let us proceed to examine into this fairytale in a consecutive and
orderly way—by geometrical progression, so to speak—linking detail
to detail in a steadily advancing and remorselessly consistent and
unassailable march upon this tinsel toy-fortress of error, the dream-
fabric of a callow imagination. To begin with, young sir, I desire to
ask you but three questions at present—*at present*. Did I understand
you to say it was your opinion that the supposititious candle was
lighted at about eight o'clock yesterday evening?"

"Yes, sir—about eight."

"Could you say exactly eight?"

"Well, no, I couldn't be that exact."

"Um. If a person had been passing along there just about that time, he would have been almost sure to encounter that assassin, do you think?"

"Yes, I should think so."

"Thank you, that is all. For the present, I say, all *for the present*."

"Dern him! he's laying for Archy," said Ferguson.

"It's so," said Ham Sandwich. "I don't like the look of it."

Stillman said, glancing at the guest,

"I was along there myself at half past eight—no, about nine."

"Indeed? This is interesting—this is very interesting. Perhaps you encountered the assassin yourself?"

"No, I encountered no one."

"Ah. Then—if you will excuse the remark—I do not quite see the relevancy of the information."

"It has none. At present. I say it has none—at present." He paused. Presently he resumed: "I did not encounter the assassin, but I am on his track, I am sure, for I believe he is in this room. I will ask you all to pass one by one in front of me—here, where there is a good light— so that I can see your feet."

A buzz of excitement swept the place, and the march began, the guest looking on with an iron attempt at gravity which was not an unqualified success. Stillman stooped, shaded his eyes with his hand, and gazed down intently at each pair of feet as it passed. Fifty men tramped monotonously by—with no result. Sixty. Seventy. The thing was beginning to look absurd. The guest remarked, with suave irony,

"Assassins appear to be scarce this evening."

The house saw the humor of it, and refreshed itself with a cordial laugh. Ten or twelve more candidates tramped by—no, *danced* by, with airy and ridiculous capers which convulsed the spectators—then suddenly Stillman put out his hand and said,

"This is the assassin!"

"Fetlock Jones, by the great Sanhedrim!" roared the crowd; and at once let fly a pyrotechnic explosion and dazzle and confusion of stirring remarks inspired by the situation.

At the height of the turmoil the guest stretched out his hand, commanding peace. The authority of a great name and a great personality laid its mysterious compulsion upon the house, and it obeyed. Out of the panting calm which succeeded, the guest spoke, saying, with dignity and feeling:

"*This* is serious. It strikes at an innocent life. Innocent beyond suspicion! Innocent beyond peradventure! Hear me *prove* it; observe how simple a fact can brush out of existence this witless lie. Listen. My friends, that lad was never out of my sight yesterday evening at *any* time!"

It made a deep impression. Men turned their eyes upon Stillman with grave inquiry in them. His face brightened, and he said,

"I *knew* there was another one!" He stepped briskly to the table and glanced at the guest's feet, then up at his face, and said: "You were *with* him! You were not fifty steps from him when he lit the candle that by and by fired the powder!" (*Sensation.*) "And what is more, you furnished the matches yourself!"

Plainly the guest seemed hit; it looked so to the public. He opened his mouth to speak; the words did not come freely.

"This—er—this is insanity—this—"

Stillman pressed his evident advantage home. He held up a charred match.

"Here is one of them. I found it in the barrel—and there's *another* one there."

The guest found his voice at once.

"*Yes*—and put them there yourself!"

It was recognized as a good shot. Stillman retorted:

"It is *wax*—a breed unknown to this camp. I am ready to be searched for the box. Are you?"

The guest was staggered this time—the dullest eye could see it. He fumbled with his hands; once or twice his lips moved, but the words did not come. The house waited and watched, in tense suspense, the stillness adding effect to the situation. Presently Stillman said, gently,

"We are waiting for your decision."

There was silence again during several moments; then the guest answered, in a low voice,

"I refuse to be searched."

There was no noisy demonstration, but all about the house one voice after another muttered:

"That settles it! He's Archy's meat."

What to do now? Nobody seemed to know. It was an embarrassing situation for the moment—merely, of course, because matters had taken such a sudden and unexpected turn that these unpracticed minds were not prepared for it, and had come to a standstill, like a stopped clock, under the shock. But after a little the machinery began to work again, tentatively, and by twos and threes the men put their heads together and privately buzzed over this and that and the other proposition. One of these propositions met with much favor; it was to confer upon the assassin a vote of thanks for removing Flint Buckner, and let him go. But the cooler heads opposed it, pointing out that addled brains in the eastern states would pronounce it a scandal, and make no end of foolish noise about it. In the end the cool heads got the upper hand, and obtained general consent to a proposition of their own, and their leader then called the house to order and stated it—to this effect: that Fetlock Jones be jailed and put upon his trial.

The motion was carried. Apparently there was nothing further to do now, and the people were glad, for, privately, they were impatient to get out and rush to the scene of the tragedy, and see whether that barrel and the other things were really there or not.

But no—the breakup got a check. The surprises were not over yet. For a while Fetlock Jones had been silently sobbing, unnoticed in the absorbing excitements which had been following one another so persistently for some time; but when his arrest and trial were decreed, he broke out despairingly, and said:

"No! it's no use. I don't wany any jail, I don't want any trial; I've had all the hard luck I want, and all the miseries. Hang me now, and let me out! It would all come out, anyway—there couldn't anything save me. He has told it all, just as if he'd been with me and seen it—*I* don't know how he found out; and you'll find the barrel and things, and then I wouldn't have any chance any more. I killed him; and *you'd* have done it too, if he'd treated you like a dog, and you only a boy, and weak and poor, and not a friend to help you."

"And served him damned well right!" broke in Ham Sandwich. "Looky here, boys—"

From the constable: "Order! Order, gentlemen!"

A voice: "Did your uncle know what you was up to?"

"No, he didn't."

"Did he give you the matches, sure enough?"

"Yes, he did; but he didn't know what I wanted them for."

"When you was out on such a business as that, how did you venture to risk having him along—and him a *detective*? How's that?"

The boy hesitated, fumbled with his buttons in an embarrassed way, then said, shyly,

"I know about detectives, on account of having them in the family; and if you don't want them to find out about a thing, it's best to have them around when you do it."

The cyclone of laughter which greeted this naïve discharge of wisdom did not modify the poor little waif's embarrassment in any large degree.

IV

From a Letter to Mrs. Stillman. Dated merely "Tuesday."

Fetlock Jones was put under lock and key in an unoccupied log cabin, and left there to await his trial. Constable Harris provided him with a couple of days' rations, instructed him to keep a good guard over himself, and promised to look in on him as soon as further supplies should be due.

Next morning a score of us went with Hillyer, out of friendship, and helped him bury his late relative, the unlamented Buckner, and I acted as first assistant pallbearer, Hillyer acting as chief. Just as we had finished our labors a ragged and melancholy stranger, carrying an old handbag, limped by with his head down, and I caught the scent I had chased around the globe! It was the odor of Paradise to my perishing hope!

In a moment I was at his side and had laid a gentle hand upon his shoulder. He slumped to the ground as if a stroke of lightning had withered him in his tracks; and as the boys came running he struggled to his knees and put up his pleading hands to me, and out of his chattering jaws he begged me to persecute him no more, and said,

"You have hunted me around the world, Sherlock Holmes, yet God is my witness I have never done any man harm!"

A glance at his wild eyes showed us that he was insane. That was my work, Mother! The tidings of your death can some day repeat the misery I felt at that moment, but nothing else can ever do it. The boys lifted him up, and gathered about him, and were full of pity of him, and said the gentlest and touchingest things to him, and said cheer up and don't be troubled, he was among friends now, and they would take care of him, and protect him, and hang any man that laid a hand on him. They are just like so many mothers, the rough mining-camp boys are, when you wake up the south side of their hearts; yes, and just like so many reckless and unreasoning children when you wake up the opposite side of that muscle. They did everything they could think of to comfort him, but nothing succeeded until Wells-Fargo Ferguson, who is a clever strategist, said,

"If it's only Sherlock Holmes that's troubling you, you needn't worry any more."

"Why?" asked the forlorn lunatic, eagerly.

"Because he's dead again."

"Dead! Dead! Oh, don't trifle with a poor wreck like me. *Is* he dead? On honor, now—is he telling me true, boys?"

"True as you're a-standing there!" said Ham Sandwich, and they all backed up the statement in a body.

"They hung him in San Bernardino last week," added Ferguson, clinching the matter, "whilst he was searching around for you. Mistook him for another man. They're sorry, but they can't help it now."

"They're a-building him a monument," said Ham Sandwich, with the air of a person who had contributed to it, and knew.

"James Walker" drew a deep sigh—evidently a sigh of relief—and said nothing; but his eyes lost something of their wildness, his countenance cleared visibly, and its drawn look relaxed a little. We all went to our cabin, and the boys cooked him the best dinner the camp could furnish the materials for, and while they were about it Hillyer and I outfitted him from hat to shoe-leather with new clothes of ours, and made a comely and presentable old gentleman of him. "Old" is the right word, and a pity, too; old by the droop of him, and the frost upon his hair, and the marks which sorrow and distress have left upon his face; though he is only in his prime in the matter of years. While he ate, we smoked and chatted; and when he was finishing he found his voice at last, and of his own accord broke out with his personal history. I cannot furnish his exact words, but I will come as near it as I can.

The "Wrong Man's" Story.

It happened like this: I was in Denver. I had been there many years; sometimes I remember how many, sometimes I don't—but it isn't any matter. All of a sudden I got a notice to leave, or I would be exposed for a horrible crime committed long before—years and years before—in the East. I knew about that crime, but I was not the criminal; it was a cousin of mine of the same name. What should I better do? My head was all disordered by fear, and I didn't know. I was allowed very little time—only one day, I think it was. I would be ruined if I was published, and the people would lynch me, and not believe what I said. It is always the way with lynchings; when they find out it is a mistake they are sorry, but it is too late—the same as it was with Mr. Holmes, you see. So I said I would sell out and get money to live on, and run away until it blew over and I could come back with my proofs. Then I escaped in the night and went a long way off in the mountains somewhere, and lived disguised and had a false name.

I got more and more troubled and worried, and my troubles made me see spirits and hear voices, and I could not think straight and clear on any subject, but got confused and involved and had to give it up, because my head hurt so. It got to be worse and worse; more spirits and more voices. They were about me all the time; at first only in the night, then in the day too. They were always whispering around my bed and plotting against me, and it broke my sleep and kept me fagged out, because I got no good rest.

And then came the worst. One night the whispers said, "We'll never manage, because we can't *see* him, and so can't point him out to the people."

They sighed; then one said: "We must bring Sherlock Holmes. He can be here in twelve days."

They all agreed, and whispered and jibbered with joy. But my heart broke; for I had read about that man, and knew what it would be to have him upon my track, with his super-human penetration and tireless energies.

The spirits went away to fetch him, and I got up at once in the middle of the night and fled away, carrying nothing but the handbag that had my money in it—thirty thousand dollars; two-thirds of it are in the bag there yet. It was forty days before that man caught up on my track. I just escaped. From habit he had written his real name on a tavern register, but had scratched it out and written "Dagget Barclay" in the place of it. But fear gives you a watchful eye and keen, and I read the true name through the scratches, and fled like a deer.

He has hunted me all over this world for three years and a half— the Pacific States, Australasia, India—everywhere you can think of; then back to Mexico and up to California again, giving me hardly any rest; but that name on the registers always saved me, and what is left of me is alive yet. And I am *so* tired! A cruel time he has given me, yet I give you my honor I have never harmed him nor any man.

That was the end of the story, and it stirred those boys to blood-heat, be sure of it. As for me—each word burnt a hole in me where it struck.

We voted that the old man should bunk with us, and be my guest and Hillyer's. I shall keep my own counsel, naturally; but as soon as he is well rested and nourished, I shall take him to Denver and rehabilitate his fortunes.

The boys gave the old fellow the bone-mashing good-fellowship handshake of the mines, and then scattered away to spread the news.

At dawn next morning Wells-Fargo Ferguson and Ham Sandwich called us softly out, and said, privately:

"That news about the way the old stranger has been treated has spread all around, and the camps are up. They are piling in from everywhere, and are going to lynch the p'fessor. Constable Harris is in a dead funk, and has telephoned the sheriff. Come along!"

We started on a run. The others were privileged to feel as they chose, but in my heart's privacy I hoped the sheriff would arrive in time, for I had small desire that Sherlock Holmes should hang for my deeds, as you can easily believe. I had heard a good deal about the sheriff, but for reassurance' sake I asked,

"Can he stop a mob?"

"Can *he* stop a mob! Can Jack *Fairfax* stop a mob! Well, I should smile! Ex-desperado—nineteen scalps on his string. Can *he!* Oh, I *say!*"

As we tore up the gulch, distant cries and shouts and yells rose faintly on the still air, and grew steadily in strength as we raced along. Roar after roar burst out, stronger and stronger, nearer and nearer; and at last, when we closed up upon the multitude massed in the open area in front of the tavern, the crash of sound was deafening. Some brutal roughs from Daly's Gorge had Holmes in their grip, and he was the calmest man there; a contemptuous smile played about his lips, and if any fear of death was in his British heart, his iron personality was master of it, and no sign of it was allowed to appear.

"Come to a vote, men!" This from one of the Daly gang, Shadbelly Higgins. "Quick! is it hang, or shoot?"

"Neither!" shouted one of his comrades. "He'd be alive again in a week; burning's the only permanency for *him*."

The gangs from all the outlying camps burst out in a thunder-crash of approval, and went struggling and surging toward the prisoner, and closed around him, shouting, "Fire! fire's the ticket!" They dragged him to the horsepost, backed him against it, chained him to it, and piled wood and pine cones around him waist-deep. Still the strong face did not blench, and still the scornful smile played about the thin lips.

"A match! fetch a match!"

Shadbelly struck it, shaded it with his hand, stooped, and held it under a pine cone. A deep silence fell upon the mob. The cone caught, a tiny flame flickered about it a moment or two. I seemed to catch the sound of distant hoofs—it grew more distinct—still more and more distinct, more and more definite, but the absorbed crowd did not appear to notice it. The match went out. The man struck another, stooped, and again the flame rose; this time it took hold and began to spread—here and there men turned away their faces. The executioner stood with the charred match in his fingers, watching his work. The hoofbeats turned a projecting crag, and now they came thundering down upon us. Almost the next moment there was a shout—

"The sheriff!"

And straightway he came tearing into the midst, stood his horse almost on his hind feet, and said,

"Fall back, you guttersnipes!"

He was obeyed. By all but their leader. He stood his ground, and his hand went to his revolver. The sheriff covered him promptly, and said:

"Drop your hand, you parlor-desperado. Kick the fire away. Now unchain the stranger."

The parlor-desperado obeyed. Then the sheriff made a speech; sitting his horse at martial ease, and not warming his words with any touch of fire, but delivering them in a measured and deliberate way, and in a tone which harmonized with their character and made them impressively disrespectful.

"You're a nice lot—now ain't you? Just about eligible to travel with this bilk here—Shadbelly Higgins—this loud-mouthed sneak that shoots people in the back and calls himself a desperado. If there's anything I do particularly despise, it's a lynching mob; I've never seen one that had a man in it. It has to tally up a hundred against one before it can pump up pluck enough to tackle a sick tailor. It's made up of cowards, and so is the community that breeds it; and ninety-nine times out of a hundred the sheriff's another one." He paused—apparently to turn that last idea over in his mind and taste the juice of it—then he went on: "The sheriff that lets a mob take a prisoner away from him is the lowest-down coward there is. By the statistics there was a hundred and eighty-two of them drawing sneak pay in America last year. By the way it's going, pretty soon there'll be a new disease in the doctor books—*sheriff complaint.*" That idea pleased him—anyone could see it. "People will say, 'Sheriff sick again?' 'Yes; got the same old thing.' And next there'll be a new title. People won't say, "He's running for sheriff of Rapaho County,' for instance; they'll say, 'He's running for Coward of Rapaho.' Lord, the idea of a grownup person being afraid of a lynch mob!"

He turned an eye on the captive, and said, "Stranger, who are you, and what have you been doing?"

"My name is Sherlock Holmes, and I have not been doing anything."

It was wonderful, the impression which the sound of that name made on the sheriff, notwithstanding he must have come posted. He spoke up with feeling, and said it was a blot on the country that a man whose marvelous exploits had filled the world with their fame and their ingenuity, and whose histories of them had won every reader's heart by the brilliancy and charm of their literary setting, should be visited under the Stars and Stripes by an outrage like this. He apologized in the name of the whole nation, and made Holmes a most handsome bow, and told Constable Harris to see him to his quarters, and hold himself personally responsible if he was molested again. Then he turned to the mob and said:

"Hunt your holes, you scum!" which they did; then he said: "Follow me, Shadbelly; I'll take care of your case myself. No—keep your popgun; whenever I see the day that I'll be afraid to have you behind me with that thing, it'll be time for me to join last year's hundred and eighty-two"; and he rode off in a walk, Shadbelly following.

When we were on our way back to our cabin, toward breakfast-time, we ran upon the news that Fetlock Jones had escaped from his lockup in the night and is gone! Nobody is sorry. Let his uncle track him if he likes; it is in his line; the camp is not interested.

V

Ten days later.—"James Walker" is all right in body now, and his mind shows improvement too. I start with him for Denver tomorrow morning.

Next night. Brief note, mailed at a way station.—As we were starting this morning, Hillyer whispered to me: "Keep this news from Walker until you think it safe and not likely to disturb his mind and check his improvement: the ancient crime he spoke of was really committed—and by his cousin, as he said. *We buried the real criminal* the other day—the unhappiest man that has lived in a century—Flint Buckner. His real name was Jacob Fuller!" There, Mother, by the help of me, an unwitting mourner, your husband and my father is in his grave. Let him rest.

The Adventure of the Oval Window (a pastiche)

JOHN H. DIRCKX

In glancing over the series of sketches in which I have recorded some of the more noteworthy investigations of my friend, Mr. Sherlock Holmes, I find that most of them refer to matters which have not otherwise come to the notice of the public. Even when he was consulted in cases which had aroused the attention of the press, Holmes' name seldom figured in the newspaper accounts. He habitually shunned popular esteem, preferring to allow the official police to take full credit for his most brilliant successes, and finding his own reward in the work itself.

Yet his powers were so remarkable, and his methods so singular and so often crowned with striking results, that they could not altogether escape the notice of the press. From his unravelling of the Jefferson Hope case in the early days of our association until his retirement, Holmes' reputation as a criminal investigator increased steadily.

During the '90s, his practice had grown so extensive that he was able to consult his own tastes in choosing which clients to serve and which inquiries to undertake. As his tastes inclined to the curious and the bizarre, the problems to which he applied his peculiar gifts became correspondingly extraordinary. My notes of the years just preceding his retirement are a veritable museum of the anomalous, the grotesque, and the macabre. Many of these cases are still of too recent date to be exposed fully to the public. Others proved to be but chimaeras, in which Holmes' special powers were summoned in vain.

I have said that Sherlock Holmes craved distraction and novelty. There was, moreover, a strong tincture of the dare-devil in his composition. Nothing engaged his interest in a case more keenly than a certain element of danger. The thrill of the chase was for him no more intense than the thrill of being chased. Other things being equal, he preferred a case fraught with hazards and pitfalls to one which could be resolved without danger or inconvenience.

It was perhaps chiefly owing to this almost morbid craving for sensation that Holmes agreed to look into the curious affair of the

404

Hanford heiress, of which I am about to give an account. The case came to our notice on a drowsy afternoon late in the summer of the year 1896. A day or two earlier, Holmes had successfully concluded the queer business of the Venetian goldsmiths, a case which had consumed all his energies for many weeks past. Now the period of reaction, whose symptoms I recognized only too well, had begun.

He had barely tasted his lunch. Lounging in a corner of the sofa, he was to all appearances sunk in the most profound lethargy. Yet, like the spider which rests motionless at the centre of its web, sensitive to the slightest disturbance in any quarter, Holmes remained perpetually alert. Even before the jangling of the bell announced the arrival of a visitor, his remarkably acute hearing had singled out, from the myriad other noises streaming in at the open window, the sounds of a cab stopping in the street and discharging its passenger at our doorstep. He was examining the cab round the edge of the blind when Mrs. Hudson knocked upon our sitting-room door.

"A gentleman to see you, sir," said she, handing in a card, which was followed immediately by its proprietor. With an impetuosity bordering upon rudeness, our caller thrust himself past our landlady and stood fidgeting and panting upon the mat. He was a dry, clerical-looking person, just turned forty. His flushed countenance and air of distraction bore testimony to the seriousness of his business, while his abrupt and restless demeanor suggested that it was a matter of some urgency as well.

"Pray take a seat, Mr. Ordway," said Holmes, indicating an armchair that stood full in the light from the window.

Our caller dropped into the proffered seat, threw open his coat as though oppressed with heat, and cast an enquiring glance from me to my companion.

"You may speak plainly before Dr. Watson," said Holmes. "He is a model of discretion, and is often good enough to assist me in my cases. His medical eye may perhaps detect some subtle clue to explain your recent loss of weight, though I confess I can suggest none besides the somewhat arduous physical labours which you have lately been obliged to perform. No doubt the commercial difficulties you have been experiencing—"

"But this is incredible!" cried our visitor, flinging himself upright in his chair and peering at Holmes with a look in which awe was mingled with distrust. "What can you know of my affairs, sir? I have not begun to state my business. You have seen nothing but my card, and yet you appear to know all."

"You are far too modest," said Holmes, sitting down and lighting his pipe. "Besides your card I have seen yourself. To a trained observer the human form—its physiognomy, its attitude, and its habiliments—presents an infinite number of suggestive points. You had scarcely entered the room when I perceived scratches on the backs of your hands, and calluses upon the palms. Yours are not the broad, muscular hands of one regularly employed in manual work. They are narrow, with long, tapering fingers—the hands of a man accustomed to hire others to do such work for him. As to the loss of weight, I am unprepared to believe your tailor so inept as to cut your coat and trousers two sizes too large."

"Those signs are plain enough, I suppose," agreed Ordway with a meditative nod. "But how came you to learn of my late financial embarrassments?"

"That is a mere trifle. I see by your card that you deal in diamonds. The papers have been full of the difficulties in the Transvaal. Surely it is no very daring inference that you have found your volume of trade much curtailed of late?"

"The accounts I have heard of your abilities have not been exaggerated, Mr. Holmes," said our visitor, pulling out a large silver watch and glancing rapidly at its dial. "But the affair about which I desire to consult you does not concern my own misfortunes. As I am much pressed for time, I must come to business at once."

"I am at your service. Please state your case as fully as you are able."

"You must know, Mr. Holmes, that when my elder brother died some years ago, he left his only daughter in my charge. The girl had lost her mother already, and would have been thrust alone upon the world had I not taken her into my own household. I am not a married man. My niece is all the family I have ever had, and she has become as dear to me as ever a daughter could be.

"My brother's wealth was immense, for he inherited nearly the whole of our father's fortune. You will have heard of Ordway and Parr, the great road-building firm?"

Holmes nodded and bade our client proceed.

"My niece, who is just nineteen, draws a generous but not opulent allowance from the estate. She will come into possession of the principal on her twenty-fifth birthday—sooner if she should marry, but Julia has shown no inclination that way, and indeed seems quite averse to the idea of ever marrying at all. To come straight to the heart of the matter, my niece has twice in the past month been the victim of murderous attacks. But for the intervention of a merciful Providence, she would not be alive at this moment."

"You amaze me," said Holmes. His eyes gleamed with the fervid light which I knew so well, and it was plain that his interest was keenly aroused. "I understand that your niece has no living relations besides yourself."

"That is true."

"You would gain a great fortune in the event of her death?"

Our visitor drew himself up with a haughty air, and fixed upon Holmes a look of the deepest indignation. "That is also perfectly true. But come, sir, if you mean to impugn me, to suggest—"

"I impugn no one and suggest nothing. I wish only to be in possession of all the relevant data. I take it that you yourself have no suspicion who is the author of these attacks?"

"None. We live a retired life. Our circle of friends is small. We go very little into society; indeed, hardly at all. It seems inconceivable how a young girl in my niece's position can have made a mortal enemy."

"Are there no rejected suitors?"

"There is a man formerly associated in my own firm. But neither his character nor the nature of their relations would permit me to entertain the slightest suspicion, if you understand me—"

"Perfectly. Still, it may be as well to have a note of the name."

Ordway consulted his watch again and thrust it away in his pocket with a gesture of impatience. "It is Lawrence, Mr. Theobald Lawrence, of Daulton Square, Soho. But my time grows shorter."

"Quite so. Pray continue with your narrative."

"The first of the attacks occurred upon a Sunday forenoon, about a month since, as we were returning from church. Since my unfortunate brother's death I have lived at Moorcroft, the family estate, near Hanford. Though the house is large, and stands in its own park, our domestic establishment is a modest one. We keep only two servants: my man Fetters, who has been with me for years, and his sister Elizabeth, who cooks our meals and serves as lady's maid to my niece.

"We had attended morning service together in the village, as is our custom, and were returning home in the dogcart when a large four-wheeled carriage drew up behind us at a great rate of speed and offered to overtake us. Fetters was driving, with me at his side, while Julia and her maid occupied the rear compartment. My first intimation of danger was the clatter of the horses' hooves. In the next instant there came a fearful explosion, which was followed immediately by the screams of the women. With great presence of mind, Fetters drew the dogcart off the road. The carriage roared quickly past and was out of sight before we had ascertained that my niece and her maid were unharmed.

"When they had regained their composure, they recited a horrifying tale. As the carriage drew nearly abreast of them, a man with his face muffled up in a dark-blue scarf had thrust a pistol out at the window and fired upon my niece at almost point-blank range. How he can have failed to inflict the slightest injury upon her is as great a mystery as who he is, or upon what motive he attempted to murder an innocent young lady in broad daylight on a public road."

"Could the police not trace the carriage?"

"No, sir. In our consternation, none of us observed any markings upon it, and the driver was as completely muffled as the blackguard who fired upon my niece."

Holmes laid aside his pipe and, placing his fingertips together and directing his gaze upwards to the ceiling, he pursued in silence some private train of thought while our visitor fairly writhed in impatience. "So much for the first attempt," remarked my friend at length. "And the other?"

"The other took place but three days ago. After the first attack I had been much alarmed for my niece's safety. She herself believed that the man was a lunatic, and that his choice of a victim had been dictated by chance and the whimsies of a disordered mind. After a time, I came to be of her opinion. The police suggested that the villian had fired a blank charge, for no bullet could be found. In short, we relaxed our vigilance, and on Tuesday I had so far overcome my fears that I permitted Julia to travel alone to London to visit the shops. As a safeguard, however, against her mysterious assailant, I required her to wear a hat with a heavy veil, and a plain drab gown borrowed from her maid.

"Well, Mr. Holmes, the scoundrel penetrated that disguise easily enough. He must have followed her up to London from Hanford. She was to have met me at one o'clock at my place of business. By half past the hour I had begun to grow uneasy, and it was after two before I learned the occasion of her delay. In alighting from her cab at Holborn Circus she was nearly run down by a heavy four-wheeled carriage which came dashing out of St. Andrew Street. The off horse shied at her and she was knocked aside by the traces, narrowly escaping serious injury."

"I suppose that the police failed again to learn anything of the carriage?"

"No, sir, they traced it at once. The driver who put Julia down at Holborn Circus noticed very particularly the markings and the numbers of the carriage. He gave the information to the police, and in less than a quarter of an hour they found the identical carriage, abandoned in an alley lying between St. Bride Street and the Farringdon Road. It belonged to a livery stable in the Poultry and had been twice hired by the same man."

"The earlier occasion being the Sunday of the first attack?"

"Exactly, sir."

"And the man?"

"He was described as a surly rogue who kept his face hidden in a scarf and provided his own driver. He gave a false name and an address which does not exist."

Holmes resumed his attitude of absorption, whereupon Ordway again gave tokens of the most acute anxiety. At length he could endure the silence no longer. "Your reputation as an unraveller of obscure puzzles is well known, Mr. Holmes," said he. "Upon learning of the second attempt I resolved to place the matter in your hands. I have been prevented from coming to you by an unfortunate turn of events, a veritable catastrophe, in fact. One of my agents on the Continent has allowed an unusually large consignment of precious stones to fall into the hands of a man who will not scruple to sell them as his own wares. All hope of recovering them will be lost unless I reach Calais tonight. My train leaves Victoria Station in less than an hour.

"Mr. Holmes, I am at my wit's end. I am half mad with fear for my niece's safety, and yet to stop at home would spell my utter ruin. Moreover, the nature of my business compels me to take Fetters with me. He is at my bankers' at this moment collecting a letter of credit. Julia refuses absolutely to accompany me. It is useless to press her, for she has her father's iron will. What am I to do, Mr. Holmes? The man who has twice attacked my niece has shown himself to be a desperate villian, who will stick at nothing. He will not fail again. To leave my niece alone is to sign her death warrant."

"She will have her maid with her."

"He will murder them both. Can you not help me, Mr. Holmes?"

"Do you wish to retain me to make inquiries, or to guard the person of your niece?"

"To do both. I shall return to England on Sunday, Monday at the latest. Can you not spend the interval at Moorcroft? Say that you will do it, Mr. Holmes! I will pay any fee which you care to name, though I should lie in debt all the rest of my days, if only you will put an end to these atrocities. It is worth all that I have, and more, to know that my niece will be safe during my absence."

"This is very short notice, Mr. Ordway. There are one or two small matters—"

"Put them aside!" cried our client, in a tone between entreaty and command. "Would you stand idly by while an innocent girl is done foully to death?"

"You are most persuasive. Let us suppose that I agree to take up the inquiry and stand guard over your niece; what are the young lady's views in the matter?"

"She knows nothing of it. She need never know. Fetters and his sister occupy the porter's lodge, which lies at some distance from the house. While Fetters and I are away, Elizabeth will stay in the house with my niece. You will find the lodge comfortable, though not luxurious."

"But," objected Holmes, "remaining at a distance from the young lady would seem to defeat the purpose of guarding her person."

"Not at all. The park is enclosed by a high wall fortified with chevaux de frise. The only entry to the grounds is through the gate and along the drive, which passes directly before the lodge. Perhaps this drawing will make the positions clear."

He drew from his breast a pocket-book and unfolded from it a plan of the estate, neatly executed upon tracing paper. Holmes took the drawing from him and smoothed it out upon the table.

"You are quite an accomplished draughtsman, sir," said he.

"That is the influence of my early training. I was employed for some years in my father's firm as a surveyor and draughtsman. Here is the lodge, built into a corner of the wall. You must not, of course, show a light in any of the windows facing the house. I have advised Elizabeth, my niece's maid, that someone will be on guard in the lodge, but Julia herself knows nothing. Fetters is a man of simple tastes, and his ideas of personal comfort run upon Spartan lines. Still, you will find in his quarters a camp-bed and a sofa, where two gentlemen may, I think, contrive to pass two or three nights in perfect ease."

"You needn't trouble yourself on that account," said Holmes. "Watson is an old campaigner, and I often spend an entire night in an arm-chair."

"Then as to meals: you will find the larder well stocked, and Elizabeth may contrive to bring you something hot in the evenings. You must make your tea with the spirit lamp, and not upon any account have a fire. Smoke rising from the chimney of the lodge is plainly visible from the house."

"The lack of a fire should prove no hardship in this season," said Holmes. "I suppose we may expect tradesmen to call at the lodge? How are we to know that they are what they say?"

"No tradesmen are expected. Whoever calls must be denied admission. I would particularly warn you against Ludwick, the land-agent in the village. He is an ingratiating but unscrupulous rogue, who covets my house. He has twice offered princely sums for it and twice been refused. At last, seeing his direct overtures fail, he had the effrontery to pay court to my niece. I have forbidden him my door."

"You do not connect him with the attempts on Miss Ordway's life?"

Our client seemed taken aback by the suggestion. "I should be surprised to learn that Ludwick is so low a dog as that," said he. "But my time is slipping away. When I think that even now—Can you go down before nightfall, Mr. Holmes? There is a train at 4.20 from Paddington Station. Here are twenty-five pounds for present expenses, the key to the lodge, and a note of my hotel in Calais."

Holmes scribbled a receipt on a page from his notebook. "You have thought of everything," said he.

"Julia is worth everything to me. I urge you to arm yourself with reliable weapons and not scruple to use them. You and your associate might take it in turns to watch through the night. A round of the park every hour or so between midnight and sunrise would be advisable. But, dear me, I have just time to catch my train."

With effusive expressions of gratitude, and repeated exhortations to caution and vigilance, our client rushed away as tempestuously as he had come.

"Well, Watson, what do you make of it?" asked Holmes, when our visitor had gone. "A curious little problem, is it not?"

"Say rather a sinister and diabolical one. I think you might have consulted me before pledging me to come down with you to Hanford to have my head blown off by a madman."

"There is no madness in this business, Watson. Our adversary may be bold and ruthless, but I should say that he is as sane as you or I. As to consulting you, I think I know my Watson well enough to see when he has fairly risen to the bait of an intriguing case. Our client was barely out of his chair before you had commenced a rapt perusal of Bradshaw's uninspired but invaluable pages. I hope that Ordway's information was correct as to the time of our train?"

"Precisely."

"Then we've just time to collect a few necessaries for our travels. You still keep your service revolver in working order, I think?"

When presently our cab left Baker Street it contained two respectable-looking gentlemen and a perfectly nefarious assortment of gear, including crepe-soled shoes, a dark lantern, and a brace of pistols. Holmes preserved a stony silence during the whole of the railway journey. Curled in his seat, with his chin sunk upon his breast, he appeared oblivious of the scenes of rural verdure that flashed constantly past the window.

At the station inn we hired a trap. I thought the driver eyed us suspiciously when he learned our destination, but perhaps it was only idle curiosity. He dropped us at the gates of Moorcroft just as the clock of some distant church was striking seven.

The Ordway estate occupied a plot of high ground in the midst of a vast marshy tract. The house, a stark, angular pile of grey stone, lay half submerged in a heavily wooded and ill-tended park. By contrast, the lodge that was to serve as our temporary diggings possessed a certain picturesque charm with its bright red shutters and neat hedges. Taking care to keep out of sight of the house, we used our key and presently found ourselves in a plain, low-ceilinged sitting-room. Fetters' sleeping chamber, which stood next to it, lay in deep shadows, for its windows, which faced the house, were tightly shuttered.

Holmes unlatched one of the shutters and opened it slightly. For a long time he stood peering intently through the aperture, while the gloom of eventide deepened around him.

Suddenly he turned away from the window with a gesture of satisfaction and walked into the sitting-room. "All is well, I think," he said, seating himself and taking out his pipe. "I have seen one of the women drawing the curtains in an upper room. Her movements were serene and untroubled. It is as well to know at once that we have not arrived too late."

The sitting-room windows looked out upon the drive and gave an uninterrupted view of the gate and the road beyond. At long intervals a solitary farm cart or a tradesman's van made its way along the lonely road. "A suitable setting for murder, is it not, Watson?" remarked my companion, amid clouds of blue smoke. "The house lies far back from the road, and the road itself is nearly deserted. The family seldom go out. They might all be massacred in their sleep, and no one the wiser."

"Have you reached any conclusions as to the attempts on the girl's life?"

"Conclusions! My dear fellow, have I never warned you against reaching conclusions without considering all the facts? It is like trying to walk to Greenwich without consulting the signposts. If you arrive there at all it will be by the merest chance, and then at the needless expense of much time and trouble."

"You seemed deeply absorbed during the journey from London."

"It was quite another matter that engaged my interests then. I was, and am, wrestling with the curious enigma of our client himself."

"You think it possible that he is the author of the attacks on his niece?"

"A pox on the attacks," replied Holmes with good-natured sarcasm. "It will be time to look into them when we have talked with Miss Ordway—not a likely eventuality until our client's return."

"Well, then, wherein lies the enigma? He seemed a decent enough chap to me, having a good deal of trouble with his business, and beside himself with worry on his niece's account."

"He did, did he? Yours is a generous and trusting nature, Watson, and your estimate of your fellow-men correspondingly favorable. You see the best in them, and I see the worst. No doubt the world is a pleasanter place by your way of viewing it, but rose-coloured spectacles are not a particularly useful piece of equipment to the criminal investigator." He finished his pipe in silence without enlarging on his views.

We dined simply on bread, cheese, and potted meat, with tea brewed with the aid of a spirit lamp. A sojourn in the country should be a soothing change after weeks of city life with its drab vistas, its grime and bustle and noise. But try as I might I could not dispel a sombre mood of gloom and foreboding, which seemed to increase as the shadows thickened and the chill of evening began to invade our fireless sitting-room.

Holmes returned to his post at the gap between the shutters, and presently reported that a light had appeared in one of the windows of the house. When the dusk was well advanced he took up his stick, a stout ash which he had chosen specially for the occasion, and slipped his revolver into his pocket. "What do you say to a moonlight excursion over the grounds?"

"I should like nothing better. The inaction of the past hour has begun to fray my nerves, and there is something hostile about an unfamiliar room without a light."

Closing the door to the bedroom, Holmes prepared the dark lantern before venturing outside. "We must keep to the shadows of the trees," said he, "for the moon is nearly full."

We began our tour of inspection with an examination of the gates. Holmes had some idea of shutting them for the night, but even without recourse to the lantern we could see that the great wrought-iron hinges had long since given way, and the gates were deeply sunken in the earth.

As we rounded the lodge and entered the grounds, the house sprang full into our view across the broad expanse of the park. The moon shed a silvery light on the high gables and threw the squat stone chimneys into jagged relief against the sable backdrop of the night. Far away to our left a round pond shone like a mirror of burnished pewter among the trees.

Keeping well in the shadow, we set our course by the simple expedient of following the wall. A high and very substantial wall it looked, and its ivied top bristled with a formidable row of iron spikes. Holmes took the lead, striking stealthily forward and looking sharply to right and left as he advanced. He made scarcely a sound as he passed over fallen boughs and a dense undergrowth of dry brushwood. Our shadows flitted and leapt grotesquely among the black trunks of the trees, but we found nothing more substantial there.

As we came nearer to the house, Holmes scanned the dark windows intently, keeping clear of the lighted ones. An inspection of the carriage house and stables showed them to be open and deserted. We had made nearly the whole circuit of the park when we arrived before a tumble-down out-building set in an angle of the wall near the pond. The shadows here lay thick as smoke. Holmes slackened his pace and signed to me to do the same. The shed possessed a single square window, nearly opaque with dirt. Opening the shade of his dark lantern, Holmes cast its beam through the glass.

"Nothing more sinister than gardener's implements and heaps of miscellaneous lumber," he observed.

We now deserted the shadows to approach the pond. Here we were in full view of the row of lighted windows on the ground floor of the house which told where the women were spending their solitary evening. Holmes' next proceeding seemed utterly without reason, for he went down upon his knees at the rocky margin of the pond and thrust his stick into the water as though to test its depth. Again and again he repeated this manoeuvre, until he had completed the circuit of the pond.

"Let us retire to that little copse," said he, shaking the water from his stick and dusting the knees of his trousers. "Our pipes won't attract any notice there, and the view of the house will be far better than from the lodge."

Selecting for our vigil a fallen tree covered with moss, we settled down for a quiet smoke. Holmes crouched motionless in the shadow, and only the rhythmic blush of the bowl of his pipe showed that he remained as watchful and alert as ever. The chime of the village church struck ten. The moon had nearly vanished behind a gable of the house, and an impalpable mist seemed to rise from the dull waters of the pond. The chill of a late summer's night had begun to seep into my marrow when I was suddenly galvanized into action by an event that was as violent as it was unexpected.

I have said that from our point of vantage we had a view of four lighted windows on the ground floor. These windows stood in a row, three of them being tall and rectangular, and the fourth small and oval. It was in this latter window that the light shone most brilliantly, and from time to time we had a glimpse of a female figure moving past the glass. On one of these occasions the figure paused in its passage as though to look out, and at that moment a deafening explosion rent the stillness of the night and sent us leaping to our feet.

Simultaneous with the shot, which seemed to issue from very near at hand, came the crash of glass and a woman's scream. The face had vanished from the window. "Quick, Watson! To the house!" cried my companion, setting off across the park at a brisk pace. He threw open the shade of his dark lantern but wasted no time in seeking the assassin. Looking towards the oval window as I ran, I saw the light from within caught and reflected by the jagged edges of the shattered panes. No human figure appeared there.

Holmes raced up the broad steps and pounced upon the bell, at which he hauled violently and repeatedly. "Did you see him, Holmes?" I asked, as I joined him in the pillared porch.

"Devil a bit of him. He must have fired from beyond the wall." His tone was one of deep chagrin, and I sensed how bitterly he regretted having to forego the pursuit of the assassin. "Pray God the lady isn't mortally wounded," he murmured, attacking the bell with renewed vigour.

The door was suddenly thrown open, and in the light of a flickering candle there appeared a young woman in a nightdress, her long hair flowing in disorder over her shoulders. "Oh, gentlemen, you must help me!" she cried, holding out her hand to us in a pathetic gesture of appeal. "My maid has been killed! Murdered!"

For an instant Holmes shone the light of his torch full in her face, and then, flinging past her without a word, he mounted a short stair that led in the direction of the apartment with the oval window. I followed more slowly, taking the candle from Miss Ordway's trembling hand and guiding her up the stair.

We found Holmes bending over the still form of the maid, who lay in a litter of broken glass. "Some brandy, Watson! She's only fainted, I think. There is no blood, and if I am not mistaken that is the ball lodged in the moulding above the door."

I snatched up a decanter and glass from the sideboard, and while Holmes and Miss Ordway chafed the maid's wrists and temples I administered a stiff dose of liquor. Presently our efforts were rewarded by the appearance of a tinge of colour in the young woman's cheeks, and a restless stirring of her limbs. We raised her gently and laid her upon the sofa.

"You are very good," said Miss Ordway. "To whom am I indebted for this kindness?"

My companion ran her over with one of his quick, all-comprehensive glances. As though aware for the first time of her deshabille, the lady retired a little into the shadows and began to adjust the disorder of her hair.

"I am Sherlock Holmes, and this is my friend and associate, Dr. Watson. We are employed by your uncle to watch the house during his absence."

"My uncle has told me nothing of this."

"It was his particular wish that we remain outside the house. You might have been spared this shocking trouble if we had been nearer."

"I spared! But it is my maid who was nearly murdered!"

"Do you not think it probable that the bullet was intended for you?"

"My uncle will have told you of the other attempts, Mr. Holmes? On the first occasion Elizabeth was seated next to me. Either of us might have been the object of the shot that was fired. When I was nearly run down in London I was wearing one of Elizabeth's gowns—an unfortunate whim of my uncle's."

"Can you suggest any reason why your maid should thrice be the victim of murderous attacks?"

"None. But neither can anyone have a reasonable motive for murdering me."

Elizabeth Fetters had by this time so far recovered herself as to sit upright upon the sofa, and now she fixed her mistress with a look of faint reproach. "You oughtn't to hide Mr. Lawrence's threats from the police, Miss, really you oughtn't, for it is all bound to come out in the end."

"Nonsense, Elizabeth. These gentlemen are not the police. Mr. Lawrence's words were spoken in the heat of anger. They came from a heart stung with disappointment, not a mind meditating revenge."

Without missing a word of this conversation, Holmes had for some moments past been examining what remained of the shattered window. The casement had been swung round on its pivots by the force of the bullet, so that it lay nearly horizontal in its frame. Of the four panes, the upper two had been broken, though the bullet had actually struck the leaden mullion between them.

"It is fortunate that the window was unlatched," observed my companion. "Otherwise we might have written a very different end to the chapter. The bullet, striking the unyielding surface of the mullion, would very likely have penetrated it instead of being deflected from its target. The police must be informed of this latest attempt, though I fear that the culprit is far away by now. Have you your revolver, Watson? Then you may stand guard while I go into the village. It cannot be half an hour's walk, and the night is fine. Bolt the door, open to no one until I return, and stay clear of the windows."

He had no sooner departed than the two women deserted me as well, retiring for the night and leaving me in possession of the sitting-room and the key to the front door. With a candle in one hand and my revolver in the other I made the round of the dark and silent house, finding everything in order. Then I sat down upon a massive carved chair in the lower hall to await Holmes' return. The time passed slowly, and I was nearly nodding when I heard the sound of wheels in the gravelled drive.

Presently Holmes called my name from the porch, and I sprang up to unfasten the bolt. A brisk, heavy-featured young man strode into the hall at Holmes' heels and examined me narrowly by the light of his torch. "Inspector Skinner, that is my associate, Dr. Watson," explained Holmes. "He is not so vicious as he looks, and a good deal wiser."

My friend's tone of banter was lost upon the Inspector, who seemed much disappointed when he learned that the ladies had retired. "That is a pretty kettle of fish, now," said he. "Here I have got out of my bed in the middle of the night to take their depositions, and I find that they are quietly tucked up in theirs. I might as well have waited until the morning, for the bird is flown, and there is nothing to be seen here that cannot be seen better by the light of day."

"Very likely," agreed Holmes. "And yet, whoever fired the shot must have left some trace upon the ground. A light fall of rain or the passage of other feet may confuse or obliterate the marks."

"Oh, yes, you may look for marks if you like, Mr. Holmes. I know your methods very well, for we read our London papers in these parts just like the gentry in Park Lane and Piccadilly. But I have little hope of finding our men by looking at their foot-prints. If we find any foot-prints at all they will lead us very shortly to wheelmarks in the lane, and then we shall have lost them properly."

"Watson and I heard no wheels in the lane. The night is exceptionally still. The sound of hooves carries half a mile on such a night."

"Well, then, they've got away through the marsh, and left no trace at all. These are wily customers, Mr. Holmes, very much abler hands at covering their tracks than at hitting the mark. This is the third time they have failed to harm the lady."

The Inspector made a careful examination of the broken window and then climbed upon a chair and extracted the bullet from the moulding with his penknife. "Brass, by Jove," said he, bouncing the projectile on his palm. "A lucky thing for the maid that this bullet was deflected, for it would surely have been lethal if it had struck any vital part." He was plainly ready to conclude his inquiries until the morrow, when the two women would be available for questioning. Holmes, however, returned to the subject of foot-prints.

"Why, sir," objected Inspector Skinner, "you might search the whole night through and find nothing. The shot could have been fired from anywhere in the park."

"The shot was fired from nowhere in the park. Though the night was clear and the moon still shining low among the trees, we saw no one. Yet the shot was fired very near to us. It must have come from beyond the wall." Holmes stepped to the oval window and stood peering out into the darkness. After a time he closed and latched the window, and cast his eye about the room. "Here is Miss Ordway's sewing basket. I think she will forgive me for the trifling theft I am about to commit."

He selected a spool of heavy black thread from among the articles in the basket and unwound four or five yards upon the floor. Having tied one end round the mullion of the window at the level of the mark made by the bullet, he carried the rest across the room and mounted the chair upon which the Inspector had stood. Finally he drew the thread taut and fastened the other extremity to a large pin which he had thrust into the centre of the bullet hole.

"There is the path of the bullet," said he, springing down and returning to the window. "Now, Watson, take the dark lantern into the park, stand next to the pond, and direct the beam towards this window. I shall signal you with the candle, and you must move in the direction that I indicate. If I raise the candle you are to move farther away, and so on."

I took up the lantern and walked out into the park to comply with his orders. Fixing the correct latitude was simple enough, but Holmes' candle went on moving upwards until I had stumbled through a dense mass of brush to the very foot of the old wall and, stretching my arm upwards, set the lantern upon its summit.

The candle disappeared from the oval window, and presently Holmes and Inspector Skinner joined me in the park. The Inspector stared up at the lantern on the wall and shook his head in dismay. "We've a weary walk before us, Mr. Holmes, if we are going to look at the other side of this wall tonight. I am not much of a climber in any case, and I don't like the look of those spikes."

"There is a ladder in the gardener's shed," said Holmes.

The ground below the lantern was soft, and thick with tangled vines, but a yard or two away there lay a broad flat stone, bare of foliage, upon which we contrived to erect the ladder. The Inspector mounted first and shone the beam of the lantern over to the far side of the wall. "There is a thicket here," he reported presently. "The ground falls away pretty sharply, and I see a bit of water at the bottom. It is just as I supposed—he has come and gone through the marsh."

"Are there no marks at the foot of the wall?" asked Holmes, chafing with impatience.

The Inspector moved a step higher and leaned forward over the wall, grasping one of the iron spikes to preserve his balance. "Why, to be sure there are, Mr. Holmes," he said. "They look in rather a muddled state, but perhaps you can read something there. The vines grow as thick and wild on the farther side of the wall as on this, and they have been disturbed just here, as though someone had climbed up."

"Let us take the lantern, and leave the ladder to mark the spot," said Holmes. Without another word he made off in the direction of the gate, so that the Inspector had little choice but to come down from the ladder and follow him. After a long walk among tangles of bracken and shallow, stagnant pools, we arrived on the outer side of the wall opposite the ladder. Here the Inspector assumed a skeptical and patronizing manner, retiring into the shadows and leaving Holmes to examine the ground alone.

Holmes, I knew, asked for nothing better. Going down on his knees in the mire, he passed the beam of the lantern rapidly back and forth over the trampled earth, reading upon that palimpsest signs invisible to other eyes. Suddenly he plucked up something that had been nearly buried in the soil, and examined it by the light of the lantern.

"What have you there, Mr. Holmes?"

"A nickle-plated screw with a large knurled head," said Holmes, handing the object to Inspector Skinner. "It has been trodden into the earth by a man springing down from the wall."

"They must be very light on their feet, these assassins," said the

Inspector. "You seemed quite certain a while ago that no carriage passed along the lane. Yet here were these fellows climbing upon the very wall not ten yards from where you sat, and you heard nothing."

"There has been only one man here," observed Holmes, too intent upon his investigation to mark the archness of the other's tone. "His boot soles are broad and short. The toes are squared, and there are lozenge-shaped metal plates upon the heels."

"Holmes," said I with considerable excitement, stepping forward to examine the foot-marks over his shoulder. "These marks—"

"—are interesting, of course, but inconclusive. Whoever made them has approached the wall from that morass below, and gone away by the same route. The marks of his coming and going are not so clear as these at the foot of the wall, but plain enough to the practised eye. Then, as to his behaviour at the wall: he has stood, he has mounted up by these vines, he has sprung down again. Curious, but hardly incriminating."

"But these marks were surely made—"

"True, Watson, they were made after that screw was dropped upon the ground. But it is probable that the screw has been lost by some chance passer-by, and has no connexion with the crime."

"As you see, Mr. Holmes," said the Inspector, "Midnight excursions for the examination of foot-marks are seldom worth the trouble." He turned up the collar of his coat and gave other tokens of a wish to return to his bed.

When he had driven off, Holmes and I returned to the sitting-room with the oval window, where I attacked him at once upon the subject of the foot-prints. "Those marks were by Ordway himself, Holmes, for I noticed the soles of his boots very particularly this afternoon, or rather yesterday afternoon."

"Excellent, Watson, excellent! You really are coming along remarkably well. There is something in what you say, though that style of boot is not such a rarity as you seem to imagine. But Ordway had set off for Calais before the shot was fired. He must have made the marks on some earlier occasion, if he made them at all. There is little point and no profit in arousing the suspicions of the police against one's client."

"Perhaps not. But we have only Ordway's word that he was bound for the Continent. He may have gone to Paddington Station instead of Victoria, and followed us down in our own train."

"'Pon my word, Watson, you grow positively cynical in the small hours. What has become of your decent enough chap, beside himself over the threats to his niece's safety?"

"But Ordway is the only man with a motive for the crime, and the foot-prints are certainly suggestive."

"So they are. Did you observe any features of interest in those leading away from the wall and into the morass?"

"They were very obscure."

"Yet they were different from all the others. The outer sides of the soles had indented the earth much more deeply than the inner sides. I commend that point to your consideration, should you prefer meditation to sleep at this wretched time of the morning. No, take the sofa, Watson. I shall do very well upon the hearth-rug."

I awoke to find the full light of day streaming in at the windows. Holmes sat curled in an armchair, smoking absorbedly. "Good morning," said he. "Coffee and scones are to be had in the morning-room. I've brought up your gear from the lodge. It is on the window seat."

"You have been abroad early."

"I have been as far as the village. I sent a cable to Ordway to apprise him of the latest events and to assure him of his niece's safety. I have also hired a trap, which is standing in the stable yard."

When I had completed a sketchy toilet and swallowed a bite of breakfast, we went out into the dewy morning. Holmes had secured a pair of our client's boots by one of those ingenious expedients with which his imagination so readily supplied him. It was the work of a moment to compare the boots with the marks and to note that they matched in every particular.

"You've lost your money by dispatching a cable to Calais," said I gloomily. "Ordway was on this spot at ten o'clock last night. He fired the shot which broke the window and nearly killed—"

"His niece's maid. Come, Watson, it won't do. Ordway is not likely to have a motive for murdering the maid, and he is scarcely capable of mistaking her for his niece, even at this distance from the house."

"But what possible interpretation do these foot-marks bear, if they do not show that Ordway came here by stealth, climbed upon the wall at the very spot from which the shot was fired, and then made off through the marsh?"

"I draw your attention once again to the differing character of this track leading down the slope," he said. "What does it suggest to you?"

"That he was carrying some heavy load which got between his knees and forced him to walk upon the outer edges of his feet."

"Capital. The faculty of reasoning analytically is a rare gift, Watson. Of course not all who possess it are equally endowed. These foot-marks are rather closer together than the others, which is against the supposition that the man who made them was walking with something between his knees. Not only does your explanation not deal with all of the facts, but it postulates others for which we have no evidence. What burden had he to carry down the hill, which he did not have when he came up? Whence did it come, and why has it left no mark or trace upon the wall or the ground?"

"I give it up, Holmes. If this jumble of marks tells any story but the obvious one, it escapes me."

"Yet I fancy the key to the mystery lay open to our view in Baker Street yesterday."

Upon our return to the house we discovered Inspector Skinner installed in the morning room with his notebook on his knee and a glass of cider at his elbow. He appeared to be upon the most familiar terms with the women of the house, and gave every indication of making a long job of taking their depositions. We left them in his charge and drove into the village. Holmes proposed that we lunch at the inn with a view to hearing some of the local gossip.

The landlord, a great red-faced man as stout as a barrel, proved to be as close and taciturn with strangers as he was free and jovial with his regular customers. When he knew that it was we who had driven to Moorcroft on the previous day in the trap belonging to the inn, he fixed us with a sardonic and by no means pleasant smile.

"Your welcome has run out quickly enough, gentlemen," said he, "but that is nothing remarkable. You'll hear no good of the Ordways hereabouts."

"What have they done, then?" asked my companion.

"It's what they have not done that's got them a black name, sir. They run up immense accounts with every tradesman in the district, and when bills are presented Ordway has the cheek to demand more credit. He hires labourers in the village and puts off paying their wages from month to month until they are grown tired of asking."

"What need has he of labourers? I understood that his man, Fetters, looked after the house and grounds."

The landlord curled up his ample lip in disdain. "Not him. Mr. Fetters is above all that, sir. Mr. Fetters is a very superior sort of servant, indeed—what you might call a private secretary. When there is labour to be done, Mr. Ordway casts about the village for some poor drifter who doesn't know the sort of man he has to deal with."

"I suppose by labour you mean gardening, and domestic chores too heavy for the maid?"

"There you ask me more than I know. Perhaps Mr. Ludwick, the estate-agent, can help you—the gentleman in the black gaiters, sir, just passing the door of the tap-room. Farms are his usual stock in trade, but I understand he has lately taken some business interest in Moorcroft."

The estate-agent responded to Holmes' overtures with open rudeness. "If you come from Ordway, sir, you shall see nothing of me but my back. But you may tell him for me that he is a wretch and a scoundrel, and that I had sooner go to my grave this day than do business with him."

"I did not say that I came from Ordway," returned Holmes, "but only that I am staying at his house."

Mr. Ludwick indulged in a laugh of savage sarcasm. "His house, did you say? It is not his house, sir, but his niece's, as I have learned to my great cost. He is neither owner, nor proprietor, nor duly appointed steward. I will tell you what he is, sir—he is a hanger-on, a parasite, a blood-sucker, and if you are wise you will have nothing whatever to do with him." He went off in great haste as though afraid of being pursued.

"This grows tiresome," said Holmes. "At least let us hope we shall meet with more courteous treatment at the post-office."

The postal clerk presented Holmes with a reply to his cable, but it proved to be only a short note from the manager of Ordway's hotel in Calais. Ordway, who was well known to the sender of the message, was not at the hotel, nor even expected.

Holmes did not seem in the least surprised at this development. On the other hand, the cable came as a thunderbolt to Inspector Skinner. It was as well that Holmes drew him into the lower hall before showing it to him, for he broke out in a perfect fury. "It is the man himself," he cried, three or four times over. "I knew it—I suspected it from the first. And so did you, too, Mr. Holmes. Miss Ordway has told me of your researches with her uncle's boots. Those are his own foot-prints, are they not?"

"These are deep waters, Inspector," replied Holmes, shaking his head slowly and solemnly, "and very murky just at present."

"You would put me off, of course, for you are in the scoundrel's pay. But I must apply for a warrant, Mr. Holmes, and I should advise you to do nothing that might impede me in the execution of my duty."

"I am beginning to feel distinctly unwelcome in this quarter of the kingdom, Watson," remarked my friend airily. "Let us retire and lament in private the absence of our host."

We saw no more of the Inspector that day, and very little of the lady who had perforce to play hostess to us for the week-end. Holmes lay coiled in a corner of the sofa, with his arms folded and his gaze fixed upon the oval window, smoking pipe after pipe and vouchsafing no reply to any of my remarks. It was plain that he did not believe in the manifest guilt of our client, and equally plain that his skepticism arose not from any misplaced loyalty but from a conviction that the evidence bore some more favourable interpretation than the obvious one.

Accustomed though I was to his unsociable ways when his mind was occupied by some insoluble riddle, I found the time lying heavily upon my hands as the shadows crept into the room and the cooler breeze of sunset stirred the curtains round the shattered window. I had nearly finished a leisurely and half-hearted perusal of a week-old newspaper when Holmes suddenly sprang out of his seat and put his pipe down upon the mantelpiece.

"I have been blind, Watson, blind!" he cried, fairly dancing across the room and peering out into the park. The thread had been taken down earlier in the day, but as I stood at his elbow it was easy enough to follow his line of sight. By the last rays of the sinking sun the little pond shone like a pool of liquid gold. Deep shadows already lay beneath the trees, but I could clearly perceive the ladder still resting on the large flat stone at the foot of the wall, where Holmes and I had placed it.

"Look at that stone," said Holmes, pointing with his forefinger through the empty sash. "Why is it bare of foliage, in a place where even the vines are entwined by other vines, and the whole is engulfed in a sea of bindweed? Come, bring the dark lantern. And not a sound."

With furtive and stealthy tread we passed out of the house and into the park, where the gloom thickened from moment to moment. Holmes made straight for the gardener's shed and without a word handed me out a spade, taking up a pick and another spade for himself. "Now, then, Watson, set the lantern upon that stump, while I shift the ladder. Be as quiet as you can, but above all let us be quick."

"What does it all mean, then, Holmes?"

"Do not the size and shape of this stone suggest anything to you? Unless I am mistaken it means murder, Watson—not murder contemplated, not murder attempted, but murder fully accomplished and concluded. Let us have this stone up, and put the matter beyond doubt."

"It is a very large and heavy stone, Holmes."

"Quite so. And yet one man put it there. Two, I fancy, can take it up again." We attacked the earth round the stone with our spades, and when the excavation had been carried to a sufficient depth Holmes inserted the pick under one edge and gave a powerful heave. As the stone shifted slightly I thrust the tip of my spade and added my strength to Holmes'.

At that moment some stir of movement near the house caught my eye. Even as our united efforts raised the stone from the earth like the lid of a coffin and tipped it back against the wall, I descried two figures crossing the porch, while a third paused for an instant, framed in the lighted doorway.

"Holmes, they are coming!"

"Who are coming?"

"The women—and another."

"Let them come."

"The fellow has a cudgel."

"Better and better."

"Holmes, it is Ordway himself."

"I doubt it." He took up the lantern and shone it into the cavity which had formerly been covered by the stone. One horrifying glimpse I had of blackened flesh and sodden garments, and then our visitors were upon us.

"So, gentlemen," said our client, "you have not been content with the duties for which you were hired, but must meddle with what does not concern you." He waved his cudgel in a vague gesture of menace, but his tone was less masterful than it might have been had not Holmes taken care to let him see that a revolver was in his hand.

"Murder is the concern of every citizen," said my companion coolly. "To ignore it or to conceal it is to be a party to it."

"Murder is a strong word, Mr. Holmes. By what right do you dig in my park, and make slanderous accusations to my face?"

"Come, sir, drop this pretence. I believe I have the honour to address Mr. Fetters?"

At this, the man with the cudgel seemed to wilt and shrink like a wounded animal. All the fight went out of him, and he nodded in dumb assent to Holmes' identification.

"And the man in the grave is Ordway?"

"Not a man, Mr. Holmes, but a monster," cried Fetters, flaring up with a new animation. "In that grave lies all that remains of the foulest blackguard who ever drew breath. You have got the better of me, fairly enough, but you said too much when you spoke of murder. If you will step into the house I shall make it all clear to you, and then you must do as you think best."

Fetters conducted us to the sitting-room and flung himself dejectedly down upon the sofa, where presently his sister Elizabeth joined him. Despite a certain similarity about the eyes, I thought them as unlike as any brother and sister I had ever known.

"How you have got hold of it by the right end, I can't think," said Fetters, "for I thought I had done a proper job of kicking sand into your eyes, Mr. Holmes."

"That is what many another has thought. The impersonation was plain to me from the first, though I confess that your motive still eludes me."

"Well, then, I shall just begin at the beginning, and if there is anything that is not quite clear you must tell me so and I shall try to put you straight. You must know, sir, that my late master was a greedy, scheming villain, though I say it before Miss Ordway. She will perhaps deny it, but I know she has cursed a thousand times the black day on which she fell into her uncle's grasp.

"She alone stood between him and his father's fortune. His business was failing. He tried to mortgage the estate without Miss Ordway's knowledge, and ran afoul of the law. He sent a pawn of his, that smirking puppy Mr. Theobald Lawrence, to make up to her and propose marriage. After she laughed him out of the house Ordway kept her shut up like a novice in a nunnery lest she marry another and so cheat him of his expectations.

"I knew my employer to be none too scrupulous in his business dealings, nor too nice in his choice of associates. But as my sister was devoted to Miss Ordway, and my duties congenial and light, I stayed with him, never dreaming that he was capable of hiring an assassin to murder his own flesh and blood.

"It was after the second attempt on Miss Ordway's life that my eyes were suddenly opened. The attack occurred, as you know, in London, when Miss Ordway was wearing a gown of my sister's—a gown that Ordway himself had particularly instructed her to wear. Through Elizabeth, I tried to warn Miss Ordway of the terrible danger in which she lay, but she would not listen.

"I resolved to take steps myself to prevent any further attempts on her life. Arming myself with a pistol, I dogged Miss Ordway's footsteps, haunted the passage outside her apartment, and at the risk of being detected and turned out for my impertinence I took to passing my nights in a linen closet near to her chamber.

"On the very second night my vigilance was rewarded. I was awakened out of a sound sleep by muffled exclamations which seemed to come from Miss Ordway's bedchamber, and without pausing to inquire into the right or wrong of what I did I snatched up my pistol and rushed into the room. Imagine, Mr. Holmes, a suckling mouse in the clutches of a hawk, a hare fallen prey to a python, and you will know what I felt upon entering that room. He was strangling her, choking out her life with an energy and force which were at once savage and deliberate. Before he knew that I was in the room I had emptied two chambers of my pistol into his brain. Only then did I see that the band which he had twisted round Miss Ordway's throat was the sash of my own dressing gown, and perceive the full extent of his treacherous purpose.

"That was four nights ago. I buried him in the park, concealing the disturbance of earth with a slab of stone which was all that remained of a watering-trough in the stable yard. Those were the labours which left their marks upon my hands.

"If you will reflect upon the position in which Miss Ordway was placed by my hasty and too thorough intervention, you will see that it was a delicate one. If Ordway had much to gain by murdering his niece, she had something to gain from his death also. By the terms of her father's will she was entitled to take possession of the entire fortune if she married at any time between the ages of eighteen and twenty-five, or if during the same period her uncle died or became legally incompetent. It was the last provision that determined our course of action.

"Miss Ordway did not choose to marry. We could scarcely pretend that her uncle's death was accidental, and years might elapse before the law would permit presumption of death if he merely disappeared. We resolved accordingly to manufacture grounds upon which a court might grant a motion to declare Ordway incompetent.

"Our plan was to stage yet another attempt upon Miss Ordway's life before reliable witnesses, and to leave traces sufficient to support the view that Ordway had made the attempt in his own proper person. To this end it was necessary to bring him to life again for a time. I am not unlike him in height and build, and you had never seen either of us. I visited your rooms in a suit of my employer's clothes, even wearing a pair of his boots and making certain that you had observed the rather distinctive pattern of the soles. After I had persuaded you to come to Moorcroft to witness the charade we had planned, I went to Victoria Station and dispatched a telegram to Ordway's firm explaining that he had been called away suddenly to the Continent. I then went on to Paddington Station and returned here by a later train than yours, walking across the downs and concealing myself in a thicket on the edge of the marsh until after nightfall.

"At the concerted time I mounted the wall and fired off a blank charge into the air. I would not, of course, take the risk of actually firing a bullet into the room. The damage to the mullion had been done in advance with a round punch. My sister insisted upon performing the role of the victim. When she heard the expected report she had only to break the glass by dashing the window inwards against that candlestick."

"And the bullet in the moulding?"

"Fired the night before last, from across the room. I had determined the exact course of the projectile with a theodolite. It was almost the only piece of truth I spoke yesterday, Mr. Holmes, when I said that I was trained as a surveyor."

"Had you been trained as an artilleryman you would have placed your bullet in the middle of the ceiling. I do not propose to demonstrate the point by actual experiment, but I assure you that if a bullet had really struck the mullion as the appearances suggested, it would have been deflected sharply upwards. Yesterday I determined the apparent path of the bullet after it struck the mullion. A continuation of that line across the park passed just over the wall. Now, the wall is at least fifty yards from the window, and the window is no more than five from the place where the bullet was lodged. If we suppose that the deflected bullet rose only twelve inches out of its original path in traversing those five yards, then that original path must have passed ten feet above the wall.

"By the way, I think you will find that there is an adjusting screw missing from your instrument. I picked it up on the far side of the wall last night and gave it to Inspector Skinner."

"Yes," said Fetters. "I stuck it into the moss on the top of the wall to mark the spot where the bullet was supposed to have passed over. I thought I was doing a clever thing in choosing so well-known a private detective to be my dupe, but it seems that it is I who am the dupe, after all. I expected that as soon as you had given a statement of the apparent facts to the police you would return to London."

"But the apparent facts were a jumble of contradictions," said Holmes. "To mention only the most glaring, the boots which Miss Ordway so willingly proffered this morning were the identical ones which had made the foot-prints beyond the wall. They must have been brought or worn into the house after the marks were made, carefully cleaned, and put into Ordway's room."

"So they were. After firing off the shot I ran into the marsh, put on my own boots, made a wide circuit over the downs, and arrived back here near dawn. My sister admitted me to the house and I have been holed up in her chamber ever since, while she has been staying with Miss Ordway.

"Have I done wrong, Mr. Holmes? Is it murder to strike down a vile beast so as to prevent his choking the life out of an innocent girl? Is it a crime to work a harmless deception so that the ends of justice may be served in justice's own despite?"

"As to the graver charge," said Holmes, "no one, I think, will call you a murderer. The British law is not an unreasonable nor a vindictive one, but it will not be trifled with. You must repeat what you have told me to the police, and you must be prepared to stand trial. If Miss Ordway and your sister confirm your story under oath, a jury may be expected to view your actions in a favourable light."

On the next morning but one, Inspector Skinner had his hour of glory in the police magistrate's court. Holmes declined to appear except in the character of a witness, and as he kept his own counsel about the curious behaviour of the bullet, the women were not brought into the case at all.

Fetters was arraigned upon charges of unlawfully disposing of a dead body and of fabricating evidence. Having pleaded guilty to both charges, he was committed for trial to the Quarter Session and released upon his recognizance.

"Are there any points in the case which are not perfectly clear to you?" asked Holmes, as we returned to London by the afternoon train.

"I can't think how you came to suspect that a body lay beneath that stone."

"Why, I was persuaded that the corpse lay concealed somewhere on the premises. The marshes would not have been chosen as a burial ground by anyone who had lived long among them. Marshland is a treacherous ally in the business of hiding bodies. Just when the murderer thinks he has put his victim forever beyond human ken, the marsh yields up a wan and watery spectre to point an accusing finger at him. The pond was too shallow, the cellars were unlikely, and there was no freshly turned earth to be seen in the park."

"But why suspect a corpse at all? You were engaged to prevent a murder, not to bring one to light."

"Quite so. But the man who engaged me was a palpable fraud."

"Come, Holmes, how could you recognize Fetters as a fraud when you knew neither him nor the man whom he impersonated? He was just a perfectly ordinary fellow, with utterly commonplace features and qualities."

"That is not altogether true. Long slender fingers like Fetters' are commonplace enough, to be sure, and so are broad, short feet like Ordway's. But their apparent concurrence in the same person is enough of an anomaly to excite not merely attention but suspicion. And then, when a man loses flesh he does not grow taller in proportion. Our client's clothing had been made for a man both stouter and shorter than himself. He said he was Ordway; then Ordway he was not, and the question arose, where *was* Ordway?"

"You might have put the matter into the hands of the police and spared yourself a great deal of trouble."

"The police would have gone about making futile inquiries for a few days, and then thrown up the whole affair. No, Watson, it was a case which demanded patience and discretion. Above all it was necessary that our client believe he had taken us in."

"But why carry on the pretence with the niece? I feared for her safety all the more after the third attempt. In your position I should have put the whole matter frankly to her."

"Where one deception has been practised, you may expect others.

You failed to appreciate the significance of the young lady's behaviour on the night of the supposed third attempt."

"I thought her remarkably composed and self-possessed, in the circumstances."

"Remarkably is the word, Watson. She was supposed not to know of our presence in the park. Yet when we rang the bell, but a few moments after a bullet had ostensibly passed through the sitting-room window and sent her maid into a dead faint, she had no hesitation about admitting us and soliciting our help."

"Fetters has little to fear, I suppose, at the Assizes?"

"I think not. I fancy that more difficult struggles await him nearer to home. If I am not mistaken, the lady is sorely smitten with her rescuer. He is scarcely the sort to set a young girl's heart a-pounding, and yet she could do worse. A stout fellow, is Fetters. Consider his injunction to us to carry firearms and not scruple to use them. It was fortunate for him that we ran to the house instead of getting upon the wall with our lantern and our revolvers. His progress must have been as slow as it was painful when he made his escape into the marsh. You recall those curious tracks? It is no simple matter to run while wearing boots which are two sizes too small."

"That was a macabre trick of his, Holmes, pretending that the shot was fired over the very place where Ordway's body lay."

"Perhaps, but I suspect that his motives were more practical than you suppose. Fetters wished to direct our attention to some spot on the other side of the wall, where we were to find a set of foot-prints made with Ordway's boots. Having selected the mullion of the oval window as one fixed point, he passed along the wall with his theodolite in search of a suitable place from which to plot the apparent course of the bullet. He might have given the game away if he had set down his apparatus on the bare earth. A tripod leaves a distinctive set of marks which would have been awkward to efface. Therefore he chose the one place along the wall where the tripod would leave no marks—the stone under which he had buried Ordway."

"You may talk of practical motives if you like, Holmes, but I cannot help seeing at least a gleam of romance in the circumstance."

"Say, rather, poetic justice," said my companion with a smile. "Truth is ever stranger than fiction, and the most improbable tale but the feeblest imitation of real life. Yet there is something in Boccaccio, is there not, that comes rather near to the present case?"

Your Appointment Is Cancelled

ANTONIA FRASER

"This is Arcangelo's Salon, Epiphany speaking. I am very sorry to inform you that your appointment is cancelled . . ." In sheer surprise, Jemima Shore looked at the receiver in her hand. But still the charming voice went on. After a brief click, the message had started all over again. "This is Arcangelo's Salon, Epiphany speaking. I am very sorry to inform you that your appointment is cancelled . . ."

In spite of the recording, Jemima imagined Epiphany herself at the other end of the telephone—the elegant black receptionist with her long neck and high cheekbones. Was she perhaps Ethiopian, Somali, or from somewhere else in Africa, which produced such beauties? Wherever she came from, Epiphany looked, and probably was, a princess. She was also, on the evidence of her voice and manner, highly educated; there was some rumor at the salon that Epiphany had been to university.

As the message continued on its level way, Jemima thought urgently: What about my hair? She touched the thick reddish-gold mass whose color and various styles had been made famous by television. Jemima thought it was professional to take as much trouble about her hair as she did about the rest of the details concerning her celebrated program looking into the social issues of the day, *Jemima Shore Investigates*. She had just returned from filming in Morocco (working title: *New Women of the Kasbah*) and her hair was in great need of the attentions of Mr. Leo, the Italian proprietor of Arcangelo's—or, failing that, those of his handsome English son-in-law, Mr. Clark.

But her appointment was cancelled and Jemima wondered what had happened at Arcangelo's.

A few hours later, the *London Evening Post* ran a brief front-page bulletin: a male hair stylist at a certain fashionable salon had been found when the salon opened that morning with his head battered in

433

by some form of blunt instrument. The police, led by Jemima's old friend, Detective Chief Inspector J. H. Portsmouth—more familiarly known as Pompey of the Yard—were investigating.

As Jemima was mulling this over, she received a phone call from Mr. Leo, who told her in a flood of Italianate English that the dead stylist was none other than his son-in-law, and that it was he, Leo, who had discovered the body when he unlocked the salon this morning, Epiphany, who normally did the unlocking, having been delayed on the Underground.

"Miss Shore," he ended brokenly, "they are thinking it is I, Leo, who am doing this dreadful thing, I who am killing Clark. Because of her, *mia cara, mia figlia, Domenica mia.* And yes, it is true, he was not a good husband, in spite of all I did for him, all she has been doing for him. In spite of the *bambino!*"

He paused and went on as though reluctantly. "A good stylist, yes, it is I who have taught him. Yes, he is good. Not as good as me, no, who would say that? But good. But he was a terrible husband. *Un marito abominabile.* I knew, of course. How could I not know? Everyone, even the juniors knew, working in the salon all day together. *My* salon! The salon *I* have created, I, Leo Vecchetti. They thought they were so clever. Clever! Bah!

"But for that I would not have killed him. She still loved him, my daughter, my only child. For her I built up everything, I did it all. My child, Domenica, and the little one, Leonella, who will come after her. Now he is dead and the police think I did it. Because I'm Italian and he's English. You Sicilians, they say. But I'm not Sicilian. I'm from the North, *sono Veneziano*—" Mr. Leo gave an angry cry and the flood poured on:

"What about *her*, then?" he almost shouted. "Maybe *she* killed him because he would not leave Domenica and marry her!" He now sounded bitter as well as enraged. "No, Clark would not leave my fine business—the business he would one day inherit. Not for one of those *savages*, not he. Maybe *she* kill him—kill him with a *spear* like in the *films!*"

From this, Jemima wondered if Leo was saying that Epiphany had been Mr. Clark's mistress.

"Mr. Leo," she said. "When the salon reopens, I want an immediate appointment."

* * *

A few days later, Jemima drew up at Arcangelo's in her white Mercedes sports car. The golden figure of an angel blowing a trumpet over the entrance made the salon impossible to miss. Jemima was put in a benign mood by being able to grab a meter directly outside the salon from under the nose of a rather flashy-looking Jaguar being propelled at a rather more dignified pace by its male driver. She glimpsed purple-faced anger, rewarded it with a ravishing smile, and was rewarded in turn by the driver's startled recognition of the famous television face.

Well, I've certainly lost a fan there, thought Jemima cheerfully. She looked through the huge plate-glass window and saw Epiphany, on the telephone, austerely beautiful in a high-necked black jersey. One of the other stylists—Mr. Roderick, she thought his name was—was bending over her. Epiphany was indeed alluring enough to make a man lose his head.

Pompey of the Yard, being a good friend of Jemima's from several previous cooperations beneficial to both sides, had filled in a few more details of the murder for Jemima. The blunt instrument had turned out to be a heavy metal hair dryer. Mr. Clark's body had been found—a macabre touch—sitting under one of the grey-and-gold automatic dryers. The medical examiner estimated the time of death as between ten and eleven the previous evening, more likely later than earlier because of the body temperature. The salon closed officially at about six, but the staff sometimes lingered until six-thirty or thereabouts, tending to each other's hair—cutting, restyling, putting in highlights, unofficial activities they had no time for during the day.

The night of the murder, Mr. Clark had offered to lock up the salon. (Being one of the senior stylists and, of course, Mr. Leo's son-in-law, he possessed his own set of keys.) At five o'clock, he had telephoned Domenica at home and told her he had a last-minute appointment: he had to streak the hair of a very important client and he might be home very late because this client was then going to take him to some film gala in aid of charity, to which she needed an escort—he couldn't offend her by refusing. Domenica, brought up in the hairdressing business and used to such last-minute arrangements, had a late supper with Mr. Clark's sister Janice, who had come to admire the baby, and went to bed alone. When she woke up in the morning and found Mr. Clark still absent, she simply assumed, said

Pompey of the Yard with a discreet cough, that the party had gone on until morning.

"Some client!" said Jemima indignantly. "I suppose you've questioned her. The client, I mean."

"I'm doing so now," Pompey had told her, with another discreet cough. "You see, the name of the famous client whose offer Mr. Clark simply could not refuse, according to his wife, was *yours*. It was you who was supposed to have come in at the last minute, needing streaks in a hurry before beginning the new series."

"Needing streaks *and* an escort, to say nothing of what else I was supposed to need," commented Jemima grimly. "Well, of all the cheek—"

"*We* think," Pompey had interposed gently into Jemima's wrath, "he had a date with the black girl there at the salon after everybody had gone. There is a beautician's room which is quite spacious and comfortable, couch and all. And very private after hours."

"All very nice and convenient," Jemima said, still smarting from the late Mr. Clark's impudence. "So that's where they were in the habit of meeting."

"We think so. And we think Mr. Leo knew that—and, being Sicilian and full of vengeance—"

"He's Venetian actually."

"Being *Venetian* and full of vengeance. There's plenty of vengeance in Venice, Jemima. Have you ever been to the place? Mrs. Portsmouth and I went once and when you encounter those gondoliers—" He broke off and resumed a more official tone. "Whatever his genesis, we believe he decided to tackle his son-in-law. That is to say, we think he killed him with several blows with a hair dryer.

"Mr. Leo has no alibi after nine o'clock. After a quick supper at home, he went out—he says—to the local pub, returning after it closed. But nobody saw him in the pub and he is, as you know, a striking-looking man. He had plenty of time to get to the salon, kill his son-in-law, and get back home."

"What about Epiphany? Mr. Leo blames her."

"She admits to having been the deceased's mistress—she could hardly deny it when everybody at the salon knew. She even admits to having an occasional liaison with him at the salon in the evening. But on this particular evening, she says very firmly that she went to the cinema—alone. She's given us the name of the film. *Gandhi*. All very pat. What's more, the commissionaire remembers her in the queue—she is, after all, a very beautiful woman—and so does the girl at the box office. The only thing is, she had plenty of time once the film was over to get back to the salon and kill her lover."

"She has no alibi for her activities after the movie?" put in Jemima.

"Not really. She lives with a girl friend off the Edgeware Road. But the friend's away—a very convenient fact if there was anything sinister going on—so according to Epiphany she just went home after the cinema, had a bit of supper, got into her lonely bed, and slept. Saw no one. Talked to no one. Telephoned no one. As for being late the next morning, that, too, was a piece of luck—stoppage on the Underground. We've checked that, of course, and it's true enough. But she could have come by a slower route, or even just left home later than usual so as to avoid opening up the shop and seeing the grisly consequences of her deed. As it was, we were there before she arrived."

With this information in her head, Jemima now entered the salon. Epiphany gave her usual calm welcome, asking the nearest junior—Jason, who had a remarkable coxcomb of multi-colored hair—to take Miss Shore's coat and lead her to the basin. But Jemima didn't think it was her imagination that made her suppose that Epiphany was frightened under her placid exterior. Of course, she could well be mourning her lover (presuming she had not killed him, and possibly even if she had) but Jemima's instinct told her there was something beyond that—something that was agitating, even terrifying Epiphany.

In the checkroom, Pearl, another junior with a multi-colored mop, took Jemima's fleecy white fur.

"Ooh, Miss Shore, how do you keep it so clean? It's white fox, is it?"

"I dump it in the bath," replied Jemima with perfect truth. "Not white fox—white nylon."

At the basin, Jason washed her hair with his usual scatty energy and later Mr. Leo set it. Mr. Leo was not scatty in any sense of the word. He did the set, as ever, perfectly, handling the thick rollers handed to him by Jason so fast and yet so deftly that Jemima, with much experience in having her hair done all over the world, doubted whether anyone could beat Mr. Leo for speed or expertise.

Nevertheless, she sensed beneath his politeness, as in Epiphany, all the tension of the situation. The natural self-discipline of the professional hairdresser able to make gentle, interested conversation with the client whatever his own personal problems: in this case, a son-in-law brutally murdered, a daughter and grandchild bereft, himself the chief suspect, to say nothing of the need to keep the salon going smoothly if the whole family business was not to collapse.

At which point Mr. Leo suddenly confounded all Jemima's theories about this unassailable professionalism by thrusting a roller abruptly back into Jason's hand.

"You finish this," he commanded. And with a very brief, muttered excuse in Jemima's general direction, he darted off toward the reception desk. In the mirror before her, Jemima was transfixed to see Mr. Leo grab a dark-haired young woman by the shoulder and shake her while Epiphany, like a carved goddess, stared enigmatically down at the appointments book on her desk as though the visitor and Mr. Leo did not exist. But it was interesting to note that the ringing telephone, which she normally answered at once, clamored for at least half a minute before it claimed her attention.

The young woman and Mr. Leo were speaking intensely in rapid Italian. Jemima spoke some Italian but this was far too quick and idiomatic for her to understand even the gist of it.

Then Jemima recognized the distraught woman—Domenica, Mr. Leo's daughter. And at the same moment she remembered that Domenica had worked as receptionist at the salon before Epiphany. Had she met Mr. Clark there? Probably. And probably left the salon to look after the baby, Leonella. It was ironic that it was Epiphany who had turned up to fill the gap. But why had Domenica come to the salon today? To attack Epiphany? Was that why Mr. Leo was hustling her away to the back of the salon with something that looked very much like force?

Jason had put in the last roller and fastened some small clips for the tendrils Jemima sometimes liked to wear at her neck. Now he fastened the special silky Arcangelo's net like a golden filigree over her red hair and led Jemima to the dryers with his usual energetic enthusiasm. Jason was a great chatterer and in the absence of Mr. Leo he really let himself go.

"I love doing your hair, Miss Shore—it's such great hair. Great styles you wear it in on the box, too. I always look for your hair style, no matter what you're talking about. I mean, even if it's abandoned wives or something heavy like that, I can still enjoy your hair style, can't I?"

Jemima flashed him one of her famously sweet smiles and sank back under the hood of the dryer.

A while later, she watched, unable to hear with the noise of the dryer, as Mr. Leo led Domenica back toward the entrance. As they passed the reception desk, Jemima saw Epiphany mouth something, possibly some words of condolence. In dumb show, Jemima saw Domenica break from her father's grip and shout in the direction of Epiphany.

"*Putana.*" In an Italian opera, the word would have been *putana*—prostitute—or something similarly insulting concerning Epiphany's moral character. Whatever the word was, Epiphany did not answer. She dropped her eyes and continued to concentrate on the appointments book in front of her as Mr. Leo led his daughter toward the front door.

"I am very sorry to inform you that your appointment is cancelled . . ." The memory of Epiphany's voice came back to Jemima. Could she really have recorded that message so levelly and impersonally after killing her lover?

Yet why had Mr. Clark lingered in the salon if not to meet Epiphany? He had certainly taken the trouble to give a false alibi to Domenica, who was expecting her sister-in-law for a late supper. Someone had known he would still be there after hours. Someone had killed him between ten and eleven, when Mr. Leo—unnoticed—was still allegedly at the pub and Epiphany was at home—alone.

Jemima closed her eyes. The dryer was getting too hot. Jason, through general enthusiasm no doubt, had a tendency to set the temperature too hot. She fiddled with the dial—and in so doing, it occurred to her to wonder under which dryer Mr. Clark's corpse had been found sitting. She began, in spite of herself, to imagine the scene. Having been struck—several times, the police said—from behind by the massive metal hair dryer, Mr. Clark had fallen onto the long grey-plush seat. The murderer had then propped him up under the plastic hood of one of the dryers to be found when the shop opened in the morning. The killer had left no fingerprints, having—another macabre touch—worn a pair of rubber gloves throughout, no doubt a pair that was missing from the tinting room. The killer had then locked the salon, presumably with Mr. Clark's own keys since these too had now vanished.

"At the bottom of the Thames now, no doubt," Pompey had said dolefully, "and the gloves along with them."

Jemima shifted restlessly, sorting images and thoughts in her head. Epiphany's solitary visit to a particularly long-drawn-out film followed by a lonely supper and bed, Mr. Leo's alibi, Domenica entertaining her sister-in-law in Mr. Clark's absence, Jason's dismissal of abandoned wives—it all began to flow together, to form and reform in a teasing kaleidoscope.

Where was Jason? She really was getting very hot.

Suddenly Jemima sat upright, hitting her head, rollers and all, on the edge of the hood as she did so. To the surprise of the clients watching (for she still attracted a few curious stares even after several years at Arcangelo's), she lifted the hood, pulled herself to her feet, and strode across the salon to where Epiphany was sitting at the reception desk. Both telephones were for once silent.

"It was true," said Jemima. "You *did* go to the cinema and then straight home. Were you angry with him? Had you quarreled? He waited here for you. But you never came."

"I told the police that, Miss Shore." It was anguish, not fear, she had sensed in Epiphany, Jemima realized. "I told them about the film. Not about the rendezvous. What was the point of telling them about that when I didn't keep it?"

"His appointment was cancelled," murmured Jemima.

"If only I *had* cancelled it," Epiphany said. "Instead, he waited. I pretended I was coming. I wanted him to wait. To suffer as I suffered, waiting for him when he was with her—with her and the baby." Epiphany's composure broke. "I could have had any job, but I stayed here like his *slave*, while she held him with her money, the business—"

"I believe you." Jemima spoke gently. "And I'm sure the police will, too."

A short while later, she was explaining it all to Pompey. The policeman, knowing the normally immaculate state of her hair and dress, was somewhat startled to be summoned to a private room at Arcangelo's by a Jemima Shore with her hair still in rollers and her elegant figure draped in a dove-grey Arcangelo's gown.

"I know, I know, Pompey," she said. "And for heaven's sake don't tell Mrs. Portsmouth you've seen me like this. But the heat of the dryer I was under a few minutes ago gave me an idea. The time of

Mr. Clark's death was all-important, wasn't it? By heating the body under the dryer and setting the time switch for an hour, the murderer made the police think that he had been killed nearer ten or eleven than the actual seven or eight when he was struck down.

"As it happened, ten or eleven was very awkward for Mr. Leo, ostensibly at the pub, but not noticed in the pub by anyone—I have a feeling that there may be an extramarital relationship there, too. Mr. Leo is still a very good-looking man. That's not our business, however, because Mr. Leo didn't kill Mr. Clark. Between eight and nine, he was in the Underground on the way home, and there we have many people to vouch for him. As for Epiphany, the girl at the box office verifies that she bought a ticket and the commissionaire that she was in the queue. The timing lets her out, lets them both out, but it lets someone else—someone who kept the appointment she knew Mr. Clark had made. The abandoned wife. Domenica.

"Domenica," Jemima went on sadly, "entertaining her sister-in-law from half past nine onward. Sitting with her, chatting with her. Spending the rest of the long evening with her, pretending to wait for her husband. And all the time he was dead here in the salon. Domenica had worked at the salon—she helped her father build it up. She knew about the rubber gloves and the keys and the hand dryers and the time switches on the stationary ones.

"Pompey," Jemima paraphrased Jason: "it's heavy being an abandoned wife. So in the end, Domenica decided to keep Epiphany's appointment. She even left her baby alone to do so—such was the passion of the woman. The woman scorned. It was she who cancelled all future appointments for Mr. Clark, with a heavy blow of a hand dryer."

Le Château de L'Arsenic

GEORGES SIMENON

He hesitated a moment. Then he stood on tiptoe and rang the bell. He was a small man and the bell was situated in an abnormally high position. The Little Doctor knew that he was being watched—not only from inside the château but from the houses in the village, where they must be wondering who, at such a time, would dare to ring this bell.

He was in a village in a clearing in the forest of Orléans, but the clearing was rather small for the château and the few surrounding cottages. The forest seemed to overflow, stifling the village, and you felt that the sun had difficulty in getting through the thick branches. A few thatched roofs, a grocer's shop, an inn—all low, narrow houses—and then the château, too large, too old, falling to ruin and looking like an impoverished aristocrat in rags, but rags which had once been well cut.

On the first floor a curtain moved. A pale face appeared for a moment at one of the windows.

Finally, a servant came to the door. She was a girl of about twenty to twenty-five, pleasant-looking, prettier than you would have expected to find in such a place.

"What do you want?" she asked him.

"I want a word with Monsieur Mordaut."

"Have you an appointment?" she asked.

"No."

"Are you from the Public Prosecutor?"

"No, but if you would be good enough to give him my card—"

She went away. A little later she came back with another servant, a woman of about fifty with a forbidding face.

"What do you want with Monsieur Mordaut?"

Then the Little Doctor, despairing of ever passing this closely guarded gate, spoke frankly. "I have come about the poisonings," he said, with the same charming smile he would have used to give someone a box of chocolates. The face had reappeared behind the first-floor window. Probably Monsieur Mordaut.

"Come in, please," he said. "Is that your car? You had better drive it in, too, or the children will soon be throwing stones at it . . ."

442

The drawing room, like the exterior of the château, was sad and dusty. So also was Monsieur Mordaut in his long, old-fashioned jacket, and with his sunken cheeks covered by a lichenlike, short, dirty grey beard.

"Good morning, sir," said the Little Doctor. "I must apologize for having almost forced an entry, particularly as you have probably never so much as heard of my name."

"No, I haven't," said Monsieur Mordaut with a shake of his head.

"Well, sir, as others are interested in handwriting or palmistry, I have a passion for human problems—for the puzzles which, in their early stages, are nearly always crimes."

"Pray continue."

"I have been extremely interested in the rumors which have been current for some time about you and this château. I came here to discover the truth; that is to say, to find out whether you murdered your aunt Émilie Duplantet; then your wife, who was Félicie Maloir before you married her; and lastly your niece, Solange Duplantet."

It was the first time that the Little Doctor had addressed such a speech to another human being, and his nervousness was aggravated by the fact that he was cut off from the world by a long corridor, with innumerable doors leading off it.

Monsieur Mordaut had not stirred. At the end of a long piece of black cord he swung an old-fashioned eyeglass; his expression was infinitely sad.

"You were right to speak frankly . . . Will you have something to drink?"

In spite of himself, the Little Doctor shivered. It is somewhat disconcerting to be offered a drink by a man you don't know, and whom, in a slightly indelicate fashion, you have just accused of being a poisoner.

"Please don't be afraid. I'll drink out of the bottle before you. Did you come by the village?"

"I stopped at the inn for a minute to book a room."

"That was unnecessary, Monsieur—Monsieur—"

"Jean Dollent."

"I would be honored, Monsieur Dollent, if you would stay here."

Monsieur Mordaut uncorked a dusty bottle of an unusual shape. Almost without thinking, the Little Doctor drank one of the best wines he had ever tasted.

"You must stay here as long as you please. You must have the run of the château, and I will answer all your questions to the best of my ability. Excuse me a moment."

He pulled a long woolen cord and somewhere in the building a reedy bell sounded. Then the old servant who had opened the door to Dollent appeared.

"Ernestine, please lay another place at the table. Also prepare the green room for monsieur. He is to be treated here as if it were his own house, and you must answer any questions he puts to you."

Once more alone with Dollent, he sighed. "You are probably surprised by this reception. But there are, Monsieur Dollent, moments when one jumps at no matter what chance of salvation. If a fortune-teller, a fakir, or a dervish offered to help me, I would treat him in the same way."

He spoke slowly, in a tired voice, fixing his eyes on the worn carpet while, with exaggerated care, he wiped the lens of the eyeglass which he never used. "I am a man who has been pursued from birth by ill luck. If there were competitions of bad luck, championships for bad luck, I would be certain to win. I was born to attract unhappiness, not only to myself, but to all those around me.

"My grandparents were extremely rich. My Grandfather Mordaut built a large part of the Haussmann area in Paris and was worth millions. The day I was born he hanged himself because of some political scandal in which he was involved. As a result of the shock, my mother developed puerperal fever and died within three days. My father tried to make good his father's losses—but of his whole fortune only this château remained. I came here when I was five. Playing in the tower I accidentally set fire to a whole wing, which was destroyed, and with it many objects of value."

This was becoming too much. It was almost comical.

"I could continue the list of my misfortunes indefinitely."

"Excuse me," interposed the Little Doctor, "but it seems to me that up to now those misfortunes seem to have fallen more on others than on yourself."

"Ah! Don't you think that it is just that which is the greatest misfortune? Eight years ago my aunt Duplantet, recently widowed, came to live with us, and six months later she was dead of a heart attack."

"They say that she had been slowly poisoned by arsenic. Hadn't she taken out a life-insurance policy in your favor, and didn't you come into a considerable sum of money through her?"

"A hundred thousand francs—scarcely enough to restore the south tower which was crumbling away. Three years later my wife—"

"Died in her turn, and again of a heart attack. She also had taken out a policy which brought you—?"

"Which brought me the accusations you know of, and a sum of two hundred thousand francs."

"Finally," said the Little Doctor, "a fortnight ago, your niece Solange Duplantet, an orphan, died here, at the age of twenty-eight, of a heart attack, leaving you the Duplantet fortune, which is nearly half a million francs."

"But in property and land—not cash," corrected the strange man.

"This time tongues were really loosened, anonymous letters poured into the Préfecture, and an official investigation was set on foot."

"The police have already been three times and found nothing. On two other occasions I was called to Orléans for questioning. I think I would be lynched if I dared appear in the village."

"Because traces of arsenic were found in the three corpses."

"It seems they always find some."

"You have a son?" asked the Little Doctor rather abruptly.

"Hector, yes. You must have heard of him. As the result of an illness in childhood, the growth of his brain was arrested. He lives here in the castle. At twenty-two he has the body of a man and the intelligence of a child of nine. But still, he's harmless."

"The person who showed me in—Ernestine—has she been here a long time?"

"Always. She was the daughter of my father's gardener. Her parents died and she stayed on."

"She never married?"

"Never."

"And the young woman?"

"Rose," said Monsieur Mordaut with a slight smile, "is Ernestine's niece. For nearly ten years now she has worked here as a maid. When she first came she was a schoolgirl of sixteen."

"Have you any other servants?"

"None. I am not rich enough to live in great style. I live among my books and my works of art. Incidentally, Ernestine hasn't got cancer," said Monsieur Mordaut, "but she talks of nothing else.

Since her sister, Rose's mother, died of cancer, she has an unshakable belief that she has also got it. At one moment it's in her back, another in her chest, another in her stomach. She spends half her time consulting doctors, and she's furious that they can't find anything. If she consults you, I advise you—"

But a furious Ernestine now appeared before them.

"Well, are you going to have any lunch or not?"

Monsieur Mordaut turned to the Little Doctor and said sadly:

"Please fear nothing. I will eat from each dish and drink out of each bottle before you touch them. It no longer means anything to me. You should know, Doctor, that I am also suffering with my heart. For the last three months I have felt the same symptoms that my aunt, my wife, and my niece all complained of at the beginning of their illnesses."

It really required a very good appetite to eat that meal. The Doctor wondered if he wouldn't have done better to eat and sleep at the inn. Hector ate gluttonously, like a badly brought-up child. It was alarming to watch this large youth with the face of a cunning urchin.

"What do you want to do this afternoon, Doctor?" asked Monsieur Mordaut. "Can I be of any help?"

"I would really like to be free to come and go as I please. I'll look round the grounds. Perhaps I'll ask the servants one or two questions."

And that is where he started. He moved off towards the kitchen where Ernestine was washing the dishes.

"What's he been telling you?" she asked immediately, with the habitual distrust of the peasant. "Did he tell you about my cancer?"

"Yes."

"Ah. He told you it wasn't true, didn't he? But he swears his heart is bad. Well, I'm certain that it's nothing of the sort. He's never had a bad heart. There's nothing wrong with him."

She talked on without stopping her work, and one was conscious of her health and strength. She must once have been a lovely girl, buxom as her niece.

"I wanted to ask you, Doctor. Can cancer be given to people by arsenic or other poisons?"

He didn't want to say yes or no, because it seemed more profitable to play on the old servant's fears.

"What do you feel?" he replied.

"Pains. As if something was being driven into me. Mostly in the bottom of my back, but sometimes also in my stomach."

He mustn't smile. It would make him an enemy.

"I'll examine you, if you like."

"As soon as I've finished the washing up," she replied with alacrity.

The examination had lasted a good quarter of an hour, and each time the Little Doctor showed signs of abandoning it Ernestine called him firmly to order.

"You haven't taken my blood-pressure."

"What was it last time?"

"Minimum nine, maximum fourteen on the Pachot apparatus."

"Well, well!" laughed the Little Doctor. "I see you know your medical terms."

"Indeed I do," she retorted. "You can't buy health, and I want to live to be a hundred and two like my grandmother."

"Have you read any medical books?"

"Gracious, yes. I had some sent from Paris only a month ago."

"I suppose your books mention poisons?"

"Of course, and I won't conceal the fact that I've read every word about them. When there have been three cases under your nose, you learn to look out. Especially when you're in a similar position.

"What did they find when Madame Duplantet died?" she went on. "That she had taken out a life insurance in favor of monsieur. And when his wife died? Another insurance. Well, I'm insured, too."

"And the money goes to your niece, I suppose?"

"No. To Monsieur Mordaut. And it's no small matter. A hundred thousand francs!"

"Your master insured your life for a hundred thousand francs! When was this?"

"At least fifteen years ago. A long time before Madame Duplantet's death so I thought nothing of it at the time."

It was before Madame Duplantet's death. This fact was immediately catalogued in a corner of the Little Doctor's mind.

"Has your master always lived in such a secluded way? Hasn't he ever had any love affairs?"

"Never."

"Er—your niece Rose is young and pretty. Do you think—"

She looked him straight in the eye before replying. "Rose would never allow it."

She had been dressed for some time and had again become the stern old cook. She seemed comforted. Her whole expression proclaimed: "Now you know as much as I do. It was my duty to tell you."

It was a strange home. Built to house at least twenty people, with an endless succession of rooms, corridors, and unexpected staircases and corners, it now sheltered only four inhabitants. And these four people, instead of living close together as would have been expected—if only to give themselves the illusion of company—seemed to have used an extraordinary amount of ingenuity in isolating themselves as much as possible. Ernestine's room was on the second floor at the farthest corner of the left wing.

The Little Doctor went in search of Rose.

He had just made a rapid calculation. Rose had been in the house for about a year when Madame Duplantet had died from arsenic—or from a weak heart. Could one conceive of a poisoner sixteen or seventeen years old?

He listened at the door of Rose's room, heard no sound, and softly turned the handle.

"Well, come on in," she said impatiently. "I've work to do."

It was obvious that she had expected him to come. She had prepared his reception. The room had been tidied and some papers had been burned in the fireplace.

"Monsieur Mordaut gave me permission to question everyone in the house. Do you mind?"

"Go ahead. I know already what you're going to ask me. My aunt told you I was Monsieur Mordaut's mistress, didn't she? The poor thing thinks of nothing else; that's because she's never been married or had a sweetheart."

The Little Doctor looked at the ashes in the fireplace and asked more slowly, "Haven't you a lover or a fiancé?"

"Wouldn't that be natural at my age?"

"Can I know his name?"

"If you can find it out . . . Since you are here to look, look. Now, I must go downstairs, because it's my day to polish the brass. Are you staying here?"

"Yes, I'll stay here if you don't object."

She was annoyed, but she went out and he heard her going down the stairs. She probably didn't know that it is possible to read the writing on burned paper. She hadn't bothered to disperse the ashes and there was an envelope which, being of thicker paper, had remained almost intact. At one corner the word "restante" could be made out, which led him to suppose that Rose fetched her mail from the village post office. On the other side the sender had written his address, of which the words "Colonial Infantry Regiment" and, lower down, "Ivory Coast" could be deciphered.

It was almost certain that Rose had a follower, a fiancé or a lover, who was at present stationed with his regiment in the tropics.

"I'm afraid I'm disturbing you once more, Monsieur Mordaut. You told me this morning that you felt pains from time to time. As a doctor I should like to make sure, above all, that there's no question of slow poisoning."

Without protest and with the trace of a bitter smile the master began to undress.

"For a long time," he sighed, "I have been expecting to suffer the same fate as my wife and aunt. When I saw Solange Duplantet die in her turn . . ."

The consultation lasted half an hour, and the Little Doctor became more and more serious.

"I wouldn't like to say anything definite until I had consulted some colleague with more experience. Nevertheless, the discomfort you have been feeling could be caused by arsenical poisoning."

"I told you so." He was neither indignant nor even afraid.

"One more question. Why did you insure Ernestine's life?"

"Did she tell you about it? Well, it's quite simple. One day, an insurance salesman called. He was a clever young man with a persuasive manner. He pointed out that there were several of us in the house and all of us getting on in years."

"I know exactly the arguments he used. Someone was bound to die first. It would be sad, of course, but why shouldn't it at least help you to restore the castle? If all your family died . . . But, excuse, me," the Little Doctor interrupted himself. "Is Hector insured, too?"

"The company won't insure mental deficients. Anyhow, I allowed myself to be persuaded, and I insured Ernestine in spite of her wonderful health."

"Another question. Did you insure yourself?"

This idea seemed to strike him for the first time.

"No," he said in a reflective voice.

Should one treat him as an inhuman monster, or just pity him? Or should one read the greatest cunning into everything he said? Why had he so willingly given the Little Doctor a free hand? Wouldn't a man who was capable of poisoning his wife and two other women also be capable of swallowing poison himself, but in insufficient quantities to do any real harm?

The Little Doctor, overcome by a kind of disgust which his curiosity only just succeeded in dominating, wandered round the château and the grounds. He was standing by the gate, wondering if a stroll to the village wouldn't be a good thing—if only for a change of atmosphere—when sounds of confusion reached him, followed by a loud cry from Ernestine.

He ran round a corner of the château.

Not far from the kitchen was an old barn containing some straw and milking utensils. Inside this building Hector lay dead, his eyes glassy, his whole face contorted. The Little Doctor did not even have to bend down to diagnose.

"A large dose of arsenic."

Near the corpse, stretched out on the straw, lay a bottle with the inscription "Jamaica Rum."

Monsieur Mordaut turned slowly away, a strange light in his eyes. Ernestine was crying, while Rose, standing a little to one side, kept her head lowered.

Half an hour later, while they were waiting for the police who had been summoned by telephone, the Little Doctor, his brow covered in a cold sweat, was wondering whether he would live to see the end of this investigation.

He had just elucidated, in part at least, the story of the bottle of rum.

"Don't you remember the conversation I had with Monsieur Mordaut after lunch?" asked Ernestine. "You were there. He asked me what there was for dinner and I said, 'A vegetable soup and a cauliflower.'"

She was quite right. The Little Doctor remembered vaguely having heard something of the sort.

"Monsieur Mordaut replied that as you were staying here it wasn't enough, and asked me to make a rum omelette."

"When you need rum," asked Dollent, "where do you get it from?"

"The cupboard in the dining room, where all the spirits are kept."

"Have you a key?"

"No, I ask for it when I want it."

"Did you return the key?"

"Yes, to Monsieur Mordaut."

"What did you do with the rum?"

"Put it on the kitchen mantelpiece, while I cleaned the vegetables."

"Did anyone come into the kitchen? Did you see Hector wandering round?"

"No."

"Did you leave the kitchen?"

"Only for a few minutes to feed the dogs."

"Was Hector in the habit of stealing drinks?"

"It has been known to happen. Not only drinks. He was terribly greedy; he stole anything he could lay his hands on and went off, like a puppy, to eat it in a corner."

What would have happened if Hector hadn't found the bottle of arsenic and supposed it to contain rum?

Ernestine would have prepared the omelette. Would anyone have noticed an unusual taste? Wouldn't any bitterness have been put down to the rum? Who would have managed not to eat the omelette—an omelette made in the kitchen, served by Rose, with Monsieur Mordaut, Hector, and the Little Doctor in the dining room?

There was no dinner at the château that evening. The police were in possession, and two of them stationed at the gate had difficulty in restraining the crowd, which was becoming noisy.

In the dilapidated drawing room Monsieur Mordaut, white and haggard, tried to understand the questions which were flung at him by the police. When the door opened after the interview, he was handcuffed. He was led into an adjacent room to remain in custody of two policemen.

How often had Dollent said to himself: "A solid fact, even one, and then, if you're not sidetracked, if you don't lose the thread, you must automatically arrive at the truth."

Solid facts. They were:

1. Monsieur Mordaut had placed no obstacle in the way of the Little Doctor's investigation and had insisted on his staying at the château.

2. Ernestine was strong and healthy. She counted on living to be a hundred and two like her grandmother, and everything she did was with this single aim in view; and she was haunted by the idea of cancer.

3. Ernestine said that her niece was not Monsieur Mordaut's mistress.

4. Rose was healthy, too, and had a lover or fiancé in the Colonial forces.

5. Rose also said that she was not Monsieur Mordaut's mistress.

6. Monsieur Mordaut showed all the symptoms of the beginnings of slow arsenical poisoning.

7. Like the three dead women, Ernestine had a life insurance which would be paid to her master.

"Would you like to know what I really think?" It was Ernestine's turn to be questioned in the ill-lit drawing room.

"Well, my idea is that my master has gone slightly mad—and when he knew that he was being found out, he preferred to finish with it all. But, as he was unbalanced and not like other people, he didn't want any of us to survive him.

"If poor Monsieur Hector hadn't drunk that rum, we should all be dead by now, including the Doctor."

This thought gave Dollent shivers down his spine.

"Monsieur," he murmured to the Police Superintendent, moving towards the door, "I'd like to have a word with you in private."

They spoke in the corridor, which was as gloomy as everywhere else in the house.

"I suppose—I hope that you have the necessary powers," the Little Doctor concluded. "There is still time—if you send an officer by car."

His work was over. The mystery was solved, and as usual it had been in a single flash. Diverse facts, little points of illumination in the fog, and then, suddenly . . .

The only way in which the Superintendent and the Little Doctor had managed to escape public curiosity was to take the banqueting chamber on the first floor of the little inn.

After an omelette, made not with rum but with *fines herbes*, they had ordered stewed rabbit, which they were now eating.

"Until we hear from the solicitor, all that I can tell you, Monsieur, is simply hypothesis.

"Well, I was struck by the fact that a man who took out a life insurance for everyone else didn't take one out for himself. If the man is a murderer, and if his object is to get the money from all those policies, what would he do to conceal his intention? First and foremost, take out a policy for himself, so as to avert suspicion . . . Monsieur Mordaut has no life insurance. For some time also he has been suffering from the effects of slow arsenical poisoning, just like the previous victims. So I ask, who will inherit on his death? Which is why I asked you to send an officer to the solicitor.

"Follow me closely now," said the Little Doctor. "It would seem that the person who inherits from Monsieur Mordaut must almost inevitably be the murderer."

"And the murderer is?"

"A moment. Do you want to know who I think is Monsieur Mordaut's heir? Rose."

"So that—"

"Not so fast. Let me follow my fantasy, if I can use such a word, until your officer returns from the solicitor. I came to the conclusion that at some time, years ago no doubt, Mordaut and Ernestine were lovers. The years went by. He married to restore his fortunes, and Ernestine didn't oppose the match.

"She just killed his wife, slowly, as she had killed the aunt whose death brought in so much money. For she was more than Mordaut's mistress, she was his heir. She knew that one day everything he possessed would come to her.

"I am sure it was she, and not some insurance agent, who was behind that long series of policies. And she had the splendid idea of making him take one out for her, so that she would appear, when the time came, as a potential victim.

"You don't understand all this? It's because you don't live, as I do, in the country, and you are not familiar with long-term schemes. Ernestine intends to live a long time. It hardly matters that she wastes twenty or thirty years with Mordaut. Afterwards she'll be free, and rich. She'll have the house of her dreams and live to be as old as her grandmother.

"That's why she's so frightened of illness. She doesn't want to have worked so hard for nothing. But the fortune she is eventually to inherit must be big enough. Emilie Duplantet, Madame Mordaut, Solange Duplantet. One by one they die, and their fortunes go to Monsieur Mordaut—and finally to Ernestine.

"What's the risk? No one will suspect her because nobody thinks she is the beneficiary of all these deaths. No one knows that she made her lover draw up a will leaving everything to her in default of direct heirs.

"She kills without any danger to herself. If anything happens, he will be the one to go to prison, to be condemned. She only starts worrying the day that she feels that her niece, whom she unwillingly brought into the house, is beginning to exert some influence. For Rose is young and pretty, and Mordaut—"

"It's disgusting," interpolated the Superintendent.

"Alas, it's life. His passion for Ernestine is transferred to her niece. Rose has a lover or a fiancé, but what does it matter to her? Rose has something of her aunt's character. She'll wait a few years. She'll wait for the inheritance her master has promised her. She doesn't have to kill anyone. Did she have any suspicions about these murders? She could ignore them, because, in the end, they fare to her benefit."

"It's been a long business, Messieurs," sighed the police officer who had had no lunch and was now confronted with the remnants of the feast.

"Apart from the son," he continued, "all Monsieur Mordaut's property is left to Mademoiselle Rose Saupiquet."

The Little Doctor's eyes shone.

"Is there no other will?" asked the Superintendent.

"There was another, in which everything was left to Mademoiselle Ernestine Saupiquet, but it was altered nearly eight years ago."

"Did Mademoiselle Ernestine know?"

"No, the change was made in secret."

The Little Doctor laughed. "So now you see it all? Ernestine didn't know about the new will. She was certain, one day, of profiting from her crimes, but she wouldn't kill Mordaut until he had amassed enough money."

"And Rose?"

"Legally she's certainly not an accomplice. But still, I wonder if she hadn't guessed what her aunt was up to."

Another bottle was placed on the table, ostensibly for the police officer. But it was the Little Doctor who helped himself first and who, after a gulp, said:

"Do you know what put me on the right track? It was when Ernestine affirmed her niece's virtue, because to doubt that would be to doubt Mordaut's virtue, and if I became suspicious of this, I might begin to suspect other things.

"In fact, we interrupted her in the middle of her work. She only killed Hector by chance in her attempt to get rid of the poison and to incriminate Mordaut. He had ordered the rum omelette for dinner. What better way to throw suspicion on him than to poison the rum? I'm sure that the rum wouldn't in fact have been poured over the omelette, but how easy to say afterwards that it seemed to have a funny smell—and so lead to the rum-bottle being examined!

"Little more would have remained to be done. And then the pretty home in the country and forty years of life lived according to her dreams."

The Little Doctor replenished his glass once more and concluded:

"There are still people, especially in the country, who make their plans far ahead. Which is why they need so desperately to live to a great age."

The Nine Mile Walk

HARRY KEMELMAN

I had made an ass of myself in a speech I had given at the Good Government Association dinner, and Nicky Welt had cornered me at breakfast at the *Blue Moon*, where we both ate occasionally, for the pleasure of rubbing it in. I had made the mistake of departing from my prepared speech to criticize a statement my predecessor in the office of District Attorney had made to the press. I had drawn a number of inferences from his statement and had thus left myself open to a rebuttal which he had promptly made and which had the effect of making me appear intellectually dishonest. I was new to this political game, having but a few months before left the Law School faculty to become the Reform Party candidate for District Attorney. I said as much in extenuation, but Nicholas Welt, who could never drop his pedagogical manner (he was Snowdon Professor of English Language and Literature), replied in much the same tone that he would dismiss a request from a sophomore for an extension on a term paper, "That's no excuse."

Although he is only two or three years older than I, in his late forties, he always treats me like a schoolmaster hectoring a stupid pupil. And I, perhaps because he looks so much older with his white hair and lined, gnome-like face, suffer it.

"They were perfectly logical inferences," I pleaded.

"My dear boy," he purred, "although human intercourse is well-nigh impossible without inference, most inferences are usually wrong. The percentage of error is particularly high in the legal profession where the intention is not to discover what the speaker wishes to convey, but rather what he wishes to conceal."

I picked up my check and eased out from behind the table.

"I suppose you are referring to cross-examination of witnesses in court. Well, there's always an opposing counsel who will object if the inference is illogical."

"Who said anything about logic?" he retorted. "An inference can be logical and still not be true."

He followed me down the aisle to the cashier's booth. I paid my

456

check and waited impatiently while he searched in an old-fashioned change purse, fishing out coins one by one and placing them on the counter beside his check, only to discover that the total was insufficient. He slid them back into his purse and with a tiny sigh extracted a bill from another compartment of the purse and handed it to the cashier.

"Give me any sentence of ten or twelve words," he said, "and I'll build you a logical chain of inferences that you never dreamed of when you framed the sentence."

Other customers were coming in, and since the space in front of the cashier's booth was small, I decided to wait outside until Nicky completed his transaction with the cashier. I remember being mildly amused at the idea that he probably thought I was still at his elbow and was going right ahead with his discourse.

When he joined me on the sidewalk I said, "A nine mile walk is no joke, especially in the rain."

"No, I shouldn't think it would be," he agreed absently. Then he stopped in his stride and looked at me sharply. "What the devil are you talking about?"

"It's a sentence and it has eleven words," I insisted. And I repeated the sentence, ticking off the words on my fingers.

"What about it?"

"You said that given a sentence of ten or twelve words—"

"Oh, yes." He looked at me suspiciously. "Where did you get it?"

"It just popped into my head. Come on now, build your inferences."

"You're serious about this?" he asked, his little blue eyes glittering with amusement. "You really want me to?"

It was just like him to issue a challenge and then to appear amused when I accepted it. And it made me angry.

"Put up or shut up," I said.

"All right," he said mildly. "No need to be huffy. I'll play. Hm—m, let me see, how did the sentence go? 'A nine mile walk is no joke, especially in the rain.' Not much to go on there."

"It's more than ten words," I rejoined.

"Very well." His voice became crisp as he mentally squared off to the problem. "First inference: the speaker is aggrieved."

"I'll grant that," I said, "although it hardly seems to be an inference. It's really implicit in the statement."

He nodded impatiently. "Next inference: the rain was unforeseen, otherwise he would have said, 'A nine mile walk in the rain is no joke,' instead of using the 'especially' phrase as an afterthought."

"I'll allow that," I said, "although it's pretty obvious."

"First inferences should be obvious," said Nicky tartly.

I let it go at that. He seemed to be floundering and I didn't want to rub it in.

"Next inference: the speaker is not an athlete or an outdoors man."

"You'll have to explain that one," I said.

"It's the 'especially' phrase again," he said. "The speaker does not say that a nine mile walk in the rain is no joke, but merely the walk— just the distance, mind you—is no joke. Now, nine miles is not such a terribly long distance. You walk more than half that in eighteen holes of golf—and golf is an old man's game," he added slyly. *I* play golf.

"Well, that would be all right under ordinary circumstances," I said, "but there are other possibilities. The speaker might be a soldier in the jungle, in which case nine miles would be a pretty good hike, rain or no rain."

"Yes," and Nicky was sarcastic, "and the speaker might be one-legged. For that matter, the speaker might be a graduate student writing a Ph.D. on humor and starting by listing all the things that are not funny. See here, I'll have to make a couple of assumptions before I continue."

"How do you mean?" I asked, suspiciously.

"Remember, I'm taking this sentence *in vacuo*, as it were. I don't know who said it or what the occasion was. Normally a sentence belongs in the framework of a situation."

"I see. What assumptions do you want to make?"

"For one thing, I want to assume that the intention was not frivolous, that the speaker is referring to a walk that was actually taken, and that the purpose of the walk was not to win a bet or something of that sort."

"That seems reasonable enough," I said.

"And I also want to assume that the locale of the walk is here."

"You mean here in Fairfield?"

"Not necessarily. I mean in this general section of the country."

"Fair enough."

"Then, if you grant those assumptions, you'll have to accept my last inference that the speaker is no athlete or outdoors man."

"Well, all right, go on."

"Then my next inference is that the walk was taken very late at night or very early in the morning—say, between midnight and five or six in the morning."

"How do you figure that one?" I asked.

"Consider the distance, nine miles. We're in a fairly well-populated section. Take any road and you'll find a community of some sort in less than nine miles. Hadley is five miles away, Hadley Falls is seven and a half, Goreton is eleven, but East Goreton is only eight and you strike East Goreton before you come to Goreton. There is local train service along the Goreton road and bus service along the others. All the highways are pretty well traveled. Would anyone have to walk nine miles in a rain unless it were late at night when no busses or trains were running and when the few automobiles that were out would hesitate to pick up a stranger on the highway?"

"He might not have wanted to be seen," I suggested.

Nicky smiled pityingly. "You think he would be less noticeable trudging along the highway than he would be riding in a public conveyance where everyone is usually absorbed in his newspaper?"

"Well, I won't press the point," I said brusquely.

"Then try this one: he was walking towards a town rather than away from one."

I nodded. "It is more likely, I suppose. If he were in a town, he could probably arrange for some sort of transportation. Is that the basis for your inference?"

"Partly that," said Nicky, "but there is also an inference to be drawn from the distance. Remember, it's a *nine* mile walk and nine is one of the exact numbers."

"I'm afraid I don't understand."

That exasperated schoolteacher-look appeared on Nicky's face again. "Suppose you say, 'I took a ten mile walk' or 'a hundred mile drive'; I would assume that you actually walked anywhere from eight to a dozen miles, or that you rode between ninety and a hundred and ten miles. In other words, *ten* and *hundred* are round numbers. You might have walked *exactly* ten miles or just as likely you might have walked *approximately* ten miles. But when you speak of walking *nine* miles, I have a right to assume that you have named an exact figure. Now, we are far more likely to know the distance of the city from a given point than we are to know the distance of a given point from the city. That is, ask anyone in the city how far out Farmer Brown lives, and if he knows him, he will say, 'Three or four miles.' But ask Farmer Brown how far he lives from the city and he will tell you. 'Three and six-tenths miles—measured it on my speedometer many a time.'"

"It's weak, Nicky," I said.

"But in conjunction with your own suggestion that he could have arranged transportation if he had been in a city—"

"Yes, that would do it," I said. "I'll pass it. Any more?"

"I've just begun to hit my stride," he boasted. "My next inference is that he was going to a definite destination and that he had to be there at a particular time. It was not a case of going off to get help because his car broke down or his wife was going to have a baby or somebody was trying to break into his house."

"Oh, come now," I said, "the car breaking down is really the most likely situation. He could have known the exact distance from having checked the mileage just as he was leaving the town."

Nicky shook his head. "Rather than walk nine miles in the rain, he would have curled up on the back seat and gone to sleep, or at least stayed by his car and tried to flag another motorist. Remember, it's nine miles. What would be the least it would take him to hike it?"

"Four hours," I offered.

He nodded. "Certainly no less, considering the rain. We've agreed that it happened very late at night or very early in the morning. Suppose he had his breakdown at one o'clock in the morning. It would be five o'clock before he would arrive. That's daybreak. You begin to see a lot of cars on the road. The busses start just a little later. In fact, the first busses hit Fairfield around 5:30. Besides, if he were going for help, he would not have to go all the way to town— only as far as the nearest telephone. No, he had a definite appointment, and it was in a town, and it was for some time before 5:30."

"Then why couldn't he have got there earlier and waited?" I asked. "He could have taken the last bus, arrived around one o'clock, and waited until his appointment. He walks nine miles in the rain instead, and you said he was no athlete."

We had arrived at the Municipal Building where my office is. Normally, any arguments begun at the *Blue Moon*, ended at the entrance to the Municipal Building. But I was interested in Nicky's demonstration and I suggested that he come up for a few minutes.

When we were seated I said, "How about it, Nicky, why couldn't he have arrived early and waited?"

"He could have," Nicky retorted. "But since he did not, we must assume that he was either detained until after the last bus left, or that he had to wait where he was for a signal of some sort, perhaps a telephone call."

"Then according to you, he had an appointment some time between midnight and 5:30—"

"We can draw it much finer than that. Remember, it takes him four hours to walk the distance. The last bus stops at 12:30 A.M. If he doesn't take that, but starts at the same time, he won't arrive at his destination until 4:30. On the other hand, if he takes the first bus in the morning, he will arrive around 5:30. That would mean that his appointment was for some time between 4:30 and 5:30."

"You mean that if his appointment were earlier than 4:30, he would have taken the last night bus, and if it were later than 5:30, he would have taken the first morning bus?"

"Precisely. And another thing: if he were waiting for a signal or a phone call, it must have come not much later than one o'clock."

"Yes, I see that," I said. "If his appointment is around five o'clock and it takes him four hours to walk the distance, he'd have to start around one."

He nodded, silent and thoughtful. For some queer reason I could not explain, I did not feel like interrupting his thoughts. On the wall was a large map of the county and I walked over to it and began to study it.

"You're right, Nicky," I remarked over my shoulder, "there's no place as far as nine miles from Fairfield that doesn't hit another town first. Fairfield is right in the middle of a bunch of smaller towns."

He joined me at the map. "It doesn't have to be Fairfield, you know," he said quietly. "It was probably one of the outlying towns he had to reach. Try Hadley."

"Why Hadley? What would anyone want in Hadley at five o'clock in the morning?"

"The Washington Flyer stops there to take on water about that time," he said quietly.

"That's right, too," I said. "I've heard that train many a night when I couldn't sleep. I'd hear it pulling in and then a minute or two later I'd hear the clock on the Methodist Church banging out five." I went back to my desk for a timetable. "The Flyer leaves Washington at 12:47 A.M. and gets into Boston at 8:00 A.M."

Nicky was still at the map measuring distances with a pencil.

"Exactly nine miles from Hadley is the Old Sumter Inn," he announced.

"Old Sumter Inn," I echoed. "But that upsets the whole theory. You can arrange for transportation there as easily as you can in a town."

He shook his head. "The cars are kept in an enclosure and you have to get an attendant to check you through the gate. The attendant would remember anyone taking out his car at a strange hour. It's a pretty conservative place. He could have waited in his room until he got a call from Washington about someone on the Flyer— maybe the number of the car and the berth. Then he could just slip out of the hotel and walk to Hadley."

I stared at him, hypnotized.

"It wouldn't be difficult to slip aboard while the train was taking on water, and then if he knew the car number and the berth—"

"Nicky," I said portentously, "as the reform District Attorney who campaigned on an economy program, I am going to waste the taxpayers' money and call Boston long distance. It's ridiculous, it's insane—but I'm going to do it!"

His little blue eyes glittered and he moistened his lips with the tip of his tongue.

"Go ahead," he said hoarsely.

I replaced the telephone in its cradle.

"Nicky," I said, "this is probably the most remarkable coincidence in the history of criminal investigation: *a man was found murdered in his berth on last night's 12:47 from Washington!* He'd been dead about three hours, which would make it exactly right for Hadley."

"I thought it was something like that," said Nicky. "But you're wrong about its being a coincidence. It can't be. Where did you get that sentence?"

"It was just a sentence. It simply popped into my head."

"It couldn't have! It's not the sort of sentence that pops into one's head. If you had taught composition as long as I have, you'd know that when you ask someone for a sentence of ten words or so, you get an ordinary statement such as 'I like milk'—with the other words made up by a modifying clause like, 'because it is good for my health.' The sentence you offered related to a *particular situation.*"

"But I tell you I talked to no one this morning. And I was alone with you at the *Blue Moon.*"

"You weren't with me all the time I paid my check," he said sharply. "Did you meet anyone while you were waiting on the sidewalk for me to come out of the *Blue Moon*?"

I shook my head. "I was outside for less than a minute before you joined me. You see, a couple of men came in while you were digging out your change and one of them bumped me, as I thought I'd wait—"

"Did you ever see them before?"

"Who?"

"The two men who came in," he said, the note of exasperation creeping into his voice again.

"Why, no—they weren't anyone I knew."

"Were they talking?"

"I guess so. Yes, they were. Quite absorbed in their conversation, as a matter of fact—otherwise, they would have noticed me and I would not have been bumped."

"Not many strangers come into the *Blue Moon*," he remarked.

"Do you think it was they?" I asked eagerly. "I think I'd know them again if I saw them."

Nicky's eyes narrowed. "It's possible. There had to be two—one to trail the victim in Washington and ascertain his berth number, the other to wait here and do the job. The Washington man would be likely to come down here afterwards. If there were theft as well as murder, it would be to divide the spoils. It it was just murder, he would probably have to come down to pay off his confederate."

I reached for the telephone.

"We've been gone less than half an hour," Nicky went on. "They were just coming in and service is slow at the *Blue Moon*. The one who walked all the way to Hadley must certainly be hungry and the other probably drove all night from Washington."

"Call me immediately if you make an arrest," I said into the phone and hung up.

Neither of us spoke a word while we waited. We paced the floor, avoiding each other almost as though we had done something we were ashamed of.

The telephone rang at last. I picked it up and listened. Then I said, "O. K." and turned to Nicky.

"One of them tried to escape through the kitchen but Winn had someone stationed at the back and they got him."

"That would seem to prove it," said Nicky with a frosty little smile.

I nodded agreement.

He glanced at his watch. "Gracious," he exclaimed, "I wanted to make an early start on my work this morning, and here I've already wasted all this time talking with you."

I let him get to the door. "Oh, Nicky," I called, "what was it you set out to prove?"

"That a chain of inferences could be logical and still not be true," he said.

"Oh."

"What are you laughing at?" he asked snappishly. And then he laughed too.

Crime in Rhyme

ROBERT BLOCH

Miss Kent approached the cottage door and rapped sharply. It was really a darling place, she decided; for some reason it reminded her of the home of the White Rabbit in *Alice in Wonderland*.

When the door opened to reveal the occupant of the cottage, Miss Kent could not restrain a gasp. Aside from the length of his ears, the man standing before her might have passed for the White Rabbit himself. He was small, pale, pink-eyed, and his face ran largely to nose; his mouth was wobbly and his chin almost negligible. Also he was wearing a checkered weskit, and even as Miss Kent gazed at him he consulted his watch.

"I'm looking for Rickie Lane," she announced.

The man blinked at her and smiled. "Won't you come in, please?"

Miss Kent entered and found herself in a paneled hallway with mid-Victorian furnishings which heightened the resemblance to the world of Lewis Carroll and Tenniel illustrations.

"I am Archibald Pope," the little man said. "You must be Miss Kent, the lady who wrote about the secretarial position."

"That is correct," she admitted. "Is Mr. Lane at home?"

The little man nodded. "If you'll be good enough to step in here—"

He waved her through a doorway and into a large parlor equipped as an office. Filing cabinets lined the walls, and the center of the room was dominated by a large desk on which stood an electric typewriter and a fluorescent lamp.

Little Mr. Pope walked over to the desk and sank into the chair behind it.

"Now, then," he said. "If I might have a look at your references, please?"

Miss Kent hesitated. "But I understand it was Mr. Lane who needed a secretary."

"So he does." The small man inclined his head. "I am Rickie Lane."

"But—"

Mr. Pope sighed. "You are disappointed because I choose to work

465

under a pseudonym?" he asked. "Considering the somewhat—er—violent nature of my writings, it seems advisable."

Miss Kent flushed slightly. "It's not that," she confessed. "I hope you don't think me rude, Mr. Pope, but you just don't *look* like a writer."

Mr. Pope uttered a delighted chuckle and leaned back, running his hands through his white hair.

"Exactly, my dear lady!" he crowed. "I *don't* look like a writer, do I? Thanks to the photographs on the back of dust jackets, we all know what a writer looks like today. He is a scowling young Neanderthal with an unshaven chin that bristles nearly as much as his crew-cut. He wears a white T-shirt, and possibly a dog tag nestles against his hairy chest. That's your modern writer, eh?"

Miss Kent nodded. "If I remember correctly," she murmured, "there is just such a photograph on the back of all the Rickie Lane books."

"Indeed there is," Mr. Pope agreed. "Posed by a professional model—or, to be specific, a Greek gentleman my agent found washing dishes in a restaurant in Soho. Although completely illiterate, it happens that he resembles a writer. In some cases, his illiteracy would increase the resemblance. At any rate, I agreed to the deception in the interests of commerce."

"I understand," said Miss Kent.

"Perhaps you're disappointed?" Mr. Pope asked, softly. "I have had that trouble with secretaries before. They come to me with visions of working with a burly young brute, a hulking he-man who responds to the sight of a blonde the way Pavlov's dogs responded to the dinner bell. If you had any idea along these lines, then perhaps you won't care to continue this interview."

Miss Kent shook her head. "On the contrary," she told him, "I'm greatly relieved." Fumbling in her purse, she drew out a sheaf of letters. "My references," she said.

"Thank you." Mr. Pope barely glanced at them before placing the correspondence on his desk. "I presume you are experienced in typing, filing, taking dictation and all the requirements my *Times* advertisement specified. But that's secondary. What I am interested in is this—if you didn't seek me out with the notion of taking a position under a virile creative man, then just what reason did you have for applying?"

"Because I am a Rickie Lane fan," Miss Kent told him, earnestly. "I've read all your books."

"Have you, indeed?" Mr. Pope glanced over at the bookshelf and smiled. "Read them all, eh? Then perhaps you'll be good enough to favor me with your opinion. What did you think of the first one?"

"*Mr. Munn Takes a Gun?*" said Miss Kent. "It hit the target, with me."

Mr. Pope smiled. "How about *Mr. Fyfe Takes a Knife?*"

"Ripping."

"And *Mr. Frazer Takes a Razor?*"

"Keen."

"Then there's *Mr. Flubb Takes a Club.*"

"Smashing."

"And my latest, have you read that—*Mr. Saxe Takes an Axe?*"

"Sharp and cutting. Penetrates deeply into your characters. Opens them up and lets the reader see what's inside."

Mr. Pope sat back and beamed.

"I am delighted to see that you are so perceptive a critic," he told her. "You may consider yourself hired as of now, if you wish. What do you say to room and board and twenty pounds a week?"

"Why, that would be wonderful, Mr. Pope." Miss Kent hesitated slightly. "But I'd intended taking a room in the village—"

"Nonsense, my dear girl! You'll stay here, of course. Plenty of room, and I can assure you I'm an excellent cook. I fancy a diet of cold mutton is not altogether to your taste, and the village inn offers little else."

"Yes, but—"

Mr. Pope glanced down at himself and smiled wryly. "I assure you there's nothing to fear from me," he said. "And if it's the neighbors you're worried about, we have none for a half mile around. I gather from your references that you are alone in the world—hence, I see no possibility of any scandal. And since I often find it necessary to work at night, your presence here will offer added convenience to us both."

Miss Kent fluffed her blonde curls nervously. "Very well," she answered. "I accept your offer. When do we begin?"

"Immediately," said Mr. Pope, rubbing his hands together briskly. "My next manuscript is due at the publisher's in a fortnight."

"How thrilling!"

Mr. Pope sighed. "I can hardly agree, inasmuch as I have yet to write a single line."

"What seems to be the problem? Can't you think of a plot?"

The little man shook his head. "I see you don't understand," he said. "To me a plot is relatively unimportant. You've read my work, and the stuff other writers turn out. What does the plot consist of? Rickie Lane is a private eye who writes in the first person singular—although not quite as singular as some others I could mention. He stumbles on the corpse of a beautiful woman, and since he is not a necrophile there is only one thing to do. He must solve the crime. During the course of the story he beats up various thugs and is in turn beaten up; he is approached by various voluptuous and full-breasted females and he approaches them in turn. Eventually he discovers that the most voluptuous female of all is the killer, and he shoots her in the end, or the naval, or the ensuing *mêlée*. The plot, you see, is secondary to the real problem."

"But I should think the real problem is finding the murderer."

"For the reader, yes. But not for the author. His problem, in writing the story, is to find the crime."

"I never thought of it that way before." Miss Kent nodded. "But it makes sense, doesn't it?"

"Of course it does. That's where I got the whole idea for my series. One day a phrase just happened to pop into my head—a common phrase which often passes unnoticed. *Poetic justice*. It was then that I began to think of crime in rhyme. My titles came about inevitably. But in each case the murder itself was the most important element."

"You had to plot perfect crimes?"

Mr. Pope shook his head. "*Im*perfect crimes," he said.

"I'm afraid I don't understand."

"There's no trick to plotting a perfect crime," he explained. "Scotland Yard tells us a murder is committed in real life once every twelve minutes. Further statistics reveal that a good half of these murders remain unsolved. *Ergo*, one unsolved murder every twenty-four minutes; sixty perfect crimes committed each and every day, or close to twenty-two thousand a year."

"You're quite an expert," Miss Kent beamed.

"I should be. After all, it's my business. And as an expert I assure you that the perfect crime is the least of my problems. It's trying to invent a crime that *looks* perfect but contains a basic flaw or error in commission—a flaw that Rickie Lane can discover and which leads to his solution of the killing."

"Now I'm beginning to see what you mean," Miss Kent said. "And that's what you're looking for now?"

"Desperately," Mr. Pope admitted.

"I'm afraid such matters are a little out of my ken," the girl told him. "But perhaps if we were to talk about it—"

Mr. Pope rose. "Later," he said. "But I see I have been a poor host. Let me get your valise from the hall and show you to your room. Undoubtedly you would like to freshen up a bit after your trip. That train from London is abominable."

He led her upstairs and into a quite comfortable apartment. "The bath is at the end of the hall," he informed her, "just past my room and the storeroom. I'll leave you to your own devices for a time while I take a turn about the garden. The sunset may provide inspiration."

He bowed and withdrew.

Miss Kent didn't bother to unpack. She waited until Mr. Pope had left the cottage and then sought out his room. For a time she was quite busy there, pausing in her efforts only to cock an ear for the sound of footsteps. Hearing nothing, she continued her activities, then transferred her attention to the storeroom.

It was necessary for her to force the lock, but this she did both expertly and effortlessly. Once inside, Miss Kent found herself amply repaid for her trouble—so much so, indeed, that she soon became completely engrossed. In fact, she forgot to listen—until it was too late.

She knew it was too late when she looked up and saw Mr. Pope standing in the doorway.

"Well, well," he observed mildly. "What have we here?"

Miss Kent faced him serenely. "What haven't we here?" she asked. She pointed to an array of objects unearthed from a small trunk in the corner. "A .38 Webley automatic—the same weapon you described in *Mr. Munn Takes a Gun*. A pearl-handled dagger with more than a suspicion of rust on the tip—just like the one mentioned in *Mr. Fyfe Takes a Knife*. And this straight-razor could not have got all these stains even if it had been legitimately used by a sufferer from chronic hemophilia. It reminds me of the murder weapon in *Mr. Frazer Takes a Razor*. Certainly there's no doubt about the blood on the end of this club—it is exactly as depicted in *Mr. Flubb Takes a Club*. As for the axe, it might be the former property of Miss Lizzie Borden, but I rather think it is the original specimen described in *Mr. Saxe Takes an Axe*."

Mr. Pope pursed his lips speculatively. "Quite right on all counts," he said. "I see there is little sense in any further attempts to conceal my methods. Like all true literary artists, I rely heavily on personal experience in my work. The autobiographical approach, you might say. I find it best to derive the bulk of my writing from life."

"From death, you mean."

"As you will, dear lady." Mr. Pope shrugged. "Let us not quibble over details."

"Details? You've virtually admitted to committing five murders."

"Over a five-year period," Mr. Pope said, gently. "Allow me to refresh your memory as to the statistics. My contribution to them is slight—merely one out of nearly twenty-two thousand per annum. And in return, my contribution to the world of crime literature is great."

He took a step forward and his voice grew stronger. "The killer instinct is basic in us all," he told her. "Even a young lady like yourself gets a vicarious thrill from reading a gory mystery, and so do beardless youths and gentle clergymen and elderly dowagers. Yours is a harmless sublimation, but the urge is there—an urge strong enough to set you reading. But consider, if you will, how much stronger the urge must be to set a man *writing* this sort of thing."

"That's no justification," Miss Kent protested.

"I do not need justification," Mr. Pope replied. "My work speaks for itself. During the past half dozen years I have moved about the country under various names and disguises, and as a result of my endeavors five women have met an untimely end. But think, for a moment, of all the lives I must have saved! Think of the girls like yourself who found harmless outlets for your own homicidal tendencies in my books; think of the young men who used me as a surrogate for their own violent impulses, and the oldsters who refrained from killing their spouses and sought satisfaction through my work. Why, I must have averted hundreds of tragedies! That's the practical way to look at it. And from the purely critical standpoint you admitted that my work was—what did you say?—ripping, keen, smashing, eh?"

"Bloody awful," Miss Kent snapped, "if you must know the truth."

"Now, now," Mr. Pope chided. "Temper, deal child! Let us have none of that. You remind me of someone I once knew in Herts. When she—"

"The widow," Miss Kent interrupted. "The one they thought shot herself while looking through her husband's gun collection. You used that situation in your first book."

"So I did."

"And there was the girl in Rainham, and the woman in Manchester, and the chorus girl in Brighton—"

"Say no more," Mr. Pope murmured. "You have told me enough. Enough to realize that it was not idle curiosity which caused you to enter my storeroom, nor accident which brought you here. You, my dear lady, are nothing but a copper's nark."

Miss Kent drew herself up proudly. "I am nothing of the sort," she snapped. "I happen to be an employee of Scotland Yard."

"Then I take it I have been under suspicion for a considerable period?"

"That is correct, Mr. Pope, or whatever your name is. The variety of names and disguises you assumed threw us off for a time. Then somebody noted that within a year after the commission of each crime a new Rickie Lane mystery appeared. Similarity of weapons gave us the clue. We've had difficulty tracking you down, because your publishers work only through your agent, and he seems singularly elusive."

"I have no agent," said Mr. Pope. "He is as fictitious as the rest of my disguises." He paused. "Where are you going?"

Miss Kent edged towards the door: "I intend to ring up the Yard," she replied firmly.

"Can I not persuade you to change your mind? After all, think of the hundreds of slayings I've prevented—"

"I am thinking of the five you committed," she told him. "I warn you," she went on, as Mr. Pope inched forward, "you'd better not try to stop me. My superiors know I'm here."

"But nobody knows *I'm* here," he reminded her. "They'll come looking for a Mr. Pope. Needless to say, I shall be long gone."

"You can't get away with it. You ran that advertisement for a secretary—"

"As bait, to draw Scotland Yard out, in the event that they suspected. It means nothing." He strode quickly to the door and slammed it shut. "Now, then," he said.

"I shall scream!"

"But not for long." Mr. Pope stepped forward. There was a moment of brisk struggle, but the little man proved surprisingly strong. Within a few minutes Miss Kent lay on the floor, arms tied behind her and the useless screams dying in her throat.

"Hot work," Mr. Pope observed. "I had better get rid of this muck before I continue." Thoughtfully he removed the white wig, disclosing his head with its close crew-cut. Off came the spectacles, the putty nose, the built-up mouth, and the protruding teeth. In another moment he peeled off his weskit, sighing gratefully as he emerged from the garments to stand before her in a T-shirt. "That's better, eh?" he said. He flexed his muscles tentatively.

Miss Kent shuddered. "Why, you look just like the pictures on the dust jackets!" she exclaimed.

"True." He smiled down at her. "The Greek dishwasher in Soho is another invention of mine. I find the role excellent protective coloration. That is why, even if your police come seeking Rickie Lane, they shall never find him. They don't know what he really looks like, or what he really is. They don't know about any of us."

"*Any* of you?"

The smile became a wolfish grin. "Yes. I told you the secret, but you didn't realize it. About those of us who write murder stories, and who gain fame and fortune because our stories are so convincing. Naturally, we all write from life. And—oddly enough—most of us look alike too. Lombroso's old theory about criminal types, you know."

"But that's impossible! I've seen photographs of—"

"Yes. Of course you have. Do you think I'm the only one who's clever enough to use a make-up kit? Or to change my name? Most of the others use pseudonyms, too." His voice sank to a whisper. "Think for a moment. Who *is* Ellery Queen, really? Or Carter Dickson, or H. H. Holmes, or—"

"You can't mean it, not *all* of them!"

"Merely a theory, my dear. I speak only for myself when I tell you that your real detective-story writer conceals his identity and the crimes on which he bases his fictional narratives. I told you before that my chief problem is to concoct an imperfect crime—fundamentally, I am so constituted that I can ordinarily think only in terms of perfection. For I am a detective-story writer, and that means I am a master criminal."

Miss Kent writhed and tugged at her wrists.

"This time you won't succeed," she threatened. "They'll find you."

"Find who?" Mr. Pope shrugged. "My present disguise is abandoned. They'll never recognize me in my new one. And if they seek out Rickie Lane, their trail will end at that restaurant in Soho.

Besides, they'll have quite a time discovering that you were the victim of foul play, not a suicide."

"Suicide?" Miss Kent gasped.

"Precisely. There will be an explanatory note downstairs—everything is arranged. I perfected my plans during a walk in the garden just now, after I remembered that I had this."

He stopped and groped for a moment in the corner of the room, coming up with a length of hempen coil in his hands.

"I shall just throw one end over the beam here," he said.

"Wait!" Miss Kent begged.

He nodded regretfully, then shook his head. "I know how you feel, dear lady," he told her. "But there really isn't any time to spare. I told you my next manuscript is due at the publisher's within a fortnight. *Ars longa vita brevis*, you know."

Bending forward, he made a knot and fastened the loop about her throat . . .

The manuscript of *Mr. Pope Takes a Rope* reached the publishers precisely on the day of the deadline. When it appeared in print the critics were enthusiastic and the public ecstatic.

If Scotland Yard failed to share in the general enthusiasm it was merely because its operatives were trying in vain to unravel a knotty problem involving a noose, an apparent suicide, an abandoned cottage, and an untraceable gentleman who looked like a White Rabbit.

Meanwhile, bloodthirsty readers of Rickie Lane mysteries await the next volume in the series. As usual, there is no hint as to what may be forthcoming.

But just recently, in Cornwall, a debonair, mustachioed gentleman took up lodgings in the boarding house of an attractive divorcee.

The other morning he had occasion to step into the shop of the neighborhood ironmonger.

"My name is Mr. Stammer," he announced, "and I should like to purchase some household tools—"

The Purloined Letter

EDGAR ALLAN POE

Nil sapientiæ odiosius acumine nimio.—*Seneca*

At Paris, just after dark one gusty evening in the autumn of 18—, I was enjoying the twofold luxury of meditation and a meerschaum, in company with my friend, C. Auguste Dupin, in his little back library, or book-closet, *au troisième*, No. 33 *Rue Dunôt, Faubourg St. Germain*. For one hour at least we had maintained a profound silence; while each, to any casual observer, might have seemed intently and exclusively occupied with the curling eddies of smoke that oppressed the atmosphere of the chamber. For myself, however, I was mentally discussing certain topics which had formed matter for conversation between us at an earlier period of the evening; I mean the affair of the Rue Morgue, and the mystery attending the murder of Marie Rogêt. I looked upon it, therefore, as something of a coincidence, when the door of our apartment was thrown open and admitted our old acquaintance, Monsieur G—, the Prefect of the Parisian police.

We gave him a hearty welcome; for there was nearly half as much of the entertaining as of the contemptible about the man, and we had not seen him for several years. We had been sitting in the dark, and Dupin now arose for the purpose of lighting a lamp, but sat down again, without doing so, upon G.'s saying that he had called to consult us, or rather to ask the opinion of my friend, about some official business which had occasioned a great deal of trouble.

"If it is any point requiring reflection," observed Dupin, as he forbore to enkindle the wick, "we shall examine it to better purpose in the dark."

"That is another of your odd notions," said the Prefect, who had the fashion of calling everything "odd" that was beyond his comprehension, and thus lived amid an absolute legion of "oddities."

"Very true," said Dupin, as he supplied his visitor with a pipe, and rolled toward him a comfortable chair.

"And what is the difficulty now?" I asked. "Nothing more in the assassination way I hope?"

"Oh, no; nothing of that nature. The fact is, the business is *very*

simple indeed, and I make no doubt that we can manage it suffi-
ciently well ourselves; but then I thought Dupin would like to hear
the details of it, because it is so excessively *odd*."

"Simple and odd," said Dupin.

"Why, yes; and not exactly that either. The fact is, we have all been
a good deal puzzled because the affair *is* so simple, and yet baffles us
altogether."

"Perhaps it is the very simplicity of the thing which puts you at
fault," said my friend.

"What nonsense you *do* talk!" replied the Prefect, laughing heartily.

"Perhaps the mystery is a little *too* plain," said Dupin.

"Oh, good heavens! who ever heard of such an idea?"

"A little *too* self-evident."

"Ha! ha! ha!—ha! ha! ha!—ho! ho! ho!" roared our visitor, profoundly amused, "oh, Dupin, you will be the death of me yet!"

"And what, after all, *is* the matter on hand?" I asked.

"Why, I will tell you," replied the Prefect, as he gave a long, steady,
and contemplative puff, and settled himself in his chair. "I will tell you in
a few words; but, before I begin, let me caution you that this is an affair
demanding the greatest secrecy, and that I should most probably lose
the position I now hold, were it known that I confided it to any one."

"Proceed," said I.

"Or not," said Dupin.

"Well, then; I have received personal information, from a very high
quarter, that a certain document of the last importance has been
purloined from the royal apartments. The individual who purloined
it is known; this beyond a doubt; he was seen to take it. It is known,
also, that it still remains in his possession."

"How is this known?" asked Dupin.

"It is clearly inferred," replied the Prefect, "from the nature of the
document, and from the non-appearance of certain results which
would at once arise from its passing *out* of the robber's possession—
that is to say, from his employing it as he must design in the end to
employ it."

"Be a little more explicit," I said.

"Well, I may venture so far as to say that the paper gives its holder
a certain power in a certain quarter where such power is immensely
valuable." The Prefect was fond of the cant of diplomacy.

"Still I do not quite understand," said Dupin.

"No? Well; the disclosure of the document to a third person, who shall be nameless, would bring in question the honor of a personage of most exalted station; and this fact gives the holder of the document an ascendancy over the illustrious personage whose honor and peace are so jeopardized."

"But this ascendancy," I interposed, "would depend upon the robber's knowledge of the loser's knowledge of the robber. Who would dare—"

"The thief," said G., "is the Minister D—, who dares all things, those unbecoming as well as those becoming a man. The method of the theft was not less ingenious than bold. The document in question—a letter, to be frank—had been received by the personage robbed while alone in the royal *boudoir*. During its perusal she was suddenly interrupted by the entrance of the other exalted personage from whom especially it was her wish to conceal it. After a hurried and vain endeavor to thrust it in a drawer, she was forced to place it, open as it was, upon a table. The address, however, was uppermost, and, the contents thus unexposed, the letter escaped notice. At this juncture enters the Minister D—. His lynx eye immediately perceives the paper, recognizes the handwriting of the address, observes the confusion of the personage addressed, and fathoms her secret. After some business transactions, hurried through in his ordinary manner, he produces a letter somewhat similar to the one in question, opens it, pretends to read it, and then places it in close juxtaposition to the other. Again he converses, for some fifteen minutes, upon the public affairs. At length, in taking leave, he takes also from the table the letter to which he had no claim. Its rightful owner saw, but, of course, dared not call attention to the act, in the presence of the third personage who stood at her elbow. The minister decamped; leaving his own letter—one of no importance—upon the table."

"Here, then," said Dupin to me, "you have precisely what you demand to make the ascendancy complete—the robber's knowledge of the loser's knowledge of the robber."

"Yes," replied the Prefect; "and the power thus attained has, for some months past, been wielded, for political purposes, to a very dangerous extent. The personage robbed is more thoroughly convinced, every day, of the necessity of reclaiming her letter. But this, of course, cannot be done openly. In fine, driven to despair, she has committed the matter to me."

"Than whom," said Dupin, amid a perfect whirlwind of smoke, "no more sagacious agent could, I suppose, be desired, or even imagined."

"You flatter me," replied the Prefect; "but it is possible that some such opinion may have been entertained."

"It is clear," said I, "as you observe, that the letter is still in the possession of the minister; since it is this possession, and not any employment of the letter, which bestows the power. With the employment the power departs."

"True," said G.; "and upon this conviction I proceeded. My first care was to make thorough search of the minister's hotel; and here my chief embarrassment lay in the necessity of searching without his knowledge. Beyond all things, I have been warned of the danger which would result from giving him reason to suspect our design."

"But," said I, "you are quite *au fait* in these investigations. The Parisian police have done this thing often before."

"Oh, yes; and for this reason I did not despair. The habits of the minister gave me, too, a great advantage. He is frequently absent from home all night. His servants are by no means numerous. They sleep at a distance from their master's apartment, and, being chiefly Neapolitans, are readily made drunk. I have keys, as you know, with which I can open any chamber or cabinet in Paris. For three months a night has not passed, during the greater part of which I have not been engaged, personally, in ransacking the D—Hotel. My honor is interested, and, to mention a great secret, the reward is enormous. So I did not abandon the search until I had become fully satisfied that the thief is a more astute man than myself. I fancy that I have investigated every nook and corner of the premises in which it is possible that the paper can be concealed."

"But is it not possible," I suggested, "that although the letter may be in possession of the minister, as it unquestionably is, he may have concealed it elsewhere than upon his own premises?"

"This is barely possible," said Dupin. "The present peculiar condition of affairs at court, and especially of those intrigues in which D— is known to be involved, would render the instant availability of the document—its susceptibility of being produced at a moment's notice—a point of nearly equal importance with its possession."

"Its susceptibility of being produced?" said I.

"'That is to say, of being *destroyed*," said Dupin.

"True," I observed; "the paper is clearly then upon the premises. As for its being upon the person of the minister, we may consider that as out of the question."

"Entirely," said the Prefect. "He has been twice waylaid, as if by footpads, and his person rigidly searched under my own inspection."

"You might have spared yourself this trouble," said Dupin. "D—, I presume, is not altogether a fool, and, if not, must have anticipated these waylayings, as a matter of course,"

"Not *altogether* a fool," said G., "but then he is a poet, which I take to be only one remove from a fool."

"True," said Dupin, after a long and thoughtful whiff from his meerschaum, "although I have been guilty of certain doggerel myself."

"Suppose you detail," said I, "the particulars of your search."

"Why, the fact is, we took our time, and we searched *everywhere*. I have had long experience in these affairs. I took the entire building, room by room; devoting the nights of a whole week to each. We examined, first, the furniture of each apartment. We opened every possible drawer; and I presume you know that, to a properly trained police-agent, such a thing as a '*secret*' drawer is impossible. Any man is a dolt who permits a '*secret*' drawer to escape him in a search of this kind. The thing is *so* plain. There is a certain amount of bulk—of space—to be accounted for in every cabinet. Then we have accurate rules. The fiftieth part of a line could not escape us. After the cabinets we took the chairs. The cushions we probed with the fine long needles you have seen me employ. From the tables we removed the tops."

"Why so?"

"Sometimes the top of a table, or other similarly arranged piece of furniture, is removed by the person wishing to conceal an article; then the leg is excavated, the article deposited within the cavity, and the top replaced. The bottoms and tops of bedposts are employed in the same way."

"But could not the cavity be detected by sounding?" I asked.

"By no means, if, when the article is deposited, a sufficient wadding of cotton be placed around it. Besides, in our case, we were obliged to proceed without noise."

"But you could not have removed—you could not have taken to pieces *all* articles of furniture in which it would have been possible to make a deposit in the manner you mention. A letter may be compressed into a thin spiral roll, not differing much in shape or bulk from a large knitting-needle, and in this form it might be inserted into the rung of a chair, for example. You did not take to pieces all the chairs?"

"Certainly not; but we did better—we examined the rungs of every chair in the hotel, and, indeed, the jointings of every description of furniture, by the aid of a most powerful microscope. Had there been any traces of recent disturbance we should not have failed to detect it instantly. A single grain of gimlet-dust, for example, would have been as obvious as an apple. Any disorder in the gluing—any unusual gaping in the joints—would have sufficed to insure detection."

"I presume you looked to the mirrors, between the boards and the plates, and you probed the beds and the bedclothes, as well as the curtains and carpets."

"That of course; and when we had absolutely completed every particle of the furniture in this way, then we examined the house itself. We divided its entire surface into compartments, which we numbered, so that none might be missed; then we scrutinized each individual square inch throughout the premises, including the two houses immediately adjoining, with the microscope, as before."

"The two houses adjoining!" I exclaimed; "you must have had a great deal of trouble."

"We had; but the reward offered is prodigious."

"You include the *grounds* about the houses?"

"All the grounds are paved with brick. They gave us comparatively little trouble. We examined the moss between the bricks, and found it undisturbed."

"You looked among D——'s papers, of course, and into the books of the library?"

"Certainly; we opened every package and parcel; we not only opened every book, but we turned over every leaf in each volume, not contenting ourselves with a mere shake, according to the fashion of some of our police officers. We also measured the thickness of every book-*cover*, with the most accurate admeasurement, and applied to each the most jealous scrutiny of the microscope. Had any of the bindings been recently meddled with, it would have been utterly impossible that the fact should have escaped observation. Some five or six volumes, just from the hands of the binder, we carefully probed, longitudinally, with the needles."

"You explored the floors beneath the carpets?"

"Beyond doubt. We removed every carpet, and examined the boards with the microscope."

"And the paper on the walls?"

"Yes."

"You looked into the cellars?"

"We did."

"Then," I said, "you have been making a miscalculation, and the letter is *not* upon the premises, as you suppose."

"I fear you are right there," said the Prefect. "And now, Dupin, what would you advise me to do?"

"To make a thorough research of the premises."

"That is absolutely needless," replied G—. "I am not more sure that I breathe than I am that the letter is not at the hotel."

"I have no better advice to give you," said Dupin. "You have, of course, an accurate description of the letter?"

"Oh, yes!"—And here the Prefect, producing a memorandum-book, proceeded to read aloud a minute account of the internal, and especially of the external, appearance of the missing document. Soon after finishing the perusal of this description, he took his departure, more entirely depressed in spirits than I had ever known the good gentleman before.

In about a month afterward he paid us another visit, and found us occupied very nearly as before. He took a pipe and a chair and entered into some ordinary conversation. At length I said:

"Well, but G., what of the purloined letter? I presume you have at last made up your mind that there is no such thing as overreaching the Minister?"

"Confound him, say I—yes; I made the re-examination, however, as Dupin suggested—but it was all labor lost, as I knew it would be."

"How much was the reward offered, did you say?" asked Dupin.

"Why, a very great deal—a *very* liberal reward—I don't like to say how much, precisely; but one thing I *will* say, that I wouldn't mind giving my individual check for fifty thousand francs to any one who could obtain me that letter. The fact is, it is becoming of more and more importance every day; and the reward has been lately doubled. If it were trebled, however, I could do no more than I have done."

"Why, yes," said Dupin, drawlingly, between the whiffs of his meerschaum, "I really—think, G., you have not exerted yourself—to the utmost in this matter. You might—do a little more, I think, eh?"

"How?—in what way?"

"Why—puff, puff—you might—puff, puff—employ counsel in the matter, eh?—puff, puff, puff. Do you remember the story they tell of Abernethy?"

"No; hang Abernethy!"

"To be sure! hang him and welcome. But, once upon a time, a certain rich miser conceived the design of spunging upon this Abernethy for a medical opinion. Getting up, for this purpose, an ordinary conversation in a private company, he insinuated his case to the physician, as that of an imaginary individual."

"'We will suppose,' said the miser, 'that his symptoms are such and such; now, doctor, what would *you* have directed him to take?'

"'Take!' said Abernethy, 'why, take *advice*, to be sure.'"

"But," said the Prefect, a little discomposed, "*I* am *perfectly* willing to take advice, and to pay for it. I would *really* give fifty thousand francs to any one who would aid me in the matter."

"In that case," replied Dupin, opening a drawer, and producing a check-book, "you may as well fill me up a check for the amount mentioned. When you have signed it, I will hand you the letter."

I was astounded. The Prefect appeared absolutely thunderstricken. For some minutes he remained speechless and motionless, looking incredulously at my friend with open mouth, and eyes that seemed starting from their sockets; then apparently recovering himself in some measure, he seized a pen, and after several pauses and vacant stares, finally filled up and signed a check for fifty thousand francs, and handed it across the table to Dupin. The latter examined it carefully and deposited it in his pocket-book; then, unlocking an *escritoire*, took thence a letter and gave it to the Prefect. This functionary grasped it in a perfect agony of joy, opened it with a trembling hand, cast a rapid glance at its contents, and then, scrambling and struggling to the door, rushed at length unceremoniously from the room and from the house, without having uttered a syllable since Dupin had requested him to fill up the check.

When he had gone, my friend entered into some explanations.

"The Parisian police," he said, "are exceedingly able in their way. They are persevering, ingenious, cunning, and thoroughly versed in the knowledge which their duties seem chiefly to demand. Thus, when G— detailed to us his mode of searching the premises at the

Hotel D—, I felt entire confidence in his having made a satisfactory investigation—so far as his labors extended."

"So far as his labors extended?" said I.

"Yes," said Dupin. "The measures adopted were not only the best of their kind, but carried out to absolute perfection. Had the letter been deposited within the range of their search, these fellows would, beyond a question, have found it."

I merely laughed—but he seemed quite serious in all that he said.

"The measures, then," he continued, "were good in their kind, and well executed; their defect lay in their being inapplicable to the case and to the man. A certain set of highly ingenious resources are, with the Prefect, a sort of Procrustean bed, to which he forcibly adapts his designs. But he perpetually errs by being too deep or too shallow for the matter in hand; and many a school-boy is a better reasoner than he. I knew one about eight years of age, whose success at guessing in the game of 'even and odd' attracted universal admiration. This game is simple, and is played with marbles. One player holds in his hand a number of these toys, and demands of another whether that number is even or odd. If the guess is right, the guesser wins one; if wrong, he loses one. The boy to whom I allude won all the marbles of the school. Of course he had some principle of guessing; and this lay in mere observation and admeasurement of the astuteness of his opponents. For example, an arrant simpleton is his opponent, and, holding up his closed hand, asks, 'Are they even or odd?' Our school-boy replies, 'Odd,' and loses; but upon the second trial he wins, for he then says to himself: 'The simpleton had them even upon the first trial, and his amount of cunning is just sufficient to make him have them odd upon the second; I will therefore guess odd';—he guesses odd, and wins. Now, with a simpleton a degree above the first, he would have reasoned thus: 'This fellow finds that in the first instance I guessed odd, and, in the second, he will propose to himself, upon the first impulse, a simple variation from even to odd, as did the first simpleton; but then a second thought will suggest that this is too simple a variation, and finally he will decide upon putting it even as before. I will therefore guess even';—he guesses even, and wins. Now this mode of reasoning in the school-boy, whom his fellows termed 'lucky,'—what, in its last analysis, is it?"

"It is merely," I said, "an identification of the reasoner's intellect with that of his opponent."

"It is," said Dupin; "and, upon inquiring of the boy by what means he effected the *thorough* identification in which his success consisted, I received answer as follows: 'When I wish to find out how wise, or how stupid, or how good, or how wicked is any one, or what are his thoughts at the moment, I fashion the expression of my face, as accurately as possible, in accordance with the expression of his, and then wait to see what thoughts or sentiments arise in my mind or heart, as if to match or correspond with the expression.' This response of the school-boy lies at the bottom of all the spurious profundity which has been attributed to Rochefoucault, to La Bougive, to Machiavelli, and to Campanella."

"And the identification," I said, "of the reasoner's intellect with that of his opponent, depends, if I understand you aright, upon the accuracy with which the opponent's intellect is admeasured."

"For its practical value it depends upon this," replied Dupin; "and the Prefect and his cohort fail so frequently, first, by default of this identification, and, secondly, by ill-admeasurement, or rather through non-admeasurement, of the intellect with which they are engaged. They consider only their *own* ideas of ingenuity; and, in searching for any thing hidden, advert only to the modes in which *they* would have hidden it. They are right in this much—that their own ingenuity is a faithful representative of that of *the mass*; but when the cunning of the individual felon is diverse in character from their own, the felon foils them, of course. This always happens when it is above their own, and very usually when it is below. They have no variation of principle in their investigations; at best, when urged by some unusual emergency—by some extraordinary reward—they extend to exaggerate their old modes of *practice*, without touching their principles. What, for example, in this case of D——, has been done to vary the principle of action? What is all this boring, and probing, and sounding, and scrutinizing with the microscope, and dividing the surface of the building into registered square inches—what is it all but an exaggeration *of the application* of the one principle or set of principles of search, which are based upon the one set of notions regarding human ingenuity, to which the Prefect, in the long routine of his duty, has been accustomed? Do you not see he has taken it for granted that *all* men proceed to conceal a letter, not exactly in a gimlet-hole bored in a chair-leg, but, at least, in *some* out-of-the-way hole or corner suggested by the same tenor of thought which would urge a man to secrete a letter in a gimlet-hole bored in a chair-leg? And do you not see also, that such *recherchés* nooks for concealment are adapted only for ordinary occasions, and would be adopted only by ordinary intellects; for, in all cases of concealment, a disposal of the article concealed—a disposal of it in this *recherché* manner,—is, in the very first instance, presumable and presumed; and thus its discovery depends, not at all upon the acumen, but altogether upon the mere care, patience, and determination of the seekers; and where the case is of importance—or, what amounts to the same thing in the political eyes, when the reward is of magnitude,—the qualities in question have *never* been known to fail. You will now understand what I meant in suggesting that, had the purloined letter been hidden anywhere within the limits of the Prefect's examination—in other words, had the principle of its concealment been comprehended within the principles of the Prefect—its discovery would have been a matter altogether beyond question. This functionary, however, has been thoroughly mystified; and the remote source of his defeat lies in the supposition that the Minister is a fool, because he has acquired renown as a poet. All fools are poets; this the Prefect *feels*; and he is merely guilty of a *non distributio medii* in thence inferring that all poets are fools."

"But is this really the poet?" I asked. "There are two brothers, I know; and both have attained reputation in letters. The Minister I believe has written learnedly on the Differential Calculus. He is a mathematician, and no poet."

"You are mistaken; I know him well; he is both. As poet *and* mathematician, he would reason well; as mere mathematician, he could not have reasoned at all, and thus would have been at the mercy of the Prefect."

"You surprise me," I said, "by these opinions, which have been contradicted by the voice of the world. You do not mean to set at naught the well-digested idea of centuries. The mathematical reason has long been regarded as *the* reason *par excellence*."

"'*Il y a à parier*,'" replied Dupin, quoting from Chamfort, "'*que toute idée publique, toute convention reçue, est une sottise, car elle a convenue au plus grand nombre*.' The mathematicians, I grant you, have done their best to promulgate the popular error to which you allude, and which is none the less an error for its promulgation as truth. With an art worthy a better cause, for example, they have insinuated the term 'analysis' into application to algebra. The French are the originators of this particular deception; but if a term is of any importance—if words derive any value from applicability—then 'analysis' conveys 'algebra' about as much as, in Latin, *'ambitus'* implies 'ambition,' *'religio'* 'religion,' or *'homines honesti'* a set of *'honorable* men.'"

"You have a quarrel on hand, I see," said I, "with some of the algebraists of Paris; but proceed."

"I dispute the availability, and thus the value, of that reason which is cultivated in any especial form other than the abstractly logical. I dispute, in particular, the reason educed by mathematical study. The mathematics are the science of form and quantity; mathematical reasoning is merely logic applied to observation upon form and quantity. The great error lies in supposing that even the truths of what is called *pure* algebra are abstract or general truths. And this error is so egregious that I am confounded at the universality with which it has been received. Mathematical axioms are *not* axioms of general truth. What is true of *relation*—of form and quantity—is often grossly false in regard to morals, for example. In this latter science it is very usually *un*true that the aggregated parts are equal to the whole. In chemistry also the axiom fails. In the consideration of motive it fails; for two motives, each of a given value, have not, necessarily, a value when united, equal to the sum of their values apart. There are numerous other mathematical truths which are only truths within the limits of *relation*. But the mathematician argues from his *finite truths*, through habit, as if they were of an absolutely general applicability—as the world indeed imagines them to be. Bryant, in his very learned 'Mythology,' mentions an analogous source of error, when he says that 'although the pagan fables are not believed, yet we forget ourselves continually, and make inferences from them as existing realities.' With the algebraists, however, who are pagans themselves, the 'pagan fables' *are* believed, and the inferences are made, not so much through lapse of memory as through an unaccountable addling of the brains. In short, I never yet encountered the mere mathematician who would be trusted out of equal roots, or one who did not clandestinely hold it as a point of his faith that $x^2 + px$ was absolutely and unconditionally equal to q. Say to one of these gentlemen, by way of experiment, if you please, that you believe occasions may occur where $x^2 + px$ is *not* altogether equal to q, and, having made him understand what you mean, get out of his reach as speedily as convenient, for, beyond doubt, he will endeavor to knock you down.

"I mean to say," continued Dupin, while I merely laughed at his last observations, "that if the Minister had been no more than a mathematician, the Prefect would have been under no necessity of giving me this check. I knew him, however, as both mathematician and poet, and my measures were adapted to his capacity, with reference to the circumstances by which he was surrounded. I knew him as a courtier, too, and as a bold *intrigant*. Such a man, I considered, could not fail to be aware of the ordinary policial modes of action. He could not have failed to anticipate—and events have proved that he did not fail to anticipate—the waylayings to which he was subjected. He must have foreseen, I reflected, the secret investigations of his premises. His frequent absences from home at night, which were hailed by the Prefect as certain aids to his success, I regarded only as *ruses*, to afford opportunity for thorough search to the police, and thus the sooner to impress them with the conviction to which G——, in fact, did finally arrive—the conviction that the letter was not upon the premises. I felt, also, that the whole train of thought, which I was at some pains in detailing to you just now, concerning the invariable principle of policial action in searches for articles concealed—I felt that this whole train of thought would necessarily pass through the mind of the minister. It would imperatively lead him to despise all the ordinary *nooks* of concealment. *He* could not, I reflected, be so weak as not to see that the most intricate and remote recess of his hotel would be as open as his commonest closets to the eyes, to the probes, to the gimlets, and to the microscopes of the Prefect. I saw, in fine, that he would be driven, as a matter of course, to *simplicity*, if not deliberately induced to it as a matter of choice. You will remember, perhaps, how desperately the Prefect laughed when I suggested, upon our first interview, that it was just possible this mystery troubled him so much on account of its being so *very* self-evident."

"Yes," said I, "I remember his merriment well. I really thought he would have fallen into convulsions."

"The material world," continued Dupin, "abounds with very strict analogies to the immaterial; and thus some color of truth has been given to the rhetorical dogma, that metaphor, or simile, may be made to strengthen an argument as well as to embellish a description. The principle of the *vis inertiæ*, for example, seems to be identical in physics and metaphysics. It is not more true in the former, that a large body is with more difficulty set in motion than a smaller one, and that its subsequent *momentum* is commensurate with this difficulty, than it is, in the latter, that intellects of the vaster capacity, while more forcible, more constant, and more eventful in their movements than those of inferior grade, are yet the less readily moved, and more embarrassed, and full of hesitation in the first few steps of their progress. Again: have you ever noticed which of the street signs, over the shop doors, are the most attractive of attention?"

"I have never given the matter a thought," I said.

"There is a game of puzzles," he resumed, "which is played upon a map. One party playing requires another to find a given word—the name of town, river, state, or empire—any word, in short, upon the motley and perplexed surface of the chart. A novice in the game generally seeks to embarrass his opponents by giving them the most minutely lettered names; but the adept selects such words as stretch, in large characters, from one end of the chart to the other. These, like the over-largely lettered signs and placards of the street, escape observation by dint of being excessively obvious; and here the physical oversight is precisely analogous with the moral inapprehension by which the intellect suffers to pass unnoticed those considerations which are too obtrusively and too palpably self-evident. But this is a point, it appears, somewhat above or beneath the understanding of the Prefect. He never once thought it probable, or possible, that the minister had deposited the letter immediately beneath the nose of the whole world, by way of best preventing any portion of that world from perceiving it.

"But the more I reflected upon the daring, dashing, and discriminating ingenuity of D——; upon the fact that the document must always have been *at hand*, if he intended to use it to good purpose; and upon the decisive evidence, obtained by the Prefect, that it was not hidden within the limits of that dignitary's ordinary search—the more satisfied I became that, to conceal this letter, the minister had resorted to the comprehensive and sagacious expedient of not attempting to conceal it at all.

"Full of these ideas, I prepared myself with a pair of green spectacles, and called one fine morning, quite by accident, at the Ministerial hotel. I found D—— at home, yawning, lounging, and dawdling, as usual, and pretending to be in the last extremity of *ennui*. He is, perhaps, the most really energetic human being now alive—but that is only when nobody sees him.

"To be even with him, I complained of my weak eyes, and lamented the necessity of the spectacles, under cover of which I cautiously and thoroughly surveyed the whole apartment, while seemingly intent only upon the conversation of my host.

"I paid especial attention to a large writing-table near which he sat, and upon which lay confusedly, some miscellaneous letters and other papers, with one or two musical instruments and a few books. Here, however, after a long and very deliberate scrutiny, I saw nothing to excite particular suspicion.

"At length my eyes, in going the circuit of the room, fell upon a trumpery filigree card-rack of pasteboard, that hung dangling by a dirty blue ribbon, from a little brass knob just beneath the middle of the mantelpiece. In this rack, which had three or four compartments, were five or six visiting cards and a solitary letter. This last was much soiled and crumpled. It was torn nearly in two, across the middle—as if a design, in the first instance, to tear it entirely up as worthless, had been altered, or stayed, in the second. It had a large black seal, bearing the D—— cipher *very* conspicuously, and was addressed, in a diminutive female hand, to D——, the minister, himself. It was thrust carelessly, and even, as it seemed, contemptuously, into one of the uppermost divisions of the rack.

"No sooner had I glanced at this letter than I concluded it to be that of which I was in search. To be sure, it was, to all appearance, radically different from the one of which the Prefect had read us so minute a description. Here the seal was large and black, with the D—— cipher; there it was small and red, with the ducal arms of the S—— family. Here, the address, to the minister, was diminutive and feminine; there the superscription, to a certain royal personage, was markedly bold and decided; the size alone formed a point of correspondence. But, then, the *radicalness* of these differences, which was excessive; the dirt; the soiled and torn condition of the paper, so inconsistent with the *true* methodical habits of D——, and so suggestive of a design to delude the beholder into an idea of the worthlessness of the document;—these things, together with the hyperobtrusive situation of this document, full in the view of every visitor, and thus exactly in accordance with the conclusions to which I had previously arrived; these things, I say, were strongly corroborative of suspicion, in one who came with the intention to suspect.

"I protracted my visit as long as possible, and, while I maintained a most animated discussion with the minister, upon a topic which I knew well had never failed to interest and excite him, I kept my attention really riveted upon the letter. In this examination, I committed to memory its external appearance and arrangement in the rack; and also fell, at length, upon a discovery which set at rest whatever trivial doubt I might have entertained. In scrutinizing the edges of the paper, I observed them to be more *chafed* than seemed necessary. They presented the *broken* appearance which is manifested when a stiff paper, having been once folded and pressed with a folder, is refolded in a reversed direction, in the same creases or edges which had formed the original fold. This discovery was sufficient. It was clear to me that the letter had been turned, as a glove, inside out, re-directed and re-sealed. I bade the minister good-morning, and took my departure at once, leaving a gold snuff-box upon the table.

"The next morning I called for the snuff-box, when we resumed, quite eagerly, the conversation of the preceding day. While thus engaged, however, a loud report, as if of a pistol, was heard immediately beneath the windows of the hotel, and was succeeded by a series of fearful screams, and the shoutings of a terrified mob. D—— rushed to a casement, threw it open, and looked out. In the meantime I stepped to the card-rack, took the letter, put it in my pocket, and replaced it by a *facsimile*, (so far as regards externals) which I had carefully prepared at my lodgings—imitating the D—— cipher, very readily, by means of a seal formed of bread.

"The disturbance in the street had been occasioned by the frantic behavior of a man with a musket. He had fired it among a crowd of women and children. It proved, however, to have been without ball, and the fellow was suffered to go his way as a lunatic or a drunkard. When he had gone, D—— came from the window, whither I had followed him immediately upon securing the object in view. Soon afterward I bade him farewell. The pretended lunatic was a man in my own pay."

"But what purpose had you," I asked, "in replacing the letter by a *facsimile*? Would it not have been better, at the first visit, to have seized it openly, and departed?"

"D——," replied Dupin, "is a desperate man, and a man of nerve. His hotel, too, is not without attendants devoted to his interests. Had I made the wild attempt you suggest, I might never have left the Ministerial presence alive. The good people of Paris might have heard of me no more. But I had an object apart from these considerations. You know my political prepossessions. In this matter, I act as a partisan of the lady concerned. For eighteen months the Minister has had her in his power. She has now him in hers—since, being unaware that the letter is not in his possession, he will proceed with his exactions as if it was. Thus will he inevitably commit himself, at once, to his political destruction. His downfall, too, will not be more precipitate than awkward. It is all very well to talk about the *facilis descensus Averni*; but in all kinds of climbing, as Catalani said of singing, it is far more easy to get up than to come down. In the present instance I have no sympathy—at least no pity—for him who descends. He is that *monstrum horrendum*, an unprincipled man of genius. I confess, however, that I should like very well to know the precise character of his thoughts, when, being defied by her whom the Prefect terms 'a certain personage,' he is reduced to opening the letter which I left for him in the card-rack."

"How? Did you put anything particular in it?"

"Why—it did not seem altogether right to leave the interior blank—that would have been insulting. D——, at Vienna once, did me an evil turn, which I told him, quite good-humoredly, that I should remember. So, as I knew he would feel some curiosity in regard to the identity of the person who had outwitted him, I thought it a pity not to give him a clew. He is well acquainted with my MS., and I just copied into the middle of the blank sheet the words—

"'——   ——Un dessein si funeste,
          S'il n'est digne d'Atrée, est digne de Thyeste.'

They are to be found in Crébillon's 'Atrée.'"

The Man With The Twisted Lip

ARTHUR CONAN DOYLE

Isa Whitney, brother of the late Elias Whitney, D.D., Principal of the Theological College of St. George's, was much addicted to opium. The habit grew upon him, as I understand, from some foolish freak when he was at college, for having read De Quincey's description of his dreams and sensations, he had drenched his tobacco with laudanum in an attempt to produce the same effects. He found, as so many more have done, that the practice is easier to attain than to get rid of, and for many years he continued to be a slave to the drug, an object of mingled horror and pity to his friends and relatives. I can see him now, with yellow, pasty face, drooping lids and pin-point pupils, all huddled in a chair, the wreck and ruin of a noble man.

One night—it was in June, '89—there came a ring to my bell, about the hour when a man gives his first yawn, and glances at the clock. I sat up in my chair, and my wife laid her needlework down in her lap and made a little face of disappointment.

"A patient!" said she. "You'll have to go out."

I groaned, for I was newly come back from a weary day.

We heard the door open, a few hurried words, and then quick steps upon the linoleum. Our own door flew open, and a lady, clad in some dark-coloured stuff, with a black veil, entered the room.

"You will excuse my calling so late," she began, and then, suddenly losing her self-control, she ran forward, threw her arms about my wife's neck, and sobbed upon her shoulder. "Oh, I'm in such trouble!" she cried; "I do so want a little help."

"Why," said my wife, pulling up her veil, "it is Kate Whitney. How you startled me, Kate! I had not an idea who you were when you came in."

"I didn't know what to do, so I came straight to you." That was always the way. Folk who were in grief came to my wife like birds to a lighthouse.

"It was very sweet of you to come. Now, you must have some wine and water, and sit here comfortably and tell us all about it. Or should you rather that I sent James off to bed?"

"Oh, no, no. I want the Doctor's advice and help too. It's about Isa. He has not been home for two days. I am so frightened about him!"

It was not the first time that she had spoken to us of her husband's trouble, to me as a doctor, to my wife as an old friend and school companion. We soothed and comforted her by such words as we could find. Did she know where her husband was? Was it possible that we could bring him back to her?

It seemed that it was. She had the surest information that of late he had, when the fit was on him, made use of an opium den in the furthest east of the City. Hitherto his orgies had always been confined to one day, and he had come back, twitching and shattered, in the evening. But now the spell had been upon him eight and forty hours, and he lay there, doubtless among the dregs of the docks, breathing in the poison or sleeping off the effects. There he was to be found, she was sure of it, at the "Bar of Gold," in Upper Swandam-lane. But what was she to do? How could she, a young and timid woman, make her way into such a place, and pluck her husband out from among the ruffians who surrounded him?

There was the case, and of course there was but one way out of it. Might I not escort her to this place? And, then, as a second thought, why should she come at all? I was Isa Whitney's medical adviser, and as such I had influence over him. I could manage it better if I were alone. I promised her on my word that I would send him home in a cab within two hours if he were indeed at the address which she had given me. And so in ten minutes I had left my arm-chair and cheery sitting-room behind me, and was speeding eastward in a hansom on a strange errand, as it seemed to me at the time, though the future only could show how strange it was to be.

But there was no great difficulty in the first stage of my adventure. Upper Swandam-lane is a vile alley lurking behind the high wharves which line the north side of the river to the east of London Bridge. Between a slop shop and a gin shop, approached by a steep flight of steps leading down to a black gap like the mouth of a cave, I found the den of which I was in search. Ordering my cab to wait, I passed down the steps, worn hollow in the centre by the ceaseless tread of drunken feet, and by the light of a flickering oil lamp above the door

I found the latch and made my way into a long, low room, thick and heavy with the brown opium smoke, and terraced with wooden berths, like the forecastle of an emigrant ship.

Through the gloom one could dimly catch a glimpse of bodies lying in strange fantastic poses, bowed shoulders, bent knees, heads thrown back and chins pointing upwards, with here and there a dark, lack-lustre eye turned upon the new comer. Out of the black shadows there glimmered little red circles of light, now bright, now faint, as the burning poison waxed or waned in the bowls of the metal pipes. The most lay silent but some muttered to themselves, and others talked together in a strange, low, monotonous voice, their conversation coming in gushes, and then suddenly tailing off into silence, each mumbling out his own thoughts, and paying little heed to the words of his neighbour. At the further end was a small brazier of burning charcoal, besides which on a three-legged wooden stool there sat a tall, thin old man with his jaw resting upon his two fists, and his elbows upon his knees, staring into the fire.

As I entered, a sallow Malay attendant had hurried up with a pipe for me and a supply of the drug, beckoning me to an empty berth.

"Thank you, I have not come to stay," said I. "There is a friend of mine here, Mr. Isa Whitney, and I wish to speak with him."

There was a movement and an exclamation from my right, and, peering through the gloom, I saw Whitney, pale, haggard, and unkempt, staring out at me.

"My God! It's Watson," said he. He was in a pitiable state of reaction, with every nerve in a twitter. "I say, Watson, what o'clock is it?"

"Nearly eleven."

"Of what day?"

"Of Friday, June 19."

"Good heavens! I thought it was Wednesday. It *is* Wednesday. What d'you want to frighten a chap for?" He sank his face on to his arms, and began to sob in a high treble key.

"I tell you that it is Friday, man. Your wife has been waiting this two days for you. You should be ashamed of yourself!"

"So I am. But you've got mixed, Watson, for I have only been here a few hours, three pipes, four pipes—I forget how many. But I'll go home with you. I wouldn't frighten Kate—poor little Kate. Give me your hand! Have you a cab?"

"Yes, I have one waiting."

"Then I shall go in it. But I must owe something. Find what I owe, Watson. I am all off colour. I can do nothing for myself."

I walked down the narrow passage between the double row of sleepers, holding my breath to keep out the vile, stupefying fumes of the drug, and looking about for the manager. As I passed the tall man who sat by the brazier I felt a sudden pluck at my skirt and a low voice whispered, "Walk past me, and then look back at me." The words fell quite distinctly upon my ear. I glanced down. They could only have come from the old man at my side, and yet he sat now as absorbed as ever, very thin, very wrinkled, bent with age, an opium pipe dangling down from between his knees, as though it had dropped in sheer lassitude from his fingers. I took two steps forward and looked back. It took all my self-control to prevent me from breaking out into a cry of astonishment. He had turned his back so that none could see him but I. His form had filled out, his wrinkles were gone, the dull eyes had regained their fire, and there, sitting by the fire, and grinning at my surprise, was none other than Sherlock Holmes. He made a slight motion to me to approach him, and instantly, as he turned his face half round to the company once more, subsided into a doddering, loose-lipped senility.

"Holmes!" I whispered, "what on earth are you doing in this den?"

"As low as you can," he answered, "I have excellent ears. If you would have the great kindness to get rid of that sottish friend of yours I should be exceedingly glad to have a little talk with you."

"I have a cab outside."

"Then pray send him home in it. You may safely trust him, for he appears to be too limp to get into any mischief. I should recommend you also to send a note by the cabman to your wife to say that you have thrown in your lot with me. If you will wait outside, I shall be with you in five minutes."

It was difficult to refuse any of Sherlock Holmes' requests, for they were always so exceedingly definite, and put forward with such a quiet air of mastery. I felt, however, that when Whitney was once confined in the cab, my mission was practically accomplished; and for the rest, I could not wish anything better than to be associated with my friend in one of those singular adventures which were the normal condition of his existence. In a few minutes I had written my note, paid Whitney's bill, led him out to the cab, and seen him driven through the darkness. In a very short time a decrepit figure had emerged from the opium den, and I was walking down the street with Sherlock Holmes. For two streets he shuffled along with a bent back and an uncertain foot. Then glancing quickly round, he straightened himself out and burst into a hearty fit of laughter.

"I suppose, Watson," said he, "that you imagine that I have added opium-smoking to cocaine injections and all the other little weaknesses on which you have favoured me with your medical views."

"I was certainly surprised to find you there."

"But not more so than I to find you."

"I came to find a friend."

"And I to find an enemy."

"An enemy?"

"Yes, one of my natural enemies, or shall I say, my natural prey. Briefly, Watson, I am in the midst of a very remarkable inquiry, and I have hoped to find a clue in the incoherent ramblings of these sots, as I have done before now. Had I been recognised in that den my life would not have been worth an hour's purchase, for I have used it before now for my own purposes, and the rascally Lascar who runs it has sworn to have vengeance upon me. There is a trap-door at the back of that building, near the corner of Paul's Wharf, which could tell some strange tales of what has passed through it upon the moonless nights."

"What! You do not mean bodies?"

"Aye, bodies, Watson. We should be rich men if we had a thousand pounds for every poor devil who has been done to death in that den. It is the vilest murder-trap on the whole river-side, and I fear that Neville St. Clair has entered it never to leave it more. But our trap should be here!" He put his two fore-fingers between his teeth and whistled shrilly, a signal which was answered by a similar whistle from the distance, followed shortly by the rattle of wheels and the clink of horses' hoofs.

"Now, Watson," said Holmes, as a tall dog-cart dashed up through the gloom, throwing out two golden tunnels of yellow light from its side lanterns. "You'll come with me, won't you?"

"If I can be of use."

"Oh, a trusty comrade is always of use. And a chronicler still more so. My room at The Cedars is a double-bedded one."

"The Cedars?"

"Yes; that is Mr. St. Clair's house. I am staying there while I conduct the inquiry."

"Where is it, then?"

"Near Lee, in Kent. We have a seven-mile drive before us."

"But I am all in the dark."

"Of course you are. You'll know all about it presently. Jump up here! All right, John, we shall not need you. Here's half-a-crown. Look out for me to-morrow, about eleven. Give her her head! So long, then!"

He flicked the horse with his whip, and we dashed away through the endless succession of sombre and deserted streets, which widened gradually, until we were flying across a broad balustraded bridge, with the murky river flowing sluggishly beneath us. Beyond lay another dull wilderness of bricks and mortar, its silence broken only by the heavy, regular footfall of the policeman, or the songs and shouts of some belated party of revellers. A dull wrack was drifting slowly across the sky, and a star or two twinkled dimly here and there through the rifts of the clouds. Holmes drove in silence, with his head sunk upon his breast, and the air of a man who is lost in thought, whilst I sat beside him, curious to learn what this new quest might be which seemed to tax his powers so sorely, and yet afraid to break in upon the current of his thoughts. We had driven several miles, and were beginning to get to the fringe of the belt of suburban villas, when he shook himself, shrugged his shoulders, and lit up his pipe with the air of a man who has satisfied himself that he is acting for the best.

"You have a grand gift of silence, Watson," said he. "It makes you quite invaluable as a companion. 'Pon my word, it is a great thing for me to have someone to talk to, for my own thoughts are not over pleasant. I was wondering what I should say to this dear little woman tonight when she meets me at the door."

"You forget that I know nothing about it."

"I shall just have time to tell you the facts of the case before we get to Lee. It seems absurdly simple, and yet, somehow, I can get nothing to go upon. There's plenty of thread, no doubt, but I can't get the end of it into my hand. Now, I'll state the case clearly and concisely to you, Watson, and maybe you may see a spark where all is dark to me."

"Proceed then."

"Some years ago—to be definite, in May, 1884—there came to Lee a gentleman, Neville St. Clair by name, who appeared to have plenty of money. He took a large villa, laid out the grounds very nicely, and lived generally in good style. By degrees he made friends in the neighbourhood, and in 1887 he married the daughter of a local brewer, by whom he has now had two children. He had no occupation, but was interested in several companies, and went into town as a rule in the morning, returning by the 5.14 from Cannon-street every night. Mr. St. Clair is now 37 years of age, is a man of temperate habits, a good husband, a very affectionate father, and a man who is popular with all who know him. I may add that his whole debts at the present moment, as far as we have been able to ascertain, amount to £88 10s., while he has £220 standing to his credit in the Capital and Counties Bank. There is no reason, therefore, to think that money troubles have been weighing upon his mind.

"Last Monday Mr. Neville St. Clair went into town rather earlier than usual, remarking before he started that he had two important commissions to perform, and that he would bring his little boy home a box of bricks. Now, by the merest chance his wife received a telegram upon this same Monday, very shortly after his departure, to the effect that a small parcel of considerable value which she had been expecting was waiting for her at the offices of the Aberdeen Shipping Company. Now, if you are well up in your London, you will know that the office of the company is in Fresno-street, which branches out of Upper Swandam-lane, where you found me to-night. Mrs. St. Clair had her lunch, started for the City, did some shopping, proceeded to the company's office, got her packet, and found herself exactly at 4.35 walking through Swandam-lane on her way back to the station. Have you follwed me so far?"

"It is very clear."

"If you remember, Monday was an exceedingly hot day, and Mrs. St. Clair walked slowly, glancing about in the hope of seeing a cab, as she did not like the neighbourhood in which she found herself. While she walked in this way down Swandam-lane she suddenly heard an ejaculation or cry, and was struck cold to see her husband looking down at her, and, as it seemed to her, beckoning to her from a second-floor window. The window was open, and she distinctly saw his face, which she describes as being terribly agitated. He waved his hands frantically to her, and then vanished from the window so suddenly that it seemed to her that he had been plucked back by some irresistible force from behind. One singular point which struck her quick feminine eye was that, although he wore some dark coat, such as he had started to town in, he had on neither collar nor necktie.

"Convinced that something was amiss with him, she rushed down the steps—for the house was none other than the opium den in which you found me to-night—and, running through the front room, she attempted to ascend the stairs which led to the first floor. At the foot of the stairs, however, she met this Lascar scoundrel of whom I have spoken, who thrust her back, and, aided by a Dane, who acts as assistant there, pushed her out into the street. Filled with the most maddening doubts and fears, she rushed down the lane, and, by rare good fortune, met, in Fresno-street, a number of constables with an inspector, all on their way to their beat. The inspector and two men accompanied her back, and, in spite of the continued resistance of the proprietor, they made their way to the room in which Mr. St. Clair had last been seen. There was no sign of him there. In fact, in the whole of that floor there was no one to be found, save a crippled wretch of hideous aspect, who, it seems, made his home there. Both he and the Lascar stoutly swore that no one else had been in the front room during the afternoon. So determined was their denial that the inspector was staggered, and had almost come to believe that Mrs. St. Clair had been deluded when, with a cry, she sprang at a small deal box which lay upon the table, and tore the lid from it. Out there fell a cascade of children's bricks. It was the toy which he had promised to bring home.

"This discovery, and the evident confusion which the cripple showed, made the inspector realise that the matter was serious. The rooms were carefully examined, and results all pointed to an abominable crime. The front room was plainly furnished as a sitting-room, and led into a small bedroom, which looked out upon the back of one of the wharves. Between the wharf and the bedroom window is a narrow strip, which is dry at low tide, but is covered at high tide with at least four and a half feet of water. The bedroom window was a broad one, and opened from below. On examination traces of blood were to be seen upon the window sill, and several scattered drops were visible upon the wooden floor of the bedroom. Thrust away behind a curtain in the front room were all the clothes of Mr. Neville St. Clair, with the exception of his coat. His boots, his socks, his hat, and his watch—all were there. There were no signs of violence upon any of these garments, and there were no other traces of Mr. Neville St. Clair. Out of the window he must apparently have gone, for no other exit could be discovered, and the ominous bloodstains upon the sill gave little promise that he could save himself by swimming, for the tide was at its very highest at the moment of the tragedy.

"And now as to the villains who seemed to be immediately implicated in the matter. The Lascar was known to be a man of the vilest antecedents, but as by Mrs. St. Clair's story he was known to have been at the foot of the stair within a very few seconds of her husband's appearance at the window, he could hardly have been more than an accessory to the crime. His defence was one of absolute ignorance, and he protested that he had no knowledge as to the doings of Hugh Boone, his lodger, and that he could not account in any way for the presence of the missing gentleman's clothes.

"So much for the Lascar manager. Now for the sinister cripple who lives upon the second floor of the opium den, and who was certainly the last human being whose eyes rested upon Neville St. Clair. His name is Hugh Boone, and his hideous face is one which is familiar to every man who goes much to the City. He is a professional beggar, though in order to avoid the police regulations he pretends to a small trade in wax vestas. Some little distance down Threadneedle-street upon the left hand side there is, as you may have remarked, a small angle in the wall. Here it is that the creature takes his daily seat, cross-legged, with his tiny stock of matches on his lap, and as he is a piteous spectacle a small rain of charity descends into the greasy leather cap which lies upon the pavement beside him. I have watched the fellow more than once, before ever I thought of making his professional acquaintance, and I have been surprised at the harvest which he has reaped in a short time. His appearance, you see, is so remarkable, that no one can pass him without observing him. A shock of orange hair, a pale face disfigured by a horrible scar, which, by its contraction, has turned up the outer edge of his upper lip, a bull-dog chin, and a pair of very penetrating dark eyes, which present a singular contrast to the colour of his hair, all mark him out from amid the common crowd of mendicants, and so, too, does his wit, for he is ever ready with a reply to any piece of chaff which may be thrown at him by the passersby. This is the man whom we now learn to have been the lodger at the opium den, And to have been the last man to see the gentleman of whom we are in quest."

"But a cripple!" said I. "What could he have done singlehanded against a man in the prime of life?"

"He is a cripple in the sense that he walks with a limp; but, in other respects, he appears to be a powerful and well-nurtured man. Surely your medical experience would tell you, Watson, that weakness in one limb is often compensated for by exceptional strength in the others."

"Pray continue your narrative."

"Mrs. St. Clair had fainted at the sight of the blood upon the window, and she was escorted home in a cab by the police, as her presence could be of no help to them in their investigations. Inspector Barton, who had charge of the case, made a very careful examination of the premises, but without finding anything which threw any light upon the matter. One mistake had been made in not arresting Boone instantly, as he was allowed some few minutes during which he might have communicated with his friend the Lascar, but this fault was soon remedied, and he was seized and searched, without anything being found which could incriminate him. There were, it is true, some bloodstains upon his right shirt-sleeve, but he pointed to his ring finger, which had been cut near the nail, and explained that the bleeding came from there, adding that he had been to the window not long before, and that the stains which had been observed there came doubtless from the same source. He denied strenuously having ever seen Mr. Neville St. Clair, and swore that the presence of the clothes in his room was as much a mystery to him as to the police. As to Mrs. St. Clair's assertion that she had actually seen her husband at the window, he declared that she must have been either mad or dreaming. He was removed, loudly protesting, to the police station, while the inspector remained upon the premises in the hope that the ebbing tide might afford some fresh clue.

"And it did, though they hardly found upon the mudbank what they had feared to find. It was Neville St. Clair's coat, and not Neville St. Clair, which lay uncovered as the tide receded. And what do you think they found in the pockets?"

"I cannot imagine."

"No, I don't think you would guess. Every pocket stuffed with pennies and half-pennies—four hundred and twenty-one pennies, and two hundred and seventy half-pennies. It was no wonder that it had not been swept away by the tide. But a human body is a different matter. There is a fierce eddy between the wharf and the house. It seemed likely enough that the weighted coat had remained when the stripped body had been sucked away into the river."

"But I understand that all the other clothes were found in the room. Would the body be dressed in a coat alone?"

"No, sir, but the facts might be met speciously enough. Suppose that this man Boone had thrust Neville St. Clair through the window, there is no human eye which could have seen the deed. What would he do then? It would of course instantly strike him that he must get rid of the tell-tale garments. He would seize the coat then, and be in the act of throwing it out when it would occur to him that it would swim and not sink. He has little time, for he has heard the scuffle downstairs when the wife tried to force her way up, and perhaps he has already heard from his Lascar confederate that the police are hurrying up the street. There is not an instant to be lost. He rushes to some secret horde, where he has accumulated the fruits of his beggary, and he stuffs all the coins upon which he can lay his hands into the pockets to make sure of the coat's sinking. He throws it out, and would have done the same with the other garments had not he heard the rush of steps below, and only just had time to close the window when the police appeared."

"It certainly sounds feasible."

"Well, we will take it as a working hypothesis for want of a better. Boone, as I have told you, was arrested and taken to the station, but it could not be shown that there had ever before been anything against him. He had for years been known as a professional beggar but his life appeared to have been a very quiet and innocent one. There the matter stands at present, and the questions which have to be solved, what Neville St. Clair was doing in the opium den, what happened to him when there, where is he now, and what Hugh Boone had to do with his disappearance, are all as far from a solution as ever. I confess that I cannot recall any case within my experience which looked at the first glance so simple, and yet which presented such difficulties."

Whilst Sherlock Holmes had been detailing this singular series of events we had been whirling through the outskirts of the great town until the last straggling houses had been left behind, and we rattled along with a country hedge upon either side of us. Just as he finished, however, we drove through two scattered villages, where a few lights still glimmered in the windows.

"We are on the outskirts of Lee," said my companion. "We have touched on three English counties in our short drive, starting in Middlesex, passing over an angle of Surrey, and ending in Kent. See that light among the trees? That is The Cedars, and beside that lamp sits a woman whose anxious ears have already, I have little doubt, caught the clink of our horse's feet."

"But why are you not conducting the case from Baker-street?" I asked.

"Because there are many inquiries which must be made out here. Mrs. St. Clair has most kindly put two rooms at my disposal, and you may rest assured that she will have nothing but a welcome for my friend and colleague. I hate to meet her, Watson, when I have no news of her husband. Here we are. Whoa, there, whoa!"

We had pulled up in front of a large villa which stood within its own grounds. A stable-boy had run out to the horse's head, and, springing down, I followed Holmes up the small, winding gravel drive which led to the house. As we approached, the door flew open, and a little blonde woman stood in the opening, clad in some sort of light mousseline de soie, with a touch of fluffy pink chiffon at her neck and wrists. She stood with her figure outlined against the flood of light, one hand upon the door, one half raised in her eagerness, her body slightly bent, her head and face protruded, with eager eyes and parted lips, a standing question.

"Well?" she cried, "well?" And then, seeing that there were two of us, she gave a cry of hope which sank into a groan as she saw that my companion shook his head and shrugged his shoulders.

"No good news?"

"None."

"No bad?"

"No."

"Thank God for that. But come in. You must be weary, for you have had a long day."

"This is my friend, Dr. Watson. He has been of most vital use to me in several of my cases, and a lucky chance has made it possible for me to bring him out and associate him with this investigation."

"I am delighted to see you," said she, pressing my hand warmly. "You will, I am sure, forgive anything which may be wanting in our arrangements, when you consider the blow which has come so suddenly upon us."

"My dear madam," said I, "I am an old campaigner, and if I were not, I can very well see that no apology is needed. If I can be of any assistance, either to you or to my friend here, I shall be indeed happy."

"Now, Mr. Sherlock Holmes," said the lady, as we entered a well-lit dining-room, upon the table of which a cold supper had been laid out. "I should very much like to ask you one or two plain questions, to which I beg that you will give a plain answer."

"Certainly, madam."

"Do not trouble about my feelings. I am not hysterical, nor given to fainting. I simply wish to hear your real, real opinion."

"Upon what point?"

"In your heart of hearts do you think that Neville is alive?"

Sherlock Holmes seemed to be embarrassed by the question. "Frankly now!" she repeated, standing upon the rug, and looking keenly down at him, as he leaned back in a basket chair.

"Frankly then, madam, I do not."

"You think that he is dead?"

"I do"

"Murdered?"

"I don't say that. Perhaps."

"And on what day did he meet his death?"

"On Monday."

"Then perhaps, Mr. Holmes, you will be good enough to explain how it is that I have received a letter from him to-day."

Sherlock Holmes sprang out of his chair as if he had been galvanised.

"What!" he roared.

"Yes, to-day." She stood smiling, holding up a little slip of paper in the air.

"May I see it?"

"Certainly."

He snatched it from her in his eagerness, and smoothing it out upon the table, he drew over the lamp, and examined it intently. I had left my chair, and was gazing at it over his shoulder. The envelope was a very coarse one, and was stamped with the Gravesend post-mark, and with the date of that very day, or rather of the day before, for it was considerably after midnight.

"Coarse writing!" murmured Holmes. "Surely this is not your husband's writing, madam."

"No, but the enclosure is."

"I perceive also that whoever addressed the envelope had to go and inquire as to the address."

"How can you tell that?"

"The name, you see, is in perfectly black ink, which has dried itself. The rest is of the greyish colour which shows that blotting-paper has been used. If it had been written straight off, and then blotted, none would be of a deep black shade. This man has written the name, and there has then been a pause before he wrote the address, which can only mean that he was not familiar with it. It is, of course, a trifle, but there is nothing so important as trifles. Let us now see the letter! Ha! there has been an enclosure here!"

"Yes, there was a ring. His signet ring."

"And you are sure that this is your husband's hand?"

"One of his hands."

"One?"

"His hand when he wrote hurriedly. It is very unlike his usual writing, and yet I know it well."

"'Dearest, do not be frightened. All will come well. There is a huge error which it may take some little time to rectify. Wait in patience.—Neville.' Written in pencil upon the fly-leaf of a book, octavo size, no watermark. Hum! Posted to-day in Gravesend by a man with a dirty thumb. Ha! And the flap has been gummed, if I am not very much in error, by a person who had been chewing tobacco. And you have no doubt that it is your husband's hand, madam?"

"None. Neville wrote those words."

"And they were posted to-day at Gravesend. Well, Mrs. St. Clair, the clouds lighten, though I should not venture to say that the danger is over."

"But he must be alive, Mr. Holmes."

"Unless this is a clever forgery to put us on the wrong scent. The ring, after all, proves nothing. It may have been taken from him."

"No, no; it is, it is, it is his very own writing!"

"Very well. It may, however, have been written on Monday, and only posted to-day."

"That is possible."

"If so, much may have happened between."

"Oh, you must not discourage me, Mr. Holmes. I know that all is well with him. There is so keen a sympathy between us that I should know if evil came upon him. On the very day that I saw him last he cut himself in the bedroom, and yet I in the dining-room rushed upstairs instantly with the utmost certainty that something had happened. Do you think that I would respond to such a trifle, and yet be ignorant of his death?"

"I have seen too much not to know that the impression of a woman may be more valuable than the conclusion of an analytical reasoner. And in this letter you certainly have a very strong piece of evidence to corroborate your view. But if your husband is alive, and able to write letters, why should he remain away from you?"

"I cannot imagine. It is unthinkable."

"And on Monday he made no remarks before leaving you?"

"No."

"And you were surprised to see him in Swandam-lane?"

"Very much so."

"Was the window open?"

"Yes."

"Then he might have called to you?"

"He might."

"He only, as I understand, gave an inarticulate cry?"

"Yes."

"A call for help, you thought?"

"Yes. He waved his hands."

"But it might have been a cry of surprise. Astonishment at the unexpected sight of you might cause him to throw up his hands?"

"It is possible."

"And you thought he was pulled back?"

"He disappeared so suddenly."

"He might have leaped back. You did not see anyone else in the room?"

"No, but this horrible man confessed to having been there, and the Lascar was at the foot of the stairs."

"Quite so. Your husband, as far as you could see, had his ordinary clothes on?"

"But without his collar or tie. I distinctly saw his bare throat."

"Had he ever spoken of Swandam-lane?"

"Never."

"Had he ever shown any signs of having taken opium?"

"Never."

"Thank you, Mrs. St. Clair. Those are the principal points about which I wished to be absolutely clear. We shall now have a little supper and then retire, for we may have a very busy day to-morrow."

A large and comfortable double-bedded room had been placed at our disposal, and I was quickly between the sheets, for I was weary after my night of adventure. Sherlock Holmes was a man, however, who when he had an unsolved problem upon his mind would go for days, and even for a week, without rest, turning it over, rearranging his facts, looking at it from every point of view, until he had either fathomed it, or convinced himself that his data were insufficient. It was soon evident to me that he was now preparing for an all night sitting. He took off his coat and waistcoat, put on a large blue dressing gown, and then wandered about the room collecting pillows from his bed, and cushions from the sofa and arm-chairs. With these he constructed a sort of Eastern divan, upon which he perched himself cross-legged, with an ounce of shag tobacco and a box of matches laid out in front of him. In the dim light of the lamp I saw him sitting there, an old brier pipe between his lips, his eyes fixed vacantly upon the corner of the ceiling, the blue smoke curling up from him, silent, motionless, with the light shining upon his strong set aquiline features. So he sat as I dropped off to sleep, and so he sat when a sudden ejaculation caused me to wake up, and I found the summer sun shining into the apartment. The pipe was still between his lips, the smoke still curled upwards, and the room was full of a dense tobacco haze, but nothing remained of the heap of shag which I had seen upon the previous night.

"Awake, Watson?" he asked.

"Yes."

"Game for a morning drive?"

"Certainly."

"Then dress. No one is stirring yet, but I know where the stable boy sleeps, and we shall soon have the trap out." He chuckled to himself as he spoke, his eyes twinkled, and he seemed a different man to the sombre thinker of the previous night.

As I dressed I glanced at my watch. It was no wonder that no one was stirring. It was twenty-five minutes past four. I had hardly finished when Holmes returned with the news that the boy was putting in the horse.

"I want to test a little theory of mine," said he, pulling on his boots.

"I think, Watson, that you are now standing in the presence of one of the most absolute fools in Europe. I deserve to be kicked from here to Charing-cross. But I think I have the key of the affair now."

"And where is it?" I asked, smiling.

"In the bath-room," he answered. "Oh, yes, I am not joking," he continued, seeing my look of incredulity. "I have just been there, and I have taken it out, and I have got it in this Gladstone bag. Come on, my boy, and we shall see whether it will not fit the lock."

We made our way downstairs as quietly as possible, and out into the bright morning sunshine. In the road stood our horse and trap, with the half-clad stable boy waiting at the head. We both sprang in, and away we dashed down the London-road. A few country carts were stirring, bearing in vegetables to the metropolis, but the lines of villas on either side were as silent and lifeless as some city in a dream.

"It has been in some points a singular case," said Holmes, flicking the horse on into a gallop. "I confess that I have been as blind as a mole, but it is better to learn wisdom late, than never to learn it at all."

In town, the earliest risers were just beginning to look sleepily from their windows as we drove through the streets of the Surrey side. Passing down the Waterloo Bridge-road we crossed over the river, and dashing up Wellington-street wheeled sharply to the right, and found ourselves in Bow-street. Sherlock Holmes was well known to the Force, and the two constables at the door saluted him. One of them held the horse's head while the other led us in.

"Who is on duty?" asked Holmes.

"Inspector Bradstreet, sir."

"Ah, Bradstreet, how are you?" A tall, stout official had come down the stone-flagged passage, in a peaked cap and frogged jacket. "I wish to have a quiet word with you, Bradstreet."

"Certainly, Mr. Holmes. Step into my room here."

It was a small office-like room, with a huge ledger upon the table, and a telephone projecting from the wall. The inspector sat down at his desk.

"What can I do for you, Mr. Holmes?"

"I called about that beggarman, Boone—the one who was charged with being concerned in the disappearance of Mr. Neville St. Clair, of Lee."

"Yes. He was brought up and remanded for further inquiries."

"So I heard. You have him here?"

"In the cells."

"Is he quiet?"

"Oh, he gives no trouble. But he is a dirty scoundrel."

"Dirty?"

"Yes, it is all we can do to make him wash his hands, and his face is as black as a tinker's. Well, when once his case has been settled he will have a regular prison bath; and I think, if you saw him, you would agree with me that he needed it."

"I should like to see him very much."

"Would you? That is easily done. Come this way. You can leave your bag."

"No, I think that I'll take it."

"Very good. Come this way, if you please." He led us down a passage, opened a barred door, passed down a winding stair, and brought us to a white-washed corridor with a line of doors on each side.

"The third on the right is his," said the inspector. "Here it is!" He quietly shot back a panel in the upper part of the door, and glanced through.

"He is asleep," said he. "You can see him very well."

We both put our eyes to the grating. The prisoner lay with his face towards us, in a very deep sleep, breathing slowly and heavily. He was a middle-sized man, coarsely clad as became his calling, with a coloured shirt protruding through the rents in his tattered coat. He was, as the inspector had said, extremely dirty, but the grime which covered his face could not conceal its repulsive ugliness. A broad wheal from an old scar ran right across it from eye to chin, and by its contraction had turned up one side of the upper lip, so that three teeth were exposed in a perpetual snarl. A shock of very bright red hair grew low over his eyes and forehead.

"He's a beauty, isn't he?" said the inspector.

"He certainly needs a wash," remarked Holmes. "I had an idea that he might, and I took the liberty of bringing the tools with me." He opened his Gladstone bag as he spoke, and took out, to my astonishment, a very large bath sponge.

"He! he! You are a funny one," chuckled the inspector.

"Now, if you will have the great goodness to open that door very quietly, we will soon make him cut a much more respectable figure."

"Well, I don't know why not," said the inspector.

"He doesn't look a credit to the Bow-street cells, does he?" He slipped his key into the lock, and we all very quietly entered the cell. The sleeper half turned, and then settled down once more into a deep slumber. Holmes stooped to the water jug, moistened his sponge, and then rubbed it twice vigorously across and down the prisoner's face.

"Let me introduce you," he shouted, "to Mr. Neville St. Clair, of Lee, in the county of Kent."

Never in my life have I seen such a sight. The man's face peeled off under the sponge like the bark from a tree. Gone was the coarse brown tint! Gone, too, the horrid scar which had seamed it across, and the twisted lip which had given the repulsive sneer to the face! A twitch brought away the tangled red hair, and there, sitting up in his bed, was a pale, sad-faced, refined-looking man, black-haired and smooth-skinned, rubbing his eyes, and staring about him with sleepy bewilderment. Then suddenly realising the exposure, he broke into a scream, and threw himself down with his face to the pillow.

"Great heaven!" cried the inspector, "it is, indeed, the missing man. I know him from the photograph."

The prisoner turned with the reckless air of a man who abandons himself to his destiny. "Be it so," said he. "And pray, what am I charged with?"

"With making away with Mr. Neville St.—— Oh, come, you can't be charged with that, unless they make a case of attempted suicide of it," said the inspector, with a grin. "Well, I have been twenty-seven years in the force, but this really takes the cake."

"If I am Mr. Neville St. Clair then it is obvious that no crime has been committed, and that, therefore, I am illegally detained."

"No crime, but a very great error has been committed," said Holmes. "You would have done better to have trusted your wife."

"It was not the wife, it was the children," groaned the prisoner. "God help me, I would not have them ashamed of their father. My God! What an exposure! What can I do?"

Sherlock Holmes sat down beside him on the couch, and patted him kindly on the shoulder.

"If you leave it to a court of law to clear the matter up," said he, "of course you can hardly avoid publicity. On the other hand, if you convince the police authorities that there is no possible case against you, I do not know that there is any reason that the details should find their way into the papers. Inspector Bradstreet would, I am sure, make notes upon anything which you might tell us, and submit it to the proper authorities. The case would then never go into court at all."

"God bless you!" cried the prisoner, passionately. "I would have endured imprisonment, aye, even execution, rather than have left my miserable secret as a family blot to my children.

"You are the first who have ever heard my story. My father was a schoolmaster in Chesterfield, where I received an excellent education. I travelled in my youth, took to the stage, and finally became a reporter on an evening paper in London. One day my editor wished to have a series of articles upon begging in the metropolis, and I volunteered to supply them. There was the point from which all my adventures started. It was only by trying begging as an amateur that I could get the facts upon which to base my articles. When an actor I had, of course, learned all the secrets of making up, and had been famous in the green-room for my skill. I took advantage now of my attainments. I painted my face, and to make myself as pitiable as possible I made a good scar and fixed one side of my lip in a twist by the aid of a small slip of flesh-coloured plaster. Then with a red head of hair, and an appropriate dress, I took my station in the busiest part of the City, ostensibly as a match-seller, but really as a beggar. For seven hours I plied my trade, and when I returned home in the evening I found, to my surprise, that I had received no less than twenty-six shillings and fourpence.

"I wrote my articles, and thought little more of the matter until, some time later, I backed a bill for a friend, and had a writ served upon me for £25. I was at my wits' end where to get the money, but a sudden idea came to me. I begged a fortnight's grace from the creditor, asked for a holiday from my employers, and spent the time in begging in the City under my disguise. In ten days I had the money, and had paid the debt.

"Well, you can imagine how hard it was to settle down to arduous work at two pounds a week, when I knew that I could earn as much in a day by smearing my face with a little paint, laying my cap on the ground, and sitting still. It was a long fight between my pride and the money, but the dollars won at last, and I threw up reporting, and sat day after day in the corner which I had first chosen, inspiring pity by my ghastly face, and filling my pockets with coppers. Only one man knew my secret. He was the keeper of a low den in which I used to lodge in Swandam-lane, where I could every morning emerge as a squalid beggar, and in the evenings transform myself into a well-dressed man about town. This fellow, a Lascar, was well paid by me for his rooms, so that I knew that my secret was safe in his possession.

"Well, very soon I found that I was saving considerable sums of money. I do not mean that any beggar in the streets of London could earn seven hundred pounds a year—which is less than my average takings—but I had exceptional advantages in my power of making up, and also in a facility in repartee, which improved by practice, and made me quite a recognised character in the City. All day a stream of pennies, varied by silver, poured in upon me, and it was a very bad day upon which I failed to take two pounds.

"As I grew richer I grew more ambitious, took a house in the country, and eventually married, without anyone having a suspicion as to my real occupation. My dear wife knew that I had business in the City. She little knew what.

"Last Monday I had finished for the day, and was dressing in my room above the opium den, when I looked out of the window, and saw, to my horror and astonishment, that my wife was standing in the street, with her eyes fixed full upon me. I gave a cry of surprise, threw up my arms to cover my face, and, rushing to my confidant, the Lascar, entreated him to prevent anyone from coming up to me. I heard her voice downstairs, but I knew that she could not ascend. Swiftly I threw off my clothes, pulled on those of a beggar, and put on my pigments and wig. Even a wife's eyes could not pierce so complete a disguise. But then it occurred to me that there might be a search in the room, and that the clothes might betray me. I threw open the window, re-opening by my violence a small cut which I had inflicted upon myself in the bedroom that morning. Then I seized my coat, which was weighted by the coppers which I had just transferred to it from the leather bag in which I carried my takings. I hurled it out of the window, and it disappeared into the Thames. The other clothes would have followed, but at that moment there was a rush of constables up the stair, and a few minutes after I found, rather, I confess, to my relief, that instead of being identified as Mr. Neville St. Clair, I was arrested as his murderer.

"I do not know that there is anything else for me to explain. I was determined to preserve my disguise as long as possible, and hence my preference for a dirty face. Knowing that my wife would be terribly anxious, I slipped off my ring, and confided it to the Lascar at a moment when no constable was watching me, together with a hurried scrawl, telling her that she had no cause to fear."

"That note only reached her yesterday," said Holmes.

"Good God! What a week she must have spent."

"The police have watched this Lascar," said Inspector Bradstreet, "and I can quite understand that he might find it difficult to post a letter unobserved. Probably he handed it to some sailor customer of his, who forgot all about it for some days."

"That was it," said Holmes, nodding approvingly, "I have no doubt of it. But have you never been prosecuted for begging?"

"Many times; but what was a fine to me?"

"It must stop here, however," said Bradstreet. "If the police are to hush this thing up, there must be no more of Hugh Boone."

"I have sworn it by the most solemn oaths which a man can take."

"In that case I think that it is probable that no further steps may be taken. But if you are found again, then all must come out. I am sure, Mr. Holmes, that we are very much indebted to you for having cleared the matter up. I wish I knew how you reach your results."

"I reached this one," said my friend, "by sitting upon five pillows and consuming an ounce of shag. I think, Watson, that if we drive to Baker-street we shall just be in time for breakfast."